P9-AFZ-412

PLAYBILL

English dramatic writing is one of the world's great literary heritages. This Mentor volume offers unabridged texts of six of the most exciting plays that have illuminated the stage of the later English theater.

Congreve's Restoration drama, *The Way of the World,* is an ebullient satire on the manners and intrigues of the idle gallants and fashionable ladies of the royal court. Lord Byron's *Cain* is a serious, searching play—a major yet little-known work that will surprise readers who think of Byron only as a nondramatic romantic poet. Goldsmith's *She Stoops to Conquer* and Wilde's *The Importance of Being Earnest* are probably the two funniest and best-loved comedies of the repertory. A burgeoning social conscience is blended with comedy and satire in Shaw's delightful piece on professional charity, *Major Barbara.*

William Golding's recent controversial play, *The Brass Butterfly,* never before published in America, brings this exciting volume to the present.

Supplementing the text are four essays by great critics of the theater, including Kenneth Tynan's recent treatise "The Angry Young Movement."

The three editors of this book hold Ph.D. degrees from Harvard University and now teach in the Boston area—Sylvan Barnet at Tufts University, Morton Berman at Boston University, and William Burto at Lowell State College.

The Genius of the LATER ENGLISH THEATER

EDITED AND WITH AN INTRODUCTION BY

Sylvan Barnet
Morton Berman
William Burto

A MENTOR BOOK from
NEW AMERICAN LIBRARY
TIMES MIRROR
New York and Toronto
The New English Library Limited, London

SECOND PRINTING

Library of Congress Catalog Card No. 62-18430

Grateful acknowledgment is made to the following for permission to quote from the works listed:

Atheneum Publishers (New York), for "The Angry Young Movement" from *Curtains* by Kenneth Tynan. Copyright © 1961 by Kenneth Tynan.

Curtis Brown, Ltd. (London & New York) for *The Brass Butterfly* by William Golding. Reprinted by permission of the author. © William Golding 1957.

William Heinemann Ltd. (London) for Sir John Gielgud's introduction to *The Importance of Being Earnest.*

Longmans, Green and Company Limited (London) for "The Angry Young Movement" from *Curtains* by Kenneth Tynan. Copyright © 1961 by Kenneth Tynan.

The Public Trustee and the Society of Authors (London) for *Major Barbara* by George Bernard Shaw.

SIGNET, SIGNET CLASSICS, MENTOR AND PLUME BOOKS
are published *in the United States* by
The New American Library, Inc.,
1301 Avenue of the Americas, New York, New York 10019,
in Canada by The New American Library of Canada Limited,
295 King Street East, Toronto 2, Ontario,
in the United Kingdom by The New English Library Limited,
Barnard's Inn, Holborn, London, E.C. 1, England

FIRST PRINTING, AUGUST, 1962

PRINTED IN THE UNITED STATES OF AMERICA

Contents

Contents

The English Theater Since 1660:

An Introduction

In 1642, when the Puritans had the upper hand, Parliament declared that "public stage-plays shall cease and be foreborne." Charles I was executed in 1649, and not until 1660, when Charles II was restored to the throne, were English theaters reopened. During this interregnum there was, of course, some theatrical activity—playlets were given in private homes, illegal performances were occasionally given in the abandoned theaters, Sir William D'Avenant was permitted to produce (as an opera) *The Siege of Rhodes,* and some plays were written that were not performed. Most of the drama of the Interregnum, like most of the Caroline drama (named for Charles I) that preceded it, can be broadly characterized as courtly and romantic, presenting an idealized image of magnanimous men and lovely ladies. When Charles II permitted the drama to be re-established in 1660, and authorized Thomas Killigrew and William D'Avenant to form two dramatic companies, the audiences and the plays at first continued the Caroline tradition.

The Elizabethan theater had drawn its audience from all levels of society, but the Restoration theater attracted only court society and their hangers-on (with their footmen in the upper gallery). Apparently this limited audience did not attend the theater with much interest or regularity. Samuel Pepys has a number of depressing entries in his diary. March 23, 1661: "To the Red Bull (where I had not been since plays come up again). . . . At last into the pit, where I think there was not above ten more than myself, and not one hundred in the whole house"; 1 August 1667: the theater is "mighty empty"; 5 October 1667: Pepys, when admitted backstage, admired Nell Gwynne as she costumed herself, "but to see how Nell cursed, for having so few people in the pit, was pretty." Most of what little audience there was came less to see a play than to exhibit themselves and make assignations. Because the audience was severely limited, a play rarely ran more than three days; most lasted only a single performance. In 1682 Killigrew's and D'Avenant's companies merged, and for the next thirteen years this single company provided London with all its plays, while the rest of England managed to get along without professional drama.

The Restoration playhouse was basically the modern playhouse—a fairly small auditorium, artificially illuminated, with a stage at one end. Though this stage jutted out past the proscenium into the audience (a vestige of the Elizabethan platform stage), the projection (the "apron") was to shrink as the decades passed, and the Restoration playhouse, with its scene at the rear, its wings, and its front curtain rising at the start of the play and descending at the end, was not well adapted to the multiplicity of scenes that the relatively unencumbered Elizabethan stage had handled so easily. The closeness of the Restoration theater to ours is further seen in its use of actresses. Women appeared in Renaissance masques (courtly entertainments) but the Elizabethan and Jacobean dramatists wrote for men and boys, the latter playing all the female roles. In December, 1660, however, an actress appeared in a revival of *Othello,* and the boy actors soon went out of fashion. Though Samuel Pepys said that Edward Kynaston made "the loveliest lady that ever I saw in my life," what was now wanted in the theater, in addition to acting, was sexual titillation. Kynaston could not compete with Nell Gwynne, who was praised for her vivacity and charm rather than for her acting. At thirteen she had been an orange-girl in Drury Lane; at fifteen she was on the stage; and at nineteen the mistress of Charles II. She was popular on and off the stage; once when her carriage was mobbed by persons who thought it contained the Catholic Duchess of Portsmouth (another mistress of the king), she announced reassuringly, "Pray, good people, be civil. I am the *Protestant* whore."

The courtly taste that dominated the Restoration theater in its first two or three decades had an elegant bent. When Shakespeare's plays were presented, therefore, they had to be purged of their alleged impurities, especially their mixture of comic with tragic material. John Dennis, who knew what he liked, explained the principle by which he had revised *The Merry Wives of Windsor*: "I have altered everything which I disliked." Nahum Tate revised *King Lear,* omitting the Fool and giving the play a happy ending. Tate's humility is as engaging as Dennis' arrogance:

> I found the whole . . . a heap of jewels, unstrung and unpolished, yet so dazzling in their disorder that I soon perceived I had seized a treasure. 'Twas my good fortune to light on one expedient to rectify what was wanting in the regularity and probability of the tale, which was to run through the whole a love betwixt Edgar and Cordelia, that never changed word with each other in the original. . . . This method necessarily threw me on making the tale conclude in a success to the innocent distressed persons; otherwise I must have encumbered the stage with dead bodies, which conduct makes many tragedies conclude with unseasonable jests. Yet was I racked with no small fears for so bold a change, till I found it well received by my audience.

When not adapting older tragedies, the dramatists, especially in the '60's and '70's, continued the Caroline tradition by composing serious plays in which impossibly heroic men in romantic lands nobly face conflicts between love and honor, and in the fifth act commonly find that they can have both. In this period authors and audience congratulated themselves on the superiority of their taste to that of the Elizabethans. "Fame was cheap" before the Restoration, Dryden says (1672) in the Epilogue to one of his heroic plays,

> And the first comer sped;
> And they have kept it since, by being dead,
> But, were they now to write, when critics weigh,
> Each line, and ev'ry word, throughout a play,
> None of 'em, no, not Jonson in his height,
> Could pass, without allowing grains for weight.
> Think it not envy, that these truths are told;
> Our poet's not malicious, though he's bold.
> 'Tis not to brand 'em that their faults are shown,
> But by their errors to excuse his own.

If Love and Honor now are higher raised,
'Tis not the poet, but the Age is praised.

There were, of course, skeptics, like Thomas Shadwell, who looked contemptuously on

A dull romantic whining play,
Where poor frail woman's made a deity,
With senseless amorous idolatry,
And sniveling heroes sigh, and pine, and cry.
Though singly they beat armies and huff kings,
Rant at the Gods, and do impossible things;
Though they can laugh at danger, blood, and wounds,
Yet if the dame once chides, the milk-sop hero swoons.
Those doughty things nor manners have, nor wit;
We ne'er saw hero fit to drink with yet.

But on the whole the theatrical public in these decades wished to see on the tragic stage an idealization of the heroic creed which courtiers supposedly held.

In addition to heroic plays and revivals or adaptations of Shakespeare and of the other Elizabethan and Jacobean dramatists, there were plunderings from Molière; and late in the seventeenth century farce and sentimental comedy appear with some frequency. But the Restoration comedy that has endured is the so-called Comedy of Manners, a witty, cynical genre so sophisticated that it did not draw the line at obscenity. The type, which flourished chiefly in the last quarter of the century, is discussed in the introduction (p. 21) to Congreve's *The Way of the World*, but a sample of the aristocratic dialogue of a comedy of manners may be given here. It is from the opening scene of Congreve's first play, *The Old Bachelor*, written when he was nineteen. "Come, come, leave business to idlers, and wisdom to fools: they have need of 'em: wit, be my faculty, and pleasure my occupation; and let father Time shake his glass."

In the early eighteenth century, tragedy, which had a few decades before been jostled by the heroic play, was elbowed by plays of pathos (notably Nicholas Rowe's "she-tragedies"). Comedy, far more popular than tragedy, was losing its witty cynicism and gaining sentimentality as comic dramatists set out (in the words of the prologue to Richard Steele's *The Conscious Lovers* [1722]) "to refine the age,/To chasten wit, and moralize the stage." The characters in Steele's play are not aristocrats but members of the bourgeoisie, yet their hearts are directed not toward money but toward other hearts. The bourgeois dramatis personae, who a few decades earlier had been presented only for ridicule, afford evidence, too, that the audience was now less exclusively aristocratic. It was largely a bourgeois audience that soon helped George Lillo to write *The London Merchant* (1731), "a tale of private woe," rather than of "royal woe." In his Dedication, Lillo suggests that a tale of "private life" may have wider relevance than a tale of "superior rank." Poetry is here displaced by prose (except for couplets at the ends of some scenes), and we are on the long road that will lead, via *drame, drame bourgeois, comédie larmoyante* (tearful comedy), *tragédie bourgeoise, bürgerliches Trauerspiel* (bourgeois tragedy)—all interchangeable terms for pathetic plays of middle-class life—and via melodrama (again, plays of domestic life, in which vice and virtue are sharply distinguished and are appropriately rewarded) to the important work of Ibsen and (to return to the English theater) such an Ibsenite as Shaw. Although the English did not eagerly follow up Lillo's lead, England's importance in establishing domestic drama is undoubted. In France, Diderot compared *The London Merchant* to plays by Sophocles and Euripides; in Germany it moved Lessing to write *Miss Sara Sampson* (appropriately set in England), a play about a girl who elopes with a blackguard, is deserted by him and poisoned by his mistress.

The English public, however, also enjoyed spectacle, and this the bourgeois drama could scarcely offer. Pantomime (not a silent performance, but an extravaganza) and opera seriously competed with spoken drama. The Puritans had allowed D'Avenant to produce *The Siege of Rhodes* (1656) as a sort of opera, but in fact the piece, which was performed in recitative, has, aside from choruses, only one song. During the Restoration, Shakespeare's *The Tempest* and *Macbeth* were outfitted with numerous musical and spectacular episodes, and in 1691 Dryden and Purcell collaborated on *King Arthur,* in which, though the mortals speak, the deities sing. In short, English opera had been a play with music. Italian opera, introduced to England in 1674, became enormously popular early in the eighteenth century, seriously threatening the English drama. The sentiments of English playwrights and performers were nicely summed up later in the century by Kitty Clive, an actress noted for her singing, who characterized the invaders as "a set of Italian squalling devils who come over to England to get our bread from us, and I say curse them all for a parcel of Italian bitches." At this distance we can be grateful to the Italian opera for provoking John Gay's parody, *The Beggar's Opera* (1728), but in other respects its impact on English drama must have been detrimental. Theatergoers customarily complain about the low state of the theater, but in the eighteenth century they were especially justified. Alexander Pope (not an impartial witness, but as shrewd as any) gives a melancholy picture of a public which preferred a drama that sacrificed the spoken word to spectacle:

> There still remains, to mortify a wit,
> The many-headed monster of the pit:
> A senseless, worthless, and unhonored crowd,
> Who, to disturb their betters mighty proud,
> Clattering their sticks before ten lines are spoke,
> Call for the farce, the bear, or the black joke.
> What dear delight to Britons farce affords!
> Ever the taste of mobs, but now of lords;
> (Taste, that eternal wanderer, which flies
> From heads to ears, and now from ears to eyes.)
> The play stands still; damn action and discourse,
> Back fly the scenes, and enter foot and horse;
> Pageants on pageants, in long order drawn,
> Peers, heralds, bishops, ermine, gold, and lawn.
> . . . .
> Ah luckless poet! Stretch thy lungs and roar,
> That bear or elephant shall heed thee more;
> While all its throats the gallery extends,
> And all the thunder of the pit ascends!
> Loud as the wolves, on Orcas' stormy steep,
> Howl to the roarings of the Northern deep.
> Such is the shout, the long-applauding note,
> At Quin's high plume, or Oldfield's petticoat.

The latter half of the century is happier, with Oliver Goldsmith and Richard Sheridan; and if we remember that the history of drama includes actors as well as playwrights, David Garrick makes this period luminous. The tradition of notable acting is continued into the early nineteenth century by John Philip Kemble, Sarah Siddons, and (later) Edward Kean, but the first three-quarters of the nineteenth century, like the last three-quarters of the eighteenth, is meager in playwrights.

The question of why there were so few important plays

between, say, *The Beggar's Opera* (1728) and Oscar Wilde's *Lady Windermere's Fan* (1892) has often been answered, but never satisfactorily. Perhaps the answer is that born playwrights weren't born, or that the novel attracted most of the literary talent that was not lyrical. The usual answers are (1) the theatrical monopoly, (2) the size of the theaters, (3) the low public taste, (4) the star system.

The theatrical monopoly, created when Charles II licensed only two theatrical companies, has been much blamed. Theaters other than the two "legitimate" theaters, prohibited from producing spoken plays, offered entertainments that were chiefly musical and spectacular. Some of these entertainments were silent or sung (instead of spoken) burlesques or burlettas of spoken plays, but burletta came to be applied to almost anything done at these houses. In fact, there was not always a noticeable difference between the repertories of the legitimate and the illegitimate theaters: the two legitimate theaters did not hesitate to offer music and spectacle (they had, in fact, been the first to perform the burlettas), and the illegitimate theaters found ways of circumventing the law. Early in the nineteenth century it was said that a burletta was wholly musical, but in the 1830's five songs per act were held sufficient to counteract the spoken dialogue. A witness to what purported to be a burletta of *Othello* testified that even this requirement was not met: he said that the play was performed to the accompaniment of a pianist, who every five minutes struck a virtually inaudible chord. The monopoly was further weakened by a license granting the Little Theater in the Haymarket the right to present plays in the summer season; in 1840 the summer season was ten months. The theatrical monopoly, which did not monopolize the theater, was sufficiently absurd so that in 1843 the Theater Regulation Act abolished whatever legal basis the patent theaters had ever had to exclusive rights to the spoken drama. Prophecies that many new theaters would be built proved unfounded; business continued much as usual, the sometime patent theaters offering fare not very different from that of the sometime illegitimate theaters. One of the patent theaters, Drury Lane, became an opera house, and the other, Covent Garden, produced a good deal of melodrama and pantomime. On the other hand, the reforms of T. W. Robertson (discussed below), some two decades after the legal abolition of the monopoly, might not have been undertaken if the law had prohibited Robertson's theater from producing spoken plays.

The second explanation commonly offered to account for the dearth of good drama is the size of the theaters. The patent theaters at first were small, but they were later enlarged several times. Covent Garden burned down in 1808, Drury Lane in 1809; each was rebuilt to hold over 3,000. The enormous capacities are said to have discouraged subtlety and encouraged spectacle, and it is indisputable that acoustics and lighting were sometimes poor. Still, when one recalls that Elizabethan theaters seem to have held about 2,500 spectators, and that some Greek theaters held about 15,000, one cannot with much confidence blame large theaters for poor drama. The abundant spectacle, for example, may be not a response to an increased auditorium that made the spoken word inaudible, but a response to the public's delight in the new methods of illumination. Gas lighting, introduced into the halls of the theaters about 1815 and into the auditoriums and stages about 1817, permitted effects previously impossible in oil- and candle-lit houses. Here is what a visitor to Covent Garden saw in 1826:

> At the rising of the curtain a thick mist covers the stage and gradually rolls off. This is remarkably well managed by means of fine gauze. In the dim light we distinguish a little cottage, the dwelling of a sorceress; in the background a lake surrounded by mountains, some of whose peaks are clothed with snow. All as yet is misty and indistinct; the sun then rises triumphantly, chases the morning dews, and the hut with the village in the distance now appears in perfect outline.

Limelight, used by 1837, made additional effects possible; and in 1859 *The Theatrical Journal* reported that "Mr. Charles Kean has shown us how, by the aid of electric light, both sun and moon are to be almost sublimely represented." In short, technical developments were such that one feels the drama was struggling to turn itself into the as yet uninvented motion picture; spectacle was provided not because words were impossible, but because spectacle could at last be effectively provided.

The third reason, low public taste, is usually justified by pointing to the plays the public liked, and by citing charges against the public taste. But the public was offered nothing better. The occasional bookish person who sought to elevate the public taste by writing a "classical" play produced nothing of value. The public did not neglect any theatrical genius. Nor, incidentally, did the public like all of the trash that it got; it was a great age for hissing. Complaints about the public's immorality and low taste are not convincing either; they can be paralleled with earnest complaints from the late sixteenth century about the morals and taste of the Elizabethan playgoers who were enjoying Shakespeare. And if the early Victorian theaters really were (as charged) "houses of ill-fame on a large scale," why did they turn out dramatists inferior to Congreve?

The star system is a more likely cause of bad drama. The Elizabethan theatrical company, apparently, functioned as a company, and its members were accustomed to performing with each other for the benefit of all. (Yet the age had its outstanding actors too. And Hamlet's fear that the clown may speak more than is set down for him suggests that Shakespeare's company may have had a comic performer who had the exhibitionistic "pitiful ambition" that Hamlet spoke of.) The nineteenth century especially was an age of stars, and that they sometimes chose plays as vehicles to display their special talents is indisputable. It is easy to find evidence in the memoirs of actors themselves, but a single statement by a playwright will suffice. Bernard Shaw wrote of Henry Irving (1838–1905):

> To the author, Irving was not an actor: he was either a rival or a collaborator who did all the real work. Therefore, he was anathema to master authors, and a godsend to journeymen authors.

In the early nineteenth century, the star system and the prestige of Shakespeare conspired to urge dramatists ambitious of fame to write "high tragedy" rather than plays of ordinary life. Today, these plays seem unbearably inflated. Keats, for example, wrote *Otho the Great* in the hope that Edmund Kean would act it. "Were it to succeed . . . it would lift me out of the mire. I mean the mire of a bad reputation which is continually rising against me. My name with the literary fashionables is vulgar—I am a weaver boy to them—a Tragedy would lift me out of this mess." (It need hardly be added that *Otho* is barely readable and utterly unactable.) Keats's choice of a tenth-century figure is symptomatic, too, of the serious dramatist's avoidance of the present during most of the nineteenth century. The neoclassicists in the late seventeenth and in the eighteenth centuries had, of course, been interested in Greece and Rome, but the Romantics added an interest in other cultures, especially that of the Middle Ages. The interest in medievalism seems to have been the result of many forces, particularly a reaction against a mechanistic world, and an increase in nationalism. In any case, it gave renewed popularity to Shakespeare's history plays. In 1823 a production of *King John* boasted that it reproduced authentic costumes; in 1857 the great scene in *Richard II* was Richard's ride through London, which Shakespeare had merely described but which now was represented on stage by a cast of 500. On the whole, tragedies became costume pieces; of plays written at this time, about all that survives is a couplet from Bulwer Lytton's *Richelieu* (1839):

> Beneath the rule of men entirely great,
> The pen is mightier than the sword.

The pomp of these costume pieces was commonly fused with swordsmanship and pathos, as in Robert Browning's *A Blot on the 'Scutcheon* (1843). This play, Browning said, has "*action* in it, drabbing, stabbing, et autres gentillesses." The hero is killed in a duel, the heroine dies of a broken heart, and the heroine's brother takes poison. The heroine's pathetic observation (several times repeated in the play), "I was so young, I loved him so, I had/ No mother, God forgot me, and I fell," filled Charles Dickens with "a perfect passion of sorrow." He wrote, "I know nothing that is so affecting, nothing in any book I have ever read, as Mildred's recurrence to that 'I was so young—I had no mother.' "

Romantic melodrama, disguised as high tragedy by its emphasis on historic detail, helped prepare the way for detailed representations of the present. In the 1830's at the Olympic Theater, managed by Mme. Vestris, a drawing room was represented not simply by wings and two chairs, but a "more perfect enclosure [that] gives the appearance of a private chamber." The exact nature of this set is unknown, but it seems close to the box set, which consists of three walls and a ceiling—in short, a room missing a wall at the proscenium. T. W. Robertson (1829–1871), who for a while was a prompter at Mme. Vestris' theater, is usually credited with introducing realism to the English stage. Basically he applied to plays of contemporary life the care that had been applied to historical plays. A few of his instructions will show the nature of his contribution:

> Throughout the Act the autumn leaves fall from the trees.
>
> The author requests this part may be played with a slight French accent. He is not to pronounce the words absurdly or duck his head toward his stomach like the conventional stage Frenchman.
>
> Sam cuts enormous slice of bread and hands it on point of knife to Hawtree. Cuts small lump of butter and hands it on point of knife to Hawtree, who looks at it through eyeglass, then takes it. Sam then helps himself. Polly meantime has poured out tea in two cups and one saucer for Sam, sugars them, and then hands cup and saucer to Hawtree, who has both hands full. He takes it awkwardly and places it on table. Polly, having only one spoon, tastes Sam's tea, then stirs Hawtree's, attracting his attention by doing so.

This last sort of stage direction gave rise to the characterization of Robertson's comedies as "cup-and-saucer drama." It is easy to dismiss them as trivial, but they helped accustom an English audience to images of contemporary life. With Robertson, drama approaches the worlds of Ibsen and Chekhov.

Ibsen's early plays were mostly romantic and historical pieces, but by 1875, when he began *Pillars of Society,* he had started on a new career as a social dramatist. In 1879 he wrote *A Doll's House,* in 1881 *Ghosts*. *Pillars of Society* had been produced in England for a single performance in 1880, but Ibsen's influence in the '80's was negligible. Henry Arthur Jones is sometimes said to show his influence, but Jones was probably right in denying that Ibsen gave him anything more than some ideas about plotting. Not until 1890, when Shaw spoke on Ibsen to the Fabian Society (the speech grew into a small book, *The Quintessence of Ibsenism*), did Ibsenism touch a major dramatist, and then of course Shaw was not yet a major dramatist—or even a produced dramatist. He turned to drama only after he had written pamphlets and novels, and then (he claimed) only because no one in England was writing the sort of play that was agitating Europe. While Oscar Wilde wrote melodrama and (in *The Importance of Being Earnest*) delightful witty comedy, Shaw turned to writing Ibsenite social dramas with a good deal of wit. When the century ended, Shaw had written four major plays; *Mrs. Warren's Profession, Arms and the Man, You Never Can Tell,* and *Caesar and Cleopatra.* Within the first five years of the twentieth century he wrote two masterpieces, *Man and Superman* and *Major Barbara.* Other playwrights, such as Henry Arthur Jones and Arthur Wing Pinero, had neither Shaw's comic sense nor his serious desire to examine social problems, and they were left behind.

Whether Shaw set the pace or was riding the wave of history, or both, the drama of ideas attracted numerous English writers in the first quarter of the twentieth century. But because they lacked Shaw's wit, exuberant imagination, and insight into society and character, their plays have not had staying power. Today it is a task to read the plays of Galsworthy, Hankin, and Granville-Barker, and even the more recent ones of, say, Mordaunt Shairp and J. B. Priestley. (Nor have the descendants of Wilde—notably Noel Coward and Somerset Maugham—equaled Wilde's achievement. Maugham's substitution of realism—or cynicism—for Wilde's fantasy is a loss, and Coward's wit has become dully dated.) It is an equal task to read the plays of the competitors of the "realistic" dramatists, the works of men who advocated a return to poetic drama. Although in Ireland some writers—notably Yeats and Synge—managed to restore to the stage the "beautiful and vivid language" that Yeats found lacking in Ibsenism, English poetic plays of the first quarter of the century sound vapid today.[1] Here is Paolo speaking in Stephen Phillips' *Paolo and Francesca,* a play much praised when produced in 1902:

> Remember how when first we met we stood
> Stung with immortal recollections.
> O face immured beside a fairy sea,
> That leaned down at dead midnight to be kissed!
> O beauty folded up in forests old!
> *Thou* wast the lovely quest of Arthur's knights.

English drama in the first half of the twentieth century, excluding Shaw, is thin stuff beside European and even American drama. A few verse plays stand out as interest-

[1] For some Irish plays of the period, see *The Genius of the Irish Theater,* ed. by S. Barnet, M. Berman, and W. Burto, New York, New American Library (Mentor Books), 1960.

ing experiments and considerable accomplishments (Eliot's *Murder in the Cathedral,* Auden and Isherwood's *The Dog Beneath the Skin,* and Spender's *The Trial of a Judge*), but the West End drama of the period is rarely interesting. An American critic, Walter Kerr, cheerfully points out in *Pieces at Eight* that the English are quite candid and relaxed about second-rate theater. They attend a thriller by Agatha Christie with no affectation and no hope of seeing more than a thriller by Agatha Christie. They attend a musical revue that is frankly (Mr. Kerr says) in a "come-if-you-have-nothing-better-to-do category." Perhaps the English tend to let Shakespeare take care of the quality drama. But England's sharpest living dramatic critic, Kenneth Tynan, will have none of it. The "culpable tolerance" of the English theatrical public, he claims, keeps the level of playwriting low. Something of the low level is indicated by a paragraph in a recent book by an English historian of the theater. One rubs one's eyes as one reads (in this rarely impassioned chronicle) the words "unforgettable," "perfectly handled," and "verve," all applied to an American import, *Oklahoma!* A second symptom of illness is revealed on the jacket of another book, this one an examination of the English theater of the late '50's: the picture is of Marlon Brando as Stanley Kowalski.

During the Second World War, however, the British theatrical public, which might have been expected to want light stuff, displayed a surprising tendency to support revivals of serious drama. The first postwar years did not produce much that now seems impressive, but they preserved the feeling that the theater is not simply show business. In the late '50's there was thus a substantial audience to welcome plays that once would have been thought avant-garde. The new playwrights have aroused considerable excitement, and there is widespread hope—even belief—that English drama is again becoming important. These playwrights (aside from Christopher Fry) can be roughly sorted into two groups, Angry Young Men (often showing the influence of Brecht and Arthur Miller) and dramatists of the Absurd (often showing the influence of Beckett and Ionesco). Both groups reveal a profound dissatisfaction with their surroundings, the first especially with the social and political world, the second especially with the cosmos. Their plays are readily available in paperbacks and on the stage, and Mr. Tynan discusses the Angry Young Men on P. 524, but a brief comparison of the two groups can be made here.[2] John Osborne, who can be taken as representative of the angry writers (though of course no writer represents another writer, and no writer is quite the same even in his own successive works), tends to use tirades; Harold Pinter, perhaps the best of the Absurd writers, in his finest work makes considerable use of silence, understatement, and comic business. Osborne's Luther proclaims that "We are living in a dangerous time"; Pinter's Davies (the old bum in *The Caretaker*) asks for a knife to cut bread with, is told to use the one he has been brandishing, but comes back with a plaintive "I picked it up somewhere. I don't know where it's been, do I?" These two schools have produced good drama; it looks as though a new English theater is beginning with a bang and a whimper.

[2] None of these writers is represented in this collection because permission to reprint a significant work could not be secured.

Part One

THE PLAYS

William Congreve:

The Way of the World

The Way of the World belongs to the dramatic species called "Restoration Comedy." The term, however, is misleading. The Restoration occurred in 1660, when the Puritan Interregnum was ended and Charles II returned from his exile in France to ascend the throne. The drama produced during the ensuing decade was mostly romantically heroic, showing the adventures and refined sentiments of courtly men and ladies who were discommoded by pirates or war but who turned their minds to thoughts of noble love. Very few if any of the plays written in the first four or five years following the Restoration are "Restoration comedies"; very few, in fact, are even comedies. Most of these plays are continuations of the courtly traditions established in the 1630's, before the Interregnum. The first characteristically Restoration comedy is Wycherley's *The Country Wife*, produced in 1675; moreover, Restoration comedy continued to be written into the first decade of the eighteenth century, almost fifty years after the Restoration, some twenty years after the death of Charles II. George Farquhar's *The Beaux' Stratagem*, for example, was written in 1707, by which time Charles had been succeeded by James II, William and Mary, and Anne.

A second name for the work of Congreve and his fellows is "Comedy of Manners," a term coined by Charles Lamb almost a century after Congreve's death. "Manners" once had—as late as the seventeenth century—ethical implications (a man's manner included his character), but Lamb used the word in its modern sense, "social code," "politeness." Restoration comedies undoubtedly make much of behavior according to a social code, but moral considerations are not always so absent as the term implies. The point will be amplified shortly.

What first strikes the student of the comedy of Etherege, Wycherley, Congreve, and Farquhar is its remoteness from the comedy of Jonson and of Shakespere. Restoration comedy (to use the familiar though historically inaccurate term) is a comedy of courtship, but lovers play only minor roles in Jonson. His two most notable plays, *Volpone* (1606) [1] and *The Alchemist* (1610) have no lovers in them; his *Every Man in His Humor* (1598) has a marriage at the end but no courting scenes. If Restoration comedy resembles Jonson's in its concentration on city life, it is nevertheless different in its central actions. It is even more remote from Shakespeare's comedy, where love is heaven on earth. The course of true love does not run smooth, but Shakespeare's lovers do not regret that they have been wounded by Cupid's arrow, and they do not conceal their condition. They could not conceal it even if they tried: to love "is to be all made of sighs and tears" or else to be all "full of joy and mirth." Shakespeare's lovers undergo something new and overpowering, that begins to melt the "cold virgin snow" upon their hearts. Take this description of Oliver and Celia, in *As You Like It*:

> Your brother and my sister no sooner met but they looked; no sooner looked but they loved; no sooner loved but they sighed; so sooner sighed but they asked one another the reason; no sooner knew the reason but they sought the remedy; and in these degrees have they made a pair of stairs to marriage.

Restoration comedy, however, is largely built on witty lovers who, old hands at the game, conceal their emotion,

[1] Printed in a companion to the present volume, *The Genius of the Early English Theater*, ed. by S. Barnet, M. Berman, and W. Burto, New York, New American Library (Mentor Books), 1962.

and effect indifference. The closest Shakespeare comes to the lovers of Restoration comedy is in *Much Ado About Nothing,* where Beatrice and Benedick wage "a kind of merry war." But, first, the affairs of Beatrice and Benedick form a subplot (the main plot deals with the love of Hero and Claudio), and, second, even Beatrice and Benedick sigh and write sonnets.

Basically, Restoration comedy deals with a small courtly society that is too well-bred to admit it loves. But this society is adept at love, and sexuality fills the air as the men and women intrigue their way toward marriage furnished with a legacy. The old, who are really out of it, do not easily admit their impotence; Lady Wishfort admits that she looks like "an old peeled wall," but Mirabel knows that she will be flattered even by a lampoon that accuses her of "an affair with a young fellow." On the whole, it is a libertine and Machiavellian society ("comedy of the manners of South-Sea islanders under city veneer" was George Meredith's summary), at war with itself, occasionally pausing to laugh at absurd clergymen, pedantic scholars, or rustic squires who are excluded from the in-group, but chiefly fencing by its wit for the possession of a spouse's legacy. Dr. Johnson said that Congreve's comedies "consist in gay remarks and unexpected answers. . . . His personages are a kind of intellectual gladiators; every sentence is to ward or strike." (Incidentally, Johnson's comment should be kept in mind if the plays seem to lack "action"; the characters do not fight with swords or even with fans; their deeds are their verbal encounters.)

The gay remarks and unexpected answers have offended many hearers, who have charged that Restoration comedies are immoral. Elizabethan drama had been steadily attacked by Puritans in the late sixteenth and early seventeenth centuries, but as the drama became increasingly associated with the court, overt hostility diminished. William Prynne charged in *Histriomastix, The Player's Scourge* (1633) that actresses were "notorious whores," but, Queen Henrietta having appeared in a court masque, he paid dearly for it: he was imprisoned and branded, and deprived of his ears and his Oxford degree. In the first decade of the Restoration, similarly, the court and the drama were so closely related that Puritans had to be braver than their Elizabethan ancestors to attack the drama. Still, attacks were not wanting; the most notable was Jeremy Collier's *A Short View of the Immorality and Profaneness of the English Stage* (1698), made long after the Restoration and at a time when Restoration comedy was petering out. Collier, attacking Congreve and others, complained about a variety of things: plays contained obsenity and profanity, clergymen were depicted unfavorably, poetic justice was not respected, etc. Collier's basic strategy, however, was to attack the plays on aesthetic grounds; he posed as an adherent of neoclassical principles of the drama, and attempted to show that the plays failed to do what the best critical theory said drama should do. Literature, he held, should be didactic; comedy should correct vice. He found things to praise even in pagan dramatists (Plautus "has some regard to the requirements of modesty and the dignity of human nature"), though Shakespeare for the most part is "too guilty to make evidence." He insisted that drama should show the vicious punished, not merely laughed at (sufficient punishment, most dramatists had held) or forgiven or invited to join in a dance. Dramatists, including Congreve, replied to Collier, but Collier was riding the crest of a new wave, and in the early eighteenth century the drama became noticebly didactic. The charge that Restoration comedy is immoral has stuck, and readers who have never looked at a page of Congreve may learn from Macaulay and Thackeray as well as from Meredith that Congreve is immoral.

But Congreve saw things differently. He insisted in several places that his comedies were moral. That his line can be quite as neoclassical as Collier's is seen in the following passage:

> Men are to be laughed out of their vices in comedy; the business of comedy is to delight, as well as to instruct; and as vicious people are made ashamed of their follies or faults, by seeing them exposed in a ridiculous manner, so are good people at once both warned and diverted at their expense.

In his dedication to *The Way of the World* he distinguishes between simpletons (who should be objects of charity) and affected asses (who are proper subjects of comedy):

> Those characters which are meant to be ridiculed in most of our comedies, are of fools so gross, that, in my humble opinion, they should rather disturb than divert the well-natured and reflecting part of an audience; they are rather objects of charity than contempt; and instead of moving our mirth, they ought very often to excite our compassion.
>
> This reflection moved me to design some characters, which

> should appear ridiculous, not so much through a natural folly (which is incorrigible, and therefore not proper for the stage) as through affected wit; a wit, which at the same time that it is affected, is also false.

Congreve goes on to explain that the reader must distinguish between the Witwouds, who are satirized, and the Truewits, who are sympathetically presented. Failure to make such a distinction is fatal to the play, and it seems that the original audience failed, as have many subsequent spectators and readers. Perhaps the fault is Congreve's; even so shrewd a satirist as Congreve's friend, Alexander Pope, wondered "if Congreve's fools are fools indeed." If we indiscriminately assume that all the characters are the author's mouthpieces, it is easy to find *The Way of the World* immoral. Witwoud says, "A wit should no more be sincere than a woman constant; one argues a decay of parts, as t'other of beauty." The speaker is not Congreve but Witwound, whom Mirabel a moment earlier has said is "a fool . . . whose conversation can never be approved; yet it is now and then to be endured." The character of a speaker, determined not only by what he says but also by his function in the plot and by what others say of him, similarly should control the way in which we hear Fainall praise cuckoldry: "Marriage is honorable, as you say; and if so, wherefore should cuckoldom be a discredit, being derived from so honorable a root?"

The charge of immorality evaporates if one keeps in mind the contrast between Mirabel and Fainall. Mirabel aptly says that Fainall is "a false and a designing lover, yet one whose wit and outward fair behavior have gained a reputation with the town." Mirabel is no chaste Shakespearean lover; he has had a mistress and then married her off to Fainall, but that was before the play began. In the play he is sensible and, in an important matter, trustworthy. Sensible because, for example, he disapproves of pretense: "I article," he tells his future wife, "that you continue to like your own face as long as I shall; and while it passes current with me, that you endeavor not to new-coin it." Trustworthy because he protects the legacy of his former mistress when he could have misused it. Furthermore, he has a generous, conciliatory spirit—at least at the end of the play when he has achieved what he wants. To the penultimate speech, Lady Wishfort's fear that her son-in-law "will pursue some desperate course," Mirabel replies, "For my part, I will contribute all that in me lies to a reunion," and he concludes with as moral a quatrain as a play can have:

> From hence let those be warned who mean to wed,
> Lest mutual falsehood stain the bridal bed;
> For each deceiver to his cost may find
> That marriage frauds too oft are paid in kind.

Finally, it should be mentioned that the play is not a sermon but a comedy, defined by Dr. Johnson as "a dramatic representation of human life as may excite mirth." The anticipated wedding and the dance near the end of *The Way of the World* suggest the joy, unity, fertility, and triumph of sex which comedy usually celebrates, but which are kept within lawful bounds. And to say that the play is a comedy is to say, also, that we regard the persons in it aesthetically as well as morally, and do not judge them exactly as we would judge the happenings if they took place outside of the theater. But this is a point that Charles Lamb defends on p. 510.

Congreve: Biographical Note.

William Congreve (1670–1729) was born in England but raised in Ireland, where his father was an army officer. In Ireland he met and formed a lifelong friendship with Jonathan Swift. Congreve returned to England to study law, but his interests were literary and social. *The Old Bachelor*, written when he was nineteen, was produced in London in 1693 with great success. His next two plays established his position as the chief comic writer of the day. His fourth play, a tragedy, was similarly successful, but today *The Mourning Bride* lives only in two quotations: "Music hath charms to sooth the savage breast," and "Heaven has no rage like love to hatred turned,/Nor Hell a fury like a woman scorned." *The Way of the World* (1700) was his last play; the cool public reception, his established place in society, and his sinecures joined to make him live the rest of his life as a gentleman. In *Lives of the Poets* Dr. Johnson puts it this way: "Having long conversed familiarly with the great, he wished to be considered rather as a man of fashion than of wit; and, when he received a visit from Voltaire, disgusted him by the despicable foppery of desiring to be considered not as an author, but a gentleman; to which the Frenchman replied, 'that if he had been only a gentleman, he should not have come to visit him.' " In his later years, apparently, the Duchess of Marlborough was his mistress; he left her his fortune, though she could not need it.

Suggested References:

Brooks, Cleanth, and Robert B. Heilman, *Understanding Drama: Twelve Plays,* New York, Henry Holt & Co., 1945; London, George G. Harrap & Co., 1945.

Fujimura, Thomas H., *The Restoration Comedy of Wit,* Princeton, Princeton University Press, 1952.

Holland, Norman N., *The First Modern Comedies,* Cambridge, Mass., Harvard University Press, 1959; London, Oxford University Press, 1959.

Mueschke, Paul, and Miriam Mueschke, *A New View of Congreve's "Way of the World,"* Ann Arbor, University of Michigan Press, 1958.

Audire est operae pretium, procedere recte
Qui maechis non vultis—
HOR. SAT. 2. 1. I.
—Metuat doti deprensa.—
IBID.[a]

[a] "It is worth while for those who do not wish well to adulterers to hear how they are hampered on all sides—"
—"Discovered in the act, the woman fears for her dowry." Horace, *Satires*, II, 1, 37–38, 131.

To the Right Honorable

RALPH, EARL OF MONTAGUE, &c.

MY LORD,

Whether the world will arraign me of vanity or not, that I have presumed to dedicate this comedy to your Lordship, I am yet in doubt; though, it may be, it is some degree of vanity even to doubt of it. One who has at any time had the honor of your Lordship's conversation, cannot be supposed to think very meanly of that which he would prefer to your perusal; yet it were to incur the imputation of too much sufficiency, to pretend to such a merit as might abide the test of your Lordship's censure.

Whatever value may be wanting to this play while yet it is mine, will be sufficiently made up to it when it is once become your Lordship's; and it is my security that I cannot have overrated it more by my dedication, than your Lordship will dignify it by your patronage.

That it succeeded on the stage, was almost beyond my expectation; for but little of it was prepared for that general taste which seems now to be predominant in the palates of our audience.

Those characters which are meant to be ridiculed in most of our comedies, are of fools so gross, that, in my humble opinion, they should rather disturb than divert the well-natured and reflecting part of an audience; they are rather objects of charity than contempt; and instead of moving our mirth, they ought very often to excite our compassion.

This reflection moved me to design some characters which should appear ridiculous, not so much through a natural folly (which is incorrigible, and therefore not proper for the stage) as through an affected wit; a wit, which at the same time that it is affected, is also false. As there is some difficulty in the formation of a character of this nature, so there is some hazard which attends the progress of its success upon the stage; for many come to a play so overcharged with criticism, that they very often let fly their censure, when through their rashness they have mistaken their aim. This I had occasion lately to observe; for this play had been acted two or three days, before some of these hasty judges could find the leisure to distinguish betwixt the character of a Witwoud[b] and a Truewit.[c]

I must beg your Lordship's pardon for this digression from the true course of this epistle; but that it may not seem altogether impertinent, I beg that I may plead the occasion of it, in part of that excuse of which I stand in need, for recommending this comedy to your protection. It is only by the countenance of your Lordship, and the *few* so qualified, that such who wrote with care and pains can hope to be distinguished; for the prostituted name of *poet* promiscuously levels all that bear it.

Terence, the most correct writer in the world, had a Scipio and a Laelius, if not to assist him, at least to support him in his reputation; and notwithstanding his extraordinary merit, it may be their countenance was not more than necessary.

The purity of his style, the delicacy of his turns, and the justness of his characters, were all of them beauties which the greater part of his audience were incapable of tasting; some of the coarsest strokes of Plautus, so severely censured by Horace, were more likely to affect the multitude; such who come with expectation to laugh at the last act of a play, and are better entertained with two or three unseasonable jests, than with the artful solution of the *fable*.

As Terence excelled in his performances, so had he great advantages to encourage his undertakings; for he built most on the foundations of Menander; his plots were generally modeled, and his characters ready drawn to his hand. He copied Menander, and Menander had no less light in the formation of his characters, from the observations of Theophrastus, of whom he was a disciple; and Theophrastus, it is known, was not only the disciple, but the immediate successor of Aristotle, the first and greatest judge of poetry. These were great models to design by; and the further advantage which Terence possessed, towards giving his plays the due ornaments of purity of style and justness of manners, was not less

[b] character in *The Way of the World*. [c] character in Ben Jonson's *Epicene* (1609)

considerable, from the freedom of conversation which was permitted him with Laelius and Scipio, two of the greatest and most polite men of his age. And indeed the privilege of such a conversation is the only certain means of attaining to the perfection of dialogue.

If it has happened in any part of this comedy, that I have gained a turn of style or expression more correct, or at least, more corrigible, than in those which I have formerly written, I must, with equal pride and gratitude, ascribe it to honor of your Lordship's admitting me into your conversation, and that of a society where everybody else was so well worthy of you, in your retirement last summer from the town; for it was immediately after that this comedy was written. If I have failed in my performance, it is only to be regretted, where there were so many, not inferior either to a Scipio or a Laelius, that there should be one wanting equal in capacity to a Terence.

If I am not mistaken, poetry is almost the only art which has not yet laid claim to your Lordship's patronage. Architecture and painting, to the great honor of our country, have flourished under your influence and protection. In the mean time, poetry, the eldest sister of all arts, and parent of most, seems to have resigned her birthright, by having neglected to pay her duty to your Lordship, and by permitting others of a later extraction, to prepossess that place in your esteem to which none can pretend a better title. Poetry, in its nature, is sacred to the good and great; the relation between them is reciprocal, and they are ever propitious to it. It is the privilege of poetry to address to them, and it is their prerogative alone to give it protection.

This received maxim is a general apology for all writers who consecrate their labors to great men; but I could wish at this time, that this address were exempted from the common pretense of all dedications; and that I can distinguish your Lordship even among the most deserving, so this offering might become remarkable by some particular instance of respect, which should assure your Lordship, that I am, with all due sense of your extreme worthiness and humanity, my Lord, your Lordship's most obedient, and most obliged humble servant,

Will. Congreve.

The Way of the World

Characters

Character	Actor
FAINALL, *in love with Mrs.*[a] *Marwood*	MR. BETTERTON
MIRABELL, *in love with Mrs. Millamant*	MR. VERBRUGGEN
WITWOUD } *followers of Mrs. Millamant*	MR. BOWEN
PETULANT } *followers of Mrs. Millamant*	MR. BOWMAN
SIR WILFULL WITWOUD, *half brother to Witwoud and nephew to Lady Wishfort*	MR. UNDERHILL
WAITWELL, *servant to Mirabell*	MR. BRIGHT
LADY WISHFORT, *enemy to Mirabell for having falsely pretended love to her*	MRS. LEIGH
MRS. MILLAMANT, *a fine lady, niece to Lady Wishfort, and loves Mirabell*	MRS. BRACEGIRDLE
MRS. MARWOOD, *friend to Mr. Fainall, and likes Mirabell*	MRS. BARRY
MRS. FAINALL, *daughter to Lady Wishfort and wife to Fainall, formerly friend to Mirabell*	MRS. BOWMAN
FOIBLE, *woman to Lady Wishfort*	MRS. WILLIS
MINCING, *woman to Mrs. Millamant*	MRS. PRINCE
[BETTY, *servant in a chocolate-house*]	
[PEG, *servant to Lady Wishfort*]	
Dancers, Footmen, and Attendants	

Scene: London
The time equal to that of the presentation.

[a] "mistress"—usual title for women, married or not

PROLOGUE

Spoken by Mr. Betterton

Of those few fools who with ill stars are cursed,
Sure scribbling fools, called poets, fare the worst;
For they're a sort of fools which Fortune makes,
And after she has made 'em fools, forsakes.
With Nature's oafs 'tis quite a different case,
For Fortune favors all her idiot-race;
In her own nest the cuckoo-eggs [e] we find,
O'er which she broods to hatch the changeling-kind.[f]
No portion for her own she has to spare,
So much she dotes on her adopted care.
   Poets are bubbles,[g] by the town drawn in,
Suffered at first some trifling stakes to win;
But what unequal hazards do they run!
Each time they write they venture all they've won;
The squire that's buttered [h] still, is sure to be undone.
This author heretofore has found your favor,
But pleads no merit from his past behavior;
To build on that might prove a vain presumption,
Should grants to poets made admit resumption; [i]
And in Parnassus he must lose his seat,
If that be found a forfeited estate.
   He owns, with toil he wrought the following scenes,
But, if they're naught, ne'er spare him for his pains;
Damn him the more; have no commiseration
For dullness on mature deliberation.
He swears he'll not resent one hissed-off scene,
Nor, like those peevish wits, his play maintain,
Who, to assert their sense, your taste arraign.

[e] the cuckoo lays its eggs in other birds' nests [f] (1) one child secretly put in the place of another (2) an idiot [g] dupes [h] gambles all his stakes on one throw [i] i.e., capable of being withdrawn

Some plot we think he has, and some new thought;
Some humor, too, no farce—but that's a fault.
Satire, he thinks, you ought not to expect;
For so reformed a town who dares correct?
To please this time has been his sole pretense;
He'll not instruct, lest it should give offense.
Should he by chance a knave or fool expose,
That hurts none here; sure, here are none of those.
In short, our play shall (with your leave to show it)
Give you one instance of a passive poet,
Who to your judgments yields all resignation;
So save or damn after your own discretion.

ACT I

Scene I: A chocolate-house

Mirabell *and* Fainall [*rising from cards*].* Betty *waiting.*

Mirabell. You are a fortunate man, Mr. Fainall.
Fainall. Have we done?
Mirabell. What you please. I'll play on to entertain you.
Fainall. No, I'll give you your revenge another time, when you are not so indifferent; you are thinking of something else now, and play too negligently. The coldness of a losing gamester lessens the pleasure of the winner. I'd no more play with a man that slighted his ill fortune than I'd make love to a woman who undervalued the loss of her reputation.
Mirabell. You have a taste extremely delicate, and are for refining on your pleasures.
Fainall. Prithee, why so reserved? Something has put you out of humor.
Mirabell. Not at all. I happen to be grave today, and you are gay; that's all.
Fainall. Confess, Millamant and you quarreled last night after I left you; my fair cousin has some humors[j] that would tempt the patience of a stoic. What, some coxcomb came in, and was well received by her, while you were by?

* Stage directions not in brackets appeared in original texts. Those in brackets were added by later editors.

[j] moods

Mirabell. Witwoud and Petulant; and what was worse, her aunt, your wife's mother, my evil genius; or to sum up all in her own name, my old Lady Wishfort came in.

Fainall. Oh, there it is then! She has a lasting passion for you, and with reason. What, then my wife was there?

Mirabell. Yes, and Mrs. Marwood, and three or four more, whom I never saw before. Seeing me, they all put on their grave faces, whispered one another; then complained aloud of the vapors[k] and after fell into a profound silence.

Fainall. They had a mind to be rid of you.

Mirabell. For which reason I resolved not to stir. At last the good old lady broke through her painful taciturnity with an invective against long visits. I would not[l] have understood her, but Millamant joining in the argument, I rose, and with a constrained smile, told her I thought nothing was so easy as to know when a visit began to be troublesome. She reddened, and I withdrew without expecting[m] her reply.

Fainall. You were to blame to resent what she spoke only in compliance with her aunt.

Mirabell. She is more mistress of herself than to be under the necessity of such a resignation.

Fainall. What! though half her fortune depends upon her marrying with my lady's approbation?

Mirabell. I was then in such a humor that I should have been better pleased if she had been less discreet.

Fainall. Now I remember, I wonder not they were weary of you; last night was one of their cabal nights. They have 'em three times a week, and meet by turns at one another's apartments, where they come together like the coroner's inquest, to sit upon the murdered reputations of the week. You and I are excluded, and it was once proposed that all the male sex should be excepted; but somebody moved that, to avoid scandal, there might be one man of the community, upon which motion Witwoud and Petulant were enrolled members.

Mirabell. And who may have been the foundress of this sect? My Lady Wishfort, I warrant, who publishes her detestation of mankind, and, full of the vigor of fifty-five, declares for a friend and ratafia;[n] and let posterity shift for itself, she'll breed no more.

Fainall. The discovery of your sham addresses to her, to

[k] the blues [l] i.e., pretended not to understand [m] awaiting [n] a liqueur

conceal your love to her niece, has provoked this separation; had you dissembled better, things might have continued in the state of nature.

Mirabell. I did as much as man could, with any reasonable conscience; I proceeded to the very last act of flattery with her, and was guilty of a song in her commendation. Nay, I got a friend to put her into a lampoon and compliment her with the imputation of an affair with a young fellow, which I carried so far that I told her the malicious town took notice that she was grown fat of a sudden; and when she lay in a dropsy, persuaded her she was reported to be in labor. The devil's in't, if an old woman is to be flattered further, unless a man should endeavor downright personally to debaunch her; and that my virtue forbade me. But for the discovery of this amour I am indebted to your friend, or your wife's friend, Mrs. Marwood.

Fainall. What should provoke her to be your enemy, unless she has made you advances which you have slighted? Women do not easily forgive omissions of that nature.

Mirabell. She was always civil to me till of late. I confess I am not one of those coxcombs who are apt to interpret a woman's good manners to her prejudice, and think that she who does not refuse 'em everything, can refuse 'em nothing.

Fainall. You are a gallant man, Mirabell; and though you may have cruelty enough not to satisfy a lady's longings, you have too much generosity not to be tender of her honor. Yet you speak with an indifference which seems to be affected and confesses you are conscious of a negligence.

Mirabell. You pursue the argument with a distrust that seems to be unaffected and confesses you are conscious of a concern for which the lady is more indebted to you than is your wife.

Fainall. Fie, fie, friend! If you grow censorious I must leave you. I'll look upon the gamesters in the next room.

Mirabell. Who are they?

Fainall. Petulant and Witwoud. [*To* Betty.] Bring me some chocolate. [*Exit* Fainall.]

Mirabell. Betty, what says your clock?

Betty. Turned of the last canonical hour,[o] sir.
Mirabell. How pertinently the jade answers me! (*Looking on his watch.*) Ha? almost one o'clock! Oh, y'are come!

Enter a Servant.

Well, is the grand affair over? You have been something[p] tedious.
Servant. Sir, there's such coupling at Pancras[q] that they stand behind one another, as 'twere in a country dance. Ours was the last couple to lead up, and no hopes appearing of dispatch—besides, the parson growing hoarse, we were afraid his lungs would have failed before it came to our turn; so we drove round to Duke's Place[r] and there they were riveted in a trice.
Mirabell. So, so! You are sure they are married?
Servant. Married and bedded, sir; I am witness.
Mirabell. Have you the certificate?
Servant. Here it is, sir.
Mirabell. Has the tailor brought Waitwell's clothes home, and the new liveries?
Servant. Yes, sir.
Mirabell. That's well. Do you go home again, d'ye hear, and adjourn the consummation till further orders. Bid Waitwell shake his ears, and Dame Partlet[s] rustle up her feathers and meet me at one o'clock by Rosamond's Pond,[t] that I may see her before she returns to her lady; and as you tender[u] your ears be secret.
[*Exit* Servant.]

Re-enter Fainall.

Fainall. Joy of your success, Mirabell; you look pleased.
Mirabell. Aye; I have been engaged in a matter of some sort of mirth, which is not yet ripe for discovery. I am glad this is not a cabal night. I wonder, Fainall, that you, who are married and of consequence should be discreet, will suffer your wife to be of such a party.
Fainall. Faith, I am not jealous. Besides, most who are engaged are women and relations; and for the men, they are of a kind too contemptible to give scandal.

[o] past noon, last hour for legal marriages [p] somewhat [q] St. Pancras Church, where marriages could be celebrated at any time without a special license [r] location of St. James Church, where marriages were also performed without a special license [s] wife of Chantecleer, in the tale of the cock and the fox [t] in St. James Park [u] i.e., value

Mirabell. I am of another opinion. The greater the coxcomb, always the more the scandal; for a woman who is not a fool, can have but one reason for associating with a man who is one.

Fainall. Are you jealous as often as you see Witwoud entertained by Millamant?

Mirabell. Of her understanding I am, if not of her person.

Fainall. You do her wrong; for, to give her her due, she has wit.

Mirabell. She has beauty enough to make any man think so; and complaisance enough not to contradict him who shall tell her so.

Fainall. For a passionate lover, methinks you are a man somewhat too discerning in the failings of your mistress.

Mirabell. And for a discerning man, somewhat too passionate a lover; for I like her with all her faults—nay, like her for her faults. Her follies are so natural, or so artful, that they become her; and those affectations which in another woman would be odious, serve but to make her more agreeable. I'll tell thee, Fainall, she once used me with that insolence, that in revenge I took her to pieces, sifted her, and separated her failings; I studied 'em, and got 'em by rote. The catalogue was so large that I was not without hopes one day or other to hate her heartily; to which end I so used myself to think of 'em that at length, contrary to my design and expectation, they gave me every hour less and less disturbance, till in a few days it became habitual to me to remember 'em without being displeased. They are now grown as familiar to me as my own frailties, and, in all probability, in a little time longer I shall like 'em as well.

Fainall. Marry her, marry her! Be half as well acquainted with her charms as you are with her defects, and my life on't, you are your own man again.

Mirabell. Say you so?

Fainall. Aye, aye, I have experience: I have a wife, and so forth.

Enter Messenger.

Messenger. Is one Squire Witwoud here?

Betty. Yes, what's your business?

Messenger. I have a letter for him from his brother Sir

Wilfull, which I am charged to deliver into his own hands.

Betty. He's in the next room, friend—that way.

[*Exit* Messenger.]

Mirabell. What, is the chief of that noble family in town —Sir Wilfull Witwoud?

Fainall. He is expected today. Do you know him?

Mirabell. I have seen him; he promises to be an extraordinary person. I think you have the honor to be related to him.

Fainall. Yes; he is half-brother to this Witwoud by a former wife, who was sister to my Lady Wishfort, my wife's mother. If you marry Millamant, you must call cousins too.

Mirabell. I had rather be his relation than his acquaintance.

Fainall. He comes to town in order to equip himself for travel.

Mirabell. For travel! Why, the man that I mean is above forty.

Fainall. No matter for that; 'tis for the honor of England, that all Europe should know we have blockheads of all ages.

Mirabell. I wonder there is not an act of parliament to save the credit of the nation, and prohibit the exportation of fools.

Fainall. By no means; 'tis better as 'tis. 'Tis better to trade with a little loss, than to be quite eaten up with being overstocked.

Mirabell. Pray, are the follies of this knight-errant and those of the squire his brother anything related?

Fainall. Not at all; Witwoud grows by the knight, like a medlar[v] grafted on a crab.[w] One will melt in your mouth, and t'other set your teeth on edge; one is all pulp, and the other all core.

Mirabell. So one will be rotten before he be ripe, and the other will be rotten without ever being ripe at all.

Fainall. Sir Wilfull is an odd mixture of bashfulness and obstinacy. But when he's drunk, he's as loving as the monster in *The Tempest,*[x] and much after the same manner. To give t'other his due, he has something of good nature, and does not always want[y] wit.

Mirabell. Not always; but as often as his memory fails

[v] a soft fruit [w] crab apple [x] Caliban (or his sister, Sycorax, in the Dryden-Davenant version of *The Tempest,* 1670) [y] lack

him, and his commonplace[z] of comparisons. He is a fool with a good memory and some few scraps of other folks' wit. He is one whose conversation can never be approved; yet it is now and then to be endured. He has indeed one good quality—he is not exceptious; for he so passionately affects the reputation of understanding raillery, that he will construe an affront into a jest, and call downright rudeness and ill language, satire and fire.

Fainall. If you have a mind to finish his picture, you have an opportunity to do it at full length. Behold the original!

Enter Witwoud.

Witwoud. Afford me your compassion, my dears! Pity me, Fainall! Mirabell, pity me!

Mirabell. I do, from my soul.

Fainall. Why, what's the matter?

Witwoud. No letters for me, Betty?

Betty. Did not the messenger bring you one but now, sir?

Witwoud. Aye, but no other?

Betty. No, sir.

Witwoud. That's hard, that's very hard. A messenger, a mule, a beast of burden! He has brought me a letter from the fool my brother, as heavy as a panegyric in a funeral sermon, or a copy of commendatory verses from one poet to another. And what's worse, 'tis as sure a forerunner of the author as an epistle dedicatory.

Mirabell. A fool—and your brother, Witwoud!

Witwoud. Aye, aye, my half-brother. My half-brother he is, no nearer, upon honor.

Mirabell. Then 'tis possible he may be but half a fool.

Witwoud. Good, good, Mirabell, *le drôle!*[a] Good, good; hang him, don't let's talk of him. Fainall, how does your lady? Gad, I say anything in the world to get this fellow out of my head. I beg pardon that I should ask a man of pleasure and the town, a question at once so foreign and domestic. But I talk like an old maid at a marriage; I don't know what I say. But she's the best woman in the world.

Fainall. 'Tis well you don't know what you say, or else

[z] a commonplace book (a collection of saws, aphorisms, etc.)
[a] the wit

your commendation would go near to make me either vain or jealous.

Witwoud. No man in town lives well with a wife but but Fainall. Your judgment, Mirabell?

Mirabell. You had better step and ask his wife if you would be credibly informed.

Witwoud. Mirabell?

Mirabell. Aye?

Witwoud. My dear, I ask ten thousand pardons—gad, I have forgot what I was going to say to you!

Mirabell. I thank you heartily, heartily.

Witwoud. No, but prithee, excuse me—my memory is such a memory.

Mirabell. Have a care of such apologies, Witwoud; for I never knew a fool but he affected to complain either of the spleen[b] or his memory.

Fainall. What have you done with Petulant?

Witwoud. He's reckoning his money—my money it was. I have no luck today.

Fainall. You may allow him to win of you at play, for you are sure to be too hard for him at repartee. Since you monopolize the wit that is between you, the fortune must be his, of course.

Mirabell. I don't find that Petulant confesses the superiority of wit to be your talent, Witwoud.

Witwoud. Come, come, you are malicious now, and would breed debates. Petulant's my friend, and a very honest fellow, and a very pretty fellow, and has a smattering—faith and troth, a pretty deal of an odd sort of a small wit. Nay, I'll do him justice. I'm his friend, I won't wrong him. And if he had any judgment in the world, he would not be altogether contemptible. Come, come, don't detract from the merits of my friend.

Fainall. You don't take your friend to be over-nicely bred?

Witwoud. No, no, hang him, the rogue has no manners at all, that I must own—no more breeding than a bumbaily[c] that I grant you—'tis pity, faith; the fellow has fire and life.

Mirabell. What, courage?

Witwoud. Hum, faith I don't know as to that; I can't say as to that. Yes, faith, in a controversy, he'll contradict anybody.

[b] ill humor [c] bailiff (contemptuous)

Mirabell. Though 'twere a man whom he feared, or a woman whom he loved?

Witwoud. Well, well, he does not always think before he speaks—we have all our failings. You're too hard upon him—you are, faith. Let me excuse him. I can defend most of his faults, except one or two. One he has, that's the truth on't; if he were my brother, I could not acquit him. That, indeed, I could wish were otherwise.

Mirabell. Aye, marry, what's that, Witwoud?

Witwoud. O pardon me! Expose the infirmities of my friend? No, my dear, excuse me there.

Fainall. What! I warrant he's unsincere, or 'tis some such trifle.

Witwoud. No, no, what if he be? 'Tis no matter for that; his wit will excuse that. A wit should no more be sincere than a woman constant; one argues a decay of parts, as t'other of beauty.

Mirabell. Maybe you think him too positive?

Witwoud. No, no, his being positive is an incentive to argument, and keeps up conversation.

Fainall. Too illiterate?

Witwoud. That? That's his happiness; his want of learning gives him the more opportunities to show his natural parts.

Mirabell. He wants words?

Witwoud. Aye, but I like him for that, now; for his want of words gives me the pleasure very often to explain his meaning.

Fainall. He's impudent?

Witwoud. No, that's not it.

Mirabell. Vain?

Witwoud. No.

Mirabell. What! He speaks unseasonable truths sometimes, because he has not wit enough to invent an evasion?

Witwoud. Truths! ha! ha! ha! No, no; since you will have it—I mean, he never speaks truth at all—that's all. He will lie like a chambermaid, or a woman of quality's porter. Now, that is a fault.

Enter Coachman.

Coachman. Is Master Petulant here, mistress?

Betty. Yes.

Coachman. Three gentlewomen in the coach would speak with him.

Fainall. O brave Petulant, three!
Betty. I'll tell him.
Coachman. You must bring two dishes of chocolate and a glass of cinnamon water.[d]
[*Exeunt* Betty *and* Coachman.]
Witwoud. That should be for two fasting strumpets, and a bawd troubled with wind. Now you may know what the three are.
Mirabell. You are very free with your friend's acquaintance.
Witwoud. Aye, aye, friendship without freedom is as dull as love without enjoyment, or wine without toasting. But to tell you a secret, these are trulls whom he allows coach-hire, and something more by the week, to call on him once a day at public places.
Mirabell. How!
Witwoud. You shall see he won't go to 'em, because there's no more company here to take notice of him. Why, this is nothing to what he used to do; before he found out this way, I have known him call for himself.
Fainall. Call for himself! What dost thou mean?
Witwoud. Mean? Why, he would slip you out of this chocolate-house just when you had been talking to him; as soon as your back was turned—whip, he was gone—then trip to his lodging, clap on a hood and scarf and a mask, slap into a hackney coach, and drive hither to the to the door again in a trice, where he would send in for himself, that is, I mean—call for himself, wait for himself; nay, and what's more, not finding himself, sometimes leave a letter for himself.
Mirabell. I confess this is something extraordinary. I believe he waits for himself now, he is so long a-coming. Oh! I ask his pardon.

Enter Petulant [*and* Betty.]

Betty. Sir, the coach stays. [*Exit.*]
Petulant. Well, well; I come. 'Sbud,[e] a man had as good be a professed midwife as a professed whoremaster, at this rate! To be knocked up and raised at all hours, and in all places! Pox on 'em, I won't come! D'ye hear, tell 'em I won't come. Let 'em snivel and cry their hearts out.
Fainall. You are very cruel, Petulant.

[d] a cordial [e] contraction of s'bodikins, i.e., God's dear body

Petulant. All's one, let it pass. I have a humor to be cruel.

Mirabell. I hope they are not persons of condition[f] that you use at this rate.

Petulant. Condition! Condition's a dried fig if I am not in humor! By this hand, if they were your—a—a—your what-d'ye-call-'ems themselves, they must wait or rub off,[g] if I want appetite.

Mirabell. What-d'ye-call-'ems! What are they, Witwoud?

Witwoud. Empresses, my dear: by your what-d'ye-call-'ems he means sultana queens.[h]

Petulant. Aye, Roxolanas.[i]

Mirabell. Cry you mercy.

Fainall. Witwoud says they are—

Petulant. What does he say th' are?

Witwoud. I? Fine ladies, I say.

Petulant. Pass on, Witwoud. Hark'ee, by this light, his relations—two co-heiresses, his cousins, and an old aunt who loves caterwauling better than a conventicle.

Witwoud. Ha, ha, ha! I had a mind to see how the rogue would come off. Ha, ha, ha! Gad, I can't be angry with him if he had said they were my mother and my sisters.

Mirabell. No?

Witwoud. No; the rogue's wit and readiness of invention charm me. Dear Petulant!

[*Re-enter Betty.*]

Betty. They are gone, sir, in great anger.

Petulant. Enough; let 'em trundle. Anger helps complexion—saves paint.

Fainall. This continence is all dissembled; this is in order to have something to brag of the next time he makes court to Millamant and swear he has abandoned the whole sex for her sake.

Mirabell. Have you not left off your impudent pretensions there yet? I shall cut your throat some time or other, Petulant, about that business.

Petulant. Aye, aye, let that pass—there are other throats to be cut.

Mirabell. Meaning mine, sir?

Petulant. Not I—I mean nobody—I know nothing. But there are uncles and nephews in the world—and they may be rivals—what then? All's one for that.

Mirabell. How! Hark'ee, Petulant, come hither. Explain,

[f] rank [g] leave [h] i.e., prostitutes [i] wife of a Turkish sultan

or I shall call your interpreter.

Petulant. Explain? I know nothing. Why, you have an uncle, have you not, lately come to town, and lodges by my Lady Wishfort's?

Mirabell. True.

Petulant. Why, that's enough—you and he are not friends; and if he should marry and have a child you may be disinherited, ha?

Mirabell. Where hast thou stumbled upon all this truth?

Petulant. All's one for that; why, then, say I know something.

Mirabell. Come, thou art an honest fellow, Petulant, and shalt make love to my mistress; thou sha't, faith. What hast thou heard of my uncle?

Petulant. I? Nothing, I. If throats are to be cut, let swords clash! snug's the word; I shrug and am silent.

Mirabell. Oh, raillery, raillery! Come, I know thou art in the women's secrets. What, you're a cabalist; I know you stayed at Millamant's last night after I went. Was there any mention made of my uncle or me? Tell me. If thou hadst but good nature equal to thy wit, Petulant, Tony Witwoud, who is now thy competitor in fame, would show as dim by [j] thee as a dead whiting's eye by a pearl of orient; [k] he would no more be seen by thee than Mercury [l] is by the sun.
Come, I'm sure thou wo't [m] tell me.

Petulant. If I do, will you grant me common sense then, for the future?

Mirabell. Faith, I'll do what I can for thee, and I'll pray that Heaven may grant it thee in the meantime.

Petulant. Well, hark'ee. [Mirabell *and* Petulant *talk apart.*]

Fainall [*to* Witwoud]. Petulant and you both will find Mirabell as warm a rival as a lover.

Witwoud. Pshaw! pshaw! That she laughs at Petulant is plain. And for my part, but that it is almost a fashion to admire her, I should—hark'ee—to tell you a secret, but let it go no further—between friends, I shall never break my heart for her.

Fainall. How!

Witwoud. She's handsome; but she's a sort of an uncertain woman.

Fainall. I thought you had died for her.

[j] beside [k] lustrous pearl [l] Mercury is too close to the sun to be visible [m] will

Witwoud. Umh—no—

Fainall. She has wit.

Witwoud. 'Tis what she will hardly allow anybody else. Now, demme![n] I should hate that, if she were as hand some as Cleopatra. Mirabell is not so sure of her as he thinks for.

Fainall. Why do you think so?

Witwoud. We stayed pretty late there last night, and heard something of an uncle to Mirabell, who is lately come to town—and is between him and the best part of his estate. Mirabell and he are at some distance,[o] as my Lady Wishfort has been told; and you know she hates Mirabell worse than a Quaker hates a parrot,[p] or than a fishmonger hates a hard frost. Whether this uncle has seen Mrs. Millamant or not, I cannot say, but there were items of such a treaty being in embryo; and if it should come to life, poor Mirabell would be in some sort unfortunately fobbed,[q] i'faith.

Fainall. 'Tis impossible Millamant should hearken to it.

Witwoud. Faith, my dear, I can't tell; she's a woman, and a kind of humorist.[r]

Mirabell [*to* Petulant]. And this is the sum of what you could collect last night?

Petulant. The quintessence. Maybe Witwoud knows more, he stayed longer. Besides, they never mind him; they say anything before him.

Mirabell. I thought you had been the greatest favorite.

Petulant. Aye, tête-à-tête, but not in public, because I make remarks.

Mirabell. Do you?

Petulant. Aye, aye; pox, I'm malicious, man! Now, he's soft, you know; they are not in awe of him—the fellow's well-bred; he's what you call a—what-d'ye-call-'em, a fine gentleman. But he's silly withal.[s]

Mirabell. I thank you. I know as much as my curiosity requires. Fainall, are you for the Mall?[t]

Fainall. Aye, I'll take a turn before dinner.

Witwoud. Aye, we'll all walk in the Park; the ladies talked of being there.

Mirabell. I thought you were obliged to watch for your brother Sir Wilfull's arrival.

Witwoud. No, no; he comes to his aunt's, my Lady Wish-

[n] damn me [o] not on good terms [p] presumably for swearing [q] cheated [r] capricious person [s] nevertheless [t] Pall Mall, a fashionable walk in St. James Park

fort. Pox on him! I shall be troubled with him, too; what shall I do with the fool?

Petulant. Beg him for his estate, that I may beg you afterwards, and so have but one trouble with you both.

Witwoud. Oh, rare Petulant! Thou art as quick as fire in a frosty morning. Thou shalt to the Mall with us, and we'll be very severe.

Petulant. Enough! I'm in a humor to be severe.

Mirabell. Are you? Pray then, walk by yourselves; let not us be accessory to your putting the ladies out of countenance with your senseless ribaldry, which you roar out aloud as often as they pass by you; and when you have made a handsome woman blush, then you think you have been severe.

Petulant. What, what? Then let 'em either show their innocence by not understanding what they hear, or else show their discretion by not hearing what they would not be thought to understand.

Mirabell. But hast not thou then sense enough to know that thou oughtest to be most ashamed thyself when thou hast put another out of countenance?

Petulant. Not I, by this hand! I always take blushing either for a sign of guilt or ill breeding.

Mirabell. I confess you ought to think so. You are in the right, that you may plead the error of your judgment in defense of your practice.

Where modesty's ill manners, 'tis but fit
That impudence and malice pass for wit.

Exeunt.

ACT II

Scene I: St. James's Park

Enter Mrs. Fainall *and* Mrs. Marwood.

Mrs. Fainall. Aye, aye, dear Marwood, if we will be happy, we must find the means in ourselves and among ourselves. Men are ever in extremes—either doting or averse. While they are lovers, if they have fire and sense, their jealousies are insupportable; and when they cease to love (we ought to think at least) they loathe; they look upon us with horror and distaste; they meet us like the ghosts of what we were, and as from such, fly from us.

Mrs. Marwood. True, 'tis an unhappy circumstance of life that love should ever die before us, and that the man so often should outlive the lover. But say what you will, 'tis better to be left than never to have been loved. To pass our youth in dull indifference, to refuse the sweets of life because they once must leave us, is as preposterous as to wish to have been born old because we one day must be old. For my part, my youth may wear and waste, but it shall never rust in my possession.

Mrs. Fainall. Then it seems you dissemble an aversion to mankind only in compliance to my mother's humor?

Mrs. Marwood. Certainly. To be free; I have no taste of those insipid dry discourses with which our sex of force must entertain themselves apart from men. We may affect endearments to each other, profess eternal friendships, and seem to dote like lovers; but 'tis not in our natures long to persevere. Love will resume his empire in our breasts, and every heart, or soon or late, receive and readmit him as its lawful tyrant.

Mrs. Fainall. Bless me, how have I been deceived? Why, you profess a libertine.

Mrs. Marwood. You see my friendship by my freedom. Come, be as sincere; acknowledge that your sentiments agree with mine.

Mrs. Fainall. Never!

Mrs. Marwood. You hate mankind?

Mrs. Fainall. Heartily, inveterately.

Mrs. Marwood. Your husband?

Mrs. Fainall. Most transcendently; aye, though I say it, meritoriously.

Mrs. Marwood. Give me your hand upon it.

Mrs. Fainall. There.

Mrs. Marwood. I join with you; what I have said has been to try you.

Mrs. Fainall. Is it possible? Dost thou hate those vipers, men?

Mrs. Marwood. I have done hating 'em, and am now come to despise 'em; the next thing I have to do is eternally to forget 'em.

Mrs. Fainall. There spoke the spirit of an Amazon, a Penthesilea.[u]

Mrs. Marwood. And yet I am thinking sometimes to carry my aversion further.

Mrs. Fainall. How?

Mrs. Marwood. Faith, by marrying; if I could but find one that loved me very well and would be thoroughly sensible of ill usage, I think I should do myself the violence of undergoing the ceremony.

Mrs. Fainall. You would not make him a cuckold?

Mrs. Marwood. No; but I'd make him believe I did, and that's as bad.

Mrs. Fainall. Why had not you as good do it?

Mrs. Marwood. Oh, if he should ever discover it, he would then know the worst and be out of his pain; but I would have him ever to continue upon the rack of fear and jealousy.

Mrs. Fainall. Ingenious mischief! Would thou wert married to Mirabell.

Mrs. Marwood. Would I were!

Mrs. Fainall. You change color.

Mrs. Marwood. Because I hate him.

Mrs. Fainall. So do I, but I can hear him named. But what reason have you to hate him in particular?

Mrs. Marwood. I never loved him; he is, and always was, insufferably proud.

Mrs. Fainall. By the reason you give for your aversion, one would think it dissembled; for you have laid a fault to his charge, of which his enemies must acquit him.

Mrs. Marwood. Oh, then it seems you are one of his favorable enemies! Methinks you look a little pale—and now you flush again.

Mrs. Fainall. Do I? I think I am a little sick o' the sudden.

Mrs. Marwood. What ails you?

Mrs. Fainall. My husband. Don't you see him? He turned short upon me unawares, and has almost overcome me.

Enter Fainall *and* Mirabell.

Mrs. Marwood. Ha, ha, ha! He comes opportunely for you.

Mrs. Fainall. For you, for he has brought Mirabell with him.

[u] queen of the Amazons

Fainall [*to* Mrs. Fainall]. My dear.

Mrs. Fainall. My soul.

Fainall. You don't look well today, child.

Mrs. Fainall. D'ye think so?

Mirabell. He is the only man that does, madam.

Mrs. Fainall. The only man that would tell me so, at least, and the only man from whom I could hear it without mortification.

Fainall. Oh, my dear, I am satisfied of your tenderness; I know you cannot resent anything from me, especially what is an effect of my concern.

Mrs. Fainall. Mr. Mirabell, my mother interrupted you in a pleasant relation last night; I would fain hear it out.

Mirabell. The persons concerned in that affair have yet a tolerable reputation. I am afraid Mr. Fainall will be censorious.

Mrs. Fainall. He has a humor more prevailing than his curiosity, and will willingly dispense with the hearing of one scandalous story, to avoid giving an occasion to make another by being seen to walk with his wife. This way, Mr. Mirabell, and I dare promise you will oblige us both. *Exeunt* Mrs. Fainall *and* Mirabell.

Fainall. Excellent creature! Well, sure if I should live to be rid of my wife, I should be a miserable man.

Mrs. Marwood. Aye?

Fainall. For having only that one hope, the accomplishment of it, of consequence, must put an end to all my hopes; and what a wretch is he who must survive his hopes! Nothing remains when that day comes but to sit down and weep like Alexander when he wanted other worlds to conquer.

Mrs. Marwood. Will you not follow 'em?

Fainall. Faith, I think not.

Mrs. Marwood. Pray, let us; I have a reason.

Fainall. You are not jealous?

Mrs. Marwood. Of whom?

Fainall. Of Mirabell.

Mrs. Marwood. If I am, is it inconsistent with my love to you that I am tender [v] of your honor?

Fainall. You would intimate, then, as if there were a fellow-feeling between my wife and him.

Mrs. Marwood. I think she does not hate him to that degree she would be thought.

Fainall. But he, I fear, is too insensible.

[v] careful

Mrs. Marwood. It may be you are deceived.

Fainall. It may be so. I do not now begin to apprehend it.

Mrs. Marwood. What?

Fainall. That I have been deceived, madam, and you are false.

Mrs. Marwood. That I am false! What mean you?

Fainall. To let you know I see through all your little arts. Come, you both love him, and both have equally dissembled your aversion. Your mutual jealousies of one another have made you clash till you have both struck fire. I have seen the warm confession reddening on your cheeks and sparkling from your eyes.

Mrs. Marwood. You do me wrong.

Fainall. I do not. 'Twas for my ease to oversee[w] and willfully neglect the gross advances made him by my wife, that by permitting her to be engaged, I might continue unsuspected in my pleasures and take you oftener to my arms in full security. But could you think, because the nodding husband would not wake, that e'er the watchful lover slept?

Mrs. Marwood. And wherewithal can you reproach me?

Fainall. With infidelity, with loving another—with love of Mirabell.

Mrs. Marwood. 'Tis false! I challenge you to show an instance that can confirm your groundless accusation. I hate him!

Fainall. And wherefore do you hate him? He is insensible, and your resentment follows his neglect. An instance. The injuries you have done him are a proof—your interposing in his love. What cause had you to make discoveries of his pretended passion? To undeceive the credulous aunt, and be the officious obstacle of his match with Millamant?

Mrs. Marwood. My obligations to my lady urged me. I had professed a friendship to her, and could not see her easy nature so abused by that dissembler.

Fainall. What, was it conscience then? Professed a friendship! Oh, the pious friendships of the female sex!

Mrs. Marwood. More tender, more sincere, and more enduring than all the vain and empty vows of men, whether professing love to us or mutual faith to one another.

[w] overlook

Fainall. Ha, ha, ha! You are my wife's friend, too.

Mrs. Marwood. Shame and ingratitude! Do you reproach me? You, you upbraid me? Have I been false to her, through strict fidelity to you, and sacrificed my friendship to keep my love inviolate? And have you the baseness to charge me with the guilt, unmindful of the merit? To you it should be meritorious that I have been vicious; and do you reflect that guilt upon me which should lie buried in your bosom?

Fainall. You misinterpret my reproof. I meant but to remind you of the slight account you once could make of strictest ties when set in competition with your love to me.

Mrs. Marwood. 'Tis false; you urged it with deliberate malice! 'Twas spoke in scorn, and I never will forgive it.

Fainall. Your guilt, not your resentment, begets your rage. If yet you loved, you could forgive a jealousy; but you are stung to find you are discovered.

Mrs. Marwood. It shall be all discovered. You too shall be discovered; be sure you shall. I can but be exposed. If I do it myself, I shall prevent[x] your baseness.

Fainall. Why, what will you do?

Mrs. Marwood. Disclose it to your wife; own what has passed between us.

Fainall. Frenzy!

Mrs. Marwood. By all my wrongs I'll do't! I'll publish to the world the injuries you have done me, both in my fame[y] and fortune! With both I trusted you—you bankrupt in honor, as indigent of wealth.

Fainall. Your fame I have preserved. Your fortune has been bestowed as the prodigality of your love would have it, in pleasures which we both have shared. Yet, had not you been false, I had ere this repaid it. 'Tis true. Had you permitted Mirabell with Millamant to have stolen their marriage, my lady had been incensed beyond all means of reconcilement; Millamant had forfeited the moiety[z] of her fortune, which then would have descended to my wife—and wherefore did I marry but to make lawful prize of a rich widow's wealth, and squander it on love and you?

Mrs. Marwood. Deceit and frivolous pretense!

Fainall. Death, am I not married? What's pretense? Am I not imprisoned, fettered? Have I not a wife? Nay, a

[x] anticipate [y] reputation [z] half

wife that was a widow, a young widow, a handsome widow; and would be again a widow, but that I have a heart of proof,[a] and something of a constitution to bustle through the ways of wedlock and this world! Will you yet be reconciled to truth and me?

Mrs. Marwood. Impossible. Truth and you are inconsistent—I hate you, and shall forever.

Fainall. For loving you?

Mrs. Marwood. I loathe the name of love after such usage; and next to the guilt with which you would asperse me, I scorn you most. Farewell!

Fainall. Nay, we must not part thus.

Mrs. Marwood. Let me go.

Fainall. Come, I'm sorry.

Mrs. Marwood. I care not—let me go—break my hands, do! I'd leave 'em to get loose.

Fainall. I would not hurt you for the world. Have I no other hold to keep you here?

Mrs. Marwood. Well, I have deserved it all.

Fainall. You know I love you.

Mrs. Marwood. Poor dissembling! Oh, that—well, it is not yet—

Fainall. What? What is it not? What is it not yet? It is not yet too late—

Mrs. Marwood. No, it is not yet too late—I have that comfort.

Fainall. It is, to love another.

Mrs. Marwood. But not to loathe, detest, abhor mankind, myself, and the whole treacherous world.

Fainall. Nay, this is extravagance! Come, I ask your pardon—no tears—I was to blame, I could not love you and be easy in my doubts. Pray, forbear—I believe you; I'm convinced I've done you wrong, and any way, every way will make amends. I'll hate my wife yet more, damn her! I'll part with her, rob her of all she's worth, and we'll retire somewhere—anywhere—to another world. I'll marry thee—be pacified—'Sdeath,[b] they come! Hide your face, your tears. You have a mask; wear it a moment. This way, this way—be persuaded.

Exeunt.

Enter Mirabell *and* Mrs. Fainall.

Mrs. Fainall. They are here yet.

Mirabell. They are turning into the other walk.

Mrs. Fainall. While I only hated my husband, I could

[a] strength [b] God's death

bear to see him; but since I have despised him, he's too offensive.

Mirabell. Oh, you should hate with prudence.

Mrs. Fainall. Yes, for I have loved with indiscretion.

Mirabell. You should have just so much disgust for your husband as may be sufficient to make you relish your lover.

Mrs. Fainall. You have been the cause that I have loved without bounds, and would you set limits to that aversion of which you have been the occasion? Why did you make me marry this man?

Mirabell. Why do we daily commit disagreeable and dangerous actions? To save that idol, reputation. If the familiarities of our loves had produced that consequence of which you were apprehensive, where could you have fixed a father's name with credit but on a husband? I knew Fainall to be a man lavish of his morals, an interested and professing friend, a false and a designing lover, yet one whose wit and outward fair behavior have gained a reputation with the town enough to make that woman stand excused who has suffered herself to be won by his addresses. A better man ought not to have been sacrificed to the occasion, a worse had not answered to the purpose. When you are weary of him, you know your remedy.

Mrs. Fainall. I ought to stand in some degree of credit with you, Mirabell.

Mirabell. In justice to you, I have made you privy to my whole design, and put it in your power to ruin or advance my fortune.

Mrs. Fainall. Whom have you instructed to represent your pretended uncle?

Mirabell. Waitwell, my servant.

Mrs. Fainall. He is an humble servant[c] to Foible, my mother's woman, and may win her to your interest.

Mirabell. Care is taken for that—she is won and worn by this time. They were married this morning.

Mrs. Fainall. Who?

Mirabell. Waitwell and Foible. I would not tempt my servant to betray me by trusting him too far. If your mother, in hopes to ruin me, should consent to marry my pretended uncle, he might, like Mosca in *The Fox*,[d] stand upon terms,[e] so I made him sure beforehand.

[c] suitor [d] the wily servant in Ben Jonson's *Volpone* [e] i.e., threaten me with blackmail

Mrs. Fainall. So if my poor mother is caught in a contract,[f] you will discover the imposture betimes,[g] and release her by producing a certificate of her gallant's former marriage.

Mirabell. Yes, upon condition that she consent to my marriage with her niece, and surrender the moiety of her fortune in her possession.

Mrs. Fainall. She talked last night of endeavoring at a match between Millamant and your uncle.

Mirabell. That was by Foible's direction and my instruction, that she might seem to carry it more privately.

Mrs. Fainall. Well, I have an opinion of your success; for I believe my lady will do anything to get a husband; and when she has this which you have provided for her, I suppose she will submit to anything to get rid of him.

Mirabell. Yes, I think the good lady would marry anything that resembled a man, though 'twere no more than what a butler could pinch out of a napkin.

Mrs. Fainall. Female frailty! We must all come to it if we live to be old and feel the craving of a false appetite when the true is decayed.

Mirabell. An old woman's appetite is depraved like that of a girl—'tis the green sickness[h] of a second childhood, and, like the faint offer[i] of a latter spring, serves but to usher in the fall, and withers in an affected bloom.

Mrs. Fainall. Here's your mistress.

Enter Mrs. Millamant, Witwoud, *and* Mincing.

Mirabell. Here she comes, i'faith, full sail, with her fan spread and her streamers out, and a shoal of fools for tenders. Ha, no, I cry her mercy!

Mrs. Fainall. I see but one poor empty sculler, and he tows her woman after him.

Mirabell [*to* Mrs. Millamant]. You seem to be unattended, madam. You used to have the beau monde[j] throng after you, and a flock of gay fine perukes[k] hovering round you.

Witwoud. Like moths about a candle. I had like to have lost my comparison for want of breath.

Mrs. Millamant. Oh, I have denied myself airs today. I have walked as fast through the crowd—

Witwoud. As a favorite just disgraced, and with as few followers.

[f] of marriage [g] in time [h] love-sickness [i] attempt [j] the world of fashion [k] wigs, i.e., men of fashion

Mrs. Millamant. Dear Mr. Witwoud, truce with your similitudes; for I'm as sick of 'em—

Witwoud. As a physician of a good air. I cannot help it, madam, though 'tis against myself.

Mrs. Millamant. Yet again! Mincing, stand between me and his wit.

Witwoud. Do, Mrs. Mincing, like a screen before a great fire. I confess I do blaze today; I am too bright.

Mrs. Fainall. But, dear Millamant, why were you so long?

Mrs. Millamant. Long! Lord, have I not made violent haste? I have asked every living thing I met for you; I have inquired after you as after a new fashion.

Witwoud. Madam, truce with your similitudes. No, you met her husband, and did not ask him for her.

Mrs. Millamant. By your leave, Witwoud, that were like inquiring after an old fashion, to ask a husband for his wife.

Witwoud. Hum, a hit! a hit! A palpable hit! I confess it.

Mrs. Fainall. You were dressed before I came abroad.[l]

Mrs. Millamant. Aye, that's true. Oh, but then I had— Mincing, what had I? Why was I so long?

Mincing. O mem, your la'ship stayed to peruse a pecquet of letters.

Mrs. Millamant. Oh, aye, letters—I had letters—I am persecuted with letters—I hate letters. Nobody knows how to write letters—and yet one has 'em, one does not know why. They serve one to pin up one's hair.

Witwoud. Is that the way? Pray, madam, do you pin up your hair with all your letters? I find I must keep copies.

Mrs. Millamant. Only with those in verse, Mr. Witwoud; I never pin up my hair with prose. I think I tried once, Mincing.

Mincing. O mem, I shall never forget it.

Mrs. Millamant. Aye, poor Mincing tift and tift[m] all the morning.

Mincing. Till I had the cremp in my fingers, I'll vow, mem; and all to no purpose. But when your la'ship pins it up with poetry, it sits so pleasant the next day as anything, and is so pure and so crips.[n]

Witwoud. Indeed, so "crips"?

Mincing. You're such a critic, Mr. Witwoud.

Mrs. Millamant. Mirabell, did you take exceptions last night? Oh, aye, and went away. Now I think on't I'm

[l] outdoors [m] arranged [n] crisp, i.e., curly

angry— No, now I think on't I'm pleased—for I believe I gave you some pain.

Mirabell. Does that please you?

Mrs. Millamant. Infinitely; I love to give pain.

Mirabell. You would affect a cruelty which is not in your nature; your true vanity is in the power of pleasing.

Mrs. Millamant. Oh, I ask your pardon for that—one's cruelty is one's power; and when one parts with one's cruelty, one parts with one's power; and when one has parted with that, I fancy one's old and ugly.

Mirabell. Aye, aye, suffer your cruelty to ruin the object of your power, to destroy your lover—and then how vain, how lost a thing you'll be! Nay, 'tis true: you are no longer handsome when you've lost your lover; your beauty dies upon the instant, for beauty is the lover's gift. 'Tis he bestows your charms—your glass is all a cheat. The ugly and the old, whom the looking glass mortifies, yet after commendation can be flattered by it and discover beauties in it; for that reflects our praises, rather than your face.

Mrs. Millamant. Oh, the vanity of these men! Fainall, d'ye hear him? If they did not commend us, we were not handsome! Now you must know they could not commend one, if one was not handsome. Beauty the lover's gift! Lord, what is a lover, that it can give? Why, one makes lovers as fast as one pleases, and they live as long as one pleases, and they die as soon as one pleases: and then, if one pleases, one makes more.

Witwoud. Very pretty. Why, you make no more of making of lovers, madam, than of making so many card matches.°

Mrs. Millamant. One no more owes one's beauty to a lover, than one's wit to an echo. They can but reflect what we look and say—vain empty things if we are silent or unseen, and want a being.

Mirabell. Yet to those two vain empty things you owe two the greatest pleasures of your life.

Mrs. Millamant. How so?

Mirabell. To your lover you owe the pleasure of hearing yourselves praised, and to an echo the pleasure of hearing yourselves talk.

Witwoud. But I know a lady that loves talking so incessantly, she won't give an echo fair play; she has that everlasting rotation of tongue, that an echo must wait

° i.e., paper matches

till she dies before it can catch her last words.

Mrs. Millamant. Oh, fiction! Fainall, let us leave these men.

Mirabell (*aside to* Mrs. Fainall). Draw off Witwoud.

Mrs. Fainall. Immediately. [*Aloud.*] I have a word or two for Mr. Witwoud.

Exeunt Witwoud *and* Mrs. Fainall.

Mirabell. I would beg a little private audience too. You had the tyranny to deny me last night, though you knew I came to impart a secret to you that concerned my love.

Mrs. Millamant. You saw I was engaged.

Mirabell. Unkind! You had the leisure to entertain [p] a herd of fools—things who visit you from their excessive idleness, bestowing on your easiness that time which is the encumbrance of their lives. How can you find delight in such society? It is impossible they should admire you; they are not capable—or if they were, it should be to you as a mortification, for sure to please a fool is some degree of folly.

Mrs. Millamant. I please myself. Besides, sometimes to converse with fools is for my health.

Mirabell. Your health! Is there a worse disease than the conversation of fools?

Mrs. Millamant. Yes, the vapors; fools are physic [q] for it, next to asafetida.

Mirabell. You are not in a course [r] of fools?

Mrs. Millamant. Mirabell, if you persist in this offensive freedom, you'll displease me. I think I must resolve, after all, not to have you. We shan't agree.

Mirabell. Not in our physic, it may be.

Mrs. Millamant. And yet our distemper, in all likelihood, will be the same; for we shall be sick of one another. I shan't endure to be reprimanded nor instructed; 'tis so dull to act always by advice, and so tedious to be told of one's faults—I can't bear it. Well, I won't have you, Mirabell—I'm resolved—I think—you may go. Ha, ha, ha! What would you give that you could help loving me?

Mirabell. I would give something that you did not know I could not help it.

Mrs Millamant. Come, don't look grave, then. Well, what do you say to me?

Mirabell. I say that a man may as soon make a friend by his wit, or a fortune by his honesty, as win a woman with plain dealing and sincerity.

[p] receive [q] medicine [r] series of remedies

Mrs. Millamant. Sententious Mirabell! Prithee, don't look with that violent and inflexible wise face, like Solomon at the dividing of the child in an old tapestry hanging.

Mirabell. You are merry, madam, but I would persuade you for a moment to be serious.

Mrs. Millamant. What, with that face? No, if you keep your countenance, 'tis impossible I should hold mine. Well, after all, there is something very moving in a lovesick face. Ha, ha, ha! Well, I won't laugh; don't be peevish. Heigho! now I'll be melancholy—as melancholy as a watch-light.[s] Well, Mirabell, if ever you will win me, woo me now. Nay, if you are so tedious, fare you well; I see they are walking away.

Mirabell. Can you not find in the variety of your disposition one moment—

Mrs. Millamant. To hear you tell me Foible's married, and your plot like to speed?[t] No.

Mirabell. But how came you to know it?

Mrs. Millamant. Without the help of the devil, you can't imagine—unless she should tell me herself. Which of the two it may have been I will leave you to consider; and when you have done thinking of that, think of me. [*Exit.*]

Mirabell. I have something more.—Gone! Think of you? To think of a whirlwind, though 'twere in a whirlwind, were a case of more steady contemplation—a very tranquillity of mind and mansion. A fellow that lives in a windmill, has not a more whimsical dwelling than the heart of a man that is lodged in a woman. There is no point of the compass to which they cannot turn, and by which they are not turned; and by one as well as another. For motion, not method, is their occupation. To know this, and yet continue to be in love, is to be made wise from the dictates of reason, and yet persevere to play the fool by the force of instinct. Oh, here come my pair of turtles![u] What, billing so sweetly! Is not Valentine's Day over with you yet?

Enter Waitwell *and* Foible.

Sirrah[v] Waitwell; why, sure you think you were married for your own recreation, and not for my conveniency.

[s] night light in a sickroom [t] succeed [u] turtledoves [v] form of address to inferiors

Waitwell. Your pardon, sir. With submission, we have indeed been solacing in lawful delights; but still with an eye to business, sir. I have instructed her as well as I could. If she can take your directions as readily as my instructions, sir, your affairs are in a prosperous way.

Mirabell. Give you joy, Mrs. Foible.

Foible. Oh, 'las, sir, I'm so ashamed! I'm afraid my lady has been in a thousand inquietudes for me. But I protest, sir, I made as much haste as I could.

Waitwell. That she did indeed, sir. It was my fault that she did not make more.

Mirabell. That I believe.

Foible. But I told my lady as you instructed me, sir, that I had a prospect of seeing Sir Rowland, your uncle; and that I would put her ladyship's picture in my pocket to show him, which I'll be sure to say has made him so enamored of her beauty, that he burns with impatience to lie at her ladyship's feet and worship the original.

Mirabell. Excellent Foible! Matrimony has made you eloquent in love.

Waitwell. I think she has profited, sir; I think so.

Foible. You have seen Madam Millamant, sir?

Mirabell. Yes.

Foible. I told her, sir, because I did not know that you might find an opportunity; she had so much company last night.

Mirabell. Your diligence will merit more—in the meantime—(*Gives money*)

Foible. O dear sir, your humble servant!

Waitwell. Spouse.

Mirabell. Stand off, sir, not a penny! Go on and prosper, Foible. The lease shall be made good and the farm stocked if we succeed.

Foible. I don't question your generosity, sir, and you need not doubt of success. If you have no more commands, sir, I'll be gone; I'm sure my lady is at her toilet, and can't dress till I come. Oh, dear (*looking out*), I'm sure that was Mrs. Marwood that went by in a mask! If she has seen me with you, I'm sure she'll tell my lady. I'll make haste home and prevent her. Your servant, sir. B'w'y,[w] Waitwell.

[*Exit* Foible.]

Waitwell. Sir Rowland, if you please. The jade's so pert upon her preferment she forgets herself.

[w] God be with you

Mirabell. Come, sir, will you endeavor to forget yourself, and transform into Sir Rowland?

Waitwell. Why, sir, it will be impossible I should remember myself. Married, knighted, and attended all in one day! 'Tis enough to make any man forget himself. The difficulty will be how to recover my acquaintance and familiarity with my former self, and fall from my transformation to a reformation into Waitwell. Nay, I shan't be quite the same Waitwell neither; for now I remember me, I'm married and can't be my own man again.

> Aye, there's the grief; that's the sad change of life,
> To lose my title, and yet keep my wife. *Exeunt.*

ACT III

Scene I: A room in Lady Wishfort's *house*
Lady Wishfort *at her toilet,* Peg *waiting.*

Lady Wishfort. Merciful! No news of Foible yet?

Peg. No, madam.

Lady Wishfort. I have no more patience. If I have not fretted myself till I am pale again, there's no veracity in me! Fetch me the red—the red, do you hear, sweetheart? An arrant ash-color, as I'm a person! Look you how this wench stirs! Why dost thou not fetch me a little red? Didst thou not hear me, Mopus? [x]

Peg. The red ratafia, does your ladyship mean, or the cherry brandy?

Lady Wishfort. Ratafia, fool! No, fool. Not the ratafia, fool—grant me patience! I mean the Spanish paper,[y] idiot—complexion, darling. Paint, paint, paint!—dost thou understand that, changeling, dangling thy hands like bobbins before thee? Why dost thou not stir, puppet? Thou wooden thing upon wires!

Peg. Lord, madam, your ladyship is so impatient! I cannot come at the paint, madam; Mrs. Foible has locked it up and carried the key with her.

Lady Wishfort. A pox take you both! Fetch me the cherry brandy then. (*Exit* Peg.) I'm as pale and as faint, I look

[x] i.e., stupid [y] cosmetics

like Mrs. Qualmsick, the curate's wife, that's always breeding. Wench! Come, come, wench, what art thou doing? Sipping? Tasting? Save thee, dost thou not know the bottle?

Enter Peg *with a bottle and china cup.*

Peg. Madam, I was looking for a cup.

Lady Wishfort. A cup, save thee, and what a cup hast thou brought! Dost thou take me for a fairy, to drink out of an acorn? Why didst thou not bring thy thimble? Hast thou ne'er a brass thimble clinking in thy pocket with a bit of nutmeg? I warrant thee. Come, fill, fill! So—again. (*One knocks.*) See who that is. Set down the bottle first. Here, here, under the table. What, wouldst thou go with the bottle in thy hand, like a tapster? As I'm a person, this wench has lived in an inn upon the road before she came to me, like Maritornes the Asturian in *Don Quixote!* No Foible yet?

Peg. No, madam, Mrs. Marwood.

Lady Wishfort. Oh, Marwood; let her come in. Come in, good Marwood.

Enter Mrs. Marwood.

Mrs. Marwood. I'm surprised to find your ladyship in dishabille at this time of day.

Lady Wishfort. Foible's a lost thing—has been abroad since morning, and never heard of since.

Mrs. Marwood. I saw her but now as I came masked through the park, in conference with Mirabell.

Lady Wishfort. With Mirabell! You call my blood into my face, with mentioning that traitor. She durst not have the confidence! I sent her to negotiate an affair in which, if I'm detected, I'm undone. If that wheedling villain has wrought upon Foible to detect me, I'm ruined. Oh, my dear friend, I'm a wretch of wretches if I'm detected.

Mrs. Marwood. O madam, you cannot suspect Mrs. Foible's integrity.

Lady Wishfort. Oh, he carries poison in his tongue that would corrupt integrity itself! If she has given him an opportunity, she has as good as put her integrity into his hands. Ah, dear Marwood, what's integrity to an opportunity? Hark! I hear her! [*To* Peg.] Go, you thing, and send her in. *Exit* Peg.

[*To* Mrs. Marwood.] Dear friend, retire into my closet,[z] that I may examine her with more freedom. You'll pardon me, dear friend; I can make bold with you. There are books over the chimney—Quarles and Prynne, and *The Short View of the Stage,* with Bunyan's works, to entertain you.[a] *Exit* Mrs. Marwood.

Enter Foible.

Lady Wishfort. O Foible, where hast thou been? What hast thou been doing?

Foible. Madam, I have seen the party.

Lady Wishfort. But what hast thou done?

Foible. Nay, 'tis your ladyship has done, and are to do; I have only promised. But a man so enamored—so transported! Well, if worshiping of pictures be a sin—poor Sir Rowland, I say.

Lady Wishfort. The miniature has been counted like—but hast thou not betrayed me, Foible? Hast thou not detected me to that faithless Mirabelle? What hadst thou to do with him in the Park? Answer me; has he got nothing out of thee?

Foible [*aside*]. So the devil has been beforehand with me. What shall I say? [*Aloud.*] Alas, madam, could I help it if I met that confident thing? Was I in fault? If you had heard how he used me, and all upon your ladyship's account, I'm sure you would not suspect my fidelity. Nay, if that had been the worst, I could have borne; but he had a fling at your ladyship too, and then I could not hold; but i'faith I gave him his own.

Lady Wishfort. Me? What did the filthy fellow say?

Foible. Oh, madam! 'tis a shame to say what he said—with his taunts and his fleers,[b] tossing up his nose. Humh! (says he) what, you are a hatching some plot (says he), you are so early abroad, or catering (says he), ferreting for some disbanded officer, I warrant. Half-pay is but thin subsistence (says he)—well, what pension does your lady propose? Let me see (says he); what, she must come down pretty deep now, she's superannuated (says he) and—

Lady Wishfort. Odds my life, I'll have him—I'll have him murdered! I'll have him poisoned! Where does he

[z] boudoir [a] Francis Quarles, a religious writer; for William Prynne and *A Short View of the Stage,* see p. 23. [b] gibes

eat? I'll marry a drawer[c] to have him poisoned in his wine. I'll send for Robin from Locket's[d] immediately.

Foible. Poison him! Poisoning's too good for him. Starve him, madam, starve him: marry Sir Rowland, and get him disinherited. Oh, you would bless yourself to hear what he said!

Lady Wishfort. A villain! Superannuated!

Foible. Humh (says he), I hear you are laying designs against me too (says he), and Mrs. Millamant is to marry my uncle (he does not suspect a word of your ladyship); but (says he) I'll fit[e] you for that, I warrant you (says he), I'll hamper you for that (says he)—you and your old frippery[f] too (says he); I'll handle you—

Lady Wishfort. Audacious villain! Handle me, would he durst! Frippery? Old frippery? Was there ever such a foul-mouthed fellow? I'll be married tomorrow; I'll be contracted tonight.

Foible. The sooner the better, madam.

Lady Wishfort. Will Sir Rowland be here, sayest thou? When, Foible?

Foible. Incontinently,[g] madam. No new sheriff's wife expects the return of her husband after knighthood with that impatience in which Sir Rowland burns for the dear hour of kissing your ladyship's hand after dinner.

Lady Wishfort. Frippery! Superannuated frippery! I'll frippery the villain; I'll reduce him to frippery and rags! a tatterdemalion! I hope to see him hung with tatters, like a Long Lane penthouse[h] or a gibbet thief.[i] A slander-mouthed railer! I warrant the spendthrift prodigal's in debt as much as the million lottery,[j] or the whole Court upon a birthday.[k] I'll spoil his credit with his tailor. Yes, he shall have my niece with her fortune, he shall.

Foible. He! I hope to see him lodge in Ludgate[l] first, and angle into Blackfriars for brass farthings with an old mitten.

Lady Wishfort. Aye, dear Foible; thank thee for that, dear Foible. He has put me out of all patience. I shall never recompose my features to receive Sir Rowland

[c] tapster [d] fashionable tavern, Charing Cross [e] fight [f] castoff clothes, i.e., old-clothes bag [g] speedily [h] stall in Long Lane, an old-clothes street [i] hanged thief [j] a government lottery in 1694, in which the payments to winners were in arrears [k] courtiers were expected to appear in new clothes on the king's birthday [l] debtors' prison; the prisoners, by lowering a mitten on a cord, could beg from passers-by

with any economy of face. This wretch has fretted me that I am absolutely decayed. Look, Foible.

Foible. Your ladyship has frowned a little too rashly, indeed, madam. There are some cracks discernible in the white varnish.

Lady Wishfort. Let me see the glass. Cracks, sayest thou? Why, I am arrantly flayed. I look like an old peeled wall. Thou must repair me, Foible, before Sir Rowland comes, or I shall never keep up to my picture.

Foible. I warrant you, madam, a little art once made your picture like you, and now a little of the same art must make you like your picture. Your picture must sit for you, madam.

Lady Wishfort. But art thou sure Sir Rowland will not fail to come? Or will he not fail when he does come? Will he be importunate, Foible, and push? For if he should not be importunate, I shall never break decorums—I shall die with confusion if I am forced to advance. Oh, no, I can never advance! I shall swoon if he should expect advances. No, I hope Sir Rowland is better bred than to put a lady to the necessity of breaking her forms. I won't be too coy, neither. I won't give him despair—but a little disdain is not amiss, a little scorn is alluring.

Foible. A little scorn becomes your ladyship.

Lady Wishfort. Yes, but tenderness becomes me best—a sort of dyingness—you see that picture has a sort of a—ha, Foible? A swimmingness in the eyes—yes, I'll look so. My niece affects it, but she wants features. Is Sir Rowland handsome? Let my toilet be removed—I'll dress above. I'll receive Sir Rowland here. Is he handsome? Don't answer me. I won't know; I'll be surprised. I'll be taken by surprise.

Foible. By storm, madam. Sir Rowland's a brisk man.

Lady Wishfort. Is he? Oh, then he'll importune, if he's a brisk man. I shall save decorums if Sir Rowland importunes. I have a mortal terror at the apprehension of offending against decorums. Oh, I'm glad he's a brisk man! Let my things be removed, good Foible.

[*Exit* Lady Wishfort.]

Enter Mrs. Fainall.

Mrs. Fainall. Oh, Foible, I have been in a fright lest I should come too late! That devil Marwood saw you in the Park with Mirabell, and I'm afraid will discover it to my lady.

Foible. Discover what, madam?

Mrs. Fainall. Nay, nay, put not on that strange face! I am privy to the whole design and know that Waitwell, to whom thou wert this morning married, is to personate Mirabell's uncle, and as such, winning my lady, to involve her in those difficulties from which Mirabell only must release her, by his making his conditions to have my cousin and her fortune left to her own disposal.

Foible. Oh, dear madam, I beg your pardon. It was not my confidence in your ladyship that was deficient, but I thought the former good correspondence between your ladyship and Mr. Mirabell might have hindered his communicating this secret.

Mrs. Fainall. Dear Foible, forget that.

Foible. O dear madam, Mr. Mirabell is such a sweet, winning gentleman—but your ladyship is the pattern of generosity. Sweet lady, to be so good! Mr. Mirabell cannot choose but be grateful. I find your ladyship has his heart still. Now, madam, I can safely tell your ladyship our success; Mrs. Marwood has told my lady, but I warrant I managed myself. I turned it all for the better. I told my lady that Mr. Mirabell railed at her; I laid horrid things to his charge, I'll vow; and my lady is so incensed that she'll be contracted to Sir Rowland tonight, she says. I warrant I worked her up, that he may have her for asking for, as they say of a Welsh maidenhead.

Mrs. Fainall. O rare Foible!

Foible. Madam, I beg your ladyship to acquaint Mr. Mirabell of his success. I would be seen as little as possible to speak to him; besides, I believe Madam Marwood watches me. She has a month's mind;[m] but I know Mr. Mirabell can't abide her. [*Enter* Footman.] John, remove my lady's toilet. Madam, your servant; my lady is so impatient I fear she'll come for me if I stay.

Mrs. Fainall. I'll go with you up the back stairs lest I should meet her. *Exeunt.*

Enter Mrs. Marwood.

Mrs. Marwood. Indeed, Mrs. Engine,[n] is it thus with you? Are you become a go-between of this importance? Yes, I shall watch you. Why, this wench is the *passe partout*, a very master key to everybody's strongbox. My friend Fainall, have you carried it so swimmingly? I

[m] strong desire (for Mirabell) [n] Schemer

thought there was something in it, but it seems it's over with you. Your loathing is not from a want of appetite, then, but from a surfeit. Else you could never be so cool to fall from a principal to be an assistant, to procure for him! A pattern of generosity, that, I confess. Well, Mr. Fainall, you have met with your match. O man, man! Woman, woman! The devil's an ass; if I were a painter, I would draw him like an idiot, a driveler with a bib and bells. Man should have his head and horns,[o] and woman the rest of him. Poor simple fiend. "Madam Marwood has a month's mind, but he can't abide her." 'Twere better for him you had not been his confessor in that affair, without you could have kept his counsel closer. I shall not prove another pattern of generosity; he has not obliged me to that with those excesses of himself! And now I'll have none of him. Here comes the good lady, panting ripe, with a heart full of hope, and a head full of care, like any chemist upon the day of projection.[p]

Enter Lady Wishfort.

Lady Wishfort. Oh, dear Marwood, what shall I say for this rude forgetfulness? But my dear friend is all goodness.

Mrs. Marwood. No apologies, dear madam; I have been very well entertained.

Lady Wishfort. As I'm a person, I am in a very chaos to think I should so forget myself: but I have such an olio[q] of affairs, really I know not what to do. [*Calls.*] Foible! I expect my nephew, Sir Wilfull, every moment, too. [*Calls again.*] Why, Foible! He means to travel for improvement.

Mrs. Marwood. Methinks Sir Wilfull should rather think of marrying than traveling, at his years. I hear he is turned of forty.

Lady Wishfort. Oh, he's in less danger of being spoiled by his travels. I am against my nephew's marrying too young. It will be time enough when he comes back and has acquired discretion to choose for himself.

Mrs. Marwood. Methinks Mrs. Millamant and he would make a very fit match. He may travel afterwards. 'Tis a thing very usual with young gentlemen.

Lady Wishfort. I promise you I have thought on't—and

[o] symbol of a cuckold [p] the day on which an alchemist attempted to transmute base metal into gold [q] hodgepodge

since 'tis your judgment, I'll think on't again. I assure you I will. I value your judgment extremely. On my word, I'll propose it.

Enter Foible.

Lady Wishfort. Come, come, Foible—I had forgot my nephew will be here before dinner. I must make haste.

Foible. Mr. Witwoud and Mr. Petulant are come to dine with your ladyship.

Lady Wishfort. Oh, dear, I can't appear till I'm dressed! Dear Marwood, shall I be free with you again, and beg you to entertain 'em? I'll make all imaginable haste. Dear friend, excuse me.

[*Exeunt* Lady Wishfort *and* Foible.]

Enter Mrs. Millamant *and* Mincing.

Mrs. Millamant. Sure never anything was so unbred as that odious man! Marwood, your servant.

Mrs. Marwood. You have a color; what's the matter?

Mrs. Millamant. That horrid fellow, Petulant, has provoked me into a flame. I have broken my fan. Mincing, lend me yours. Is not all the powder out of my hair?

Mrs. Marwood. No. What has he done?

Mrs. Millamant. Nay, he has done nothing; he has only talked—nay, he has said nothing neither, but he has contradicted everything that has been said. For my part, I thought Witwoud and he would have quarreled.

Mincing. I vow, mem, I thought once they would have fit.

Mrs. Millamant. Well, 'tis a lamentable thing, I swear, that one has not the liberty of choosing one's acquaintance as one does one's clothes.

Mrs. Marwood. If we had that liberty, we should be as weary of one set of acquaintance, though never so good, as we are of one suit, though never so fine. A fool and a doily stuff[r] would now and then find days of grace, and be worn for variety.

Mrs. Millamant. I could consent to wear 'em if they would wear alike; but fools never wear out—they are such *drap-de-Berry*[s] things. Without one could give 'em to one's chambermaid after a day or two!

Mrs. Marwood. 'Twere better so indeed. Or what think you of the playhouse? A fine, gay, glossy fool should be

[r] cheap woolen cloth [s] heavy woolen cloth

given there, like a new masking habit, after the masquerade is over and we have done with the disguise. For a fool's visit is always a disguise, and never admitted by a woman of wit but to blind her affair with a lover of sense. If you would but appear barefaced now, and own Mirabell, you might as easily put off Petulant and Witwoud as your hood and scarf. And indeed, 'tis time, for the town has found it; the secret is grown too big for the pretense. 'Tis like Mrs. Primly's great belly; she may lace it down before, but it burnishes on her hips. Indeed, Millamant, you can no more conceal it than my Lady Strammel can her face—that goodly face, which, in defiance of her Rhenish-wine tea,[t] will not be comprehended[u] in a mask.

Mrs. Millamant. I'll take my death, Marwood, you are more censorious than a decayed beauty or a discarded toast.[v] Mincing, tell the men they may come up. My aunt is not dressing here; their folly is less provoking than your malice. *Exit* Mincing. The town has found it! what has it found? That Mirabell loves me is no more a secret than it is a secret that you discovered it to my aunt, or than the reason why you discovered it is a secret.

Mrs. Marwood. You are nettled.

Mrs. Millamant. You're mistaken. Ridiculous!

Mrs. Marwood. Indeed, my dear, you'll tear another fan if you don't mitigate those violent airs.

Mrs. Millamant. Oh, silly! Ha, ha, ha! I could laugh immoderately. Poor Mirabell. His constancy to me has quite destroyed his complaisance for all the world beside. I swear, I never enjoined it him to be so coy. If I had the vanity to think he would obey me, I would command him to show more gallantry—'tis hardly well-bred to be so particular on one hand, and so insensible on the other. But I despair to prevail, and so let him follow his own way. Ha, ha, ha! Pardon me, dear creature, I must laugh—ha, ha, ha!—though I grant you 'tis a little barbarous—ha, ha, ha!

Mrs. Marwood. What pity 'tis, so much fine raillery and delivered with so significant gesture, should be so unhappily directed to miscarry.

Mrs. Millamant. Ha? Dear creature, I ask your pardon. I swear, I did not mind[w] you.

[t] for the figure and the complexion [u] enclosed [v] i.e., to a former beauty [w] listen to

Mrs. Marwood. Mr. Mirabell and you both may think it a thing impossible, when I shall tell him by telling you—

Mrs. Millamant. Oh dear, what? For it is the same thing if I hear it—ha, ha, ha!

Mrs. Marwood. That I detest him, hate him, madam.

Mrs. Millamant. O, madam! why, so do I—and yet the creature loves me—ha, ha, ha! How can one forbear laughing to think of it. I am a sibyl[x] if I am not amazed to think what he can see in me. I'll take my death, I think you are handsomer—and within a year or two as young; if you could but stay for me, I should overtake you—but that cannot be. Well, that thought makes me melancholic. Now I'll be sad.

Mrs. Marwood. Your merry note may be changed sooner than you think.

Mrs. Millamant. D'ye say so? Then I'm resolved I'll have a song to keep up my spirits.

Enter Mincing.

Mincing. The gentlemen stay but to comb, madam, and will wait on you.

Mrs. Millamant. Desire Mrs. ——— that is in the next room to sing the song I would have learned yesterday. You shall hear it, madam—not that there's any great matter in it, but 'tis agreeable to my humor.

SONG

Set by Mr. John Eccles, and sung by Mrs. Hodgson.

1

Love's but the frailty of the mind,
When 'tis not with ambition joined;
A sickly flame, which, if not fed, expires,
And feeding, wastes in self-consuming fires.

2

'Tis not to wound a wanton boy
Or amorous youth, that gives the joy;
But 'tis the glory to have pierced a swain,
For whom inferior beauties sighed in vain.

3

Then I alone the conquest prize,
When I insult a rival's eyes:
If there's delight in love, 'tis when I see
That heart, which others bleed for, bleed for me.

[x] a hag

Enter Petulant *and* Witwoud.

Mrs. Millamant. Is your animosity composed, gentlemen?

Witwoud. Raillery, raillery, madam; we have no animosity—we hit off a little wit now and then, but no animosity. The falling out of wits is like the falling out of lovers. We agree in the main, like treble and bass. Ha, Petulant?

Petulant. Aye, in the main—but when I have a humor to contradict—

Witwould. Aye, when he has a humor to contradict, then I contradict, too. What! I know my cue. Then we contradict one another like two battledores;[y] for contradictions beget one another like Jews.

Petulant. If he says black's black—if I have a humor to say 'tis blue—let that pass—all's one for that. If I have a humor to prove it, it must be granted.

Witwoud. Not positively must—but it may—it may.

Petulant. Yes, it positively must, upon proof positive.

Witwoud. Aye, upon proof positive it must; but upon proof presumptive it only may. That's a logical distinction now, madam.

Mrs. Marwood. I perceive your debates are of importance and very learnedly handled.

Petulant. Importance is one thing, and learning's another. But a debate's a debate; that I assert.

Witwoud. Petulant's an enemy to learning; he relies altogether on his parts.[z]

Petulant. No, I'm no enemy to learning. It hurts not me.

Mrs. Marwood. That's a sign indeed 'tis no enemy to you.

Petulant. No, no, 'tis no enemy to anybody but them that have it.

Mrs. Millamant. Well, an illiterate man's my aversion. I wonder at the impudence of any illiterate man to offer to make love.

Witwoud. That I confess I wonder at, too.

Mrs. Millamant. Ah! To marry an ignorant that can hardly read or write!

Petulant. Why should a man be any further from being married, though he can't read, than he is from being hanged? The ordinary's[a] paid for setting the psalm,

[y] paddles [z] talents [a] prison chaplains who read a psalm before a hanging

and the parish priest for reading the ceremony. And for the rest which is to follow in both cases, a man may do it[b] without book—so all's one for that.

Mrs. Millamant. D'ye hear the creature? Lord, here's company, I'll be gone.

[*Exeunt* Mrs. Millamant *and* Mincing.]

Enter Sir Wilfull Witwoud *in a country riding habit, and* Servant *to* Lady Wishfort.

Witwoud. In the name of Bartlemew and his fair,[c] what have we here?

Mrs. Marwood. 'Tis your brother, I fancy. Don't you know him?

Witwoud. Not I. Yes, I think it is he—I've almost forgot him; I have not seen him since the Revolution.[d]

Servant [*to* Sir Wilfull]. Sir, my lady's dressing. Here's company; if you please towalk in, in the meantime.

Sir Wilfull. Dressing! What, 'tis but morning here I warrant, with you in London; we should count it towards afternoon in our parts, down in Shropshire. Why, then belike, my aunt han't dined yet, ha, friend?

Servant. Your aunt, sir?

Sir Wilfull. My aunt, sir! Yes, my aunt, sir, and your lady, sir; your lady is my aunt, sir. Why, what! Dost thou not know me, friend? Why, then send somebody hither that does. How long hast thou lived with thy lady, fellow, ha?

Servant. A week, sir—longer than anybody in the house, except my lady's woman.

Sir Wilfull. Why, then belike thou dost not know thy lady, if thou seest her, ha, friend?

Servant. Why, truly, sir, I cannot safely swear to her face in a morning, before she is dressed. 'Tis like I may give a shrewd guess at her by this time.

Sir Wilfull. Well, prithee try what thou canst do; if thou canst not guess, inquire her out, dost hear, fellow? And tell her, her nephew, Sir Wilfull Witwoud, is in the house.

Servant. I shall, sir.

Sir Wilfull. Hold ye; hear me, friend; a word with you in your ear. Prithee, who are these gallants?

[b] i.e., either marry or not [c] freaks were exhibited in Smithfield at the annual Bartholomew Fair [d] Revolution of 1688 (which deposed James II)

Servant. Really, sir, I can't tell; here come so many here, 'tis hard to know 'em all. [*Exit* Servant.]

Sir Wilfull. Oons,[e] this fellow knows less than a starling; I don't think a'[f] knows his own name.

Mrs. Marwood. Mr. Witwoud, your brother is not behindhand in forgetfulness—I fancy he has forgot you too.

Witwoud. I hope so—the devil take him that remembers first, I say.

Sir Wilfull. Save you, gentlemen and lady!

Mrs. Marwood. For shame, Mr. Witwoud; why don't you speak to him? And you, sir.

Witwoud. Petulant, speak.

Petulant. And you, sir.

Sir Wilfull. No offense, I hope. (*Salutes*[g] Mrs. Marwood.)

Mrs. Marwood. No, sure, sir.

Witwoud [*aside*]. This is a vile dog, I see that already. No offense! Ha, ha, ha! To him; to him, Petulant, smoke[h] him.

Petulant [*surveying him round*]. It seems as if you had come a journey, sir; hem, hem.

Sir Wilfull. Very likely, sir, that it may seem so.

Petulant. No offense, I hope, sir.

Witwoud [*aside*]. Smoke the boots, the boots, Petulant, the boots! Ha, ha, ha!

Sir Wilfull. May be not, sir; thereafter, as 'tis meant, sir.

Petulant. Sir, I presume upon the information of your boots.

Sir Wilfull. Why, 'tis like you may, sir; if you are not satisfied with the information of my boots, sir, if you will step to the stable, you may inquire further of my horse, sir.

Petulant. Your horse, sir? Your horse is an ass, sir!

Sir Wilfull. Do you speak by way of offense, sir?

Mrs. Marwood. The gentleman's merry, that's all, sir. (*Aside.*) 'Slife,[i] we shall have a quarrel betwixt an horse and an ass before they find one another out. (*Aloud.*) You must not take anything amiss from your friends, sir. You are among your friends here, though it may be you don't know it. If I am not mistaken, you are Sir Wilfull Witwoud.

[e] God's wounds [f] he [g] kisses [h] tease [i] God's life

Sir Wilfull. Right, lady; I am Sir Wilful Witwoud—so I write myself. No offense to anybody, I hope—and nephew to the Lady Wishfort of this mansion.

Mrs. Marwood. Don't you know this gentleman, sir?

Sir Wilfull. Hum! What, sure 'tis not—yea, by'r Lady, but 'tis—'sheart,[j] I know not whether 'tis or no—yea, but 'tis, by the Wrekin[k] Brother Anthony. What, Tony, i'faith! What, dost thou not know me? By'r Lady, nor I thee, thou art so be-cravated, and so be-periwigged! 'Sheart, why dost not speak? Art thou overjoyed?

Witwoud. Odso,[l] brother, is it you? Your servant, brother.

Sir Wilfull Your servant! Why yours, sir. Your servant again—'sheart, and your friend and servant to that—and a (*puff*)—and a—flap-dragon[m] for your service, sir, and a hare's foot and a hare's scut[n] for your service, sir, an[o] you be so cold and so courtly.

Witwoud. No offense, I hope, brother.

Sir Wilfull. 'Sheart, sir, but there is, and much offense! A pox, is this your Inns o' Court breeding,[p] not to know your friends and your relations, your elders, and your betters?

Witwoud. Why, brother Wilfull of Salop,[q] you may be as short as a Shrewsbury cake,[r] if you please. But I tell you 'tis not modish to know relations in town. You think you're in the country, where great lubberly brothers slabber and kiss one another when they meet, like a call of sergeants[s]—'tis not the fashion here; 'tis not indeed, dear brother.

Sir Wilfull. The fashion's a fool; and you're a fop, dear brother. 'Sheart, I've suspected this—by'r Lady, I conjectured you were a fop since you began to change the style of your letters, and write in a scrap of paper gilt round the edges, no bigger than a subpoena. I might expect this when you left off "Honored Brother," and "hoping you are in good health," and so forth—to begin with a "Rat me,[t] knight, I'm so sick of a last night's debauch—'ods heart," and then tell a familiar tale of a cock and a bull, and a whore and a bottle, and so conclude. You could write news before you were out of

[j] God's heart [k] a Shropshire hill [l] Godso [m] raisin (contemptuous) [n] tail [o] if [p] i.e., law training [q] Shropshire [r] a shortcake [s] lawyers newly appointed to the rank of sergeant-at-law [t] rot me (i.e., God rot me)

your time,[u] when you lived with honest Pumple[v] Nose, the attorney of Furnival's Inn—you could entreat to be remembered then to your friends round the Wrekin. We could have gazettes, then, and Dawks's Letter,[w] and the Weekly Bill,[x] till of late days.

Petulant. 'Slife, Witwoud, were you ever an attorney's clerk? Of the family of the Furnivals? Ha, ha, ha!

Witwoud. Aye, aye, but that was but for a while—not long, not long. Pshaw! I was not in my own power then; an orphan, and this fellow was my guardian. Aye, aye, I was glad to consent to that man to come to London. He had the disposal of me then. If I had not agreed to that, I might have been bound 'prentice to a felt-maker in Shrewsbury; this fellow would have bound me to a maker of felts.

Sir Wilfull. 'Sheart, and better than to be bound to a maker of fops—where, I suppose, you have served your time, and now you may set up for yourself.

Mrs. Marwood. You intend to travel, sir, as I'm informed.

Sir Wilfull. Belike I may, madam. I may chance to sail upon the salt seas, if my mind hold.

Petulant. And the wind serve.

Sir Wilfull. Serve or not serve, I shan't ask license of you, sir; nor the weathercock your companion. I direct my discourse to the lady, sir. 'Tis like my aunt may have told you, madam—yes, I have settled my concerns, I may say now, and am minded to see foreign parts—if an' how that the peace holds, whereby, that is, taxes abate.

Mrs. Marwood. I thought you had designed for France at all adventures.[y]

Sir Wilfull. I can't tell that; 'tis like I may, and 'tis like I may not. I am somewhat dainty in making a resolution because when I make it I keep it. I don't stand shill I, shall I,[z] then; if I say't, I'll do't. But I have thoughts to tarry a small matter in town to learn somewhat of your lingo first, before I cross the seas. I'd gladly have a spice of your French, as they say, whereby to hold discourse in foreign countries.

Mrs. Marwood. Here's an academy in town for that use.

Sir Wilfull. There is? 'Tis like there may.

[u] apprenticeship [v] pimple [w] a weekly news summary [x] London mortality lists [y] anyway [z] i.e., I don't shilly-shally

Mrs. Marwood. No doubt you will return very much improved.

Witwoud. Yes, refined, like a Dutch skipper from a whale-fishing.

Enter Lady Wishfort *and* Fainall.

Lady Wishfort. Nephew, you are welcome.

Sir Wilfull. Aunt, your servant.

Fainall. Sir Wilfull, your most faithful servant.

Sir Wilfull. Cousin Fainall, give me your hand.

Lady Wishfort. Cousin Witwoud, your servant; Mr. Petulant, your servant. Nephew, you are welcome again. Will you drink anything after your journey, nephew, before you eat? Dinner's almost ready.

Sir Wilfull. I'm very well, I thank you, aunt—however, I thank you for your courteous offer. 'Sheart, I was afraid you would have been in the fashion, too, and have remembered to have forgot your relations. Here's your cousin Tony; belike, I mayn't call him brother for fear of offense.

Lady Wishfort. Oh, he's a rallier, nephew—my cousin's a wit. And your great wits always rally[a] their best friends to choose.[b] When you have been abroad, nephew, you'll understand raillery better.

Fainall *and* Mrs. Marwood *talk apart.*

Sir Wilfull. Why then, let him hold his tongue in the meantime, and rail when that day comes.

Enter Mincing.

Mincing. Mem, I am come to acquaint your la'ship that dinner is impatient.

Sir Wilfull. Impatient! why, then, belike it won't stay till I pull off my boots. Sweetheart, can you help me to a pair of slippers? My man's with his horses, I warrant.

Lady Wishfort. Fie, fie, nephew! You would not pull off your boots here! Go down into the hall—dinner shall stay for you. [*Exit* Sir Wilfull.] My nephew's a little unbred; you'll pardon him, madam. Gentlemen, will you walk? Marwood?

Mrs. Marwood. I'll follow you, madam—before Sir Wilfull is ready.

[a] tease [b] as they please

Manent[c] Mrs. Marwood *and* Fainall.

Fainall. Why then, Foible's a bawd, an arrant, rank, matchmaking bawd. And I, it seems, am a husband, a rank husband; and my wife a very errant, rank wife—all in the way of the world. 'Sdeath, to be an anticipated cuckold, a cuckold in embryo! Sure, I was born with budding antlers, like a young satyr or a citizen's child.[d] 'Sdeath! to be outwitted, to be out-jilted—out-matrimony'd! If I had kept my speed like a stag, 'twere somewhat—but to crawl after with my horns like a snail, and be outstripped by my wife—'tis scurvy wedlock.

Mrs. Marwood. Then shake it off. You have often wished for an opportunity to part, and now you have it. But first prevent their plot—the half of Millamant's fortune is too considerable to be parted with to a foe, to Mirabell.

Fainall. Damn him! That had been mine, had you not made that fond[e] discovery. That had been forfeited, had they been married. My wife had added luster to my horns by that increase of fortune; I could have worn 'em tipped with gold, though my forehead had been furnished like a deputy-lieutenant's hall.[f]

Mrs. Marwood. They may prove a cap of maintenance[g] to you still, if you can away with[h] your wife. And she's no worse than when you had her—I dare swear she had given up her game before she was married.

Fainall. Hum! that may be. She might throw up her cards, but I'll be hanged if she did not put pam[i] in her pocket.

Mrs. Marwood. You married her to keep you; and if you can contrive to have her keep you better than you expected, why should you not keep her longer than you intended?

Fainall. The means, the means?

Mrs. Marwood. Discover to my lady your wife's conduct; threaten to part with her! My lady loves her, and will come to any composition[j] to save her reputation. Take the opportunity of breaking it just upon the discovery of this imposture. My lady will be enraged

[c] remain [d] i.e., the bastard born of a courtier's seduction of a bourgeois wife [e] foolish [f] i.e., with numerous antlers [g] a heraldic term (here, a pointed cap) [h] endure [i] the Jack of clubs, i.e., the trump card [j] agreement

beyond bounds, and sacrifice niece, and fortune, and all, at that conjuncture. And let me alone[k] to keep her warm; if she should flag in her part, I will not fail to prompt her.

Fainall. Faith, this has an appearance.

Mrs. Marwood. I'm sorry I hinted to my lady to endeavor a match between Millamant and Sir Wilfull; that may be an obstacle.

Fainall. Oh, for that matter, leave me to manage him. I'll disable him for that; he will drink like a Dane. After dinner I'll set his hand in.[l]

Mrs. Marwood. Well, how do you stand affected towards your lady?

Fainall. Why, faith, I'm thinking of it. Let me see—I am married already, so that's over. My wife has played the jade with me—well, that's over, too. I never loved her, or if I had, why, that would have been over, too, by this time. Jealous[m] of her I cannot be, for I am certain; so there's an end of jealousy. Weary of her I am, and shall be—no, there's no end of that—no, no, that were too much to hope. Thus far concerning my repose; now for my reputation. As to my own, I married not for it, so that's out of the question; and as to my part in my wife's—why, she had parted with hers before; so bringing none to me, she can take none from me. 'Tis against all rule of play that I should lose to one who has not wherewithal to stake.

Mrs. Marwood. Besides, you forgot marriage is honorable.

Fainall. Hum, faith, and that's well thought on. Marriage is honorable, as you say; and if so, wherefore should cuckoldom be a discredit, being derived from so honorable a root?

Mrs. Marwood. Nay, I know not; if the root be honorable, why not the branches?

Fainall. So, so; why, this, point's clear. Well, how do we proceed?

Mrs. Marwood. I will contrive a letter which shall be delivered to my lady at the time when that rascal who is to act Sir Rowland is with her. It shall come as from an unknown hand—for the less I appear to know of the truth, the better I can play the incendiary. Besides, I would not have Foible provoked if I could help it—because you know she knows some passages—nay, I

[k] leave it to me [l] start him [m] suspicious

expect all will come out. But let the mine be sprung first, and then I care not if I am discovered.

Fainall. If the worst come to the worst, I'll turn my wife to grass. I have already a deed of settlement of the best part of her estate, which I wheedled out of her, and that you shall partake at least.

Mrs. Marwood. I hope you are convinced that I hate Mirabell. Now you'll be no more jealous?

Fainall. Jealous! No, by this kiss. Let husbands be jealous, but let the lover still believe; or, if he doubt, let it be only to endear his pleasure, and prepare the joy that follows when he proves his mistress true. But let husbands' doubts convert to endless jealousy; or, if they have belief, let it corrupt to superstition and blind credulity. I am single, and will herd no more with 'em. True, I wear the badge,[n] but I'll disown the order. And since I take my leave of 'em, I care not if I leave 'em a common motto to their common crest:

> All husbands must or pain or shame endure;
> The wise too jealous are, fools too secure.

Exeunt.

ACT IV

Scene I: [*A room in* Lady Wishfort's *house*]

Enter Lady Wishfort *and* Foible.

Lady Wishfort. Is Sir Rowland coming, sayest thou Foible? And are things in order?

Foible. Yes, madam, I have put wax lights in the sconces, and placed the footmen in a row in the hall, in their best liveries, with the coachman and postilion to fill up the equipage.

Lady Wishfort. Have you pulvilled[o] the coachman and postilion, that they may not stink of the stable when Sir Rowland comes by?

Foible. Yes, madam.

Lady Wishfort. And are the dancers and the music

[n] i.e., my cuckold's horns [o] scented with powder

ready, that he may be entertained in all points with correspondence to his passion?

Foible. All is ready, madam.

Lady Wishfort. And—well—how do I look, Foible?

Foible. Most killing well, madam.

Lady Wishfort. Well, and how shall I receive him? In what figure shall I give his heart the first impression? There is a great deal in the first impression. Shall I sit? No, I won't sit—I'll walk—aye, I'll walk from the door upon his entrance, and then turn full upon him—no, that will be too sudden. I'll lie—aye, I'll lie down—I'll receive him in my little dressing room; there's a couch—yes, yes, I'll give the first impression on a couch. I won't lie neither, but loll and lean upon one elbow with one foot a little dangling off, jogging in a thoughtful way—yes—and then as soon as he appears, start, aye, start and be surprised, and rise to meet him in a pretty disorder—yes. Oh, nothing is more alluring than a levee[p] from a couch, in some confusion; it shows the foot to advantage, and furnishes with blushes and recomposing airs beyond comparison. Hark! There's a coach.

Foible. 'Tis he, madam.

Lady Wishfort. Oh, dear, has my nephew made his addresses to Millamant? I ordered him.

Foible. Sir Wilfull is set to[q] in drinking, madam, in the parlor.

Lady Wishfort. Odds my life, I'll send him to her. Call her down, Foible; bring her hither. I'll send him as I go. When they are together, then come to me, Foible, that I may not be too long alone with Sir Rowland.

[*Exit* Lady Wishfort.]

Enter Mrs. Millamant *and* Mrs. Fainall.

Foible. Madam, I stayed here to tell your ladyship that Mr. Mirabell has waited this half-hour for an opportunity to talk with you—though my lady's orders were to leave you and Sir Wilfull together. Shall I tell Mr. Mirabell that you are at leisure?

Mrs. Millamant. No. What would the dear man have? I am thoughtful, and would amuse myself. Bid him come another time. (*Repeating, and walking about.*)

> There never yet was a woman made
> Nor shall, but to be cursed.

[p] reception [q] started

That's hard!

Mrs. Fainall. You are very fond of Sir John Suckling[r] today, Millamant, and the poets.

Mrs. Millamant. He? Aye, and filthy verses—so I am.

Foible. Sir Wilfull is coming, madam. Shall I send Mr. Mirabell away?

Mrs. Millamant. Aye, if you please, Foible, send him away, or send him hither—just as you will, dear Foible. I think I'll see him—shall I? Aye, let the wretch come.

[*Exit* Foible.]

(*Repeating.*)

Thyrsis, a youth of the inspired train.[s]

Dear Fainall, entertain Sir Wilfull—thou hast philosophy to undergo a fool. Thou art married and hast patience. I would confer with my own thoughts.

Mrs. Fainall. I am obliged to you that you would make me your proxy in this affair, but I have business of my own.

Enter Sir Wilfull.

O Sir Wilfull, you are come at the critical instant. There's your mistress up to the ears in love and contemplation; pursue your point now or never.

Sir Wilfull. Yes; my aunt will have it so. I would gladly have been encouraged with a bottle or two, because I'm somewhat wary at first before I am acquainted. (*This while* Millamant *walks about repeating to herself.*) But I hope, after a time, I shall break my mind—that is, upon further acquaintance. So for the present, cousin, I'll take my leave. If so be you'll be so kind to make my excuse, I'll return to my company—

Mrs. Fainall. Oh, fie, Sir Wilfull! What! You must not be daunted.

Sir Wilfull. Daunted! No, that's not it; it is not so much for that—for if it so be that I set on't, I'll do't. But only for the present, 'tis sufficient till further acquaintance, that's all—your servant.

Mrs. Fainall. Nay, I'll swear you shall never lose so fa-

[r] English poet (1609–1642) [s] opening lines of "The Story of Phoebus and Daphne, Applied," by Edmund Waller (1606–1687)

vorable an opportunity if I can help it. I'll leave you together, and lock the door.

Exit.

Sir Wilfull. Nay, nay, cousin—I have forgot my gloves! What d'ye do? 'Sheart, a' has locked the door indeed, I think. Nay, Cousin Fainall, open the door! Pshaw, what a vixen trick is this? Nay, now a' has seen me too. Cousin, I made bold to pass through as it were—I think this door's enchanted!

Mrs. Millamant (*repeating*).

> I prithee spare me, gentle boy,
> Press me no more for that slight toy.[t]

Sir Wilfull. Anan?[u] Cousin, your servant.

Mrs. Millamant.

> That foolish trifle of a heart—

Sir Wilfull!

Sir Wilfull. Yes—your servant. No offense, I hope, cousin.

Mrs. Millamant (*repeating*).

> I swear it will not do its part,
> Though thou dost thine, employ'st thy power and art.

Natural, easy Suckling!

Sir Wilfull. Anan? Suckling? No such suckling neither, cousin, nor stripling; I thank heaven, I'm no minor.

Mrs. Millamant. Ah, rustic, ruder than Gothic![v]

Sir Wilfull. Well, well, I shall understand your lingo one of these days, cousin; in the meanwhile I must answer in plain English.

Mrs. Millamant. Have you any business with me, Sir Wilfull?

Sir Wilfull. Not at present, cousin. Yes, I made bold to see, to come and know if that how you were disposed to fetch a walk this evening; if so be that I might not be troublesome, I would have sought a walk with you.

Mrs. Millamant. A walk! What then?

Sir Wilfull. Nay, nothing—only for the walk's sake, that's all.

Mrs. Millamant. I nauseate walking; 'tis a country di-

[t] trifle [u] what's that? [v] i.e., a barbarian

version. I loathe the country and everything that relates to it.

Sir Wilfull. Indeed! Ha! Look ye, look ye—you do? Nay, 'tis like you may—here are choice of pastimes here in town, as plays and the like; that must be confessed, indeed.

Mrs. Millamant. *Ah, l'étourdie!*[w] I hate the town too.

Sir Wilfull. Dear heart, that's much. Ha! That you should hate 'em both! Ha! 'Tis like you may; there are some can't relish the town, and others can't away with the country—'tis like you may be one of those, cousin.

Mrs. Millamant. Ha, ha, ha! Yes, 'tis like I may. You have nothing further to say to me?

Sir Wilfull. Not at present, cousin. 'Tis like when I have an opportunity to be more private, I may break my mind in some measure—I conjecture you partly guess—however, that's as time shall try—but spare to speak and spare to speed, as they say.

Mrs. Millamant. If it is of no great importance, Sir Wilfull, you will oblige me to leave me; I have just now a little business—

Sir Wilfull. Enough, enough, cousin; yes, yes, all a case.[x] When you're disposed, when you're disposed. Now's as well as another time, and another time as well as now. All's one of that— Yes, yes, if your concerns call you, there's no haste; it will keep cold, as they say. Cousin, your servant. I think this door's locked.

Mrs. Millamant. You may go this way, sir.

Sir Wilfull. Your servant; then with your leave I'll return to my company.

Exit.

Mrs. Millamant. Aye, aye; ha, ha, ha!

Like Phœbus sung the no less amorous boy.

Enter Mirabell.

Mirabell. "Like Daphne she, as lovely and as coy." Do you lock yourself up from me to make my search more curious,[y] or is this pretty artifice contrived to signify that here the chase must end, and my pursuit be crowned? For you can fly no further.

Mrs. Millamant. Vanity! No—I'll fly and be followed to

[w] the giddy (town) [x] all the same [y] complicated

the last moment. Though I am upon the very verge of matrimony, I expect you should solicit me as much as if I were wavering at the grate of a monastery,[z] with one foot over the threshold. I'll be solicited to the very last—nay, and afterwards.

Mirabell. What, after the last?

Mrs. Millamant. Oh, I should think I was poor and had nothing to bestow, if I were reduced to an inglorious ease and freed from the agreeable fatigues of solicitation.

Mirabell. But do not know that when favors are conferred upon instant[a] and tedious solicitation, that they diminish in their value, and that both the giver loses the grace, and the receiver lessens his pleasure?

Mrs. Millamant. It may be in things of common application; but never, sure, in love. Oh, I hate a lover that can dare to think he draws a moment's air, independent of the bounty of his mistress. There is not so impudent a thing in nature as the saucy look of an assured man, confident of success. The pedantic arrogance of a very husband has not so pragmatical[b] an air. Ah! I'll never marry unless I am first made sure of my will and pleasure.

Mirabell. Would you have 'em both before marriage? Or will you be contented with the first now, and stay for the other till after grace?[c]

Mrs. Millamant. Ah! Don't be impertinent. My dear liberty, shall I leave thee? My faithful solitude, my darling contemplation, must I bid you then adieu? Ay-h adieu—my morning thoughts, agreeable wakings, indolent slumbers, all ye *douceurs,* ye *sommeils du matin,*[d] *adieu.* I can't do't, 'tis more than impossible. Positively, Mirabell, I'll lie abed in a morning as long as I please.

Mirabell. Then I'll get up in a morning as early as I please.

Mrs. Millamant. Ah? Idle creature, get up when you will—and d'ye hear, I won't be called names after I'm married; positively, I won't be called names.

Mirabell. Names!

Mrs. Millamant. Aye, as wife, spouse, my dear, joy, jewel, love, sweetheart, and the rest of that nauseous cant, in which men and their wives are so fulsomely familiar—I shall never bear that. Good Mirabell, don't let us be familiar or fond, nor kiss before folks, like my Lady Fadler

[z] barred window of a convent [a] insistent [b] officious [c] i.e., the marriage ceremony [d] comforts, morning slumbers

and Sir Francis; nor go to Hyde Park together the first Sunday in a new chariot, to provoke eyes and whispers, and then never be seen there together again, as if we were proud of one another the first week, and ashamed of one another ever after. Let us never visit together, nor go to a play together; but let us be very strange[e] and well-bred. Let us be as strange as if we had been married a great while, and as well-bred as if we were not married at all.

Mirabell. Have you any more conditions to offer? Hitherto your demands are pretty reasonable.

Mrs. Millamant. Trifles—as liberty to pay and receive visits to and from whom I please; to write and receive letters, without interrogatories or wry faces on your part; to wear what I please, and choose conversation with regard only to my own taste; to have no obligation upon me to converse with wits that I don't like, because they are your acquaintance; or to be intimate with fools, because they may be your relations. Come to dinner when I please; dine in my dressing room when I'm out of humor, without giving a reason. To have my closet[f] inviolate; to be sole empress of my tea table, which you must never presume to approach without first asking leave. And lastly, wherever I am, you shall always knock at the door before you come in. These articles subscribed, if I continue to endure you a little longer, I may by degrees dwindle into a wife.

Mirabell. Your bill of fare is something advanced[g] in this latter account, Well, have I liberty to offer conditions—that when you are dwindled into a wife, I may not be beyond measure enlarged into a husband?

Mrs. Millamant. You have free leave. Propose your utmost; speak and spare not.

Mirabell. I thank you. *Imprimis*[h] then, I covenant that your acquaintance be general; that you admit no sworn confidante or intimate of your own sex—no she-friend to screen her affairs under your countenance,[i] and tempt you to make trial of a mutual secrecy. No decoy-duck to wheedle you a fop-scrambling to the play in a mask, then bring you home in a pretended fright, when you think you shall be found out, and rail at me for missing the play and disappointing the frolic which you had, to pick me up and prove my constancy.

[e] reserved [f] boudoir [g] somewhat increased [h] in the first place
[i] approval

Mrs. Millamant. Detestable *imprimis!* I go to the play in a mask!

Mirabell. *Item,* I article that you continue to like your own face as long as I shall; and while it passes current with me, that you endeavor not to new-coin it. To which end, together with all vizards[j] for the day, I prohibit all masks[k] for the night, made of oiled-skins and I know not what—hog's bones, hare's gall, pig-water, and the marrow of a roasted cat. In short, I forbid all commerce with the gentlewoman in what-d'ye-call-it Court.[l] *Item,* I shut my doors against all bawds with baskets, and pennyworths of muslin, china, fans, atlases,[m] etc. *Item,* when you shall be breeding—

Mrs. Millamant. Ah! Name it not.

Mirabell. Which may be presumed, with a blessing on our endeavors—

Mrs. Millamant. Odious endeavors!

Mirabell. I denounce against all strait lacing, squeezing for a shape, till you mold my boy's head like a sugar loaf, and instead of a man-child, make me father to a crooked billet. Lastly, to the dominion of the tea table I submit—but with proviso, that you exceed not in your province, but restrain yourself to native and simple tea-table drinks, as tea, chocolate, and coffee; as likewise to genuine and authorized tea-table talk—such as mending of fashions, spoiling reputations, railing at absent friends, and so forth—but that on no account you encroach upon the men's prerogative, and presume to drink healths, or toast fellows; for prevention of which I banish all foreign forces, all auxiliaries to the tea table, as orange-brandy, all aniseed, cinnamon, citron, and Barbadoes waters, together with ratafia, and the most noble spirit of clary,[n] but for[o] cowslip wine, poppy water, and all dormitives,[p] those I allow. These provisos admitted, in other things I may prove a tractable and complying husband.

Mrs. Millamant. O horrid provisos! filthy strong-waters! I toast fellows! odious men! I hate your odious provisos.

Mirabell. Then we're agreed. Shall I kiss your hand upon the contract? And here comes one to be a witness to the sealing of the deed.

[j] masks [k] facial creams [l] presumably a cosmetics dealer [m] a kind of satin [n] all highly alcoholic drinks [o] as for [p] sleeping potions

Enter Mrs. Fainall.

Mrs. Millamant. Fainall, what shall I do? Shall I have him? I think I must have him.
Mrs. Fainall. Aye, aye, take him, take him; what should you do?
Mrs. Millamant. Well then—I'll take my death, I'm in a horrid fright. Fainall, I shall never say it—well—I think —I'll endure you.
Mrs. Fainall. Fie! fie! Have him, have him, and tell him so in plain terms; for I am sure you have a mind to him.
Mrs. Millamant. Are you? I think I have—and the horrid man looks as if he thought so too. Well, you ridiculous thing you, I'll have you—I won't be kissed, nor I won't be thanked—here, kiss my hand though. So, hold your tongue now; don't say a word.
Mrs. Fainall. Mirabell, there's a necessity for your obedience; you have neither time to talk nor stay. My mother is coming, and in my conscience if she should see you, would fall into fits, and maybe not recover time enough to return to Sir Rowland, who, as Foible tells me, is in a fair way to succeed. Therefore spare your ecstasies for another occasion, and slip down the back-stairs, where Foible waits to consult you.
Mrs. Millamant. Aye, go, go. In the meantime I suppose you have said something to please me.
Mirabell. I am all obedience.

[*Exit* Mirabell.]

Mrs. Fainall. Yonder, Sir Wilfull's drunk, and so noisy that my mother has been forced to leave Sir Rowland to appease him; but he answers her only with singing and drinking. What they may have done by this time I know not, but Petulant and he were upon quarreling as I came by.
Mrs. Millamant. Well, if Mirabell should not make a good husband, I am a lost thing, for I find I love him violently.
Mrs. Fainall. So it seems, for you mind not what's said to you. If you doubt him, you had best take up with Sir Wilfull.
Mrs. Millamant. How can you name that superannuated lubber? Foh!

Enter Witwoud *from drinking.*

Mrs. Fainall. So! Is the fray made up, that you have left 'em?

Witwoud. Left 'em? I could stay no longer. I have laughed like ten christ'nings—I am tipsy with laughing. If I had stayed any longer I should have burst—I must have been let out and pieced in the sides like an unfixed camlet.[q] Yes, yes, the fray is composed; my lady came in like a *nolle prosequi,*[r] and stopped their proceedings.

Mrs. Millamant. What was the dispute?

Witwoud. That's the jest; there was no dispute. They could neither of 'em speak for rage, and so fell a sputtering at one another like two roasting apples.

Enter Petulant, *drunk.*

Now, Petulant, all's over, all's well. Gad, my head begins to whim it about— Why dost thou not speak? Thou art both as drunk and mute as a fish.

Petulant. Look you, Mrs. Millamant—if you can love me, dear nymph, say it—and that's the conclusion. Pass on, or pass off—that's all.

Witwoud. Thou hast uttered volumes, folios, in less than *decimo sexto,*[s] *my dear Lacedemonian.*[t] Sirrah Petulant, thou art an epitomizer of words.

Petulant. Witwoud—you are an annihilator of sense.

Witwoud. Thou art a retailer of phrases, and dost deal in remnants of remnants, like a maker of pincushions—thou art in truth (metaphorically speaking) a speaker of shorthand.

Petulant. Thou art (without a figure) just one-half of an ass, and Baldwin[u] yonder, thy half-brother, is the rest. A Gemini[v] of asses split would make just four of you.

Witwoud. Thou dost bite, my dear mustard seed; kiss me for that.

Petulant. Stand off! I'll kiss no more males—I have kissed your twin yonder in a humor of reconciliation, till he (*hiccup*) rises upon my stomach like a radish.

Mrs. Millamant. Eh! filthy creature! What was the quarrel?

Petulant. There was no quarrel—there might have been a quarrel.

Witwoud. If there had been words enow[w] between 'em to have expressed provocation, they had gone together

[q] unstiffened material [r] to prosecute (legal term) [s] a tiny book [t] Spartans were noted for their terseness [u] the ass in *Reynard the Fox* [v] pair [w] enough

by the ears like a pair of castanets.

Petulant. You were the quarrel.

Mrs. Millamant. Me!

Petulant. If I have a humor to quarrel, I can make less matters conclude premises.[x] If you are not handsome, what then, if I have a humor to prove it? If I shall have my reward, say so; if not, fight for your face the next time yourself. I'll go sleep.

Witwoud. Do; wrap thyself up like a wood-louse, and dream revenge—and hear me; if thou canst learn to write by tomorrow morning, pen me a challenge. I'll carry it for thee.

Petulant. Carry your mistress' monkey a spider! Go, flea dogs, and read romances! I'll go to bed to my maid.

Exit [Petulant.]

Mrs. Fainall. He's horridly drunk. How came you all in this pickle?

Witwoud. A plot, a plot, to get rid of the knight—your husband's advice, but he sneaked off.

Enter Lady [Wishfort], *and* Sir Wilfull, *drunk.*

Lady Wishfort. Out upon't, out upon't! At years of discretion, and comport yourself at this rantipole[y] rate!

Sir Wilfull. No offense, aunt.

Lady Wishfort. Offense? As I'm a person, I'm ashamed of you. Foh! How you stink of wine! D'ye think my niece will ever endure such a borachio![z] You're an absolute borachio.

Sir Wilfull. Borachio?

Lady Wishfort. At a time when you should commence an amour and put your best foot foremost—

Sir Wilfull. 'Sheart, and you grutch[a] me your liquor, make a bill—give me more drink, and take my purse. (*Sings.*)

Prithee fill me the glass,
Till it laugh in my face,
With ale that is potent and mellow;
He that whines for a lass,
Is an ignorant ass,
For a bumper has not its fellow.

But if you would have me marry my cousin—say the word, and I'll do't. Wilfull will do't; that's the word. Wilfull will do't; that's my crest. My motto I have forgot.

[x] bring matters to a head [y] ill-mannered [z] winebag [a] begrudge

Lady Wishfort [*to* Mrs. Millamant]. My nephew's a little overtaken, cousin, cousin, but 'tis with drinking your health. O' my word, you are obliged to him.

Sir Wilfull. *In vino veritas,*[b] aunt. If I drunk your health today, cousin, I am a borachio. But if you have a mind to be married, say the word, and send for the piper; Wilfull will do't. If not, dust it away,[c] and let's have t'other round. Tony? Odds heart, where's Tony? Tony's an honest fellow; but he spits after a bumper, and that's a fault. (*Sings.*)

> We'll drink, and we'll never ha' done, boys,
>   Put the glass then around with the sun, boys,
> Let Apollo's example invite us;
>   For he's drunk every night,
>   And that makes him so bright,
> That he's able next morning to light us.

The sun's a good pimple,[d] an honest soaker; he has a cellar at your Antipodes. If I travel, aunt, I touch at your Antipodes. Your Antipodes are a good, rascally sort of topsy-turvy fellow: if I had a bumper, I'd stand upon my head and drink a health to 'em. A match or no match, cousin with the hard name—Aunt, Wilfull will do't. If she has her maidenhead, let her look to't; if she has not, let her keep her own counsel in the meantime, and cry out at the nine months' end.

Mrs. Millamant. Your pardon, madam, I can stay no longer—Sir Wilfull grows very powerful. Eh! how he smells! I shall be overcome, if I stay. Come, cousin.

Exeunt Mrs. Millamant *and* Mrs. Fainall.

Lady Wishfort. Smells! He would poison a tallow-chandler and his family! Beastly creature, I know not what to do with him! Travel, quotha! Aye, travel, travel—get thee gone; get thee gone; get thee but far enough, to the Saracens, or the Tartars, or the Turks—for thou art not fit to live in a Christian commonwealth, thou beastly pagan!

Sir Wilfull. Turks? No; no Turks, aunt. Your Turks are infidels, and believe not in the grape. Your Mahometan, your Mussulman, is a dry stinkard—no offense, aunt. My map says that your Turk is not so honest a man as [illegible] your [illegible] that [illegible] com-

orthodox is a hard word, aunt, and (hiccup)—Greek for claret. (*Sings.*)

> To drink is a Christian diversion,
> Unknown to the Turk or the Persian:
>   Let Mahometan fools
>   Live by heathenish rules,
> And be damned over teacups and coffee.
>   But let British lads sing,
>   Crown a health to the king,
> And a fig for your sultan and sophy![f]

Ah, Tony!

Enter Foible, *and whispers* [*to*] Lady Wishfort.

Lady Wishfort (*aside to* Foible). Sir Rowland impatient? Good lack! What shall I do with this beastly tumbril? (*Aloud.*) Go lie down and sleep, you sot—or, as I'm a person, I'll have you bastinadoed with broomsticks. Call up the wenches.

Exit Foible.

Sir Wilfull. Ahey! Wenches; where are the wenches?

Lady Wishfort. Dear Cousin Witwoud, get him away, and you will bind me to you inviolably. I have an affair of moment that invades me with some precipitation. You will oblige me to all futurity.

Witwoud. Come, knight. Pox on him, I don't know what to say to him. Will you go to a cock-match?

Sir Wilfull. With a wench, Tony? Is she a shakebag,[g] sirrah? Let me bite your cheek for that.

Witwoud. Horrible! He has a breath like a bagpipe— Aye, aye; come, will you march, my Salopian?

Sir Wilfull. Lead on, little Tony—I'll follow thee, my Anthony, my Tantony. Sirrah, thou shalt be my Tantony, and I'll be thy pig.[h] (*Sings.*)

> And a fig for your sultan and sophy.

Exit singing with Witwoud.

Lady Wishfort. This will never do. It will never make a match—at least before he has been abroad.

Enter Waitwell, *disguised as* Sir Rowland.

Lady Wishfort. Dear Sir Rowland, I am confounded with confusion at the retrospection of my own rudeness! I have more pardons to ask than the pope distrib-

[f] Shah of Persia [g] i.e., plump [h] St. Anthony was patron of swineherds

utes in the year of jubilee. But I hope, where there is likely to be so near an alliance, we may unbend the severity of decorum and dispense with a little ceremony.

Waitwell. My impatience, madam, is the effect of my transport; and till I have the possession of your adorable person, I am tantalized on the rack; and do but hang, madam, on the tenter[i] of expectation.

Lady Wishfort. You have excess of gallantry, Sir Rowland, and press things to a conclusion with a most prevailing vehemence. But a day or two for decency of marriage—

Waitwell. For decency of funeral, madam! The delay will break my heart—or, if that should fail, I shall be poisoned. My nephew will get an inkling of my designs, and poison me; and I would willingly starve him before I die—I would gladly go out of the world with that satisfaction. That would be some comfort to me, if I could but live so long as to be revenged on that unnatural viper!

Lady Wishfort. Is he so unnatural, say you? Truly, I would contribute much, both to the saving of your life and the accomplishment of your revenge—not that I respect[j] myself, though he has been a perfidious wretch to me.

Waitwell. Perfidious to you!

Lady Wishfort. O Sir Rowland, the hours that he has died away at my feet, the tears that he has shed, the oaths that he has sworn, the palpitations that he has left, the trances and the tremblings, the ardors and the ecstasies, the kneelings and the risings, the heart-heavings and the handgrippings, the pangs and the pathetic regards of his protesting eyes! Oh, no memory can register!

Waitwell. What, my rival! Is the rebel my rival? A' dies!

Lady Wishfort. No, don't kill him at once, Sir Rowland; starve him gradually, inch by inch.

Waitwell. I'll do't. In three weeks he shall be barefoot; in a month out at knees with begging an alms. He shall starve upward and upward, till he has nothing living but his head, and then go out in a stink like a candle's end upon a save-all.[k]

Lady Wishfort. Well, Sir Rowland, you have the way

[i] tenterhook [j] regard [k] holder that allows a candle to burn to the end

—you are no novice in the labyrinth of love; you have the clue. But as I am a person, Sir Rowland, you must not attribute my yielding to any sinister appetite, or indigestion of widowhood; nor impute my complacency to any lethargy of continence. I hope you do not think me prone to any iteration of nuptials—

Waitwell. Far be it from me—

Lady Wishfort. If you do, I protest I must recede—or think that I have made a prostitution of decorums; but[l] in the vehemence of compassion, and to save the life of a person of so much importance—

Waitwell. I esteem it so—

Lady Wishfort. Or else you wrong my condescension.

Waitwell. I do not, I do not—

Lady Wishfort. Indeed you do.

Waitwell. I do not, fair shrine of virtue!

Lady Wishfort. If you think the least scruple of carnality was an ingredient—

Waitwell. Dear madam, no. You are all camphire[m] and frankincense, all chastity and odor.

Lady Wishfort. Or that—

Enter Foible.

Foible. Madam, the dancers are ready; and there's one with a letter, who must deliver it into your own hands.

Lady Wishfort. Sir Rowland, will you give me leave? Think favorably, judge candidly, and conclude you have found a person who would suffer racks in honor's cause, dear Sir Rowland, and will wait on you incessantly.[n] [*Exit* Lady Wishfort.]

Waitwell. Fie, fie! What a slavery have I undergone! Spouse, hast thou any cordial? I want[o] spirits.

Foible. What a washy rogue art thou, to pant thus for a quarter of an hour's lying and swearing to a fine lady!

Waitwell. Oh, she is the antidote to desire! Spouse, thou wilt fare the worse for't—I shall have no appetite to iteration of nuptials this eight-and-forty hours. By this hand I'd rather be a chairman[p] in the dog days than act Sir Rowland till this time tomorrow!

Enter Lady Wishfort, *with a letter.*

Lady Wishfort. Call in the dancers. Sir Rowland, we'll

[l] except [m] camphor (supposedly an antiaphrodisiac) [n] without delay [o] lack [p] sedan-chair bearer

sit, if you please, and see the entertainment. (*A dance.*) Now, with your permission, Sir Rowland, I will peruse my letter. I would open it in your presence, because I would not make you uneasy. If it should make you uneasy, I would burn it. Speak, if it does—but you may see the superscription is like a woman's hand.

Foible (*aside to* Waitwell). By heaven! Mrs. Marwood's, I know it. My heart aches—get it from her.

Waitwell. A woman's hand? No, madam, that's no woman's hand; I see that already. That's somebody whose throat must be cut.

Lady Wishfort. Nay, Sir Rowland, since you give me a proof of your passion by your jealousy, I promise you I'll make a return by a frank communication. You shall see it—we'll open it together—look you here. (*Reads.*) "Madam, though unknown to you"—look you there, 'tis from nobody that I know—"I have that honor for your character, that I think myself obliged to let you know you are abused. He who pretends to be Sir Rowland, is a cheat and a rascal." Oh, heavens! What's this?

Foible (*aside*). Unfortunate, all's ruined!

Waitwell. How, how! Let me see, let me see! (*Reads.*) "A rascal, and disguised and suborned for that imposture"—O villainy! O villainy!—"by the contrivance of—"

Lady Wishfort. I shall faint! I shall die! Oh!

Foible (*aside to* Waitwell). Say 'tis your nephew's hand —quickly, his plot—swear swear it!

Waitwell. Here's a villain! Madam, don't you perceive it? Don't you see it?

Lady Wishfort. Too well, too well! I have seen too much.

Waitwell. I told you at first I knew the hand. A woman's hand! The rascal writes a sort of a large hand—your Roman hand.[a] I saw there was a throat to be cut presently. If he were my son, as he is my nephew, I'd pistol him!

Foible. O treachery! But are you sure, Sir Rowland, it is his writing?

Waitwell. Sure? Am I here? Do I live? Do I love this pearl of India? I have twenty letters in my pocket from him in the same character.

Lady Wishfort. How!

Foible. Oh, what luck it is, Sir Rowland, that you were present at this juncture! This was the business that

[a] i.e., written in large letters

brought Mr. Mirabell disguised to Madam Millamant this afternoon. I thought something was contriving when he stole by me and would have hid his face.

Lady Wishfort. How, how! I heard the villain was in the house, indeed; and now I remember, my niece went away abruptly when Sir Wilfull was to have made his addresses.

Foible. Then, then, madam, Mr. Mirabell waited for her in her chamber; but I would not tell your ladyship to discompose you when you were to receive Sir Rowland.

Waitwell. Enough; his date is short.

Foible. No, good Sir Rowland, don't incur the law.

Waitwell. Law! I care not for law. I can but die and 'tis in a good cause. My lady shall be satisfied of my truth and innocence, though it cost me my life.

Lady Wishfort. No, dear Sir Rowland, don't fight. If you should be killed, I must never show my face; or hanged—oh, consider my reputation, Sir Rowland! No, you shan't fight. I'll go in and examine my niece; I'll make her confess. I conjure you, Sir Rowland, by all your love, not to fight.

Waitwell. I am charmed, madam; I obey. But some proof you must let me give you; I'll go for a black box which contains the writings of my whole estate, and deliver that into your hands.

Lady Wishfort. Aye, dear Sir Rowland, that will be some comfort. Bring the black box.

Waitwell. And may I presume to bring a contract to be signed this night? May I hope so far?

Lady Wishfort. Bring what you will, but come alive, pray, come alive! Oh, this is a happy discovery!

Waitwell. Dead or alive I'll come—and married we will be in spite of treachery; aye, and get an heir that shall defeat the last remaining glimpse of hope in my abandoned nephew. Come, my buxom widow:

> Ere long you shall substantial proofs receive,
> That I'm an errant knight—

Foible. (*aside*). Or arrant knave.

Exeunt.

ACT V

Scene I: [*A room in* Lady Wishfort's *house*]

[*Enter*] Lady Wishfort *and* Foible.

Lady Wishfort. Out of my house! Out of my house, thou viper, thou serpent, that I have fostered! Thou bosom traitress, that I raised from nothing! Begone, begone, begone, go! go! That I took from washing of old gauze and weaving of dead hair,[r] with a bleak blue nose over a chafing-dish of starved embers, and dining behind a traverse rag, in a shop no bigger than a bird cage! Go, go! Starve again! Do, do!

Foible. Dear madam, I'll beg pardon on my knees.

Lady Wishfort. Away! out, out! Go, set up for yourself again! Do, drive a trade, do, with your three-pennyworth of small ware, flaunting upon a packthread under a brandy-seller's bulk,[s] or against a dead wall by a balladmonger! Go, hang out an old Frisoneer gorget,[t] with a yard of yellow colbertine[u] again, do! An old gnawed mask, two rows of pins, and a child's fiddle; a glass necklace with the beads broken, and a quilted nightcap with one ear! Go, go, drive a trade! These were your commodities, you treacherous trull! this was the merchandise you dealt in when I took you into my house, placed you next myself, and made you governante[v] of my whole family! You have forgot this, have you, now you have feathered your nest?

Foible. No, no, dear madam. Do but hear me; have but a moment's patience. I'll confess all. Mr. Mirabell seduced me. I am not the first he has wheedled with his dissembling tongue, your ladyship's own wisdom has been deluded by him—then how should I, a poor ignorant, defend myself? O madam, if you knew but what he promised me, and how he assured me your ladyship should come to no damage! Or else the wealth of the Indies

[r] i.e., wigmaker [s] stall [t] a coarse woolen scarf [u] cheap lace
[v] housekeeper

should not have bribed me to conspire against so good, so sweet, so kind a lady as you have been to me.

Lady Wishforth. No damage! What, to betray me, and marry me to a cast servingman! To make me a receptacle, an hospital for a decayed pimp! No damage! O thou frontless[w] impudence, more than a big-bellied actress!

Foible. Pray, do but hear me, madam! He could not marry your ladyship, madam. No, indeed; his marriage was to have been void in law, for he was married to me first, to secure your ladyship. He could not have bedded your ladyship; for if he had consummated with your ladyship, he must have run the risk of the law, and been put upon his clergy.[x] Yes, indeed, I inquired of the law in that case before I would meddle or make.

Lady Wishfort. What, then I have been your property, have I? I have been convenient to you, it seems! While you were catering for Mirabell, I have been broker for you! What, have you made a passive bawd of me? This exceeds all precedent! I am brought to fine uses, to become a botcher[y] of second-hand marriages between Abigails and Andrews.[z] I'll couple you! Yes, I'll baste you together, you and your Philander.[a] I'll Duke's-place you, as I'm a person! Your turtle is in custody already: you shall coo in the same cage if there be a constable or warrant in the parish. *Exit* Lady Wishfort.

Foible. Oh, that ever I was born! Oh, that I was ever married! A bride! Aye, I shall be a Bridewell-bride.[b] Oh!

Enter Mrs. Fainall.

Mrs. Fainall. Poor Foible, what's the matter?

Foible. O madam, my lady's gone for a constable! I shall be had to a justice and put to Bridewell to beat hemp. Poor Waitwell's gone to prison already.

Mrs. Fainall. Have a good heart, Foible; Mirabell's gone to give security for him. This is all Marwood's and my husband's doing.

Foible. Yes, yes; I know it, madam. She was in my lady's closet, and overheard all that you said to me before dinner. She sent the letter to my lady, and that missing effect, Mr. Fainall laid this plot to arrest Waitwell when

[w] shameless [x] plead benefit of clergy—not limited only to the clergy at this time—i.e., get off by showing that he could read [y] tailor [z] stock servant names [a] lover [b] Bridewell, a prison

he pretended to go for the papers, and in the meantime Mrs. Marwood declared all to my lady.

Mrs. Fainall. Was there no mention made of me in the letter? My mother does not suspect my being in the confederacy? I fancy Marwood has not told her, though she has told my husband.

Foible. Yes, madam, but my lady did not see that part; we stifled the letter before she read so far. Has that mischievous devil told Mr. Fainall of your ladyship, then?

Mrs. Fainall. Aye, all's out, my affair with Mirabell—everything discovered. This is the last day of our living together, that's my comfort.

Foible. Indeed, madam; and so 'tis a comfort if you knew all—he has been even with your ladyship, which I could have told you long enough since, but I love to keep peace and quietness by my good will. I had rather bring friends together than set 'em at distance. But Mrs. Marwood and he are nearer related than ever their parents thought for.

Mrs. Fainall. Sayest thou so, Foible? Canst thou prove this?

Foible. I can take my oath of it, madam; so can Mrs. Mincing. We have had many a fair word from Madam Marwood, to conceal something that passed in our chamber one evening when you were at Hyde Park, and we were thought to have gone a-walking, but we went up unawares—though we were sworn to secrecy, too; Madam Marwood took a book and swore us upon it, but it was but a book of poems. So long as it was not a Bible oath, we may break it with a safe conscience.

Mrs. Fainall. This discovery is the most opportune thing I could wish. Now, Mincing!

Enter Mincing.

Mincing. My lady would speak with Mrs. Foible, mem. Mr. Mirabell is with her; he has set your spouse at liberty, Mrs. Foible, and would have you hide yourself in my lady's closet till my old lady's anger is abated. Oh, my old lady is in a perilous passion at something Mr. Fainall has said; he swears, and my old lady cries. There's a fearful hurricane, I vow. He says, mem, how that he'll have my lady's fortune made over to him, or he'll be divorced.

Mrs. Fainall. Does your lady or Mirabell know that?

Mincing. Yes, mem; they have sent me to see if Sir Wilfull be sober, and to bring him to them. My lady is resolved to have him, I think, rather than lose such a vast sum as six thousand pound. Oh, come, Mrs. Foible, I hear my old lady.

Mrs. Fainall. Foible, you must tell Mincing that she must prepare to vouch when I call her.

Foible. Yes, yes, madam.

Mincing. Oh, yes! Mem, I'll vouch anything for your ladyship's service, be what it will.

[*Exeunt* Mincing *and* Foible.]

Enter Lady Wishfort *and* Mrs. Marwood.

Lady Wishfort. Oh, my dear friend, how can I enumerate the benefits that I have received from your goodness! To you I owe the timely discovery of the false vows of Mirabell; to you I owe the detection of the imposter Sir Rowland. And now you are become an intercessor with my son-in-law, to save the honor of my house and compound for the frailties of my daughter. Well, friend, you are enough to reconcile me to the bad world, or else I would retire to deserts and solitudes, and feed harmless sheep by groves and purling streams. Dear Marwood, let us leave the world, and retire by ourselves and be shepherdesses.

Mrs. Marwood. Let us first dispatch the affair in hand, madam. We shall have leisure to think of retirement afterwards. Here is one who is concerned in the treaty.

Lady Wishfort. Oh, daughter, daughter! Is it possible thou shouldst be my child, bone of my bone, and flesh of my flesh, and, as I may say, another me, and yet transgress the most minute particle of severe virtue? Is it possible you should lean aside to iniquity, who have been cast in the direct mold of virtue? I have not only been a mold but a pattern for you and a model for you, after you were brought into the world.

Mrs. Fainall. I don't understand your ladyship.

Lady Wishfort. Not understand? Why, have you not been naught?[c] Have you not been sophisticated?[d] Not understand! Here I am ruined to compound[e] for your caprices and your cuckoldoms. I must pawn my plate and my jewels, and ruin my niece, and all little enough—

[c] wicked [d] corrupted [e] pay

Mrs. Fainall. I am wronged and abused, and so are you. 'Tis a false accusation—as false as hell, as false as your friend there, aye, or your friend's friend, my false husband!

Mrs. Marwood. My friend, Mrs. Fainall! Your husband my friend? What do you mean?

Mrs. Fainall. I know what I mean, madam, and so do you; and so shall the world at a time convenient.

Mrs. Marwood. I am sorry to see you so passionate, madam. More temper[f] would look more like innocence. But I have done. I am sorry my zeal to serve your ladyship and family should admit of misconstruction, or make me liable to affronts. You will pardon me, madam, if I meddle no more with an affair in which I am not personally concerned.

Lady Wishfort. O dear friend, I am so ashamed that you should meet with such returns! [*To* Mrs. Fainall.] You ought to ask pardon on your knees, ungrateful creature; she deserves more from you than all your life can accomplish. [*To* Mrs. Marwood.] Oh, don't leave me destitute in this perplexity! No, stick to me, my good genius.

Mrs. Fainall. I tell you, madam, you're abused. Stick to you! Aye, like a leech, to suck your best blood—she'll drop off when she's full. Madam, you shan't pawn a bodkin, nor part with a brass counter,[g] in composition for me. I defy 'em all. Let 'em prove their aspersions; I know my own innocence, and dare stand a trial.

[*Exit* Mrs. Fainall.]

Lady Wishfort. Why, if she should be innocent, if she should be wronged after all, ha? I don't know what to think—and I promise you her education has been unexceptionable—I may say it; for I chiefly made it my own care to initiate her very infancy in the rudiments of virtue, and to impress upon her tender years a young odium and aversion to the very sight of men. Aye, friend, she would ha' shrieked if she had but seen a man, till she was in her teens. As I am a person, 'tis true—she was never suffered to play with a male child, though but in coats; nay, her very babies[h] were of the feminine gender. Oh, she never looked a man in the face but her own father, or the chaplain, and him we made a shift[i] to put upon her for a woman, by the help of his long garments and his sleek face, till she was going in her fifteen.

[f] composure [g] token [h] dolls [i] trick

Mrs. Marwood. 'Twas much she should be deceived so long.

Lady Wishfort. I warrant you, or she would never have borne to have been catechized by him; and have heard his long lectures against singing and dancing, and such debaucheries; and going to filthy plays, and profane music meetings, where the lewd trebles squeak nothing but bawdy, and the basses roar blasphemy. Oh, she would have swooned at the sight or name of an obscene playbook! And can I think, after all this, that my daughter can be naught? What, a whore? And thought it excommunication to set her foot within the door of a playhouse! O dear friend, I can't believe it. No, no! As she says, let him prove it—let him prove it.

Mrs. Marwood. Prove it, madam? What, and have your name prostituted in a public court—yours and your daughter's reputation worried at the bar by a pack of bawling lawyers? To be ushered in with an "O yez" of scandal, and have your case opened by an old fumbling lecher in a quoif[j] like a man-midwife; to bring your daughter's infamy to light; to be a theme for legal punsters and quibblers by the statute; and become a jest against a rule of court, where there is no precedent for a jest in any record—not even in Domesday Book;[k] to discompose the gravity of the bench, and provoke naughty interrogatories in more naughty law Latin; while the good judge, tickled with the proceeding, simpers under a grey beard, and fidges[l] off and on his cushion as if he had swallowed cantharides,[m] or sat upon cow-itch.[n]

Lady Wishfort. Oh, 'tis very hard!

Mrs. Marwood. And then to have my young revelers of the Temple[o] take notes, like 'prentices at a conventicle,[p] and after, talk it all over again in commons,[q] or before drawers in an eating house.

Lady Wishfort. Worse and worse!

Mrs. Marwood. Nay, this is nothing; if it would end here, 'twere well. But it must after this be consigned by the shorthand writers to the public press; and from thence be transferred to the hands, nay, into the throats and lungs of hawkers, with voices more licentious than the loud flounder-man's, or the woman that cries gray

[j] lawyer's wig [k] William the Conqueror's record of English landholdings [l] fidgets [m] an aphrodisiac [n] cowhage, a vine whose hairy pods cause itching [o] i.e., law students [p] apprentices were quizzed by their masters about the sermon [q] dining halls

peas. And this you must hear till you are stunned—nay, you must hear nothing else for some days.

Lady Wishfort. Oh, 'tis insupportable! No, no, dear friend, make it up, make it up; aye, aye, I'll compound. I'll give up all, myself and my all, my niece and her all—anything, everything for composition.

Mrs. Marwood. Nay, madam, I advise nothing; I only lay before you, as a friend, the inconveniences which perhaps you have overseen.[r] Here comes Mr. Fainall. If he will be satisfied to huddle up all in silence, I shall be glad. You must think I would rather congratulate than condole with you.

Lady Wishfort. Aye, aye, I do not doubt it, dear Marwood; no, no, I do not doubt it.

Enter Fainall.

Fainall. Well, madam, I have suffered myself to be overcome by the importunity of this lady, your friend; and am content you shall enjoy your own proper estate during life, on condition you oblige yourself never to marry, under such penalty as I think convenient.

Lady Wishfort. Never to marry!

Fainall. No more Sir Rowlands; the next imposture may not be so timely detected.

Mrs. Marwood. That condition, I dare answer, my lady will consent to without difficulty; she has already but too much experienced the perfidiousness of men. Besides, madam, when we retire to our pastoral solitude we shall bid adieu to all other thoughts.

Lady Wishfort. Aye, that's true; but in case of necessity, as of health, or some such emergency—

Fainall. Oh, if you are prescribed marriage, you shall be considered; I only will reserve to myself the power to choose for you. If your physic be wholesome, it matters not who is your apothecary. Next, my wife shall settle on me the remainder of her fortune not made over already, and for her maintenance depend entirely on my discretion.

Lady Wishfort. This is most inhumanly savage, exceeding the barbarity of a Muscovite husband.

Fainall. I learned it from his Czarish majesty's[s] retinue, in a winter evening's conference over brandy and pepper, amongst other secrets of matrimony and policy

[r] overlooked [s] Peter the Great visited England in 1697

as they are at present practiced in the northern hemisphere. But this must be agreed unto, and that positively. Lastly, I will be endowed, in right of my wife, with that six thousand pounds which is the moiety of Mrs. Millamant's fortune in your possession, and which she has forfeited (as will appear by the last will and testament of your deceased husband, Sir Jonathan Wishfort) by her disobedience in contracting herself against your consent or knowledge and by refusing the offered match with Sir Wilfull Witwoud, which you, like a careful aunt, had provided for her.

Lady Wishfort. My nephew was *non compos*,[t] and could not make his addresses.

Fainall. I come to make demands—I'll hear no objections.

Lady Wishfort. You will grant me time to consider?

Fainall. Yes, while the instrument is drawing, to which you must set your hand till more sufficient deeds can be perfected, which I will take care shall be done with all possible speed. In the meanwhile I will go for the said instrument, and till my return you may balance this matter in your own discretion. [*Exit* Fainall.]

Lady Wishfort. This insolence is beyond all precedent, all parallel. Must I be subject to this merciless villain?

Mrs. Marwood. 'Tis severe indeed, madam, that you should smart for your daughter's wantonness.

Lady Wishfort. 'Twas against my consent that she married this barbarian, but she would have him, though her year[u] was not out. Ah! her first husband, my son Languish, would not have carried it[v] thus! Well, that was my choice, this is hers: she is matched now with a witness.[w] I shall be mad! Dear friend, is there no comfort for me? Must I live to be confiscated at this rebel-rate?[x] Here come two more of my Egyptian plagues too.

Enter Mrs. Millamant *and* Sir Wilfull Witwoud.

Sir Wilfull. Aunt, your servant.

Lady Wishfort. Out, caterpillar! Call not me aunt! I know thee not!

Sir Wilfull. I confess I have been a little in disguise,[y] as they say. 'Sheart! and I'm sorry for't. What would you have? I hope I committed no offense, aunt—and if I did

[t] not in his right mind [u] of mourning [v] behaved [w] i.e., without a doubt [x] the property of rebels was totally confiscated [y] drunk

I am willing to make satisfaction; and what can a man say fairer? If I have broke anything, I'll pay for't, an it cost a pound. And so let that content for what's past, and make no more words. For what's to come, to pleasure you I'm willing to marry my cousin; so pray let's all be friends. She and I are agreed upon the matter before a witness.

Lady Wishfort. How's this, dear niece? Have I any comfort? Can this be true?

Mrs. Millamant. I am content to be a sacrifice to your repose, madam; and to convince you that I had no hand in the plot, as you were misinformed, I have laid my commands on Mirabell to come in person and be a witness that I give my hand to this flower of knighthood; and for the contract that passed between Mirabell and me, I have obliged him to make a resignation of it in your ladyship's presence. He is without, and waits your leave for admittance.

Lady Wishfort. Well, I'll swear I am something revived at this testimony of your obedience, but I cannot admit that traitor—I fear I cannot fortify myself to support his appearance. He is as terrible to me as a gorgon, if I see him I fear I shall turn to stone, petrify incessantly.

Mrs. Millamant. If you disoblige him, he may resent your refusal and insist upon the contract still. Then 'tis the last time he will be offensive to you.

Lady Wishfort. Are you sure it will be the last time? If I were sure of that—shall I never see him again?

Mrs. Millamant. Sir Wilfull, you and he are to travel together, are you not?

Sir Wilfull. 'Sheart, the gentleman's a civil gentleman, aunt; let him come in. Why, we are sworn brothers and fellow travelers. We are to be Pylades and Orestes,[z] he and I. He is to be my interpreter in foreign parts. He has been overseas once already, and with proviso that I marry my cousin, will cross 'em once again only to bear me company. 'Sheart, I'll call him in. An I set on't once, he shall come in; and see who'll hinder him.

[*Exit* Sir Wilfull.]

Mrs. Marwood. This is precious fooling, if it would pass; but I'll know the bottom of it.

Lady Wishfort. O dear Marwood, you are not going?

Mrs. Marwood. Not far, madam; I'll return immediately.

[z] legendary faithful friends

[*Exit* Mrs. Marwood.]

Re-enter Sir Wilfull *and* Mirabell.

Sir Wilfull. Look up, man, I'll stand by you. 'Sbud, an she do frown, she can't kill you; besides—harkee, she dare not frown desperately, because her face is none of her own. 'Sheart, an she should, her forehead would wrinkle like the coat of a cream cheese; but mum for that, fellow traveler.

Mirabell. If a deep sense of the many injuries I have offered to so good a lady, with a sincere remorse and a hearty contrition, can but obtain the least glance of compassion, I am too happy. Ah, madam, there was a time—but let it be forgotten—I confess I have deservedly forfeited the high place I once held, of sighing at your feet. Nay, kill me not by turning from me in disdain. I come not to plead for favor—nay, not for pardon; I am a suppliant only for your pity. I am going where I never shall behold you more—

Sir Wilfull. How, fellow traveler! you shall go by yourself then.

Mirabell. Let me be pitied first, and afterwards forgotten. I ask no more.

Sir Wilfull. By'r Lady, a very reasonable request, and will cost you nothing, aunt! Come, come, forgive and forget, aunt. Why, you must, an you are a Christian.

Mirabell. Consider, madam, in reality you could not receive much prejudice. It was an innocent device; though I confess it had a face of guiltiness, it was at most an artifice which love contrived—and errors which love produces have ever been accounted venial. At least think it is punishment enough that I have lost what in my heart I hold most dear, that to your cruel indignation I have offered up this beauty, and with her my peace and quiet—nay, all my hopes of future comfort.

Sir Wilfull. An he does not move me, would I may never be o' the quorum![a] An it were not as good a deed as to drink, to give her to him again, I would might never take shipping! Aunt, if you don't forgive quickly, I shall melt, I can tell you that. My contract went no farther than a little mouth glue,[b] and that's hardly dry

[a] a justice of the peace required for court sessions [b] i.e., a verbal agreement

—one doleful sigh more from my fellow traveler, and 'tis dissolved.

Lady Wishfort. Well, nephew, upon your account— Ah, he has a false insinuating tongue! Well, sir, I will stifle my just resentment at my nephew's request. I will endeavor what I can to forget, but on proviso that you resign the contract with my niece immediately.

Mirabell. It is in writing, and with papers of concern; but I have sent my servant for it, and will deliver it to you with all acknowledgments for your transcendent goodness.

Lady Wishfort (*aside*). Oh, he has witchcraft in his eyes and tongue! When I did not see him, I could have bribed a villain to his assassination; but his appearance rakes the embers which have so long lain smothered in my breast.

Enter Fainall *and* Mrs. Marwood.

Fainall. Your date of deliberation, madam, is expired. Here is the instrument; are you prepared to sign?

Lady Wishfort. If I were prepared, I am not impowered. My niece exerts a lawful claim, having matched herself by my direction to Sir Wilfull.

Fainall. That sham is too gross to pass on me—though 'tis imposed on you, madam.

Mrs. Millamant. Sir, I have given my consent.

Mirabell. And, sir, I have resigned my pretensions.

Sir Wilfull. And, sir, I assert my right and will maintain it in defiance of you, sir, and of your instrument. 'Sheart, an you talk of an instrument, sir, I have an old fox by my thigh shall hack your instrument of ram vellum to shreds, sir! It shall not be sufficient for a mittimus[c] or a tailor's measure.[d] Therefore withdraw your instrument, sir, or by'r Lady, I shall draw mine.

Lady Wishfort. Hold, nephew, hold!

Mrs. Millamant. Good Sir Wilfull, respite your valor!

Fainall. Indeed! Are you provided of a guard, with your single beefeater[e] there? But I'm prepared for you, and insist upon my first proposal. You shall submit your own estate to my management, and absolutely make over my wife's to my sole use, as pursuant to the purport and tenor of this other covenant. [*To* Mrs. Millamant.] I suppose, madam, your consent is not

[c] warrant for arrest [d] sheet on which a tailor writes his measurements [e] guard of the Tower of London

requisite in this case; nor, Mr. Mirabell, your resignation; nor, Sir Wilfull, your right. You may draw your fox if you please, sir, and make a bear garden flourish somewhere else, for here it will not avail. This, my Lady Wishfort, must be subscribed, or your darling daughter's turned adrift, like a leaky hulk, to sink or swim, as she and the current of this lewd town can agree.

Lady Wishfort. Is there no means, no remedy to stop my ruin? Ungrateful wretch! Dost thou not owe thy being, thy subsistence, to my daughter's fortune?

Fainall. I'll answer you when I have the rest of it in my possession.

Mirabell. But that you would not accept of a remedy from my hands—I own I have not deserved you should owe any obligation to me; or else perhaps I could advise—

Lady Wishfort. Oh, what? What? To save me and my child from ruin, from want, I'll forgive all that's past; nay, I'll consent to anything to come, to be delivered from this tyranny.

Mirabell. Aye, madam, but that is too late; my reward is intercepted. You have disposed of her who only could have made me a compensation for all my services. But be it as it may, I am resolved I'll serve you! You shall not be wronged in this savage manner.

Lady Wishfort. How! Dear Mr. Mirabell, can you be so generous at last? But it is not possible. Harkee, I'll break my nephew's match; you shall have my niece yet, and all her fortune, if you can but save me from this imminent danger.

Mirabell. Will you? I'll take you at your word. I ask no more. I must have leave for two criminals to appear.

Lady Wishfort. Aye, aye; anybody, anybody!

Mirabell. Foible is one, and a penitent.

Enter Mrs. Fainall, Foible, *and* Mincing.

Mrs. Marwood [*aside*]. Oh, my shame! (*To* Fainall.) These corrupt things are brought hither to expose me.

(Mirabell *and* Lady Wishfort *go to* Mrs. Fainall *and* Foible.)

Fainall. If it must all come out, why let 'em know it; 'tis but the way of the world. That shall not urge me to relinquish or abate one tittle of my terms; no, I will insist the more.

Foible. Yes, indeed, madam, I'll take my Bible oath of it.

Mincing. And so will I, mem.

Lady Wishfort. O Marwood, Marwood, art thou false? My friend deceive me? Hast thou been a wicked accomplice with that profligate man?

Mrs. Marwood. Have you so much ingratitude and injustice to give credit against your friend to the aspersions of two such mercenary trulls?

Mincing. Mercenary, mem? I scorn your words. 'Tis true we found you and Mr. Fainall in the blue garret; by the same token, you swore us to secrecy upon Messalina's poems.[f] Mercenary? No, if we would have been mercenary, we should have held our tongues; you would have bribed us sufficiently.

Fainall. Go, you are an insignificant thing! Well, what are you the better for this? Is this Mr. Mirabell's expedient? I'll be put off no longer. You, thing that was a wife, shall smart for this! I will not leave thee wherewithal to hide thy shame; your body shall be naked as your reputation.

Mrs. Fainall. I despise you and defy your malice! You have aspersed me wrongfully—I have proved your falsehood! Go, you and your treacherous—I will not name it, but, starve together. Perish!

Fainall. Not while you are worth a groat, indeed, my dear. Madam, I'll be fooled no longer.

Lady Wishfort. Ah, Mr. Mirabell, this is small comfort, the detection of this affair.

Mirabell. Oh, in good time. Your leave for the other offender and penitent to appear, madam.

Enter Waitwell *with a box of writings.*

Lady Wishfort. O Sir Rowland! Well, rascal!

Waitwell. What your ladyship pleases. I have brought the black box at last, madam.

Mirabell. Give it me. Madam, you remember your promise?

Lady Wishfort. Aye, dear sir.

Mirabell. Where are the gentlemen?

[f] probably a malapropism for *Miscellaneous Poems*

Waitwell. At hand, sir, rubbing their eyes—just risen from sleep.

Fainall. 'Sdeath, what's this to me? I'll not wait your private concerns.

Enter Petulant *and* Witwoud.

Petulant. How now! What's the matter? Whose hand's out?

Witwoud. Heyday! What, are you all got together like players at the end of the last act?

Mirabell. You may remember, gentlemen, I once requested your hands as witnesses to a certain parchment.

Witwoud. Aye, I do; my hand I remember—Petulant set his mark.

Mirabell. You wrong him. His name is fairly written, as shall appear. (*Undoing the box.*) You do not remember, gentlemen, anything of what that parchment contained?

Witwoud. No.

Petulant. Not I; I writ, I read nothing.

Mirabell. Very well, now you shall know. Madam, your promise.

Lady Wishfort. Aye, aye, sir, upon my honor.

Mirabell. Mr. Fainall, it is now time that you should know that your lady, while she was at her own disposal, and before you had by your insinuations wheedled her out of a pretended settlement of the greatest part of her fortune—

Fainall. Sir! Pretended!

Mirabell. Yes, sir. I say that this lady while a widow, having, it seems, received some cautions respecting your inconstancy and tyranny of temper, which from her own partial opinion and fondness of you she could never have suspected—she did, I say, by the wholesome advice of friends and of sages learned in the laws of this land, deliver this same as her act and deed to me in trust, and to the uses within mentioned. You may read if you please—(*holding out the parchment*) though perhaps what is written on the back may serve your occasions.

Fainall. Very likely, sir. What's here? Damnation! (*Reads.*) "A deed of conveyance of the whole estate real of Arabella Languish, widow, in trust to Edward Mirabell." Confusion!

Mirabell. Even so, sir; 'tis the way of the world, sir—of the widows of the world. I suppose this deed may bear an elder date than what you have obtained from your lady?

Fainall. Perfidious fiend! then thus I'll be revenged. (*Offers*[g] *to run at* Mrs. Fainall.)

Sir Wilfull. Hold, sir! Now you may make your bear garden flourish somewhere else, sir.

Fainall. Mirabell, you shall hear of this, sir, be sure you shall. Let me pass, oaf! [*Exit* Fainall.]

Mrs. Fainall. Madam, you seem to stifle your resentment; you had better give it vent.

Mrs. Marwood. Yes, it shall have vent—and to your confusion, or I'll perish in the attempt. [*Exit* Mrs. Marwood.]

Lady Wishfort. O daughter, daughter! 'Tis plain thou has inherited thy mother's prudence.

Mrs. Fainall. Thank Mr. Mirabell, a cautious friend, to whose advice all is owing.

Lady Wishfort. Well, Mr. Mirabell, you have kept your promise—and I must perform mine. First, I pardon, for your sake, Sir Rowland there, and Foible. The next thing is to break the matter to my nephew—and how to do that—

Mirabell. For that, madam, give yourself no trouble; let me have your consent. Sir Wilfull is my friend. He has had compassion upon lovers, and generously engaged a volunteer in this action for our service, and now designs to prosecute his travels.

Sir Wilfull. 'Sheart, aunt, I have no mind to marry. My cousin's a fine lady, and the gentleman loves her, and she loves him, and they deserve one another. My resolution is to see foreign parts—I have set on't—and when I'm set on't I must do't. And if these two gentlemen would travel too, I think they may be spared.

Petulant. For my part, I say little—I think things are best off or on.[h]

Witwoud. 'Ygad, I understand nothing of the matter; I'm in a maze yet, like a dog in a dancing school.

Lady Wishfort. Well, sir, take her, and with her all the joy I can give you.

Mrs. Millamant. Why does not the man take me? Would you have me give myself to you over again?

[g] attempts [h] either way

Mirabell. Aye, and over and over again. (*Kisses her hand.*) I would have you as often as possibly I can. Well, Heaven grant I love you not too well; that's all my fear.

Sir Wilfull. 'Sheart, you'll have time enough to toy after you're married; or if you will toy now, let us have a dance in the meantime, that we who are not lovers may have some other employment besides looking on.

Mirabell. With all my heart, dear Sir Wilfull. What shall we do for music?

Foible. Oh, sir, some that were provided for Sir Rowland's entertainment are yet within call. (*A dance.*)

Lady Wishfort. As I am a person, I can hold out no longer. I have wasted my spirits so today already, that I am ready to sink under the fatigue, and I cannot but have some fears upon me yet, that my son Fainall will pursue some desperate course.

Mirabell. Madam, disquiet not yourself on that account; to my knowledge his circumstances are such he must of force comply. For my part, I will contribute all that in me lies to a reunion; in the meantime, madam—(*to* Mrs. Fainall) let me before these witnesses restore to you this deed of trust. It may be a means, well managed, to make you live easily together.

From hence let those be warned who mean to wed,
Lest mutual falsehood stain the bridal bed;
For each deceiver to his cost may find
That marriage frauds too oft are paid in kind.

Exeunt omnes.

EPILOGUE

Spoken by Mrs. Bracegirdle

After our epilogue this crowd dismisses,
I'm thinking how this play'll be pulled to pieces;
But pray consider, ere you doom its fall,
How hard a thing 'twould be to please you all.
There are some critics so with spleen[1] diseased,
They scarcely come inclining to be pleased;

[1] thought to be the seat of spite

And sure he must have more than mortal skill,
Who pleases anyone against his will.
Then all bad poets, we are sure, are foes,
And how their number's swelled the town well knows;
In shoals I've marked 'em judging in the pit;
Though they're on no pretense for judgment fit,
But that they have been damned for want of wit.
Since then, they by their own offenses taught,
Set up for spies on plays, and finding fault.
Others there are whose malice we'd prevent;
Such who watch plays with scurrilous intent
To mark out who by characters are meant;
And though no perfect likeness they can trace,
Yet each pretends to know the copied face.
These with false glosses[j] feed their own ill nature,
And turn to libel what was meant a satire.
May such malicious fops this fortune find,
To think themselves alone the fools designed,
If any are so arrogantly vain,
To think they singly can support a scene,
And furnish fool enough to entertain.
For well the learn'd and the judicious know
That satire scorns to stoop so meanly low
As any one abstracted[k] fop to show.
For, as when painters form a matchless face,
They from each fair one catch some different grace,
And shining features in one portrait blend,
To which no single beauty must pretend,
So poets oft do in one piece expose
Whole *belles-assemblées*[l] of coquettes and beaux.

[j] interpretations [k] separate [l] fashionable gatherings

Oliver Goldsmith:

She Stoops to Conquer

or, The Mistakes of a Night

Because Dr. Johnson's connection with Goldsmith was close—he arranged for the sale of *The Vicar of Wakefield,* he contributed some lines to "The Deserted Village," he helped get *She Stoops to Conquer* onto the stage, he was the dedicatee of the play, and he wrote Goldsmith's epitaph —it is appropriate to let Johnson set the play in its age: "I know of no comedy for many years that has so much exhilarated an audience, that has answered so much the great end of comedy—making an audience merry."

That a comedy ought to make an audience merry seems obvious enough, but the history of comic theory contains numerous competing theories, including, for example, the astonishing statements by Sir Philip Sidney and by Ben Jonson (based on a misunderstanding of Aristotle) that a comedy which evokes laughter is likely to be a poor thing. Indeed, the burden of much early comic theory was a variation on Cicero's theme that comedy displays human follies so that man may learn what to avoid. But Dr. Johnson, immersed in what Boswell called "habitual gloom," knew how to value laughter properly, and knew that a comedy is done no service by being transformed into a moral. Some two decades before his comment on *She Stoops to Conquer,* Johnson in an essay in *The Rambler* had summarized a number of theories of comedy, pointing out that some critics say this, some say that, and others say the other thing; his own definition was simple:

a comedy is "such dramatic representation of human life, as may excite mirth."

Goldsmith himself seems to have demanded no more: when a friend hesitated to evaluate *She Stoops to Conquer,* Goldsmith asked if it had made him laugh. It had; "then that is all I require." Goldsmith was wise enough to choose for his plot an absurd situation (two young gentlemen mistake an old house for an inn, and order their host about), and to conjure up a world in which there are the two Miss Hoggs, a Mrs. Oddfish, a young man who is shy with genteel ladies but rakish among barmaids, a young lady who is enough taken with the young man to pretend to be a barmaid in her own home, and an incomparable booby—Tony Lumpkin—who is simple enough to outwit his intellectual superiors. Such happy fooling, such robust pointlessness, is rare in any age, and Johnson's tribute to Goldsmith was no mere friendly puff. Probably John Gay's *The Begger's Opera* (1728) is the only consistently funny play between Farquhar's *The Beaux' Stratagem* (1707) and *She Stoops to Conquer* (1773), and probably not since the early seventeenth century had there been so consistently genial a play as Goldsmith's.

Even before Goldsmith was born, Restoration comedy—of which Congreve's *The Way of the World* may be the crown—had run its course. An unmistakable weariness is evident at the end of the seventeenth century, and John Dryden must have spoken for many when he wrote in his *Secular Masque* (a dramatic performance of 1700 designed to welcome the eighteenth century) that if in the days following the restoration of the monarchy "Joy ruled the day, and Love the night," the trouble was that the "Lovers were all untrue." His conclusion:

> 'Tis well an old age is out,
> And time to begin a new.

Something of the spirit of the Restoration continues, of course, into the eighteenth century: some of the early plays of the century have Restoration wit and Restoration dramatis personae. But as the century continues, benevolism increasingly replaces ridicule, and ethical instruction and tenderheartedness replace high spirits. Richard Steele, who said that the intent of his newspaper *The Tatler* was "to expose the false arts of life, to pull off the disguises of cunning, vanity, and affectation, and to recommend a general simplicity in our dress, our discourse, and our behavior," furnished his comedy, *The Lying Lover* (1703), with a prologue announcing that the play did not offer mere idle laughter, "a distorted passion" of which we are later ashamed, but offered rather pity, a quality which "makes us ourselves both more approve and know." Steele was a little ahead of his time, and his play (whose object, he said, was to stimulate "simplicity of mind, good-nature, friendship, and honor") failed, but he continued to work this vein and by 1722, when his *The Conscious Lovers* was produced, the public had caught up with him and granted him its applause. Even Fielding's Parson Adams approved of *The Conscious Lovers,* finding in it "some things almost solemn enough for a sermon."

In short, as Restoration comedy dwindled, sentimental comedy (preaching benevolism and eschewing bawdry) became increasingly popular, and the stage became peopled with tender lovers, repentant profligates, and charitable elderly gentlemen. Steele and Addison were not wholly innocent victims of Joseph Dorman, who wrote a sticky two-act piece (1740) about their famous invention, *Sir Roger de Coverley*. A short passage will be enough:

> *Sir Roger:* Be sure, Prudence, you take care to let us have plenty today. —Beef, pudding, plum-porridge, and mince pies in abundance. —My honest neighbors love them; and today's the day they make me happy.
>
> *Prudence:* The day your Honor makes them so, rather, Sir.
>
> *Sir Roger:* That's what I mean, Prudence. The making them happy makes me so too. I'm always delighted at the felicity of others; but more especially, if I myself have been the cause on't
>
> *Prudence:* Best of men!

Goldsmith, though not untouched by sentimentalism (the vicar of Wakefield is distressingly kindly, the deserted village seems to have been free from the serpent, and the rural setting of *She Stoops to Conquer* is cozily idyllic), several times took issue with the sentimentalists, notably in his "An Essay on the Theater" (p. 506) and in *She Stoops to Conquer*. In the essay he explains that among the ingredients of a sentimental comedy are "mighty good hearts" and "a pathetic scene or two, with a sprinkling of tender melancholy conversation through the whole." In the play, or rather in his dedicatory note to Johnson, Goldsmith stiffly comments that he has written a play which, by being funny rather than sentimental, has evoked the manager's skepticism. Garrick, in the prologue he contributed to the play, sees Goldsmith as the doctor attempting to revive the moribund comic muse, so thoroughly have sentimental plays replaced comic ones. In the play itself, Goldsmith occasionally jibes at the literature of sentiment ("Let her cry. It's the comfort of her heart. I have seen her and sister cry over a book for an hour together, and they said they liked the book the better the more it made them cry"). But because he is writing a comedy rather than a treatise or a satire, he attacks sentimental drama chiefly by ignoring it and by writing a play whose claim on us is not that it edifies or melts to tears but that it entertains. Some of the titles Goldsmith attached to the play before he settled on the present one—*The Mistakes of a Night,* and *The Novel,* i.e., "the fiction," "the invention" —give a good idea of the play's nature. Goldsmith was trying to go back to the Shakespearean tradition suggested in such titles as *The Comedy of Errors, All's Well That Ends Well,* and *Much Ado About Nothing.* A spirit of fun animates the play, and people are finally brought into unanimity by laughing rather than by weeping. "An hour or two's laughing with my daughter will set all to rights again," Hardcastle genially predicts in the fifth act, and the play concludes with comedy's traditional invitation to supper and the prospect of weddings and "a merry morning."

Doctor Goldsmith's potion of farce with some wit did not restore the English comic muse, as Garrick hoped it would, but *She Stoops to Conquer* has itself been remarkably healthy and shows no signs of age as it completes its second century.

Goldsmith: Biographical Note.

Oliver Goldsmith (1728–1774) was born in Ireland, the son of a poor rector who provided the model for Dr. Primrose in *The Vicar of Wakefield.* After being graduated from Trinity College, Dublin, he seems to have idled (1750–1752) until he began the study of medicine at Edinburgh. He next toured Europe, attending several universities and acquiring (though it is not certainly known where) a medical degree. He then engaged in various pursuits in London, but by the end of 1759 he was established there as a hack writer. He produced an enormous amount, including histories, translations, and compilations, sometimes easing his task by plagiarizing. Though he turned out several dozen volumes, he wrote only two plays, *The Good-Natured Man* (1768) and *She Stoops to Conquer* (1773). Dr. Johnson's Latin epitaph summarizing Goldsmith's productivity and excellence may be translated thus: "There was hardly one branch of literature he did not touch; none, that he touched and failed to adorn."

Suggested References:

Jeffares, A. Norman, *Oliver Goldsmith,* London, Longmans, Green, 1959.

Wardle, Ralph M., *Oliver Goldsmith,* Lawrence, Kansas, University of Kansas Press, 1957; London: Constable & Co., 1958.

She Stoops to Conquer

Characters

Sir Charles Marlow
Young Marlow, his son
Hardcastle
Hastings
Tony Lumpkin
Diggory
Mrs. Hardcastle
Miss Hardcastle
Miss Neville
Maid
Landlord, Servants, *etc.*

To Samuel Johnson, L.L.D.

Dear Sir,

By inscribing this slight performance to you, I do not mean so much to compliment you as myself. It may do me some honor to inform the public, that I have lived many years in intimacy with you. It may serve the interests of mankind also to inform them, that the greatest wit may be found in a character, without impairing the most unaffected piety.

I have, particularly, reason to thank you for your partiality to this performance. The undertaking a comedy, not merely sentimental, was very dangerous; and Mr. Colman,[a] who saw this piece in its various stages, always thought it so. However, I ventured to trust it to the public; and though it was necessarily delayed till late in the season, I have every reason to be grateful.

I am, Dear Sir,
Your most sincere friend,
And admirer,
Oliver Goldsmith.

[a] George Colman, manager of Covent Garden

PROLOGUE

By David Garrick, Esq.

Enter Mr. Woodward,[b] *dressed in black, and holding a handkerchief to his eyes.*

Excuse me, sirs, I pray—I can't yet speak—
  I'm crying now—and have been all the week!
" 'Tis not alone this mourning suit," good masters;
  "I've that within" [c]—for which there are no plasters!
Pray would you know the reason why I'm crying?
  The Comic Muse, long sick, is now a-dying!
And if she goes, my tears will never stop;
  For as a player, I can't squeeze out one drop:
I am undone, that's all—shall lose my bread—
  I'd rather, but that's nothing—lose my head.
When the sweet maid is laid upon the bier,
  Shuter and I shall be chief mourners here.
To her a mawkish drab of spurious breed,
  Who deal in sentimentals will succeed!
Poor Ned and I are dead to all intents;
  We can as soon speak Greek as sentiments.
Both nervous grown, to keep our spirits up,
  We now and then take down a hearty cup.
What shall we do? —If Comedy forsake us!
  They'll turn us out, and no one else will take us.
But, why can't I be moral? —Let me try—
  My heart thus pressing—fixed my face and eye—
With a sententious look, that nothing means
  (Faces are blocks, in sentimental scenes),

[b] a popular London actor; Edward "Ned" Shuter, mentioned in the prologue, was another popular actor, of low comedy [c] paraphrase of *Hamlet*, I. ii. 77ff.

Thus I begin—"All is not gold that glitters,
Pleasure seems sweet, but proves a glass of bitters.
When ign'rance enters, folly is at hand;
Learning is better far than house and land.
Let not your virtue trip, who trips may stumble,
And virtue is not virtue, if she tumble."
I give it up—morals won't do for me;
To make you laugh, I must play tragedy.
One hope remains—hearing the maid was ill,
A doctor comes this night to show his skill.
To cheer her heart, and give your muscles motion,
He in five draughts prepared, presents a potion:
A kind of magic charm—for be assured,
If you will swallow it, the maid is cured.
But desp'rate the doctor, and her case is,
If you reject the dose, and make wry faces!
This truth he boasts, will boast it while he lives,
No pois'nous drugs are mixed in what he gives.
Should he succeed, you'll give him his degree;
If not, within he will receive no fee!
The college, you, must his pretensions back,
Pronounce him regular, or dub him quack.

ACT I

Scene I: A chamber in an old-fashioned house.

Enter Mrs. Hardcastle *and* Mr. Hardcastle.

Mrs. Hardcastle. I vow, Mr. Hardcastle, you're very particular. Is there a creature in the whole country, but ourselves, that does not take a trip to town now and then, to rub off the rust a little? There's the two Miss Hoggs, and our neighbor, Mrs. Grigsby, go to take a month's polishing every winter.

Hardcastle. Aye, and bring back vanity and affectation to last them the whole year. I wonder why London cannot keep its own fools at home. In my time, the follies of the town crept slowly among us, but now they travel faster than a stagecoach. Its fopperies come down, not only as inside passengers, but in the very basket.[d]

[d] an outside compartment, usually for luggage, at the rear of a stagecoach

Mrs. Hardcastle. Aye, *your* times were fine times, indeed; you have been telling us of *them* for many a long year. Here we live in an old rumbling mansion, that looks for all the world like an inn, but that we never see company. Our best visitors are old Mrs. Oddfish, the curate's wife, and little Cripplegate, the lame dancing master: and all our entertainment your old stories of Prince Eugene[e] and the Duke of Marlborough. I hate such old-fashioned trumpery.

Hardcastle. And I love it. I love everything that's old: old friends, old times, old manners, old books, old wine; and, I believe, Dorothy (*taking her hand*), you'll own I have been pretty fond of an old wife.

Mrs. Hardcastle. Lord, Mr. Hardcastle, you're forever at your Dorothy's and your old wife's. You may be a Darby, but I'll be no Joan,[f] I promise you. I'm not so old as you'd make me, by more than one good year. Add twenty to twenty, and make money of that.

Hardcastle. Let me see; twenty added to twenty makes just fifty and seven.

Mrs. Hardcastle. It's false, Mr. Hardcastle: I was but twenty when I was brought to bed of Tony, that I had by Mr. Lumpkin, my first husband; and he's not come to years of discretion yet.

Hardcastle. Nor ever will, I dare answer for him. Ay, you have taught *him* finely!

Mrs. Hardcastle. No matter. Tony Lumpkin has a good fortune. My son is not to live by his learning. I don't think a boy wants much learning to spend fifteen hundred a year.

Hardcastle. Learning, quotha! A mere composition of tricks and mischief!

Mrs. Hardcastle. Humor, my dear; nothing but humor. Come, Mr. Hardcastle, you must allow the boy a little humor.

Hardcastle. I'd sooner allow him a horsepond! If burning the footmen's shoes, frightening the maids, and worrying the kittens be humor, he has it. It was but yesterday he fastened my wig to the back of my chair, and when I went to make a bow, I popped my bald head in Mrs. Frizzle's face!

Mrs. Hardcastle. And am I to blame? The poor boy was always too sickly to do any good. A school would be his

[e] Marlborough's ally at the Battle of Blenheim (1704) [f] in the eighteenth century, stock names for a happy couple

death. When he comes to be a little stronger, who knows what a year or two's Latin may do for him?

Hardcastle. Latin for him! A cat and fiddle! No, no, the alehouse and the stable are the only schools he'll ever go to.

Mrs. Hardcastle. Well, we must not snub the poor boy now, for I believe we shan't have him long among us. Anybody that looks in his face may see he's consumptive.

Hardcastle. Aye, if growing too fat be one of the symptoms.

Mrs. Hardcastle. He coughs sometimes.

Hardcastle. Yes, when his liquor goes the wrong way.

Mrs. Hardcastle. I'm actually afraid of his lungs.

Hardcastle. And truly, so am I; for he sometimes whoops like a speaking trumpet—(Tony *hallooing behind the scenes*) O, there he goes—a very consumptive figure, truly!

Enter Tony, *crossing the stage.*

Mrs. Hardcastle. Tony, where are going, my charmer? Won't you give papa and I a little of your company, lovee?

Tony. I'm in haste, mother; I cannot stay.

Mrs. Hardcastle. You shan't venture out this raw evening, my dear; you look most shockingly.

Tony. I can't stay, I tell you. The Three Pigeons expects me down every moment. There's some fun going forward.

Hardcastle. Aye; the alehouse, the old place: I thought so.

Mrs. Hardcastle. A low, paltry set of fellows.

Tony. Not so low, neither. There's Dick Muggins, the exciseman; Jack Slang the horse doctor; Little Aminadab, that grinds the music box; and Tom Twist, that spins the pewter platter.

Mrs. Hardcastle. Pray, my dear, disappoint them for one night at least.

Tony. As for disappointing *them,* I should not so much mind; but I can't abide to disappoint *myself.*

Mrs. Hardcastle (*detaining him*). You shan't go.

Tony. I will, I tell you.

Mrs. Hardcastle. I say you shan't.

Tony. We'll see which is strongest, you or I.

Exit, hauling her out.

Hardcastle *solus.*[g]

Hardcastle. Aye, there goes a pair that only spoil each other. But is not the whole age in a combination to drive sense and discretion out of doors? There's my pretty darling Kate; the fashions of the times have almost infected her too. By living a year or two in town, she is as fond of gauze and French frippery as the best of them.

Enter Miss Hardcastle.

Hardcastle. Blessings on my pretty innocence! Dressed out as usual, my Kate. Goodness! What a quantity of superfluous silk hast thou got about thee, girl! I could never teach the fools of this age that the indigent world could be clothed out of the trimmings of the vain.

Miss Hardcastle. You know our agreement, sir. You allow me the morning to receive and pay visits, and to dress in my own manner; and in the evening I put on my housewife's dress to please you.

Hardcastle. Well, remember, I insist on the terms of our agreement; and, by the bye, I believe I shall have occasion to try your obedience this very evening.

Miss Hardcastle. I protest, sir, I don't comprehend your meaning.

Hardcastle. Then, to be plain with you, Kate, I expect the young gentleman I have chosen to be your husband from town this very day. I have his father's letter, in which he informs me his son is set out, and that he intends to follow himself shortly after.

Miss Hardcastle. Indeed! I wish I had known something of this before. Bless me, how shall I behave? It's a thousand to one I shan't like him; our meeting will be so formal, and so like a thing of business, that I shall find no room for friendship or esteem.

Hardcastle. Depend upon it, child, I'll never control your choice; but Mr. Marlow, whom I have pitched upon, is the son of my old friend, Sir Charles Marlow, of whom you have heard me talk so often. The young gentleman has been bred a scholar, and is designed for an employment in the service of his country. I am told he's a man of an excellent understanding.

Miss Hardcastle. Is he?

Hardcastle. Very generous.

[g] alone

Miss Hardcastle. I believe I shall like him.

Hardcastle. Young and brave.

Miss Hardcastle. I'm sure I shall like him.

Hardcastle. And very handsome.

Miss Hardcastle. My dear papa, say no more (*kissing his hand*). He's mine, I'll have him!

Hardcastle. And, to crown all, Kate, he's one of the most bashful and reserved young fellows in all the world.

Miss Hardcastle. Eh! you have frozen me to death again. That word "reserved" has undone all the rest of his accomplishments. A reserved lover, it is said, always makes a suspicious husband.

Hardcastle. On the contrary, modesty seldom resides in a breast that is not enriched with nobler virtues. It was the very feature in his character that first struck me.

Miss Hardcastle. He must have more striking features to catch me, I promise you. However, if he be so young, so handsome, and so everything as you mention, I believe he'll do still. I think I'll have him.

Hardcastle. Aye, Kate, but there is still an obstacle. It is more than an even wager, he may not have *you.*

Miss Hardcastle. My dear papa, why will you mortify one so? Well, if he refuses, instead of breaking my heart at his indifference, I'll only break my glass for its flattery, set my cap to some newer fashion, and look out for some less difficult admirer.

Hardcastle. Bravely resolved! In the meantime I'll go prepare the servants for his reception; as we seldom see company, they want as much training as a company of recruits the first day's muster. *Exit.*

Miss Hardcastle (*sola*). Lud, this news of papa's puts me all in a flutter. Young, handsome; these he put last; but I put them foremost. Sensible, good-natured; I like all that. But then reserved, and sheepish; that's much against him. Yet can't he be cured of his timidity by being taught to be proud of his wife? Yes, and can't I— but I vow I'm disposing of the husband before I have secured the lover.

Enter Miss Neville.

Miss Hardcastle. I'm glad you're come, Neville, my dear. Tell me, Constance, how do I look this evening? Is there anything whimsical about me? Is it one of my well-looking days, child? Am I in face today?

Miss Neville. Perfectly, my dear. Yet, now I look again

—bless me!—sure, no accident has happened among the canary birds or the goldfishes? Has your brother or the cat been meddling? Or has the last novel been too moving?

Miss Hardcastle. No; nothing of all this. I have been threatened—I can scarce get it out—I have been threatened with a lover.

Miss Neville. And his name?

Miss Hardcastle. Is Marlow.

Miss Neville. Indeed!

Miss Hardcastle. The son of Sir Charles Marlow.

Miss Neville. As I live, the most intimate friend of Mr. Hastings, *my* admirer. They are never asunder. I believe you must have seen him when we lived in town.

Miss Hardcastle. Never.

Miss Neville. He's a very singular character, I assure you. Among women of reputation and virtue, he is the modestest man alive; but his acquaintance give him a very different character among creatures of another stamp: you understand me.

Miss Hardcastle. An odd character, indeed. I shall never be able to manage him. What shall I do? Pshaw, think no more of him, but trust to occurrences for success. But how goes on your own affair, my dear? Has my mother been courting you for my brother Tony as usual?

Miss Neville. I have just come from one of our agreeable tête-à-têtes. She has been saying a hundred tender things, and setting off her pretty monster as the very pink of perfection.

Miss Hardcastle. And her partiality is such that she actually thinks him so. A fortune like yours is no small temptation. Besides, as she has the sole management of it, I'm not surprised to see her unwilling to let it go out of the family.

Miss Neville. A fortune like mine, which chiefly consists in jewels, is no such mighty temptation. But at any rate, if my dear Hastings be but constant, I make no doubt to be too hard for her at last. However, I let her suppose that I am in love with her son; and she never once dreams that my affections are fixed upon another.

Miss Hardcastle. My good brother holds out stoutly. I could almost love him for hating you so.

Miss Neville. It is a good-natured creature at bottom, and I'm sure would wish to see me married to anybody but himself. But my aunt's bell rings for our afternoon's walk round the improvements. *Allons.* Courage is necessary, as our affairs are critical.

Miss Hardcastle. "Would it were bed-time and all were well."[h]

Exeunt.

Scene II: An alehouse room

Several shabby fellows with punch and tobacco. Tony *at the head of the table, a little higher than the rest, a mallet in his hand.*

Omnes. Hurrea! hurrea! hurrea! bravo!

First Fellow. Now, gentlemen, silence for a song. The squire is going to knock himself down[i] for a song.

Omnes. Aye, a song, a song.

Tony. Then I'll sing you, gentlemen, a song I made upon this alehouse, the Three Pigeons.

Song

Let schoolmasters puzzle their brain
With grammar, and nonsense, and learning;
Good liquor, I stoutly maintain,
Gives genius a better discerning.
Let them brag of their heathenish gods,
Their Lethes, their Styxes, and Stygians;
Their Quis, and their Quaes, and their Quods,[j]
They're all but a parcel of pigeons.
Toroddle, toroddle, toroll!

When Methodist preachers come down,
A-preaching that drinking is sinful,
I'll wager the rascals a crown,
They always preach best with a skinful.
But when you come down with your pence,
For a slice of their scurvy religion,
I'll leave it to all men of sense,
But you, my good friend, are the pigeon.
Toroddle, toroddle, toroll!

Then come, put the jorum[k] about,
And let us be merry and clever,
Our hearts and our liquors are stout,

[h] Cf. Falstaff in *1 Henry IV*, V. i. 125. [i] Tony, as chairman, is calling upon himself for a song [j] Latin relative pronouns [k] drinking bowl

Here's the Three Jolly Pigeons for ever.
Let some cry up woodcock or hare,
Your bustards, your ducks, and your widgeons;
But of all the birds in the air,
Here's a health to the Three Jolly Pigeons.
Toroddle, toroddle, toroll!

Omnes. Bravo, bravo!

First Fellow. The squire has got spunk in him.

Second Fellow. I loves to hear him sing, bekeays he never gives us nothing that's *low*.

Third Fellow. O damn anything that's *low*, I cannot bear it.

Fourth Fellow. The genteel thing is the genteel thing at any time; if so be that a gentleman bees in a concatenation accordingly.

Third Fellow. I like the maxum of it, Master Muggins. What, though I am obligated to dance a bear, a man may be a gentleman for all that. May this be my poison if my bear ever dances but to the very genteelest of tunes: "Water Parted," or the minuet in *Ariadne*.

Second Fellow. What a pity it is the squire is not come to his own. It would be well for all the publicans within ten miles round of him.

Tony. Ecod, and so it would, Master Slang. I'd then show what it was to keep choice of company.

Second Fellow. Oh, he takes after his own father for that. To be sure, old squire Lumpkin was the finest gentleman I ever set my eyes on. For winding the straight horn, or beating a thicket for a hare, or a wench, he never had his fellow. It was a saying in the place, that he kept the best horses, dogs, and girls, in the whole county.

Tony. Ecod, and when I'm of age I'll be no bastard, I promise you. I have been thinking of Bet Bouncer and the miller's gray mare to begin with. But come, my boys, drink about and be merry, for you pay no reckoning. Well, Stingo, what's the matter?

Enter Landlord.

Landlord. There be two gentlemen in a post chaise at the door. They have lost their way upo' the forest; and they are talking something about Mr. Hardcastle.

Tony. As sure as can be, one of them must be the gentleman that's coming down to court my sister. Do they seem to be Londoners?

Landlord. I believe they may. They look woundily[1] like Frenchmen.

Tony. Then desire them to step this way, and I'll set them right in a twinkling. (*Exit* Landlord.) Gentlemen, as they mayn't be good enough company for you, step down for a moment, and I'll be with you in the squeezing of a lemon. *Exeunt Mob.*

Tony (*solus*). Father-in-law has been calling me whelp and hound this half year. Now, if I pleased, I could be so revenged upon the old grumbletonian. But then I'm afraid—afraid of what? I shall soon be worth fifteen hundred a year, and let him frighten me out of *that* if he can!

Enter Landlord, *conducting* Marlow *and* Hastings.

Marlow. What a tedious, uncomfortable day have we had of it! We were told it was but forty miles across the country, and we have come above threescore!

Hastings. And all, Marlow, from that unaccountable reserve of yours that would not let us enquire more frequently on the way.

Marlow. I own, Hastings, I am unwilling to lay myself under an obligation to everyone I meet, and often stand the chance of an unmannerly answer.

Hastings. At present, however, we are not likely to receive any answer.

Tony. No offense, gentlemen. But I'm told you have been enquiring for one Mr. Hardcastle in these parts. Do you know what part of the country you are in?

Hastings. Not in the least, sir, but should thank you for information.

Tony. Nor the way you came?

Hastings. No, sir; but if you can inform us—

Tony. Why, gentlemen, if you know neither the road you are going, nor where you are, nor the road you came, the first thing I have to inform you is, that—you have lost your way.

Marlow. We wanted no ghost to tell us that.[m]

Tony. Pray, gentlemen, may I be so bold as to ask the place from whence you came?

Marlow. That's not necessary towards directing us where we are to go.

[1] extremely [m] Cf. Horatio in *Hamlet,* I. v. 125.

Tony. No offense; but question for question is all fair, you know. Pray, gentlemen, is not this same Hardcastle a cross-grained, old-fashioned, whimsical fellow with an ugly face, a daughter, and a pretty son?

Hastings. We have not seen the gentleman; but he has the family you mention.

Tony. The daughter, a tall, trapesing, trolloping, talkative maypole—the son, a pretty, well-bred, agreeable youth, that everybody is fond of?

Marlow. Our information differs in this. The daughter is said to be well-bred, and beautiful; the son, an awkward booby, reared up and spoiled at his mother's apron string.

Tony. He-he-hem!—Then, gentlemen, all I have to tell you is, that you won't reach Mr. Hardcastle's house this night, I believe.

Hastings. Unfortunate!

Tony. It's a damned long, dark, boggy, dirty, dangerous way. Stingo, tell the gentlemen the way to Mr. Hardcastle's. (*Winking upon the* Landlord.) Mr. Hardcastle's of Quagmire Marsh, you understand me.

Landlord. Master Hardcastle's! Lack-a-daisy, my masters, you're come a deadly deal wrong! When you came to the bottom of the hill, you should have crossed down Squash Lane.

Marlow. Cross down Squash Lane!

Landlord. Then you were to keep straight forward, until you came to four roads.

Marlow. Come to where four roads meet!

Tony. Aye, but you must be sure to take only one of them.

Marlow. O, sir, you're facetious!

Tony. Then, keeping to the right, you are to go sideways till you come upon Crack-skull Common: there you must look sharp for the track of the wheel, and go forward, till you come to Farmer Murrain's barn. Coming to the farmer's barn, you are to turn to the right, and then to the left, and then to the right about again, till you find out the old mill—

Marlow. Zounds, man! We could as soon find out the longitude!

Hastings. What's to be done, Marlow?

Marlow. This house promises but a poor reception; though perhaps the landlord can accommodate us.

Landlord. Alack, master, we have but one spare bed in the whole house.

Tony. And to my knowledge, that's taken up by three lodgers already. (*After a pause, in which the rest seem disconcerted.*) I have hit it. Don't you think, Stingo, our landlady could accommodate the gentlemen by the fireside, with—three chairs and a bolster?

Hastings. I hate sleeping by the fireside.

Marlow. And I detest your three chairs and a bolster.

Tony. You do, do you?—then let me see—what if you go on a mile further, to the Buck's Head; the old Buck's Head on the hill, one of the best inns in the whole country?

Hastings. Oho! so we have escaped an adventure for this night, however.

Landlord (*apart to* Tony). Sure, you ben't sending them to your father's as an inn, be you?

Tony. Mum, you fool, you. Let *them* find that out. (*To them.*) You have only to keep on straight forward, till you come to a large old house by the roadside. You'll see a pair of large horns over the door. That's the sign. Drive up the yard, and call stoutly about you.

Hastings. Sir, we are obliged to you. The servants can't miss the way?

Tony. No, no: but I tell you, though, the landlord is rich, and going to leave off business; so he wants to be thought a gentleman, saving your presence, he! he! he! He'll be for giving you his company, and, ecod, if you mind him, he'll persuade you that his mother was an alderman, and his aunt a justice of peace!

Landlord. A troublesome old blade, to be sure; but 'a keeps as good wines and beds as any in the whole country.

Marlow. Well, if he supplies us with these, we shall want no further connection. We are to turn to the right, did you say?

Tony. No, no; straight forward. I'll just step myself, and show you a piece of the way. (*To the* Landlord.) Mum.

Landlord. Ah, bless your heart for a sweet, pleasant—damned mischievous son of a whore. *Exeunt.*

ACT II

An old-fashioned house.

(*Enter* Hardcastle, *followed by three or four awkward* Servants.)

Hardcastle. Well, I hope you're perfect in the table exercise I have been teaching you these three days. You all know your posts and your places, and can show that you have been used to good company, without ever stirring from home.

Omnes. Aye, aye.

Hardcastle. When company comes, you are not to pop out and stare, and then run in again, like frightened rabbits in a warren.

Omnes. No, no.

Hardcastle. You, Diggory, whom I have taken from the barn, are to make a show at the side table; and you, Roger, whom I have advanced from the plow, are to place yourself behind *my* chair. But you're not to stand so, with your hands in your pockets. Take your hands from your pockets, Roger; and from your head, you blockhead, you. See how Diggory carries his hands. They're a little too stiff, indeed, but that's no great matter.

Diggory. Aye, mind how I hold them. I learned to hold my hands this way, when I was upon drill for the militia. And so being upon drill—

Hardcastle. You must not be so talkative, Diggory. You must be all attention to the guests. You must hear us talk, and not think of talking; you must see us drink, and not think of drinking; you must see us eat, and not think of eating.

Diggory. By the laws, your worship, that's parfectly unpossible. Whenever Diggory sees yeating going forward, ecod, he's always wishing for a mouthful himself.

Hardcastle. Blockhead! Is not a bellyful in the kitchen as good as a bellyful in the parlor? Stay your stomach with that reflection.

Diggory. Ecod, I thank your worship, I'll make a shift to stay my stomach with a slice of cold beef in the pantry.

Hardcastle. Diggory, you are too talkative. Then, if I happen to say a good thing, or tell a good story at table, you must not all burst out a-laughing, as if you made part of the company.

Diggory. Then, ecod, your worship must not tell the story of old Grouse in the gun room: I can't help laughing at that—he! he! he!—for the soul of me! We have laughed at that these twenty years—ha! ha! ha!

Hardcastle. Ha! ha! ha! The story is a good one. Well, honest Diggory, you may laugh at that—but still remember to be attentive. Suppose one of the company should call for a glass of wine, how will you behave? A glass of wine, sir, if you please. (*To* Diggory.) Eh, why don't you move?

Diggory. Ecod, your worship, I never have courage till I see the eatables and drinkables brought upo' the table, and then I'm as bauld as a lion.

Hardcastle. What, will nobody move?

First Servant. I'm not to leave this pleace.

Second Servant. I'm sure it's no pleace of mine.

Third Servant. Nor mine, for sartain.

Diggory. Wauns, and I'm sure it canna be mine.

Hardcastle. You numskulls! and so while, like your betters, you are quarreling for places, the guests must be starved. O, you dunces! I find I must begin all over again.—But don't I hear a coach drive into the yard? To your posts, you blockheads. I'll go in the meantime and give my old friend's son a hearty reception at the gate. *Exit* Hardcastle.

Diggory. By the elevens, my pleace is gone quite out of my head.

Roger. I know that my pleace is to be everywhere!

First Servant. Where the devil is mine?

Second Servant. My pleace is to be nowhere at all; and so I'ze go about my business!

Exeunt Servants, *running about as if frighted, different ways.*

Enter Servant *with candles, showing in* Marlow *and* Hastings.

Servant. Welcome, gentlemen, very welcome! This way.

Hastings. After the disappointments of the day, welcome

once more, Charles, to the comforts of a clean room and a good fire. Upon my word, a very well-looking house; antique but creditable.

Marlow. The usual fate of a large mansion. Having first ruined the master by good housekeeping, it at last comes to levy contributions as an inn.

Hastings. As you say, we passengers are to be taxed to pay for all these fineries. I have often seen a good side-board, or a marble chimney piece, though not actually put in the bill, inflame a reckoning confoundedly.

Marlow. Travelers, George, must pay in all places. The only difference is, that in good inns you pay dearly for luxuries, in bad inns, you are fleeced and starved.

Hastings. You have lived pretty much among them. In truth, I have been often surprised that you, who have seen so much of the world, with your natural good sense, and your many opportunities, could never yet acquire a requisite share of assurance.

Marlow. The Englishman's malady. But tell me, George, where could I have learned that assurance you talk of? My life has been chiefly spent in a college or an inn, in seclusion from that lovely part of the creation that chiefly teach men confidence. I don't know that I was ever familiarly acquainted with a single modest woman —except my mother. But among females of another class, you know—

Hastings. Aye, among them you are impudent enough of all conscience!

Marlow. They are of *us*, you know.

Hastings. But in the company of women of reputation I never saw such an idiot, such a trembler; you look for all the world as if you wanted an opportunity of stealing out of the room.

Marlow. Why, man, that's because I *do* want to steal out of the room. Faith, I have often formed a resolution to break the ice, and rattle away at any rate. But I don't know how, a single glance from a pair of fine eyes has totally overset my resolution. An impudent fellow may counterfeit modesty, but I'll be hanged if a modest man can ever counterfeit impudence.

Hastings. If you could but say half the fine things to them, that I have heard you lavish upon the barmaid of an inn, or even a college bed-maker—

Marlow. Why, George, I can't say fine things to them. They freeze, they petrify me. They may talk of a comet, or a burning mountain, or some such bagatelle; but to me, a modest woman, dressed out in all her finery, is the most tremendous object of the whole creation.

Hastings. Ha! ha! ha! At this rate, man, how can you ever expect to marry?

Marlow. Never; unless, as among kings and princes, my bride were to be courted by proxy. If, indeed, like an Eastern bridegroom, one were to be introduced to a wife he never saw before, it might be endured. But to go through all the terrors of a formal courtship, together with the episode of aunts, grandmothers, and cousins, and at last to blurt out the broad staring question of, Madam, will you marry me? No, no, that's a strain much above me, I assure you!

Hastings. I pity you. But how do you intend behaving to the lady you are come down to visit at the request of your father?

Marlow. As I behave to all other ladies. Bow very low; answer yes, or no, to all her demands. But for the rest, I don't think I shall venture to look in her face till I see my father's again.

Hastings. I'm surprised that one who is so warm a friend can be so cool a lover.

Marlow. To be explicit, my dear Hastings, my chief inducement down was to be instrumental in forwarding your happiness, not my own. Miss Neville loves you; the family don't know you; as my friend you are sure of a reception; and let honor do the rest.

Hastings. My dear Marlow! But I'll suppress the emotion. Were I a wretch, meanly seeking to carry off a fortune, you should be the last man in the world I would apply to for assistance. But Miss Neville's person is all I ask, and that is mine, both from her deceased father's consent, and her own inclination.

Marlow. Happy man! You have talents and art to captivate any woman. I'm doomed to adore the sex, and yet to converse with the only part of it I despise. This stammer in my address, and this awkward unprepossessing visage of mine, can never permit me to soar above the reach of a milliner's prentice, or one of the duchesses of Drury Lane.[n] Pshaw! this fellow here to interrupt us.

Enter Hardcastle.

[n] women of the town

Hardcastle. Gentlemen, once more you are heartily welcome. Which is Mr. Marlow? Sir, you're heartily welcome. It's not my way, you see, to receive my friends with my back to the fire. I like to give them a hearty reception in the old style at my gate. I like to see their horses and trunks taken care of.

Marlow (*aside*). He has got our names from the servants already. (*To him.*) We approve your caution and hospitality, sir. (*To* Hastings.) I have been thinking, George, of changing our traveling dresses in the morning. I am grown confoundedly ashamed of mine.

Hardcastle. I beg, Mr. Marlow, you'll use no ceremony in this house.

Hastings. I fancy, [Charles], you're right: the first blow is half the battle. I intend opening the campaign with the white and gold.

Hardcastle. Mr. Marlow—Mr. Hastings—gentlemen—pray be under no constraint in this house. This is Liberty Hall, gentlemen. You may do just as you please here.

Marlow. Yet, George, if we open the campaign too fiercely at first, we may want ammunition before it is over. I think to reserve the embroidery to secure a retreat.

Hardcastle. Your talking of a retreat, Mr. Marlow, puts me in mind of the Duke of Marlborough, when we went to besiege Denain. He first summoned the garrison—

Marlow. Don't you think the *ventre d'or* waistcoat will do with the plain brown?

Hardcastle. He first summoned the garrison, which might consist of about five thousand men—

Hastings. I think not: brown and yellow mix but very poorly.

Hardcastle. I say, gentlemen, as I was telling you, he summoned the garrison, which might consist of about five thousand men—

Marlow. The girls like finery.

Hardcastle. Which might consist of about five thousand men, well appointed with stores, ammunition, and other implements of war. "Now," says the Duke of Marlborough to George Brooks, that stood next to him—you must have heard of George Brooks—"I'll pawn my Dukedom," says he, "but I take that garrison without spilling a drop of blood." So—

Marlow. What, my good friend, if you gave us a glass of

punch in the meantime, it would help us to carry on the siege with vigor.

Hadcastle. Punch, sir! (*Aside.*) This is the most unaccountable kind of modesty I ever met with.

Marlow. Yes, sir, punch! A glass of warm punch, after our journey, will be comfortable. This is Liberty Hall, you know.

Hardcastle. Here's a cup, sir.

Marlow (*aside*). So this fellow, in his Liberty Hall, will only let us have just what he pleases.

Hardcastle (*taking the cup*). I hope you'll find it to your mind. I have prepared it with my own hands, and I believe you'll own the ingredients are tolerable. Will you be so good as to pledge me, sir? Here, Mr. Marlow, here is our better acquaintance. (*Drinks.*)

Marlow (*aside*). A very impudent fellow this! But he's a character, and I'll humor him a little. Sir, my service to you. (*Drinks.*)

Hastings (*aside*). I see this fellow wants to give us his company, and forgets that he's an innkeeper, before he has learned to be a gentleman.

Marlow. From the excellence of your cup, my old friend, I suppose you have a good deal of business in this part of the country. Warm work, now and then, at elections, I suppose?

Hardcastle. No, sir, I have long given that work over. Since our betters have hit upon the expedient of electing each other, there's no business "for us that sell ale." [o]

Hastings. So, then you have no turn for politics, I find.

Hardcastle. Not in the least. There was a time, indeed, I fretted myself about the mistakes of government, like other people; but finding myself every day grow more angry, and the government growing no better, I left it to mend itself. Since that, I no more trouble my head about Heyder Ally or Ally Cawn than about "Ally Croaker." [p] Sir, my service to you.

Hastings. So that with eating above stairs, and drinking below, with receiving your friends within, and amusing them without, you lead a good, pleasant, bustling life of it.

Hardcastle. I do stir about a great deal, that's certain.

[o] ordinary people [p] Ally and Cawn were Indian sultans; "Ally Croaker," a popular Irish song

Half the differences of the parish are adjusted in this very parlor.

Marlow (*after drinking*). And you have an argument in your cup, old gentleman, better than any in Westminster Hall.[q]

Hardcastle. Aye, young gentleman, that, and a little philosophy.

Marlow (*aside*). Well, this is the first time I ever heard of an innkeeper's philosophy.

Hastings. So then, like an experienced general, you attack them on every quarter. If you find their reason manageable, you attack it with your philosophy; if you find they have no reason, you attack them with this. Here's your health, my philosopher. (*Drinks.*)

Hardcastle. Good, very good, thank you; ha! ha! Your generalship puts me in mind of Prince Eugene, when he fought the Turks at the battle of Belgrade. You shall hear—

Marlow. Instead of the battle of Belgrade, I believe it's almost time to talk about supper. What has your philosophy got in the house for supper?

Hardcastle. For supper, sir! (*Aside.*) Was ever such a request to a man in his own house!

Marlow. Yes, sir, supper, sir; I begin to feel an appetite. I shall make devilish work tonight in the larder, I promise you.

Hardcastle (*aside*). Such a brazen dog sure never my eyes beheld. (*To him.*) Why, really, sir, as for supper I can't well tell. My Dorothy, and the cook-maid, settle these things between them. I leave these kind of things entirely to them.

Marlow. You do, do you?

Hardcastle. Entirely. By the bye, I believe they are in actual consultation upon what's for supper this moment in the kitchen.

Marlow. Then I beg they'll admit *me* as one of their privy council. It's a way I have got. When I travel I always chose to regulate my own supper. Let the cook be called. No offense, I hope, sir.

Hardcastle. Oh no, sir, none in the least; yet, I don't know how: our Bridget, the cook-maid, is not very communicative upon these occasions. Should we send for her, she might scold us all out of the house.

Hastings. Let's see your list of the larder, then. I ask it

[q] seat of Law Courts

as a favor. I always match my appetite to my bill of fare.

Marlow (*to* Hardcastle, *who looks at them with surprise*). Sir, he's very right, and it's my way, too.

Hardcastle. Sir, you have a right to command here. Here, Roger, bring us the bill of fare for tonight's supper; I believe it's drawn out. [*Exit* Roger.] Your manner, Mr. Hastings, puts me in mind of my uncle, Colonel Wallop. It was a saying of his, that no man was sure of his supper till he had eaten it.

Hastings (*aside*). All upon the high ropes! His uncle a colonel! We shall soon hear of his mother being a justice of peace. [*Re-enter* Roger.] But let's hear the bill of fare.

Marlow (*perusing*). What's here? For the first course; for the second course; for the dessert. The devil, sir, do you think we have brought down the whole Joiners' Company, or the Corporation of Bedford, to eat up such a supper? Two or three little things, clean and comfortable, will do.

Hastings. But let's hear it.

Marlow (*reading*). For the first course at the top, a pig, and prune sauce.

Hastings. Damn your pig, I say!

Marlow. And damn your prune sauce, say I!

Hardcastle. And yet, gentlemen, to men that are hungry, pig with prune sauce is very good eating.

Marlow. At the bottom a calf's tongue and brains.

Hastings. Let your brains be knocked out, my good sir, I don't like them.

Marlow. Or you may clap them on a plate by themselves. I do.

Hardcastle (*aside*). Their impudence confounds me. (*To them.*) Gentlemen, you are my guests, make what alterations you please. Is there anything else you wish to retrench or alter, gentlemen?

Marlow. Item: A pork pie, a boiled rabbit and sausages, a florentine,[r] a shaking pudding, and a dish of tiff-taff-taffety cream!

Hastings. Confound your made dishes; I shall be as much at a loss in this house as at a green and yellow dinner at the French ambassador's table. I'm for plain eating.

Hardcastle. I'm sorry, gentlemen, that I have nothing you

[r] a baked pie

like, but if there be anything you have a particular fancy to—

Marlow. Why really, sir, your bill of fare is so exquisite, that any one part of it is full as good as another. Send us what you please. So much for supper. And now to see that our beds are aired, and properly taken care of.

Hardcastle. I entreat you'll leave all that to me. You shall not stir a step.

Marlow. Leave that to you! I protest, sir, you must excuse me; I always look to these things myself.

Hardcastle. I must insist, sir, you'll make yourself easy on that head.

Marlow. You see I'm resolved on it. (*Aside.*) A very troublesome fellow this, as ever I met with.

Hardcastle. Well, sir, I'm resolved at least to attend you. (*Aside.*) This may be modern modesty, but I never saw anything look so like old-fashioned impudence.

Exeunt Marlow *and* Hardcastle.

Hastings (*solus*). So I find this fellow's civilities begin to grow troublesome. But who can be angry at those assiduities which are meant to please him? Ha! what do I see? Miss Neville, by all that's happy!

Enter Miss Neville.

Miss Neville. My dear Hastings! To what unexpected good fortune, to what accident, am I to ascribe this happy meeting?

Hastings. Rather let me ask the same question, as I could never have hoped to meet my dearest Constance at an inn.

Miss Neville. An inn! Sure you mistake; my aunt, my guardian, lives here. What could induce you to think this house an inn?

Hastings. My friend, Mr. Marlow, with whom I came down, and I, have been sent here as to an inn, I assure you. A young fellow, whom we accidentally met at a house hard by, directed us thither.

Miss Neville. Certainly it must be one of my hopeful cousin's tricks, of whom you have heard me talk so often: ha! ha! ha!

Hastings. He whom your aunt intends for you? He of whom I have such just apprehensions?

Miss Neville. You have nothing to fear from him, I assure you. You'd adore him if you knew how heartily he despises me. My aunt knows it, too, and has undertaken to court me for him, and actually begins to think she has made a conquest.

Hastings. Thou dear dissembler! You must know, my Constance, I have just seized this happy opportunity of my friend's visit here to get admittance into the family. The horses that carried us down are now fatigued with their journey, but they'll soon be refreshed; and then, if my dearest girl will trust in her faithful Hastings, we shall soon be landed in France, where even among slaves the laws of marriage are respected.

Miss Neville. I have often told you that though ready to obey you, I yet should leave my little fortune behind with reluctance. The greatest part of it was left me by my uncle, the India Director, and chiefly consists in jewels. I have been for some time persuading my aunt to let me wear them. I fancy I'm very near succeeding. The instant they are put into my possession you shall find me ready to make them and myself yours.

Hastings. Perish the baubles! Your person is all I desire. In the meantime, my friend Marlow must not be let into his mistake. I know the strange reserve of his temper is such that, if abruptly informed of it, he would instantly quit the house before our plan was ripe for execution.

Miss Neville. But how shall we keep him in the deception? Miss Hardcastle is just returned from walking; what if we still continue to deceive him? —This, this way—(*They confer.*)

Enter Marlow.

Marlow. The assiduities of these good people tease me beyond bearing. My host seems to think it ill manners to leave me alone, and so he claps not only himself, but his old-fashioned wife on my back. They talk of coming to sup with us, too; and then, I suppose, we are to run the gantlet through all the rest of the family. —What have we got here?—

Hastings. My dear Charles! Let me congratulate you!—The most fortunate accident! —Who do you think is just alighted?

Marlow. Cannot guess.

Hastings. Our mistresses, boy, Miss Hardcastle and Miss Neville. Give me leave to introduce Miss Constance Neville to your acquaintance. Happening to dine in the neighborhood, they called, on their return, to take fresh horses here. Miss Hardcastle has just stepped into the next room, and will be back in an instant. Wasn't it lucky? eh!

Marlow (*aside*). I have just been mortified enough of all conscience, and here comes something to complete my embarrassment.

Hastings. Well! but wasn't it the most fortunate thing in the world?

Marlow. Oh! yes. Very fortunate—a most joyful encounter. —But our dresses, George, you know, are in disorder. —What if we should postpone the happiness till tomorrow? —Tomorrow at her own house.—It will be every bit as convenient—and rather more respectful. —Tomorrow let it be. (*Offering to go.*)

Miss Neville. By no means, sir. Your ceremony will displease her. The disorder of your dress will show the ardor of your impatience. Besides, she knows you are in the house, and will permit you to see her.

Marlow. Oh! the devil! how shall I support it? Hem! hem! Hastings, you must not go. You are to assist me, you know. I shall be confoundedly ridiculous. Yet, hang it! I'll take courage. Hem!

Hastings. Pshaw, man! it's but the first plunge, and all's over. She's but a woman, you know.

Marlow. And of all women, she that I dread most to encounter!

Enter Miss Hardcastle, *as returned from walking, a bonnet, etc.*

Hastings (*introducing them*). Miss Hardcastle. Mr. Marlow. I'm proud of bringing two persons of such merit together, that only want to know, to esteem each other.

Miss Hardcastle (*aside*). Now, for meeting my modest gentleman with a demure face, and quite in his own manner. (*After a pause, in which he appears very uneasy and disconcerted.*) I'm glad of your safe arrival, sir—I'm told you had some accidents by the way.

Marlow. Only a few, madam. Yes, we had some. Yes, madam, a good many accidents, but should be sorry—madam—or rather glad of any accidents—that are so agreeably concluded. Hem!

Hastings (*to him*). You never spoke better in your whole life. Keep it up, and I'll insure you the victory.

Miss Hardcastle. I'm afraid you flatter, sir. You that have seen so much of the finest company can find little entertainment in an obscure corner of the country.

Marlow (*gathering courage*). I have lived, indeed, in the world, madam; but I have kept very little company. I have been but an observer upon life, madam, while others were enjoying it.

Miss Neville. But that, I am told, is the way to enjoy it at last.

Hastings (*to him*). Cicero never spoke better. Once more, and you are confirmed in assurance forever.

Marlow (*to him*). Hem! Stand by me, then, and when I'm down, throw in a word or two to set me up again.

Miss Hardcastle. An observer, like you, upon life, were, I fear, disagreeably employed, since you must have had much more to censure than to approve.

Marlow. Pardon me, madam. I was always willing to be amused. The folly of most people is rather an object of mirth than uneasiness.

Hastings (*to him*). Bravo, bravo. Never spoke so well in your whole life. Well, Miss Hardcastle, I see that you and Mr. Marlow are going to be very good company. I believe our being here will but embarrass the interview.

Marlow. Not in the least, Mr. Hastings. We like your company of all things. (*To him.*) Zounds! George, sure you won't go? How can you leave us?

Hastings. Our presence will but spoil conversation, so we'll retire to the next room. (*To him.*) You don't consider, man, that we are to manage a little tête-à-tête of our own.

Exeunt [Hastings *and* Miss Neville.]

Miss Hardcastle (*after a pause*). But you have not been wholly an observer, I presume, sir. The ladies, I should hope, have employed some part of your addresses.

Marlow (*relapsing into timidity*). Pardon me, madam, I—I—I—as yet have studied—only—to—deserve them.

Miss Hardcastle. And that some say is the very worst way to obtain them.

Marlow. Perhaps so, madam. But I love to converse only with the more grave and sensible part of the sex.—But I'm afraid I grow tiresome.

Miss Hardcastle. Not at all, sir; there is nothing I like so much as grave conversation myself; I could hear it forever. Indeed, I have often been surprised how a man of sentiment could ever admire those light airy pleasures, where nothing reaches the heart.

Marlow. It's—a disease—of the mind, madam. In the variety of tastes there must be some who, wanting a relish for—um-a-um.

Miss Hardcastle. I understand you, sir. There must be some, who, wanting a relish for refined pleasures, pretend to despise what they are incapable of tasting.

Marlow. My meaning, madam, but infinitely better expressed. And I can't help observing—a—

Miss Hardcastle (*aside*). Who could ever suppose this fellow impudent upon some occasions. (*To him.*) You were going to observe, sir—

Marlow. I was observing, madam—I protest, madam, I forget what I was going to observe.

Miss Hardcastle (*aside*). I vow and so do I. (*To him.*) You were observing, sir, that in this age of hypocrisy—something about hypocrisy, sir.

Marlow. Yes, madam. In this age of hypocrisy, there are few who upon strict inquiry do not—a—a—a—

Miss Hardcastle. I understand you perfectly, sir.

Marlow (*aside*). Egad! and that's more than I do myself!

Miss Hardcastle. You mean that in this hypocritical age there are few that do not condemn in public what they practise in private, and think they pay every debt to virtue when they praise it.

Marlow. True, madam; those who have most virtue in their mouths, have least of it in their bosoms. But I'm sure I tire you, madam.

Miss Hardcastle. Not in the least, sir; there's something so agreeable and spirited in your manner, such life and force—pray, sir, go on.

Marlow. Yes, madam. I was saying—that there are some occasions—when a total want of courage, madam, destroys all the—and puts us—upon a—a—a—

Miss Hardcastle. I agree with you entirely, a want of courage upon some occasions assumes the appearance of ignorance, and betrays us when we most want to excel. I beg you'll proceed.

Marlow. Yes, madam. Morally speaking, madam—but I see Miss Neville expecting us in the next room. I would not intrude for the world.

Miss Hardcastle. I protest, sir, I never was more agreeably entertained in all my life. Pray go on.

Marlow. Yes, madam. I was—but she beckons us to join her. Madam, shall I do myself the honor to attend you?

Miss Hardcastle. Well then, I'll follow.

Marlow (*aside*). This pretty smooth dialogue has done for me. *Exit.*

Miss Hardcastle (*sola*). Ha! ha! ha! Was there ever such a sober, sentimental interview? I'm certain he scarce looked in my face the whole time. Yet the fellow, but for his unaccountable bashfulness, is pretty well, too. He has good sense, but then so buried in his fears, that it fatigues one more than ignorance. If I could teach him a little confidence, it would be doing somebody that I know of a piece of service. But who is that somebody?—That, faith, is a question I can scarce answer. *Exit.*

Enter Tony *and* Miss Neville, *followed by* Mrs. Hardcastle *and* Hastings.

Tony. What do you follow me for, cousin Con? I wonder you're not ashamed to be so very engaging.

Miss Neville. I hope, cousin, one may speak to one's own relations, and not be to blame.

Tony. Aye, but I know what sort of a relation you want to make me, though; but it won't do. I tell you, cousin Con, it won't do; so I beg you'll keep your distance, I want no nearer relationship. (*She follows, coquetting him to the back scene.*)

Mrs. Hardcastle. Well! I vow, Mr. Hastings, you are very entertaining. There's nothing in the world I love to talk of so much as London, and the fashions, though I was never there myself.

Hastings. Never there! You amaze me! From your air and manner, I concluded you had been bred all your life either at Ranelagh, St. James's, or Tower Wharf.[8]

Mrs. Hardcastle. Oh! sir, you're only pleased to say so. We country persons can have no manner at all. I'm in love with the town, and that serves to raise me above some of our neighboring rustics; but who can have a manner, that has never seen the Pantheon, the Grotto Gardens, the Borough, and such places where the nobility chiefly resort? All I can do is to enjoy London at second hand. I take care to know every tête-à-tête from the *Scandalous Magazine,* and have all the fashions as they come out, in a letter from the two Miss Rickets of Crooked Lane. Pray how do you like this head, Mr. Hastings?

[8] Tower Wharf, and the Borough in the following speech, were unfashionable places; the other names refer to resorts of the nobility

Hastings. Extremely elegant and *dégagée,* upon my word, madam. Your *friseur* is a Frenchman, I suppose?

Mrs. Hardcastle. I protest, I dressed it myself from a print in the *Ladies' Memorandum-book* for the last year.

Hastings. Indeed. Such a head in a side box, at the play-house, would draw as many gazers as my Lady Mayoress at a city ball.

Mrs. Hardcastle. I vow, since inoculation began, there is no such thing to be seen as a plain woman; so one must dress a little particular, or one may escape in the crowd.

Hastings. But that can never be your case, madam, in any dress! (*Bowing.*)

Mrs. Hardcastle. Yet, what signifies *my* dressing when I have such a piece of antiquity by my side as Mr. Hard-castle? All I can say will never argue down a single but-ton from his clothes. I have often wanted him to throw off his great flaxen wig, and where he was bald, to plaster it over like my Lord Pately, with powder.

Hastings. You are right, madam; for, as among the ladies there are none ugly, so among the men there are none old.

Mrs. Hardcastle. But what do you think his answer was? Why, with his usual Gothic vivacity, he said I only wanted him to throw off his wig to convert it into a *tête*[t] for my own wearing!

Hastings. Intolerable! At your age you may wear what you please, and it must become you.

Mrs. Hardcastle. Pray, Mr. Hastings, what do you take to be the most fashionable age about town?

Hastings. Some time ago forty was all the mode; but I'm told the ladies intend to bring up fifty for the ensuing winter.

Mrs. Hardcastle. Seriously? Then I shall be too young for the fashion!

Hastings. No lady begins now to put on jewels till she's past forty. For instance, Miss there, in a polite circle would be considered as a child, as a mere maker of sam-plers.

Mrs. Hardcastle. And yet Mrs.[u] Niece thinks herself as much a woman, and is as fond of jewels as the oldest of us all.

Hastings. Your niece, is she? And that young gentleman, a brother of yours, I should presume?

[t] a lady's wig [u] mistress, applied to unmarried as well as to married women

Mrs. Hardcastle. My son, sir. They are contracted to each other. Observe their little sports. They fall in and out ten times a day, as if they were man and wife already. (*To them.*) Well, Tony, child, what soft things are you saying to your cousin Constance this evening?

Tony. I have been saying no soft things; but that it's very hard to be followed about so! Ecod! I've not a place in the house now that's left to myself but the stable.

Mrs. Hardcastle. Never mind him, Con, my dear. He's in another story behind your back.

Miss Neville. There's something generous in my cousin's manner. He falls out before faces to be forgiven in private.

Tony. That's a damned confounded—crack.[v]

Mrs. Hardcastle. Ah! he's a sly one. Don't you think they're like each other about the mouth, Mr. Hastings? The Blenkinsop mouth to a *T*. They're of a size, too. Back to back, my pretties, that Mr. Hastings may see you. Come, Tony.

Tony. You had as good not make me, I tell you. (*Measuring.*)

Miss Neville. Oh lud! he has almost cracked my head.

Mrs. Hardcastle. Oh, the monster! For shame, Tony. You a man, and behave so!

Tony. If I'm a man, let me have my fortin. Ecod! I'll not be made a fool of no longer.

Mrs. Hardcastle. Is this, ungrateful boy, all that I'm to get for the pains I have taken in your education? I that have rocked you in your cradle, and fed that pretty mouth with a spoon! Did not I work that waistcoat to make you genteel? Did not I prescribe for you every day, and weep while the receipt was operating?

Tony. Ecod! you had reason to weep, for you have been dosing me ever since I was born. I have gone through every receipt in *The Complete Housewife* ten times over; and you have thoughts of coursing me through Quincy[w] next spring. But, ecod! I tell you, I'll not be made a fool of no longer.

Mrs. Hardcastle. Wasn't it all for your good, viper? Wasn't it all for your good?

Tony. I wish you'd let me and my good alone, then. Snubbing this way when I'm in spirits. If I'm to have any good, let it come of itself; not to keep dinging it, dinging it into one so.

[v] lie [w] author of *Complete English Dispensatory*

Mrs. Hardcastle. That's false; I never see you when you're in spirits. No, Tony, you then go to the alehouse or kennel. I'm never to be delighted with your agreeable wild notes, unfeeling monster!

Tony. Ecod! Mamma, your own notes are the wildest of the two.

Mrs. Hardcastle. Was ever the like? But I see he wants to break my heart, I see he does.

Hastings. Dear Madam, permit me to lecture the young gentleman a little. I'm certain I can persuade him to his duty.

Mrs. Hardcastle. Well, I must retire. Come, Constance, my love. You see, Mr. Hastings, the wretchedness of my situation. Was ever poor woman so plagued with a dear, sweet, pretty, provoking, undutiful boy?

Exeunt Mrs. Hardcastle *and* Miss Neville.

Hastings, Tony

Tony (*singing*). "There was a young man riding by, and fain would have his will. Rang do didlo dee."
Don't mind her. Let her cry. It's the comfort of her heart. I have seen her and sister cry over a book for an hour together, and they said they liked the book the better the more it made them cry.

Hastings. Then you're no friend to the ladies, I find, my pretty young gentleman?

Tony. That's as I find 'um.

Hastings. Not to her of your mother's choosing, I dare answer! And yet she appears to me a pretty, well-tempered girl.

Tony. That's because you don't know her as well as I. Ecod! I know every inch about her; and there's not a more bitter cantankerous toad in all Christendom!

Hastings (*aside*). Pretty encouragement this for a lover!

Tony. I have seen her since the height of that. She has as many tricks as a hare in a thicket, or a colt the first day's breaking.

Hastings. To me she appears sensible and silent.

Tony. Aye, before company. But when she's with her playmates, she's as loud as a hog in a gate.

Hastings. But there is a meek modesty about her that charms me.

Tony. Yes, but curb her never so little, she kicks up, and you're flung in a ditch.

Hastings. Well, but you must allow her a little beauty.—Yes, you must allow her some beauty.

Tony. Bandbox! She's all a made-up thing, mun. Ah! could you but see Bet Bouncer of these parts, you might then talk of beauty. Ecod, she has two eyes as black as sloes, and cheeks as broad and red as a pulpit cushion. She'd make two of she.

Hastings. Well, what say you of a friend that would take this bitter bargain off your hands?

Tony. Anon?*

Hastings. Would you thank him that would take Miss Neville, and leave you to happiness and your dear Betsy?

Tony. Aye; but where is there such a friend, for who would take *her*?

Hastings. I am he. If you but assist me, I'll engage to whip her off to France, and you shall never hear more of her.

Tony. Assist you! Ecod, I will, to the last drop of my blood. I'll clap a pair of horses to your chaise that shall trundle you off in a twinkling, and may be get you a part of her fortin beside in jewels that you little dream of.

Hastings. My dear squire, this looks like a lad of spirit.

Tony. Come along then, and you shall see more of my spirit before you have done with me.
(*Singing.*)

We are the boys
That fears no noise
Where the thundering cannons roar.

Exeunt.

ACT III

Enter Hardcastle *solus.*

Hardcastle. What could my old friend Sir Charles mean by recommending his son as the modestest young man in town? To me he appears the most impudent piece of brass that ever spoke with a tongue. He has taken possession of the easy chair by the fireside already. He took off his boots in the parlor, and desired me to see them

* "What?"

taken care of. I'm desirous to know how his impudence affects my daughter. —She will certainly be shocked at it.

Enter Miss Hardcastle, *plainly dressed.*

Hardcastle. Well, my Kate, I see you have changed your dress, as I bid you; and yet, I believe, there was no great occasion.

Miss Hardcastle. I find such a pleasure, sir, in obeying your commands, that I take care to observe them without ever debating their propriety.

Hardcastle. And yet, Kate, I sometimes give you some cause, particularly when I recommended my *modest* gentleman to you as a lover today.

Miss Hardcastle. You taught me to expect something extraordinary, and I find the original exceeds the description!

Hardcastle. I was never so surprised in my life! He has quite confounded all my faculties!

Miss Hardcastle. I never saw anything like it: and a man of the world, too!

Hardcastle. Aye, he learned it all abroad—what a fool was I, to think a young man could learn modesty by traveling. He might as soon learn wit at a masquerade.

Miss Hardcastle. It seems all natural to him.

Hardcastle. A good deal assisted by bad company and a French dancing master.

Miss Hardcastle. Sure, you mistake papa! A French dancing master could never have taught him that timid look—that awkward address—that bashful manner—

Hardcastle. Whose look? whose manner, child?

Miss Hardcastle. Mr. Marlow's: his *mauvaise honte,*[y] his timidity, struck me at the first sight.

Hardcastle. Then your first sight deceived you; for I think him one of the most brazen first sights that ever astonished my senses!

Miss Hardcastle. Sure, sir, you rally! I never saw anyone so modest.

Hardcastle. And can you be serious! I never saw such a bouncing, swaggering puppy since I was born. Bully Dawson [z] was but a fool to him.

Miss Hardcastle. Surprising! He met me with a respect-

[y] bashfulness [z] a ruffian

ful bow, a stammering voice, and a look fixed on the ground.

Hardcastle. He met me with a loud voice, a lordly air, and a familiarity that made my blood freeze again.

Miss Hardcastle. He treated me with diffidence and respect; censured the manners of the age; admired the prudence of girls that never laughed; tired me with apologies for being tiresome; then left the room with a bow, and "Madam, I would not for the world detain you."

Hardcastle. He spoke to me as if he knew me all his life before; asked twenty questions, and never waited for an answer; interrupted my best remarks with some silly pun; and when I was in my best story of the Duke of Marlborough and Prince Eugene, he asked if I had not a good hand at making punch. Yes, Kate, he asked your father if he was a maker of punch!

Miss Hardcastle. One of us must certainly be mistaken.

Hardcastle. If he be what he has shown himself, I'm determined he shall never have my consent.

Miss Hardcastle. And if he be the sullen thing I take him, he shall never have mine.

Hardcastle. In one thing then we are agreed—to reject him.

Miss Hardcastle. Yes: but upon conditions. For if you should find him less impudent, and I more presuming; if you find him more respectful, and I more importunate—I don't know—the fellow is well enough for a man. Certainly we don't meet many such at a horse race in the country.

Hardcastle. If we should find him so—but that's impossible. The first appearance has done my business. I'm seldom deceived in that.

Miss Hardcastle. And yet there may be many good qualities under that first appearance.

Hardcastle. Aye, when a girl finds a fellow's outside to her taste, she then sets about guessing the rest of his furniture. With her, a smooth face stands for good sense, and a genteel figure for every virtue.

Miss Hardcastle. I hope, sir, a conversation begun with a compliment to my good sense won't end with a sneer at my understanding?

Hardcastle. Pardon me, Kate. But if young Mr. Brazen can find the art of reconciling contradictions, he may please us both, perhaps.

Miss Hardcastle. And as one of us must be mistakaen, what if we go to make further discoveries?

Hardcastle. Agreed. But depend on't I'm in the right.

Miss Hardcastle. And depend on't I'm not much in the wrong. *Exeunt.*

Enter Tony, *running in with a casket.*

Tony. Ecod! I have got them. Here they are. My cousin Con's necklaces, bobs and all. My mother shan't cheat the poor souls out of their fortin neither. Oh! my genius, is that you?

Enter Hastings.

Hastings. My dear friend, how have you managed with your mother? I hope you have amused her with pretending love for your cousin, and that you are willing to be reconciled at last? Our horses will be refreshed in a short time, and we shall soon be ready to set off.

Tony. And here's something to bear your charges by the way (*Giving the casket.*) Your sweetheart's jewels. Keep them, and hang those, I say, that would rob you of one of them.

Hastings. But how have you procured them from your mother?

Tony. Ask me no questions, and I'll tell you no fibs. I procured them by the rule of thumb. If I had not a key to every drawer in mother's bureau, how could I go to the alehouse so often as I do? An honest man may rob himself of his own at any time.

Hastings. Thousands do it every day. But to be plain with you, Miss Neville is endeavoring to procure them from her aunt this very instant. If she succeeds, it will be the most delicate way at least of obtaining them.

Tony. Well, keep them, till you know how it will be. But I know how it will be well enough; she'd as soon part with the only sound tooth in her head!

Hastings. But I dread the effects of her resentment, when she finds she has lost them.

Tony. Never you mind her resentment, leave *me* to manage that. I don't value her resentment the bounce of a cracker.[a] Zounds! here they are! Morrice![b] prance!

[a] explosion of a firecracker [b] "Move on"

Exit Hastings.

Tony, Mrs. Hardcastle, *and* Miss Neville.

Mrs. Hardcastle. Indeed, Constance, you amaze me. Such a girl as you want jewels? It will be time enough for jewels, my dear, twenty years hence, when your beauty begins to want repairs.

Miss Neville. But what will repair beauty at forty, will certainly improve it at twenty, madam.

Mrs. Hardcastle. Yours, my dear, can admit of none. That natural blush is beyond a thousand ornaments. Besides, child, jewels are quite out at present. Don't you see half the ladies of our acquaintance, my Lady Kill-daylight, and Mrs. Crump, and the rest of them, carry their jewels to town, and bring nothing but paste and marcasites [c] back?

Miss Neville. But who knows, madam, but somebody that shall be nameless would like me best with all my little finery about me?

Mrs. Hardcastle. Consult your glass, my dear, and then see, if with such a pair of eyes, you want any better sparklers. What do you think, Tony, my dear, does your cousin Con want any jewels, in your eyes, to set off her beauty?

Tony. That's as thereafter may be.

Miss Neville. My dear aunt, if you knew how it would oblige me.

Mrs. Hardcastle. A parcel of old-fashioned rose and table-cut things.[d] They would make you look like the court of King Solomon at a puppet show. Besides, I believe I can't readily come at them. They may be missing, for aught I know to the contrary.

Tony (*apart to* Mrs. Hardcastle). Then why don't you tell her so at once, as she's so longing for them. Tell her they're lost. It's the only way to quiet her. Say they're lost, and call me to bear witness.

Mrs. Hardcastle (*apart to* Tony). You know, my dear, I'm only keeping them for you. So if I say they're gone, you'll bear me witness, will you? He! he! he!

Tony. Never fear me. Ecod! I'll say I saw them taken out with my own eyes.

Miss Neville. I desire them but for a day, madam. Just

[c] ornaments of crystallized iron pyrites [d] i.e., gems cut in a manner no longer fashionable

to be permitted to show them as relics, and then they may be locked up again.

Mrs. Hardcastle. To be plain with you, my dear Constance, if I could find them, you should have them. They're missing, I assure you. Lost, for aught I know; but we must have patience wherever they are.

Miss Neville. I'll not believe it; this is but a shallow pretense to deny me. I know they're too valuable to be so slightly kept, and as you are to answer for the loss—

Mrs. Hardcastle. Don't be alarmed, Constance. If they be lost, I must restore an equivalent. But my son knows they are missing, and not to be found.

Tony. That I can bear witness to. They are missing, and not to be found, I'll take my oath on't.

Mrs. Hardcastle. You must learn resignation, my dear; for though we lose our fortune, yet we should not lose our patience. See me, how calm I am.

Miss Neville. Aye, people are generally calm at the misfortunes of others.

Mrs. Hardcastle. Now, I wonder a girl of your good sense should waste a thought upon such trumpery. We shall soon find them; and, in the meantime, you shall make use of my garnets till your jewels be found.

Miss Neville. I detest garnets.

Mrs. Hardcastle. The most becoming things in the world to set off a clear complexion. You have often seen how well they look upon me. You *shall* have them. *Exit.*

Miss Neville. I dislike them of all things. You shan't stir. Was ever anything so provoking to mislay my own jewels, and force me to wear her trumpery.

Tony. Don't be a fool. If she gives you the garnets, take what you can get. The jewels are your own already. I have stolen them out of her bureau, and she does not know it. Fly to your spark, he'll tell you more of the matter. Leave me to manage *her.*

Miss Neville. My dear cousin!

Tony. Vanish. She's here, and has missed them already. [*Exit* Miss Neville.] Zounds! how she fidgets and spits about like a catherine wheel!

Enter Mrs. Hardcastle.

Mrs. Hardcastle. Confusion! thieves! robbers! We are cheated, plundered, broke open, undone!

Tony. What's the matter, what's the matter, mamma? I hope nothing has happened to any of the good family!

Mrs. Hardcastle. We are robbed. My bureau has been broke open, the jewels taken out, and I'm undone!

Tony. Oh! is that all! Ha! ha! ha! By the laws, I never saw it better acted in my life. Ecod, I thought you was ruined in earnest, ha, ha, ha!

Mrs. Hardcastle. Why, boy, I *am* ruined in earnest. My bureau has been broke open, and all taken away.

Tony. Stick to that; ha, ha, ha! stick to that. I'll bear witness, you know, call me to bear witness.

Mrs. Hardcastle. I tell you, Tony, by all that's precious, the jewels are gone, and I shall be ruined forever.

Tony. Sure I know they're gone, and I am to say so.

Mrs. Hardcastle. My dearest Tony, but hear me. They're gone, I say.

Tony. By the laws, mamma, you make me for to laugh, ha! ha! I know who took them well enough, ha! ha! ha!

Mrs. Hardcastle. Was there ever such a blockhead, that can't tell the difference between jest and earnest? I tell you I'm not in jest, booby!

Tony. That's right, that's right! You must be in a bitter passion, and then nobody will suspect either of us. I'll bear witness that they are gone.

Mrs. Hardcastle. Was there ever such a cross-grained brute, that won't hear me? Can you bear witness that you're no better than a fool? Was ever poor woman so beset with fools on one hand, and thieves on the other?

Tony. I can bear witness to that.

Mrs. Hardcastle. Bear witness again, you blockhead you, and I'll turn you out of the room directly. My poor niece, what will become of *her*? Do you laugh, you unfeeling brute, as if you enjoyed my distress?

Tony. I can bear witness to that.

Mrs. Hardcastle. Do you insult me, monster? I'll teach you to vex your mother, I will.

Tony. I can bear witness to that. (*He runs off, she follows him.*)

Enter Miss Hardcastle *and* Maid.

Miss Hardcastle. What an unaccountable creature is that brother of mine, to send them to the house as an inn, ha! ha! I don't wonder at his impudence.

Maid. But what is more, madam, the young gentleman as you passed by in your present dress, asked me if you were the barmaid. He mistook you for the barmaid, madam!

Miss Hardcastle. Did he? Then as I live I'm resolved to keep up the delusion. Tell me, Pimple, how do you like my present dress? Don't you think I look something like Cherry in *The Beaux' Stratagem?* [e]

Maid. It's the dress, madam, that every lady wears in the country, but when she visits or receives company.

Miss Hardcastle. And are you sure he does not remember my face or person?

Maid. Certain of it.

Miss Hardcastle. I vow, I thought so; for though we spoke for some time together, yet his fears were such, that he never once looked up during the interview. Indeed, if he had, my bonnet would have kept him from seeing me.

Maid. But what do you hope from keeping him in his mistake?

Miss Hardcastle. In the first place, I shall be *seen,* and that is no small advantage to a girl who brings her face to market. Then I shall perhaps make an acquaintance, and that's no small victory gained over one who never addresses any but the wildest of her sex. But my chief aim is to take my gentleman off his guard, and like an invisible champion of romance, examine the giant's force before I offer to combat.

Maid. But you are sure you can act your part, and disguise your voice, so that he may mistake that, as he has already mistaken your person?

Miss Hardcastle. Never fear me. I think I have got the true bar cant. Did your honor call?—Attend the Lion [f] there. —Pipes and tobacco for the Angel. —The Lamb has been outrageous this half hour.

Maid. It will do, madam. But he's here. *Exit* Maid.

Enter Marlow.

Marlow. What a bawling in every part of the house; I have scarce a moment's repose. If I go to the best room, there I find my host and his story. If I fly to the gallery, there we have my hostess with her curtsy down to the ground. I have at last got a moment to myself, and now for recollection. (*Walks and muses.*)

Miss Hardcastle. Did you call, sir? Did your honor call?

Marlow (*musing*). As for Miss Hardcastle, she's too grave and sentimental for me.

[e] the landlord's daughter in Farquhar's play [f] typical names of inn rooms

Miss Hardcastle. Did your honor call? (*She still places herself before him, he turning away.*)

Marlow. No, child. (*Musing.*) Besides from the glimpse I had of her, I think she squints.

Miss Hardcastle. I'm sure, sir, I heard the bell ring.

Marlow. No, no. (*Musing.*) I have pleased my father, however, by coming down, and I'll tomorrow please myself by returning. (*Taking out his tablets,*[g] *and perusing.*)

Miss Hardcastle. Perhaps the other gentleman called, sir?

Marlow. I tell you, no.

Miss Hardcastle. I should be glad to know, sir. We have such a parcel of servants.

Marlow. No, no, I tell you. (*Looks full in her face.*) Yes, child, I think I did call. I wanted—I wanted—I vow, child, you are vastly handsome.

Miss Hardcastle. O la, sir, you'll make one ashamed.

Marlow. Never saw a more sprightly, malicious eye. Yes, yes, my dear, I did call. Have you got any of your—a—what d'ye call it in the house?

Miss Hardcastle. No, sir, we have been out of that these ten days.

Marlow. One may call in this house, I find, to very little purpose. Suppose I should call for a taste, just by way of trial, of the nectar of your lips; perhaps I might be disappointed in that, too.

Miss Hardcastle. Nectar! nectar! that's a liquor there's no call for in these parts. French, I suppose. We keep no French wines here, sir.

Marlow. Of true English growth, I assure you.

Miss Hardcastle. Then it's odd I should not know it. We brew all sorts of wines in this house, and I have lived here these eighteen years.

Marlow. Eighteen years! Why one would think, child, you kept the bar before you were born. How old are you?

Miss Hardcastle. O! sir, I must not tell my age. They say women and music should never be dated.

Marlow. To guess at this distance, you can't be much above forty. (*Approaching.*) Yet nearer I don't think so much. (*Approaching.*) By coming close to some women they look younger still; but when we come very close indeed— (*Attempting to kiss her.*)

Miss Hardcastle. Pray, sir, keep your distance. One

[g] memorandum book

would think you wanted to know one's age as they do horses, by mark of mouth.

Marlow. I protest, child, you use me extremely ill. If you keep me at this distance, how is it possible you and I can be ever acquainted?

Miss Hardcastle. And who wants to be acquainted with you? I want no such acquaintance, not I. I'm sure you did not treat Miss Hardcastle that was here awhile ago in this obstropalous manner. I'll warrant me, before her you looked dashed, and kept bowing to the ground, and talked, for all the world, as if you was before a justice of peace.

Marlow (*aside*). Egad! she has hit it, sure enough. (*To her.*) In awe of her, child? Ha! ha! ha! A mere awkward, squinting thing! No, no! I find you don't know me. I laughed, and rallied her a little; but I was unwilling to be too severe. No, I could not be too severe, curse me!

Miss Hardcastle. Oh! then, sir, you are a favorite, I find, among the ladies?

Marlow. Yes, my dear, a great favorite. And yet, hang me, I don't see what they find in me to follow. At the Ladies' Club in town I'm called their agreeable Rattle. Rattle, child, is not my real name, but one I'm known by. My name is Solomons. Mr. Solomons, my dear, at your service. (*Offering to salute her.*)

Miss Hardcastle. Hold, sir; you are introducing me to your club, not to yourself. And you're so great a favorite there, you say?

Marlow. Yes, my dear. There's Mrs. Mantrap, Lady Betty Blackleg, the Countess of Sligo, Mrs. Langhorns, old Miss Biddy Buckskin and your humble servant, keep up the spirit of the place.

Miss Hardcastle. Then it's a very merry place, I suppose?

Marlow. Yes, as merry as cards, suppers, wine, and old women can make us.

Miss Hardcastle. And their agreeable Rattle, ha! ha! ha!

Marlow (*aside*). Egad! I don't quite like this chit. She looks knowing, methinks. You laugh, child!

Miss Hardcastle. I can't but laugh to think what time they all have for minding their work or their family.

Marlow (*aside*). All's well, she don't laugh at me. (*To her.*) Do you ever work, child?

Miss Hardcastle. Aye, sure. There's not a screen or a

quilt in the whole house but what can bear witness to that.

Marlow. Odso! Then you must show me your embroidery. I embroider and draw patterns myself a little. If you want a judge of your work you must apply to me. (*Seizing her hand.*)

Enter Hardcastle, *who stands in surprise.*

Miss Hardcastle. Aye, but the colors don't look well by candlelight. You shall see all in the morning. (*Struggling.*)

Marlow. And why not now, my angel? Such beauty fires beyond the power of resistance. —Pshaw! the father here! My old luck: I never nicked seven that I did not throw ames-ace three times following.[h]

Exit Marlow.

Hardcastle. So, madam. So I find *this* is your *modest* lover. This is your humble admirer that kept his eyes fixed on the ground, and only adored at humble distance. Kate, Kate, art thou not ashamed to deceive your father so?

Miss Hardcastle. Never trust me, dear papa, but he's still the modest man I first took him for, you'll be convinced of it as well as I.

Hardcastle. By the hand of my body, I believe his impudence is infectious! Didn't I see him seize your hand? Didn't I see him haul you about like a milkmaid? And now you talk of his respect and his modesty, forsooth!

Miss Hardcastle. But if I shortly convince you of his modesty that he has only the faults that will pass off with time, and the virtues that will improve with age, I hope you'll forgive him.

Hardcastle. The girl would actually make one run mad! I tell you I'll not be convinced. I am convinced. He has scarcely been three hours in the house, and he has already encroached on all my prerogatives. You may like his impudence, and call it modesty. But my son-in-law, madam, must have very different qualifications.

Miss Hardcastle. Sir, I ask but this night to convince you.

Hardcastle. You shall not have half the time, for I have thoughts of turning him out this very hour.

Miss Hardcastle. Give me that hour then, and I hope to satisfy you.

[h] dicing terms

Hardcastle. Well, an hour let it be then. But I'll have no trifling with your father. All fair and open, do you mind me?

Miss Hardcastle. I hope, sir, you have ever found that I considered your commands as my pride; for your kindness is such, that my duty as yet has been inclination.

ACT IV

Enter Hastings *and* Miss Neville.

Hastings. You surprise me! Sir Charles Marlow expected here this night! Where have you had your information?

Miss Neville. You may depend upon it. I just saw his letter to Mr. Hardcastle, in which he tells him he intends setting out a few hours after his son.

Hastings. Then, my Constance, all must be completed before he arrives. He knows me; and should he find me here, would discover my name, and perhaps my designs, to the rest of the family.

Miss Neville. The jewels, I hope, are safe?

Hastings. Yes, yes. I have sent them to Marlow, who keeps the keys of our baggage. In the meantime, I'll go to prepare matters for our elopment. I have had the squire's promise of a fresh pair of horses; and, if I should not see him again, will write him further directions. *Exit.*

Miss Neville. Well! success attend you. In the meantime, I'll go amuse my aunt with the old pretense of a violent passion for my cousin. *Exit.*

Enter Marlow, *followed by* Servant.

Marlow. I wonder what Hastings could mean by sending me so valuable a thing as a casket to keep for him, when he knows the only place I have is the seat of a post coach at an inn door. Have you deposited the casket with the landlady, as I ordered you? Have you put it into her own hands?

Servant. Yes, your honor.

Marlow. She said she'd keep it safe, did she?

Servant. Yes, she said she'd keep it safe enough; she

asked me how I came by it, and she said she had a great mind to make me give an account of myself.

Exit Servant.

Marlow. Ha! ha! ha! They're safe, however. What an unaccountable set of beings have we got amongst! This little barmaid, though, runs in my head most strangely, and drives out the absurdities of all the rest of the family. She's mine, she must be mine, or I'm greatly mistaken.

Enter Hastings.

Hastings. Bless me! I quite forgot to tell her that I intended to prepare at the bottom of the garden. Marlow here, and in spirits too!

Marlow. Give me joy, George! Crown me, shadow me with laurels! Well, George, after all, we modest fellows don't want for success among the women.

Hastings. Some women, you mean. But what success has your honor's modesty been crowned with now, that it grows so insolent upon us?

Marlow. Didn't you see the tempting, brisk, lovely little thing that runs about the house with a bunch of keys to its girdle?

Hastings. Well! and what then?

Marlow. She's mine, you rogue you. Such fire, such motions, such eyes, such lips—but, egad! she would not let me kiss them though.

Hastings. But are you so sure, so very sure of her?

Marlow. Why man, she talked of showing me her work above stairs and I am to improve the pattern.

Hastings. But how can *you*, Charles, go about to rob a woman of her honor?

Marlow. Pshaw! pshaw! We all know the honor of a barmaid of an inn. I don't intend to *rob* her, take my word for it; there's nothing in this house I shan't honestly *pay* for.

Hastings. I believe the girl has virtue.

Marlow. And if she has, I should be the last man in the world that would attempt to corrupt it.

Hastings. You have taken care, I hope, of the casket I sent you to lock up? It's in safety?

Marlow. Yes, yes. It's safe enough. I have taken care of it. But how could you think the seat of a post coach at an inn door a place of safety? Ah! numskull! I have taken better precautions for you than you did for yourself. I have—

Hastings. What?

Marlow. I have sent it to the landlady to keep for you.

Hastings. To the landlady!

Marlow. The landlady.

Hastings. You did?

Marlow. I did. She's to be answerable for its forthcoming, you know.

Hastings. Yes, she'll bring it forth with a witness.

Marlow. Wasn't I right? I believe you'll allow that I acted prudently upon this occasion?

Hastings (*aside*). He must not see my uneasiness.

Marlow. You seem a little disconcerted, though, methinks. Sure nothing has happened?

Hastings. No, nothing. Never was in better spirits in all my life. And so you left it with the landlady, who, no doubt, very readily undertook the charge?

Marlow. Rather too readily. For she not only kept the casket, but, through her great precaution, was going to keep the messenger too. Ha! ha! ha!

Hastings. He! he! he! They're safe, however.

Marlow. As a guinea in a miser's purse.

Hastings (*aside*). So now all hopes of fortune are at an end, and we must set off without it. (*To him.*) Well, Charles, I'll leave you to your meditations on the pretty barmaid, and, he! he! he! may you be as successful for yourself as you have been for me. *Exit.*

Marlow. Thank ye, George! I ask no more. Ha! ha! ha!

Enter Hardcastle.

Hardcastle. I no longer know my own house. It's turned all topsy-turvy. His servants have got drunk already. I'll bear it no longer, and yet, from my respect for his father, I'll be calm. (*To him.*) Mr. Marlow, your servant. I'm your very humble servant. (*Bowing low.*)

Marlow. Sir, your humble servant. (*Aside.*) What's to be the wonder now?

Hardcastle. I believe, sir, you must be sensible, sir, that no man alive ought to be more welcome than your father's son, sir. I hope you think so?

Marlow. I do, from my soul, sir. I don't want much entreaty. I generally make my father's son welcome wherever he goes.

Hardcastle. I believe you do, from my soul, sir. But

though I say nothing to your own conduct, that of your servants is insufferable. Their manner of drinking is setting a very bad example in this house, I assure you.

Marlow. I protest, my very good sir, that's no fault of mine. If they don't drink as they ought, *they* are to blame. I ordered them not to spare the cellar. I did, I assure you. (*To the side scene.*) Here, let one of my servants come up. (*To him.*) My positive directions were, that as I did not drink myself, they should make up for my deficiencies below.

Hardcastle. Then they had your orders for what they do! I'm satisfied!

Marlow. They had, I assure you. You shall hear from one of themselves.

Enter Servant, *drunk.*

Marlow. You, Jeremy! Come forward, sirrah! What were my orders? Were you not told to drink freely, and call for what you thought fit, for the good of the house?

Hardcastle (*aside*). I begin to lose my patience.

Jeremy (*staggering forward*). Please your honor, liberty and Fleet Street[1] forever! Though I'm but a servant, I'm as good as another man. I'll drink for no man before supper, sir, dammy! Good liquor will sit upon a good supper, but a good supper will not sit upon—hiccup—upon my conscience, sir. *Exit.*

Marlow. You see, my old friend, the fellow is as drunk as he can possibly be. I don't know what you'd have more, unless you'd have the poor devil soused in a beer barrel.

Hardcastle. Zounds! He'll drive me distracted if I contain myself any longer. Mr. Marlow, sir; I have submitted to your insolence for more than four hours, and I see no likelihood of its coming to an end. I'm now resolved to be master here, sir, and I desire that you and your drunken pack may leave my house directly.

Marlow. Leave your house!—Sure, you jest, my good friend! What, when I'm doing what I can to please you!

Hardcastle. I tell you, sir, you don't please me; so I desire you'll leave my house.

Marlow. Sure, you cannot be serious! At this time o' night, and such a night! You only mean to banter me!

Hardcastle. I tell you, sir, I'm serious; and, now that my

[1] London street, known for taverns

passions are roused, I say this house is mine, sir; this house is mine, and I command you to leave it directly.

Marlow. Ha! ha! ha! A puddle in a storm. I shan't stir a step, I assure you. (*In a serious tone*.) This your house, fellow! It's my house. This is my house. Mine, while I choose to stay. What right have you to bid me leave this house, sir? I never met with such impudence, curse me, never in my whole life before.

Hardcastle. Nor I, confound me if ever I did! To come to my house, to call for what he likes, to turn me out of my own chair, to insult the family, to order his servants to get drunk, and then to tell me *This house is mine, sir*. By all that's impudent, it makes me laugh. Ha! ha! ha! Pray sir (*bantering*), as you take the house, what think you of taking the rest of the furniture? There's a pair of silver candlesticks, and there's a firescreen, and here's a pair of brazen-nosed bellows, perhaps you may take a fancy to them?

Marlow. Bring me your bill, sir, bring me your bill, and let's make no more words about it.

Hardcastle. There are a set of prints, too. What think you of "The Rake's Progress" [j] for your own apartment?

Marlow. Bring me your bill, I say; and I'll leave you and your infernal house directly.

Hardcastle. Then there's a mahogany table, that you may see your own face in.

Marlow. My bill, I say.

Hardcastle. I had forgot the great chair, for your own particular slumbers, after a hearty meal.

Marlow. Zounds! bring me my bill, I say, and let's hear no more on't.

Hardcastle. Young man, young man, from your father's letter to me, I was taught to expect a well-bred modest man as a visitor here, but now I find him no better than a coxcomb and a bully; but he will be down here presently, and shall hear more of it. *Exit*.

Marlow. How's this! Sure I have not mistaken the house! Everything looks like an inn. The servants cry "Coming"; the attendance is awkward; the barmaid, too, to attend us. But she's here, and will further inform me. Whither so fast, child? A word with you.

Enter Miss Hardcastle.

[j] Hogarth's series of engravings (1735)

Miss Hardcastle. Let it be short, then. I'm in a hurry. (*Aside.*) I believe he begins to find out his mistake. But it's too soon quite to undeceive him.

Marlow. Pray, child, answer me one question. What are you, and what may your business in this house be?

Miss Hardcastle. A relation of the family, sir.

Marlow. What, a poor relation?

Miss Hardcastle. Yes, sir. A poor relation appointed to keep the keys, and to see that the guests want nothing in my power to give them.

Marlow. That is, you act as the barmaid of this inn.

Miss Hardcastle. Inn. O law! What brought that in your head? One of the best families in the country keep an inn! Ha, ha, ha, old Mr. Hardcastle's house an inn!

Marlow. Mr. Hardcastle's house! Is this house Mr. Hardcastle's house, child?

Miss Hardcastle. Aye, sure. Whose else should it be?

Marlow. So then all's out, and I have been damnably imposed on. O, confound my stupid head, I shall be laughed at over the whole town. I shall be stuck up in caricatura in all the print shops. "The Dullissimo Maccaroni." To mistake this house of all others for an inn, and my father's old friend for an innkeeper. What a swaggering puppy must he take me for. What a silly puppy do I find myself. There again, may I be hanged, my dear, but I mistook you for the barmaid.

Miss Hardcastle. Dear me! dear me! I'm sure there's nothing in my *behavour* [k] to put me upon a level with one of that stamp.

Marlow. Nothing, my dear, nothing. But I was in for a list of blunders, and could not help making you a subscriber. My stupidity saw everything the wrong way. I mistook your assiduity for assurance, and your simplicity for allurement. But it's over. This house I no more show my face in!

Miss Hardcastle. I hope, sir, I have done nothing to disoblige you. I'm sure I should be sorry to affront any gentleman who has been so polite, and said so many civil things to me. I'm sure I should be sorry (*pretending to cry*) if he left the family upon my account. I'm sure I should be sorry people said anything amiss, since I have no fortune but my character.

Marlow (*aside*). By heaven, she weeps. This is the first mark of tenderness I ever had from a modest woman,

[k] Miss Hardcastle continues to affect a vulgar speech

and it touches me. (*To her.*) Excuse me, my lovely girl, you are the only part of the family I leave with reluctance. But to be plain with you, the difference of our birth, fortune and education, make an honorable connection impossible, and I can never harbor a thought of seducing simplicity that trusted in my honor, or bringing ruin upon one whose only fault was being too lovely.

Miss Hardcastle (*aside*). Generous man! I now begin to admire him. (*To him.*) But I'm sure my family is as good as Miss Hardcastle's, and though I'm poor, that's no great misfortune to a contented mind, and, until this moment, I never thought that it was bad to want fortune.

Marlow. And why now, my pretty simplicity?

Miss Hardcastle. Because it puts me at a distance from one, that if I had a thousand pound I would give it all to.

Marlow (*aside*). This simplicity bewitches me, so that if I stay I'm undone. I must make one bold effort, and leave her. (*To her.*) Your partiality in my favor, my dear, touches me most sensibly, and were I to live for myself alone, I could easily fix my choice. But I owe too much to the opinion of the world, too much to the authority of a father, so that—I can scarcely speak it—it affects me. Farewell. *Exit.*

Miss Hardcastle. I never knew half his merit till now. He shall not go, if I have power or art to detain him. I'll still preserve the character in which I stooped to conquer, but will undeceive my papa, who, perhaps, may laugh him out of his resolution. *Exit.*

Enter Tony, Miss Neville.

Tony. Aye, you may steal for yourselves the next time. I have done my duty. She has got the jewels again, that's a sure thing; but she believes it was all a mistake of the servants.

Miss Neville. But, my dear cousin, sure, you won't forsake us in this distress. If she in the least suspects that I am going off, I shall certainly be locked up, or sent to my Aunt Pedigree's which is ten times worse.

Tony. To be sure, aunts of all kinds are damned bad things. But what can I do? I have got you a pair of horses that will fly like Whistlejacket, and I'm sure you can't say but I have courted you nicely before her face. Here she comes, we must court a bit or two more, for fear she should suspect us. (*They retire, and seem to fondle.*)

Enter Mrs. Hardcastle.

Mrs. Hardcastle. Well, I was greatly fluttered, to be sure. But my son tells me it was all a mistake of the servants. I shan't be easy, however, till they are fairly married, and then let her keep her own fortune. But what do I see? Fondling together, as I'm alive! I never saw Tony so sprightly before. Ah! have I caught you, my pretty doves? What, billing, exchanging stolen glances, and broken murmurs! Ah!

Tony. As for murmurs, mother, we grumble a little now and then, to be sure. But there's no love lost between us.

Mrs. Hardcastle. A mere sprinkling, Tony, upon the flame, only to make it burn brighter.

Miss Neville. Cousin Tony promises to give us more of his company at home. Indeed, he shan't leave us any more. It won't leave us, cousin Tony, will it?

Tony. O! it's a pretty creature. No, I'd sooner leave my horse in a pound, than leave you when you smile upon one so. Your laugh makes you so becoming.

Miss Neville. Agreeable cousin! Who can help admiring that natural humor, that pleasant, broad, red, thoughtless (*patting his cheek*) ah! it's a bold face.

Mrs. Hardcastle. Pretty innocence!

Tony. I'm sure I always loved cousin Con's hazel eyes, and her pretty long fingers, that she twists this way and that, over the haspicholls,[1] like a parcel of bobbins.

Mrs. Hardcastle. Ah, he would charm the bird from the tree. I was never so happy before. My boy takes after his father, poor Mr. Lumpkin, exactly. The jewels, my dear Con, shall be yours incontinently. You shall have them. Isn't he a sweet boy, my dear? You shall be married to-morrow, and we'll put off the rest of his education, like Dr. Drowsy's sermons, to a fitter opportunity.

Enter Diggory.

Diggory. Where's the squire? I have got a letter for your worship.

Tony. Give it to my mamma. She reads all my letters first.

[1] harpsichord

Diggory. I had orders to deliver it into your own hands.

Tony. Who does it come from?

Diggory. Your worship mun ask that o' the letter itself.

Tony. I could wish to know, though. (*Turning the letter, and gazing on it.*) [*Exit* Diggory.]

Miss Neville (*aside*). Undone, undone. A letter to him from Hastings. I know the hand. If my aunt sees it, we are ruined forever. I'll keep her employed a little if I can. (*To* Mrs. Hardcastle.) But I have not told you, madam, of my cousin's smart answer just now to Mr. Marlow. We so laughed. You must know, madam. This way a little, for he must not hear us. (*They confer.*)

Tony (*still gazing*). A damned cramp piece of penmanship, as ever I saw in my life. I can read your print-hand very well. But here there are such handles, and shakes, and dashes, that one can scarce tell the head from the tail. "To Anthony Lumpkin, Esquire." It's very odd, I can read the outside of my letters, where my own name is, well enough. But when I come to open it, it's all—buzz. That's hard, very hard; for the inside of the letter is always the cream of the correspondence.

Mrs. Hardcastle. Ha! ha! ha! Very well, very well. And so my son was too hard for the philosopher.

Miss Neville. Yes, madam; but you must hear the rest, madam. A little more this way, or he may hear us. You'll hear how he puzzled him again.

Mrs. Hardcastle. He seems strangely puzzled now himself, methinks.

Tony (*still gazing*). A damned up-and-down hand, as if it was disguised in liquor. (*Reading.*) "Dear Sir." Aye, that's that. Then there's an *M*, and a *T*, and an *S*, but whether the next be an "izzard" [m] or an *R*, confound me, I cannot tell.

Mrs. Hardcastle. What's that, my dear? Can I give you any assistance?

Miss Neville. Pray, aunt, let me read it. Nobody reads a cramp hand better than I (*twitching the letter from her*). Do you know who it is from?

Tony. Can't tell, except from Dick Ginger the feeder.

Miss Neville. Aye, so it is. (*Pretending to read.*) Dear Squire, Hoping that you're in health, as I am at this present. The gentlemen of the Shakebag club has cut the gentlemen of Goose-green quite out of feather.

[m] the letter *Z*

The odds—um—odd battle—um—long fighting—um, here, here, it's all about cocks, and fighting; it's of no consequence, here, put it up, put it up. (*Thrusting the crumpled letter upon him.*)

Tony. But I tell you, miss, it's of all the consequence in the world. I would not lose the rest of it for a guinea. Here, mother, do you make it out? Of no consequence! (*Giving* Mrs. Hardcastle *the letter.*)

Mrs. Hardcastle. How's this! (*Reads.*) "Dear Squire, I'm now waiting for Miss Neville, with a post chaise and pair, at the bottom of the garden but I find my horses yet unable to perform the journey. I expect you'll assist us with a pair of fresh horses, as you promised. Dispatch is necessary, as the hag"—aye, the hag—"your mother, will otherwise suspect us. Yours, Hastings." Grant me patience. I shall run distracted. My rage chokes me.

Miss Neville. I hope, madam, you'll suspend your resentment for a few moments, and not impute to me any impertinence, or sinister design, that belongs to another.

Mrs. Hardcastle (*curtsying very low*). Fine spoken, madam, you are most miraculously polite and engaging, and quite the very pink of courtesy and circumspection, madam. (*Changing her tone.*) And you, you great ill-fashioned oaf, with scarce sense enough to keep your mouth shut. Were you, too, joined against me? But I'll defeat all your plots in a moment. As for you, madam, since you have got a pair of fresh horses ready, it would be cruel to disappoint them. So, if you please, instead of running away with your spark, prepare, this very moment, to run off with *me*. Your old Aunt Pedigree will keep you secure, I'll warrant me. You, too, sir, may mount your horse, and guard us upon the way. Here, Thomas, Roger, Diggory, I'll show you that I wish you better than you do yourselves. *Exit.*

Miss Neville. So now I'm completely ruined.

Tony. Aye, that's a sure thing.

Miss Neville. What better could be expected from being connected with such a stupid fool, and after all the nods and signs I made him.

Tony. By the laws, miss, it was your own cleverness, and not my stupidity, that did your business. You were so nice and so busy with your Shakebags and Goosegreens, that I thought you could never be making believe.

Enter Hastings.

Hastings. So, sir, I find by my servant, that you have shown my letter, and betrayed us. Was this well done, young gentleman?

Tony. Here's another. Ask Miss there who betrayed you. Ecod, it was her doing, not mine.

Enter Marlow.

Marlow. So I have been finely used here among you. Rendered contemptible, driven into ill manners, despised, insulted, laughed at.

Tony. Here's another. We shall have old Bedlam broke loose presently.

Miss Neville. And there, sir, is the gentleman to whom we all owe every obligation.

Marlow. What can I say to him, a mere boy, an idiot, whose ignorance and age are a protection.

Hastings. A poor contemptible booby, that would but disgrace correction.

Miss Neville. Yet with cunning and malice enough to make himself merry with all our embarrassments.

Hastings. An insensible cub.

Marlow. Replete with tricks and mischief.

Tony. Baw! damme, but I'll fight you both one after the other—with baskets.

Marlow. As for him, he's below resentment. But your conduct, Mr. Hastings, requires an explanation. You knew of my mistakes, yet would not undeceive me.

Hastings. Tortured as I am with my own disappointments, is this a time for explanations? It is not friendly, Mr. Marlow.

Marlow. But, sir—

Miss Neville. Mr. Marlow, we never kept on your mistake, till it was too late to undeceive you. Be pacified.

Enter Servant.

Servant. My mistress desires you'll get ready immediately, madam. The horses are putting to. Your hat and things are in the next room. We are to go thirty miles before morning. *Exit* Servant.

Miss Neville. Well, well; I'll come presently.

Marlow (*to* Hastings). Was it well done, sir, to assist in rendering me ridiculous? To hang me out for the scorn of all my acquaintance? Depend upon it, sir, I shall expect an explanation.

Hastings. Was it well done, sir, if you're upon that subject, to deliver what I entrusted to yourself, to the care of another, sir?

Miss Neville. Mr. Hastings, Mr. Marlow. Why will you increase my distress by this groundless dispute? I implore, I entreat you—

Enter Servant.

Servant. Your cloak, madam. My mistress is impatient.

Miss Neville. I come. [*Exit* Servant.] Pray be pacified. If I leave you thus, I shall die with apprehension!

Enter Servant.

Servant. Your fan, muff, and gloves, madam. The horses are waiting. [*Exit* Servant.]

Miss Neville. O, Mr. Marlow! if you knew what a scene of constraint and ill-nature lies before me, I'm sure it would convert your resentment into pity.

Marlow. I'm so distracted with a variety of passions, that I don't know what I do. Forgive me, madam. George, forgive me. You know my hasty temper, and should not exasperate it.

Hastings. The torture of my situation is my only excuse.

Miss Neville. Well, my dear Hastings, if you have that esteem for me that I think, that I am sure you have, your constancy for three years will but increase the happiness of our future connection. If—

Mrs. Hardcastle (*within*). Miss Neville. Constance, why, Constance, I say!

Miss Neville. I'm coming. Well, constancy. Remember, constancy is the word. *Exit.*

Hastings. My heart! How can I support this? To be so near happiness, and such happiness!

Marlow (*to* Tony). You see now, young gentleman, the effects of your folly. What might be amusement to you, is here disappointment, and even distress.

Tony (*from a reverie*). Ecod, I have hit it. It's here. Your hands. Yours and yours, my poor Sulky. My boots there, ho! Meet me two hours hence at the bottom of the garden; and if you don't find Tony Lumpkin a more good-natur'd fellow than you thought for, I'll give you leave to take my best horse, and Bet Bouncer into the bargain. Come along. My boots, ho! *Exeunt.*

ACT V

Scene I: Scene continues.

Enter Hastings *and* Servant.

Hastings. You saw the old lady and Miss Neville drive off, you say?
Servant. Yes, your honor. They went off in a post coach, and the young squire went on horseback. They're thirty miles off by this time.
Hastings. Then all my hopes are over.
Servant. Yes, sir. Old Sir Charles is arrived. He and the old gentleman of the house have been laughing at Mr. Marlow's mistake this half hour. They are coming this way.
Hastings. Then I must not be seen. So now to my fruitless appointment at the bottom of the garden. This is about the time. *Exit.*

Enter Sir Charles *and* Hardcastle.

Hardcastle. Ha! ha! ha! The peremptory tone in which he sent forth his sublime commands.
Sir Charles. And the reserve with which I suppose he treated all your advances.
Hardcastle. And yet he might have seen something in me above a common innkeeper, too.
Sir Charles. Yes, Dick, but he mistook you for an uncommon innkeeper, ha! ha! ha!
Hardcastle. Well, I'm in too good spirits to think of anything but joy. Yes, my dear friend, this union of our families will make our personal friendships hereditary; and though my daughter's fortune is but small—
Sir Charles. Why, Dick, will you talk of fortune to me? My son is possessed of more than a competence already, and can want nothing but a good and virtuous girl to share his happiness and increase it. If they like each other, as you say they do—
Hardcastle. *If*, man! I tell you they *do* like each other. My daughter as good as told me so.
Sir Charles. But girls are apt to flatter themselves, you know.
Hardcastle. I saw him grasp her hand in the warmest

manner myself; and here he comes to put you out of your *ifs*, I warrant him.

Enter Marlow.

Marlow. I come, sir, once more, to ask pardon for my strange conduct. I can scarce reflect on my insolence without confusion.

Hardcastle. Tut, boy, a trifle. You take it too gravely. An hour or two's laughing with my daughter will set all to rights again. She'll never like you the worse for it.

Marlow. Sir, I shall be always proud of her approbation.

Hardcastle. Approbation is but a cold word, Mr. Marlow; if I am not deceived, you have something more than approbation thereabouts. You take me?

Marlow. Really, sir, I have not that happiness.

Hardcastle. Come, boy, I'm an old fellow, and know what's what, as well as you that are younger. I know what has past between you; but mum.

Marlow. Sure, sir, nothing has passed between us but the most profound respect on my side, and the most distant reserve on hers. You don't think, sir, that my impudence has been passed upon all the rest of the family.

Hardcastle. Impudence! No, I don't say that—not quite impudence—though girls like to be played with, and rumpled a little too, sometimes. But she has told no tales, I assure you.

Marlow. I never gave her the slightest cause.

Hardcastle. Well, well, I like modesty in its place well enough. But this is overacting, young gentleman. You may be open. Your father and I will like you the better for it.

Marlow. May I die, sir, if I ever—

Hardcastle. I tell you, she don't dislike you; and as I'm sure you like her—

Marlow. Dear sir—I protest, sir—

Hardcastle. I see no reason why you should not be joined as fast as the parson can tie you.

Marlow. But hear me, sir—

Hardcastle. Your father approves the match, I admire it, every moment's delay will be doing mischief; so—

Marlow. But why won't you hear me? By all that's just and true, I never gave Miss Hardcastle the slightest mark of my attachment, or even the most distant hint to suspect me of affection. We had but one interview, and that was formal, modest, and uninteresting.

Hardcastle (*aside*). This fellow's formal, modest impudence is beyond bearing.

Sir Charles. And you never grasped her hand, or made any protestations!

Marlow. As heaven is my witness, I came down in obedience to your commands. I saw the lady without emotion, and parted without reluctance. I hope you'll exact no further proofs of my duty, nor prevent me from leaving a house in which I suffer so many mortifications. *Exit.*

Sir Charles. I'm astonished at the air of sincerity with which he parted.

Hardcastle. And I'm astonished at the deliberate intrepidity of his assurance.

Sir Charles. I dare pledge my life and honor upon his truth.

Hardcastle (*looking out to right*). Here comes my daughter, and I would stake my happiness upon her veracity.

Enter Miss Hardcastle.

Hardcastle. Kate, come hither, child. Answer us sincerely, and without reserve; has Mr. Marlow made you any professions of love and affection?

Miss Hardcastle. The question is very abrupt, sir! But since you require unreserved sincerity, I think he has.

Hardcastle (*to* Sir Charles). You see.

Sir Charles. And pray, madam, have you and my son had more than one interview?

Miss Hardcastle. Yes, sir, several.

Hardcastle (*to* Sir Charles). You see.

Sir Charles. But did he profess any attachment?

Miss Hardcastle. A lasting one.

Sir Charles. Did he talk of love?

Miss Hardcastle. Much, sir.

Sir Charles. Amazing! And all this formally?

Miss Hardcastle. Formally.

Hardcastle. Now, my friend, I hope you are satisfied.

Sir Charles. And how did he behave, madam?

Miss Hardcastle. As most professed admirers do. Said some civil things of my face, talked much of his want of merit, and the greatness of mine; mentioned his heart, gave a short tragedy speech, and ended with pretended rapture.

Sir Charles. Now I'm perfectly convinced, indeed. I know his conversation among women to be modest and submissive. This forward, canting, ranting manner by no means describes him, and I am confident he never sat for the picture.

Miss Hardcastle. Then what, sir, if I should convince you to your face of my sincerity? If you and my papa, in about half an hour, will place yourselves behind that screen, you shall hear him declare his passion to me in person.

Sir Charles. Agreed. And if I find him what you describe, all my happiness in him must have an end. *Exit.*

Miss Hardcastle. And if you don't find him what I describe—I fear my happiness must never have a beginning.

Exeunt.

[*Scene II:*] *Scene changes to the back of the garden.*

Enter Hastings.

Hastings. What an idiot am I, to wait here for a fellow, who probably takes a delight in mortifying me. He never intended to be punctual, and I'll wait no longer. What do I see? It is he, and perhaps with news of my Constance.

Enter Tony, *booted and spattered.*

Hastings. My honest squire! I now find you a man of your word. This looks like friendship.

Tony. Aye, I'm your friend, and the best friend you have in the world, if you knew but all. This riding by night, by the bye, is cursedly tiresome. It has shook me worse than the basket of a stagecoach.

Hastings. But how? Where did you leave your fellow travelers? Are they in safety? Are they housed?

Tony. Five and twenty miles in two hours and a half is no such bad driving. The poor beasts have smoked for it: rabbit me, but I'd rather ride forty miles after a fox, than ten with such varment.

Hastings. Well, but where have you left the ladies? I die with impatience.

Tony. Left them? Why, where should I leave them, but where I found them?

Hastings. This is a riddle.

Tony. Riddle me this, then. What's that goes round the house, and round the house, and never touches the house?

Hastings. I'm still astray.

Tony. Why, that's it, mon. I have led them astray. By

jingo, there's not a pond or slough within five miles of the place but they can tell the taste of.

Hastings. Ha, ha, ha, I understand; you took them in a round, while they supposed themselves going forward. And so you have at last brought them home again.

Tony. You shall hear. I first took them down Feather-Bed Lane, where we stuck fast in the mud. I then rattled them crack over the stones of Up-and-Down Hill—I then introduced them to the gibbet on Heavy-Tree Heath, and from that, with a circumbendibus, I fairly lodged them in the horsepond at the bottom of the garden.

Hastings. But no accident, I hope.

Tony. No, no. Only mother is confoundedly frightened. She thinks herself forty miles off. She's sick of the journey, and the cattle can scarce crawl. So, if your own horses be ready, you may whip off with cousin, and I'll be bound that no soul here can budge a foot to follow you.

Hastings. My dear friend, how can I be grateful?

Tony. Aye, now it's dear friend, noble squire. Just now, it was all idiot, cub, and run me through the guts. Damn *your* way of fighting, I say. After we take a knock in this part of the country, we kiss and be friends. But if you had run me through the guts, then I should be dead, and you might go kiss the hangman.

Hastings. The rebuke is just. But I must hasten to relieve Miss Neville; if you keep the old lady employed, I promise to take care of the young one.

Tony. Never fear me. Here she comes. Vanish. [*Exit* Hastings.] She's got from the pond, and draggled up to the waist like a mermaid.

Enter Mrs. Hardcastle.

Mrs. Hardcastle. Oh, Tony, I'm killed. Shook. Battered to death. I shall never survive it. That last jolt that laid us against the quickset hedge has done my business.

Tony. Alack, mamma, it was all your own fault. You would be for running away by night, without knowing one inch of the way.

Mrs. Hardcastle. I wish we were at home again. I never met so many accidents in so short a journey. Drenched in the mud, overturned in a ditch, stuck fast in a slough, jolted to a jelly, and at last to lose our way. Whereabouts do you think we are, Tony?

Tony. By my guess we should be upon Crackskull Common, about forty miles from home.

Mrs. Hardcastle. O lud! O lud! the most notorious spot in all the country. We only want a robbery to make a complete night on't.

Tony. Don't be afraid, mamma, don't be afraid. Two of the five that kept here[n] are hanged, and the other three may not find us. Don't be afraid. Is that a man that's galloping behind us? No; it's only a tree. Don't be afraid.

Mrs. Hardcastle. The fright will certainly kill me.

Tony. Do you see any thing like a black hat moving behind the thicket?

Mrs. Hardcastle. O death!

Tony. No, it's only a cow. Don't be afraid, mamma, don't be afraid.

Mrs. Hardcastle. As I'm alive, Tony, I see a man coming towards us. Ah! I'm sure on't. If he perceives us, we are undone.

Tony (*aside*). Father-in-law, by all that's unlucky, come to take one of his night walks. (*To her*.) Ah, it's a highwayman, with pistols as long as my arm. A damned ill-looking fellow.

Mrs. Hardcastle. Good Heaven defend us! He approaches.

Tony. Do you hide yourself in that thicket and leave me to manage him. If there be any danger I'll cough and cry hem. When I cough be sure to keep close.

Mrs. Hardcastle *hides behind a tree in the back scene*.

Enter Hardcastle.

Hardcastle. I'm mistaken, or I heard voices of people in want of help. Oh, Tony, is that you? I did not expect you so soon back. Are your mother and her charge in safety?

Tony. Very safe, sir, at my Aunt Pedigree's. Hem.

Mrs. Hardcastle (*from behind*). Ah, death! I find there's danger.

Hardcastle. Forty miles in three hours; sure, that's too much, my youngster.

Tony. Stout horses and willing minds make short journeys, as they say. Hem.

Mrs. Hardcastle (*from behind*). Sure he'll do the dear boy no harm.

Hardcastle. But I heard a voice here; I should be glad to know from whence it came?

[n] frequented the place

Tony. It was I, sir, talking to myself, sir. I was saying that forty miles in four hours was very good going. Hem. As to be sure it was. Hem. I have got a sort of cold by being out in the air. We'll go in if you please. Hem.

Hardcastle. But if you talked to yourself, you did not answer yourself. I am certain I heard two voices, and am resolved (*raising his voice*) to find the other out.

Mrs. Hardcastle (*from behind*). Oh! he's coming to find me out. Oh!

Tony. What need you go, sir, if I tell you? Hem. I'll lay down my life for the truth—hem—I'll tell you all, sir. (*Detaining him.*)

Hardcastle. I tell you I will not be detained. I insist on seeing. It's in vain to expect I'll believe you.

Mrs. Hardcastle (*running forward from behind*). O lud, he'll murder my poor boy, my darling. Here, good gentleman, whet your rage upon me. Take my money, my life, but spare that young gentleman, spare my child, if you have any mercy.

Hardcastle. My wife! as I'm a Christian. From whence can she come, or what does she mean?

Mrs. Hardcastle (*kneeling*). Take compassion on us, good Mr. Highwayman. Take our money, our watches, all we have, but spare our lives. We will never bring you to justice, indeed, we won't, good Mr. Highwayman.

Hardcastle. I believe the woman's out of her senses. What, Dorothy, don't you know me?

Mrs. Hardcastle. Mr. Hardcastle, as I'm alive! My fears blinded me. But who, my dear, could have expected to meet you here, in this frightful place, so far from home. What has brought you to follow us?

Hardcastle. Sure, Dorothy, you have not lost your wits. So far from home, when you are within forty yards of your own door! (*To him.*) This is one of your old tricks, you graceless rogue, you! (*To her.*) Don't you know the gate, and the mulberry tree; and don't you remember the horsepond, my dear?

Mrs. Hardcastle. Yes, I shall remember the horsepond as long as I live; I have caught my death in it. (*To* Tony.) And it is to you, you graceless varlet, I owe all this? I'll teach you to abuse your mother, I will.

Tony. Ecod, mother, all the parish says you have spoiled me, and so you may take the fruits on't.

Mrs. Hardcastle. I'll spoil you, I will. *Follows him off the stage.*

Hardcastle. There's morality, however, in his reply. *Exit.*

Enter Hastings *and* Miss Neville.

Hastings. My dear Constance, why will you deliberate thus? If we delay a moment, all is lost forever. Pluck up a little resolution, and we shall soon be out of the reach of her malignity.

Miss Neville. I find it impossible. My spirits are so sunk with the agitations I have suffered, that I am unable to face any new danger. Two or three years' patience will at last crown us with happiness.

Hastings. Such a tedious delay is worse than inconstancy. Let us fly, my charmer. Let us date our happiness from this very moment. Perish fortune. Love and content will increase what we possess beyond a monarch's revenue. Let me prevail.

Miss Neville. No, Mr. Hastings, no. Prudence once more comes to my relief, and I will obey its dictates. In the moment of passion, fortune may be despised, but it ever produces a lasting repentance. I'm resolved to apply to Mr. Hardcastle's compassion and justice for redress.

Hastings. But though he had the will, he has not the power to relieve you.

Miss Neville. But he has influence, and upon that I am resolved to rely.

Hastings. I have no hopes. But since you persist, I must reluctantly obey you. *Exeunt.*

Scene III: Scene changes [*the house.*]

Enter Sir Charles *and* Miss Hardcastle.

Sir Charles. What a situation am I in. If what you say appears, I shall then find a guilty son. If what he says be true, I shall then lose one that, of all others, I most wished for a daughter.

Miss Hardcastle. I am proud of your approbation, and, to show I merit it, if you place yourselves as I directed, you shall hear his explicit declaration. But he comes.

Sir Charles. I'll to your father, and keep him to the appointment. *Exit* Sir Charles.

Enter Marlow.

Marlow. Though prepared for setting out, I come once more to take leave, nor did I, till this moment, know the pain I feel in the separation.

Miss Hardcastle (*in her own natural manner*). I believe

sufferings cannot be very great, sir, which you can so easily remove. A day or two longer, perhaps, might lessen your uneasiness, by showing the little value of what you think proper to regret.

Marlow (*aside*). This girl every moment improves upon me. (*To her.*) It must not be, madam. I have already trifled too long with my heart. My very pride begins to submit to my passion. The disparity of education and fortune, the anger of a parent, and the contempt of my equals begin to lose their weight; and nothing can restore me to myself but this painful effort of resolution.

Miss Hardcastle. Then go, sir. I'll urge nothing more to detain you. Though my family be as good as hers you came down to visit, and my education, I hope, not inferior, what are these advantages without equal affluence? I must remain contented with the slight approbation of imputed merit; I must have only the mockery of your addresses, while all your serious aims are fixed on fortune.

Enter Hardcastle *and* Sir Charles *from behind.*

Sir Charles. Here, behind this screen.

Hardcastle. Aye, aye, make no noise. I'll engage my Kate covers him with confusion at last.

Marlow. By heavens, madam, fortune was ever my smallest consideration. Your beauty at first caught my eye; for who could see that without emotion? But every moment that I converse with you, steals in some new grace, heightens the picture, and gives it stronger expression. What at first seemed rustic plainness, now appears refined simplicity. What seemed forward assurance, now strikes me as the result of courageous innocence and conscious virtue.

Sir Charles. What can it mean! He amazes me!

Hardcastle. I told you how it would be. Hush!

Marlow. I am now determined to stay, madam, and I have too good an opinion of my father's discernment, when he sees you, to doubt his approbation.

Miss Hardcastle. No, Mr. Marlow, I will not, cannot detain you. Do you think I could suffer a connection, in which there is the smallest room for repentance? Do you think I would take the mean advantage of a transient passion, to load you with confusion? Do you think I could ever relish that happiness, which was acquired by lessening yours!

Marlow. By all that's good, I can have no happiness but what's in your power to grant me. Nor shall I ever feel repentance, but in not having seen your merits before. I will stay, even contrary to your wishes; and though you should persist to shun me, I will make my respectful assiduities atone for the levity of my past conduct.

Miss Hardcastle. Sir, I must entreat you'll desist. As our acquaintance began, so let it end, in indifference. I might have given an hour or two to levity; but, seriously, Mr. Marlow, do you think I could ever submit to a connection, where *I* must appear mercenary, and *you* imprudent? Do you think, I could ever catch at the confident addresses of a secure admirer?

Marlow (*kneeling*). Does this look like security? Does this look like confidence? No, madam, every moment that shows me your merit, only serves to increase my diffidence and confusion. Here let me continue—

Sir Charles. I can hold it no longer. Charles, Charles, how hast thou deceived me! Is this your indifference, your uninteresting conversation!

Hardcastle. Your cold contempt; your formal interview. What have you to say now?

Marlow. That I'm all amazement! What can it mean?

Hardcastle. It means that you can say and unsay things at pleasure; that you can address a lady in private, and deny it in public; that you have one story for us, and another for my daughter!

Marlow. Daughter! This lady your daughter!

Hardcastle. Yes, sir, my only daughter, my Kate; whose else should she be?

Marlow. Oh, the devil!

Miss Hardcastle. Yes, sir, that very identical tall, squinting lady you were pleased to take me for. (*Curtsying.*) She that you addressed as the mild, modest, sentimental man of gravity, and the bold, forward, agreeable Rattle of the Ladies' Club: ha, ha, ha.

Marlow. Zounds, there's no bearing this; it's worse than death.

Miss Hardcastle. In which of your characters, sir, will you give us leave to address you? As the faltering gentleman, with looks on the ground, that speaks just to be heard, and hates hypocrisy: or the loud, confident creature, that keeps it up with Mrs. Mantrap, and old Miss Biddy Buckskin, till three in the morning? Ha, ha, ha!

Marlow. Oh, curse on my noisy head. I never attempted

to be impudent yet, that I was not taken down. I must be gone.

Hardcastle. By the hand of my body, but you shall not. I see it was all a mistake, and I am rejoiced to find it. You shall not, sir, I tell you. I know she'll forgive you. Won't you forgive him, Kate? We'll all forgive you. Take courage, man. (*They retire, she tormenting him, to the back scene.*)

Enter Mrs. Hardcastle *and* Tony.

Mrs. Hardcastle. So, so, they're gone off. Let them go, I care not.

Hardcastle. Who gone?

Mrs. Hardcastle. My dutiful niece and her gentleman, Mr. Hastings, from town. He who came down with our modest visitor here.

Sir Charles. Who, my honest George Hastings? As worthy a fellow as lives, and the girl could not have made a more prudent choice.

Hardcastle. Then, by the hand of my body, I'm proud of the connection.

Mrs. Hardcastle. Well, if he has taken away the lady, he has not taken her fortune; that remains in this family to console us for her loss.

Hardcastle. Sure, Dorothy, you would not be so mercenary?

Mrs. Hardcastle. Aye, that's my affair, not yours.

Hardcastle. But you know, if your son, when of age, refuses to marry his cousin, her whole fortune is then at her own disposal.

Mrs. Hardcastle. Ah, but he's not of age, and she has not thought proper to wait for his refusal.

Enter Hastings *and* Miss Neville.

Mrs. Hardcastle (*aside*). What, returned so soon! I begin not to like it.

Hastings (*to* Hardcastle). For my late attempt to fly off with your niece, let my present confusion be my punishment. We are now come back, to appeal from your justice to your humanity. By her father's consent, I first paid her my addresses, and our passions were first founded in duty.

Miss Neville. Since his death, I have been obliged to stoop to dissimulation to avoid oppression. In an hour of levity, I was ready even to give up my fortune to secure my choice. But I'm now recovered from the delusion, and hope from your tenderness what is denied me from a nearer connection.

Mrs. Hardcastle. Pshaw, pshaw, this is all but the whining end of a modern novel.

Hardcastle. Be it what it will, I'm glad they're come back to reclaim their due. Come hither, Tony, boy. Do you refuse this lady's hand whom I now offer you?

Tony. What signifies my refusing? You know I can't refuse her till I'm of age, father.

Hardcastle. While I thought concealing your age, boy, was likely to conduce to your improvement, I concurred with your mother's desire to keep it secret. But since I find she turns it to a wrong use, I must now declare, you have been of age these three months.

Tony. Of age! Am I of age, father?

Hardcastle. Above three months.

Tony. Then you'll see the first use I'll make of my liberty. (*Taking* Miss Neville's *hand.*) Witness all men by these presents, that I, Anthony Lumpkin, Esquire, of BLANK place, refuse you, Constantia Neville, spinster, of no place at all, for my true and lawful wife. So Constance Neville may marry whom she pleases and Tony Lumpkin is his own man again!

Sir Charles. O brave squire!

Hastings. My worthy friend!

Mrs. Hardcastle. My undutiful offspring!

Marlow. Joy, my dear George, I give you joy, sincerely. And could I prevail upon my little tyrant here to be less arbitrary, I should be the happiest man alive, if you would return me the favor.

Hastings (*to* Miss Hardcastle). Come, madam, you are now driven to the very last scene of all your contrivances. I know you like him, I'm sure he loves you, and you must and shall have him.

Hardcastle (*joining their hands*). And I say so, too. And Mr. Marlow, if she makes as good a wife as she has a daughter, I don't believe you'll ever repent your bargain. So now to supper. Tomorrow we shall gather all the poor of the parish about us, and the mistakes of the night shall be crowned with a merry morning; so, boy, take her; and as you have been mistaken in the mistress, my wish is, that you may never be mistaken in the wife.

EPILOGUE

By Dr. Goldsmith

WELL, having stooped to conquer with success,
And gained a husband without aid from dress,
Still as a barmaid, I could wish it too,
As I have conquered him to conquer you:
And let me say, for all your resolution,
That pretty barmaids have done execution.
Our life is all a play, composed to please,
"We have our exits and our entrances." [o]
The first act shows the simple country maid,
Harmless and young, of everything afraid;
Blushes when hired, and with unmeaning action,
"I hopes as how to give you satisfaction."
Her second act displays a livelier scene,—
Th' unblushing barmaid of a country inn,
Who whisks about the house, at market caters,
Talks loud, coquets the guests, and scolds the waiters.
Next the scene shifts to town, and there she soars,
The chophouse toast of ogling connoisseurs.
On squires and cits she there displays her arts,
And on the gridiron broils her lovers' hearts—
And as she smiles, her triumphs to complete,
Even common councilmen forget to eat.
The fourth act shows her wedded to the squire,
And madam now begins to hold it higher;
Pretends to taste, at operas cries *caro*,
And quits her "Nancy Dawson,"[p] for *Che Faro*.[q]
Dotes upon dancing, and in all her pride,
Swims round the room, the Heinel[r] of Cheapside:
Ogles and leers with artificial skill,
Till having lost in age the power to kill,
She sits all night at cards, and ogles at spadille.[s]
Such, through our lives, th' eventful history—
The fifth and last act still remains for me.
The barmaid now for your protection prays,
Turns female barrister, and pleads for Bayes.[t]

[o] Cf. *As You Like It*, II. vii. 141. [p] a popular song [q] an aria in Glück's opera, *Orfeo* [r] popular German dancer [s] leading trump in ombre, a card game [t] i.e., the author (cf. Bayes in Buckingham's *The Rehearsal*)

George Gordon, Lord Byron:

CAIN

A Mystery

During most of the nineteenth century, when a poet wrote a serious play he usually took Shakespeare as his model, consciously or unconsciously. While Shelley, for example, was working on *Charles I*, he told a friend that his play was modeled on *King Lear* and that his aim was to "approach as near our great dramatist as my feeble powers will permit." In general, the situations and the verse of nineteenth-century poetic tragedies contain unmistakable echoes of Shakespeare, though somehow in their new form they are usually dull or ludicrous. The bookish tendency of verse drama was heightened by the playwrights' failure to gain public approval. When their plays were rejected by managers or (if the managers accepted them) by audiences, the poets commonly rejected the playhouse and wrote closet drama, plays designed not to be staged but to be read in the privacy of the study.

The pernicious influence of Shakespeare was clearly seen by Thomas Lovell Beddoes, a poet contemporary with Byron:

> The man who is to awaken the drama must be a bold trampling fellow—no creeper into worm-holes—no reviser even—however good. These reanimations are vampire-cold. . . . With the greatest reverence for all the antiquities of the drama, I still think that we had better beget than revive—attempt to give the literature of this age an idiosyncrasy and spirit of its own and only raise a ghost

to gaze on not to live with—just now the drama is a haunted ruin.

Byron was certainly a trampling fellow. When his first book of poems was unfavorably reviewed, he wrote a second in which he trampled on his critics. He then trampled across Europe to get material for a third book, returned to England, made an unhappy marriage, and, age twenty-eight, left England to spend the remainder of his life abroad. His critical pronouncements were equally vigorous: Shakespeare is "the *worst* of models, though the most extraordinary of writers." Byron often spoke slightingly of Shakespeare, preferring (or affecting to prefer) the Greeks, Ben Jonson, Alfieri, and other "classical" writers more to a lord's taste. Some of Byron's plays follow the allegedly classical "unities" of time, place, and action (a play covers no more than twenty-four hours; has only one locale; has only one plot, wholly tragic or wholly comic), but Byron denied in letters and prefaces that even these plays were designed for the stage. His plays, he said, were designed for the closet (some, he said, were for the water closet), but he had a keen interest in the theater and when in 1815 he was a member of the managing committee of Drury Lane, he eagerly sought plays better than those it had been doing. One cannot help feeling that his ardent protests (he boasts, for example, that one of his plays is "quite *impossible* for the stage, for which my intercourse with Drury Lane has given me the greatest contempt") do not quite jibe with his numerous experiments in playwriting. One cannot help feeling, in short, that although he despised the popular stage he would not have minded if posterity recorded him as the stage's reformer.

In *Cain* (1821) Byron is sufficiently classical (and for that matter Shakespearean) to write in verse. The beginning of the play, in which five speakers each briefly invoke God, is ritualistic and incantatory, but on the whole the language of the play is not hypnotic nor is it richly connotative. It is verse that one looks *through* rather than *at*, to use T. S. Eliot's distinction. Byron's verse is highly suited to argumentation, or to "thought," which Aristotle distinguishes from "character." "Thought" is a man's intellectual quality, "character" his moral nature. Byron, in contrast for example to Wordsworth, is chiefly concerned with "thought"; Wordsworth said that in writing his tragedy *The Borderers* his concern "was almost exclusively given to the passions and character." Byron's concern with thought makes his play more modern than almost any other of the period. Some idea of Byron's modernity (though the modern play, from Ibsen and Chekhov on, is in prose) can be got from Shaw's distinction between a modern play and an old-fashioned one: "A play with a discussion is a modern play. A play with only an emotional situation is an old-fashioned one." Wordsworth's play is old-fashioned; Byron's, though in verse (Shaw obviously had Ibsen's prose plays and his own in mind), is modern.

The modernity of *Cain* begins with the Preface. Though Byron calls it "A Mystery," intending to link it to medieval dramatizations of the Bible (see *The Genius of the Early English Theater*[1]), the Preface argues that traditional views of Cain are wrongheaded; it goes on to say that he has made use of recent scientific thought, specifically that of Cuvier. The interest in *Cain* is not primarily in character revealing itself through interesting language, but in ideas, to which language is subservient. The play is largely a discussion, largely talk. Shaw, commenting on the charge that his own plays are largely talk, helps put Byron's plays in proper perspective:

> It is quite true that my plays are all talk, just as Raphael's pictures are all paint, Michael Angelo's statues all marble, Beethoven's symphonies all noise. Mr. Rattigan, not being a born fool, does not complain of this, but, being an irrational genius, does let himself in for the more absurd complaint that, though plays must be all talk, the talk should have no ideas behind it, though he knows as well as I do when, if ever, he thinks for a moment, that without a stock of ideas, mind cannot operate and plays cannot exist. The quality of a play is the quality of its ideas.

The quality of Byron's ideas was such that it caused an outburst in England. In Shaw's plays the ideas are customarily thrashed out by antagonists sitting around a table. Byron chooses a different method, one that has exposed the play to the charge of being undramatic. The ideas in the play are chiefly presented by Lucifer and Cain, both of whom take the same side. Lucifer is Cain's tutor; Cain is often Lucifer's straight-man. But this does not mean that there is little tension—little drama—in the

[1] Ed. by S. Barnet M. Berman, and W. Burto, New York, New American Library (Mentor Books), 1962.

play. There is abundant drama in the questions and answers, especially because they strike against the traditional ideas presumably held by—or at least familiar to—most readers. Nor, of course, is Cain's education conducted simply by questions and answers. Consider as an example the beginning of Act II, set in "The Abyss of Space":

> *Cain.* I tread on air, and sink not; yet I fear
> To sink.
> *Lucifer.* Have faith in me, and thou shalt be
> Borne on the air, of which I am the prince.
> *Cain.* Can I do so without impiety?
> *Lucifer.* Believe—and sink not! doubt—and perish!
> This would run the edict of the other God. . . .
> Worship or worship not, thou shalt behold
> The worlds beyond thy little world.

To Cain's fear Lucifer replies with a demand for faith, and to Cain's question whether such faith is impious Lucifer at first replies with a command. But a moment later he reveals that this command is not his but his foe's, "the other God"; Lucifer goes on to assure Cain that he will be safe whether he believes or not. Lucifer's speech, that is, holds our interest, adds meaning to meaning, effectively presents an issue by using—with a difference—the New Testament's report that faith will enable Jesus' followers to walk on the waves.

There is tension and conflict, too, between Cain and his family. Cain is set apart from them by an awareness of the horror of death, which makes life to him a cruel divine joke. To Abel's suggestion that he give thanks for living, he replies, "Must I not die?" He cannot humbly bow before God as Adam and Abel bow, nor can he joyfully accept the domestic life that delights Adah. Like the traditional tragic hero, he stands apart from and above his fellow men, more sensitive to apparent injustice and less fit to thrive in the world:

> My father is
> Tamed down; my mother has forgot the mind
> Which made her thirst for knowledge at the risk
> Of an eternal curse; my brother is
> A watching shepherd boy, who offers up
> The firstlings of the flock to him who bids
> The earth yield nothing to us without sweat;
> My sister Zillah sings an earlier hymn
> Than the birds' matins; and my Adah, my

Own and belovèd, she, too, understands not
The mind which overwhelms me.

Appalled at the thought of the suffering of the guiltless, Cain sees no good in the deity to whom Abel sacrifices the innocent sheep.

The tragedy (the play is a tragedy as well as a problem play) is that this man—so far from the coarse, stingy Cain of the medieval plays—who is repelled by bloodshed should commit the first murder. Adam's disobedience to God seems to most men a slighter thing than Cain's assault on Abel; to Byron's Cain, at least, Adam's disobedience is no crime at all, but the slaughter of a brother is monstrous. The murder—vaguely motivated in the Bible—in the play is motivated chiefly by Cain's despair and hatred for a Creator who has placed a death penalty on the innocent, born and unborn. Stung by the injustice, and angered by Abel's submission, Cain strikes, and does the deed which seems most foreign to him. The deed here, as in most tragedies (think, for example, of Othello's murder of the woman he loves), is one that in large part arises out of the doer's nature, and yet seems contrary to what is central to that nature. Behind these motives of dejection and anger, however, there is—as in most tragedy—the shadow of destiny, the suggestion that actions seem free but are nevertheless mysteriously destined. Cain has inherited the taint of death from his parents' fault; he was begot too soon after the Fall, "ere yet my mother's mind subsided from/ The serpent." Exile, the punishment now inflicted on him (along with internal torment), is the consequence of his deed, and yet the deed is and is not wholly his. He was an exile from Paradise before the play began.

The preceding paragraph has discussed *Cain* in terms of the usual tragedy—a man does a deed and suffers for it, internally as well as externally. But the play clearly tries to be more than a tragedy. Its Promethean heroes force the reader to think about God, about power, about suffering, about the meaning of life and death. They force the reader to re-examine the account in Genesis. In Genesis he finds that civilization—the wearing of clothes, the tilling of the soil, the building of cities (specifically attributed to Cain), and the development of metallurgy (by Cain's descendants), a development which can be both creative and destructive—proceeds from violations of divine law. Byron's *Cain* is a profound reinterpretation of this insight.

Byron: Biographical Note.

George Noel Gordon, Lord Byron (1788–1824) is chiefly known as a nondramatic poet. His father was a libertine, his mother an heiress who was deserted by her husband when her money ran out. When Byron was ten the death of a great-uncle made him the sixth Baron Byron. He was rebellious in childhood and in later years, but he put his rebelliousness to good use in his satiric and in his narrative poems, and in his political actions at home and abroad. Rumors of incest between him and his half-sister caused him to be virtually banished from England in 1816. He spent most of his few remaining years in Italy, where he wrote several plays as well as his satiric narrative, *Don Juan*. He died of fever at Missolonghi, in western Greece, where he was seeking to aid the Greeks in their struggle for freedom from the Turks. Of his plays, only *Marino Faliero* (1820) was produced in his lifetime, but they have attracted increasing attention. *Werner* (first produced in 1830) has been expecially popular, furnishing William Macready with his most acclaimed role, a role played later in the nineteenth century by Henry Irving. In 1920 Stanislavsky offered a notable production of *Cain* at the Moscow Art Theater.

Suggested References:

Chew, Samuel, *The Dramas of Lord Byron,* Göttingen, Vandenhoeck and Ruprecht, 1915.

Knight, G. Wilson, "Shakespeare and Byron's Plays," *Shakespeare Jahrbuch,* XCV (1959), 82–97.

Magarshack, David, *Stanislavsky,* New York, Chanticleer Press, 1951; London, MacGibbon & Kee, 1951.

Marchand, Leslie, *Byron*: *A Biography*, 3 vols., New York, Alfred A. Knopf, 1957; London, John Murray, 1958.

Cain

Characters

Men — ADAM, CAIN, ABEL

Spirits — ANGEL OF THE LORD, LUCIFER

Women — EVE, ADAH, ZILLAH

"Now the Serpent was more subtil than any beast of the field which the Lord God had made." [Genesis 3:1]

TO
SIR WALTER SCOTT, BART.
THIS MYSTERY OF CAIN
IS INSCRIBED,
BY HIS OBLIGED FRIEND,
AND FAITHFUL SERVANT,
THE AUTHOR.

PREFACE

The following scenes are entitled "A Mystery," in conformity with the ancient title annexed to dramas upon similar subjects, which were styled "Mysteries, or Moralities."[a] The

[a] Byron fails to distinguish between the medieval mystery play, which was a dramatization of a Biblical episode, and the late-medieval morality play, which was an allegorical dramatization of the conflict between good and evil. For examples of each, see *The Genius of the Early English Theater*.

author has by no means taken the same liberties with his subject which were common, formerly, as may be seen by any reader curious enough to refer to those very profane productions, whether in English, French, Italian, or Spanish. The author has endeavored to preserve the language adapted to his characters, and where it is (and this is but rarely) taken from actual *Scripture,* he has made as little alteration, even of words, as the rhythm would permit. The reader will recollect that the book of Genesis does not state that Eve was tempted by a demon, but by "the Serpent"; and that only because he was "the most subtil of all the beasts of the field." Whatever interpretation the Rabbins[b] and the Fathers may have put upon this, I take the words as I find them, and reply, with Bishop Watson upon similar occasions, when the Fathers were quoted to him, as Moderator in the schools of Cambridge, "Behold the Book"—holding up the Scripture. It is to be recollected that my present subject has nothing to do with the *New Testament,* to which no reference can be here made without anachronism. With the poems upon similar topics, I have not been recently familiar. Since I was twenty I have never read Milton; but I had read him so frequently before, that this may make little difference. Gesner's *Death of Abel* I have never read since I was eight years of age, at Aberdeen. The general impression of my recollection is delight; but of the contents I remember only that Cain's wife was called Mahala, and Abel's Thirza: in the following pages I have called them "Adah" and "Zillah," the earliest female names which occur in Genesis; they were those of Lamech's wives:[c] those of Cain and Abel are not called by their names. Whether, then, a coincidence of subject may have caused the same in expression, I know nothing, and care as little.

The reader will please to bear in mind (what few choose to recollect), that there is no allusion to a future state in any of the books of Moses, nor indeed in the Old Testament. For a reason for this extraordinary omission he may consult Warburton's *Divine Legation;* whether satisfactory or not, no better has yet been assigned. I have therefore supposed it new to Cain, without, I hope, any perversion of Holy Writ.

With regard to the language of Lucifer, it was difficult for me to make him talk like a clergyman upon the same subjects; but I have done what I could to restrain him within the bounds of spiritual politeness. If he disclaims having tempted Eve in the shape of the Serpent, it is only because the book of Genesis, has not the most distant allusion to anything of the kind, but merely to the Serpent in his serpentine capacity.

[b] Rabbis [c] Genesis 4:19

Note.—The reader will perceive that the author has partly adopted in this poem the notion of Cuvier, [d] that the world had been destroyed several times before the creation of man. This speculation, derived from the different strata and the bones of enormous and unknown animals found in them, is not contrary to the Mosaic account, but rather confirms it; as no human bones have yet been discovered in those strata, although those of many known animals are found near the remains of the unknown. The assertion of Lucifer, that the pre-Adamite world was also peopled by rational beings much more intelligent than man, and proportionably powerful to the mammoth, etc., etc., is, of course, a poetical fiction to help him to make out his case.

I ought to add, that there is a "tramelogedia" of Alfieri, called *Abele*. [e]—I have never read that, nor any other of the posthumous works of the writer, except his Life.

RAVENNA, *Sept. 20, 1821.*

ACT I

Scene I: The Land without[f] Paradise.—Time, Sunrise.

Adam, Eve, Cain, Abel, Adah, Zillah, offering a Sacrifice.

Adam. God, the Eternal! Infinite! All-wise!—
Who out of darkness on the deep didst make
Light on the waters with a word—all hail!
Jehovah, with returning light, all hail!
Eve. God! who didst name the day, and separate
Morning from night, till then divided never,
Who didst divide the wave from wave, and call
Part of thy work the firmament—all hail!
Abel. God! who didst call the elements into
Earth—ocean—air—and fire, and with the day 10
And night, and worlds which these illuminate
Or shadow, madest beings to enjoy them,
And love both them and thee—all hail! all hail!
Adah. God, the Eternal! Parent of all things!
Who didst create these best and beauteous beings,
To be belovèd more than all save thee—
Let me love thee and them:—all hail! all hail!

[d] Baron Georges Cuvier (1769–1832) French paleontologist, naturalist, and zoologist [e] Vittorio Alfieri (1749–1803) preferred to call his play *Abele* a "tramelogedia," i.e., a tragedy with music (Greek: *melos*—"song"). [f] outside

Zillah. Oh, God! who loving, making, blessing all,
Yet didst permit the Serpent to creep in,
And drive my father forth from Paradise, 20
Keep us from further evil:—Hail! all hail!
Adam. Son Cain, my first-born, wherefore art thou silent?
Cain. Why should I speak?
Adam. To pray.
Cain. Have ye not prayed?
Adam. We have, most fervently.
Cain. And loudly: I
Have heard you.
Adam. So will God, I trust.
Abel. Amen!
Adam. But thou, my eldest born, art silent still.
Cain. 'Tis better I should be so.
Adam. Wherefore so?
Cain. I have nought to ask.
Adam. Nor aught to thank for?
Cain. No.
Adam. Dost thou not live?
Cain. Must I not die?
Eve. Alas!
The fruit of our forbidden tree begins 30
To fall.
Adam. And we must gather it again.
Oh, God! why didst thou plant the Tree of Knowledge?
Cain. And wherefore plucked ye not the Tree of Life?
Ye might have then defied him.
Adam. Oh! my son,
Blaspheme not: these are serpent's words.
Cain. Why not?
The snake spoke *truth:* it *was* the Tree of Knowledge;
It *was* the Tree of Life: knowledge is good,
And life is good; and how can both be evil?
Eve. My boy! thou speakest as I spoke, in sin,
Before thy birth: let me not see renewed 40
My misery in thine. I have repented.
Let me not see my offspring fall into
The snares beyond the walls of Paradise,
Which e'en in Paradise destroyed his parents.
Content thee with what *is*. Had we been so,
Thou now hadst been contented.—Oh, my son!
Adam. Our orisons completed, let us hence,
Each to his task of toil—not heavy, though

[f] outside

Needful: the earth is young, and yields us kindly
Her fruits with little labor.

Eve. Cain, my son, 50
Behold thy father cheerful and resigned,
And do as he doth. *Exeunt* Adam *and* Eve.

Zillah. Wilt thou not, my brother?

Abel. Why wilt thou wear this gloom upon thy brow,
Which can avail thee nothing, save to rouse
The Eternal anger?

Adah. My belovèd Cain,
Wilt thou frown even on me?

Cain. No, Adah! no;
I fain would be alone a little while.
Abel, I'm sick at heart: but it will pass.
Precede me, brother—I will follow shortly.
And you, too, sisters, tarry not behind; 60
Your gentleness must not be harshly met:
I'll follow you anon.[g]

Adah. If not, I will
Return to seek you here.

Abel. The peace of God
Be on your spirit, brother!

Exeunt Abel, Zillah, *and* Adah.

Cain (*solus*[h]). And this is
Life—Toil! and wherefore should I toil?—because
My father could not keep his place in Eden.
What had *I* done in this?—I was unborn:
I sought not to be born; nor love the state
To which that birth has brought me. Why did he
Yield to the serpent and the woman? or, 70
Yielding, why suffer? What was there in this?
The tree was planted, and why not for him?
If not, why place him near it, where it grew,
The fairest in the center? They have but
One answer to all questions, " 'Twas *his* will,
And *he* is good." How know I that? Because
He is all-powerful, must all-good, too, follow?
I judge but by the fruits—and they are bitter—
Which I must feed on for a fault not mine.
Whom have we here?—A shape like to the angels, 80
Yet of a sterner and a sadder aspect
Of spiritual essence: why do I quake?
Why should I fear him more than other spirits,
Whom I see daily wave their fiery swords

[g] presently [h] alone

Before the gates round which I linger oft,
In twilight's hour, to catch a glimpse of those
Gardens which are my just inheritance,
Ere the night closes o'er the inhibited walls
And the immortal trees which overtop
The cherubim-defended battlements? 90
If I shrink not from these, the fire-armed angels,
Why should I quail from him who now approaches?
Yet he seems mightier far than them, nor less
Beauteous, and yet not all as beautiful
As he hath been, and might be: sorrow seems
Half of his immortality. And is it
So? and can aught grieve save humanity?
He cometh.

Enter Lucifer.

Lucifer. Mortal!
Cain. Spirit, who art thou?
Lucifer. Master of spirits.
Cain. And being so, canst thou
Leave them, and walk with dust?
Lucifer. I know the thoughts 100
Of dust, and feel for it, and with you.
Cain. How!
You know my thoughts?
Lucifer. They are the thoughts of all
Worthy of thought;—'tis your immortal part
Which speaks within you.
Cain. What immortal part?
This has not been revealed: the Tree of Life
Was withheld from us by my father's folly,
While that of Knowledge, by my mother's haste,
Was plucked too soon; and all the fruit is death!
Lucifer. They have deceived thee; thou shalt live.
Cain. I live,
But live to die: and, living, see no thing 110
To make death hateful, save an innate clinging,
A loathsome, and yet all invincible
Instinct of life, which I abhor, as I
Despise myself, yet cannot overcome—
And so I live. Would I had never lived!
Lucifer. Thou livest, and must live for ever: think not
The earth, which is thine outward cov'ring, is
Existence—it will cease, and thou wilt be
No less than thou art now.

Cain. No *less!* and why
No more?
Lucifer. It may be thou shalt be as we. 120
Cain. And ye?
Lucifer. Are everlasting.
Cain. Are ye happy?
Lucifer. We are mighty.
Cain. Are ye happy?
Lucifer. No; art thou?
Cain. How should I be so? Look on me!
Lucifer. Poor clay!
And thou pretendest to be wretched! Thou!
Cain. I am:—and thou, with all thy might, what art
thou?
Lucifer. One who aspired to be what made thee, and
Would not have made thee what thou art.
Cain. Ah!
Thou look'st almost a god; and—
Lucifer. I am none:
And having failed to be one, would be nought
Save what I am. He conquered; let him reign! 130
Cain. Who?
Lucifer. Thy sire's Maker and the earth's.
Cain. And heaven's,
And all that in them is. So I have heard
His seraphs sing; and so my father saith.
Lucifer. They say—what they must sing and say on pain
Of being that which I am—and thou art—
Of spirits and of men.
Cain. And what is that?
Lucifer. Souls who dare use their immortality—
Souls who dare look the Omnipotent tyrant in
His everlasting face, and tell him that
His evil is not good! If he has made, 140
As he saith—which I know not, nor believe—
But, if he made us—he cannot unmake:
We are immortal!—nay, he 'd *have* us so,
That he may torture:—let him! He is great—
But, in his greatness, is no happier than
We in our conflict! Goodness would not make
Evil; and what else hath he made? But let him
Sit on his vast and solitary throne,
Creating worlds, to make eternity
Less burthensome to his immense existence 150
And unparticipated solitude;
Let him crowd orb on orb: he is alone

Indefinite, indissoluble tyrant;
Could he but crush himself, 'twere the best boon
He ever granted: but let him reign on,
And multiply himself in misery!
Spirits and men, at least we sympathize—
And, suffering in concert, make our pangs,
Innumerable, more endurable,
By the unbounded sympathy of all 160
With all! But *He!* so wretched in his height,
So restless in his wretchedness, must still
Create, and re-create—

Cain. Thou speak'st to me of things which long have swum
In visions through my thought: I never could
Reconcile what I saw with what I heard.
My father and my mother talk to me
Of serpents, and of fruits and trees: I see
The gates of what they call their Paradise
Guarded by fiery-sworded cherubim, 170
Which shut them out, and me: I feel the weight
Of daily toil and constant thought: I look
Around a world where I seem nothing, with
Thoughts which arise within me, as if they
Could master all things:—but I thought alone
This misery was *mine*.—My father is
Tamed down; my mother has forgot the mind
Which made her thirst for knowledge at the risk
Of an eternal curse; my brother is
A watching shepherd boy, who offers up 180
The firstlings of the flock to him who bids
The earth yield nothing to us without sweat;
My sister Zillah sings an earlier hymn
Than the birds' matins; and my Adah, my
Own and belovèd, she, too, understands not
The mind which overwhelms me: never till
Now met I aught to sympathize with me.
'Tis well—I rather would consort with spirits.

Lucifer. And hadst thou not been fit by thine own soul
For such companionship, I would not now 190
Have stood before thee as I am: a serpent
Had been enough to charm ye, as before.

Cain. Ah! didst *thou* tempt my mother?

Lucifer. I tempt none,
Save with the truth: was not the Tree, the Tree
Of Knowledge? and was not the Tree of Life
Still fruitful? Did *I* bid her pluck them not?

Did *I* plant things prohibited within
The reach of beings innocent, and curious
By their own innocence? I would have made ye
Gods; and even He who thrust ye forth, so thrust ye 200
Because "ye should not eat the fruits of life,
And become gods as we." Were those his words?

Cain. They were, as I have heard from those who heard them,
In thunder.

Lucifer. Then who was the demon? He
Who would not let ye live, or he who would
Have made ye live for ever in the joy
And power of knowledge?

Cain. Would they had snatched both
The fruits, or neither!

Lucifer. One is yours already;
The other may be still.

Cain. How so?

Lucifer. By being
Yourselves, in your resistance. Nothing can 210
Quench the mind, if the mind will be itself
And center of surrounding things—'tis made
To sway.

Cain. But didst thou tempt my parents?

Lucifer. I?
Poor clay! what should I tempt them for, or how?

Cain. They say the serpent was a spirit.

Lucifer. Who
Saith that? It is not written so on high:
The proud One will not so far falsify,
Though man's vast fears and little vanity
Would make him cast upon the spiritual nature
His own low failing. The snake *was* the snake— 220
No more; and yet not less than those he tempted,
In nature being earth also—*more* in *wisdom,*
Since he could overcome them, and foreknew
The knowledge fatal to their narrow joys.
Think'st thou I'd take the shape of things that die?

Cain. But the thing had a demon?[1]

Lucifer. He but woke one
In those he spake to with his forky tongue.
I tell thee that the serpent was no more
Than a mere serpent: ask the cherubim
Who guard the tempting tree. When thousand ages 230
Have rolled o'er your dead ashes, and your seed's,

[1] i.e., daimon, governing spirit

The seed of the then world may thus array
Their earliest fault in fable, and attribute
To them a shape I scorn, as I scorn all
That bows to him who made things but to bend
Before his sullen, sole eternity;
But we, who see the truth, must speak it. Thy
Fond[j] parents listened to a creeping thing,
And fell. For what should spirits tempt them? What
Was there to envy in the narrow bounds 240
Of Paradise, that spirits who pervade
Space—but I speak to thee of what thou know'st not,
With all thy Tree of Knowledge.

Cain. But thou canst not
Speak aught of knowledge which I would not know,
And do not thirst to know, and bear a mind
To know.

Lucifer. And heart to look on?

Cain. Be it proved.

Lucifer. Darest thou to look on Death?

Cain. He has not yet
Been seen.

Lucifer. But must be undergone.

Cain. My father
Says he is something dreadful, and my mother
Weeps when he 's named; and Abel lifts his eyes 250
To heaven, and Zillah casts hers to the earth,
And sighs a prayer; and Adah looks on me,
And speaks not.

Lucifer. And thou?

Cain. Thoughts unspeakable
Crowd in my breast to burning, when I hear
Of this almighty Death, who is, it seems,
Inevitable. Could I wrestle with him?
I wrestled with the lion, when a boy,
In play, till he ran roaring from my gripe.[k]

Lucifer. It has no shape; but will absorb all things
That bear the form of earth-born being.

Cain. Ah! 260
I thought it was a being: who could do
Such evil things to beings save a being?

Lucifer. Ask the Destroyer.

Cain. Who?

Lucifer. The Maker—call him
Which name thou wilt: he makes but to destroy.

[j] foolish [k] grasp

Cain. I knew not that, yet thought it, since I heard
Of Death; although I know not what it is,
Yet it seems horrible. I have looked out
In the vast desolate night in search of him;
And when I saw gigantic shadows in
The umbrage of the walls of Eden, chequered 270
By the far-flashing of the cherubs' swords,
I watched for what I thought his coming; for
With fear rose longing in my heart to know
What 'twas which shook us all—but nothing came.
And then I turned my weary eyes from off
Our native and forbidden Paradise,
Up to the lights above us, in the azure,
Which are so beautiful: shall they, too, die?

Lucifer. Perhaps—but long outlive both thine and thee.

Cain. I'm glad of that: I would not have them die— 280
They are so lovely. What is Death? I fear,
I feel, it is a dreadful thing; but what,
I cannot compass: 'tis denounced against us,
Both them who sinn'd and sinn'd not, as an ill—
What ill?

Lucifer To be resolved into the earth.

Cain. But shall I know it?

Lucifer. As I know not death,
I cannot answer.

Cain. Were I quiet earth
That were no evil: would I ne'er had been
Aught else but dust!

Lucifer. That is a groveling wish,
Less than thy father's, for he wish'd to know. 290

Cain. But not to live, or wherefore pluck'd he not
The Life-tree?

Lucifer. He was hindered.

Cain. Deadly error!
Not to snatch first that fruit:—but ere he plucked
The knowledge, he was ignorant of death.
Alas! I scarcely now know what it is,
And yet I fear it—fear I know not what!

Lucifer. And I, who know all things, fear nothing: see
What is true knowledge.

Cain. Wilt thou teach me all?

Lucifer. Aye, upon one condition.

Cain. Name it.

Lucifer. That
Thou dost fall down and worship me—thy Lord. 300

Cain. Thou art not the Lord my father worships.

Lucifer. No.
Cain. His equal?
Lucifer. No;—I have nought in common with him!
Nor would: I would be aught above—beneath—
Aught save a sharer or a servant of
His power. I dwell apart; but I am great:—
Many there are who worship me, and more
Who shall—be thou amongst the first.
Cain. I never
As yet have bowed unto my father's God,
Although my brother Abel oft implores
That I would join with him in sacrifice:— 310
Why should I bow to thee?
Lucifer. Hast thou ne'er bowed
To him?
Cain. Have I not said it?—need I say it?
Could not thy mighty knowledge teach thee that?
Lucifer. He who bows not to him has bowed to me!
Cain. But I will bend to neither.
Lucifer Ne'er the less,
Thou art my worshiper: not worshiping
Him makes thee mine the same.
Cain. And what is that?
Lucifer. Thou 'lt know here—and hereafter.
Cain. Let me but
Be taught the mystery of my being.
Lucifer. Follow
Where I will lead thee.
Cain. But I must retire 320
To till the earth—for I had promised—
Lucifer. What?
Cain. To cull some first-fruits.
Lucifer. Why?
Cain. To offer up.
With Abel on an altar.
Lucifer. Saidst thou not.
Thou ne'er hadst bent to him who made thee?
Cain. Yes—
But Abel's earnest prayer has wrought upon me;
The offering is more his than mine—and Adah—
Lucifer. Why dost thou hesitate?
Cain. She is my sister,
Born on the same day, of the same womb; and
She wrung from me, with tears, this promise; and
Rather than see her weep, I would, methinks, 330
Bear all—and worship aught.

Lucifer. Then follow me!
Cain. I will.

Enter Adah.

Adah. My brother, I have come for thee;
It is our hour of rest and joy—and we
Have less without thee. Thou hast labored not
This morn; but I have done thy task: the fruits
Are ripe, and glowing as the light which ripens:
Come away.
Cain. Seest thou not?
Adah. I see an angel;
We have seen many: will he share our hour
Of rest?—he is welcome.
Cain. But he is not like
The angels we have seen.
Adah. Are there, then, others? 340
But he is welcome, as they were: they deigned
To be our guests—will he?
Cain (*to* Lucifer). Wilt thou?
Lucifer. I ask
Thee to be mine.
Cain. I must away with him.
Adah. And leave us?
Cain. Aye.
Adah. And *me?*
Cain. Belovèd Adah!
Adah. Let me go with thee.
Lucifer. No, she must not.
Adah Who
Art thou that steppest between heart and heart?
Cain. He is a god.
Adah. How know'st thou?
Cain. He speaks like
A god.
Adah. So did the serpent, and it lied.
Lucifer. Thou errest, Adah!—was not the Tree that
Of Knowledge?
Adah. Aye—to our eternal sorrow. 350
Lucifer. And yet that grief is knowledge—so he lied not:
And if he did betray you, 'twas with Truth;
And Truth in its own essence cannot be
But good.
Adah. But all we know of it has gathered
Evil on ill: expulsion from our home,

And dread, and toil, and sweat, and heaviness;
Remorse of that which was—and hope of that
Which cometh not. Cain! walk not with this spirit.
Bear with what we have borne, and love me—I
Love thee.

Lucifer. More than thy mother and thy sire? 360

Adah. I do. Is that a sin, too?

Lucifer. No, not yet.
It one day will be in your children.

Adah. What!
Must not my daughter love her brother Enoch?

Lucifer. Not as thou lovest Cain.

Adah. Oh, my God!
Shall they not love and bring forth things that love
Out of their love? have they not drawn their milk
Out of this bosom? was not he, their father,
Born of the same sole womb, in the same hour
With me? did we not love each other? and
In multiplying our being multiply 370
Things which will love each other as we love
Them?—And as I love thee, my Cain! go not
Forth with this spirit; he is not of ours.

Lucifer. The sin I speak of is not of my making,
And cannot be a sin in you—whate'er
It seem in those who will replace ye in
Mortality.

Adah. What is the sin which is not
Sin in itself? Can circumstance make sin
Or virtue?—if it doth, we are the slaves
Of—

Lucifer. Higher things than ye are slaves: 380
Than them or ye would be so, did they not
Prefer an independency of torture
To the smooth agonies of adulation,
In hymns and harpings, and self-seeking prayers,
To that which is omnipotent, because
It is omnipotent, and not from love,
But terror and self-hope.

Adah. Omnipotence
Must be all goodness.

Lucifer. Was it so in Eden?

Adah. Fiend! tempt me not with beauty; thou art fairer
Than was the serpent, and as false.

Lucifer. As true. 390
Ask Eve, your mother: bears she not the knowledge
Of good and evil?

Adah. Oh, my mother! thou
Hast plucked a fruit more fatal to thine offspring
Than to thyself; thou at the least hast passed
Thy youth in Paradise, in innocent
And happy intercourse with happy spirits:
But we, thy children, ignorant of Eden,
Are girt about by demons, who assume
The words of God and tempt us with our own
Dissatisfied and curious thoughts—as thou 400
Wert worked on by the snake in thy most flushed
And heedless, harmless wantonness of bliss.
I cannot answer this immortal thing
Which stands before me; I cannot abhor him;
I look upon him with a pleasing fear,
And yet I fly not from him: in his eye
There is a fastening attraction which
Fixes my fluttering eyes on his; my heart
Beats quick; he awes me, and yet draws me near,
Nearer, and nearer:—Cain—Cain—save me from 410
him!

Cain. What dreads my Adah? This is no ill spirit.

Adah. He is not God—nor God's: I have beheld
The cherubs and the seraphs; he looks not
Like them.

Cain. But there are spirits loftier still—
The archangels.

Lucifer. And still loftier than the archangels.

Adah. Ay—but not blessèd.

Lucifer. If the blessedness
Consists in slavery—no.

Adah. I have heard it said,
The seraphs *love most*—cherubim *know most;*
And this should be a cherub—since he loves not.

Lucifer. And if the higher knowledge quenches love, 420
What must *he be* you cannot love when known?
Since the all-knowing cherubim love least,
The seraphs' love can be but ignorance:
That they are not compatible, the doom
Of thy fond parents, for their daring, proves.
Choose betwixt love and knowledge—since there is
No other choice. Your sire has chosen already;
His worship is but fear.

Adah. Oh, Cain! choose love.

Cain. For thee, my Adah, I choose not—it was
Born with me—but I love nought else.

Adah. Our parents? 430

Cain. Did they love us when they snatched from the Tree
That which hath driven us all from Paradise?

Adah. We were not born then—and if we had been,
Should we not love them and our children, Cain?

Cain. My little Enoch! and his lisping sister!
Could I but deem them happy, I would half
Forget—but it can never be forgotten
Through thrice a thousand generations! never
Shall men love the remembrance of the man
Who sowed the seed of evil and mankind 440
In the same hour! They plucked the tree of science,
And sin—and not content with their own sorrow,
Begot *me*—*thee*—and all the few that are,
And all the unnumbered and innumerable
Multitudes, millions, myriads, which may be,
To inherit agonies accumulated
By ages!—And *I* must be sire of such things!
Thy beauty and thy love—my love and joy,
The rapturous moment and the placid hour,
All we love in our children and each other, 450
But lead them and ourselves through many years
Of sin and pain—or few, but still of sorrow,
Interchecked with an instant of brief pleasure,
To Death—the unknown! Methinks the Tree of
Knowledge
Hath not fulfilled its promise:—if they sinned,
At least they ought to have known all things that are
Of knowledge—and the mystery of death.
What do they know?—that they are miserable.
What need of snakes and fruits to teach us that?

Adah. I am not wretched, Cain, and if thou 460
Wert happy—

Cain. Be thou happy, then, alone—
I will have nought to do with happiness,
Which humbles me and mine.

Adah. Alone I could not,
Nor *would* be happy: but with those around us
I think I could be so, despite of death,
Which, as I know it not, I dread not, though
It seems an awful shadow—if I may
Judge from what I have heard.

Lucifer. And thou couldst not
Alone, thou say'st, be happy?

Adah. Alone! Oh, my God!
Who could be happy and alone, or good? 470
To me my solitude seems sin; unless

When I think how soon I shall see my brother,
His brother, and our children, and our parents.
Lucifer. Yet thy God is alone; and is he happy,
Lonely, and good?
Adah. He is not so; he hath
The angels and the mortals to make happy,
And thus becomes so in diffusing joy.
What else can joy be, but the spreading joy?
Lucifer. Ask of your sire, the exile fresh from Eden;
Or of his first-born son: ask your own heart; 480
It is not tranquil.
Adah. Alas, no! and you—
Are you of heaven?
Lucifer. If I am not, enquire
The cause of this all-spreading happiness
(Which you proclaim) of the all-great and good
Maker of life and living things; it is
His secret, and he keeps it. *We* must bear,
And some of us resist, and both in vain,
His seraphs say; but it is worth the trial,
Since better may not be without. There is
A wisdom in the spirit, which directs 490
To right, as in the dim blue air the eye
Of you, young mortals, lights at once upon
The star which watches, welcoming the morn.
Adah. It is a beautiful star; I love it for
Its beauty.
Lucifer. And why not adore?
Adah. Our father
Adores the Invisible only.
Lucifer. But the symbols
Of the Invisible are the loveliest
Of what is visible; and yon bright star
Is leader of the host of heaven.
Adah. Our father
Saith that he has beheld the God himself 500
Who made him and our mother.
Lucifer. Hast *thou* seen him?
Adah. Yes—in his works.
Lucifer. But in his being?
Adah. No—
Save in my father, who is God's own image;
Or in his angels, who are like to thee—
And brighter, yet less beautiful and powerful
In seeming: as the silent sunny noon,
All light they look upon us; but thou seem'st

Like an ethereal night, where long white clouds
Streak the deep purple, and unnumbered stars
Spangle the wonderful mysterious vault 510
With things that look as if they would be suns;
So beautiful, unnumbered, and endearing,
Not dazzling, and yet drawing us to them,
They fill my eyes with tears, and so dost thou.
Thou seem'st unhappy: do not make us so,
And I will weep for thee.

Lucifer. Alas! those tears!
Couldst thou but know what oceans will be shed—

Adah. By me?

Lucifer. By all.

Adah. What all?

Lucifer. The million millions—
The myriad myriads—the all-peopled earth—
The unpeopled earth—and the o'erpeopled Hell, 520
Of which thy bosom is the germ.

Adah. O Cain!
This spirit curseth us.

Cain. Let him say on;
Him will I follow.

Adah. Wither?

Lucifer. To a place
Whence he shall come back to thee in an hour;
But in that hour see things of many days.

Adah. How can that be?

Lucifer. Did not your Maker make
Out of old worlds this new one in few days?
And cannot I, who aided in this work,
Show in an hour what he hath made in many,
Or hath destroyed in few?

Cain. Lead on.

Adah. Will he, 530
In sooth, return within an hour?

Lucifer. He shall.
With us acts are exempt from time, and we
Can crowd eternity into an hour,
Or stretch an hour into eternity:
We breathe not by a mortal measurement—
But that's a mystery. Cain, come on with me.

Adah. Will he return?

Lucifer. Aye, woman! he alone
Of mortals from that place (the first and last
Who shall return, save ONE) shall come back to thee,
To make that silent and expectant world 540

As populous as this: at present there
Are few inhabitants.

Adah. Where dwellest thou?

Lucifer. Throughout all space. Where should I dwell?
Where are
Thy God or Gods—there am I: all things are
Divided with me; life and death—and time—
Eternity—and heaven and earth—and that
Which is not heaven nor earth, but peopled with
Those who once peopled or shall people both—
These are my realms! So that I do divide
His, and possess a kingdom which is not 550
His. If I were not that which I have said,
Could I stand here? His angels are within
Your vision.

Adah. So they were when the fair serpent
Spoke with our mother first.

Lucifer. Cain! thou hast heard.
If thou dost long for knowledge, I can satiate
That thirst; nor ask thee to partake of fruits
Which shall deprive thee of a single good
The conqueror has left thee. Follow me.

Cain. Spirit, I have said it. 560

Exeunt Lucifer *and* Cain.

Adah (*follows, exclaiming*). Cain! my brother! Cain!

ACT II

Scene I: The Abyss of Space

Cain. I tread on air, and sink not; yet I fear
To sink.

Lucifer. Have faith in me, and thou shalt be
Borne on the air, of which I am the prince.

Cain. Can I do so without impiety?

Lucifer. Believe—and sink not! doubt—and perish!
Thus would run the edict of the other God,
Who names me demon to his angels; they
Echo the sound to miserable things,
Which, knowing nought beyond their shallow senses,
Worship the word which strikes their ear, and deem 10
Evil or good what is proclaimed to them
In their abasement. I will have none such:
Worship or worship not, thou shalt behold
The worlds beyond thy little world, nor be

Amerced[1] for doubts beyond thy little life,
With torture of *my* dooming. There will come
An hour, when, tossed upon some water-drops,
A man shall say to a man, "Believe in me,
And walk the waters;" and the man shall walk
The billows and be safe. *I* will not say, 20
Believe in *me,* as a conditional creed
To save thee; but fly with me o'er the gulf
Of space an equal flight, and I will show
What thou dar'st not deny,—the history
Of past, and present, and of future worlds.

Cain. Oh, god, or demon, or whate'er thou art,
Is yon our earth?

Lucifer. Dost thou not recognize
The dust which formed your father?

Cain. Can it be?
Yon small blue circle, swinging in far ether,
With an inferior circlet near it still, 30
Which looks like that which lit our earthly night?
Is this our Paradise? Where are its walls,
And they who guard them?

Lucifer. Point me out the site
Of Paradise.

Cain. How should I? As we move
Like sunbeams onward, it grows small and smaller,
And as it waxes little, and then less,
Gathers a halo round it, like the light
Which shone the roundest of the stars, when I
Beheld them from the skirts of Paradise:
Methinks they both, as we recede from them, 40
Appear to join the innumerable stars
Which are around us; and, as we move on,
Increase their myriads.

Lucifer. And if there should be
Worlds greater than thine own, inhabited
By greater things, and they themselves far more
In number than the dust of thy dull earth,
Though multiplied to animated atoms,
All living, and all doomed to death, and wretched,
What wouldst thou think?

Cain. I should be proud of thought
Which knew such things.

Lucifer. But if that high thought were 50
Linked to a servile mass of matter, and,

[1] penalized

Knowing such things, aspiring to such things,
And science still beyond them, were chained down
To the most gross and petty paltry wants,
All foul and fulsome, and the very best
Of thine enjoyments a sweet degradation,
A most enervating and filthy cheat
To lure thee on to the renewal of
Fresh souls and bodies, all foredoomed to be
As frail and few so happy—

Cain. Spirit! I 60
Know nought of death, save as a dreadful thing
Of which I have heard my parents speak, as of
A hideous heritage I owe to them
No less than life; a heritage not happy,
If I may judge, till now. But, spirit! if
It be as thou hast said (and I within
Feel the prophetic torture of its truth),
Here let me die: for to give birth to those
Who can but suffer many years, and die,
Methinks is merely propagating death, 70
And multiplying murder.

Lucifer. Thou canst not
All die—there is what must survive.

Cain. The Other
Spake not of this unto my father, when
He shut him forth from Paradise, with death
Written upon his forehead. But at least
Let what is mortal of me perish, that
I may be in the rest as angels are.

Lucifer. *I* am angelic: wouldst thou be as I am?

Cain. I know not what thou art: I see thy power,
And see thou show'st me things beyond *my* power, 80
Beyond all power of my born faculties,
Although inferior still to my desires
And my conceptions.

Lucifer. What are they which dwell
So humbly in their pride, as to sojourn
With worms in clay?

Cain. And what art thou who dwellest
So haughtily in spirit, and canst range
Nature and immortality—and yet
Seem'st sorrowful?

Lucifer. I seem that which I am;
And therefore do I ask of thee, if thou
Wouldst be immortal?

Cain. Thou hast said, I must be 90
Immortal in despite of me. I knew not
This until lately—but since it must be,
Let me, or happy or unhappy, learn
To anticipate my immortality.
Lucifer. Thou didst before I came upon thee.
Cain. How?
Lucifer. By suffering.
Cain. And must torture be immortal?
Lucifer. We and thy sons will try. But now, behold!
Is it not glorious?
Cain. Oh, thou beautiful
And unimaginable ether! and
Ye multiplying masses of increased 100
And still increasing lights! what are ye? what
Is this blue wilderness of interminable
Air, where ye roll along, as I have seen
The leaves along the limpid streams of Eden?
Is your course measured for ye? Or do ye
Sweep on in your unbounded revelry
Through an aërial universe of endless
Expansion—at which my soul aches to think—
Intoxicated with eternity?
Oh God! Oh Gods! or whatsoe'er ye are! 110
How beautiful ye are! how beautiful
Your works, or accidents, or whatsoe'er
They may be! Let me die as atoms die
(If that they die), or know ye in your might
And knowledge! My thoughts are not in this hour
Unworthy what I see, though my dust is;—
Spirit! let me expire, or see them nearer.
Lucifer. Art thou not nearer? look back to thine earth!
Cain. Where is it? I see nothing save a mass
Of most innumerable lights.
Lucifer. Look there! 120
Cain. I cannot see it.
Lucifer. Yet it sparkles still.
Cain. That!—yonder!
Lucifer. Yea.
Cain. And wilt thou tell me so?
Why, I have seen the fire-flies and fire-worms
Sprinkle the dusky groves and the green banks
In the dim twilight, brighter than yon world
Which bears them.
Lucifer. Thou hast seen both worms and worlds,
Each bright and sparkling—what dost think of them?

Cain. That they are beautiful in their own sphere,
And that the night, which makes both beautiful,
The little shining fire-fly in its flight, 130
And the immortal star in its great course,
Must both be guided—
Lucifer. But by whom or what?
Cain. Show me.
Lucifer. Dar'st thou behold?
Cain. How know I what
I *dare* behold? As yet, thou hast shown nought
I dare not gaze on further.
Lucifer. On, then, with me.
Wouldst thou behold things mortal or immortal?
Cain. Why, what are things?
Lucifer. Both partly; but what doth
Sit next thy heart?
Cain. The things I see.
Lucifer. But what
Sate nearest it?
Cain. The things I have not seen,
Nor ever shall—the mysteries of death. 140
Lucifer. What, if I show to thee things which have died,
As I have shown thee much which cannot die?
Cain. Do so.
Lucifer. Away, then, on our mighty wings!
Cain. Oh, how we cleave the blue! The stars fade from us!
The earth! where is my earth? Let me look on it,
For I was made of it.
Lucifer. 'Tis now beyond thee,
Less, in the universe, than thou in it;
Yet deem not that thou canst escape it; thou
Shalt soon return to earth, and all its dust:
'Tis part of thy eternity, and mine. 150
Cain. Where dost thou lead me?
Lucifer. To what was before thee!
The phantasm of the world; of which thy world
Is but the wreck.
Cain. What! is it not then new?
Lucifer. No more than life is; and that was ere thou
Or I were, or the things which seem to us
Greater than either. Many things will have
No end; and some, which would pretend to have
Had no beginning, have had one as mean
As thou; and mightier things have been extinct
To make way for much meaner than we can 160
Surmise; for *moments* only and the *space*

Have been and must be all *unchangeable*.
But changes make not death, except to clay;
But thou art clay, and canst but comprehend
That which was clay, and such thou shalt behold.

Cain. Clay—spirit—what thou wilt—I can survey.

Lucifer. Away, then!

Cain. But the lights fade from me fast,
And some till now grew larger as we approached
And wore the look of worlds.

Lucifer. And such they are.

Cain. And Edens in them?

Lucifer. It may be.

Cain. And men? 170

Lucifer. Yea, or things higher.

Cain. Ay? and serpents too?

Lucifer. Wouldst thou have men without them? must no reptiles
Breathe save the erect ones?

Cain. How the lights recede!
Where fly we?

Lucifer. To the world of phantoms, which
Are beings past, and shadows still to come.

Cain. But it grows dark and dark—the stars are gone!

Lucifer. And yet thou seest.

Cain. 'Tis a fearful light!
No sun, no moon, no lights innumerable—
The very blue of the empurpled night
Fades to a dreary twilight, yet I see 180
Huge dusky masses: but unlike the worlds
We were approaching, which, begirt with light,
Seemed full of life even when their atmosphere
Of light gave way, and showed them taking shapes
Unequal, of deep valleys and vast mountains;
And some emitting sparks, and some displaying
Enormous liquid plains, and some begirt
With luminous belts, and floating moons, which took
Like them the features of fair earth:—instead,
All here seems dark and dreadful.

Lucifer. But distinct. 190
Thou seekest to behold Death and dead things?

Cain. I seek it not; but as I know there are
Such, and that my sire's sin makes him and me,
And all that we inherit, liable
To such, I would behold at once what I
Must one day see perforce.

Lucifer. Behold!

Cain. 'Tis darkness.
Lucifer. And so it shall be ever; but we will
Unfold its gates!
Cain. Enormous vapors roll
Apart—what's this?
Lucifer. Enter!
Cain. Can I return?
Lucifer. Return! be sure: how else should Death be peopled? 200
Its present realm is thin to what it will be,
Through thee and thine.
Cain. The clouds still open wide
And wider, and make widening circles round us.
Lucifer. Advance!
Cain. And thou?
Lucifer. Fear not—without me thou
Couldst not have gone beyond thy world. On! on!
They disappear through the clouds.

Scene II: Hades

Enter Lucifer *and* Cain.

Cain. How silent and how vast are these dim worlds!
For they seem more than one, and yet more peopled
Than the huge brilliant luminous orbs which swung
So thickly in the upper air, that I
Had deemed them rather the bright populace
Of some all unimaginable Heaven
Than things to be inhabited themselves,
But that on drawing near them I beheld
Their swelling into palpable immensity
Of matter, which seemed made for life to dwell on, 10
Rather than life itself. But here, all is
So shadowy and so full of twilight, that
It speaks of a day past.
Lucifer. It is the realm
Of Death.—Wouldst have it present?
Cain. Till I know
That which it really is, I cannot answer.
But if it be as I have heard my father
Deal out in his long homilies, 'tis a thing—
Oh God! I dare not think on 't! Cursèd be
He who invented life that leads to death!

Or the dull mass of life, that, being life, 20
Could not retain, but needs must forfeit it—
Even for the innocent!

Lucifer. Dost thou curse thy father?

Cain. Cursed he not me in giving me my birth?
Cursed he not me before my birth, in daring
To pluck the fruit forbidden?

Lucifer. Thou say'st well:
The curse is mutual 'twixt thy sire and thee—
But for thy sons and brother?

Cain. Let them share it
With me, their sire and brother! What else is
Bequeathed to me? I leave them my inheritance.
Oh, ye interminable gloomy realms 30
Of swimming shadows and enormous shapes,
Some fully shown, some indistinct, and all
Mighty and melancholy—what are ye?
Live ye, or have ye lived?

Lucifer. Somewhat of both.

Cain. Then what is Death?

Lucifer. What? Hath not he who made ye
Said 'tis another life?

Cain. Till now he hath
Said nothing, save that all shall die.

Lucifer. Perhaps
He one day will unfold that further secret.

Cain. Happy the day!

Lucifer. Yes; happy! when unfolded,
Through agonies unspeakable, and clogged 40
With agonies eternal, to innumerable
Yet unborn myriads of unconscious atoms,
All to be animated for this only!

Cain. What are these mighty phantoms which I see
Floating around me?—They wear not the form
Of the Intelligences I have seen
Round our regretted and unentered Eden,
Nor wear the form of man as I have view'd it
In Adam's, and in Abel's, and in mine,
Nor in my sister-bride's, nor in my children's: 50
And yet they have an aspect, which, though not
Of men nor angels, looks like something which,
If not the last, rose higher than the first,
Haughty, and high, and beautiful, and full
Of seeming strength, but of inexplicable
Shape; for I never saw such. They bear not
The wing of seraph, nor the face of man,

Nor form of mightiest brute, nor aught that is
Now breathing; mighty yet and beautiful
As the most beautiful and mighty which 60
Live, and yet so unlike them, that I scarce
Can call them living.

Lucifer. Yet they lived.

Cain. Where?

Lucifer. Where
Thou livest.

Cain. When?

Lucifer. On what thou callest earth
They did inhabit.

Cain. Adam is the first.

Lucifer. Of thine, I grant thee—but too mean to be
The last of these.

Cain. And what are they?

Lucifer. That which
Thou shalt be.

Cain. But what *were* they?

Lucifer. Living, high,
Intelligent, good, great, and glorious things,
As much superior unto all thy sire,
Adam, could e'er have been in Eden, as 70
The sixty-thousandth generation shall be,
In its dull damp degeneracy, to
Thee and thy son;—and how weak they are, judge
By thy own flesh.

Cain. Ah me! and did *they* perish?

Lucifer. Yes, from their earth, as thou wilt fade from
thine.

Cain. But was *mine* theirs?

Lucifer. It was.

Cain. But not as now.
It is too little and too lowly to
Sustain such creatures.

Lucifer. True, it was more glorious.

Cain. And wherefore did it fall?

Lucifer. Ask him who fells.

Cain. But how?

Lucifer. By a most crushing and inexorable 80
Destruction and disorder of the elements,
Which struck a world to chaos, as a chaos
Subsiding has struck out a world: such things,
Though rare in time, are frequent in eternity.—
Pass on, and gaze upon the past.

Cain. 'Tis awful!

Lucifer. And true. Behold these phantoms! they were once
Material as thou art.
Cain. And must I be
Like them?
Lucifer. Let He who made thee answer that.
I show thee what thy predecessors are,
And what they *were* thou feelest, in degree 90
Inferior as thy petty feelings and
Thy pettier portion of the immortal part
Of high intelligence and earthly strength.
What ye in common have with what they had
Is life, and what ye *shall* have—death: the rest
Of your poor attributes is such as suits
Reptiles engendered out of the subsiding
Slime of a mighty universe, crushed into
A scarcely-yet shaped planet, peopled with
Things whose enjoyment was to be in blindness— 100
A Paradise of Ignorance, from which
Knowledge was barred as poison. But behold
What these superior beings are or were;
Or, if it irk thee, turn thee back and till
The earth, thy task—I 'll waft thee there in safety.
Cain. No; I 'll stay here.
Lucifer. How long?
Cain. For ever! Since
I must one day return here from the earth,
I rather would remain; I am sick of all
That dust has shown me—let me dwell in shadows.
Lucifer. It cannot be: thou now beholdest as 110
A vision that which is reality.
To make thyself fit for this dwelling, thou
Must pass through what the things thou seest have passed—
The gates of death—
Cain. By what gate have we entered
Even now?
Lucifer. By mine! But, plighted to return,
My spirit buoys thee up to breathe in regions
Where all is breathless save thyself. Gaze on;
But do not think to dwell here till thine hour
Is come.
Cain. And these, too; can they ne'er repass
To earth again?
Lucifer. *Their* earth is gone for ever— 120
So changed by its convulsion, they would not

Be conscious to a single present spot
Of its new scarcely hardened surface—'twas—
Oh, what a beautiful world it *was!*

Cain. And is.
It is not with the earth, though I must till it,
I feel at war, but that I may not profit
By what it bears of beautiful, untoiling,
Nor gratify my thousand swelling thoughts
With knowledge, nor allay my thousand fears
Of death and life.

Lucifer. What thy world is, thou seest, 130
But canst not comprehend the shadow of
That which it was.

Cain. And those enormous creatures,
Phantoms inferior in intelligence
(At least so seeming) to the things we have passed,
Resembling somewhat the wild habitants
Of the deep woods of earth, the hugest which
Roar nightly in the forest, but ten-fold
In magnitude and terror; taller than
The cherub-guarded walls of Eden, with
Eyes flashing like the fiery swords which fence them, 140
And tusks projecting like the trees stripped of
Their bark and branches—what were they?

Lucifer. That which
The Mammoth is in thy world;—but these lie
By myriads underneath its surface.

Cain. But
None on it?

Lucifer. No; for thy frail race to war
With them would render the curse on it useless—
'Twould be destroyed so early.

Cain. But why *war?*

Lucifer. You have forgotten the denunciation
Which drove your race from Eden—war with all things,
And death to all things, and disease to most things, 150
And pangs, and bitterness; these were the fruits
Of the forbidden tree.

Cain. But animals—
Did they, too, eat of it, that they must die?

Lucifer. Your Maker told ye, *they* were made for you,
As you for him.—You would not have their doom
Superior to your own? Had Adam not
Fallen, all had stood.

Cain. Alas! the hopeless wretches!
They too must share my sire's fate, like his sons;

Like them, too, without having shared the apple;
Like them, too, without the so dear-bought *knowledg* 160
It was a lying tree—for we *know* nothing.
At least it *promised knowledge* at the *price*
Of death—but *knowledge* still: but what *knows* man?

Lucifer. It may be death leads to the *highest* knowledge;
And being of all things the sole thing certain,
At least leads to the *surest* science: therefore
The tree was true, though deadly.

Cain. These dim realms!
I see them, but I know them not.

Lucifer. Because
Thy hour is yet afar, and matter cannot
Comprehend spirit wholly—but 'tis something 170
To know there are such realms.

Cain. We knew already
That there was Death.

Lucifer. But not what was beyond it.

Cain. Nor know I now.

Lucifer. Thou knowest that there is
A state, and many states beyond thine own—
And this thou knewest not this morn.

Cain. But all
Seems dim and shadowy.

Lucifer. Be content; it will
Seem clearer to thine immortality.

Cain. And yon immeasurable liquid space
Of glorious azure which floats on beyond us,
Which looks like water, and which I should deem 180
The river which flows out of Paradise
Past my own dwelling, but that it is bankless
And boundless, and of an ethereal hue—
What is it?

Lucifer. There is still some such on earth,
Although inferior, and thy children shall
Dwell near it—'tis the phantasm of an ocean.

Cain. 'Tis like another world; a liquid sun—
And those inordinate creatures sporting o'er
Its shining surface?

Lucifer. Are its habitants,
The past leviathans.

Cain. And yon immense 190
Serpent, which rears his dripping mane and vasty
Head ten times higher than the haughtiest cedar
Forth from the abyss, looking as he could coil
Himself around the orbs we lately looked on—

Is he not of the kind which basked beneath
The tree in Eden?

Lucifer. Eve, thy mother, best
Can tell what shape of serpent tempted her.

Cain. This seems too terrible. No doubt the other
Had more of beauty.

Lucifer. Hast thou ne'er beheld him?

Cain. Many of the same kind (at least so called), 200
But never that precisely which persuaded
The fatal fruit, nor even of the same aspect.

Lucifer. Your father saw him not?

Cain. No; 'twas my mother
Who tempted him—she tempted by the serpent.

Lucifer. Good man! whene'er thy wife, or thy sons' wives,
Tempt thee or them to aught that 's new or strange,
Be sure thou seest first who hath tempted *them*.

Cain. Thy precept comes too late: there is no more
For serpents to tempt woman to.

Lucifer. But there
Are some things still which woman may tempt man to, 210
And man tempt woman:—let thy sons look to it!
My counsel is a kind one; for 'tis even
Given chiefly at my own expense; 'tis true,
'Twill not be followed, so there's little lost.

Cain. I understand not this.

Lucifer. The happier thou!—
Thy world and thou are still too young! Thou thinkest
Thyself most wicked and unhappy: is it
Not so?

Cain. For crime, I know not; but for pain,
I have felt much.

Lucifer. First-born of the first man!
Thy present state of sin—and thou art evil, 220
Of sorrow—and thou sufferest, are both Eden
In all its innocence compared to what
Thou shortly may'st be; and that state again,
In its redoubled wretchedness, a Paradise
To what thy sons' sons' sons, accumulating
In generations like to dust (which they
In fact but add to), shall endure and do.—
Now let us back to earth!

Cain. And wherefore didst thou
Lead me only to inform me this?

Lucifer. Was not thy quest for knowledge?

Cain. Yes, as being 230
The road to happiness.
Lucifer. If truth be so,
Thou hast it.
Cain. Then my father's God did well
When he prohibited the fatal tree.
Lucifer. But had done better in not planting it.
But ignorance of evil doth not save
From evil; it must still roll on the same,
A part of all things.
Cain. Not of all things. No;
I 'll not believe it—for I thirst for good.
Lucifer. And who and what doth not? *Who* covets evil
For its own bitter sake? *None*—nothing! 'tis 240
The leaven of all life, and lifelessness.
Cain. Within those glorious orbs which we beheld,
Distant, and dazzling, and innumerable,
Ere we came down into this phantom realm,
Ill cannot come: they are too beautiful.
Lucifer. Thou hast seen them from afar.
Cain. And what of that?
Distance can but diminish glory—they,
When nearer, must be more ineffable.
Lucifer. Approach the things of earth most beautiful,
And judge their beauty near.
Cain. I have done this— 250
The loveliest thing I know is loveliest nearest.
Lucifer. Then there must be delusion.—What is that,
Which being nearest to thine eyes is still
More beautiful than beauteous things remote?
Cain. My sister Adah.—All the stars of heaven,
The deep blue noon of night, lit by an orb
Which looks a spirit, or a spirit's world—
The hues of twilight—the sun's gorgeous coming—
His setting indescribable, which fills
My eyes with pleasant tears as I behold 260
Him sink, and feel my heart float softly with him
Along that western paradise of clouds—
The forest shade—the green bough—the bird's voice,
The vesper[m] bird's which seems to sing of love,
And mingles with the song of cherubim,
As the day closes over Eden's walls;—
All these are nothing, to my eyes and heart,
Like Adah's face: I turn from earth and heaven

[m] evening

To gaze on it.
Lucifer. 'Tis fair as frail mortality,
In the first dawn and bloom of young creation, 270
And earliest embraces of earth's parents
Can make its offspring; still it is delusion.
Cain. You think so, being not her brother.
Lucifer. Mortal!
My brotherhood 's with those who have no children.
Cain. Then thou canst have no fellowship with us.
Lucifer. It may be that thine own shall be for me.
But if thou dost possess a beautiful
Being beyond all beauty in thine eyes,
Why art thou wretched?
Cain. Why do I exist?
Why art *thou* wretched? why are all things so? 280
Ev'n he who made us must be, as the maker
Of things unhappy! To produce destruction
Can surely never be the task of joy,
And yet my sire says he 's omnipotent:
Then why is evil—he being good? I asked
This question of my father; and he said,
Because this evil only was the path
To good. Strange good, that must arise from out
Its deadly opposite. I lately saw
A lamb stung by a reptile: the poor suckling 290
Lay foaming on the earth, beneath the vain
And piteous bleating of its restless dam;
My father plucked some herbs, and laid them to
The wound: and by degrees the helpless wretch
Resumed its careless[n] life, and rose to drain
The mother's milk, who o'er it tremulous
Stood licking its reviving limbs with joy.
Behold, my son! said Adam, how from evil
Springs good!
Lucifer. What didst thou answer?
Cain. Nothing; for
He is my father; but I thought, that 'twere 300
A better portion for the animal
Never to have been *stung at all*, than to
Purchase renewal of its little life
With agonies unutterable, though
Dispelled by antidotes.
Lucifer. But as thou saidst
Of all belovèd things thou lovest her

[n] i.e., without care

Who shared thy mother's milk, and giveth hers
Unto thy children—

Cain. Most assuredly:
What should I be without her?

Lucifer. What am I?

Cain. Dost thou love nothing?

Lucifer. What does thy God love? 310

Cain. All things, my father says; but I confess
I see it not in their allotment here.

Lucifer. And, therefore, thou canst not see if *I* love
Or no, except some vast and general purpose,
To which particular things must melt like snows.

Cain. Snows! what are they?

Lucifer. Be happier in not knowing
What thy remoter offspring must encounter;
But bask beneath the clime which knows no winter!

Cain. But dost thou not love something like thyself?

Lucifer. And dost thou love *thyself?*

Cain. Yes, but love more 320
What makes my feelings more endurable,
And is more than myself because I love it.

Lucifer. Thou lovest it, because 'tis beautiful,
As was the apple in thy mother's eye;
And when it ceases to be so, thy love
Will cease, like any other appetite.

Cain. Cease to be beautiful! how can that be?

Lucifer. With time.

Cain. But time has past, and hitherto
Even Adam and my mother both are fair:
Not fair like Adah and the seraphim— 330
But very fair.

Lucifer. All that must pass away
In them and her.

Cain. I'm sorry for it; but
Cannot conceive my love for her the less.
And when her beauty disappears, methinks
He who creates all beauty will lose more
Than me in seeing perish such a work.

Lucifer. I pity thee who lovest what must perish.

Cain. And I thee who lov'st nothing.

Lucifer. And thy brother—
Sits he not near thy heart?

Cain. Why should he not?

Lucifer. Thy father loves him well—so does thy 340
God.

Cain. And so do I.

Lucifer. 'Tis well and meekly done.
Cain. Meekly!
Lucifer. He is the second born of flesh,
And is his mother's favorite.
Cain. Let him keep
Her favor, since the serpent was the first
To win it.
Lucifer. And his father's?
Cain. What is that
To me? should I not love that which all love?
Lucifer. And the Jehovah—the indulgent Lord
And bounteous planter of barred Paradise—
He, too, looks smilingly on Abel.
Cain. I
Ne'er saw him, and I know not if he smiles. 350
Lucifer. But you have seen his angels.
Cain. Rarely.
Lucifer. But
Sufficiently to see they love your brother:
His sacrifices are acceptable.
Cain. So be they! wherefore speak to me of this?
Lucifer. Because thou hast thought of this ere now.
Cain. And if
I *have* thought, why recall a thought that—(*he pauses, as agitated*)—Spirit!
Here we are in *thy* world; speak not of *mine*.
Thou hast shown me wonders; thou hast shown me those
Mighty pre-Adamites who walked the earth
Of which ours is the wreck; thou hast pointed out 360
Myriads of starry worlds, of which our own
Is the dim and remote companion, in
Infinity of life; thou hast shown me shadows
Of that existence with the dreaded name
Which my sire brought us—Death; thou hast shown me much—
But not all: show me where Jehovah dwells,
In his especial Paradise,—or *thine:*
Where is it?
Lucifer. *Here*, and o'er all space.
Cain. But ye
Have some allotted dwelling—as all things:
Clay has its earth, and other worlds their tenants; 370
All temporary breathing creatures their
Peculiar element; and things which have
Long ceased to breathe *our* breath, have theirs, thou say'st;

And the Jehovah and thyself have thine—
Ye do not dwell together?
Lucifer. No, we reign
Together; but our dwellings are asunder.
Cain. Would there were only one of ye! perchance
An unity of purpose might make union
In elements which seem now jarred in storms.
How came ye, being spirits wise and infinite, 380
To separate? Are ye not as brethren in
Your essence, and your nature, and your glory?
Lucifer. Art thou not Abel's brother?
Cain. We are brethren,
And so we shall remain; but were it not so,
Is spirit like to flesh? can it fall out—
Infinity with Immortality?
Jarring and turning space to misery—
For what?
Lucifer. To reign.
Cain. Did ye not tell me that
Ye are both eternal?
Lucifer. Yea!
Cain. And what I have seen,
Yon blue immensity, is boundless?
Lucifer. Aye. 390
Cain. And cannot ye both *reign* then?—is there not
Enough?—why should ye differ?
Lucifer. We *both* reign.
Cain. But one of you makes evil.
Lucifer. Which?
Cain. Thou! for
If thou canst do man good, why dost thou not?
Lucifer. And why not he who made? *I* made ye not;
Ye are *his* creatures, and not mine.
Cain. Then leave us
His creatures, as thou say'st we are, or show me
Thy dwelling, or *his* dwelling.
Lucifer. I could show thee
Both; but the time will come thou shalt see one
Of them for evermore.
Cain. And why not now? 400
Lucifer. Thy human mind hath scarcely grasp to gather
The little I have shown thee into calm
And clear thought; and *thou* wouldst go on aspiring
To the great double Mysteries! the *two Principles!*
And gaze upon them on their secret thrones!
Dust! limit thy ambition; for to see

Either of these, would be for thee to perish!
Cain. And let me perish, so I see them!
Lucifer. There
The son of her who snatched the apple spake!
But thou wouldst only perish, and not see them; 410
That sight is for the other state.
Cain. Of death?
Lucifer. That is the prelude.
Cain. Then I dread it less,
Now that I know it leads to something definite.
Lucifer. And now I will convey thee to thy world,
Where thou shalt multiply the race of Adam,
Eat, drink, toil, tremble, laugh, weep, sleep, and die.
Cain. And to what end have I beheld these things
Which thou hast shown me?
Lucifer. Didst thou not require
Knowledge? And have I not, in what I showed,
Taught thee to know thyself?
Cain. Alas! I seem 420
Nothing.
Lucifer. And this should be the human sum
Of knowledge, to know mortal nature's nothingness:
Bequeath that science to thy children, and
'Twill spare them many tortures.
Cain. Haughty spirit!
Thou speak'st it proudly; but thyself, though proud,
Hast a superior.
Lucifer. No! by Heaven, which He
Holds, and the abyss, and the immensity
Of worlds and life, which I hold with him—No!
I have a victor—true; but no superior.
Homage he has from all—but none from me: 430
I battle it against him, as I battled
In highest heaven. Through all eternity,
And the unfathomable gulfs of Hades,
And the interminable realms of space,
And the infinity of endless ages,
All, all, will I dispute! And world by world,
And star by star, and universe by universe,
Shall tremble in the balance, till the great
Conflict shall cease, if ever it shall cease,
Which it ne'er shall, till he or I be quenched! 440
And what can quench our immortality,
Or mutual and irrevocable hate?
He as a conqueror will call the conquered
Evil; but what will be the *good* he gives?

Were I the victor, *his* works would be deemed
The only evil ones. And you, ye new
And scarce-born mortals, what have been his gifts
To you already, in your little world?

Cain. But few! and some of those but bitter.

Lucifer. Back
With me, then, to thine earth, and try the rest 450
Of his celestial boons to you and yours.
Evil and good are things in their own essence,
And not made good or evil by the giver;
But if he gives you good—so call him: if
Evil springs from *him*, do not name it *mine*,
Till ye know better its true fount; and judge
Not by words, though of spirits, but the fruits
Of your existence, such as it must be.
One good gift has the fatal apple given—
Your *reason*:—let it not be over-swayed 460
By tyrannous threats to force you into faith
'Gainst all external sense and inward feeling:
Think and endure,—and form an inner world
In your own bosom—where the outward fails;
So shall you nearer be the spiritual
Nature, and war triumphant with your own.

They disappear.

ACT III

Scene I: The Earth near Eden, as in Act I

Enter Cain *and* Adah.

Adah. Hush! tred softly, Cain.

Cain. I will; but wherefore?

Adah. Our little Enoch sleeps upon yon bed
Of leaves, beneath the cypress.

Cain. Cypress! 'tis
A gloomy tree, which looks as if it mourned
O'er what it shadows; wherefore didst thou choose it
For our child's canopy?

Adah. Because its branches
Shut out the sun like night, and therefore seemed
Fitting to shadow slumber.

Cain. Aye, the last—
And longest; but no matter—lead me to him.

They go up to the child.

How lovely he appears! his little cheeks, 10
In their pure incarnation,° vying with
The rose leaves strewn beneath them.
Adah. And his lips, too,
How beautifully parted! No; you shall not
Kiss him, at least not now: he will awake soon—
His hour of mid-day rest is nearly over;
But it were pity to disturb him till
'Tis closed.
Cain. You have said well; I will contain
My heart till then. He smiles and sleeps!—Sleep on
And smile, thou little, young inheritor
Of a world scarce less young: sleep on, and smile! 20
Thine are the hours and days when both are cheering
And innocent! *thou* hast not plucked the fruit—
Thou know'st not that thou art naked! Must the time
Come thou shalt be amerced for sins unknown,
Which were not thine nor mine? But now sleep on!
His cheeks are reddening into deeper smiles,
And shining lids are trembling o'er his long
Lashes, dark as the cypress which waves o'er them;
Half open, from beneath them the clear blue
Laughs out, although in slumber. He must dream— 30
Of what? Of Paradise!—Aye! dream of it,
My disinherited boy! 'Tis but a dream;
For never more thyself, thy sons, nor fathers,
Shall walk in that forbidden place of joy!
Adah. Dear Cain! Nay, do not whisper o'er our son
Such melancholy yearnings o'er the past:
Why wilt thou always mourn for Paradise?
Can we not make another?
Cain. Where?
Adah. Here, or
Where'er thou wilt: where'er thou art, I feel not
The want of this so much regretted Eden. 40
Have I not thee, our boy, our sire, and brother,
And Zillah—our sweet sister, and our Eve,
To whom we owe so much besides our birth?
Cain. Yes—death, too, is amongst the debts we owe her.
Adah. Cain! that proud spirit who withdrew thee hence,
Hath saddened thine still deeper. I had hoped
The promised wonders which thou hast beheld,

° carnation (i.e., flesh-color)

Visions, thou say'st, of past and present worlds,
Would have composed thy mind into the calm
Of a contented knowledge; but I see 50
Thy guide hath done thee evil: still I thank him,
And can forgive him all, that he so soon
Hath given thee back to us.

Cain. So soon?

Adah. 'Tis scarcely
Two hours since ye departed: two *long* hours
To *me*, but only *hours* upon the sun.

Cain. And yet I have approached that sun, and seen
Worlds which he once shone on, and never more
Shall light; and worlds he never lit: methought
Years had rolled o'er my absence.

Adah. Hardly hours.

Cain. The mind then hath capacity of time 60
And measures it by that which it beholds,
Pleasing or painful, little or almighty.
I had beheld the immemorial works
Of endless beings; skirred[p] extinguished worlds;
And, gazing on eternity, methought
I had borrowed more by a few drops of ages
From its immensity; but now I feel
My littleness again. Well said the spirit,
That I was nothing!

Adah. Wherefore said he so?
Jehovah said not that.

Cain. No; *he* contents him 70
With making us the *nothing* which we are;
And after flattering dust with glimpses of
Eden and Immortality, resolves
It back to dust again—for what?

Adah. Thou know'st—
Even for our parents' error.

Cain. What is that
To us? they sinned, then *let them* die!

Adah. Thou hast not spoken well, nor is that thought
Thy own, but of the spirit who was with thee.
Would *I* could die for them, so *they* might live!

Cain. Why, so say I—provided that one victim 80
Might satiate the insatiable of life,
And that our little rosy sleeper there
Might never taste of death nor human sorrow,
Nor hand it down to those who spring from him.

[p] scoured

Adah. How know we that some such atonement one day
May not redeem our race?
Cain. By sacrificing
The harmless for the guilty? what atonement
Were there? Why, *we* are innocent: what have we
Done, that we must be victims for a deed
Before our birth, or need have victims to 90
Atone for this mysterious, nameless sin—
If it be such a sin to seek for knowledge?
Adah. Alas! thou sinnest now, my Cain: thy words
Sound impious in mine ears.
Cain. Then leave me!
Adah. Never,
Though thy God left thee.
Cain. Say, what have we here?
Adah. Two altars, which our brother Abel made
During thine absence, whereupon to offer
A sacrifice to God on thy return.
Cain. And how knew *he*, that *I* would be so ready
With the burnt offerings, which he daily brings 100
With a meek brow, whose base humility
Shows more of fear than worship, as a bribe
To the Creator?
Adah. Surely, 'tis well done.
Cain. One altar may suffice; *I* have no offering.
Adah. The fruits of the earth, the early, beautiful
Blossom and bud and bloom of flowers and fruits,
These are a goodly offering to the Lord,
Given with a gentle and a contrite spirit.
Cain. I have toiled, and tilled, and sweaten in the sun
According to the curse:—must I do more? 110
For what should I be gentle? for a war
With all the elements ere they will yield
The bread we eat? For what must I be grateful?
For being dust, and groveling in the dust,
Till I return to dust? If I am nothing—
For nothing shall I be an hypocrite,
And seem well-pleased with pain? For what should I
Be contrite? for my father's sin, already
Expiate with what we all have undergone,
And to be more than expiated by 120
The ages prophesied, upon our seed.
Little deems our young blooming sleeper there,
The germs of an eternal misery
To myriads is within him! better 'twere
I snatched him in his sleep, and dashed him 'gainst

The rocks, than let him live to—
Adah. Oh, my God!
Touch not the child—my child! *thy* child! Oh, Cain!
Cain. Fear not! for all the stars, and all the power
Which sways them, I would not accost yon infant
With ruder greeting than a father's kiss. 130
Adah. Then, why so awful in thy speech?
Cain. I said,
'Twere better that he ceased to live, than give
Life to so much of sorrow as he must
Endure, and, harder still, bequeath; but since
That saying jars you, let us only say—
'Twere better that he never had been born.
Adah. Oh, do not say so! Where were then the joys,
The mother's joys of watching, nourishing,
And loving him? Soft! he awakes. Sweet Enoch!

She goes to the child.

Oh Cain! look on him; see how full of life, 140
Of strength, of bloom, of beauty, and of joy,
How like to me—how like to thee, when gentle,
For *then* we are *all* alike; is 't not so, Cain?
Mother, and sire, and son, our features are
Reflected in each other; as they are
In the clear waters, when *they* are *gentle*, and
When *thou* art *gentle*. Love us, then, my Cain!
And love thyself for our sakes, for we love thee.
Look! how he laughs and stretches out his arms,
And opens wide his blue eyes upon thine, 150
To hail his father; while his little form
Flutters as winged with joy. Talk not of pain!
The childless cherubs well might envy thee
The pleasures of a parent! Bless him, Cain!
As yet he hath no words to thank thee, but
His heart will, and thine own too.
Cain. Bless thee, boy!
If that a mortal blessing may avail thee,
To save thee from the serpent's curse!
Adah. It shall.
Surely a father's blessing may avert
A reptile's subtlety.
Cain. Of that I doubt; 160
But bless him ne'er the less.
Adah. Our brother comes.
Cain. Thy brother Abel.

Enter Abel.

Abel. Welcome, Cain!
My brother,
The peace of God be on thee!
Cain. Abel, hail!
Abel. Our sister tells me that thou hast been wandering,
In high communion with a spirit, far
Beyond our wonted range. Was he of those
We have seen and spoken with, like to our father?
Cain. No.
Abel. Why then commune with him? he may be
A foe to the Most High.
Cain. And friend to man.
Has the Most High been so—if so you term him? 170
Abel. *Term him!* your words are strange today, my brother.
My sister Adah, leave us for awhile—
We mean to sacrifice.
Adah. Farewell, my Cain;
But first embrace thy son. May his soft spirit,
And Abel's pious ministry, recall thee
To peace and holiness! *Exit* Adah, *with her child.*
Abel. Where hast thou been?
Cain. I know not.
Abel. Nor what thou hast seen?
Cain. The dead,
The immortal, the unbounded, the omnipotent,
The overpowering mysteries of space—
The innumerable worlds that were and are— 180
A whirlwind of such overwhelming things,
Suns, moons, and earths, upon their loud-voiced spheres
Singing in thunder round me, as have made me
Unfit for mortal converse: leave me, Abel.
Abel. Thine eyes are flashing with unnatural light—
Thy cheek is flushed with an unnatural hue—
Thy words are fraught with an unnatural sound—
What may this mean?
Cain. It means—I pray thee, leave me.
Abel. Not till we have prayed and sacrificed together.
Cain. Abel, I pray thee, sacrifice alone— 190
Jehovah loves thee well.
Abel. *Both* well, I hope.
Cain. But thee the better: I care not for that;

Thou art fitter for his worship than I am;
Revere him, then—but let it be alone—
At least, without me.

Abel. Brother, I should ill
Deserve the name of our great father's son,
If, as my elder, I revered thee not,
And in the worship of our God called not
On thee to join me, and precede me in
Our priesthood—'tis thy place.

Cain. But I have ne'er 200
Asserted it.

Abel. The more my grief; I pray thee
To do so now: thy soul seems laboring in
Some strong delusion; it will calm thee.

Cain. No;
Nothing can calm me more. *Calm!* say I? Never
Knew I what calm was in the soul, although
I have seen the elements stilled. My Abel, leave me!
Or let me leave thee to thy pious purpose.

Abel. Neither; we must perform our task together.
Spurn me not.

Cain. If it must be so—well, then,
What shall I do?

Abel. Choose one of those two altars. 210

Cain. Choose for me: they to me are so much turf
And stone.

Abel. Choose thou!

Cain. I have chosen.

Abel. 'Tis the highest,
And suits thee, as the elder. Now prepare
Thine offerings.

Cain. Where are thine?

Abel. Behold them here—
The firstlings of the flock, and fat thereof—
A shepherd's humble offering.

Cain. I have no flocks;
I am a tiller of the ground, and must
Yield what it yieldeth to my toil—its fruit: *He gathers fruits.*
Behold them in their various bloom and ripeness.

They dress their altars, and kindle a flame upon them.

Abel. My brother, as the elder, offer first 220
Thy prayer and thanksgiving with sacrifice.

Cain. No—I am new to this; lead thou the way,
And I will follow—as I may.
Abel (*kneeling*). Oh God!
Who made us, and who breathed the breath of life
Within our nostrils, who hath blessèd us,
And spared, despite our father's sin, to make
His children all lost, as they might have been,
Had not thy justice been so tempered with
The mercy which is thy delight as to
Accord a pardon like a Paradise 230
Compared with our great crimes:—Sole Lord of light!
Of good, and glory, and eternity;
Without whom all were evil, and with whom
Nothing can err, except to some good end
Of thine omnipotent benevolence—
Inscrutable, but still to be fulfilled—
Accept from out thy humble first of shepherd's
First of the first-born flocks—an offering,
In itself nothing—as what offering can be
Aught unto thee?—but yet accept it for 240
The thanksgiving of him who spreads it in
The face of thy high heaven, bowing his own
Even to the dust, of which he is, in honor
Of thee, and of thy name, for evermore!
Cain (*standing erect during this speech*). Spirit! whate'er or whosoe'er thou art,
Omnipotent, it may be—and, if good,
Shown in the exemption of thy deeds from evil;
Jehovah upon earth! and God in heaven!
And it may be with other names, because
Thine attributes seem many, as thy works— 250
If thou must be propitiated with prayers,
Take them! If thou must be induced with altars,
And softened with a sacrifice, receive them!
Two beings here erect them unto thee.
If thou lov'st blood, the shepherd's shrine, which smokes
On my right hand, hath shed it for thy service
In the first of his flock whose limbs now reek
In sanguinary incense to thy skies;
Or if the sweet and blooming fruits of earth
And milder seasons, which the unstained turf 260
I spread them on now offers in the face
Of the broad sun which ripened them, may seem
Good to thee, inasmuch as they have not
Suffered in limb or life, and rather form
A sample of thy works than supplication

To look on ours! If a shrine without victim,
And altar without gore, may win thy favor,
Look on it! and for him who dresseth it,
He is—such as thou mad'st him; and seeks nothing
Which must be won by kneeling; if he 's evil, 270
Strike him! thou art omnipotent and may'st—
For what can he oppose? If he be good,
Strike him, or spare him, as thou wilt! since all
Rests upon thee; and good and evil seem
To have no power themselves, save in thy will;
And whether that be good or ill I know not,
Not being omnipotent, nor fit to judge
Omnipotence, but merely to endure
Its mandate; which thus far I have endured.

The fire upon the altar of Abel *kindles into a column of the brightest flame, and ascends to heaven; while a whirlwind throws down the altar of* Cain, *and scatters the fruits abroad upon the earth.*

Abel (*kneeling*). Oh, brother, pray! Jehovah's wroth
with thee. 280
Cain. Why so?
Abel. Thy fruits are scattered on the earth.
Cain. From earth they came, to earth let them return;
Their seed will bear fresh fruit there ere the summer:
Thy burnt flesh-off'ring prospers better; see
How heav'n licks up the flames when thick with blood!
Abel. Think not upon my offering's acceptance,
But make another of thine own before
It is too late.
Cain. I will build no more altars,
Nor suffer[a] any.
Abel (*rising*). Cain! what meanest thou?
Cain. To cast down yon vile flatt'rer of the clouds, 290
The smoky harbinger of thy dull pray'rs—
Thine altar, with its blood of lambs and kids,
Which fed on milk, to be destroyed in blood.
Abel (*opposing him*). Thou shalt not:—add not impious
works to impious
Words! let that altar stand—'tis hallowed now
By the immortal pleasure of Jehovah,
In his acceptance of the victims.
Cain. *His!*

[a] allow

His pleasure! what was his high pleasure in
The fumes of scorching flesh and smoking blood,
To the pain of the bleating mothers which 300
Still yearn for their dead offspring? or the pangs
Of the sad ignorant victims underneath
Thy pious knife? Give way! this bloody record
Shall not stand in the sun, to shame creation!

Abel. Brother, give back! thou shalt not touch my altar
With violence: if that thou wilt adopt it,
To try another sacrifice, 'tis thine.

Cain. Another sacrifice! Give way, or else
That sacrifice may be—

Abel. What mean'st thou?

Cain. Give—
Give way!—thy God loves blood!—then look to it: 310
Give way, ere he hath *more!*

Abel. In *his* great name,
I stand between thee and the shrine which hath
Had his acceptance.

Cain. If thou lov'st thyself,
Stand back till I have strew'd this turf along
Its native soil:—else—

Abel (*opposing him*). I love God far more
Than life.

Cain (*striking him with a brand, on the temples, which he snatches from the altar*). Then take thy life unto thy God,
Since he loves lives.

Abel (*falls*). What hast thou done, my brother?

Cain. Brother!

Abel. Oh, God! receive thy servant, and
Forgive his slayer, for he knew not what
He did—Cain, give me—give me thy hand; and tell 320
Poor Zillah—

Cain (*after a moment's stupefaction*). *My* hand! 'tis all red, and with—
What? *A long pause.—Looking slowly round.*
Where am I? alone! Where's Abel? where
Cain? Can it be that I am he? My brother,
Awake!—why liest thou so on the green earth?
'Tis not the hour of slumber:—why so pale?
What hast thou!—thou wert full of life this morn!
Abel! I pray thee, mock me not! I smote
Too fiercely, but not fatally. Ah, why
Wouldst thou oppose me? This is mockery;
And only done to daunt me:—'twas a blow— 330

And but a blow. Stir—stir—nay, only stir!
Why, so—that 's well—thou breath'st! breathe upon me!
Oh God! Oh God!

Abel (*very faintly*). What 's he who speaks of God?

Cain. Thy murderer.

Abel. Then may God forgive him! Cain,
Comfort poor Zillah:—she has but one brother
Now. Abel *dies*.

Cain. And I none!—Who makes me brotherless?
His eyes are open! then he is not dead!
Death is like sleep; and sleep shuts down our lids.
His lips, too, are apart; why then he breathes!
And yet I feel it not.—His heart! his heart!— 340
Let me see, doth it beat? methinks—No!—no!
This is a vision, else I am become
The native of another and worse world.
The earth swims round me:—what is this?—'tis wet;

Puts his hand to his brow, and then looks at it.

And yet there are no dews! 'Tis blood—my blood—
My brother's and my own, and shed by me!
Then what have I further to do with life,
Since I have taken life from my own flesh?
But he cannot be dead!—Is silence death?
No; he will wake; then let me watch by him. 350
Life cannot be so slight, as to be quenched
Thus quickly!—he hath spoken to me since—
What shall I say to him?—My brother!—No:
He will not answer to that name; for brethren
Smite not each other. Yet—yet—speak to me.
Oh, for a word more of that gentle voice,
That I may bear to hear my own again!

Enter Zillah.

Zillah. I heard a heavy sound; what can it be?
'Tis Cain; and watching by my husband. What
Dost thou there, brother? Doth he sleep? Oh, 360
heav'n!
What means this paleness, and yon stream?—No, no!
It is not blood; for who would shed his blood?
Abel! what 's this?—who hath done this? He moves
not;
He breathes not; and his hands drop down from mine
With stony lifelessness! Ah, cruel Cain!
Why cam'st thou not in time to save him from

This violence? Whatever hath assail'd him,
Thou wert the stronger, and shouldst have stepped in
Between him and aggression! Father!—Eve!—
Adah!—come hither! Death is in the world! 370

Exit Zillah, *calling on her Parents, etc.*

Cain (*solus*). And who hath brought him there?—I— who abhor
The name of Death so deeply, that the thought
Empoisoned all my life before I knew
His aspect—I have led him here, and giv'n
My brother to his cold and still embrace,
As if he would not have asserted his
Inexorable claim without my aid.
I am awake at last—a dreary dream
Had madden'd me;—but *he* shall ne'er awake!

Enter Adam, Eve, Adah, *and* Zillah.

Adam. A voice of woe from Zillah brings me here. 380
What do I see?—'Tis true!—My son! my son!
Woman, behold the serpent's work and thine! *To* Eve.

Eve. Oh! Speak not of it now; the serpent's fangs
Are in my heart. My best beloved, Abel!
Jehovah! this is punishment beyond
A mother's sin, to take *him* from me!

Adam. Who,
Or what hath done this deed?—speak, Cain, since thou
Wert present; was it some more hostile angel,
Who walks not with Jehovah? or some wild
Brute of the forest?

Eve. Ah! a livid light 390
Breaks through, as from a thunder-cloud! yon brand,
Massy and bloody! snatched from off the altar,
And black with smoke, and red with—

Adam. Speak, my son!
Speak, and assure us, wretched as we are,
That we are not more miserable still.

Adah. Speak, Cain! and say it was not *thou!*

Eve. It was,
I see it now—he hangs his guilty head,
And covers his ferocious eye with hands
Incarnadine.

Adah. Mother, thou dost him wrong—
Cain! clear thee from this horrible accusal, 400
Which grief wrings from our parent.

Eve. Hear, Jehovah!

May the eternal serpent's curse be on him!
For he was fitter for his seed than ours.
May all his days be desolate! May—

Adah. Hold!
Curse him not, mother, for he is thy son—
Curse him not, mother, for he is my brother,
And my betrothed.

Eve. He hath left thee no brother—
Zillah no husband—me *no son!*—for thus
I curse him from my sight for evermore!
All bonds I break between us, as he broke 410
That of his nature, in yon—Oh Death! Death!
Why didst thou not take *me,* who first incurred thee?
Why dost thou not so now?

Adam. Eve! let not this,
Thy natural grief, lead to impiety!
A heavy doom was long forespoken to us;
And now that it begins, let it be borne
In such sort as may show our God that we
Are faithful servants to his holy will.

Eve (*pointing to* Cain). *His will!* the will of yon incarnate spirit
Of death, whom I have brought upon the earth 420
To strew it with the dead. May all the curses
Of life be on him! and his agonies
Drive him forth o'er the wilderness, like us
From Eden, till his children do by him
As he did by his brother! May the swords
And wings of fiery cherubim pursue him
By day and night—snakes spring up in his path—
Earth's fruits be ashes in his mouth—the leaves
On which he lays his head to sleep be strewed
With scorpions! May his dreams be of his victim! 430
His waking a continual dread of Death!
May the clear rivers turn to blood as he
Stoops down to stain them with his raging lip!
May every element shun or change to him!
May he live in the pangs which others die with!
And Death itself wax something worse than Death
To him who first acquainted him with man!
Hence, fratricide! henceforth that word is *Cain,*
Through all the coming myriads of mankind,
Who shall abhor three though thou wert their sire! 440
May the grass wither from thy feet! the woods
Deny thee shelter! earth a home! the dust
A grave! the sun his light! and heaven her God! *Exit* Eve.

Adam. Cain! get thee forth: we dwell no more together.
Depart and leave the dead to me—I am
Henceforth alone—we never must meet more.
Adah. Oh, part not with him thus, my father: do not
Add thy deep curse to Eve's upon his head!
Adam. I curse him not: his spirit be his curse.
Come, Zillah!
Zillah. I must watch my husband's corse.[r] 450
Adam. We will return again, when he is gone
Who hath provided for us this dread office.[s]
Come, Zillah!
Zillah. Yet one kiss on yon pale clay,
And those lips once so warm—my heart! my heart!
Exeunt Adam *and* Zillah, *weeping.*
Adah. Cain! thou hast heard, we must go forth. I am ready,
So shall our children be. I will bear Enoch,
And you his sister. Ere the sun declines
Let us depart, nor walk the wilderness
Under the cloud of night.—Nay, speak to me,
To *me—thine own.*
Cain. Leave me!
Adah. Why, all have left thee. 460
Cain. And wherefore lingerest thou? Dost thou not fear
To dwell with one who hath done this?
Adah. I fear
Nothing except to leave thee, much as I
Shrink from the deed which leaves thee brotherless.
I must not speak of this—it is between thee
And the great God.
A Voice from within exclaims, Cain! Cain!
Adah. Hear'st thou that voice?
The Voice within. Cain! Cain!
Adah. It soundeth like an angel's tone.

Enter the Angel of the Lord.

Angel. Where is thy brother Abel?
Cain. Am I then
My brother's keeper?
Angel. Cain! what hast thou done?
The voice of thy slain brother's blood cries out, 470
Even from the ground, unto the Lord!—Now art thou
Cursed from the earth, which opened late her mouth

[r] corpse [s] duty

To drink thy brother's blood from thy rash hand.
Henceforth, when thou shalt till the ground, it shall not
Yield thee her strength; a fugitive shalt thou
Be from this day, and vagabond on earth! 480

Adah. This punishment is more than he can bear.
Behold, thou drivest him from the face of earth,
And from the face of God shall he be hid.
A fugitive and vagabond on earth,
'Twill come to pass, that whoso findeth him
Shall slay him.

Cain. Would they could! but who are they
Shall slay me? Where are these on the lone earth
As yet unpeopled?

Angel. Thou hast slain thy brother,
And who shall warrant thee against thy son?

Adah. Angel of Light! be merciful, nor say
That this poor aching breast now nourishes
A murderer in my boy, and of his father.

Angel. Then he would but be what his father is.
Did not the milk of Eve give nutriment 490
To him thou now see'st so besmeared with blood?
The fratricide might well engender parricides.—
But it shall not be so—the Lord thy God
And mine commandeth me to set his seal
On Cain, so that he may go forth in safety.
Who slayeth Cain, a sevenfold vengeance shall
Be taken on his head. Come hither!

Cain. What
Wouldst thou with me?

Angel. To mark upon thy brow
Exemption from such deeds as thou hast done.

Cain. No, let me die!

Angel. It must not be.

The Angel *sets the mark on* Cain's *brow.*

Cain. It burns 500
My brow, but nought to that which is within it.
Is there more? let me meet it as I may.

Angel. Stern hast thou been and stubborn from the womb,
As the ground thou must henceforth till; but he
Thou slew'st was gentle as the flocks he tended.

Cain. After the fall too soon was I begotten;
Ere yet my mother's mind subsided from
The serpent, and my sire still mourned for Eden.

That which I am, I am; I did not seek
For life, nor did I make myself; but could I 510
With my own death redeem him from the dust—
And why not so? let him return today,
And I lie ghastly! so shall be restored
By God the life to him he loved; and taken
From me a being I ne'er loved to bear.

Angel. Who shall heal murder? what is done is done;
Go forth! fulfil thy days! and be thy deeds
Unlike the last!

The Angel *disappears.*

Adah. He's gone, let us go forth;
I hear our little Enoch cry within
Our bower.

Cain. Ah, little knows he what he weeps for! 520
And I who have shed blood cannot shed tears!
But the four rivers[t] would not cleanse my soul.
Think'st thou my boy will bear to look on me?

Adah. If I thought that he would not, I would—

Cain (*interrupting her*). No,
No more of threats: we have had too many of them:
Go to our children; I will follow thee.

Adah. I will not leave thee lonely with the dead;
Let us depart together.

Cain. Oh, thou dead
And everlasting witness! whose unsinking
Blood darkens earth and heaven! what thou *now* art 530
I know not! but if *thou* see'st what *I* am,
I think thou wilt forgive him, whom his God
Can ne'er forgive, nor his own soul.—Farewell!
I must not, dare not touch what I have made thee.
I, who sprung from the same womb with thee, drained
The same breast, clasped thee often to my own,
In fondness brotherly and boyish, I
Can never meet thee more, nor even dare
To do that for thee, which thou shouldst have done
For me—compose thy limbs into their grave— 540
The first grave yet dug for mortality.
But who hath dug that grave? Oh, earth! Oh, earth!
For all the fruits thou has rendered to me, I
Give thee back this.—Now for the wilderness.

[t] i.e., of Eden (Genesis 2:10–14)

Adah *stoops down and kisses the body of* Abel.

Adah. A dreary, and an early doom, my brother,
Has been thy lot! Of all who mourn for thee,
I alone must not weep. My office is
Henceforth to dry up tears, and not to shed them:
But yet, of all who mourn, none mourn like me,
Not only for thyself, but him who slew thee. 550
Now, Cain! I will divide thy burden with thee.
Cain. Eastward from Eden will we take our way;
'Tis the most desolate, and suits my steps.
Adah. Lead! thou shalt be my guide, and may our God
Be thine! Now let us carry forth our children.
Cain. And *he* who lieth there was childless. I
Have dried the fountain of a gentle race,
Which might have graced his recent marriage couch,
And might have tempered this stern blood of mine,
Uniting with our children Abel's offspring! 560
O Abel!
Adah. Peace be with him!
Cain. But with *me!* *Exeunt.*

Oscar Wilde:

THE IMPORTANCE OF BEING EARNEST

A Trivial Comedy for Serious People

When Oscar Wilde was young, like most other literary men of his century he wrote a tragedy; this tragedy, like most that were written during the century, is pseudo-Shakespearean. After Shakespeare's Duncan has been killed, Lady Macbeth says, "Who would have thought the old man to have had so much blood in him," but she cheers herself with the thought that "a little water clears us of this deed." After Wilde's Duke has been killed, the Duchess therefore says,

> I did not think he would have bled so much,
> But I can wash my hands in water after.

In a decade Wilde moved away from this sort of thing, and wrote three plays that are much more indebted to the commercial theater of his day, and much better. *Lady Windermere's Fan* (1892), *A Woman of No Importance* (1893), and *An Ideal Husband* (1895) are domestic melodramas—melodramas with the fisticuffs left out—of the sort that had for more than a decade been popular on the English stage. These plays have a wit that their predecessors lack ("I can resist everything except temptation"; "The only thing to do with good advice is to pass it on"), but basically the plots are meant to be serious. In *Lady Windermere's Fan,* for instance, a woman who has twenty years earlier deserted her child and husband for a lover returns to the scene to find her daughter about to make the same dreadful mistake:

No! Go back, Lady Windermere, to the husband who loves you, whom you love. You have a child, Lady Windermere. Go back to that child who even now, in pain or in joy, may be calling you.

Here is the end of the third act of *A Woman of No Importance.* (Gerald, the illegitimate son of Lord Illingworth, does not know that Illingworth is his father.)

Gerald (*he is quite beside himself with rage and indignation*). Lord Illingworth, you have insulted the purest thing on God's earth, a thing as pure as my own mother. You have insulted the woman I love most in the world with my own mother. As there is a God in Heaven, I will kill you!
Mrs. Arbuthnot (*rushing across and catching hold of him*). No! no!
Gerald (*thrusting her back*). Don't hold me, Mother. Don't hold me—I'll kill him!
Mrs. Arbuthnot. Gerald!
Gerald. Let me go, I say!
Mrs. Arbuthnot. Stop, Gerald, stop! He is your own father!

Now, ignorance of one's parentage can be the stuff of tragedy (in Gerald's assault on his father we have a situation close to that in Sophocles' *Oedipus the King*), but it is hard to take Wilde's scene seriously. Aristotle highly praised tragedies with situations of this sort (a man in ignorance is about to do a terrible deed to a friend or kinsman, but recognizes him in time), but we can scarcely help feeling that this is the material of melodrama and of comedy, comedy usually having the improbable plot and flat characters of melodrama but having mirth in addition.

In *The Importance of Being Earnest,* Wilde has jettisoned the melodrama and given us only comedy. The mystery of Jack's parentage is suffused not with pathos but with laughter: "To be born, or at any rate, bred in a handbag, whether it had handles or not, seems to me to display a contempt for the ordinary decencies of family life that remind one of the worst excesses of the French Revolution." Following the traditional comic formula the mystery is cleared up by a series of amusing coincidences and the play ends with the union of lovers—three pairs of them here. Such a union, implying a fertile community, is usual in late Greek comedy, in Roman comedy, and of course in most comedy from the Renaissance onward. This celebration of fertility, of the triumph of life over obstacles, is kept within acceptable moral bounds: the lovers presumably have been chaste, and they will presumably make for the church. The epigrams invert moral values, but for all the outrageous talk (which never really outrages, because it amuses), no one does anything offensive. When Algernon first meets Cecily, he denies he is "wicked." She rebukes him: "If you are not, then you have certainly been deceiving us all in a very inexcusable manner. I hope you have not been leading a double life, pretending to be wicked and being really good all the time. That would be hypocrisy." In its wit the play resembles the comedy of manners (see p. 22), and certainly Lady Bracknell owes something to Lady Wishfort; but in its freedom from obscenity and in its playfulness it is something else. Its nonsensical paradoxes and its absurd situations push it toward farce, but farce performed with high gravity, making it the funnier.

Wilde called his play "A Trivial Comedy for Serious People." *The Importance of Being Earnest* amuses, and that ought to be enough, but serious people sometimes want it "to mean," as well as to entertain. A case can be made that the play is an attack on Victorian society, and because Wilde did kick at his society openly in his private life, some have felt that he needled it covertly in the epigrams of his public life. André Gide, who met Wilde in North Africa when *Earnest* was in rehearsal (shortly before Wilde became involved in the lawsuits that ultimately sent him to jail), recorded that Wilde's witty conversation was not mere nonsense: "People do not always realize how much truth, wisdom, and seriousness were concealed under the mask of the jester." Was a comic plot the disguise or jester's garment that allowed him to indict society? The idea is appealing, but it loses substance when one sees the play, or reads it, or rereads it. Can we really feel that Wilde is attacking the aristocracy's morals of social irresponsibility when Algernon says of his butler, "Lane's views on marriage seem somewhat lax. Really, if the lower orders don't set us a good example, what on earth is the use of them?" If satire is supposed to wound susceptibilities, or to allow the innocent to enjoy the exposure of vice, surely *Earnest* fails as a satire. But it is ungracious to castigate *Earnest* for ineffectual satire when it is such effective absurdity. Let Max Beerbohm have the last word: "The fun depends mainly on what the characters say, rather than on what they do. They speak a kind of beautiful nonsense—the language of high comedy twisted into fantasy."

Wilde: Biographical Note.

Oscar Wilde (1854–1900) was born in Dublin. He distinguished himself as a student at Trinity College, Dublin, and at Oxford, and then turned to a career of writing, lecturing, and in other ways making himself a public figure in England: his posture as an aesthete (he was alleged to have walked down Piccadilly with a flower in his hand) was caricatured by Gilbert and Sullivan in *Patience*. But it became no laughing matter when in 1895 he was arrested and convicted of homosexuality. After serving two years at hard labor, he was released from jail. He then went to France, where he lived under an assumed name until he died. His Irish birth did not ally him to the Irish Renaissance at the end of the nineteenth century; when W. B. Yeats was writing plays on Irish legends, Wilde was writing drawing-room comedies.

Suggested References:

Auden, W. H., "A Playboy of the Western World: St. Oscar, the Homintern Martyr," *Partisan Review*, XVII (April, 1950), 390-394.

Beerbohm, Max, *Around Theatres*, New York, Simon & Schuster, 1954; London, Rupert Hart-Davis, 1953.

Bentley, Eric, *The Playwright as Thinker*, New York, Reynal and Hitchcock, 1946; New York, Meridian Books, 1955.

Reinert, Otto, "Satiric Strategy in *The Importance of Being Earnest*," *College English*, XVIII (October, 1956), 14-18.

Shaw, George Bernard, *Our Theatres in the Nineties*, London, Constable, & Co., 1932, Vol. I, pp. 41-44.

Woodcock, George R., *The Paradox of Oscar Wilde*, New York, Macmillan, 1950; London, T. V. Boardman, & Co., 1949.

The Importance of Being Earnest

Characters

JOHN WORTHING, J.P.
ALGERNON MONCRIEFF
REV. CANON CHASUBLE, D.D.
MERRIMAN, *butler*
LANE, *manservant*
LADY BRACKNELL
HON. GWENDOLEN FAIRFAX
CECILY CARDEW
MISS PRISM, *governess*

ACT I

Morning room in Algernon's flat in Half-Moon Street. The room is luxuriously and artistically furnished. The sound of a piano is heard in the adjoining room.
Lane *is arranging afternoon tea on the table, and after the music has ceased,* Algernon *enters.*

Algernon. Did you hear what I was playing, Lane?
Lane. I didn't think it polite to listen, sir.
Algernon. I'm sorry for that, for your sake. I don't play accurately—any one can play accurately—but I play with wonderful expression. As far as the piano is concerned, sentiment is my forte. I keep science for Life.
Lane. Yes, sir.
Algernon. And, speaking of the science of Life, have you got the cucumber sandwiches cut for Lady Bracknell?
Lane. Yes, sir. (*Hands them on a salver.*)
Algernon (*inspects them, takes two, and sits down on the sofa*). Oh! . . . by the way, Lane, I see from your book that on Thursday night, when Lord Shoreman and Mr. Worthing were dining with me, eight bottles of champagne are entered as having been consumed.
Lane. Yes, sir; eight bottles and a pint.
Algernon. Why is it that at a bachelor's establishment the servants invariably drink the champagne? I ask merely for information.
Lane. I attribute it to the superior quality of the wine, sir. I have often observed that in married households the champagne is rarely of a first-rate brand.
Algernon. Good heavens! Is marriage so demoralizing as that?
Lane. I believe it *is* a very pleasant state, sir. I have had very little experience of it myself up to the present. I have only been married once. That was in consequence of a misunderstanding between myself and a young person.
Algernon (*languidly*). I don't know that I am much interested in your family life, Lane.
Lane. No, sir; it is not a very interesting subject. I never think of it myself.

Algernon. Very natural, I am sure. That will do, Lane, thank you.

Lane. Thank you, sir.

Lane *goes out.*

Algernon. Lane's views on marriage seem somewhat lax. Really, if the lower orders don't set us a good example, what on earth is the use of them? They seem, as a class, to have absolutely no sense of moral responsibility.

Enter Lane.

Lane. Mr. Ernest Worthing.

Enter Jack. Lane *goes out.*

Algernon. How are you, my dear Ernest? What brings you up to town?

Jack. Oh, pleasure, pleasure! What else should bring one anywhere? Eating as usual, I see, Algy!

Algernon (*stiffly*). I believe it is customary in good society to take some slight refreshment at five o'clock. Where have you been since last Thursday?

Jack (*sitting down on the sofa*). In the country.

Algernon. What on earth do you do there?

Jack (*pulling off his gloves*). When one is in town one amuses oneself. When one is in the country one amuses other people. It is excessively boring.

Algernon. And who are the people you amuse?

Jack (*airily*). Oh, neighbors, neighbors.

Algernon. Got nice neighbors in your part of Shropshire?

Jack. Perfectly horrid! Never speak to one of them.

Algernon. How immensely you must amuse them! (*Goes over and takes sandwich.*) By the way, Shropshire is your county, is it not?

Jack. Eh? Shropshire? Yes, of course. Hallo! Why all these cups? Why cucumber sandwiches? Why such reckless extravagance in one so young? Who is coming to tea?

Algernon. Oh! merely Aunt Augusta and Gwendolen.

Jack. How perfectly delightful!

Algernon. Yes, that is all very well; but I am afraid Aunt Augusta won't quite approve of your being here.

Jack. May I ask why?

Algernon. My dear fellow, the way you flirt with Gwendolen is perfectly disgraceful. It is almost as bad as the way Gwendolen flirts with you.

Jack. I am in love with Gwendolen. I have come up to town expressly to propose to her.

Algernon. I thought you had come up for pleasure? . . . I call that business.

Jack. How utterly unromantic you are!

Algernon. I really don't see anything romantic in proposing. It is very romantic to be in love. But there is nothing romantic about a definite proposal. Why, one may be accepted. One usually is, I believe. Then the excitement is all over. The very essence of romance is uncertainty. If ever I get married, I'll certainly try to forget the fact.

Jack. I have no doubt about that, dear Algy. The Divorce Court was specially invented for people whose memories are so curiously constituted.

Algernon. Oh! there is no use speculating on that subject. Divorces are made in Heaven—(Jack *puts out his hand to take a sandwich.* Algernon *at once interferes.*) Please don't touch the cucumber sandwiches. They are ordered specially for Aunt Augusta. (*Takes one and eats it.*)

Jack. Well, you have been eating them all the time.

Algernon. That is quite a different matter. She is my aunt. (*Takes plate from below.*) Have some bread and butter. The bread and butter is for Gwendolen. Gwendolen is devoted to bread and butter.

Jack (*advancing to table and helping himself*). And very good bread and butter it is too.

Algernon. Well, my dear fellow, you need not eat as if you were going to eat it all. You behave as if you were married to her already. You are not married to her already, and I don't think you ever will be.

Jack. Why on earth do you say that?

Algernon. Well, in the first place, girls never marry the men they flirt with. Girls don't think it right.

Jack. Oh, that is nonsense!

Algernon. It isn't. It is a great truth. It accounts for the extraordinary number of bachelors that one sees all over the place. In the second place, I don't give my consent.

Jack. Your consent!

Algernon. My dear fellow, Gwendolen is my first cousin. And before I allow you to marry her, you will have to clear up the whole question of Cecily. (*Rings bell.*)

Jack. Cecily! What on earth do you mean? What do you mean, Algy, by Cecily! I don't know any one of the name of Cecily.

Enter Lane.

Algernon. Bring me that cigarette case Mr. Worthing left in the smoking room the last time he dined here.

Lane. Yes, sir.

Lane *goes out.*

Jack. Do you mean to say you have had my cigarette case all this time? I wish to goodness you had let me know. I have been writing frantic letters to Scotland Yard about it. I was very nearly offering a large reward.

Algernon. Well, I wish you would offer one. I happen to be more than usually hard up.

Jack. There is no good offering a large reward now that the thing is found.

Enter Lane *with the cigarette case on a salver.* Algernon *takes it at once.* Lane *goes out.*

Algernon. I think that is rather mean of you, Ernest, I must say. (*Opens case and examines it.*) However, it makes no matter, for, now that I look at the inscription inside, I find that the thing isn't yours after all.

Jack. Of course it's mine. (*Moving to him.*) You have seen me with it a hundred times, and you have no right whatsoever to read what is written inside. It is a very ungentlemanly thing to read a private cigarette case.

Algernon. Oh! it is absurd to have a hard and fast rule about what one should read and what one shouldn't. More than half of modern culture depends on what one shouldn't read.

Jack. I am quite aware of the fact, and I don't propose to discuss modern culture. It isn't the sort of thing one should talk of in private. I simply want my cigarette case back.

Algernon. Yes; but this isn't your cigarette case. This cigarette case is a present from someone of the name of Cecily, and you said you didn't know anyone of that name.

Jack. Well, if you want to know, Cecily happens to be my aunt.

Algernon. Your aunt!

Jack. Yes. Charming old lady she is, too. Lives at Tunbridge Wells. Just give it back to me, Algy.

Algernon (*retreating to back of sofa*). But why does she call herself little Cecily if she is your aunt and lives at

Tunbridge Wells. (*Reading.*) "From little Cecily with her fondest love."

Jack (*moving to sofa and kneeling upon it*). My dear fellow, what on earth is there in that? Some aunts are tall, some aunts are not tall. That is a matter that surely an aunt may be allowed to decide for herself. You seem to think that every aunt should be exactly like your aunt! That is absurd. For Heaven's sake give me back my cigarette case. (*Follows* Algernon *round the room.*)

Algernon. Yes. But why does your aunt call you her uncle? "From little Cecily, with her fondest love to her dear Uncle Jack." There is no objection, I admit, to an aunt being a small aunt, but why an aunt, no matter what her size may be, should call her own nephew her uncle, I can't quite make out. Besides, your name isn't Jack at all; it is Ernest.

Jack. It isn't Ernest; it's Jack.

Algernon. You have always told me it was Ernest. I have introduced you to every one as Ernest. You answer to the name of Ernest. You look as if your name was Ernest. You are the most earnest-looking person I ever saw in my life. It is perfectly absurd your saying that your name isn't Ernest. It's on your cards. Here is one of them (*taking it from case*). "Mr. Ernest Worthing, B.4, The Albany." I'll keep this as a proof that your name is Ernest if ever you attempt to deny it to me, or to Gwendolen, or to any one else. (*Puts the card in his pocket.*)

Jack. Well, my name is Ernest in town and Jack in the country, and the cigarette case was given to me in the country.

Algernon. Yes, but that does not account for the fact that your small Aunt Cecily, who lives at Tunbridge Wells, calls you her dear uncle. Come, old boy, you had much better have the thing out at once.

Jack. My dear Algy, you talk exactly as if you were a dentist. It is very vulgar to talk like a dentist when one isn't a dentist. It produces a false impression.

Algernon. Well, that is exactly what dentists always do. Now, go on! Tell me the whole thing. I may mention that I have always suspected you of being a confirmed and secret Bunburyist; and I am quite sure of it now.

Jack. Bunburyist? What on earth do you mean by a Bunburyist?

Algernon. I'll reveal to you the meaning of that incomparable expression as soon as you are kind enough to inform me why you are Ernest in town and Jack in the country.

Jack. Well, produce my cigarette case first.

Algernon. Here it is. (*Hands cigarette case.*) Now produce your explanation, and pray make it improbable. (*Sits on sofa.*)

Jack. My dear fellow, there is nothing improbable about my explanation at all. In fact it's perfectly ordinary. Old Mr. Thomas Cardew, who adopted me when I was a little boy, made me in his will guardian to his granddaughter, Miss Cecily Cardew. Cecily, who addresses me as her uncle from motives of respect that you could not possibly appreciate, lives at my place in the country under the charge of her admirable governess, Miss Prism.

Algernon. Where is that place in the country, by the way?

Jack. That is nothing to you, dear boy. You are not going to be invited. . . . I may tell you candidly that the place is not in Shropshire.

Algernon. I suspected that, my dear fellow! I have Bunburyed all over Shropshire on two separate occasions. Now, go on. Why are you Ernest in town and Jack in the country?

Jack. My dear Algy, I don't know whether you will be able to understand my real motives. You are hardly serious enough. When one is placed in the position of guardian, one has to adopt a very high moral tone on all subjects. It's one's duty to do so. And as a high moral tone can hardly be said to conduce very much to either one's health or one's happiness, in order to get up to town I have always pretended to have a younger brother of the name of Ernest, who lives in the Albany, and gets into the most dreadful scrapes. That, my dear Algy, is the whole truth pure and simple.

Algernon. The truth is rarely pure and never simple. Modern life would be very tedious if it were either, and modern literature a complete impossibility!

Jack. That wouldn't be at all a bad thing.

Algernon. Literary criticism is not your forte, my dear fellow. Don't try it. You should leave that to people who haven't been at a University. They do it so well in the daily papers. What you really are is a Bunburyist. I was quite right in saying you were a Bunburyist. You are one of the most advanced Bunburyists I know.

Jack. What on earth do you mean?

Algernon. You have invented a very useful younger brother called Ernest, in order that you may be able to come up to town as often as you like. I have invented an invaluable permanent invalid called Bunbury, in order that I may be able to go down into the country whenever I choose. Bunbury is perfectly invaluable. If it wasn't for Bunbury's extraordinary bad health, for instance, I wouldn't be able to dine with you at Willis's tonight, for I have been really engaged to Aunt Augusta for more than a week.

Jack. I haven't asked you to dine with me anywhere tonight.

Algernon. I know. You are absurdly careless about sending out invitations. It is very foolish of you. Nothing annoys people so much as not receiving invitations.

Jack. You had much better dine with your Aunt Augusta.

Algernon. I haven't the smallest intention of doing anything of the kind. To begin with, I dined there on Monday, and once a week is quite enough to dine with one's own relations. In the second place, whenever I do dine there I am always treated as a member of the family, and sent down with either no woman at all, or two. In the third place, I know perfectly well whom she will place me next to, tonight. She will place me next Mary Farquhar, who always flirts with her own husband across the dinner table. That is not very pleasant. Indeed, it is not even decent . . . and that sort of thing is enormously on the increase. The amount of women in London who flirt with their own husbands is perfectly scandalous. It looks so bad. It is simply washing one's clean linen in public. Besides, now that I know you to be a confirmed Bunburyist I naturally want to talk to you about Bunburying. I want to tell you the rules.

Jack. I'm not a Bunburyist at all. If Gwendolen accepts me, I am going to kill my brother, indeed I think I'll kill him in any case. Cecily is a little too much interested in him. It is rather a bore. So I am going to get rid of Ernest. And I strongly advise you to do the same with Mr. . . . with your invalid friend who has the absurd name.

Algernon. Nothing will induce me to part with Bunbury, and if you ever get married, which seems to me extremely problematic, you will be very glad to know Bunbury. A man who marries without knowing Bunbury has a very tedious time of it.

Jack. That is nonsense. If I marry a charming girl like

Gwendolen, and she is the only girl I ever saw in my life that I would marry, I certainly won't want to know Bunbury.

Algernon. Then your wife will. You don't seem to realize, that in married life three is company and two is none.

Jack (sententiously). That, my dear young friend, is the theory that the corrupt French Drama has been propounding for the last fifty years.

Algernon. Yes; and that the happy English home has proved in half the time.

Jack. For heaven's sake, don't try to be cynical. It's perfectly easy to be cynical.

Algernon. My dear fellow, it isn't easy to be anything nowadays. There's such a lot of beastly competition about. (*The sound of an electric bell is heard.*) Ah! that must be Aunt Augusta. Only relatives, or creditors, ever ring in that Wagnerian manner. Now, if I get her out of the way for ten minutes, so that you can have an opportunity for proposing to Gwendolen, may I dine with you tonight at Willis's?

Jack. I suppose so, if you want to.

Algernon. Yes, but you must be serious about it. I hate people who are not serious about meals. It is so shallow of them.

Enter Lane.

Lane. Lady Bracknell and Miss Fairfax.

Algernon *goes forward to meet them. Enter* Lady Bracknell *and* Gwendolen.

Lady Bracknell. Good afternoon, dear Algernon, I hope you are behaving very well.

Algernon. I'm feeling very well, Aunt Augusta.

Lady Bracknell. That's not quite the same thing. In fact the two things rarely go together. (*Sees* Jack *and bows to him with icy coldness.*)

Algernon (to Gwendolen*).* Dear me, you are smart!

Gwendolen. I am always smart! Am I not, Mr. Worthing?

Jack. You're quite perfect, Miss Fairfax.

Gwendolen. Oh! I hope I am not that. It would leave no room for developments, and I intend to develop in many directions. (Gwendolen *and* Jack *sit down together in the corner.*)

Lady Bracknell. I'm sorry if we are a little late, Algernon, but I was obliged to call on dear Lady Harbury. I hadn't been there since her poor husband's death. I never saw a woman so altered; she looks quite twenty years younger. And now I'll have a cup of tea and one of those nice cucumber sandwiches you promised me.

Algernon. Certainly, Aunt Augusta. (*Goes over to tea table.*)

Lady Bracknell. Won't you come and sit here, Gwendolen?

Gwendolen. Thanks, mamma, I'm quite comfortable where I am.

Algernon (*picking up empty plate in horror*). Good heavens! Lane! Why are there no cucumber sandwiches? I ordered them specially.

Lane (*gravely*). There were no cucumbers in the market this morning, sir. I went down twice.

Algernon. No cucumbers!

Lane. No, sir. Not even for ready money.

Algernon. That will do, Lane, thank you.

Lane. Thank you, sir. (*Goes out.*)

Algernon. I am greatly distressed, Aunt Augusta, about there being no cucumbers, not even for ready money.

Lady Bracknell. It really makes no matter, Algernon. I had some crumpets with Lady Harbury, who seems to me to be living entirely for pleasure now.

Algernon. I hear her hair has turned quite gold from grief.

Lady Bracknell. It certainly has changed its color. From what cause I, of course, cannot say. (Algernon *crosses and hands tea.*) Thank you. I've quite a treat for you tonight, Algernon. I am going to send you down with Mary Farquhar. She is such a nice woman, and so attentive to her husband. It's delightful to watch them.

Algernon. I am afraid, Aunt Augusta, I shall have to give up the pleasure of dining with you tonight after all.

Lady Bracknell (*frowning*). I hope not, Algernon. It would put my table completely out. Your uncle would have to dine upstairs. Fortunately he is accustomed to that.

Algernon. It is a great bore, and, I need hardly say, a terrible disappointment to me, but the fact is I have just had a telegram to say that my poor friend Bunbury is very ill again. (*Exchanges glances with* Jack.) They seem to think I should be with him.

Lady Bracknell. It is very strange. This Mr. Bunbury seems to suffer from curiously bad health.

Algernon. Yes; poor Bunbury is a dreadful invalid.

Lady Bracknell. Well, I must say, Algernon, that I think it is high time that Mr. Bunbury made up his mind whether he was going to live or to die. This shilly-shallying with the question is absurd. Nor do I in any way approve of the modern sympathy with invalids. I consider it morbid. Illness of any kind is hardly a thing to be encouraged in others. Health is the primary duty of life. I am always telling that to your poor uncle, but he never seems to take much notice . . . as far as any improvement in his ailments goes. I should be much obliged if you would ask Mr. Bunbury, from me, to be kind enough not to have a relapse on Saturday, for I rely on you to arrange my music for me. It is my last reception, and one wants something that will encourage conversation, particularly at the end of the season when every one has practically said whatever they had to say, which, in most cases, was probably not much.

Algernon. I'll speak to Bunbury, Aunt Augusta, if he is still conscious, and I think I can promise you he'll be all right by Saturday. Of course the music is a great difficulty. You see, if one plays good music, people don't listen, and if one plays bad music, people don't talk. But I'll run over the program I've drawn out, if you will kindly come into the next room for a moment.

Lady Bracknell. Thank you, Algernon. It is very thoughtful of you. (*Rising, and following* Algernon.) I'm sure the program will be delightful, after a few expurgations. French songs I cannot possibly allow. People always seem to think that they are improper, and either look shocked, which is vulgar, or laugh, which is worse. But German sounds a thoroughly respectable language, and, indeed I believe is so. Gwendolen, you will accompany me.

Gwendolen. Certainly, mamma.

Lady Bracknell *and* Algernon *go into the music room;* Gwendolen *remains behind.*

Jack. Charming day it has been, Miss Fairfax.

Gwendolen. Pray don't talk to me about the weather, Mr. Worthing. Whenever people talk to me about the weather, I always feel quite certain that they mean something else. And that makes me so nervous.

Jack. I do mean something else.

Gwendolen. I thought so. In fact, I am never wrong.

Jack. And I would like to be allowed to take advantage of Lady Bracknell's temporary absence. . . .

Gwendolen. I would certainly advise you to do so. Mamma has a way of coming back suddenly into a room that I have often had to speak to her about.

Jack (*nervously*). Miss Fairfax, ever since I met you I have admired you more than any girl . . . I have ever met since . . . I met you.

Gwendolen. Yes, I am quite aware of the fact. And I often wish that in public, at any rate, you had been more demonstrative. For me you have always had an irresistiible fascination. Even before I met you I was far from indifferent to you. (Jack *looks at her in amazement.*) We live, as I hope you know, Mr. Worthing, in an age of ideals. The fact is constantly mentioned in the more expensive monthly magazines, and has reached the provincial pulpits, I am told; and my ideal has always been to love someone of the name of Ernest. There is something in that name that inspires absolute confidence. The moment Algernon first mentioned to me that he had a friend called Ernest, I knew I was destined to love you.

Jack. You really love me, Gwendolen?

Gwendolen. Passionately!

Jack. Darling! You don't know how happy you've made me.

Gwendolen. My own Ernest!

Jack. But you don't really mean to say that you couldn't love me if my name wasn't Ernest?

Gwendolen. But your name is Ernest.

Jack. Yes, I know it is. But supposing it was something else? Do you mean to say you couldn't love me then?

Gwendolen (*glibly*). Ah! that is clearly a metaphysical speculation, and like most metaphysical speculations has very little reference at all to the actual facts of real life, as we know them.

Jack. Personally, darling, to speak quite candidly, I don't much care about the name of Ernest. . . . I don't think the name suits me at all.

Gwendolen. It suits you perfectly. It is a divine name. It has a music of its own. It produces vibrations.

Jack. Well, really, Gwendolen, I must say that I think there are lots of other much nicer names. I think Jack, for instance, a charming name.

Gwendolen. Jack? . . . No, there is very little music in the name Jack, if any at all, indeed. It does not thrill. It produces absolutely no vibrations. . . . I have known several Jacks, and they all, without exception, were more than usually plain. Besides, Jack is a notorious domesticity for John! And I pity any woman who is married to a man called John. She would probably never be allowed to know the entrancing pleasure of a single moment's solitude. The only really safe name is Ernest.

Jack. Gwendolen, I must get christened at once—I mean we must get married at once. There is no time to be lost.

Gwendolen. Married, Mr. Worthing?

Jack (astounded). Well . . . surely. You know that I love you, and you led me to believe, Miss Fairfax, that you were not absolutely indifferent to me.

Gwendolen. I adore you. But you haven't proposed to me yet. Nothing has been said at all about marriage. The subject has not even been touched on.

Jack. Well . . . may I propose to you now?

Gwendolen. I think it would be an admirable opportunity. And to spare you any possible disappointment, Mr. Worthing, I thing it only fair to tell you quite frankly beforehand that I am fully determined to accept you.

Jack. Gwendolen!

Gwendolen. Yes, Mr. Worthing, what have you got to say to me?

Jack. You know what I have got to say to you.

Gwendolen. Yes, but you don't say it.

Jack. Gwendolen, will you marry me? (*Goes on his knees.*)

Gwendolen. Of course I will, darling. How long you have been about it! I am afraid you have had very little experience in how to propose.

Jack. My own one, I have never loved anyone in the world but you.

Gwendolen. Yes, but men often propose for practice. I know my brother Gerald does. All my girl friends tell me so. What wonderfully blue eyes you have, Ernest! They are quite, quite blue. I hope you will always look at me just like that, especially when there are other people present.

Enter Lady Bracknell.

Lady Bracknell. Mr. Worthing! Rise sir, from this semi-recumbent posture. It is most indecorous.

Gwendolen. Mamma! (*He tries to rise; she restrains*

him.) I must beg you to retire. This is no place for you. Besides, Mr. Worthing has not quite finished yet.

Lady Bracknell. Finished what, may I ask?

Gwendoen. I am engaged to Mr. Worthing, Mamma. (*They rise together.*)

Lady Bracknell. Pardon me, you are not engaged to any one. When you do become engaged to someone, I, or your father, should his health permit him, will inform you of the fact. An engagement should come on a young girl as a surprise, pleasant or unpleasant, as the case may be. It is hardly a matter that she could be allowed to arrange for herself. . . . And now I have a few questions to put to you, Mr. Worthing. While I am making these inquiries, you, Gwendolen, will wait for me below in the carriage.

Gwendolen (*reproachfully*). Mamma!

Lady Bracknell. In the carriage, Gwendolen! (Gwendolen *goes to the door. She and* Jack *blow kisses to each other behind* Lady Bracknell's *back.* Lady Bracknell *looks vaguely about as if she could not understand what the noise was. Finally turns round.*) Gwendolen, the carriage!

Gwendolen. Yes, mamma. (*Goes out, looking back at* Jack.)

Lady Bracknell (*sitting down*). You can take a seat, Mr. Worthing. (*Looks in her pocket for notebook and pencil.*)

Jack. Thank you, Lady Bracknell, I prefer standing.

Lady Bracknell (*pencil and notebook in hand*). I feel bound to tell you that you are not down on my list of eligible young men, although I have the same list as the dear Duchess of Bolton has. We work together, in fact. However, I am quite ready to enter your name, should your answers be what a really affectionate mother requires. Do you smoke?

Jack. Well, yes, I must admit I smoke.

Lady Bracknell. I am glad to hear it. A man should always have an occupation of some kind. There are far too many idle men in London as it is. How old are you?

Jack. Twenty-nine.

Lady Bracknell. A very good age to be married at. I have always been of opinion that a man who desires to get married should know either everything or nothing. Which do you know?

Jack (*after some hesitation*). I know nothing, Lady Bracknell.

Lady Bracknell. I am pleased to hear it. I do not approve of anything that tampers with natural ignorance. Ignorance is like a delicate exotic fruit; touch it and the bloom is gone. The whole theory of modern education is radically unsound. Fortunately in England, at any rate, education produces no effect whatsoever. If it did, it would prove a serious danger to the upper classes, and probably lead to acts of violence in Grosvenor Square. What is your income?

Jack. Between seven and eight thousand a year.

Lady Bracknell (*makes a note in her book*). In land, or in investments?

Jack. In investments, chiefly.

Lady Bracknell. That is satisfactory. What between the duties expected of one during one's lifetime, and the duties exacted from one after one's death, land has ceased to be either a profit or a pleasure. It gives one position, and prevents one from keeping it up. That's all that can be said about land.

Jack. I have a country house with some land, of course, attached to it, about fifteen hundred acres, I believe; but I don't depend on that for my real income. In fact, as far as I can make out, the poachers are the only people who make anything out of it.

Lady Bracknell. A country house! How many bedrooms? Well, that point can be cleared up afterwards. You have a town house, I hope? A girl with a simple, unspoiled nature, like Gwendolen, could hardly be expected to reside in the country.

Jack. Well, I own a house in Belgrave Square, but it is let by the year to Lady Bloxham. Of course, I can get it back whenever I like, at six months' notice.

Lady Bracknell. Lady Bloxham? I don't know her.

Jack. Oh, she goes about very little. She is a lady considerably advanced in years.

Lady Bracknell. Ah, nowadays that is no guarantee of respectability of character. What number in Belgrave Square?

Jack. 149.

Lady Bracknell (*shaking her head*). The unfashionable side. I thought there was something. However, that could easily be altered.

Jack. Do you mean the fashion, or the side?

Lady Bracknell (*sternly*). Both, if necessary, I presume. What are your politics?

Jack. Well, I am afraid I really have none. I am a Liberal Unionist.

Lady Bracknell. Oh, they count as Tories. They dine with us. Or come in the evening, at any rate. Now to minor matters. Are your parents living?

Jack. I have lost both my parents.

Lady Bracknell. To lose one parent, Mr. Worthing, may be regarded as a misfortune; to lose both looks like carelessness. Who was your father? He was evidently a man of some wealth. Was he born in what the Radical papers call the purple of commerce, or did he rise from the ranks of the aristocracy?

Jack. I am afraid I really don't know. The fact is, Lady Bracknell, I said I had lost my parents. It would be nearer the truth to say that my parents seem to have lost me. . . . I don't actually know who I am by birth. I was . . . well, I was found.

Lady Bracknell. Found!

Jack. The late Mr. Thomas Cardew, an old gentleman of a very charitable and kindly disposition, found me, and gave me the name of Worthing, because he happened to have a first-class ticket for Worthing in his pocket at the time. Worthing is a place in Sussex. It is a seaside resort.

Lady Bracknell. Where did the charitable gentleman who had a first-class ticket for this seaside resort find you?

Jack (*gravely*). In a handbag.

Lady Bracknell. A handbag?

Jack (*very seriously*). Yes, Lady Bracknell. I was in a handbag—a somewhat large, black leather handbag, with handles to it—an ordinary handbag in fact.

Lady Bracknell. In what locality did this Mr. James, or Thomas, Cardew come across this ordinary handbag?

Jack. In the cloakroom at Victoria Station. It was given to him in mistake for his own.

Lady Braknell. The cloakroom at Victoria Station?

Jack. Yes. The Brighton line.

Lady Bracknell. The line is immaterial. Mr. Worthing, I confess I feel somewhat bewildered by what you have just told me. To be born, or at any rate bred, in a handbag, whether it had handles or not, seems to me to display a contempt for the ordinary decencies of family life that reminds one of the worst excesses of the French Revolution. And I presume you know what that unfortunate movement led to? As for the particular locality in which the handbag was found, a cloakroom at a railway station might serve to conceal a social indiscretion—has probably, indeed, been used for that purpose before now—but it could hardly be regarded as an assured basis for a recognized position in good society.

Jack. May I ask you then what you would advise me to do? I need hardly say I would do anything in the world to ensure Gwendolen's happiness.

Lady Bracknell. I would strongly advise you, Mr. Worthing, to try and acquire some relations as soon as possible, and to make a definite effort to produce at any rate one parent, of either sex, before the season is quite over.

Jack. Well, I don't see how I could possibly manage to do that. I can produce the handbag at any moment. It is in my dressing room at home. I really think that should satisfy you, Lady Bracknell.

Lady Bracknell. Me, sir! What has it to do with me? You can hardly imagine that I and Lord Bracknell would dream of allowing our only daughter—a girl brought up with the utmost care—to marry into a cloakroom, and form an alliance with a parcel. Good morning, Mr. Worthing!

(Lady Bracknell *sweeps out in majestic indignation.*)

Jack. Good morning! (Algernon, *from the other room, strikes up the Wedding March.* Jack *looks perfectly furious, and goes to the door.*) For goodness' sake don't play that ghastly tune, Algy! How idiotic you are!

The music stops and Algernon *enters cheerily.*

Algernon. Didn't it go off all right, old boy? You don't mean to say Gwendolen refused you? I know it is a way she has. She is always refusing people. I think it is most ill-natured of her.

Jack. Oh, Gwendolen is as right as a trivet. As far as she is concerned, we are engaged. Her mother is perfectly unbearable. Never met such a Gorgon. . . . I don't really know what a Gorgon is like, but I am quite sure that Lady Bracknell is one. In any case, she is a monster, without being a myth, which is rather unfair. . . . I beg your pardon, Algy, I suppose I shouldn't talk about your own aunt in that way before you.

Algernon. My dear boy, I love hearing my relations abused. It is the only thing that makes me put up with them at all. Relations are simply a tedious pack of people, who haven't got the remotest knowledge of how to live, nor the smallest instinct about when to die.

Jack. Oh, that is nonsense!

Algernon. It isn't!

Jack. Well, I won't argue about the matter. You always want to argue about things.

Algernon. That is exactly what things were originally made for.

Jack. Upon my word, if I thought that, I'd shoot myself. . . . (*A pause.*) You don't think there is any chance of Gwendolen becoming like her mother in about a hundred and fifty years, do you, Algy?

Algernon. All women become like their mothers. That is their tragedy. No man does. That's his.

Jack. Is that clever?

Alegernon. It is perfectly phrased! and quite as true as any observation in civilized life should be.

Jack. I am sick to death of cleverness. Everybody is clever nowadays. You can't go anywhere without meeting clever people. The thing has become an absolute public nuisance. I wish to goodness we had a few fools left.

Algernon. We have.

Jack. I should extremely like to meet them. What dò they talk about?

Algernon. The fools? Oh! about the clever people, of course.

Jack. What fools.

Algernon. By the way, did you tell Gwendolen the truth about your being Ernest in town, and Jack in the country?

Jack (*in a very patronizing manner*). My dear fellow, the truth isn't quite the sort of thing one tells to a nice, sweet, refined girl. What extraordinary ideas you have about the way to behave to a woman!

Algernon. The only way to behave to a woman is to make love to her, if she is pretty, and to someone else, if she is plain.

Jack. Oh, that is nonsense.

Algernon. What about your brother? What about the profligate Ernest?

Jack. Oh, before the end of the week I shall have got rid of him. I'll say he died in Paris of apoplexy. Lots of people die of apoplexy, quite suddenly, don't they?

Algernon. Yes, but it's hereditary, my dear fellow. It's a sort of thing that runs in families. You had much better say a severe chill.

Jack. You are sure a severe chill isn't hereditary, or anything of that kind?

Algernon. Of course it isn't!

Jack. Very well, then. My poor brother Ernest is carried off suddenly, in Paris, by a severe chill. That gets rid of him.

Algernon. But I thought you said that . . . Miss Cardew was a little too much interested in your poor brother Ernest? Won't she feel his loss a good deal?

Jack. Oh, that is all right. Cecily is not a silly romantic girl, I am glad to say. She has got a capital appetite, goes long walks, and pays no attention at all to her lessons.

Algernon. I would rather like to see Cecily.

Jack. I will take very good care you never do. She is excessively pretty, and she is only just eighteen.

Algernon. Have you told Gwendolen yet that you have an excessively pretty ward who is only just eighteen?

Jack. Oh! one doesn't blurt these things out to people. Cecily and Gwendolen are perfectly certain to be extremely great friends. I'll bet you anything you like that half an hour after they have met, they will be calling each other sister.

Algernon. Women only do that when they have called each other a lot of other things first. Now, my dear boy, if we want to get a good table at Willis's, we really must go and dress. Do you know it is nearly seven?

Jack (*irritably*). Oh! it always is nearly seven.

Algernon. Well, I'm hungry.

Jack. I never knew you when you weren't. . . .

Algernon. What shall we do after dinner? Go to a theater?

Jack. Oh no! I loathe listening.

Algernon. Well, let us go to the Club?

Jack. Oh, no! I hate talking.

Algernon. Well, we might trot round to the Empire at ten?

Jack. Oh, no! I can't bear looking at things. It is so silly.

Algernon. Well, what shall we do?

Jack. Nothing!

Algernon. It is awfully hard work doing nothing. However, I don't mind hard work where there is no definite object of any kind.

Enter Lane.

Lane. Miss Fairfax.

Enter Gwendolen. Lane *goes out.*

Algernon. Gwendolen, upon my word!
Gwendolen. Algy, kindly turn your back. I have something very particular to say to Mr. Worthing.
Algernon. Really, Gwendolen, I don't think I can allow this at all.
Gwendolen. Algy, you always adopt a strictly immoral attitude towards life. You are not quite old enough to do that. (Algernon *retires to the fireplace.*)
Jack. My own darling!
Gwendolen. Ernest, we may never be married. From the expression on mamma's face I fear we never shall. Few parents nowadays pay any regard to what their children say to them. The old-fashioned respect for the young is fast dying out. Whatever influence I ever had over mamma, I lost at the age of three. But although she may prevent us from becoming man and wife, and I may marry someone else, and marry often, nothing that she can possibly do can alter my eternal devotion to you.
Jack. Dear Gwendolen!
Gwendolen. The story of your romantic origin, as related to me by mamma, with unpleasing comments, has naturally stirred the deeper fibers of my nature. Your Christian name has an irresistible fascination. The simplicity of your character makes you exquisitely incomprehensible to me. Your town address at the Albany I have. What is your address in the country?
Jack. The Manor House, Woolton, Hertfordshire.

Algernon, *who has been carefully listening, smiles to himself, and writes the address on his shirt cuff. Then picks up the* Railway Guide.

Gwendolen. There is a good postal service, I suppose? It may be necessary to do something desperate. That of course will require serious consideration. I will communicate with you daily.
Jack. My own one!
Gwendolen. How long do you remain in town?
Jack. Till Monday.
Gwendolen. Good! Algy, you may turn round now.
Algernon. Thanks, I've turned round already.
Gwendolen. You may also ring the bell.
Jack. You will let me see you to your carriage, my own darling?

Gwendolen. Certainly.

Jack (*to* Lane, *who now enters*). I will see Miss Fairfax out.

Lane. Yes, sir. (Jack *and* Gwendolen *go off.*)

Lane *presents several letters on a salver to* Algernon. *It is to be surmised that they are bills, as* Algernon, *after looking at the envelopes, tears them up.*

Algernon. A glass of sherry, Lane.

Lane. Yes, sir.

Algernon. Tomorrow, Lane, I'm going Bunburying.

Lane. Yes, sir.

Algernon. I shall probably not be back till Monday. You can put up my dres- clothes, my smoking jacket, and all the Bunbury suits . . .

Lane. Yes, sir. (*Handing sherry.*)

Algernon. I hope tomorrow will be a fine day, Lane.

Lane. It never is, sir.

Algernon. Lane, you're a perfect pessimist.

Lane. I do my best to give satisfaction, sir.

Enter Jack. Lane *goes off.*

Jack. There's a sensible, intellectual girl! the only girl I ever cared for in my life. (Algernon *is laughing immoderately.*) What on earth are you so amused at?

Algernon. Oh, I'm a little anxious about poor Bunbury, that is all.

Jack. If you don't take care, your friend Bunbury will get you into a serious scrape some day.

Algernon. I love scrapes. They are the only things that are never serious.

Jack. Oh, that's nonsense, Algy. You never talk anything but nonsense.

Algernon. Nobody ever does.

Jack looks indignantly at him, and leaves the room. Algernon *lights a cigarette, reads his shirt-cuff, and smiles.*

ACT II

Garden at the Manor House. A flight of gray stone steps leads up to the house. The garden, an old-fashioned one, full of roses. Time of year, July. Basket chairs, and a table covered with books, are set under a large yew tree.

Miss Prism *discovered seated at the table.* Cecily *is at the back, watering flowers.*

Miss Prism (*calling*). Cecily, Cecily! Surely such a ultilitarian occupation as the watering of flowers is rather Moulton's duty than yours? Especially at a moment when intellectual pleasures await you. Your German grammar is on the table. Pray open it at page fifteen. We will repeat yesterday's lesson.

Cecily (*coming over very slowly*). But I don't like German. It isn't at all a becoming language. I know perfectly well that I look quite plain after my German lesson.

Miss Prism. Child, you know how anxious your guardian is that you should improve yourself in every way. He laid particular stress on your German, as he was leaving for town yesterday. Indeed, he always lays stress on your German when he is leaving for town.

Cecily. Dear Uncle Jack is so very serious! Sometimes he is so serious that I think he cannot be quite well.

Miss Prism (*drawing herself up*). Your guardian enjoys the best of health, and his gravity of demeanor is especially to be commended in one so comparatively young as he is. I know no one who has a higher sense of duty and responsibility.

Cecily. I suppose that is why he often looks a little bored when we three are together.

Miss Prism. Cecily! I am surprised at you. Mr. Worthing has many troubles in his life. Idle merriment and triviality would be out of place in his conversation. you must remember his constant anxiety about that unfortunate young man his brother.

Cecily. I wish Uncle Jack would allow that unfortunate

young man, his brother, to come down here sometimes. We might have a good influence over him, Miss Prism. I am sure you certainly would. You know German, and geology, and things of that kind influence a man very much. (Cecily *begins to write in her diary.*)

Miss Prism (*shaking her head*). I do not think that even I could produce any effect on a character that according to his own brother's admission is irretrievably weak and vacillating. Indeed I am not sure that I would desire to reclaim him. I am not in favor of this modern mania for turning bad people into good people at a moment's notice. As a man sows so let him reap. You must put away your diary, Cecily. I really don't see why you should keep a diary at all.

Cecily. I keep a diary in order to enter the wonderful secrets of my life. If I didn't write them down, I should probably forget all about them.

Miss Prism. Memory, my dear Cecily, is the diary that we all carry about with us.

Cecily. Yes, but it usually chronicles the things that have never happened, and couldn't possibly have happened. I believe that Memory is responsible for nearly all the three-volume novels that Mudie sends us.

Miss Prism. Do not speak slightingly of the three-volume novel, Cecily. I wrote one myself in earlier days.

Cecily. Did you really, Miss Prism? How wonderfully clever you are! I hope it did not end happily? I don't like novels that end happily. They depress me so much.

Miss Prism. The good ended happily, and the bad unhappily. That is what Fiction means.

Cecily. I suppose so. But it seems very unfair. And was your novel ever published?

Miss Prism. Alas! no. The manuscript unfortunately was abandoned. (Cecily *starts.*) I used the word in the sense of lost or mislaid. To your work, child, these speculations are profitless.

Cecily (*smiling*). But I see dear Dr. Chasuble coming up through the garden.

Miss Prism (*rising and advancing*). Dr. Chasuble! This is indeed a pleasure.

Enter Canon Chasuble.

Chasuble. And how are we this morning? Miss Prism, you are, I trust, well?

Cecily. Miss Prism has just been complaining of a slight

headache. I think it would do her so much good to have a short stroll with you in the Park, Dr. Chasuble.

Miss Prism. Cecily, I have not mentioned anything about a headache.

Cecily. No, dear Miss Prism, I know that, but I felt instinctively that you had a headache. Indeed I was thinking about that, and not about my German lesson, when the Rector came in.

Chasuble. I hope, Cecily, you are not inattentive.

Cecily. Oh, I am afraid I am.

Chasuble. That is strange. Were I fortunate enough to be Miss Prism's pupil, I would hang upon her lips. (Miss Prism *glares.*) I spoke metaphorically.—My metaphor was drawn from bees. Ahem! Mr. Worthing, I suppose, has not returned from town yet?

Miss Prism. We do not expect him till Monday afternoon.

Chasuble. Ah yes, he usually likes to spend his Sunday in London. He is not one of those whose sole aim is enjoyment, as, by all accounts, that unfortunate young man his brother seems to be. But I must not disturb Egeria and her pupil any longer.

Miss Prism. Egeria? My name is Laetitia, Doctor.

Chasuble (*bowing*). A classical allusion merely, drawn from the Pagan authors. I shall see you both no doubt at Evensong?

Miss Prism. I think, dear Doctor, I will have a stroll with you. I find I have a headache after all, and a walk might do it good.

Chasuble. With pleasure, Miss Prism, with pleasure. We might go as far as the schools and back.

Miss Prism. That would be delightful. Cecily, you will read your Political Economy in my absence. The chapter on the Fall of the Rupee you may omit. It is somewhat too sensational. Even these metallic problems have their melodramatic side. (*Goes down the garden with* Dr. Chasuble).

Cecily (*picks up books and throws them back on table*). Horrid Political Economy! Horrid Geography! Horrid, horrid German!

Enter Merriman *with a card on a salver.*

Merriman. Mr. Ernest Worthing has just driven over from the station. He has brought his luggage with him.

Cecily (*takes the card and reads it*). "Mr. Ernest Worthing,

B.4, The Albany, W." Uncle Jack's brother! Did you tell him Mr. Worthing was in town?

Merriman. Yes, Miss. He seemed very much disappointed. I mentioned that you and Miss Prism were in the garden. He said he was anxious to speak to you privately for a moment.

Cecily. Ask Mr. Ernest Worthing to come here. I suppose you had better talk to the housekeeper about a room for him.

Merriman. Yes, Miss. (Merriman *goes off.*)

Cecily. I have never met any really wicked person before. I feel rather frightened. I am so afraid he will look just like every one else.

Enter Algernon, *very gay and debonair.*

He does!

Algernon (*raising his hat*). You are my little cousin Cecily, I'm sure.

Cecily. You are under some strange mistake. I am not little. In fact, I believe I am more than usually tall for my age. (Algernon *is rather taken aback.*) But I am your cousin Cecily. You, I see from your card, are Uncle Jack's brother, my cousin Ernest, my wicked cousin Ernest.

Algernon. Oh! I am not really wicked at all, Cousin Cecily. You mustn't think that I am wicked.

Cecily. If you are not, then you have certainly been deceiving us all in a very inexcusable manner. I hope you have not been leading a double life, pretending to be wicked and being really good all the time. That would be hypocrisy.

Algernon (*looks at her in amazement*). Oh! Of course I have been rather reckless.

Cecily. I am glad to hear it.

Algernon. In fact, now you mention the subject, I have been very bad in my own small way.

Cecily. I don't think you should be so proud of that, though I am sure it must have been very pleasant.

Algernon. It is much pleasanter being here with you.

Cecily. I can't understand how you are here at all. Uncle Jack won't be back till Monday afternoon.

Algernon. That is a great disappointment. I am obliged to go up by the first train on Monday morning. I have a business appointment that I am anxious . . . to miss!

Cecily. Couldn't you miss it anywhere but in London?

Algernon. No: the appointment is in London.

Cecily. Well, I know, of course, how important it is not to keep a business engagement, if one wants to retain any sense of the beauty of life, but still I think you had better wait till Uncle Jack arrives. I know he wants to speak to you about your emigrating.

Algernon. About my what?

Cecily. Your emigrating. He has gone up to buy your outfit.

Algernon. I certainly wouldn't let Jack buy my outfit. He has no taste in neckties at all.

Cecily. I don't think you will require neckties. Uncle Jack is sending you to Australia.

Algernon. Australia! I'd sooner die.

Cecily. Well, he said at dinner on Wednesday night, that you would have to choose between this world, the next world, and Australia.

Algernon. Oh, well! The accounts I have received of Australia and the next world are not particularly encouraging. This world is good enough for me, Cousin Cecily.

Cecily. Yes, but are you good enough for it?

Algernon. I'm afraid I'm not that. That is why I want you to reform me. You might make that your mission, if you don't mind, cousin Cecily.

Cecily. I'm afraid I've no time, this afternoon.

Algernon. Well, would you mind my reforming myself this afternoon?

Cecily. It is rather Quixotic of you. But I think you should try.

Algernon. I will. I feel better already.

Cecily. You are looking a little worse.

Algernon. That is because I am hungry.

Cecily. How thoughtless of me. I should have remembered that when one is going to lead an entirely new life, one requires regular and wholesome meals. Won't you come in?

Algernon. Thank you. Might I have a buttonhole first? I never have any appetite unless I have a buttonhole first.

Cecily. A Maréchal Niel? (*Picks up scissors.*)

Algernon. No, I'd sooner have a pink rose.

Cecily. Why? (*Cuts a flower.*)

Algernon. Because you are like a pink rose, Cousin Cecily.

Cecily. I don't think it can be right for you to talk to me like that. Miss Prism never says such things to me.

Algernon. Then Miss Prism is a shortsighted old lady.

(Cecily *puts the rose in his buttonhole.*) You are the prettiest girl I ever saw.

Cecily. Miss Prism says that all good looks are a snare.

Algernon. They are a snare that every sensible man would like to be caught in.

Cecily. Oh, I don't think I would care to catch a sensible man. I shouldn't know what to talk to him about.

They pass into the house. Miss Prism *and* Dr. Chasuble *return.*

Miss Prism. You are too much alone, dear Dr. Chasuble. You should get married. A misanthrope I can understand—a womanthrope, never!

Chasuable (with a scholar's shudder). Believe me, I do not deserve so neologistic a phrase. The precept as well as the practice of the Primitive Church was distinctly against matrimony.

Miss Prism (sententiously). That is obviously the reason why the Primitive Church has not lasted up to the present day. And you do not seem to realize, dear Doctor, that by persistently remaining single, a man converts himself into a permanent public temptation. Men should be more careful; this very celibacy leads weaker vessels astray.

Chasuble. But is a man not equally attractive when married?

Miss Prism. No married man is ever attractive except to his wife.

Chasuble. And often, I've been told, not even to her.

Miss Prism. That depends on the intellectual sympathies of the woman. Maturity can always be depended on. Ripeness can be trusted. Young women are green. (Dr. Chasuble *starts.*) I spoke horticulturally. My metaphor was drawn from fruits. But where is Cecily?

Chasuble. Perhaps she followed us to the schools.

Enter Jack *slowly from the back of the garden. He is dressed in the deepest mourning, with crepe hatband and black gloves.*

Miss Prism. Mr. Worthing!

Chasuble. Mr. Worthing?

Miss Prism. This is indeed a surprise. We did not look for you till Monday afternoon.

Jack (shakes Miss Prism's *hand in a tragic manner).*

have returned sooner than I expected. Dr. Chasuble, I hope you are well?

Chasuble. Dear Mr. Worthing, I trust this garb of woe does not betoken some terrible calamity?

Jack. My brother.

Miss Prism. More shameful debts and extravagance?

Chasuble. Still leading his life of pleasure?

Jack (*shaking his head*). Dead!

Chasuble. Your brother Ernest dead?

Jack. Quite dead.

Miss Prism. What a lesson for him! I trust he will profit by it.

Chasuble. Mr. Worthing, I offer you my sincere condolence. You have at least the consolation of knowing that you were always the most generous and forgiving of brothers.

Jack. Poor Ernest! He had many faults, but it is a sad, sad blow.

Chasuble. Very sad indeed. Were you with him at the end?

Jack. No. He died abroad; in Paris, in fact. I had a telegram last night from the manager of the Grand Hotel.

Chasuble. Was the cause of death mentioned?

Jack. A severe chill, it seems.

Miss Prism. As a man sows, so shall he reap.

Chasuble (*raising his hand*). Charity, dear Miss Prism, charity! None of us are perfect. I myself am peculiarly susceptible to draughts. Will the interment take place here?

Jack. No. He seems to have expressed a desire to be buried in Paris.

Chasuble. In Paris! (*Shakes his head.*) I fear that hardly points to any very serious state of mind at the last. You would no doubt wish me to make some slight allusion to this tragic domestic affliction next Sunday. (Jack *presses his hand convulsively.*) My sermon on the meaning of the manna in the wilderness can be adapted to almost any occasion, joyful, or, as in the present case, distressing. (*All sigh.*) I have preached it at harvest celebrations, christening, confirmations, on days of humiliation and festal days. The last time I delivered it was in the Cathedral, as a charity sermon on behalf of the Society for the Prevention of Discontent among the Upper Orders. The Bishop, who was present, was much struck by some of the analogies I drew.

Jack. Ah! that reminds me, you mentioned christenings

I think, Dr. Chasuble? I suppose you know how to christen all right? (Dr. Chasuble *looks astounded.*) I mean, of course, you are continually christening, aren't you?

Miss Prism. It is, I regret to say, one of the Rector's most constant duties in this parish. I have often spoken to the poorer classes on the subject. But they don't seem to know what thrift is.

Chasuble. But is there any particular infant in whom you are interested, Mr. Worthing? Your brother was, I believe, unmarried, was he not?

Jack. Oh yes.

Miss Prism (*bitterly*). People who live entirely for pleasure usually are.

Jack. But it is not for any child, dear Doctor. I am very fond of children. No! the fact is, I would like to be christened myself, this afternoon, if you have nothing better to do.

Chasuble. But surely, Mr. Worthing, you have been christened already?

Jack. I don't remember anything about it.

Chasuble. But have you any grave doubts on the subject?

Jack. I certainly intend to have. Of course I don't know if the thing would bother you in any way, or if you think I am a little too old now.

Chasuble. Not at all. The sprinkling, and, indeed, the immersion of adults is a perfectly canonical practice.

Jack. Immersion!

Chasuble. You need have no apprehensions. Sprinkling is all that is necessary, or indeed I think advisable. Our weather is so changeable. At what hour would you wish the ceremony performed?

Jack. Oh, I might trot round about five if that would suit you.

Chasuble. Perfectly, perfectly! In fact I have two similar ceremonies to perform at that time. A case of twins that occurred recently in one of the outlying cottages on your own estate. Poor Jenkins the carter, a most hard-working man.

Jack. Oh! I don't see much fun in being christened along with other babies. It would be childish. Would half-past five do?

Chasuble. Admirably! Admirably! (*Takes out watch.*) And now, dear Mr. Worthing, I will not intrude any longer into a house of sorrow. I would merely beg you not to be too much bowed down by grief. What seems to us bitter trials are often blessings in disguise.

Miss Prism. This seems to me a blessing of an extremely obvious kind.

Enter Cecily *from the house.*

Cecily. Uncle Jack! Oh, I am pleased to see you back. But what horrid clothes you have got on. Do go and change them.

Miss Prism. Cecily!

Chasuble. My child! My child! (Cecily *goes towards* Jack; *he kisses her brow in a melancholy manner.*)

Cecily. What is the matter, Uncle Jack? Do look happy! You look as if you had toothache, and I have got such a surprise for you. Who do you think is in the dining room? Your brother!

Jack. Who?

Cecily. Your brother Ernest. He arrived about half an hour ago.

Jack. What nonsense! I haven't got a brother.

Cecily. Oh, don't say that. However badly he may have behaved to you in the past he is still your brother. You couldn't be so heartless as to disown him. I'll tell him to come out. And you will shake hands with him, won't you, Uncle Jack? (*Runs back into the house.*)

Chasuble. These are very joyful tidings.

Miss Prism. After we had all been resigned to his loss, his sudden return seems to me peculiarly distressing.

Jack. My brother is in the dining room? I don't know what it all means. I think it is perfectly absurd.

Enter Algernon *and* Cecily *hand in hand. They come slowly up to* Jack.

Jack. Good heavens! (*Motions* Algernon *away.*)

Algernon. Brother John, I have come down from town to tell you that I am very sorry for all the trouble I have given you, and that I intend to lead a better life in the future. (Jack *glares at him and does not take his hand.*)

Cecily. Uncle Jack, you are not going to refuse your own brother's hand?

Jack. Nothing will induce me to take his hand. I think his coming down here disgraceful. He knows perfectly well why.

Cecily. Uncle Jack, do be nice. There is some good in

everyone. Ernest has just been telling me about his poor invalid friend Mr. Bunbury whom he goes to visit so often. And surely there must be much good in one who is kind to an invalid, and leaves the pleasures of London to sit by a bed of pain.

Jack. Oh! he has been talking about Bunbury, has he?

Cecily. Yes, he has told me all about poor Mr. Bunbury, and his terrible state of health.

Jack. Bunbury! Well, I won't have him talk to you about Bunbury or about anything else. It is enough to drive one perfectly frantic.

Algernon. Of course I admit that the faults were all on my side. But I must say that I think that Brother John's coldness to me is peculiarly painful. I expected a more enthusiastic welcome, especially considering it is the first time I have come here.

Cecily. Uncle Jack, if you don't shake hands with Ernest I will never forgive you.

Jack. Never forgive me?

Cecily. Never, never, never!

Jack. Well, this is the last time I shall ever do it. (*Shakes hands with* Algernon *and glares.*)

Chasuble. It's pleasant, is it not, to see so perfect a reconciliation? I think we might leave the two brothers together.

Miss Prism. Cecily, you will come with us.

Cecily. Certainly, Miss Prism. My little task of reconciliation is over.

Chasuble. You have done a beautiful action today, dear child.

Miss Prism. We must not be premature in our judgments.

Cecily. I feel very happy. (*They all go off except* Jack *and* Algernon.)

Jack. You young scoundrel, Algy, you must get out of this place as soon as possible. I don't allow any Bunburying here.

Enter Merriman.

Merriman. I have put Mr. Ernest's things in the room next to yours, sir. I suppose that is all right?

Jack. What?

Merriman. Mr. Ernest's luggage, sir. I have unpacked it and put it in the room next to your own.

Jack. His luggage?

Merriman. Yes, sir. Three portmanteaus, a dressing case, two hatboxes, and a large luncheon basket.

Algernon. I am afraid I can't stay more than a week this time.

Jack. Merriman, order the dogcart at once. Mr. Ernest has been suddenly called back to town.

Merriman. Yes, sir. (*Goes back into the house.*)

Algernon. What a fearful liar you are, Jack. I have not been called back to town at all.

Jack. Yes, you have.

Algernon. I haven't heard anyone call me.

Jack. Your duty as a gentleman calls you back.

Algernon. My duty as a gentleman has never interfered with my pleasures in the smallest degree.

Jack. I can quite understand that.

Algernon. Well, Cecily is a darling.

Jack. You are not to talk of Miss Cardew like that. I don't like it.

Algernon. Well, I don't like your clothes. You look perfectly ridiculous in them. Why on earth don't you go up and change? It is perfectly childish to be in deep mourning for a man who is actually staying for a whole week with you in your house as a guest. I call it grotesque.

Jack. You are certainly not staying with me for a whole week as a guest or anything else. You have got to leave . . . by the four-five train.

Algernon. I certainly won't leave you so long as you are in mourning. It would be most unfriendly. If I were in mourning you would stay with me, I suppose. I should think it very unkind if you didn't.

Jack. Well, will you go if I change my clothes?

Algernon. Yes, if you are not too long. I never saw anybody take so long to dress, and with such little result.

Jack. Well, at any rate, that is better than being always overdressed as you are.

Algernon. If I am occasionally a little overdressed, I make up for it by being always immensely overeducated.

Jack. Your vanity is ridiculous, your conduct an outrage, and your presence in my garden utterly absurd. However, you have got to catch the four-five, and I hope you will have a pleasant journey back to town. This Bunburying, as you call it, has not been a great success for you. (*Goes into the house.*)

Algernon. I think it has been a great success. I'm in love with Cecily, and that is everything.

Enter Cecily *at the back of the garden. She picks up the can and begins to water the flowers.*

But I must see her before I go, and make arrangements for another Bunbury. Ah, there she is.

Cecily. Oh, I merely came back to water the roses. I thought you were with Uncle Jack.

Algernon. He's gone to order the dogcart for me.

Cecily. Oh, is he going to take you for a nice drive?

Algernon. He's going to send me away.

Cecily. Then have we got to part?

Algernon. I am afraid so. It's a very painful parting.

Cecily. It is always painful to part from people whom one has known for a very brief space of time. The absence of old friends one can endure with equanimity. But even a momentary separation from anyone to whom one has just been introduced is almost unbearable.

Algernon. Thank you.

Enter Merriman.

Merriman. The dogcart is at the door, sir.

(Algernon *looks appealing at* Cecily.)

Cecily. It can wait, Merriman . . . for . . . five minutes.

Merriman. Yes, miss.

Exit Merriman.

Algernon. I hope, Cecily, I shall not offend you if I state quite frankly and openly that you seem to me to be in every way the visible personification of absolute perfection.

Cecily. I think your frankness does you great credit, Ernest. If you will allow me, I will copy your remarks into my diary. (*Goes over to table and begins writing in diary.*)

Algernon. Do you really keep a diary? I'd give anything to look at it. May I?

Cecily. Oh no. (*Puts her hand over it.*) You see, it is simply a very young girl's record of her own thoughts and impressions, and consequently meant for publication. When it appears in volume form I hope you will order a copy. But pray, Ernest, don't stop. I delight in taking down from dictation. I have reached "absolute perfection." You can go on. I am quite ready for more.

Algernon (*somewhat taken aback*). Ahem! Ahem!

Cecily. Oh, don't cough, Ernest. When one is dictating one should speak fluently and not cough. Besides, I don't know how to spell a cough. (*Writes as* Algernon *speaks.*)

Algernon (*speaking very rapidly*). Cecily, ever since I first looked upon your wonderful and incomparable beauty, I have dared to love you wildly, passionately, devotedly, hopelessly.

Cecily. I don't think that you should tell me that you love me wildly, passionately, devotedly, hopelessly. Hopelessly doesn't seem to make much sense, does it?

Algernon. Cecily.

Enter Merriman.

Merriman. The dogcart is waiting, sir.

Algernon. Tell it to come round next week, at the same hour.

Merriman (*looks at* Cecily, *who makes no sign*). Yes, sir.

Merriman *retires.*

Cecily. Uncle Jack would be very much annoyed if he knew you were staying on till next week, at the same hour.

Algernon. Oh, I don't care about Jack. I don't care for anybody in the whole world but you. I love you, Cecily. You will marry me, won't you?

Cecily. You silly boy! Of course. Why, we have been engaged for the last three months.

Algernon. For the last three months?

Cecily. Yes, it will be exactly three months on Thursday.

Algernon. But how did we become engaged?

Cecily. Well, ever since dear Uncle Jack first confessed to us that he had a younger brother who was very wicked and bad, you of course have formed the chief topic of conversation between myself and Miss Prism. And of course a man who is much talked about is always very attractive. One feels there must be something in him, after all. I daresay it was foolish of me, but I fell in love with you, Ernest.

Algernon. Darling. And when was the engagement actually settled?

Cecily. On the 14th of February last. Worn out by your entire ignorance of my existence, I determined to end the matter one way or the other, and after a long struggle with myself I accepted you under this dear old tree here. The next day I bought this little ring in your name, and this is the little bangle with the true lovers' knot I promised you always to wear.

Algernon. Did I give you this? It's very pretty, isn't it?

Cecily. Yes, you've wonderfully good taste, Ernest. It's the excuse I've always given for your leading such a bad life. And this is the box in which I keep all your dear letters. (*Kneels at table, opens box, and produces letters tied up with blue ribbon.*)

Algernon. My letters! But, my own sweet Cecily, I have never written you any letters.

Cecily. You need hardly remind me of that, Ernest. I remember only too well that I was forced to write your letters for you. I wrote always three times a week, and sometimes oftener.

Algernon. Oh, do let me read them, Cecily?

Cecily. Oh, I couldn't possibly. They would make you far too conceited. (*Replaces box.*) The three you wrote me after I had broken off the engagement are so beautiful, and so badly spelled, that even now I can hardly read them without crying a little.

Algernon. But was our engagement ever broken off?

Cecily. Of course it was. On the 22nd of last March. You can see the entry if you like. (*Shows diary.*) "Today I broke off my engagement with Ernest. I feel it is better to do so. The weather still continues charming."

Algernon. But why on earth did you break it off? What had I done? I had done nothing at all. Cecily, I am very much hurt indeed to hear you broke it off. Particularly when the weather was so charming.

Cecily. It would hardly have been a really serious engagement if it hadn't been broken off at least once. But I forgave you before the week was out.

Algernon (*crossing to her, and kneeling*). What a perfect angel you are, Cecily.

Cecily. You dear romantic boy. (*He kisses her, she puts her fingers through his hair.*) I hope your hair curls naturally, does it?

Algernon. Yes, darling, with a little help from others.

Cecily. I am so glad.

Algernon. You'll never break off our engagement again. Cecily?

Cecily. I don't think I could break it off now that I have actually met you. Besides, of course, there is the question of your name.

Algernon. Yes, of course. (*Nervously*.)

Cecily. You must not laugh at me, darling, but it had always been a girlish dream of mine to love someone whose name was Ernest. (Algernon *rises*, Cecily *also*.) There is something in that name that seems to inspire absolute confidence. I pity any poor married woman whose husband is not called Ernest.

Algernon. But, my dear child, do you mean to say you could not love me if I had some other name?

Cecily. But what name?

Algernon. Oh, any name you like—Algernon—for instance . . .

Cecily. But I don't like the name of Algernon.

Algernon. Well, my own dear, sweet, loving little darling, I really can't see why you should object to the name of Algernon. It is not at all a bad name. In fact, it is rather an aristocratic name. Half of the chaps who get into the Bankruptcy Court are called Algernon. But seriously, Cecily . . . (*moving to her*) if my name was Algy, couldn't you love me?

Cecily (*rising*). I might respect you, Ernest, I might admire your character, but I fear that I should not be able to give you my undivided attention.

Algernon. Ahem! Cecily! (*Picking up hat*.) Your Rector here is, I suppose, thoroughly experienced in the practice of all the rites and ceremonials of the Church?

Cecily. Oh, yes. Dr. Chasuble is a most learned man. He has never written a single book, so you can imagine how much he knows.

Algernon. I must see him at once on a most important christening—I mean on most important business.

Cecily. Oh!

Algernon. I shan't be away more than half an hour.

Cecily. Considering that we have been engaged since February the 14th, and that I only met you today for the first time, I think it is rather hard that you should leave me for so long a period as half an hour. Couldn't you make it twenty minutes?

Algernon. I'll be back in no time. (*Kisses her and rushes down the garden*.)

Cecily. What an impetuous boy he is! I like his hair so much. I must enter his proposal in my diary.

Enter Merriman.

Merriman. A Miss Fairfax just called to see Mr. Worthing. On very important business, Miss Fairfax states.
Cecily. Isn't Mr. Worthing in his library?
Merriman. Mr. Worthing went over in the direction of the Rectory some time ago.
Cecily. Pray ask the lady to come out here; Mr. Worthing is sure to be back soon. And you can bring tea.
Merriman. Yes, Miss. (*Goes out.*)
Cecily. Miss Fairfax! I suppose one of the many good elderly women who are associated with Uncle Jack in some of his philanthropic work in London. I don't quite like women who are interested in philanthropic work. I think it is so forward of them.

Enter Merriman.

Merriman. Miss Fairfax.

Enter Gwendolen. *Exit* Merriman.

Cecily (*advancing to meet her*). Pray let me introduce myself to you. My name is Cecily Cardew.
Gwendolen. Cecily Cardew? (*Moving to her and shaking hands.*) What a very sweet name! Something tells me that we are going to be great friends. I like you already more than I can say. My first impressions of people are never wrong.
Cecily. How nice of you to like me so much after we have known each other such a comparatively short time. Pray sit down.
Gwendolen (*still standing up*). I may call you Cecily, may I not?
Cecily. With pleasure!
Gwendolen. And you will always call me Gwendolen, won't you?
Cecily. If you wish.
Gwendolen. Then that is all quite settled, is it not?
Cecily. I hope so. (*A pause. They both sit down together.*)
Gwendolen. Perhaps this might be a favorable opportunity for my mentioning who I am. My father is Lord

Bracknell. You have never heard of papa, I suppose?

Cecily. I don't think so.

Gwendolen. Outside the family circle, papa, I am glad to say, is entirely unknown. I think that is quite as it should be. The home seems to me to be the proper sphere for the man. And certainly once a man begins to neglect his domestic duties he becomes painfully effeminate, does he not? And I don't like that. It makes men so very attractive. Cecily, mamma, whose views on education are remarkably strict, has brought me up to be extremely shortsighted; it is part of her system; so do you mind my looking at you through my glasses?

Cecily. Oh! not at all, Gwendolen. I am very fond of being looked at.

Gwendolen (*after examining* Cecily *carefully through a lorgnette*). You are here on a short visit, I suppose.

Cecily. Oh no! I live here.

Gwendolen (*severely*). Really? Your mother, no doubt, or some female relative of advanced years, resides here also?

Cecily. Oh no! I have no mother, nor, in fact, any relations.

Gwendolen. Indeed?

Cecily. My dear guardian, with the assistance of Miss Prism, has the arduous task of looking after me.

Gwendolen. Your guardian?

Cecily. Yes, I am Mr. Worthing's ward.

Gwendolen. Oh! It is strange he never mentioned to me that he had a ward. How secretive of him! He grows more interesting hourly. I am not sure, however, that the news inspires me with feelings of unmixed delight. (*Rising and going to her.*) I am very fond of you, Cecily; I have liked you ever since I met you! But I am bound to state that now that I know that you are Mr. Worthing's ward, I cannot help expressing a wish you were—well, just a little older than you seem to be—and not quite so very alluring in appearance. In fact, if I may speak candidly—

Cecily. Pray do! I think that whenever one has anything unpleasant to say, one should always be quite candid.

Gwendolen. Well, to speak with perfect candor, Cecily, I wish that you were fully forty-two, and more than usually plain for your age. Ernest has a strong upright nature. He is the very soul of truth and honor. Disloyalty would be as impossible to him as deception. But even men of the noblest possible moral character are extremely susceptible to the influence of the physical charms of others. Modern, no less than Ancient History, supplies us with many most painful examples of what I refer to. If it were not so, indeed, History would be quite unreadable.

Cecily. I beg your pardon, Gwendolen, did you say Ernest?

Gwendolen. Yes.

Cecily. Oh, but it is not Mr. Ernest Worthing who is my guardian. It is his brother—his elder brother.

Gwendolen (*sitting down again*). Ernest never mentioned to me that he had a brother.

Cecily. I am sorry to say they have not been on good terms for a long time.

Gwendolen. Ah! that accounts for it. And now that I think of it I have never heard any man mention his brother. The subject seems distasteful to most men. Cecily, you have lifted a load from my mind. I was growing almost anxious. It would have been terrible if any cloud had come across a friendship like ours, would it not? Of course you are quite, quite sure that it is not Mr. Ernest Worthing who is your guardian?

Cecily. Quite sure. (*A pause.*) In fact, I am going to be his.

Gwendolen (*inquiringly*). I beg your pardon?

Cecily (*rather shy and confidingly*). Dearest Gwendolen, there is no reason why I should make a secret of it to you. Our little country newspaper is sure to chronicle the fact next week. Mr. Ernest Worthing and I are engaged to be married.

Gwendolen (*quite politely, rising*). My darling Cecily, I think there must be some slight error. Mr. Ernest Worthing is engaged to me. The announcement will appear in the *Morning Post* on Saturday at the latest.

Cecily (*very politely, rising*). I am afraid you must be under some misconception. Ernest proposed to me exactly ten minutes ago. (*Shows diary.*)

Gwendolen (*examines diary through her lorgnette carefully*). It is very curious, for he asked me to be his wife yesterday afternoon at 5:30. If you would care to verify the incident, pray do so. (*Produces diary of her own.*) I never travel without my diary. One should always have something sensational to read in the train. I am so sorry, dear Cecily, if it is any disappointment to you, but I am afraid I have the prior claim.

Cecily. It would distress me more than I can tell you, dear Gwendolen, if it caused you any mental or physical anguish, but I feel bound to point out that since Ernest proposed to you he clearly has changed his mind.

Gwendolen (*meditatively*). If the poor fellow has been entrapped into any foolish promise I shall consider it my duty to rescue him at once, and with a firm hand.

Cecily (*thoughtfully and sadly*). Whatever unfortunate entanglement my dear boy may have got into, I will never reproach him with it after we are married.

Gwendolen. Do you allude to me, Miss Cardew, as an entanglement? You are presumptuous. On an occasion of this kind it becomes more than a moral duty to speak one's mind. It becomes a pleasure.

Cecily. Do you suggest, Miss Fairfax, that I entrapped Ernest into an engagement? How dare you? This is no time for wearing the shallow mask of manners. When I see a spade I call it a spade.

Gwendolen (*satirically*). I am glad to say that I have never seen a spade. It is obvious that our social spheres have been widely different.

Enter Merriman, *followed by the footman. He carries a salver, tablecloth, and plate stand.* Cecily *is about to retort. The presence of the servants exercises a restraining influence, under which both girls chafe.*

Merriman. Shall I lay tea here as usual, Miss?

Cecily (*sternly, in a calm voice*). Yes, as usual. (Merriman *begins to clear table and lay cloth. A long pause.* Cecily *and* Gwendolen *glare at each other.*)

Gwendolen. Are there many interesting walks in the vicinity, Miss Cardew?

Cecily. Oh! yes! a great many. From the top of one of the hills quite close one can see five counties.

Gwendolen. Five counties! I don't think I should like that; I hate crowds.

Cecily (*sweetly*). I suppose that is why you live in town? (Gwendolen *bites her lip, and beats her foot nervously with her parasol.*)

Gwendolen (*looking round*). Quite a well-kept garden this is, Miss Cardew.

Cecily. So glad you like it, Miss Fairfax.

Gwendolen. I had no idea there were any flowers in the country.

Cecily. Oh, flowers are as common here, Miss Fairfax, as people are in London.

Gwendolen. Personally I cannot understand how anybody manages to exist in the country, if anybody who is anybody does. The country always bores me to death.

Cecily. Ah! This is what the newspapers call agricultural depression, is it not? I believe the aristocracy are suffering very much from it just at present. It is almost an epidemic amongst them, I have been told. May I offer you some tea, Miss Fairfax?

Gwendolen (*with elaborate politeness*). Thank you. (*Aside.*) Detestable girl! But I require tea!

Cecily (*sweetly*). Sugar?

Gwendolen (*superciliously*). No, thank you. Sugar is not fashionable any more. (Cecily *looks angrily at her, takes up the tongs and puts four lumps of sugar into the cup.*)

Cecily (*severely*). Cake or bread and butter?

Gwendolen (*in a bored manner*). Bread and butter, please. Cake is rarely seen at the best houses nowdays.

Cecily (*cuts a very large slice of cake and puts it on the tray*). Hand that to Miss Fairfax.

Merriman *does so, and goes out with footman.* Gwendolen *drinks the tea and makes a grimace. Puts down cup at once, reaches out her hand to the bread and butter, looks at it, and finds it is cake. Rises in indignation.*

Gwendolen. You have filled my tea with lumps of sugar, and though I asked most distinctly for bread and butter, you have given me cake. I am known for the gentleness of my disposition, and the extraordinary sweetness of my nature, but I warn you, Miss Cardew, you may go too far.

Cecily (*rising*). To save my poor, innocent, trusting boy from the machinations of any other girl there are no lengths to which I would not go.

Gwendolen. From the moment I saw you I distrusted you. I felt that you were false and deceitful. I am never deceived in such matters. My first impressions of people are invariably right.

Cecily. It seems to me, Miss Fairfax, that I am trespassing on your valuable time. No doubt you have many other calls of a similar character to make in the neighborhood.

Enter Jack.

Gwendolen (*catches sight of him*). Ernest! My own Ernest!

Jack. Gwendolen! Darling! (*Offers to kiss her*.)

Gwendolen (*drawing back*). A moment! May I ask if you are engaged to be married to this young lady? (*Points to* Cecily.)

Jack (*laughing*). To dear little Cecily! Of course not! What could have put such an idea into your pretty little head?

Gwendolen. Thank you. You may! (*Offers her cheek*.)

Cecily (*very sweetly*). I knew there must be some misunderstanding, Miss Fairfax. The gentleman whose arm is at present round your waist is my dear guardian, Mr. John Worthing.

Gwendolen. I beg your pardon?

Cecily. This is Uncle Jack.

Gwendolen (*receding*). Jack! Oh!

Enter Algernon.

Cecily. Here is Ernest.

Algernon (*goes straight over to* Cecily *without noticing anyone else*). My own love! (*Offers to kiss her*.)

Cecily (*drawing back*). A moment, Ernest! May I ask you —are you engaged to be married to this young lady?

Algernon (*looking round*). To what young lady? Good heavens! Gwendolen!

Cecily. Yes: to good heavens, Gwendolen, I mean to Gwendolen.

Algernon (*laughing*). Of course not. What could have put such an idea into your pretty little head?

Cecily. Thank you. (*Presenting her cheek to be kissed*.) You may. (Algernon *kisses her*.)

Gwendolen. I felt there was some slight error, Miss Cardew. The gentleman who is now embracing you is my cousin, Mr. Algernon Moncrieff.

Cecily (*breaking away from* Algernon). Algernon Moncrieff! Oh! (*The two girls move towards each other and put their arms round each other's waists as if for protection*.)

Cecily. Are you called Algernon?

Algernon. I cannot deny it.

Cecily. Oh!

Gwendolen. Is your name really John?

Jack (*standing rather proudly*). I could deny it if I liked. I could deny anything if I liked. But my name certainly is John. It has been John for years.

Cecily (*to* Gwendolen). A gross deception has been practiced on both of us.

Gwendolen. My poor wounded Cecily!

Cecily. My sweet wronged Gwendolen!

Gwendolen (*slowly and seriously*). You will call me sister, will you not? (*They embrace.* Jack *and* Algernon *groan and walk up and down.*)

Cecily (*rather brightly*). There is just one question I would like to be allowed to ask my guardian.

Gwendolen. An admirable idea! Mr. Worthing, there is just one question I would like to be permitted to put to you. Where is your brother Ernest? We are both engaged to be married to your brother Ernest, so it is a matter of some importance to us to know where your brother Ernest is at present.

Jack (*slowly and hesitatingly*). Gwendolen—Cecily—it is very painful for me to be forced to speak the truth. It is the first time in my life that I have ever been reduced to such a painful position, and I am really quite inexperienced in doing anything of the kind. However, I will tell you quite frankly that I have no brother Ernest. I have no brother at all. I never had a brother in my life, and I certainly have not the smallest intention of ever having one in the future.

Cecily (*surprised*). No brother at all?

Jack (*cheerily*). None!

Gwendolen (*severely*). Had you never a brother of any kind?

Jack (*pleasantly*). Never. Not even of any kind.

Gwendolen. I am afraid it is quite clear, Cecily, that neither of us is engaged to be married to anyone.

Cecily. It is not a very pleasant position for a young girl suddenly to find herself in. Is it?

Gwendolen. Let us go into the house. They will hardly venture to come after us there.

Cecily. No, men are so cowardly, aren't they?

They retire into the house with scornful looks.

Jack. This ghastly state of things is what you call Bunburying, I suppose?

Algernon. Yes, and a perfectly wonderful Bunbury it

is. The most wonderful Bunbury I have ever had in my life.

Jack. Well, you've no right whatsoever to Bunbury here.

Algernon. That is absurd. One has a right to Bunbury anywhere one chooses. Every serious Bunburyist knows that.

Jack. Serious Bunburyist? Good heavens!

Agernon. Well, one must be serious about something, if one wants to have any amusement in life. I happen to be serious about Bunburying. What on earth you are serious about I haven't got the remotest idea. About everything, I should fancy. You have such an absolutely trivial nature.

Jack. Well, the only small satisfaction I have in the whole of this wretched business is that your friend Bunbury is quite exploded. You won't be able to run down to the country quite so often as you used to do, dear Algy. And a very good thing too.

Algernon. Your brother is a little off color, isn't he, dear Jack? You won't be able to disappear to London quite so frequently as your wicked custom was. And not a bad thing either.

Jack. As for your conduct towards Miss Cardew, I must say that your taking in a sweet, simple, innocent girl like that is quite inexcusable. To say nothing of the fact that she is my ward.

Algernon. I can see no possible defense at all for your deceiving a brilliant, clever, thoroughly experienced young lady like Miss Fairfax. To say nothing of the fact that she is my cousin.

Jack. I wanted to be engaged to Gwendolen, that is all. I love her.

Algernon. Well, I simply wanted to be engaged to Cecily. I adore her.

Jack. There is certainly no chance of your marrying Miss Cardew.

Agernon. I don't think there is much likelihood, Jack, of you and Miss Fairfax being united.

Jack. Well, that is no business of yours.

Algernon. If it was my business, I wouldn't talk about it. (*Begins to eat muffins.*) It is very vulgar to talk about one's business. Only people like stockbrokers do that, and then merely at dinner parties.

Jack. How you can sit there, calmly eating muffins when we are in this horrible trouble, I can't make out. You seem to me to be perfectly heartless.

Algernon. Well, I can't eat muffins in an agitated manner. The butter would probably get on my cuffs. One should always eat muffins quite calmly. It is the only way to eat them.

Jack. I say it's perfectly heartless your eating muffins at all, under the circumstances.

Algernon. When I am in trouble, eating is the only thing that consoles me. Indeed, when I am in really great trouble, as any one who knows me intimately will tell you, I refuse everything except food and drink. At the present moment I am eating muffins because I am unhappy. Besides, I am particularly fond of muffins. (*Rising.*)

Jack (*rising*). Well, there is no reason why you should eat them all in that greedy way. (*Takes muffins from* Algernon.)

Algernon (*offering teacake*). I wish you would have teacake instead. I don't like teacake.

Jack. Good heavens! I suppose a man may eat his own muffins in his own garden.

Algernon. But you have just said it was perfectly heartless to eat muffins.

Jack. I said it was perfectly heartless of you, under the circumstances. That is a very different thing.

Algernon. That may be. But the muffins are the same. (*He seizes the muffin dish from* Jack.)

Jack. Algy, I wish to goodness you would go.

Algernon. You can't possibly ask me to go without having some dinner. It's absurd. I never go without my dinner. No one ever does, except vegetarians and people like that. Besides I have just made arrangements with Dr. Chasuble to be christened at a quarter to six under the name of Ernest.

Jack. My dear fellow, the sooner you give up that nonsense the better. I made arrangements this morning with Dr. Chasuble to be christened myself at 5:30, and I naturally will take the name of Ernest. Gwendolen would wish it. We can't both be christened Ernest. It's absurd. Besides, I have a perfect right to be christened if I like. There is no evidence at all that I have ever been christened by anybody. I should think it extremely probably I never was, and so does Dr. Chasuble. It is entirely different in your case. You have been christened already.

Algernon. Yes, but I have not been christened for years.

Jack. Yes, but you have been christened. That is the important thing.

Algernon. Quite so. So I know my constitution can stand it. If you are not quite sure about your ever having been christened, I must say I think it rather dangerous your venturing on it now. It might make you very unwell. You can hardly have forgotten that someone very closely connected with you was very nearly carried off this week in Paris by a severe chill.

Jack. Yes, but you said yourself that a severe chill was not hereditary.

Algernon. It usen't to be, I know—but I daresay it is now. Science is always making wonderful improvements in things.

Jack (*picking up the muffin dish*). Oh, that is nonsense; you are always talking nonsense.

Algernon. Jack, you are at the muffins again! I wish you wouldn't. There are only two left. (*Takes them.*) I told you I was particularly fond of muffins.

Jack. But I hate teacake.

Algernon. Why on earth then do you allow teacake to be served up for your guests? What ideas you have of hospitality!

Jack. Algernon! I have already told you to go. I don't want you here. Why don't you go!

Algernon. I haven't quite finished my tea yet! and there is still one muffin left. (Jack *groans, and sinks into a chair.* Algernon *still continues eating.*)

ACT III

Morning room at the Manor House. Gwendolen *and* Cecily *are at the window, looking out into the garden.*

Gwendolen. The fact that they did not follow us at once into the house, as any one else would have done, seems to me to show that they have some sense of shame left.

Cecily. They have been eating muffins. That looks like repentance.

Gwendolen (*after a pause*). They don't seem to notice us at all. Couldn't you cough?

Cecily. But I haven't got a cough.

Gwendolen. They're looking at us. What effrontery!

Cecily. They're approaching. That's very forward of them.

Gwendolen. Let us preserve a dignified silence.

Cecily. Certainly. It's the only thing to do now.

Enter Jack *followed by* Algernon. *They whistle some dreadful popular air from a British opera.*

Gwendolen. This dignified silence seems to produce an unpleasant effect.

Cecily. A most distasteful one.

Gwendolen. But we will not be the first to speak.

Cecily. Certainly not.

Gwendolen. Mr. Worthing, I have something very particular to ask you. Much depends on your reply.

Cecily. Gwendolen, your common sense is invaluable. Mr. Moncrieff, kindly answer me the following question. Why did you pretend to be my guardian's brother?

Algernon. In order that I might have an opportunity of meeting you.

Cecily (*to* Gwendolen). That certainly seems a satisfactory explanation, does it not?

Gwendolen. Yes, dear, if you can believe him.

Cecily. I don't. But that does not affect the wonderful beauty of his answer.

Gwendolen. True. In matters of grave importance, style, not sincerity, is the vital thing. Mr. Worthing, what explanation can you offer to me for pretending to have a brother? Was it in order that you might have an opportunity of coming up to town to see me as often as possible?

Jack. Can you doubt it, Miss Fairfax?

Gwendolen. I have the gravest doubts upon the subject. But I intend to crush them. This is not the moment for German skepticism. (*Moving to* Cecily.) Their explanations appear to be quite satisfactory, especially Mr. Worthing's. That seems to me to have the stamp of truth upon it.

Cecily. I am more than content with what Mr. Moncrieff said. His voice alone inspires one with absolute credulity.

Gwendolen. Then you think we should forgive them?

Cecily. Yes. I mean no.

Gwendolen. True! I had forgotten. There are principles

at stake that one cannot surrender. Which of us should tell them? The task is not a pleasant one.

Cecily. Could we not both speak at the same time?

Gwendolen. An excellent idea! I nearly always speak at the same time as other people. Will you take the time from me?

Cecily. Certainly. (Gwendolen *beats time with uplifted finger.*)

Gwendolen and Cecily (*speaking together*). Your Christian names are still an insuperable barrier. That is all!

Jack and Algernon (*speaking together*). Our Christian names! Is that all? But we are going to be christened this afternoon.

Gwendolen (*to* Jack). For my sake you are prepared to do this terrible thing?

Jack. I am.

Cecily (*to* Algernon). To please me you are ready to face this fearful ordeal?

Alegrnon. I am!

Gwendolen. How absurd to talk of the equality of the sexes! Where questions of self-sacrifice are concerned, men are infinitely beyond us.

Jack. We are. (*Clasps hands with* Algernon.)

Cecily. They have moments of physical courage of which we women know absolutely nothing.

Gwendolen (*to* Jack). Darling!

Algernon (*to* Cecily). Darling! (*They fall into each other's arms.*)

Enter Merriman. *When he enters he coughs loudly, seeing the situation.*

Merriman. Ahem! Ahem! Lady Bracknell.

Jack. Good heavens!

Enter Lady Bracknell. *The couples separate in alarm.*

Exit Merriman.

Lady Bracknell. Gwendolen! What does this mean?

Gwendolen. Merely that I am engaged to be married to Mr. Worthing, mamma.

Lady Bracknell. Come here. Sit down. Sit down immediately. Hesitation of any kind is a sign of mental decay in the young, of physical weakness in the old. (*Turns to* Jack.) Apprised, sir, of my daughter's sudden flight by her trusty maid, whose confidence I purchased by means of a small coin, I followed her at once by a luggage train. Her unhappy father is, I am glad to say, under the impression that she is attending a more than usually lengthy lecture by the University Extension Scheme on the Influence of a permanent income on Thought. I do not propose to undeceive him. Indeed I have never undeceived him on any question. I would consider it wrong. But of course, you will clearly understand that all communication between yourself and my daughter must cease immediately from this moment. On this point, as indeed on all points, I am firm.

Jack. I am engaged to be married to Gwendolen, Lady Bracknell!

Lady Bracknell. You are nothing of the kind, sir. And now as regards Algernon! . . . Algernon!

Algernon. Yes, Aunt Augusta.

Lady Bracknell. May I ask if it is in this house that your invalid friend Mr. Bunbury resides?

Algernon (*stammering*). Oh! No! Bunbury doesn't live here. Bunbury is somewhere else at present. In fact, Bunbury is dead.

Lady Bracknell. Dead! When did Mr. Bunbury die? His death must have been extremely sudden.

Algernon (*airily*). Oh! I killed Bunbury this afternoon. I mean poor Bunbury died this afternoon.

Lady Bracknell. What did he die of?

Algernon. Bunbury? Oh, he was quite exploded.

Lady Bracknell. Exploded! Was he the victim of a revolutionary outrage? I was not aware that Mr. Bunbury was interested in social legislation. If so, he is well punished for his morbidity.

Algernon. My dear Aunt Augusta, I mean he was found out! The doctors found out that Bunbury could not live, that is what I mean—so Bunbury died.

Lady Bracknell. He seems to have had great confidence in the opinion of his physicians. I am glad, however, that he made up his mind at the last to some definite course of action, and acted under proper medical advice. And now that we have finally got rid of this Mr. Bunbury, may I ask, Mr. Worthing, who is that young person whose hand my nephew Algernon is now holding in what seems to me a peculiarly unnecessary manner?

Jack. That lady is Miss Cecily Cardew, my ward. (Lady Bracknell *bows coldly to* Cecily.)

Algernon. I am engaged to be married to Cecily, Aunt Augusta.

Lady Bracknell. I beg your pardon?

Cecily. Mr. Moncrieff and I are engaged to be married, Lady Bracknell.

Lady Bracknell (*with a shiver, crossing to the sofa and sitting down*). I do not know whether there is anything peculiarly exciting in the air of this particular part of Hertfordshire, but the number of engagements that go on seems to me considerably above the proper average that statistics have laid down for our guidance. I think some preliminary inquiry on my part would not be out of place. Mr. Worthing, is Miss Cardew at all connected with any of the larger railway stations in London? I merely desire information. Until yesterday I had no idea that there were any families or persons whose origin was a Terminus. (Jack *looks perfectly furious, but restrains himself.*)

Jack (*in a cold, clear voice*). Miss Cardew is the granddaughter of the late Mr. Thomas Cardew of 149 Belgrave Square, S.W.; Gervase Park, Dorking, Surrey; and the Sporran, Fifeshire, N.B.

Lady Bracknell. That sounds not unsatisfactory. Three addresses always inspire confidence, even in tradesmen. But what proof have I of their authenticity?

Jack. I have carefully preserved the Court Guides of the period. They are open to your inspection, Lady Bracknell.

Lady Bracknell (*grimly*). I have known strange errors in that publication.

Jack. Miss Cardew's family solicitors are Messrs. Markby, Markby, and Markby.

Lady Bracknell. Markby, Markby, and Markby? A firm of the very highest position in their profession. Indeed I am told that one of the Mr. Markbys is occasionally to be seen at dinner parties. So far I am satisfied.

Jack (*very irritably*). How extremely kind of you, Lady Bracknell! I have also in my possession, you will be pleased to hear, certificates of Miss Cardew's birth, baptism, whooping cough, registration, vaccination, confirmation, and the measles; both the German and the English variety.

Lady Bracknell. Ah! A life crowded with incident, I see; though perhaps somewhat too exciting for a young girl.

I am not myself in favour of premature experiences. (*Rises, looks at her watch.*) Gwendolen! the time approaches for our departure. We have not a moment to lose. As a matter of form, Mr. Worthing, I had better ask you if Miss Cardew has any little fortune?

Jack. Oh! about a hundred and thirty thousand pounds in the Funds. That is all. Good-by, Lady Bracknell. So pleased to have seen you.

Lady Bracknell (*sitting down again*). A moment, Mr. Worthing. A hundred and thirty thousand pounds! And in the Funds! Miss Cardew seems to me a most attractive young lady, now that I look at her. Few girls of the present day have any really solid qualities, any of the qualities that last, and improve with time. We live, I regret to say, in an age of surfaces. (*To* Cecily.) Come over here, dear. (Cecily *goes across.*) Pretty child! your dress is sadly simple, and your hair seems almost as Nature might have left it. But we can soon alter all that. A thoroughly experienced French maid produces a really marvelous result in a very brief space of time. I remember recommending one to young Lady Lancing, and after three months her own husband did not know her.

Jack. And after six months nobody knew her.

Lady Bracknell (*glares at* Jack *for a few moments. Then bends, with a practiced smile, to* Cecily). Kindly turn round, sweet child. (Cecily *turns completely round.*) No, the side view is what I want. (Cecily *presents her profile.*) Yes, quite as I expected. There are distinct social possibilities in your profile. The two weak points in our age are its want of principle and its want of profile. The chin a little higher, dear. Style largely depends on the way the chin is worn. They are worn very high, just at present. Algernon!

Algernon. Yes, Aunt Augusta!

Lady Bracknell. There are distinct social possibilities in Miss Cardew's profile.

Algernon. Cecily is the sweetest, dearest, prettiest girl in the whole world. And I don't care twopence about social possibilities.

Lady Bracknell. Never speak disrespectfully of Society, Algernon. Only people who can't get into it do that. (*To* Cecily.) Dear child, of course you know that Algernon has nothing but his debts to depend upon. But I do not approve of mercenary marriages. When I married Lord Bracknell I had no fortune of any kind. But I never dreamed for a moment of allowing that to stand in my way. Well, I suppose I must give my consent.

Algernon. Thank you, Aunt Augusta.

Lady Bracknell. Cecily, you may kiss me!

Cecily (*kisses her*). Thank you, Lady Bracknell.

Lady Bracknell. You may also address me as Aunt Augusta for the future.

Cecily. Thank you, Aunt Augusta.

Lady Bracknell. The marriage, I think, had better take place quite soon.

Algernon. Thank you, Aunt Augusta.

Cecily. Thank you, Aunt Augusta.

Lady Bracknell. To speak frankly, I am not in favor of long engagements. They give people the opportunity of finding out each other's character before marriage, which I think is never advisable.

Jack. I beg your pardon for interrupting you, Lady Bracknell, but this engagement is quite out of the question. I am Miss Cardew's guardian, and she cannot marry without my consent until she comes of age. That consent I absolutely decline to give.

Lady Bracknell. Upon what grounds, may I ask? Algernon is an extremely, I may almost say an ostentatiously, eligible young man. He has nothing, but he looks everything. What more can one desire?

Jack. It pains me very much to have to speak frankly to you, Lady Bracknell, about your nephew, but the fact is that I do not approve at all of his moral character. I suspect him of being untruthful. (Algernon *and* Cecily *look at him in indignant amazement.*)

Lady Bracknell. Untruthful! My nephew Algernon? Impossible! He is an Oxonian.

Jack. I fear there can be no possible doubt about the matter. This afternoon during my temporary absence in London on an important question of romance, he obtained admission to my house by means of the false pretense of being my brother. Under an assumed name he drank, I've just been informed by my butler, an entire pint bottle of my Perrier-Jouet, Brut, '89; wine I was specially reserving for myself. Continuing his disgraceful deception, he succeeded in the course of the afternoon in alienating the affections of my only ward. He subsequently stayed to tea, and devoured every single muffin. And what makes his conduct all the more heartless is, that he was perfectly well aware from the first that I have no brother, that I never had a brother, and that I don't intend to have a brother, not even of any kind. I distinctly told him so myself yesterday afternoon.

Lady Bracknell. Ahem! Mr. Worthing, after careful consideration I have decided entirely to overlook my nephew's conduct to you.

Jack. That is very generous of you, Lady Bracknell. My own decision, however, is unalterable. I decline to give my consent.

Lady Bracknell (*to* Cecily). Come here, sweet child. (Cecily *goes over.*) How old are you, dear?

Cecily. Well, I am really only eighteen, but I always admit to twenty when I go to evening parties.

Lady Bracknell. You are perfectly right in making some slight alteration. Indeed, no woman should ever be quite accurate about her age. It looks so calculating. . . . (*In a meditative manner.*) Eighteen, but admitting to twenty at evening parties. Well, it will not be very long before you are of age and free from the restraints of tutelage. So I don't think your guardian's consent is, after all, a matter of any importance.

Jack. Pray excuse me, Lady Bracknell, for interrupting you again, but it is only fair to tell you that according to the terms of her grandfather's will Miss Cardew does not come legally of age till she is thirty-five.

Lady Bracknell. That does not seem to me to be a grave objection. Thirty-five is a very attractive age. London society is full of women of the very highest birth who have, of their own free choice, remained thirty-five for years. Lady Dumbleton is an instance in point. To my own knowledge she has been thirty-five ever since she arrived at the age of forty, which was many years ago now. I see no reason why our dear Cecily should not be even still more attractive at the age you mention than she is at present. There will be a large accumulation of property.

Cecily. Algy, could you wait for me till I was thirty-five?

Algernon. Of course I could, Cecily. You know I could.

Cecily. Yes, I felt it instinctively, but I couldn't wait all that time. I hate waiting even five minutes for anybody. It always makes me rather cross. I am not punctual myself, I know, but I do like punctuality in others, and waiting, even to be married, is quite out of the question.

Algernon. Then what is to be done, Cecily?

Cecily. I don't know, Mr. Moncrieff.

Lady Bracknell. My dear Mr. Worthing, as Miss Cardew

states positively that she cannot wait till she is thirty-five—a remark which I am bound to say seems to me to show a somewhat impatient nature—I would beg of you to reconsider your decision.

Jack. But my dear Lady Bracknell, the matter is entirely in your own hands. The moment you consent to my marriage with Gwendolen, I will most gladly allow your nephew to form an alliance with my ward.

Lady Bracknell (*rising and drawing herself up*). You must be quite aware that what you propose is out of the question.

Jack. Then a passionate celibacy is all that any of us can look forward to.

Lady Bracknell. That is not the destiny I propose for Gwendolen. Algernon, of course, can choose for himself. (*Pulls out her watch.*) Come, dear (Gwendolen *rises*), we have already missed five, if not six, trains. To miss any more might expose us to comment on the platform.

Enter Dr. Chasuble.

Chasuable. Everything is quite ready for the christenings.

Lady Bracknell. The christenings, sir! Is not that somewhat premature?

Chasuble (*looking rather puzzled, and pointing to* Jack *and* Algernon). Both these gentlemen have expressed a desire for immediate baptism.

Lady Bracknell. At their age? The idea is grotesque and irreligious! Algernon, I forbid you to be baptized. I will not hear of such excesses. Lord Bracknell would be highly displeased if he learned that that was the way in which you wasted your time and money.

Chasuble. Am I to understand then that there are to be no christenings at all this afternoon?

Jack. I don't think that, as things are now, it would be of much practical value to either of us, Dr. Chasuble.

Chasuble. I am grieved to hear such sentiments from you, Mr. Worthing. They savor of the heretical views of the Anabaptists, views that I have completely refuted in four of my unpublished sermons. However, as your present mood seems to be one peculiarly secular, I will return to the church at once. Indeed, I have just been informed by the pew-opener that for the last hour and a half Miss Prism has been waiting for me in the vestry.

Lady Bracknell (starting.) Miss Prism! Did I hear you mention a Miss Prism?

Chasuble. Yes, Lady Bracknell. I am on my way to join her.

Lady Bracknell. Pray allow me to detain you for a moment. This matter may prove to be one of vital importance to Lord Bracknell and myself. Is this Miss Prism a female of repellent aspect, remotely connected with education?

Chasuble (somewhat indignantly). She is the most cultivated of ladies, and the very picture of respectability.

Lady Bracknell. It is obviously the same person. May I ask what position she holds in your household?

Chasuble (severely). I am a celibate, madam.

Jack (interposing). Miss Prism, Lady Bracknell, has been for the last three years Miss Cardew's esteemed governess and valued companion.

Lady Bracknell. In spite of what I hear of her, I must see her at once. Let her be sent for.

Chasuble (looking off). She approaches; she is nigh.

Enter Miss Prism *hurriedly.*

Miss Prism. I was told you expected me in the vestry, dear Canon. I have been waiting for you there for an hour and three-quarters. (*Catches sight of* Lady *Bracknell, who has fixed her with a stony glare.* Miss Prism *grows pale and quails. She looks anxiously round as if desirous to escape.*)

Lady Bracknell (in a severe, judicial voice). Prism! (Miss Prism *bows her head in shame.*) Come here, Prism! (Miss Prism *approaches in a humble manner.*) Prism! Where is that baby? (*General consternation. The* Canon *starts back in horror.* Algernon *and* Jack *pretend to be anxious to shield* Cecily *and* Gwendolen *from hearing the details of a terrible public scandal.*) Twenty-eight years ago, Prism, you left Lord Bracknell's house, Number 104, Upper Grosvenor Square, in charge of a perambulator that contained a baby of the male sex. You never returned. A few weeks later, through the elaborate investigations of the Metropolitan police, the perambulator was discovered at midnight standing by itself in a remote corner of Bayswater. It contained the manuscript of a three-volume novel of more than usually revolting sentimentality. (Miss Prism *starts in involuntary indig-*

nation.) But the baby was not there. (*Everyone looks at* Miss Prism.) Prism! Where is that baby? (*A pause*.)

Miss Prism. Lady Bracknell, I admit with shame that I do not know. I only wish I did. The plain facts of the case are these. On the morning of the day you mention, a day that is forever branded on my memory, I prepared as usual to take the baby out in its perambulator. I had also with me a somewhat old, but capacious handbag in which I had intended to place the manuscript of a work of fiction that I had written during my few unoccupied hours. In a moment of mental abstraction, for which I can never forgive myself, I deposited the manuscript in the bassinette and placed the baby in the handbag.

Jack (*who has been listening attentively*). But where did you deposit the handbag?

Miss Prism. Do not ask me, Mr. Worthing.

Jack. Miss Prism, this is a matter of no small importance to me. I insist on knowing where you deposited the handbag that contained that infant.

Miss Prism. I left it in the cloakroom of one of the larger railway stations in London.

Jack. What railway station?

Miss Prism (*quite crushed*). Victoria. The Brighton line. (*Sinks into a chair*.)

Jack. I must retire to my room for a moment. Gwendolen, wait here for me.

Gwendolen. If you are not too long, I will wait here for you all my life. (*Exit* Jack *in great excitement*.)

Chasuble. What do you think this means, Lady Bracknell?

Lady Bracknell. I dare not even suspect, Dr. Chasuble. I need hardly tell you that in families of high position strange coincidences are not supposed to occur. They are hardly considered the thing.

Noises heard overhead as if someone was throwing trunks about. Every one looks up.

Cecily. Uncle Jack seems strangely agitated.

Chasuble. Your guardian has a very emotional nature.

Lady Bracknell. This noise is extremely unpleasant. It sounds as if he was having an argument. I dislike arguments of any kind. They are always vulgar, and often convincing.

Chasuble (*looking up*). It has stopped now. (*The noise is redoubled.*)

Lady Bracknell. I wish he would arrive at some conclusion.

Gwendolen. This suspense is terrible. I hope it will last.

Enter Jack *with a handbag of black leather in his hand.*

Jack (*rushing over to Miss Prism*). Is this the handbag, Miss Prism? Examine it carefully before you speak. The happiness of more than one life depends on your answer.

Miss Prism (*calmly*). It seems to be mine. Yes, here is the injury it received through the upsetting of a Gower Street omnibus in younger and happier days. Here is the stain on the lining caused by the explosion of a temperance beverage, an incident that occurred at Leamington. And here, on the lock, are my initials. I had forgotten that in an extravagant mood I had had them placed there. The bag is undoubtedly mine. I am delighted to have it so unexpectedly restored to me. It has been a great inconvenience being without it all these years.

Jack (*in a pathetic voice*). Miss Prism, more is restored to you than this handbag. I was the baby you placed in it.

Miss Prism (*amazed*). You?

Jack (*embracing her*). Yes . . . mother!

Miss Prism (*recoiling in indignant astonishment*). *Mr.* Worthing. I am unmarried!

Jack. Unmarried! I do not deny that is a serious blow. But after all, who has the right to cast a stone against one who has suffered? Cannot repentance wipe out an act of folly? Why should there be one law for men, and another for women? Mother, I forgive you. (*Tries to embrace her again.*)

Miss Prism (*still more indignant*). Mr. Worthing, there is some error. (*Pointing to* Lady Bracknell.) There is the lady who can tell you who you really are.

Jack (*after a pause*). Lady Bracknell, I hate to seem inquisitive, but would you kindly inform me who I am?

Lady Bracknell. I am afraid that the news I have to give you will not altogether please you. You are the son of my poor sister, Mrs. Moncrieff, and consequently Algernon's elder brother.

Jack. Algy's elder brother! Then I have a brother after all. I knew I had a brother! I always said I had a brother! Cecily—how could you have ever doubted that I had a brother? (*Seizes hold of* Algernon.) Dr. Chasuble, my unfortunate brother. Miss Prism, my unfortunate brother. Gwendolen, my unfortunate brother. Algy, you young scoundrel, you will have to treat me with more respect in the future. You have never behaved to me like a brother in all your life.

Algernon. Well, not till today, old boy, I admit. I did my best, however, though I was out of practice. (*Shakes hands.*)

Gwendolen (*to* Jack). My own! But what own are you? What is your Christian name, now that you have become someone else?

Jack. Good heavens! . . . I had quite forgotten that point. Your decision on the subject of my name is irrevocable, I suppose?

Gwendolen. I never change, except in my affections.

Cecily. What a noble nature you have, Gwendolen!

Jack. Then the question had better be cleared up at once. Aunt Augusta, a moment. At the time when Miss Prism left me in the handbag, had I been christened already?

Lady Bracknell. Every luxury that money could buy, including christening, had been lavished on you by your fond and doting parents.

Jack. Then I was christened! That is settled. Now, what name was I given? Let me know the worst.

Lady Bracknell. Being the eldest son you were naturally christened after your father.

Jack (*irritably*). Yes, but what was my father's Christian name?

Lady Bracknell (*meditatively*). I cannot at the present moment recall what the General's Christian name was. But I have no doubt he had one. He was eccentric, I admit. But only in later years. And that was the result of the Indian climate, and marriage, and indigestion, and other things of that kind.

Jack. Algy! Can't you recollect what our father's Christian name was?

Algernon. My dear boy, we were never even on speaking terms. He died before I was a year old.

Jack. His name would appear in the Army Lists of the period, I suppose, Aunt Augusta?

Lady Bracknell. The General was essentially a man of peace, except in his domestic life. But I have no doubt his name would appear in any military directory.

Jack. The Army Lists of the last forty years are here. These delightful records should have been my constant study. (*Rushes to bookcase and tears the books out.*) M. Generals . . . Mallam, Maxbohm, Magley—what ghastly names they have—Markby, Migsby, Mobbs, Moncrieff! Lieutenant 1840, Captain, Lieutenant-Colonel, Colonel, General 1869, Christian names, Ernest John. (*Puts book very quietly down and speaks quite calmly.*) I always told you, Gwendolen, my name was Ernest, didn't I? Well, it is Ernest after all. I mean it naturally is Ernest.

Lady Bracknell. Yes, I remember now that the General was called Ernest. I knew I had some particular reason for disliking the name.

Gwendolen. Ernest! My own Ernest! I felt from the first that you could have no other name!

Jack. Gwendolen, it is a terrible thing for a man to find out suddenly that all his life he has been speaking nothing but the truth. Can you forgive me?

Gwendolen. I can. For I feel that you are sure to change.

Jack. My own one!

Chasuble (*to* Miss Prism). Laetitia! (*Embraces her.*)

Miss Prism (*enthusiastically*). Frederick! At last!

Algernon. Cecily! (*Embraces her.*) At last!

Jack. Gwendolen! (*Embraces her.*) At last!

Lady Bracknell. My nephew, you seem to be displaying signs of triviality.

Jack. On the contrary, Aunt Augusta, I've now realized for the first time in my life the vital Importance of Being Earnest.

TABLEAU

George Bernard Shaw:

MAJOR BARBARA

When we think of comedy we think of humor and happy endings. *Major Barbara* has both. The ending will here be left unspoiled for the reader, who will reach it soon enough; the humor is sufficiently abundant that a little may be thrown away in these introductory comments. On the whole it is close to that of Congreve and Wilde; commonly Shaw reverses a platitude, or presents a paradox. Like Wilde's Lady Bracknell, Shaw's Lady Britomart, an enormously self-possessed woman, entertains us by her imperious and sententious remarks: "I know your quiet, simple, refined poetic people like Adolphus: quite content with the best of everything." "Really, Barbara, you go on as if religion were a pleasant subject. Do have some sense of propriety." "I couldn't forgive Andrew for preaching immorality: while he practised morality."

These amusing lines barely veil their social criticism. The social criticism in Shaw's comedy, however, is different from that in most earlier comedies, for it is not directed at deviations from the norm but at the norm itself. On the whole dramatic comedy is conservative, criticizing present eccentricities—and occasionally vices—and suggesting or preaching a return to society's established norms. Beginning with the oldest comic dramatist, Aristophanes, who ridiculed the new politicians, the new philosophers, the new poets, and proceeding through Jonson and Molière, one finds in general a dissatisfaction with innovations. Shaw says something like this in his remarks accompanying *Back to Methuselah*:

> Comedy, as a destructive, derisory, critical, negative art, kept the theatre open when sublime tragedy perished. From Molière to Oscar Wilde we had a line of comedic playwrights who, if they had nothing fundamentally positive to say, were at least in revolt against falsehood and imposture, and were not only, as they claimed, "chastening morals by ridicule," but, in Johnson's phrase, clearing our minds of cant, and thereby shewing an uneasiness in the presence of error which is the surest symptom of intellectual vitality.

But Shaw turns from destructive, negative criticism to constructive, positive proposals. He ridicules the ideas of today and yesterday, so that he may offer a new idea for tomorrow. For Shaw the theater differed from the soapbox and the lecture platform he had earlier mounted to disseminate Fabian Socialism chiefly in that the theater was a more effective pulpit. In the Preface to an early play, *Mrs. Warren's Profession,* he confessed his didactic aim:

> I am convinced that fine art is the subtlest, the most seductive, the most effective instrument of moral propaganda in the world, excepting only the example of personal conduct; and then I waive even this exception in favor of the stage, because it works by exhibiting examples of personal conduct made intelligible and moving to crowds of unobservant unreflecting people to whom real life means nothing.

Fifteen years later, in the Preface to *The Shewing-up of Blanco Posnet,* he said that the theater is "a most powerful instrument for teaching the nation how to and what to think and feel."

To teach people how and what he wanted them to think and feel, Shaw had first to destroy what they had (however casually) been thinking and feeling. Comedy—which he characterized as "the fine art of disillusionment"—was the appropriate instrument. And in *Major Barbara* his strategy is to show us the disillusionment of the heroine, and the consequent beginnings of a new life founded on more profound Shavian insights. The shattering of illusions is the material of comedy as well as tragedy, but on the whole in a comedy it comes late and seems unimportant. The comic miser's illusion that money is life entertains us for four acts; he may learn in the fifth act that he is wrong, but his late enlightenment is not what makes the play entertaining or memorable. On the other hand, the disillusionment of Oedipus or Lear is the core of the play. Oedipus thought he knew all, Lear thought he was all; both kings painfully find that things are other, and their hard process of enlightenment runs through the play. Furthermore, the illusions or ideals of the comic character are usually presented as trivial and ridiculous: avarice, hypochondria, pedantry. But in *Major Barbara* Shaw gives Barbara an ideal that commands respect: the salvation of souls. And when her world collapses, she does not cry out for her money box, her pills, or her Greek lexicon; she uses the words (from the Twenty-second Psalm) that Christ had used on the Cross: "My God: why hast thou forsaken me?" She is in a world akin to Othello's, when Desdemona seemed false, or to Hamlet's, when his mother took a second husband soon after Hamlet's father had died, or to Lear's, when his daughters turned on him; the universe seems to have fallen apart, chaos is come again. Barbara describes her sense of loss, in a speech close to the language of tragedy:

> I stood on the rock I thought was eternal; and without a word of warning it reeled and crumbled under me. I was safe with an infinite wisdom watching me, an army marching to Salvation with me; and in a moment, at a strike of your pen in a cheque book, I stood alone; and the heavens were empty. That was the first shock of the earthquake: I am waiting for the second.

But Barbara's father immediately begins to dissipate the tragic effect: "Come, come, my daughter! don't make too much of your little tinpot tragedy." A tragic hero sees his world collapse, and faces it, recognizing what Whitehead calls "the remorseless working of things"; Barbara sees her world collapse, and is offered the possibility of a better one, which she accepts. The problems of the existence of evil and pain, which tragedy almost always raises and which there seem inscrutable, are converted by Shaw from metaphysical to sociologic and economic problems with available solutions. The momentary "Tragedy of Barbara," then, has its place in the comedy of *Major Barbara*: the disenchantment is the beginning of a new-found, well-founded joyous life.

The solutions Shaw offers, because they are new rather than traditional, must be presented at some length (most of the plays have long prefaces, too), hence the charge that Shaw's plays are "all talk." But through the talk, ideas are brilliantly set forth, allowed to clash, and are resolved. In an essay written only a few months before he died, Shaw said that opera (his mother had been an excellent singer, and he had for several years been a music critic) had taught him to shape his plays into "recitatives, arias, duets, trios, ensemble finales, and bravura pieces." Sometimes the dialogue is cut and thrust:

Barbara. Take care. It may end in your giving up the cannons for the sake of the Salvation Army.
Undershaft. Are you sure it will not end in your giving up the Salvation Army for the sake of the cannons?
Barbara. I will take my chance of that.
Undershaft. And I will take my chance of the other. (*They shake hands on it.*) Where is your shelter?
Barbara. In West Ham. At the sign of the cross. Ask anybody in Canning Town. Where are your works?
Undershaft. In Perivale St Andrews. At the sign of the sword. Ask anybody in Europe.

Sometimes it soars—but it is pointless to quote an example when the thing itself is at hand.

Shaw: Biographical Note. George Bernard Shaw (1856–1950) was born in Dublin; because he was of Protestant English stock, because he left Dublin for England before he was twenty (thus spending only about one-fifth of his life in Ireland), and because almost all of his plays were written for the English stage, his Irish birth cannot disqualify him from this collection. His formal schooling ceased when he was fifteen, but he read widely, especially in English literature and in economics, and from his mother he learned much about music. In 1884 he joined the new Fabian Society (his *Intelligent Woman's Guide to Socialism and Capitalism* is a detailed presentation of the society's principles). He wrote novels, journalism, music criticism, and pamphlets before he wrote his first play (*Widowers' Houses,* 1892); he said he turned to playwriting in order to help out a producer who was looking for the enlightened drama Shaw had been clamoring for. From 1895 to 1898, while writing dramatic criticism for the *Saturday Review* (London), Shaw wrote such notable plays as *You Never Can Tell, Candida,* and *The Devil's Disciple.* In 1905 he wrote

Major Barbara. By the time he died he had written more than fifty plays.

Suggested References:

Bentley, Eric, *Bernard Shaw*, rev. ed., Norfolk, Conn., New Directions, 1957.

Chesterton, G. K., *George Bernard Shaw*, New York, Devin-Adair, 1950; New York, Hill and Wang, 1956; London, Bodley Head, 1948.

Henderson, Archibald, *George Bernard Shaw: Man of the Century*, New York, Appleton-Century-Crofts, 1956.

Mander, Raymond, and Joe Mitchenson, *Theatrical Companion to Shaw*, New York, Pitman Publishing Corp., 1955; London, Rockliff Publishing Corp., 1955.

Ussher, Arland, *Three Great Irishmen: Shaw, Yeats, Joyce*, New York, Devin-Adair, 1953; New York, New American Library (Mentor Books), 1957.

NOTE: Because orthography was one of Shaw's serious interests, the editors have not altered his spelling to conform to American usage.

Preface to Major Barbara

First Aid to Critics

Before dealing with the deeper aspects of Major Barbara, let me, for the credit of English literature, make a protest against an unpatriotic habit into which many of my critics have fallen. Whenever my view strikes them as being at all outside the range of, say, an ordinary suburban churchwarden, they conclude that I am echoing Schopenhauer, Nietzsche, Ibsen, Strindberg, Tolstoy, or some other heresiarch in northern or eastern Europe.

I confess there is something flattering in this simple faith in my accomplishment as a linguist and my erudition as a philosopher. But I cannot countenance the assumption that life and literature are so poor in these islands that we must go abroad for all dramatic material that is not common and all ideas that are not superficial. I therefore venture to put my critics in possession of certain facts concerning my contact with modern ideas:

About half a century ago, an Irish novelist, Charles Lever, wrote a story entitled A Day's Ride: A Life's Romance. It was published by Charles Dickens in Household Words, and proved so strange to the public taste that Dickens pressed Lever to make short work of it. I read scraps of this novel when I was a child; and it made an enduring impression on me. The hero was a very romantic hero, trying to live bravely, chivalrously, and powerfully by dint of mere romance-fed imagination, without courage, without means, without knowledge, without skill, without anything real except his bodily appetites. Even in my childhood I found in this poor devil's unsuccessful encounters with the facts of life, a poignant quality that romantic fiction lacked. The book, in spite of its first failure, is not dead: I saw its title the other day in the catalogue of Tauchnitz.

Now why is it that when I also deal in the tragi-comic irony of the conflict between real life and the romantic imagination, critics never affiliate me to my countryman and immediate forerunner, Charles Lever, whilst they confidently derive me from a Norwegian author of whose language I do not know three words, and of whom I knew nothing until years after the Shavian *Anschauung* was already unequivocally declared in books full of what came, ten years later, to be perfunctorily labelled Ibsenism? I was not Ibsenist even at second hand; for Lever, though he may have read Henri Beyle, *alias* Stendhal, certainly never read Ibsen. Of the books that made Lever popular, such as Charles O'Malley and Harry Lorrequer, I know nothing but the names and some of the illustrations. But the story of the day's ride and life's romance of Potts (claiming alliance with Pozzo di Borgo) caught me and fascinated me as something strange and significant, though I already knew all about Alnaschar and Don Quixote and Simon Tappertit and many another romantic hero mocked by reality. From the plays of Aristophanes to the tales of Stevenson that mockery has been made familiar to all who are properly saturated with letters.

Where, then, was the novelty in Lever's tale? Partly, I think, in a new seriousness in dealing with Potts's disease. Formerly, the contrast between madness and sanity was deemed comic: Hogarth shews us how fashionable people went in parties to Bedlam to laugh at the lunatics. I myself have had a village idiot exhibited to me as something irresistibly funny. On the stage the madman was once a regular comic figure: that was how Hamlet got his opportunity before Shakespear touched him. The originality of Shakespear's version lay in his taking the lunatic sympathetically and seriously, and thereby making an advance towards the eastern consciousness of the fact that lunacy may be inspiration in disguise, since a man who has more brains than his fellows necessarily appears as mad to them as one who has less. But Shakespear did not do for Pistol and Parolles what he did for Hamlet. The particular sort of madman they represented, the romantic make-believer, lay outside the pale of sympathy in literature: he was pitilessly despised and ridiculed here as he was in the east under the name of Alnaschar, and was doomed to be, centuries later, under the name of Simon Tappertit. When Cervantes relented over Don Quixote, and Dickens relented over Pickwick, they did not become impartial: they simply changed sides, and became friends and apologists where they had formerly been mockers.

In Lever's story there is a real change of attitude. There is no relenting towards Potts: he never gains our affections like Don Quixote and Pickwick: he has not even the infatuate courage of Tappertit. But we dare not laugh at him, because, somehow, we recognize ourselves in Potts. We may, some of us, have enough nerve, enough muscle, enough luck, enough tact or skill or address or knowledge to carry things off better than he did; to impose on the people who saw through him; to fascinate Katinka (who cut Potts so ruthlessly at the end of the story); but for all that, we know that Potts plays an enormous part in ourselves and in the world, and that the social problem is not a problem of story-book heroes of the older pattern, but a problem of Pottses, and of how to make men of them. To fall back on my old phrase, we have the feeling—one that Alnaschar, Pistol, Parolles, and Tappertit never gave us—that Potts is a piece of really scientific natural history as distinguished from funny story telling. His author is not throwing a stone at a creature of another and inferior order, but making a confession, with the effect that the stone hits each of us full in the conscience and causes our self-esteem to smart very sorely. Hence the failure of Lever's book to please the readers of Household Words. That pain in the self-esteem nowadays causes critics to raise a cry of Ibsenism. I therefore assure them that the sensation first came to me from Lever and may have come to him from Beyle, or at least out of the Stendhalian atmosphere. I exclude the hypothesis of complete originality on Lever's part, because a man can no more be completely original in that sense than a tree can grow out of air.

Another mistake as to my literary ancestry is made whenever I violate the romantic convention that all women are angels when they are not devils; that they are better looking than men; that their part in courtship is entirely passive; and that the human female form is the most beautiful object in nature. Schopenhauer wrote a splenetic essay which, as it is neither polite nor profound, was probably intended to knock this nonsense violently on the head. A sentence denouncing the idolized form as ugly has been largely quoted. The English critics have read that sentence; and I must here affirm, with as much gentleness as the implication will bear, that it has yet to be proved that they have dipped any deeper. At all events, whenever an

English playwright represents a young and marriageable woman as being anything but a romantic heroine, he is disposed of without further thought as an echo of Schopenhauer. My own case is a specially hard one, because, when I implore the critics who are obsessed with the Schopenhauerian formula to remember that playwrights, like sculptors, study their figures from life, and not from philosophic essays, they reply passionately that I am not a playwright and that my stage figures do not live. But even so, I may and do ask them why, if they must give the credit of my plays to a philosopher, they do not give it to an English philosopher? Long before I ever read a word by Schopenhauer, or even knew whether he was a philosopher or a chemist, the Socialist revival of the eighteen-eighties brought me into contact, both literary and personal, with Ernest Belfort Bax, an English Socialist and philosophic essayist, whose handling of modern feminism would provoke romantic protests from Schopenhauer himself, or even Strindberg. As a matter of fact I hardly noticed Schopenhauer's disparagements of women when they came under my notice later on, so thoroughly had Bax familiarized me with the homoist attitude, and forced me to recognize the extent to which public opinion, and consequently legislation and jurisprudence, is corrupted by feminist sentiment.

Belfort Bax's essays were not confined to the Feminist question. He was a ruthless critic of current morality. Other writers have gained sympathy for dramatic criminals by eliciting the alleged "soul of goodness in things evil"; but Bax would propound some quite undramatic and apparently shabby violation of our commercial law and morality, and not merely defend it with the most disconcerting ingenuity, but actually prove it to be a positive duty that nothing but the certainty of police persecution should prevent every right-minded man from at once doing on principle. The Socialists were naturally shocked, being for the most part morbidly moral people; but at all events they were saved later on from the delusion that nobody but Nietzsche had ever challenged our mercanto-Christian morality. I first heard the name of Nietzsche from a German mathematician, Miss Borchardt, who had read my Quintessence of Ibsenism, and told me that she saw what I had been reading: namely, Nietzsche's Jenseits von Gut und Böse. Which I protest I had never seen, and could not have read with any comfort, for want of the necessary German, if I had seen it.

Nietzsche, like Schopenhauer, is the victim in England of a single much quoted sentence containing the phrase 'big blonde beast'. On the strength of this alliteration it is assumed that Nietzsche gained his European reputation by a senseless glorification of selfish bullying as the rule of life, just as it is assumed, on the strength of the single word Superman (Übermensch) borrowed by me from Nietzsche, that I look for the salvation of society to the despotism of a single Napoleonic Superman, in spite of my careful demonstration of the folly of that outworn infatuation. But even the less recklessly superficial critics seem to believe that the modern objection to Christianity as a pernicious slave-morality was first put forward by Nietzsche. It was familiar to me before I ever heard Nietzsche. The late Captain Wilson, author of several queer pamphlets, propagandist of a metaphysical system called Comprehensionism, and inventor of the term "Crosstianity" to distinguish the retrograde element in Christendom, was wont thirty years ago, in the discussions of the Dialectical Society, to protest earnestly against the beatitudes of the Sermon on the Mount as excuses for cowardice and servility, as destructive of our will, and consequently of our honour and manhood. Now it is true that Captain Wilson's moral criticism of Christianity was not a historical theory of it, like Nietzsche's; but this objection cannot be made to Stuart-Glennie, the successor of Buckle as a philosophic historian, who devoted his life to the elaboration and propagation of his theory that Christianity is part of an epoch (or rather an aberration, since it began as recently as 6000 B.C. and is already collapsing) produced by the necessity in which the numerically inferior white races found themselves to impose their domination on the colored races by priestcraft, making a virtue and a popular religion of drudgery and submissiveness in this world not only as a means of achieving saintliness of character but of securing a reward in heaven. Here was the slave-morality view formulated by a Scotch philosopher of my acquaintance long before we all began chattering about Nietzsche.

As Stuart-Glennie traced the evolution of society to the conflict of races, his theory made some sensation among Socialists—that is, among the only people who were seriously thinking about historical evolution at all—by its collision with the class-conflict theory of Karl Marx. Nietzsche, as I gather, regarded the slave-morality as having been invented and imposed on the world by slaves making a virtue of necessity and a religion of their servitude. Stuart-Glennie regarded the slave-morality as an invention of the superior white race to subjugate the minds of the inferior races whom they wished to exploit, and who would have destroyed them by force of numbers if their minds had not been subjugated. As this process is in operation still, and can be studied at first hand not only in our Church schools and in the struggle between our modern proprietary classes and the proletariat, but in the part played by Christian missionaries in reconciling the black races of Africa to their subjugation by European Capitalism, we can judge for ourselves whether the initiative came from above or below. My object here is not to argue the historical point, but simply to make our theatre critics ashamed of their habit of treating Britain as an intellectual void, and assuming that every philosophical idea, every historic theory, every criticism of our moral, religious and juridical institutions, must necessarily be either a foreign import, or else a fantastic sally (in rather questionable taste) totally unrelated to the existing body of thought. I urge them to remember that this body of thought is the slowest of growths and the rarest of blossomings, and that if there be such a thing on the philosophic plane as a matter of course, it is that no individual can make more than a minute contribution to it. In fact, their conception of clever persons parthenogenetically bringing forth complete original cosmogonies by dint of sheer 'brilliancy' is part of that ignorant credulity which is the despair of the honest philosopher, and the opportunity of the religious impostor.

The Gospel of St. Andrew Undershaft

It is this credulity that drives me to help my critics out with Major Barbara by telling them what to say about it. In the millionaire Undershaft I have represented a man who has become intellectually and spiritually as well as practically conscious of the irresistible natural truth which we all abhor and repudiate: to wit, that the greatest of our evils, and the worst of our crimes is poverty, and that our first duty, to which every other consideration should be sacrificed, is not to be poor. "Poor but honest," "the respectable poor," and such phrases are as intolerable and as immoral as "drunken but amiable," "fraudulent but a good after-dinner speaker," "splendidly criminal," or the like. Security, the chief pretence of civilization, cannot exist where the worst of dangers, the danger of poverty, hangs over everyone's head, and where the alleged protection of our persons from violence is only an accidental result of the existence of a police force whose real business is to force the poor man to see his children starve whilst idle people overfeed pet dogs with the money that might feed and clothe them.

It is exceedingly difficult to make people realize that an evil is an evil. For instance, we seize a man and deliberately do him a malicious injury: say, imprison him for years. One would not suppose that it needed any exceptional clearness of wit to recognize in this an act of diabolical cruelty. But in England such a recognition provokes a stare of surprise, followed by an explanation that the outrage is punishment or justice or something else that is all right, or perhaps by a heated attempt to argue that we should all be robbed and murdered in our beds if such stupid villainies as sentences of imprisonment were not committed daily. It is useless to argue that even if this were true, which it is not, the alternative to adding crimes of our own to the crimes from which we suffer is not helpless submission. Chickenpox is an evil; but if I were to declare that we must either submit to it or else repress it sternly by seizing everyone who suffers from it and punishing them by inoculation with smallpox, I should be laughed at; for though nobody could deny that the result would be to prevent chickenpox to some extent by making people avoid it much more carefully, and to effect a further apparent prevention by making them conceal it very anxiously, yet people would have sense enough to see that the deliberate propagation of smallpox was a creation of evil, and must therefore be ruled out in favor of purely humane and hygienic measures. Yet in the precisely parallel case of a man breaking into my house and stealing my wife's diamonds I am expected as a matter of course to steal ten years of his life, torturing him all the time. If he tries to defeat that monstrous retaliation by shooting me, my survivors hang him. The net result suggested by the police statistics is that we inflict atrocious injuries on the burglars we catch in order to make the rest take effectual precautions against detection; so that instead of saving our wives' diamonds from burglary we only greatly decrease our chances of ever getting them back, and increase our chances of being shot by the robber if we are unlucky enough to disturb him at his work.

But the thoughtless wickedness with which we scatter sentences of imprisonment, torture in the solitary cell and on the plank bed, and flogging, on moral invalids and energetic rebels, is as nothing compared to the silly levity with which we tolerate poverty as if it were either a wholesome tonic for lazy people or else a virtue to be embraced as St Francis embraced it. If a man is indolent, let him be poor. If he is drunken, let him be poor. If he is not a gentleman, let him be poor. If he is addicted to the fine arts or to pure science instead of to trade and finance, let him be poor. If he chooses to spend his urban eighteen shillings a week or his agricultural thirteen shillings a week on his beer and his family instead of saving it up for his old age, let him be poor. Let nothing be done for "the undeserving": let him be poor. Serve him right! Also—somewhat inconsistently—blessed are the poor!

Now what does this Let Him Be Poor mean? It means let him be weak. Let him be ignorant. Let him become a nucleus of disease. Let him be a standing exhibition and example of ugliness and dirt. Let him have rickety children. Let him be cheap, and drag his fellows down to his own price by selling himself to do their work. Let his habitations turn our cities into poisonous congeries of slums. Let his daughters infect our young men with the diseases of the streets, and his sons revenge him by turning the nation's manhood into scrofula, cowardice, cruelty, hypocrisy, political imbecility, and all the other fruits of oppression and malnutrition. Let the undeserving become still less deserving; and let the deserving lay up for himself, not treasures in heaven, but horrors in hell upon earth. This being so, is it really wise to let him be poor? Would he not do ten times less harm as a prosperous burglar, incendiary, ravisher or murderer, to the utmost limits of humanity's comparatively negligible impulses in these directions? Suppose we were to abolish all penalties for such activities, and decide that poverty is the one thing we will not tolerate—that every adult with less than, say, £365 a year, shall be painlessly but inexorably killed, and every hungry half naked child forcibly fattened and clothed, would not that be an enormous improvement on our existing system, which has already destroyed so many civilizations, and is visibly destroying ours in the same way?

Is there any radicle of such legislation in our parliamentary system? Well, there are two measures just sprouting in the political soil, which may conceivably grow to something valuable. One is the institution of a Legal Minimum Wage. The other, Old Age Pensions. But there is a better plan than either of these. Some time ago I mentioned the subject of Universal Old Age Pensions to my fellow Socialist Cobden-Sanderson, famous as an artist-craftsman in bookbinding and printing. "Why not Universal Pensions for Life?" said Cobden-Sanderson. In saying this, he solved the industrial problem at a stroke. At present we say callously to each citizen "If you want money, earn it" as if his having or not having it were a matter that concerned himself alone. We do not even secure for him the opportunity of earning it: on the contrary, we allow our industry to be organized in open dependence on the maintenance of "a reserve army of unemployed" for the sake of "elasticity." The sensible course would be Cobden-Sanderson's: that is, to give every man enough to live well on, so as to guarantee the community against the possibility of a case of the malignant disease of poverty, and then (necessarily) to see that he earned it.

Undershaft, the hero of Major Barbara, is simply a man who, having grasped the fact that poverty is a crime, knows that when society offered him the alternative of poverty or a lucrative trade in death and destruction, it offered him, not a choice between opulent villainy and humble virtue, but between energetic enterprise and cowardly infamy. His conduct stands the Kantian test, which Peter Shirley's does not. Peter Shirley is what we call the honest poor man. Undershaft is what we call the wicked rich one: Shirley is Lazarus, Undershaft Dives. Well, the misery of the world is due to the fact that the great mass of men act and believe as Peter Shirley acts and believes. If they acted and believed as Undershaft acts and believes, the immediate result would be a revolution of incalculable beneficence. To be wealthy, says Undershaft, is with me a point of honor for which I am prepared to kill at the risk of my own life. This preparedness is, as he says, the final test of sincerity. Like Froissart's medieval hero, who saw that "to rob and pill was a good life" he is not the dupe of that public sentiment against killing which is propagated and endowed by people who would otherwise be killed themselves, or of the mouth-honor paid to poverty and obedience by rich and insubordinate do-nothings who want to rob the poor without courage and command them without superiority. Froissart's knight, in placing the achievement of a good life before all the other duties—which indeed are not duties at all when they conflict with it, but plain wickedness—behaved bravely, admirably, and, in the final analysis, public-spiritedly. Medieval society, on the other hand, behaved very badly indeed in organizing itself so stupidly that a good life could be achieved by robbing and pilling. If the knight's contemporaries had been all as resolute as he, robbing and pilling would have been the shortest way to the gallows, just as, if we were all as resolute and clearsighted as Undershaft, an attempt to live by means of what is called "an independent income" would be the shortest way to the lethal chamber. But as, thanks to our political imbecility and personal cowardice (fruits of poverty, both), the best imitation of a good life now procurable is life on an independent income, all sensible people aim at securing such an income, and are, of course, careful to legalize and moralize both it and all the actions and sentiments which lead to it and support it as an institution. What else can they do? They know, of course, that they are rich because others are poor. But they cannot help that: it is for the poor to repudiate poverty when they have had enough of it. The thing can be done easily enough: the demonstrations to the contrary made by the economists, jurists, moralists and sentimentalists hired by the rich to defend them, or even doing the work gratuitously out of sheer folly and abjectness, imposed only on those who want to be imposed on.

The reason why the independent income-tax payers are not solid in defence of their position is that since we are not medieval rovers through a sparsely populated country, the poverty of those we rob prevents our having the good life for which we sacrifice them. Rich men or aristocrats with a developed sense of life—men like Ruskin and William Morris and Kropotkin—have enormous social appetites and very fastidious personal ones. They are not content with handsome houses: they want handsome cities. They are not content with bediamonded wives and blooming daughters: they complain because the charwoman is badly dressed, because the laundress smells of gin, because the sempstress is anemic, because every man they meet is not a friend and every woman not a romance. They turn up their noses at their neighbor's drains, and are made ill by the architecture of their neighbor's houses. Trade patterns made to suit vulgar people do not please them (and they can get nothing else): they cannot sleep nor sit at ease upon "slaughtered" cabinet makers' furniture. The very air is not good enough for them: there is too much factory smoke in it. They even demand abstract conditions: justice, honor, a noble moral atmosphere, a mystic nexus to replace the cash nexus. Finally they declare that though to rob and pill with your own hand on horseback and in steel coat may have been a good life, to rob and pill by the hands of the policeman, the bailiff, and the soldier, and to underpay them meanly for doing it, is not a good life, but rather fatal to all possibility of even a tolerable one. They call on the poor to revolt, and, finding the poor shocked at their ungentlemanliness, despairingly revile the proletariat for its "damned wantlessness" (*verdammte Bedürfnislosigkeit*).

So far, however, their attack on society has lacked simplicity. The poor do not share their tastes nor understand their art-criticisms. They do not want the simple life, nor the esthetic life; on the contrary, they want very much to wallow in all the costly vulgarities from which the elect souls among the rich turn away with loathing. It is by surfeit and not by abstinence that they will be cured of their hankering after unwholesome sweets. What they do dislike and despise and are ashamed of is poverty. To ask them to fight for the difference between the Christmas number of the Illustrated London News and the Kelmscott Chaucer is silly: they prefer the News. The difference between a stock-broker's cheap and dirty starched white shirt and collar and the comparatively costly and carefully dyed blue shirt of William Morris is a difference so disgraceful to Morris in their eyes that if they fought on the subject at all, they would fight in defence of the starch. "Cease to be slaves, in order that you may become cranks" is not a very inspiring call to arms; nor is it really improved by substituting saints for cranks. Both terms denote men of genius; and the common man does not want to live the life of a man of genius: he would much rather live the life of a pet collie if that were the only alternative. But he does want more money. Whatever else he may be vague about, he is clear about that. He may or may not prefer Major Barbara to the Drury Lane pantomime; but he always prefers five hundred pounds to five hundred shillings.

Now to deplore this preference as sordid, and teach children that it is sinful to desire money, is to strain towards the extreme possible limit of impudence in lying and corruption in hypocrisy. The universal regard for money is the one hopeful fact in our civilization, the one sound spot in our social conscience. Money is the most important thing in the world. It represents health, strength, honor, generosity and beauty as conspicuously and undeniably as the want of it represents illness, weakness, disgrace, meanness and ugliness. Not the least of its virtues is that it destroys base people as certainly as it fortifies and dignifies noble people. It is only when it is cheapened to worthlessness for some and made impossibly dear to others, that it becomes a curse. In short, it is a curse only in such foolish social conditions that life itself is a curse. For the two things are inseparable: money is the counter that enables life to be distributed socially: it *is* life as truly as sovereigns and bank notes are money. The first duty of every citizen is to insist on having money on reasonable terms; and this demand is not complied with by giving four men three shillings each for ten or twelve hours' drudgery and one man a thousand pounds for nothing. The crying need of the nation is not for better morals, cheaper bread, temperance, liberty, culture, redemption of fallen sisters and erring brothers, nor the grace, love and fellowship of the Trinity, but simply for enough money. And the evil to be attacked is not sin, suffering, greed, priestcraft, kingcraft, demagogy, monopoly, ignorance, drink, war, pestilence, nor any other of the scapegoats which reformers sacrifice, but simply poverty.

Once take your eyes from the ends of the earth and fix them on this truth just under your nose; and Andrew Undershaft's views will not perplex you in the least. Unless indeed his constant sense that he is only the instrument of a Will or Life Force which uses him for purposes wider than his own, may puzzle you. If so, that is because you are walking either in artificial Darwinian darkness, or in mere stupidity. All genuinely religious people have that consciousness. To them Undershaft the Mystic will be quite intelligible, and his perfect comprehension of his daughter the Salvationist and her lover the Euripidean republican natural and inevitable. That, however, is not new, even on the stage. What is new, as far as I know, is that article in Undershaft's religion which recognizes in Money the first need and in poverty the vilest sin of man and society.

This dramatic conception has not, of course, been attained *per saltum*. Nor has it been borrowed from Nietzsche or from any man born beyond the Channel. The late Samuel Butler, in his own department the greatest English writer of the latter half of the XIX century, steadily inculcated the necessity and morality of a conscientious Laodiceanism in religion and of an earnest and constant sense of the importance of money. It drives one almost to despair of English literature when one sees so extraordinary a study of English life as Butler's posthumous Way of All Flesh making so little impression that when, some years later, I produce plays in which Butler's extraordinarily fresh, free and future-piercing suggestions have an obvious share, I am met with nothing but vague cacklings about Ibsen and Nietzsche, and am only too thankful that they are not about Alfred de Musset and Georges Sand. Really, the English do not deserve to have great men. They allowed Butler to die practically unknown, whilst I, a comparatively insignificant Irish journalist, was leading them by the nose into an advertisement of me which has made my own life a burden. In Sicily there is a Via Samuele Butler. When an English tourist sees it, he either asks "Who the devil was Samuele Butler?" or wonders why the Sicilians should perpetuate the memory of the author of Hudibras.

Well, it cannot be denied that the English are only too anxious to recognize a man of genius if somebody will kindly point him out to them. Having pointed myself out in this manner with some success, I now point out Samuel Butler, and trust that in consequence I shall hear a little less in future of the novelty and foreign origin of the ideas which are now making their way into the English theatre through plays written by Socialists. There are living men whose originality and power are as obvious as Butler's and when they die that fact will be discovered. Meanwhile I recommend them to insist on their own merits as an important part of their own business.

The Salvation Army

When Major Barbara was produced in London, the second act was reported in an important northern newspaper as a withering attack on the Salvation Army, and the despairing ejaculation of Barbara deplored by a London daily as a tasteless blasphemy. And they were set right, not by the professed critics of the theatre, but by religious and philosophical publicists like Sir Oliver Lodge and Dr Stanton Coit, and strenuous Nonconformist journalists like William Stead, who not only understood the act as well as the Salvationists themselves, but also saw it in its relation to the religious life of the nation, a life which seems to lie not only outside the sympathy of many of our theatre critics, but actually outside their knowledge of society. Indeed nothing could be more ironically curious than the confrontation Major Barbara effected of the theatre enthusiasts with the religious enthusiasts. On the one hand was the playgoer, always seeking pleasure, paying exorbitantly for it, suffering unbearable discomforts for it, and hardly every getting it. On the other hand was the Salvationist, repudiating gaiety and courting effort and sacrifice, yet always in the wildest spirits, laughing, joking, singing, rejoicing, drumming, and tambourining: his life flying by in a flash of excitement, and his death arriving as a climax of triumph. And, if you please, the playgoer despising the Salvationist as a joyless person, shut out from the heaven of the theatre, self-condemned to a life of hideous gloom; and the Salvationist mourning over the playgoer as over a prodigal with vine leaves in his hair, careering outrageously to hell amid the popping of champagne corks and the ribald laughter of sirens! Could misunderstanding be more complete, or sympathy worse misplaced?

Fortunately, the Salvationists are more accessible to the religious character of the drama than the playgoers to the gay energy and artistic fertility of religion. They can see, when it is pointed out to them, that a theatre, as a place where two or three are gathered together, takes from that divine presence an inalienable sanctity of which the grossest and profanest farce can no more deprive it than a hypocritical sermon by a snobbish bishop can desecrate Westminster Abbey. But in our professional playgoers this indispensable preliminary conception of sanctity seems wanting. They talk of actors as mimes and mummers, and, I fear, think of dramatic authors as liars and pandars, whose main business is the voluptuous soothing of the tired city speculator when what he calls the serious business of the day is over. Passion, the life of drama, means nothing to them but primitive sexual excitement: such phrases as "impassioned poetry" or "passionate love of truth" have fallen quite out of their vocabulary and been replaced by "passional crime" and the like. They assume, as far as I can gather, that people in whom passion has a larger scope are passionless and therefore uninteresting. Consequently they come to think of religious people as people who are not interesting and not amusing. And so, when Barbara cuts the regular Salvation Army jokes, and snatches a kiss from her lover across his drum, the devotees of the theatre think they ought to appear shocked, and conclude that the whole play is an elaborate mockery of the Army. And then either hypocritically rebuke me for mocking, or foolishly take part in the supposed mockery!

Even the handful of mentally competent critics got into difficulties over my demonstration of the economic deadlock in which the Salvation Army finds itself. Some of them thought that the Army would not have taken money from a distiller and a cannon founder: others thought it should not have taken it: all assumed more or less definitely that it reduced itself to absurdity or hypocrisy by taking it. On the first point the reply of the Army itself was prompt and conclusive. As one of its officers said, they would take money from the devil himself and be only too glad to get it out of his hands and into God's. They gratefully acknowledged that publicans not only give them money but allow them to collect it in the bar—sometimes even when there is a Salvation meeting outside preaching teetotalism. In fact, they questioned the verisimilitude of the play, not because Mrs Baines took the money, but because Barbara refused it.

On the point that the Army ought not to take such money, its justification is obvious. It must take the money because it cannot exist without money, and there is no other money to be had. Practically all the spare money in the country consists of a mass of rent, interest, and profit, every penny of which is bound up with crime, drink, prostitution, disease, and all the evil fruits of poverty, as inextricably as with enterprise, wealth, commercial probity, and national prosperity. The notion that you can earmark certain coins as tainted is an unpractical individualist superstition. None the less the fact that all our money is tainted gives a very severe shock to earnest young souls when some dramatic instance of the taint first makes them conscious of it. When an enthusiastic young clergyman of the Established Church first realizes that the Ecclesiastical Commissioners receive the rents of sporting public houses, brothels, and sweating dens; or that the most generous contributor at his last charity sermon was an employer trading in female labor cheapened by prostitution as unscrupulously as a hotel keeper trades in waiters' labor cheapened by tips, or commissionaires' labor cheapened by pensions; or that the only patron who can afford to rebuild his church or his schools or give his boys' brigade a gymnasium or a library is the son-in-law of a Chicago meat King, that young clergyman has, like Barbara, a very bad quarter hour. But he cannot help himself by refusing to accept money from anybody except sweet old ladies with independent incomes and gentle and lovely ways of life. He has only to follow up the income of the sweet ladies to its industrial source, and there he will find Mrs Warren's profession and the poisonous canned meat and all the rest of it. His own stipend has the same root. He must either share the world's guilt or go to another planet. He must save the world's honor if he is to save his own. This is what all the Churches find just as the Salvation Army and Barbara find it in the play. Her discovery that she is her father's accomplice; that the Salvation Army is the accomplice of the distiller and the dynamite maker; that they can no more escape one another than they can escape the air they breathe; that there is no salvation for them through personal righteousness, but only through the redemption of the whole nation from its vicious, lazy, competitive anarchy: this discovery has been made by everyone except the Pharisees and (apparently) the professional playgoers, who still wear their Tom Hood shirts and underpay their washerwoman without the slightest misgiving as to the elevation of their private characters, the purity of their private atmospheres, and their right to repudiate as foreign to themselves the coarse depravity of the garret and the slum. Not that they mean any harm: they only desire to be, in their little private way, what they call gentlemen. They do not understand Barbara's lesson because they have not, like her, learnt it by taking their part in the larger life of the nation.

Barbara's Return to the Colors

Barbara's return to the colors may yet provide a subject for the dramatic historian of the future. To get back to the Salvation Army with the knowledge that even the Salvationists themselves are not saved yet; that poverty is not blessed, but a most damnable sin; and that when General Booth chose Blood and Fire for the emblem of Salvation instead of the Cross, he was perhaps better inspired than he knew: such knowledge, for the daughter of Andrew Undershaft, will clearly lead to something hopefuller than distributing bread and treacle at the expense of Bodger.

It is a very significant thing, this instinctive choice of the military form of organization, this substitution of the drum for the organ, by the Salvation Army. Does it not suggest that the Salvationists divine that they must actually fight the devil instead of merely praying at him? At present, it is true, they have not quite ascertained his correct address. When they do, they may give a very rude shock to that sense of security which he has gained from his experience of the fact that hard words, even when uttered by eloquent essayists and lecturers, or carried unanimously at enthusiastic public meetings on the motion of eminent reformers, break no bones. It has been said that the French Revolution was the work of Voltaire, Rousseau and the Encyclopedists. It seems to me to have been the work of men who had observed that virtuous indignation, caustic criticism, conclusive argument and instructive pamphleteering, even when done by the most earnest and witty literary geniuses, were as useless as praying, things going steadily from bad to worse whilst the Social Contract and the pamphlets of Voltaire were at the height of their vogue. Eventually, as we know, perfectly respectable citizens and earnest philanthropists connived at the September massacres because hard experience had convinced them that if they contented themselves with appeals to humanity and patriotism, the aristocracy, though it would read their appeals with the greatest enjoyment and appreciation, flattering and admiring the writers, would none the less continue to conspire with foreign monarchists to undo the revolution and restore the old system with every circumstance of savage vengeance and ruthless repression of popular liberties.

The nineteenth century saw the same lesson repeated in England. It had its Utilitarians, its Christian Socialists, its Fabians (still extant): it had Bentham, Mill, Dickens, Ruskin, Carlyle, Butler, Henry George, and Morris. And the end of all their efforts is the Chicago described by Mr Upton Sinclair, and the London in which the people who pay to be amused by my dramatic representation of Peter Shirley turned out to starve at forty because there are younger slaves to be had for his wages, do not take, and have not the slightest intention of taking, any effective step to organize society in such a way as to make that everyday infamy impossible. I, who have preached and pamphleteered like any Encyclopedist, have to confess that my methods are no use, and would be no use if I were Voltaire, Rousseau, Bentham, Marx, Mill, Dickens, Carlyle, Ruskin, Butler, and Morris all rolled into one, with Euripides, More, Montaigne, Molière, Beaumarchais, Swift, Goethe, Ibsen, Tolstoy, Jesus and the prophets all thrown in (as indeed in some sort I actually am, standing as I do on all their shoulders). The problem being to make heroes out of cowards, we paper apostles and artist-magicians have succeeded only in giving cowards all the sensations of heroes whilst they tolerate every abomination, accept every plunder, and submit to every oppression. Christianity, in making a merit of such submission, has marked only that depth in the abyss at which the very sense of shame is lost. The Christian has been like Dickens' doctor in the debtor's prison, who tells the newcomer of its ineffable peace and security: no duns; no tyrannical collectors of rates, taxes, and rent; no importunate hopes nor exacting duties; nothing but the rest and safety of having no farther to fall.

Yet in the poorest corner of this soul-destroying Christendom vitality suddenly begins to germinate again. Joyousness, a sacred gift long dethroned by the hellish laughter of derision and obscenity, rises like a flood miraculously out of the fetid dust and mud of the slums; rousing marches and impetuous dithyrambs rise to the heavens from people among whom the depressing noise called "sacred music" is a standing joke; a flag with Blood and Fire on it is unfurled, not in murderous rancor, but because fire is beautiful and blood a vital and splendid red; Fear, which we flatter by calling Self, vanishes; and transfigured men and women carry their gospel through a transfigured world, calling their leader General, themselves captains and brigadiers, and their whole body an Army: praying, but praying only for refreshment, for strength to fight, and for needful MONEY (a notable sign, that); preaching, but not preaching submission; daring ill-usage and abuse, but not putting up with more of it than is inevitable; and practising what the world will let them practise, including soap and water, color and music. There is danger in such activity; and where there is danger there is hope. Our present security is nothing, and can be nothing, but evil made irresistible.

Weaknesses of the Salvation Army

For the present, however, it is not my business to flatter the Salvation Army. Rather must I point out to it that it has almost as many weaknesses as the Church of England itself. It is building up a business organization which will compel it eventually to see that its present staff of enthusiast-commanders shall be succeeded by a bureaucracy of men of business who will be no better than bishops, and perhaps a good deal more unscrupulous. That has always happened sooner or later to great orders founded by saints;

and the order founded by St William Booth is not exempt from the same danger. It is even more dependent than the Church on rich people who would cut off supplies at once if it began to preach that indispensable revolt against poverty which must also be a revolt against riches. It is hampered by a heavy contingent of pious elders who are not really Salvationists at all, but Evangelicals of the old school. It still, as Commissioner Howard affirms, "sticks to Moses," which is flat nonsense at this time of day if the Commissioner means, as I am afraid he does, that the Book of Genesis contains a trustworthy scientific account of the origin of species, and that the god to whom Jephthah sacrificed his daughter is any less obviously a tribal idol than Dagon or Chemosh.

Further, there is still too much other-worldliness about the Army. Like Frederick's grenadier, the Salvationist wants to live for ever (the most monstrous way of crying for the moon); and though it is evident to anyone who has ever heard General Booth and his best officers that they would work as hard for human salvation as they do at present if they believed that death would be the end of them individually, they and their followers have a bad habit of talking as if the Salvationists were heroically enduring a very bad time on earth as an investment which will bring them in dividends later on in the form, not of a better life to come for the whole world, but of an eternity spent by themselves personally in a sort of bliss which would bore any active person to a second death. Surely the truth is that the Salvationists are unusually happy people. And is it not the very diagnostic of true salvation that it shall overcome the fear of death? Now the man who has come to believe that there is no such thing as death, the change so called being merely the transition to an exquisitely happy and utterly careless life, has not overcome the fear of death at all: on the contrary, it has overcome him so completely that he refuses to die on any terms whatever. I do not call a Salvationist really saved until he is ready to lie down cheerfully on the scrap heap, having paid scot and lot and something over, and let his eternal life pass on to renew its youth in the battalions of the future.

Then there is the nasty lying habit called confession, which the Army encourages because it lends itself to dramatic oratory, with plenty of thrilling incident. For my part, when I hear a convert relating the violences and oaths and blasphemies he was guilty of before he was saved, making out that he was a very terrible fellow then and is the most contrite and chastened of Christians now, I believe him no more than I believe the millionaire who says he came up to London or Chicago as a boy with only three halfpence in his pocket. Salvationists have said to me that Barbara in my play would never have been taken in by so transparent a humbug as Snobby Price; and certainly I do not think Snobby could have taken in any experienced Salvationist on a point on which the Salvationist did not wish to be taken in. But on the point of conversion all Salvationists wish to be taken in; for the more obvious the sinner the more obvious the miracle of his conversion. When you advertize a converted burglar or reclaimed drunkard as one of the attractions at an experience meeting, your burglar can hardy have been too burglarious or your drunkard too drunken. As long as such attractions are relied on, you will have your Snobbies claiming to have beaten their mothers when they were as a matter of prosaic fact habitually beaten by them, and your Rummies of the tamest respectability pretending to a past of reckless and dazzling vice. Even when confessions are sincerely autobiographic we should beware of assuming that the impulse to make them was pious or that the interest of the hearers is wholesome. As well might we assume that the poor people who insist on shewing disgusting ulcers to district visitors are convinced hygienists, or that the curiosity which sometimes welcomes such exhibitions is a pleasant and creditable one. One is often tempted to suggest that those who pester our police superintendents with confessions of murder might very wisely be taken at their word and executed, except in the few cases in which a real murderer is seeking to be relieved of his guilt by confession and expiation. For though I am not, I hope, an unmerciful person, I do not think that the inexorability of the deed once done should be disguised by any ritual, whether in the confessional or on the scaffold.

And here my disagreement with the Salvation Army, and with all propagandists of the Cross (which I loathe as I loathe all gibbets) becomes deep indeed. Forgiveness, absolution, atonement, are figments: punishment is only a pretence of cancelling one crime by another; and you can no more have forgiveness without vindictiveness than you can have a cure without a disease. You will never get a high morality from people who conceive that their misdeeds are revocable and pardonable, or in a society where absolution and expiation are officially provided for us all. The demand may be very real; but the supply is spurious. Thus Bill Walker, in my play, having assaulted the Salvation Lass, presently finds himself overwhelmed with an intolerable conviction of sin under the skilled treatment of Barbara. Straightway he begins to try to unassault the lass and deruffianize his deed, first by getting punished for it in kind, and, when that relief is denied him, by fining himself a pound to compensate the girl. He is foiled both ways. He finds the Salvation Army is inexorable as fact itself. It will not punish him: it will not take his money. It will not tolerate a redeemed ruffian: it leaves him no means of salvation except ceasing to be a ruffian. In doing this, the Salvation Army instinctively grasps the central truth of Christianity and discards its central superstition: that central truth being the vanity of revenge and punishment, and that central superstition the salvation of the world by the gibbet.

For, be it noted, Bill has assaulted an old and starving woman also; and for this worse offence he feels no remorse whatever, because she makes it clear that her malice is as great as his own. "Let her have the law of me, as she said she would," says Bill: "what I done to her is no more on what you might call my conscience than sticking a pig." This shews a perfectly natural and wholesome state of mind on his part. The old woman, like the law she threatens him with, is perfectly ready to play the game of retaliation with him: to rob him if he steals, to flog him if he strikes, to murder him if he kills. By example and precept the law and public opinion teach him to impose his will on others by anger, violence, and cruelty, and to wipe off the moral score by punishment. That is sound Crosstianity. But this Crosstianity has got entangled with something which Barbara calls Christianity, and which unexpectedly causes her to refuse to play the hangman's game of Satan casting out Satan. She refuses to prosecute a drunken ruffian; she converses on equal terms with a blackguard to whom no lady should be seen speaking in the public street: in short, she imitates Christ. Bill's conscience reacts to this just as naturally as it does to the old woman's threats. He is placed in a position of unbearable moral inferiority, and strives by every means in his power to escape from it, whilst he is still quite ready to meet the abuse of the old woman by attempting to smash a mug on her face. And that is the triumphant justification of Barbara's Christianity as against our system of judicial punishment and the vindictive villainthrashings and "poetic justice" of the romantic stage.

For the credit of literature it must be pointed out that the situation is only partly novel. Victor Hugo long ago gave us the epic of the convict and the bishop's candlesticks, of the Crosstian policeman annihilated by his encounter with the Christian Valjean. But Bill Walker is not, like Valjean, romantically changed from a demon into an angel. There are millions of Bill Walkers in all classes of society today; and the point which I, as a professor of natural psychology, desire to demonstrate, is that Bill, without any change in his character or circumstances whatsoever, will react one way to one sort of treatment and another way to another.

In proof I might point to the sensational object lesson provided by our commercial millionaires today. They begin as brigands: merciless, unscrupulous, dealing out ruin and death and slavery to their competitors and employees, and facing desperately the worst that their competitors can do to them. The history of the English factories, the American Trusts, the exploitation of African gold, diamonds, ivory and rubber, outdoes in villainy the worst that has ever been imagined of the buccaneers of the Spanish Main. Captain Kidd would have marooned a modern Trust magnate for conduct unworthy of a gentleman of fortune. The law every day seizes on unsuccessful scoundrels of this type and punishes them with a cruelty worse than their own, with the result that they come out of the torture house more dangerous than they went in, and renew their evil doing (nobody will employ them at anything else) until they are again seized, again tormented, and again let loose, with the same result.

But the successful scoundrel is dealt with very differently, and very Christianly. He is not only forgiven: he is idolized, respected, made much of, all but worshipped. Society returns him good for evil in the most extravagant overmeasure. And with what result? He begins to idolize himself, to respect himself, to live up to the treatment he receives. He preaches sermons; he writes books of the most edifying advice to young men, and actually persuades himself that he got on by taking his own advice; he endows educational institutions; he supports charities; he dies finally in the odor of sanctity, leaving a will which is a monument of public spirit and bounty. And all this without any change in his character. The spots of the leopard and the stripes of the tiger are as brilliant as ever; but the conduct of the world towards him has changed; and his conduct has changed accordingly. You have only to reverse your attitude towards him—to lay hands on his property, revile him, assault him, and he will be a brigand again in a moment, as ready to crush you as you are to crush him, and quite as full of pretentious moral reasons for doing it.

In short, when Major Barbara says that there are no scoundrels, she is right: there are no absolute scoundrels, though there are impracticable people of whom I shall treat presently. Every reasonable man (and woman) is a potential scoundrel and a potential good citizen. What a man is depends on his character; but what he does, and what we think of what he does, depends on his circumstances. The characteristics that ruin a man in one class make him eminent in another. The characters that behave differently in different circumstances behave alike in similiar circumstances. Take a common English character like that of Bill Walker. We meet Bill everywhere: on the judicial bench, on the episcopal bench, in the Privy Council, at the War Office and Admiralty, as well as in the Old Bailey dock or in the ranks of casual unskilled labor. And the morality of Bill's characteristics varies with these various circumstances. The faults of the burglar are the qualities of the financier: the manners and habits of a duke would cost a city clerk his situation. In short, though character is independent of circumstances, conduct is not; and our moral judgments of character are not: both are circumstantial. Take any condition of life in which the circumstances are for a mass of men practically alike: felony, the House of Lords, the factory, the stables, the gipsy encampment or where you please! In spite of diversity of character and temperament, the conduct and morals of the individuals in each group are as predicable and as alike in the main as if they were a flock of sheep, morals being mostly only social habits and circumstantial necessities. Strong people know this and count upon it. In nothing have the master-minds of the world been distinguished from the ordinary suburban season-ticket holder more than in their straightforward perception of the fact that mankind is practically a single species, and not a menagerie of gentlemen and bounders, villains and heroes, cowards and daredevils, peers and peasants, grocers and aristocrats, artisans and laborers, washerwomen and duchesses, in which all the grades of income and caste represent distinct animals who must not be introduced to one another or intermarry. Napoleon constructing a galaxy of generals and courtiers, and even of monarchs, out of his collection of social nobodies; Julius Cæsar appointing as governor of Egypt the son of a freedman—one who but a short time before would have been legally disqualified for the post even of a private soldier in the Roman army; Louis XI making his barber his privy councillor: all these had in their different ways a firm hold of the scientific fact of human equality, expressed by Barbara in the Christian formula that all men are children of one father. A man who believes that men are naturally divided into upper and lower and middle classes morally is making exactly the same mistake as the man who believes that they are naturally divided in the same way socially. And just as our persistent attempts to found political institutions on a basis of social inequality have always produced long periods of destructive friction relieved from time to time by violent explosions of revolution; so the attempt—will Americans please note—to found moral institutions on a basis of moral inequality can lead to nothing but unnatural Reigns of the Saints relieved by licentious Restorations; to Americans who have made divorce a public institution turning the face of Europe into one huge sardonic smile by refusing to stay in the same hotel with a Russian man of genius who has changed wives without the sanction of South Dakota; to grotesque hypocrisy, cruel persecution, and final utter confusion of conventions and compliances with benevolence and respectability. It is quite useless to declare that all men are born free if you deny that they are born good. Guarantee a man's goodness and his liberty will take care of itself. To guarantee his freedom on condition that you approve of his moral character is formally to abolish all freedom whatsoever, as every man's liberty is at the mercy of a moral indictment which any fool can trump up against everyone who violates custom, whether as a prophet or as a rascal. This is the lesson Democracy has to learn before it can become anything but the most oppressive of all the priesthoods.

Let us now return to Bill Walker and his case of conscience against the Salvation Army. Major Barbara, not being a modern Tetzel, or the treasurer of a hospital, refuses to sell absolution to Bill for a sovereign. Unfortunately, what the Army can afford to refuse in the case of Bill Walker, it cannot refuse in the case of Bodger. Bodger is master of the situation because he holds the purse strings. "Strive as you will," says Bodger, in effect: "me you cannot do without. You cannot save Bill Walker without my money." And the Army answers, quite rightly under the circumstances, "We will take money from the devil himself sooner than abandon the work of Salvation." So Bodger plays his conscience-money and gets the absolution that is refused to Bill. In real life Bill would perhaps never know this. But I, the dramatist whose business it is to shew the connexion between things that seem apart and unrelated in the haphazard order of events in real life, have contrived to make it known to Bill, with the result that the Salvation Army loses its hold of him at once.

But Bill may not be lost, for all that. He is still in the grip of the facts and of his own conscience, and may find his taste for blackguardism permanently spoiled. Still, I cannot guarantee that happy ending. Walk through the poorer quarters of our cities on Sunday when the men are not working, but resting and chewing the cud of their reflections. You will find one expression common to every mature face: the expression of cynicism. The discovery made by Bill Walker about the Salvation Army has been made by everyone there. They have found that every man has his price; and they have been foolishly or corruptly taught to mistrust and despise him for that necessary and salutary condition of social existence. When they learn that General Booth, too, has his price, they do not admire him because it is a high one, and admit the need of organizing society so that he shall get it in an honorable way: they conclude that his character is unsound and that all religious men are hypocrites and allies of their sweaters and oppressors. They know that the large subscriptions which help to support the Army are endowments, not of religion, but of the wicked doctrine of docility in poverty and humility under oppression; and they are rent by the most agonizing of all the doubts of the soul, the doubt whether their true salvation must not come from their most abhorrent passions, from murder, envy, greed, stubbornness, rage, and terrorism, rather than from public spirit, reasonableness, humanity, generosity, tenderness, delicacy, pity and kindness. The confirmation of that doubt, at which our newspapers have been working so hard for years past, is the morality of militarism; and the justification of militarism is that circumstances may at any time make it the true morality of the moment. It is by producing such moments that we produce violent and sanguinary revolutions, such as the one now in progress in Russia and the one which Capitalism in England and America is daily and diligently provoking.

At such moments it becomes the duty of the Churches to evoke all the powers of destruction against the existing order. But if they do this, the existing order must forcibly suppress them. Churches are suffered to exist only on condition that they preach submission to the State as at present capitalistically organized. The Church of England itself is compelled to add to the thirtysix articles in which it formulates its religious tenets, three more in which it apologetically protests that the moment any of these articles comes in conflict with the State it is to be entirely renounced, abjured, violated, abrogated and abhorred, the policeman being a much more important person than any of the Persons of the Trinity. And this is why no tolerated Church nor Salvation Army can ever win the entire confidence of the poor. It must be on the side of the police and the military, no matter what it believes or disbelieves; and as the police and the military are the instruments by which the rich rob and oppress the poor (on legal and moral principles made for the purpose), it is not possible to be on the side of the poor and of the police at the same time. Indeed the religious bodies, as the almoners of the rich, become a sort of auxiliary police, taking off the insurrectionary edge of poverty with coals and blankets, bread and treacle, and soothing and cheering the victims with hopes of immense and inexpensive happiness in another world when the process of working them to premature death in the service of the rich is complete in this.

Christianity and Anarchism

Such is the false position from which neither the Salvation Army nor the Church of England nor any other religious organization whatever can escape except through a reconstition of society. Nor can they merely endure the State passively, washing their hands of its sins. The State is constantly forcing the consciences of men by violence and cruelty. Not content with exacting money from us for the maintenance of its soldiers and policemen, its gaolers and executioners, it forces us to take an active personal part in its proceedings on pain of becoming ourselves the victims of its violence. As I write these lines, a sensational example is given to the world. A royal marriage has been celebrated, first by sacrament in a cathedral, and then by a bullfight having for its main amusement the spectacle of horses gored and disembowelled by the bull, after which, when the bull is so exhausted as to be no longer dangerous, he is killed by a cautious matador. But the ironic contrast between the bullfight and the sacrament of marriage does not move anyone. Another contrast—that between the splendor, the happiness, the atmosphere of kindly admiration surrounding the young couple, and the price paid for it under our abominable social arrangements in the misery, squalor and degradation of millions of other young couples—is drawn at the same moment by a novelist, Mr Upton Sinclair, who chips a corner of the veneering from the huge meat packing industries of Chicago, and shews it to us as a sample of what is going on all over the world underneath the top layer of prosperous plutocracy. One man is sufficiently moved by that contrast to pay his own life as the price of one terrible blow at the responsible parties. His poverty has left him ignorant enough to be duped by the pretence that the innocent young bride and bridegroom, put forth and crowned by plutocracy as the heads of a State in which they have less personal power than any policeman, and less influence than any Chairman of a Trust, are responsible. At them accordingly he launches his sixpennorth of fulminate, missing his mark, but scattering the bowels of as many horses as any bull in the arena, and slaying twentythree persons, besides wounding ninetynine. And of all these, the horses alone are innocent of the guilt he is avenging: had he blown all Madrid to atoms with every adult person in it, not one could have escaped the charge of being an accessory, before, at, and after the fact, to poverty and prostitution, to such wholesale massacre of infants as Herod never dreamt of, to plague, pestilence and famine, battle, murder and lingering death—perhaps not one who had not helped, through example, precept, connivance, and even clamor, to teach the dynamiter his well-learnt gospel of hatred and vengeance, by approving every day of sentences of years of imprisonment so infernal in their unnatural stupidity and panic-stricken cruelty, that their advocates can disavow neither the dagger nor the bomb without stripping the mask of justice and humanity from themselves also.

Be it noted that at this very moment there appears the biography of one of our dukes, who, being a Scot, could argue about politics, and therefore stood out as a great brain among our aristocrats. And what, if you please, was his grace's favorite historical episode, which he declared he never read without intense satisfaction? Why, the young General Bonapart's pounding of the Paris mob to pieces in 1795, called in playful approval by our respectable classes "the whiff of grapeshot," though Napoleon, to do him justice, took a deeper view of it, and would fain have had it forgotten. And since the Duke of Argyll was not a demon, but a man of like passions with ourselves, by no means rancorous or cruel as men go, who can doubt that all over the world proletarians of the ducal kidney are now revelling in "the whiff of dynamite" (the flavor of the joke seems to evaporate a little, does it not?) because it was aimed at the class they hate even as our argute duke hated what he called the mob.

In such an atmosphere there can be only one sequel to the Madrid explosion. All Europe burns to emulate it. Vengeance! More blood! Tear "the Anarchist beast" to shreds. Drag him to the scaffold. Imprison him for life. Let all civilized States band together to drive his like off the face of the earth; and if any State refuses to join, make war on it. This time the leading London newspaper, anti-Liberal and therefore anti-Russian in politics, does not say "Serve you right" to the victims, as it did, in effect, when Bobrikoff, and De Plehve, and Grand Duke Sergius, were in the same manner unofficially fulminated into fragments. No: fulminate our rivals in Asia by all means, ye brave Russian revolutionaries; but to aim at an English princess! monstrous! hideous! hound down the wretch to his doom; and observe, please, that we are a civilized and merciful people, and, however much we may regret it, must not treat him as Ravaillac and Damiens were treated. And meanwhile, since we have not yet caught him, let us soothe our quivering nerves with the bullfight, and comment in a courtly way on the unfailing tact and good taste of the ladies of our royal houses, who, though presumably of full normal natural tenderness, have been so effectually broken in to fashionable routine that they can be taken to see the horses slaughtered as helplessly as they could no doubt be taken to a gladiator show, if that happened to be the mode just now.

Strangely enough, in the midst of this raging fire of

malice, the one man who still has faith in the kindness and intelligence of human nature is the fulminator, now a hunted wretch, with nothing, apparently, to secure his triumph over all the prisons and scaffolds of infuriate Europe except the revolver in his pocket and his readiness to discharge it at a moment's notice into his own or any other head. Think of him setting out to find a gentleman and a Christian in the multitude of human wolves howling for his blood. Think also of this: that at the very first essay he finds what he seeks, a veritable grandee of Spain, a noble, high-thinking, unterrified, malice-void soul, in the guise—of all masquerades in the world!—of a modern editor. The Anarchist wolf, flying from the wolves of plutocracy, throws himself on the honor of the man. The man, not being a wolf (nor a London editor), and therefore not having enough sympathy with his exploit to be made bloodthirsty by it, does not throw him back to the pursuing wolves—gives him, instead, what help he can to escape, and sends him off acquainted at last with a force that goes deeper than dynamite, though you cannot buy so much of it for sixpence. That righteous and honorable high human deed is not wasted on Europe, let us hope, though it benefits the fugitive wolf only for a moment. The plutocratic wolves presently smell him out. The fugitive shoots the unlucky wolf whose nose is nearest; shoots himself; and then convinces the world, by his photograph, that he was no monstrous freak of reversion to the tiger, but a good looking young man with nothing abnormal about him except his appalling courage and resolution (that is why the terrified shriek Coward at him): one to whom murdering a happy young couple on their wedding morning would have been an unthinkably unnatural abomination under rational and kindly human circumstances.

Then comes the climax of irony and blind stupidity. The wolves, balked of their meal of fellow-wolf, turn on the man, and proceed to torture him, after their manner, by imprisonment, for refusing to fasten his teeth in the throat of the dynamiter and hold him down until they came to finish him.

Thus, you see, a man may not be a gentleman nowadays even if he wishes to. As to being a Christian, he is allowed some latitude in that matter, because, I repeat, Christianity has two faces. Popular Christianity has for its emblem a gibbet, for its chief sensation a sanguinary execution after torture, for its central mystery an insane vengeance bought off by a trumpery expiation. But there is a nobler and profounder Christianity which affirms the sacred mystery of Equality, and forbids the glaring futility and folly of vengeance, often politely called punishment or justice. The gibbet part of Christianity is tolerated. The other is criminal felony. Connoisseurs in irony are well aware of the fact that the only editor in England who denounces punishment as radically wrong, also repudiates Christianity; calls his paper The Freethinker; and has been imprisoned for "bad taste" under the law against blasphemy.

Sane Conclusions

And now I must ask the excited reader not to lose his head on one side or the other, but to draw a sane moral from these grim absurdities. It is not good sense to propose that laws against crime should apply to principals only and not to accessories whose consent, counsel, or silence may secure impunity to the principal. If you institute punishment as part of the law, you must punish people for refusing to punish. If you have a police, part of its duty must be to compel everybody to assist the police. No doubt if your laws are unjust, and your policemen agents of oppression, the result will be an unbearable violation of the private consciences of citizens. But that cannot be helped: the remedy is, not to license everybody to thwart the law if they please, but to make laws that will command the public assent, and not to deal cruelly and stupidly with law-breakers. Everybody disapproves of burglars; but the modern burglar, when caught and overpowered by a householder, usually appeals, and often, let us hope, with success, to his captor not to deliver him over to the useless horrors of penal servitude. In other cases the lawbreaker escapes because those who could give him up do not consider his breach of the law a guilty action. Sometimes, even, private tribunals are formed in opposition to the official tribunals; and these private tribunals employ assassins as executioners, as was done, for example, by Mahomet before he had established his power officially, and by the Ribbon lodges of Ireland in their long struggle with the landlords. Under such circumstances, the assassin goes free although everybody in the district knows who he is and what he has done. They do not betray him, partly because they justify him exactly as the regular Government justifies its official executioner, and partly because they would themselves be assassinated if they betrayed him: another method learnt from the official government. Given a tribunal, employing a slayer who has no personal quarrel with the slain; and there is clearly no moral difference between official and unofficial killing.

In short, all men are anarchists with regard to laws which are against their consciences, either in the preamble or in the penalty. In London our worst anarchists are the magistrates, because many of them are so old and ignorant that when they are called upon to administer any law that is based on ideas or knowledge less than half a century old, they disagree with it, and being mere ordinary home-bred private Englishmen without any respect for law in the abstract, naïvely set the example of violating it. In this instance the man lags behind the law; but when the law lags behind the man, he becomes equally an anarchist. When some huge change in social conditions, such as the industrial revolution of the eighteenth and nineteenth centuries, throws our legal and industrial institutions out of date, Anarchism becomes almost a religion. The whole force of the most energetic geniuses of the time in philosophy, economics, and art, concentrates itself on demonstrations and reminders that morality and law are only conventions, fallible and continually obsolescing. Tragedies in which the heroes are bandits, and comedies in which law-abiding and conventionally moral folk are compelled to satirize themselves by outraging the conscience of the spectators every time they do their duty, appear simultaneously with economic treatises entitled "What is Property? Theft!" and with histories of "The Conflict between Religion and Science."

Now this is not a healthy state of things. The advantages of living in society are proportionate, not to the freedom of the individual from a code, but to the complexity and subtlety of the code he is prepared not only to accept but to uphold as a matter of such vital importance that a law-breaker at large is hardly to be tolerated on any plea. Such an attitude becomes impossible when the only men who can make themselves heard and remembered throughout the world spend all their energy in raising our gorge against current law, current morality, current respectability, and legal property. The ordinary man, uneducated in social theory even when he is schooled in Latin verse, cannot be set against all the laws of his country and yet persuaded to regard law in the abstract as vitally necessary to society. Once he is brought to repudiate the laws and institutions he knows, he will repudiate the very conception of law and the very groundwork of institutions, ridiculing human rights, extolling brainless methods as "historical," and tolerating nothing except pure empiricism in conduct, with dynamite as the basis of politics and vivisection as the basis of science. That is hideous; but what is to be done? Here am I, for instance, by class a respectable man, by common sense a hater of waste and disorder, by intellectual constitution legally minded to the verge of pedantry, and by temperament apprehensive and economically disposed to the limit of old-maidishness; yet I am, and have always been, and shall now always be, a revolutionary writer, because our laws make law impossible; our liberties destroy all freedom; our property is organized robbery; our morality is an impudent hypocrisy; our wisdom is administered by inexperienced or malexperienced dupes, our power wielded by cowards and weaklings, and our honor false in all its points. I am an enemy of the existing order for good reasons; but that does not make my attacks any less encouraging or helpful to people who are its enemies for bad reasons. The existing order may shriek that if I tell the truth about it, some foolish person may drive it to become still worse by trying to assassinate it. I cannot help that, even if I could see what worse it could do than it is already doing. And the disadvantage of that worst even from its own point of view is that society, with all its prisons and bayonets and whips and ostracisms and starvations, is powerless in the face of the Anarchist who is prepared to sacrifice his own life in the battle with it. Our natural safety from the cheap and devastating explosives which every Russian student can make, and every Russian grenadier has learnt to handle in Manchuria, lies in the fact that brave and resolute men, when they are rascals, will not risk their skins for the good of humanity, and, when they are not, are sympathetic enough to care for humanity, abhorring murder, and never committing it until their consciences are outraged beyond endurance. The remedy is, then, simply not to outrage their consciences.

Do not be afraid that they will not make allowances. All men make very large allowances indeed before they stake their own lives in a war to the death with society. Nobody demands or expects the millennium. But there are two things that must be set right, or we shall perish, like Rome, of soul atrophy disguised as empire.

The first is, that the daily ceremony of dividing the

wealth of the country among its inhabitants shall be so conducted that no crumb shall, save as a criminal's ration, go to any able-bodied adults who are not producing by their personal exertions not only a full equivalent for what they take, but a surplus sufficient to provide for their superannuation and pay back the debt due for their nurture.

The second is that the deliberate infliction of malicious injuries which now goes on under the name of punishment be abandoned; so that the thief, the ruffian, the gambler, and the beggar, may without inhumanity be handed over to the law, and made to understand that a State which is too humane to punish will also be too thrifty to waste the life of honest men in watching or restraining dishonest ones. That is why we do not imprison dogs. We even take our chance of their first bite. But if a dog delights to bark and bite, it goes to the lethal chamber. That seems to me sensible. To allow the dog to expiate his bite by a period of torment, and then let him loose in a much more savage condition (for the chain makes a dog savage) to bite again and expiate again, having meanwhile spent a great deal of human life and happiness in the task of chaining and feeding and tormenting him, seems to me idiotic and superstitious. Yet that is what we do to men who bark and bite and steal. It would be far more sensible to put up with their vices, as we put up with their illnesses, until they give more trouble than they are worth, at which point we should, with many apologies and expressions of sympathy, and some generosity in complying with their last wishes, place them in the lethal chamber and get rid of them. Under no circumstances should they be allowed to expiate their misdeeds by a manufactured penalty, to subscribe to a charity, or to compensate the victims. If there is to be no punishment there can be no forgiveness. We shall never have real moral responsibility until everyone knows that his deeds are irrevocable, and that his life depends on his usefulness. Hitherto, alas! humanity has never dared face these hard facts. We frantically scatter conscience money and invent systems of conscience banking, with expiatory penalties, atonements, redemptions, salvations, hospital subscription lists and what not, to enable us to contract-out of the moral code. Not content with the old scapegoat and sacrificial lamb, we deify human saviors, and pray to miraculous virgin intercessors. We attribute mercy to the inexorable; soothe our consciences after committing murder by throwing ourselves on the bosom of divine love;

and shrink even from our own gallows because we are forced to admit that it, at least, is irrevocable—as if one hour of imprisonment were not as irrevocable as any execution!

If a man cannot look evil in the face without illusion, he will never know what it really is, or combat it effectually. The few men who have been able (relatively) to do this have been called cynics, and have sometimes had an abnormal share of evil in themselves, corresponding to the abnormal strength of their minds; but they have never done mischief unless they intended to do it. That is why great scoundrels have been beneficent rulers whilst amiable and privately harmless monarchs have ruined their countries by trusting to the hocus-pocus of innocence and guilt, reward and punishment, virtuous indignation and pardon, instead of standing up to the facts without either malice or mercy. Major Barbara stands up to Bill Walker in that way, with the result that the ruffian who cannot get hated, has to hate himself. To relieve this agony he tries to get punished; but the Salvationist whom he tries to provoke is as merciless as Barbara, and only prays for him. Then he tries to pay, but can get nobody to take his money. His doom is the doom of Cain, who, failing to find either a savior, a policeman, or an almoner to help him to pretend that his brother's blood no longer cried from the ground, had to live and die a murderer. Cain took care not to commit another murder, unlike our railway shareholders (I am one) who kill and maim shunters by hundreds to save the cost of automatic couplings, and make atonement by annual subscriptions to deserving charities. Had Cain been allowed to pay off his score, he might possibly have killed Adam and Eve for the mere sake of a second luxurious reconciliation with God afterwards. Bodger, you may depend on it, will go on to the end of his life poisoning people with bad whisky, because he can always depend on the Salvation Army or the Church of England to negotiate a redemption for him in consideration of a trifling percentage of his profits.

There is a third condition too, which must be fulfilled before the great teachers of the world will cease to scoff at its religions. Creeds must become intellectually honest. At present there is not a single credible established religion in the world. That is perhaps the most stupendous fact in the whole world-situation. This play of mine, Major Barbara, is, I hope, both true and inspired; but whoever says that it all happened, and that faith in it and understanding of it consist in believing that it is a record of an actual occurrence, is, to speak according to Scripture, a fool and a liar, and is hereby solemnly denounced and cursed as such by me, the author, to all posterity.

London, June 1906

Major Barbara

Characters

STEPHEN UNDERSHAFT
LADY BRITOMART
BARBARA UNDERSHAFT
SARAH UNDERSHAFT
ANDREW UNDERSHAFT
JENNY HILL
BILL WALKER
MORRISON
ADOLPHUS CUSINS
CHARLES LOMAX
RUMMY MITCHENS
SNOBBY PRICE
PETER SHIRLEY
BILTON
MRS. BAINES

N.B. The Euripidean verses in the second act of Major Barbara are not by me, nor even directly by Euripides. They are by Professor Gilbert Murray, whose English version of The Bacchae came into our dramatic literature with all the impulsive power of an original work shortly before Major Barbara was begun. The play, indeed, stands indebted to him in more ways than one.

G.B.S.

ACT I

It is after dinner in January 1906, in the library in Lady Britomart Undershaft's *house in Wilton Crescent. A large and comfortable settee is in the middle of the room, upholstered in dark leather. A person sitting on it (it is vacant at present) would have, on his right,* Lady Britomart's *writing table, with the lady herself busy at it; a smaller writing table behind him on his left; the door behind him on* Lady Britomart's *side; and a window with a window seat directly on his left. Near the window is an armchair.*

Lady Britomart *is a woman of fifty or thereabouts, well dressed and yet careless of her dress, well bred and quite reckless of her breeding, well mannered and yet appallingly outspoken and indifferent to the opinion of her interlocutors, amiable and yet peremptory, arbitrary, and high-tempered to the last bearable degree, and withal a very typical managing matron of the upper class, treated as a naughty child until she grew into a scolding mother, and finally settling down with plenty of practical ability and worldly experience, limited in the oddest way with domestic and class limitations, conceiving the universe exactly as if it were a large house in Wilton Crescent, though handling her corner of it very effectively on that assumption, and being quite enlightened and liberal as to the books in the library, the pictures on the walls, the music in the portfolios, and the articles in the papers.*

Her son, Stephen, *comes in. He is a gravely correct young man under 25, taking himself very seriously, but still in some awe of his mother, from childish habit and bachelor shyness rather than from any weakness of character.*

Stephen. Whats the matter?
Lady Britomart. Presently, Stephen.

Stephen submissively walks to the settee and sits down. He takes up a Liberal weekly called The Speaker.

Lady Britomart. Dont begin to read, Stephen. I shall require all your attention.

Stephen. It was only while I was waiting—

Lady Britomart. Dont make excuses, Stephen. (*He puts down The Speaker.*) Now! (*She finishes her writing; rises; and comes to the settee.*) I have not kept you waiting very long, I think.

Stephen. Not at all, mother.

Lady Britomart. Bring me my cushion. (*He takes the cushion from the chair at the desk and arranges it for her as she sits down on the settee.*) Sit down. (*He sits down and fingers his tie nervously.*) Dont fiddle with your tie, Stephen: there is nothing the matter with it.

Stephen. I beg your pardon. (*He fiddles with his watch chain instead.*)

Lady Britomart. Now are you attending to me, Stephen?

Stephen. Of course, mother.

Lady Britomart. No: it's not of course. I want something much more than your everyday matter-of-course attention. I am going to speak to you very seriously, Stephen. I wish you would let that chain alone.

Stephen (*hastily relinquishing the chain*). Have I done anything to annoy you, mother? If so, it was quite unintentional.

Lady Britomart (*astonished*). Nonsense! (*With some remorse.*) My poor boy, did you think I was angry with you?

Stephen. What is it, then, mother? You are making me very uneasy.

Lady Britomart (*squaring herself at him rather aggressively*). Stephen: may I ask how soon you intend to realize that you are a grown-up man, and that I am only a woman?

Stephen (*amazed*). Only a—

Lady Britomart. Dont repeat my words, please: it is a most aggravating habit. You must learn to face life seriously, Stephen. I really cannot bear the whole burden of our family affairs any longer. You must advise me: you must assume the responsibility.

Stephen. I!

Lady Britomart. Yes, you, of course. You were 24 last June. Youve been at Harrow and Cambridge. Youve been to India and Japan. You must know a lot of things now; unless you have wasted your time most scandalously. Well, advise me.

Stephen (much perplexed). You know I have never interfered in the household—

Lady Britomart. No: I should think not. I dont want you to order the dinner.

Stephen. I mean in our family affairs.

Lady Britomart. Well, you must interfere now; for they are getting quite beyond me.

Stephen (troubled). I have thought sometimes that perhaps I ought; but really, mother, I know so little about them; and what I do know is so painful! it is so impossible to mention some things to you—(*he stops, ashamed*).

Lady Britomart. I suppose you mean your father.

Stephen (almost inaudibly). Yes.

Lady Britomart. My dear: we cant go on all our lives not mentioning him. Of course you were quite right not to open the subject until I asked you to; but you are old enough now to be taken into my confidence, and to help me to deal with him about the girls.

Stephen. But the girls are all right. They are engaged.

Lady Britomart (complacently). Yes: I have made a very good match for Sarah. Charles Lomax will be a millionaire at 35. But that is ten years ahead; and in the meantime his trustees cannot under the terms of his father's will allow him more than £800 a year.

Stephen. But the will says also that if he increases his income by his own exertions, they may double the increase.

Lady Britomart. Charles Lomax's exertions are much more likely to decrease his income than to increase it. Sarah will have to find at least another £800 a year for the next ten years; and even then they will be as poor as church mice. And what about Barbara? I thought Barbara was going to make the most brilliant career of all of you. And what does she do? Joins the Salvation Army; discharges her maid; lives on a pound a week; and walks in one evening with a professor of Greek whom she has picked up in the street, and who pretends to be a Salvationist, and actually plays the big drum for her in public because he has fallen head over ears in love with her.

Stephen. I was certainly rather taken aback when I heard they were engaged. Cusins is a very nice fellow, certainly: nobody would ever guess that he was born in Australia; but—

Lady Britomart. Oh, Adolphus Cusins will make a very

good husband. After all, nobody can say a word against Greek: it stamps a man at once as an educated gentleman. And my family, thank Heaven, is not a pigheaded Tory one. We are Whigs, and believe in liberty. Let snobbish people say what they please: Barbara shall marry, not the man they like, but the man *I* like.

Stephen. Of course I was thinking only of his income. However, he is not likely to be extravagant.

Lady Britomart. Don't be too sure of that, Stephen. I know your quiet, simple, refined, poetic people like Adolphus: quite content with the best of everything! They cost more than your extravagant people, who are always as mean as they are second rate. No: Barbara will need at least £2000 a year. You see it means two additional households. Besides, my dear, y o u must marry soon. I don't approve of the present fashion of philandering bachelors and late marriages; and I am trying to arrange something for you.

Stephen. It's very good of you, mother; but perhaps I had better arrange that for myself.

Lady Britomart. Nonsense! you are much too young to begin matchmaking: you would be taken in by some pretty little nobody. Of course I don't mean that you are not to be consulted: you know that as well as I do. (*Stephen closes his lips and is silent.*) Now dont sulk, Stephen.

Stephen. I am not sulking, mother. What has all this got to do with—with—with my father?

Lady Britomart. My dear Stephen: where is the money to come from? It is easy enough for you and the other children to live on my income as long as we are in the same house; but I cant keep four families in four separate houses. You know how poor my father is: he has barely seven thousand a year now; and really, if he were not the Earl of Stevenage, he would have to give up society. He can do nothing for us. He says, naturally enough, that it is absurd that he should be asked to provide for the children of a man who is rolling in money. You see, Stephen, your father must be fabulously wealthy, because there is always a war going on somewhere.

Stephen. You need not remind me of that, mother. I have hardly ever opened a newspaper in my life without seeing our name in it. The Undershaft torpedo! The Undershaft quick firers! The Undershaft ten inch! the Undershaft disappearing rampart gun! the Undershaft submarine! and now the Undershaft aerial battleship! At Harrow they called me the Woolwich Infant. At Cambridge it was the same. A little brute at King's who was always trying to get up revivals, spoilt my Bible—your first birthday present to me—by writing under my name, "Son and heir to Undershaft and Lazarus, Death and Destruction Dealers: address Christendom and Judea." But that was not so bad as the way I was kowtowed to everywhere because my father was making millions by selling cannons.

Lady Britomart. It is not only the cannons, but the war loans that Lazarus arranges under cover of giving credit for the cannons. You know, Stephen, it's perfectly scandalous. Those two men, Andrew Undershaft and Lazarus, positively have Europe under their thumbs. That is why your father is able to behave as he does. He is above the law. Do you think Bismarck or Gladstone or Disraeli could have openly defied every social and moral obligation all their lives as your father has? They simply wouldnt have dared. I asked Gladstone to take it up. I asked The Times to take it up. I asked the Lord Chamberlain to take it up. But it was just like asking them to declare war on the Sultan. They w o u l d n t. They said they couldnt touch him. I believe they were afraid.

Stephen. What could they do? He does not actually break the law.

Lady Britomart. Not break the law! He is always breaking the law. He broke the law when he was born: his parents were not married.

Stephen. Mother! Is that true?

Lady Britomart. Of course it's true: that was why we separated.

Stephen. He married without letting you know this!

Lady Britomart (*rather taken aback by this inference*). Oh no. To do Andrew justice, that was not the sort of thing he did. Besides, you know the Undershaft motto: Unashamed. Everybody knew.

Stephen. But you said that was why you separated.

Lady Britomart. Yes, because he was not content with being a foundling himself: he wanted to disinherit you for another foundling. That was what I couldnt stand.

Stephen (*ashamed*). Do you mean for—for—for—

Lady Britomart. Don't stammer, Stephen. Speak distinctly.

Stephen. But this is so frightful to me, mother. To have to speak to you about such things!

Lady Britomart. It's not pleasant for me, either, especially if you are still so childish that you must make it worse by a display of embarrassment. It is only in the middle classes, Stephen, that people get into a state of dumb helpless horror when they find that there are wicked people in the world. In our class, we have to decide what is to be done with wicked people; and nothing should disturb our self-possession. Now ask your question properly.

Stephen. Mother: have you no consideration for me? For Heaven's sake either treat me as a child, as you always do, and tell me nothing at all; or tell me everything and let me take it as best I can.

Lady Britomart. Treat you as a child! What do you mean? It is most unkind and ungrateful of you to say such a thing. You know I have never treated any of you as children. I have always made you my companions and friends, and allowed you perfect freedom to do and say whatever you liked, so long as you liked what I could approve of.

Stephen (*desperately*). I daresay we have been the very imperfect children of a very perfect mother; but I do beg you to let me alone for once, and tell me about this horrible business of my father wanting to set me aside for another son.

Lady Britomart (*amazed*). Another son! I never said anything of the kind. I never dreamt of such a thing. This is what comes of interrupting me.

Stephen. But you said—

Lady Britomart (*cutting him short*). Now be a good boy, Stephen, and listen to me patiently. The Undershafts are descended from a foundling in the parish of St Andrew Undershaft in the city. That was long ago, in the reign of James the First. Well, this foundling was adopted by an armorer and gun-maker. In the course of time the foundling succeeded to the business; and from some notion of gratitude, or some vow or something, he adopted another foundling, and left the business to him. And that foundling did the same. Ever since that, the cannon business has always been left to an adopted foundling named Andrew Undershaft.

Stephen. But did they never marry? Were there no legitimate sons?

Lady Britomart. Oh yes: they married just as your father

did; and they were rich enough to buy land for their own children and leave them well provided for. But they always adopted and trained some foundling to succeed them in the business; and of course they always quarrelled with their wives furiously over it. Your father was adopted in that way; and he pretends to consider himself bound to keep up the tradition and adopt somebody to leave the business to. Of course I was not going to stand that. There may have been some reason for it when the Undershafts could only marry women in their own class, whose sons were not fit to govern great estates. But there could be no excuse for passing over my son.

Stephen (*dubiously*). I am afraid I should make a poor hand of managing a cannon foundry.

Lady Britomart. Nonsense! you could easily get a manager and pay him a salary.

Stephen. My father evidently had no great opinion of my capacity.

Lady Britomart. Stuff, child! you were only a baby: it had nothing to do with your capacity. Andrew did it on principle, just as he did every perverse and wicked thing on principle. When my father remonstrated, Andrew actually told him to his face that history tells us of only two successful institutions: one the Undershaft firm, and the other the Roman Empire under the Antonines. That was because the Antonine emperors all adopted their successors. Such rubbish! The Stevenages are as good as the Antonines, I hope; and you are a Stevenage. But that was Andrew all over. There you have the man! Always clever and unanswerable when he was defending nonsense and wickedness: always awkward and sullen when he had to behave sensibly and decently!

Stephen. Then it was on my account that your home life was broken up, mother. I am sorry.

Lady Britomart. Well, dear, there were other differences. I really cannot bear an immoral man. I am not a Pharisee, I hope; and I should not have minded his merely doing wrong things: we are none of us perfect. But your father didnt exactly d o wrong things: he said them and thought them: that was what was so dreadful. He really had a sort of religion of wrongness. Just as one doesnt mind men practising immorality so long as they own that they are in the wrong by preaching morality; so I couldnt forgive Andrew for preaching immorality while he practised morality. You would all have grown up without principles, without any knowledge of right and wrong, if he had been in the house. You know, my dear, your father was a very attractive man in some ways. Children did not dislike him; and he took advantage of it to put the wickedest ideas into their heads, and make them quite unmanageable. I did not dislike him myself: very far from it; but nothing can bridge over moral disagreement.

Stephen. All this simply bewilders me, mother. People may differ about matters of opinion, or even about religion; but how can they differ about right and wrong? Right is right; and wrong is wrong; and if a man cannot distinguish them properly, he is either a fool or a rascal: thats all.

Lady Britomart (*touched*). Thats my own boy (*she pats his cheek*)! Your father never could answer that: he used to laugh and get out of it under cover of some affectionate nonsense. And now that you understand the situation, what do you advise me to do?

Stephen. Well, what c a n you do?

Lady Britomart. I must get the money somehow.

Stephen. We cannot take money from him. I had rather go and live in some cheap place like Bedford Square or even Hampstead than take a farthing of his money.

Lady Britomart. But after all, Stephen, our present income comes from Andrew.

Stephen (*shocked*). I never knew that.

Lady Britomart. Well, you surely didnt suppose your grandfather had anything to give me. The Stevenages could not do everything for you. We gave you social position. Andrew had to contribute s o m e t h i n g. He had a very good bargain, I think.

Stephen (*bitterly*). We are utterly dependent on him and his cannons, then?

Lady Britomart. Certainly not: the money is settled. But he provided it. So you see it is not a question of taking money from him or not: it is simply a question of how much. I dont want any more for myself.

Stephen. Nor do I.

Lady Britomart. But Sarah does; and Barbara does. That is, Charles Lomax and Adolphus Cusins will cost them more. So I must put my pride in my pocket and ask for it, I suppose. That is your advice, Stephen, is it not?

Stephen. No.

Lady Britomart (*sharply*). Stephen!

Stephen. Of course if you are determined—

Lady Britomart. I am not determined: I ask your advice; and I am waiting for it. I will not have all the responsibility thrown on my shoulders.

Stephen (*obstinately*). I would die sooner than ask him for another penny.

Lady Britomart (*resignedly*). You mean that *I* must ask him. Very well, Stephen: it shall be as you wish. You will be glad to know that your grandfather concurs. But he thinks I ought to ask Andrew to come here and see the girls. After all, he must have some natural affection for them.

Stephen. Ask him here!!!

Lady Britomart. Do not repeat my words, Stephen. Where else can I ask him?

Stephen. I never expected you to ask him at all.

Lady Britomart. Now dont tease, Stephen. Come! you see that it is necessary that he should pay us a visit, dont you?

Stephen (*reluctantly*). I suppose so, if the girls cannot do without his money.

Lady Britomart. Thank you, Stephen: I knew you would give me the right advice when it was properly explained to you. I have asked your father to come this evening. (*Stephens bounds from his seat.*) Dont jump, Stephen: it fidgets me.

Stephen (*in utter consternation*). Do you mean to say that my father is coming here tonight—that he may be here at any moment?

Lady Britomart (*looking at her watch*). I said nine. (*He gasps. She rises.*) Ring the bell, please. (Stephen *goes to the smaller writing table; presses a button on it; and sits at it with his elbows on the table and his head in his hands, outwitted and overwhelmed.*) It is ten minutes to nine yet; and I have to prepare the girls. I asked Charles Lomax and Adolphus to dinner on purpose that they might be here. Andrew had better see them in case he should cherish any delusions as to their being capable of supporting their wives. (*The butler enters:* Lady Britomart *goes behind the settee to speak to him.*) Morrison: go up to the drawing room and tell everybody to come down here at once. (Morrison *withdraws.* Lady Britomart *turns to* Stephen.) Now remember, Stephen: I shall need all your countenance and authority. (*He rises and tries to recover some vestige of these attributes.*) Give me a chair, dear. (*He pushes a chair forward from the wall to where she stands, near the smaller writing table. She sits down; and he goes to the armchair, into which he throws himself.*) I dont know how Barbara will take it. Ever since they made her a major in the Salvation Army she has developed a propensity to have her own way and order people about which quite cows me sometimes. It's not ladylike: I'm sure I dont know where she picked it up. Anyhow, Barbara shant bully me, but still it's just as well that your father should be here before she has time to refuse to meet him or make a fuss. Dont look nervous, Stephen: it will only encourage Barbara to make difficulties. *I* am nervous enough, goodness knows; but I dont shew it.

Sarah *and* Barbara *come in with their respective young men,* Charles Lomax *and* Adolphus Cusins. Sarah *is slender, bored, and mundane. Barbara is robuster, jollier, much more energetic. Sarah is fashionably dressed:* Barbara *is in Salvation Army uniform.* Lomax, *a young man about town, is like many other young men about town. He is afflicted with a frivolous sense of humor which plunges him at the most inopportune moments into paroxysms of imperfectly suppressed laughter.* Cusins *is a spectacled student, slight, thin haired, and sweet voiced, with a more complex form of* Lomax's *complaint. His sense of humor is intellectual and subtle, and is complicated by an appalling temper. The lifelong struggle of a benevolent temperament and a high conscience against impulses of inhuman ridicule and fierce impatience has set up a chronic strain which has visibly wrecked his constitution. He is a most implacable, determined, tenacious, intolerant person who by mere force of character presents himself as—and indeed actually is—considerate, gentle, explanatory, even mild and apologetic, capable possibly of murder, but not of cruelty or coarseness. By the operation of some instinct which is not merciful enough to blind him with the illusions of love, he is obstinately bent on marrying* Barbara. Lomax *likes Sarah and thinks it will be rather a lark to marry her. Consequently he has not attempted to resist* Lady Britomart's *arrangements to that end.*

All four look as if they had been having a good deal of

fun in the drawing room. The girls enter first, leaving the swains outside. Sarah *comes to the settee.* Barbara *comes in after her and stops at the door.*

Barbara. Are Cholly and Dolly to come in?

Lady Britomart (forcibly). Barbara: I will not have Charles called Cholly: the vulgarity of it positively makes me ill.

Barbara. It's all right, mother: Cholly is quite correct nowadays. Are they to come in?

Lady Britomart. Yes, if they will behave themselves.

Barbara (through the door). Come in, Dolly; and behave yourself.

Barbara *comes to her mother's writing table.* Cusins *enters smiling, and wanders towards* Lady Britomart.

Sarah (calling). Come in, Cholly. (Lomax *enters, controlling his features very imperfectly, and places himself vaguely between* Sarah *and* Barbara.)

Lady Britomart (peremptorily). Sit down, all of you. (*They sit.* Cusins *crosses to the window and seats himself there.* Lomax *takes a chair.* Barbara *sits at the writing table and* Sarah *on the settee.*) I don't in the least know what you are laughing at, Adolphus. I am surprised at you, though I expected nothing better from Charles Lomax.

Cusins (in a remarkably gentle voice). Barbara has been trying to teach me the West Ham Salvation March.

Lady Britomart. I see nothing to laugh at in that; nor should you if you are really converted.

Cusins (sweetly). You were not present. It was really funny, I believe.

Lomax. Ripping.

Lady Britomart. Be quiet, Charles. Now listen to me, children. Your father is coming here this evening.

General stupefaction. Lomax, Sarah, *and* Barbara *rise:* Sarah *scared, and* Barbara *amused and expectant.*

Lomax (remonstrating). Oh I say!

Lady Britomart. You are not called on to say anything, Charles.

Sarah. Are you serious, mother?

Lady Britomart. Of course I am serious. It is on your account, Sarah, and also on Charles's. (*Silence.* Sarah *sits, with a shrug.* Charles *looks painfully unworthy.*) I hope you are not going to object, Barbara.

Barbara. I! why should I? My father has a soul to be saved like anybody else. He's quite welcome as far as I am concerned. (*She sits on the table, and softly whistles "Onward, Christian Soldiers."*)

Lomax (*still remonstrant*). But really, don't you know! Oh I say!

Lady Britomart (*frigidly*). What do you wish to convey, Charles?

Lomax. Well, you must admit that this is a bit thick.

Lady Britomart (*turning with ominous suavity to* Cusins). Adolphus: you are a professor of Greek. Can you translate Charles Lomax's remarks into reputable English for us?

Cusins (*cautiously*). If I may say so, Lady Brit, I think Charles has rather happily expressed what we all feel. Homer, speaking of Autolycus, uses the same phrase. πυκινὸν δόμον ἐλθεῖν means a bit thick.

Lomax (*handsomely*). Not that I mind, you know, if Sarah dont. (*He sits.*)

Lady Britomart (*crushingly*). Thank you. Have I your permission, Adolphus, to invite my own husband to my own house?

Cusins (*gallantly*). You have my unhesitating support in everything you do.

Lady Britomart. Tush! Sarah: have you nothing to say?

Sarah. Do you mean that he is coming regularly to live here?

Lady Britomart. Certainly not. The spare room is ready for him if he likes to stay for a day or two and see a little more of you; but there are limits.

Sarah. Well, he cant eat us, I suppose. *I* dont mind.

Lomax (*chuckling*). I wonder how the old man will take it.

Lady Britomart. Much as the old woman will, no doubt, Charles.

Lomax (*abashed*). I didn't mean—at least—

Lady Britomart. You didn't t h i n k, Charles. You never do; and the result is, you never mean anything. And now please attend to me, children. Your father will be quite a stranger to us.

Lomax. I suppose he hasn't seen Sarah since she was a little kid.

Lady Britomart. Not since she was a little kid, Charles, as you express it with that elegance of diction and refinement of thought that seem never to desert you. Accordingly—er—(*impatiently*) Now I have forgotten what I was going to say. That comes of your provoking me to be sarcastic, Charles. Adolphus: will you kindly tell me where I was.

Cusins (sweetly). You were saying that as Mr Undershaft has not seen his children since they were babies, he will form his opinion of the way you have brought them up from their behavior tonight, and that therefore you wish us all to be particularly careful to conduct ourselves well, especially Charles.

Lady Britomart (with emphatic approval). Precisely.

Lomax. Look here, Dolly: Lady Brit didnt say that.

Lady Britomart (vehemently). I did, Charles. Adolphus's recollection is perfectly correct. It is most important that you should be good; and I do beg you for once not to pair off into opposite corners and giggle and whisper while I am speaking to your father.

Barbara. All right, mother. We'll do you credit. (*She comes off the table, and sits in her chair with ladylike elegance.*)

Lady Britomart. Remember, Charles, that Sarah will want to feel proud of you instead of ashamed of you.

Lomax. Oh I say! theres nothing to be exactly proud of, dont you know.

Lady Britomart. Well, try and look as if there was.

Morrison, *pale and dismayed, breaks into the room in unconcealed disorder.*

Morrison. Might I speak a word to you, my lady?

Lady Britomart. Nonsense! Shew him up.

Morrison. Yes, my lady. (*He goes.*)

Lomax. Does Morrison know who it is?

Lady Britomart. Of course, Morrison has always been with us.

Lomax. It must be a regular corker for him, don't you know.

Lady Britomart. Is this a moment to get on my nerves, Charles, with your outrageous expressions?

Lomax. But this is something out of the ordinary, really—

Morrison (at the door). The—er—Mr Undershaft. (*He retreats in confusion.*)

Andrew Undershaft *comes in. All rise.* Lady Britomart *meets him in the middle of the room behind the settee.*

Andrew *is, on the surface, a stoutish, easygoing elderly man, with kindly patient manners, and an engaging simplicity of character. But he has a watchful, deliberate, waiting, listening face, and formidable reserves of power, both bodily and mental, in his capacious chest and long head. His gentleness is partly that of a strong man who has learnt by experience that his natural grip hurts ordinary people unless he handles them very carefully, and partly the mellowness of age and success. He is also a little shy in his present very delicate situation.*

Lady Britomart. Good evening, Andrew.

Undershaft. How d'ye do, my dear.

Lady Britomart. You look a good deal older.

Undershaft (apologetically). I am somewhat older. (*Taking her hand with a touch of courtship*). Time has stood still with you.

Lady Britomart (throwing away his hand). Rubbish! This is your family.

Undershaft (surprised). Is it so large? I am sorry to say my memory is failing very badly in some things. (*He offers his hand with paternal kindness to* Lomax.)

Lomax (jerkily shaking his hand). Ahdedoo.

Undershaft. I can see you are my eldest. I am very glad to meet you again, my boy.

Lomax (remonstrating). No, but look here dont you know— (*Overcome.*) Oh I say!

Lady Britomart (recovering from momentary speechlessness). Andrew: do you mean to say that you dont remember how many children you have?

Undershaft. Well, I am afraid I—. They have grown so much—er. Am I making any ridiculous mistake? I may as well confess: I recollect only one son. But so many things have happened since, of course—er—

Lady Britomart (decisively). Andrew: you are talking nonsense. Of course you have only one son.

Undershaft. Perhaps you will be good enough to introduce me, my dear.

Lady Britomart. That is Charles Lomax, who is engaged to Sarah.

Undershaft. My dear sir, I beg your pardon.

Lomax. Notatall. Delighted, I assure you.

Lady Britomart. This is Stephen.

Undershaft (bowing). Happy to make your acquaintance, Mr Stephen. Then (*going to* Cusins) you must be my son. (*Taking* Cusins' *hands in his.*) How are you, my young friend? (*To* Lady Britomart.) He is very like you, my love.

Cusins. You flatter me, Mr Undershaft. My name is Cusins: engaged to Barbara. (*Very explicitly.*) That is Major Barbara Undershaft, of the Salvation Army. That is Sarah, your second daughter. This is Stephen Undershaft, your son.

Undershaft. My dear Stephen, I beg your pardon.

Stephen. Not at all.

Undershaft. Mr Cusins: I am much indebted to you for explaining so precisely. (*Turning to* Sarah.) Barbara, my dear—

Sarah (*prompting him*). Sarah.

Undershaft. Sarah, of course. (*They shake hands. He goes over to* Barbara) Barbara—I am right this time, I hope?

Barbara. Quite right. (*They shake hands.*)

Lady Britomart (*resuming command*). Sit down, all of you. Sit down, Andrew. (*She comes forward and sits on the settee.* Cusins *also brings his chair forward on her left.* Barbara *and* Stephen *resume their seats.* Lomax *gives his chair to* Sarah *and goes for another.*)

Undershaft. Thank you, my love.

Lomax (*conversationally, as he brings a chair forward between the writing table and the settee, and offers it to* Undershaft). Takes you some time to find out exactly where you are, dont it?

Undershaft (*accepting the chair, but remaining standing*). That is not what embarrasses me, Mr Lomax. My difficulty is that if I play the part of a father, I shall produce the effect of an intrusive stranger; and if I play the part of a discreet stranger, I may appear a callous father.

Lady Britomart. There is no need for you to play any part at all, Andrew. You had much better be sincere and natural.

Undershaft (*submissively*). Yes, my dear: I daresay that will be best. (*He sits down comfortably.*) Well, here I am. Now what can I do for you all?

Lady Britomart. You need not do anything, Andrew. You are one of the family. You can sit with us and enjoy yourself.

A painfully conscious pause. Barbara *makes a face at* Lomax, *whose too long suppressed mirth immediately explodes in agonized neighings.*

Lady Britomart (*outraged*). Charles Lomax: if you can behave yourself, behave yourself. If not, leave the room.

Lomax. I'm awfully sorry, Lady Brit; but really you know, upon my soul! (*He sits on the settee between* Lady Britomart *and* Undershaft, *quite overcome.*)

Barbara. Why don't you laugh if you want to, Cholly? It's good for your inside.

Lady Britomart. Barbara: you have had the education of a lady. Please let your father see that; and don't talk like a street girl.

Undershaft. Never mind me, my dear. As you know, I am not a gentleman; and I was never educated.

Lomax (*encouragingly*). Nobody'd know it, I assure you. You look all right, you know.

Cusins. Let me advise you to study Greek, Mr. Undershaft. Greek scholars are privileged men. Few of them know Greek; and none of them know anything else; but their position is unchallengeable. Other languages are the qualifications of waiters and commercial travellers: Greek is to a man of position what the hallmark is to silver.

Barbara. Dolly: dont be insincere. Cholly: fetch your concertina and play something for us.

Lomax (*jumps up eagerly, but checks himself to remark doubtfully to* Undershaft). Perhaps that sort of thing isnt in your line, eh?

Undershaft. I am particularly fond of music.

Lomax (*delighted*). Are you? Then I'll get it. (*He goes upstairs for the instrument.*)

Undershaft. Do you play, Barbara?

Barbara. Only the tambourine. But Cholly's teaching me the concertina.

Undershaft. Is Cholly also a member of the Salvation Army?

Barbara. No: he says it's bad form to be a dissenter. But I don't despair of Cholly. I made him come yesterday to a meeting at the dock gates, and take the collection in his hat.

Undershaft (*looks whimsically at his wife*) !!

Lady Britomart. It is not my doing, Andrew. Barbara is old enough to take her own way. She has no father to advise her.

Barbara. Oh yes she has. There are no orphans in the Salvation Army.

Undershaft. Your father there has a great many children and plenty of experience, eh?

Barbara (*looking at him with quick interest and nodding*). Just so. How did you come to understand that? (Lomax *is heard at the door trying the concertina.*)

Lady Britomart. Come in, Charles. Play us something at once.

Lomax. Righto! (*He sits down in his former place, and preludes.*)

Undershaft. One moment, Mr Lomax. I am rather interested in the Salvation Army. Its motto might be my own: Blood and Fire.

Lomax (*shocked*). But not your sort of blood and fire, you know.

Undershaft. My sort of blood cleanses: my sort of fire purifies.

Barbara. So do ours. Come down tomorrow to my shelter—the West Ham shelter—and see what we're doing. We're going to march to a great meeting in the Assembly Hall at Mile End. Come and see the shelter and then march with us: it will do you a lot of good. Can you play anything?

Undershaft. In my youth I earned pennies, and even shillings occasionally, in the streets and in public house parlors by my natural talent for stepdancing. Later on, I became a member of the Undershaft orchestral society, and performed passably on the tenor trombone.

Lomax (*scandalized—putting down the concertina*). Oh I say!

Barbara. Many a sinner has played himself into heaven on the trombone, thanks to the Army.

Lomax (*to* Barbara, *still rather shocked*). Yes; but what about the cannon business, don't you know? (*To* Undershaft.) Getting into heaven is not exactly in your line, is it?

Lady Britomart. Charles!!!

Lomax. Well; but it stands to reason, dont it? The cannon business may be necessary and all that: we cant get on without cannons; but it isnt right, you know. On the other hand, there may be a certain amount of tosh about the Salvation Army—I belong to the Established Church myself—but still you cant deny that it's religion; and you cant go against religion, can you? At least unless youre downright immoral, dont you know.

Undershaft. You hardly appreciate my position, Mr Lomax—

Lomax (*hastily*). I'm not saying anything against you personally—

Undershaft. Quite so, quite so. But consider for a moment. Here I am, a profiteer in mutilation and murder. I find myself in a specially amiable humor just now because, this morning, down at the foundry, we blew twenty-seven dummy soldiers into fragments with a gun which formerly destroyed only thirteen.

Lomax (*leniently*). Well, the more destructive war becomes, the sooner it will be abolished, eh?

Undershaft. Not at all. The more destructive war becomes the more fascinating we find it. No, Mr Lomax: I am obliged to you for making the usual excuse for my trade; but I am not ashamed of it. I am not one of those men who keep their morals and their business in watertight compartments. All the spare money my trade rivals spend on hospitals, cathedrals, and other receptacles for conscience money, I devote to experiments and researches in improved methods of destroying life and property. I have always done so; and I always shall. Therefore your Christmas card moralities of peace on earth and goodwill among men are of no use to me. Your Christianity, which enjoins you to resist not evil, and to turn the other cheek, would make me a bankrupt. My morality—my religion—must have a place for cannons and torpedoes in it.

Stephen (*coldly—almost sullenly*). You speak as if there were half a dozen moralities and religions to choose from, instead of one true morality and one true religion.

Undershaft. For me there is only one true morality; but it might not fit you, as you do not manufacture aerial battleships. There is only one true morality for every man; but every man has not the same true morality.

Lomax (*overtaxed*). Would you mind saying that again? I didnt quite follow it.

Cusins. It's quite simple. As Euripides says, one man's meat is another man's poison morally as well as physically.

Undershaft. Precisely.

Lomax. Oh, t h a t! Yes, yes, yes. True. True.

Stephen. In other words, some men are honest and some are scoundrels.

Barbara. Bosh! There are no scoundrels.

Undershaft. Indeed? Are there any good men?

Barbara. No. Not one. There are neither good men nor scoundrels: there are just children of one Father; and the sooner they stop calling one another names the better. You neednt talk to me: I know them. I've had scores of them through my hands: scoundrels, criminals, infidels, philanthropists, missionaries, county councillors, all sorts. Theyre all just the same sort of sinner; and theres the same salvation ready for them all.

Undershaft. May I ask have you ever saved a maker of cannons?

Barbara. No. Will you let me try?

Undershaft. Well, I will make a bargain with you. If I go to see you tomorrow in your Salvation Shelter, will you come the day after to see me in my cannon works?

Barbara. Take care. It may end in your giving up the cannons for the sake of the Salvation Army.

Undershaft. Are you sure it will not end in your giving up the Salvation Army for the sake of the cannons?

Barbara. I will take my chance of that.

Undershaft. And I will take my chance of the other. (*They shake hands on it.*) Where is your shelter?

Barbara. In West Ham. At the sign of the cross. Ask anybody in Canning Town. Where are your works?

Undershaft. In Perivale St Andrews. At the sign of the sword. Ask anybody in Europe.

Lomax. Hadnt I better play something?

Barbara. Yes. Give us Onward, Christian Soldiers.

Lomax. Well, thats rather a strong order to begin with, dont you know. Suppose I sing Thourt passing hence, my brother. It's much the same tune.

Barbara. It's too melancholy. You get saved, Cholly; and youll pass hence, my brother, without making such a fuss about it.

Lady Britomart. Really, Barbara, you go on as if religion were a pleasant subject. Do have some sense of propriety.

Undershaft. I do not find it an unpleasant subject, my dear. It is the only one that capable people really care for.

Lady Britomart (*looking at her watch*). Well, if you are determined to have it, I insist on having it in a proper and respectable way. Charles: ring for prayers.

General amazement. Stephen *rises in dismay.*

Lomax (*rising*). Oh I say!

Undershaft (*rising*). I am afraid I must be going.

Lady Britomart. You cannot go now, Andrew: it would be most improper. Sit down. What will the servants think?

Undershaft. My dear: I have conscientious scruples. May I suggest a compromise? If Barbara will conduct a little service in the drawing room, with Mr Lomax as organist, I will attend it willingly. I will even take part, if a trombone can be procured.

Lady Britomart. Dont mock, Andrew.

Undershaft (*shocked—to* Barbara). You don't think I am mocking, my love, I hope.

Barbara. No, of course not; and it wouldnt matter if you were: half the Army came to their first meeting for a lark. (*Rising.*) Come along. (*She throws her arm round her father and sweeps him out, calling to the others from the threshold.*) Come, Dolly. Come, Cholly.

Cusins *rises.*

Lady Britomart. I will not be disobeyed by everybody. Adolphus: sit down. (*He does not.*) Charles: you may go. You are not fit for prayers: you cannot keep your countenance.

Lomax. Oh I say! (*He goes out.*)

Lady Britomart (*continuing*). But you, Adolphus, can behave yourself if you choose to. I insist on your staying.

Cusins. My dear Lady Brit: there are things in the family prayer book that I couldnt bear to hear you say.

Lady Britomart. What things, pray?

Cusins. Well, you would have to say before all the servants that we have done things we ought not to have done, and left undone things we ought to have done, and that there is no health in us. I cannot bear to hear you doing yourself such an injustice, and Barbara such an injustice. As for myself, I flatly deny it: I have done my best. I shouldnt dare to marry Barbara—I couldnt look you in the face—if it were true. So I must go to the drawing room.

Lady Britomart (*offended*). Well, go. (*He starts for the door.*) And remember this, Adolphus (*he turns to listen*): I have a very strong suspicion that you went to the Salvation Army to worship Barbara and nothing else. And I quite appreciate the very clever way in which you systematically humbug me. I have found you out. Take care Barbara doesnt. Thats all.

Cusins (*with unruffled sweetness*). Don't tell on me, (*He steals out.*)

Lady Britomart. Sarah: if you want to go, go. Anything's better than to sit there as if you wished you were a thousand miles away.

Sarah (*lauguidly*). Very well, mamma. (*She goes.*)

Lady Britomart, *with a sudden flounce, gives way to a little gust of tears.*

Stephen (*going to her*). Mother: whats the matter?

Lady Britomart (*swishing away her tears with her handkerchief*). Nothing. Foolishness. You can go with him, too, if you like, and leave me with the servants.

Stephen. Oh, you mustnt think that, mother. I—I don't like him.

Lady Britomart. The others do. That is the injustice of a woman's lot. A woman has to bring up her children; and that means to restrain them, to deny them things they want, to set them tasks, to punish them when they do wrong, to do all the unpleasant things. And then the father, who has nothing to do but pet them and spoil them, comes in when all her work is done and steals their affection from her.

Stephen. He has not stolen our affection from you. It is only curiosity.

Lady Britomart (*violently*). I wont be consoled, Stephen. There is nothing the matter with me. (*She rises and goes towards the door.*)

Stephen. Where are you going, mother?

Lady Britomart. To the drawing room, of course. (*She goes out. Onward, Christian Soldiers, on the concertina, with tambourine accompaniment, is heard when the door opens.*) Are you coming, Stephen?

Stephen. No. Certainly not. (*She goes. He sits down on the settee, with compressed lips and an expression of strong dislike.*)

ACT II

The yard of the West Ham shelter of the Salvation Army is a cold place on a January morning. The building itself, an old warehouse, is newly whitewashed. Its gabled end projects into the yard in the middle, with a door on the ground floor, and another in the loft above it without any balcony or ladder, but with a pulley rigged over it for hoisting sacks. Those who come from this central gable end into the yard have the gateway leading to the street on their left, with a stone horse-trough just beyond it, and, on the right, a penthouse shielding a table from the weather. There are forms at the table; and on them are seated a man and a woman, both much down on their luck, finishing a meal of bread (one thick slice each, with margarine and golden syrup) and diluted milk.

The man, a workman out of employment, is young, agile, a talker, a poser, sharp enough to be capable of anything in reason except honesty or altruistic considerations of any kind. The woman is a commonplace old bundle of poverty and hard-worn humanity. She looks sixty and probably is forty-five. If they were rich people, gloved and muffed and well wrapped up in furs and overcoats, they would be numbed and miserable; for it is a grindingly cold raw January day; and a glance at the background of grimy warehouses and leaden sky visible over the whitewashed walls of the yard would drive any idle rich person straight to the Mediterranean. But these two, being no more troubled with visions of the Mediterranean than of the moon, and being compelled to keep more of their clothes in the pawnshop, and less on their persons, in winter than in summer, are not depressed by the cold: rather are they stung into vivacity, to which their meal has just now given an almost jolly turn. The man takes a pull at his mug, and then gets up and moves about the yard with his hands deep in his pockets, occasionally breaking into a stepdance.

The Woman. Feel better arter your meal, sir?

The Man. No. Call that a meal! Good enough for you, praps; but wot is it to me, an intelligent workin man.

The Woman. Workin man! Wot are you?

The Man. Painter.

The Woman (sceptically). Yus, I dessay.

The Man. Yus, you dessay! I know. Every loafer that cant do nothink calls isself a painter. Well, I'm a real painter: grainer, finisher, thirty-eight bob a week when I can get it.

The Woman. Then why dont you go and get it?

The Man. I'll tell you why. Fust: I'm intelligent—fffff! it's rotten cold here (*he dances a step or two*)—yes: intelligent beyond the station o life into which it has pleased the capitalists to call me; and they dont like a man that sees through em. Second, an intelligent bein needs a doo share of appiness; so I drink somethink cruel when I get the chawnce. Third, I stand by my class and do as little as I can so's to leave arf the job for me fellow workers. Fourth, I'm fly enough to know wots inside the law and wots outside it; and inside it I do as the capitalists do: pinch wot I can lay me ands on. In a proper state of society I am sober, industrious and honest: in Rome, so to speak, I do as the Romans do. Wots the consequence? When trade is bad—and it's rotten bad just now—and the employers az to sack arf their men, they generally start on me.

The Woman. Whats your name?

The Man. Price. Bronterre O'Brien Price. Usually called Snobby Price, for short.

The Woman. Snobby's a carpenter, aint it? You said you was a painter.

Price. Not that kind of snob, but the genteel sort. I'm too uppish, owing to my intelligence, and my father being a Chartist and a reading, thinking man: a stationer, too. I'm none of your common hewers of wood and drawers of water; and dont you forget it. (*He returns to his seat at the table, and takes up his mug.*) Wots your name?

The Woman. Rummy Mitchens, sir.

Price (*quaffing the remains of his milk to her*). Your elth, Miss Mitchens.

Rummy (*correcting him*). Missis Mitchens.

Price. Wot! Oh Rummy, Rummy! Respectable married woman, Rummy, gittin rescued by the Salvation Army by pretendin to be a bad un. Same old game!

Rummy. What am I to do? I cant starve. Them Salvation lasses is dear good girls; but the better you are, the worse they likes to think you were before they rescued you. Why shouldnt they av a bit o credit, poor loves? theyre worn to rags by their work. And where would they get the money to rescue us if we was to let on we're no worse than other people? You know what ladies and gentlemen are.

Price. Thievin swine! Wish I ad their job, Rummy, all the same. Wot does Rummy stand for? Pet name praps?

Rummy. Short for Romola.

Price. For wot!?

Rummy. Romola. It was out of a new book. Somebody me mother wanted me to grow up like.

Price. We're companions in misfortune, Rummy. Both on us got names that nobody cawnt pronounce. Consequently I'm Snobby and youre Rummy because Bill and Sally wasnt good enough for our parents. Such is life!

Rummy. Who saved you, Mr Price? Was it Major Barbara?

Price. No: I come here on my own. I'm going to be Bronterre O'Brien Price, the converted painter. I know wot they like. I'll tell em how I blasphemed and gambled and wopped my poor old mother—

Rummy (*shocked*). Used you to beat your mother?

Price. Not likely. She used to beat me. No matter: you come and listen to the converted painter, and youll hear how she was a pious woman that taught me me prayers at er knee, an how I used to come home drunk and drag her out o bed be er snow white airs, an lam into er with the poker.

Rummy. Thats whats so unfair to us women. Your confessions is just as big lies as ours: you dont tell what you really done no more than us; but you men can tell your lies right out at the meetins and be made much of for it; while the sort o confessions we az to make az to be wispered to one lady at a time. It aint right, spite of all their piety.

Price. Right! Do you spose the Army'd be allowed if it went and did right? Not much. It combs our air and makes us good little blokes to be robbed and put upon. But I'll play the game as good as any of em. I'll see somebody struck by lightnin, or hear a voice sayin 'Snobby Price: where will you spend eternity?' I'll av a time of it, I tell you.

Rummy. You wont be let drink, though.

Price. I'll take it out in gorspellin, then. I dont want to drink if I can get fun enough any other way.

Jenny Hill, *a pale, overwrought, pretty Salvation lass of 18, comes in through the yard gate, leading* Peter Shirley, *a half hardened, half worn-out elderly man, weak with hunger.*

Jenny (*supporting him*). Come! pluck up. I'll get you something to eat. Youll be all right then.

Price (*rising and hurrying officiously to take the old man off* Jenny's *hands*). Poor old man! Cheer up, brother: youll find rest and peace and appiness ere. Hurry up with the food, miss: e's fair done. (Jenny *hurries into the shelter.*) Ere, buck up, daddy! she's fetchin y'a thick slice o breadn treacle, an a mug o skyblue. (*He seats him at the corner of the table.*)

Rummy (*gaily*). Keep up your old art! Never say die!

Shirley. I'm not an old man. I'm only 46. I'm as good as ever I was. The grey patch come in my hair before I was thirty. All it wants is three pennorth o hair dye: am I to be turned on the streets to starve for it? Holy God! Ive worked ten to twelve hours a day since I was thirteen, and paid my way all through; and now am I to be thrown into the gutter and my job given to a young man that can do it no better than me because Ive black hair that goes white at the first change?

Price (*cheerfully*). No good jawrin about it. Youre ony a jumped-up, jerked-off, orspittle-turned-out incurable of an ole workin man: who cares about you? Eh? Make the thievin swine give you a meal: theyve stole many a one from you. Get a bit o your own back. (Jenny *returns with the usual meal.*) There you are, brother. Awsk a blessin an tuck that into you.

Shirley (*looking at it ravenously but not touching it, and crying like a child*). I never took anything before.

Jenny (*petting him*). Come, come! the Lord sends it to you: he wasnt above taking bread from his friends; and why should you be? Besides, when we find you a job you can pay us for it if you like.

Shirley (*eagerly*). Yes, yes: thats true. I can pay you back: it's only a loan. (*Shivering.*) Oh Lord! oh Lord! (*He turns to the table and attacks the meal ravenously.*)

Jenny. Well, Rummy, are you more comfortable now?

Rummy. God bless you, lovey! youve fed my body and saved my soul, havnt you? (Jenny, *touched, kisses her.*) Sit down and rest a bit: you must be ready to drop.

Jenny. Ive been going hard since morning. But there's more work than we can do. I mustnt stop.

Rummy. Try a prayer for just two minutes. Youll work all the better after.

Jenny (*her eyes lighting up*). Oh isnt it wonderful how a few minutes prayer revives you! I was quite lightheaded at twelve o'clock, I was so tired; but Major Barbara just sent me to pray for five minutes; and I was able to go on as if I had only just begun. (*To* Price.) Did you have a piece of bread?

Price (*with unction*). Yes, miss; but Ive got the piece that I value more; and thats the peace that passeth hall hannerstennin.

Rummy (*fervently*). Glory Hallelujah!

Bill Walker, *a rough customer of about 25, appears at the yard gate and looks malevolently at* Jenny.

Jenny. That makes me so happy. When you say that, I feel wicked for loitering here. I must get to work again.

She is hurrying to the shelter, when the new-comer moves quickly up to the door and intercepts her. His manner is so threatening that she retreats as he comes at her truculently, driving her down the yard.

Bill. Aw knaow you. Youre the one that took awy maw girl. Youre the one that set er agen me. Well, I'm gowin to ev er aht. Not that Aw care a carse for er or you: see? Bat Aw'll let er knaow; and Aw'll let you knaow. Aw'm gowing to give her a doin thatll teach er to cat awy from me. Nah in wiv you and tell er to cam aht afore Aw cam in and kick er aht. Tell her Bill Walker wants er. She'll knaow wot thet means; and if she keeps me witin itll be worse. You stop to jawr beck at me; and Aw'll stawt on you: d'ye eah? Theres your wy. In you gow. (*He takes her by the arm and slings her towards the door of the shelter. She falls on her hand and knee.* Rummy *helps her up again.*)

Price (*rising, and venturing irresolutely towards* Bill). Easy there, mate. She aint doin you no arm.

Bill. Oo are you callin mite? (*Standing over him threateningly.*) Youre gowin to stend ap for er, aw yer? Put ap your ends.

Rummy (*running indignantly to him to scold him*). Oh, you great brute—(*He instantly swings his left hand back against her face. She screams and reels back to the trough, where she sits down, covering her bruised face with her hands and rocking herself and moaning with pain.*)

Jenny (*going to her*). Oh, God forgive you! How could you strike an old woman like that?

Bill (*seizing her by the hair so violently that she also screams, and tearing her away from the old woman*). You Gawd forgimme again an Aw'll Gawk forgive you one on the jawr thetll stop you pryin for a week. (*Holding her and turning fiercely on* Price.) Ev you ennything to sy agen it?

Price (*intimidated*). No, matey: she aint anything to do with me.

Bill. Good job for you! Aw'd pat two meals into you and fawt you with one finger arter, you stawved cur. (*To* Jenny.) Nah are you gowin to fetch aht Mog Ebbijem; or em Aw to knock your fice off you and fetch her meself?

Jenny (*writhing in his grasp*). Oh please someone go in and tell Major Barbara—(*she screams again as he wrenches her head down; and* Price *and* Rummy *flee into the shelter*.)

Bill. You want to gow in and tell your Mijor of me, do you?

Jenny. Oh please dont drag my hair. Let me go.

Bill. Do you or downt you? (*She stifles a scream.*) Yus or nao?

Jenny. God give me strength—

Bill (*striking her with his fist in the face*). Gow an shaow her thet, and tell her if she wants one lawk it to cam and interfere with me. (Jenny, *crying with pain, goes into the shed. He goes to the form and addresses the old man.*) Eah: finish you mess; an git aht o maw wy.

Shirley (*springing up and facing him fiercely, with the mug in his hand*). You take a liberty with me, and I'll smash you over the face with the mug and cut your eye out. Aint you satisfied—young whelps like you—with takin the bread out o the mouths of your elders that have brought you up and slaved for you, but you must come shovin and cheekin and bullyin in here, where the bread o charity is sickenin in our stummicks?

Bill (*contemptuously, but backing a little*). Wot good are you, you aold palsy mag? Wot good are you?

Shirley. As good as you and better. I'll do a day's work agen you or any fat young soaker of your age. Go and take my job at Horrockses, where I worked for ten year. They want young men there: they cant afford to keep men over forty-five. Theyre very sorry—give you a character and happy to help you to get anything suited to your years—sure a steady man wont be long out of a job. Well, let em try you. Theyll find the differ. What do y o u know? Not as much as how to beeyave yourself—layin your dirty fist across the mouth of a respectable woman!

Bill. Downt provowk me to ly it acrost yours: d'ye eah?

Shirley (*with blighting contempt*). Yes: you like an old man to hit, dont you, when youve finished with the women. I aint seen you hit a young one yet.

Bill (*stung*). You loy, you aold soupkitchener, you. There was a yang menn eah. Did Aw offer to itt him or did Aw not?

Shirley. Was he starvin or was he not? Was he a man or only a crosseyed thief an a loafer? Would you hit my son-in-law's brother?

Bill. Oo's ee?

Shirley. Todger Fairmile o Balls Pond. Him that won £20 off the Japanese wrastler at the music hall by standin out 17 minutes 4 seconds agen him.

Bill (*sullenly*). Aw'm nao music awl wrastler. Ken he box?

Shirley. Yes: an you cant.

Bill. Wot! Aw cawnt, cawnt Aw? Wots thet you sy (*threatening him*)?

Shirley (*not budging an inch*). Will you box Todger Fairmile if I put him on to you? Say the word.

Bill (*subsiding with a slouch*). Aw'll stend ap to enny menn alawv, if he was ten Todger Fairmawls. But Aw dont set ap to be a perfeshnal.

Shirley (*looking down on him with unfathomable disdain*). You box! Slap an old woman with the back o your hand! You hadnt even the sense to hit her where a magistrate couldn't see the mark of it, you silly young lump of conceit and ignorance. Hit a girl in the jaw and ony make her cry! If Todger Fairmile'd done it, she wouldnt a got up inside o ten minutes, no more than you would if he got on to you. Yah! I'd set about you myself if I had a week's feedin in me instead o two months' starvation. (*He turns his back on him and sits down moodily at the table.*)

Bill (*following him and stooping over him to drive the taunt in*). You loy! youve the bread and treacle in you that you cam eah to beg.

Shirley (*bursting into tears*). Oh God! it's true: I'm only an old pauper on the scrap heap. (*Furiously.*) But youll come to it yourself; and then youll know. Youll come to it sooner than a teetotaller like me, fillin yourself with gin at this hour o the mornin!

Bill. Aw'm nao gin drinker, you oald lawr; bat wen Aw want to give my girl a bloomin good awdin Aw lawk to ev a bit o devil in me: see? An eah Aw emm, talkin to a rotten aold blawter like you sted o givin her wot for. (*Working himself into a rage.*) Aw'm gowin in there to fetch her aht. (*He makes vengefully for the shelter door.*)

Shirley. Youre going to the station on a stretcher, more likely; and theyll take the gin and the devil out of you there when they get you inside. You mind what youre about: the major here is the Earl o Stevenage's granddaughter.

Bill (*checked*). Garn!

Shirley. Youll see.

Bill (*his resolution oozing*). Well, Aw aint dan nathin to er.

Shirley. Spose she said you did! who'd believe you?

Bill (*very uneasy, skulking back to the corner of the penthouse*). Gawd! theres no jastice in this cantry. To think wot them people can do! Aw'm as good as er.

Shirley. Tell her so. It's just what a fool like you would do.

Barbara, *brisk and businesslike, comes from the shelter with a note book, and addresses herself to* Shirley. Bill, *cowed, sits down in the corner on a form, and turns his back on them.*

Barbara. Good morning.

Shirley (*standing up and taking off his hat*). Good morning, miss.

Barbara. Sit down: make yourself at home. (*He hesitates; but she puts a friendly hand on his shoulder and makes him obey.*) Now then! since youve made friends with us, we want to know all about you. Names and addresses and trades.

Shirley. Peter Shirley. Fitter. Chucked out two months ago because I was too old.

Barbara (*not at all surprised*). Youd pass still. Why didnt you dye your hair?

Shirley. I did. Me age come out at a coroner's inquest on me daughter.

Barbara. Steady?

Shirley. Teetotaller. Never out of a job before. Good worker. And sent to the knackers like an old horse!

Barbara. No matter: if you did your part God will do his.

Shirley (*suddenly stubborn*). My religion's no concern of anybody but myself.

Barbara (*guessing*). *I* know. Secularist?

Shirley (*hotly*). Did I offer to deny it?

Barbara. Why should you? My own father's a Secularist, I think. Our Father—yours and mine—fulfils himself in many ways; and I daresay he knew what he was about when he made a Secularist of you. So buck up, Peter! we can always find a job for a steady man like you. (Shirley, *disarmed and a little bewildered, touches his hat. She turns from him to* Bill.) Whats your name?

Bill (*insolently*). Wots thet to you?

Barbara (*calmly making a note*). Afraid to give his name. Any trade?

Bill. Oo's afride to give is nime? (*Doggedly, with a sense of heroically defying the House of Lords in the person of Lord Stevenage.*) If you want to bring a chawge agen me, bring it. (*She waits, unruffled.*) Moy nime's Bill Walker.

Barbara (*as if the name were familiar: trying to remember how*). Bill Walker? (*Recollecting.*) Oh, I know: youre the man that Jenny Hill was praying for inside just now. (*She enters his name in her note book.*)

Bill. Oo's Jenny Ill? And wot call as she to pry for me?

Barbara. I dont know. Perhaps it was you that cut her lip.

Bill (*defiantly*). Yus, it was me that cat her lip. Aw aint afride o you.

Barbara. How could you be, since youre not afraid of God? Youre a brave man, Mr Walker. It takes some pluck to do o u r work here; but none of us dare lift our hand against a girl like that, for fear of her father in heaven.

Bill (*sullenly*). I want nan o your kentin jawr. I spowse you think Aw cam eah to beg from you, like this demmiged lot eah. Not me. Aw downt want your bread and scripe and ketlep. Aw dont blieve in your Gawd, no more than you do yourself.

Barbara (*sunnily apologetic and ladylike, as on a new footing with him*). Oh, I beg your pardon for putting your name down, Mr Walker. I didnt understand. I'll strike it out.

Bill (*taking this as a slight, and deeply wounded by it*). Eah! you let maw nime alown. Aint it good enaff to be in your book?

Barbara (*considering*). Well, you see, theres no use putting down your name unless I can do something for you, is there? Whats your trade?

Bill (*still smarting*). Thets nao concern o yours.

Barbara. Just so. (*Very businesslike.*) I'll put you down as (*writing*) the man who—struck—poor little Jenny Hill—in the mouth.

Bill (*rising threateningly*). See eah. Awve ed enaff o this.

Barbara (*quite sunny and fearless*). What did you come to us for?

Bill. Aw cam for maw gel, see? Aw cam to tike her aht o this and to brike er jawr for er.

Barbara (*complacently*). You see I was right about your trade. (Bill, *on the point of retorting furiously, finds himself, to his great shame and terror, in danger of crying instead. He sits down again suddenly.*) Whats her name?

Bill (*dogged*). Er nime's Mog Ebbijem: thets wot her nime is.

Barbara. Mog Habbijam! Oh, she's gone to Canning Town, to our barracks there.

Bill (*fortified by his resentment of Mog's perfidy*). Is she? (*Vindictively.*) Then Aw'm gowin to Kennintahn arter her. (*He crosses to the gate; hesitates; finally comes back at* Barbara.) Are you loyin to me to git shat o me?

Barbara. I dont want to get shut of you. I want to keep you here and save your soul. Youd better stay: youre going to have a bad time today, Bill.

Bill. Oo's gowin to give it to me? You, preps?

Barbara. Someone you dont believe in. But youll be glad afterwards.

Bill (*slinking off*). Aw'll gow to Kennintahn to be aht o reach o your tangue. (*Suddenly turning on her with intense malice.*) And if Aw downt fawnd Mog there, Aw'll cam beck and do two years for you, selp me Gawd if Aw downt!

Barbara (*a shade kindlier, if possible*). It's no use, Bill. She's got another bloke.

Bill. Wot!

Barbara. One of her own converts. He fell in love with her when he saw her with her soul saved, and her face clean, and her hair washed.

Bill (*surprised*). Wottud she wash it for, the carroty slat? It's red.

Barbara. It's quite lovely now, because she wears a new look in her eyes with it. It's a pity youre too late. The new bloke has put your nose out of joint, Bill.

Bill. Aw'll put his nowse aht o joint for him. Not that Aw care a carse for er, mawnd thet. But Aw'll teach her to drop me as if Aw was dirt. And Aw'll teach him to meddle with maw judy. Wots iz bleedin nime?

Barbara. Sergeant Todger Fairmile.

Shirley (*rising with grim joy*). I'll go with him, miss. I want to see them two meet. I'll take him to the infirmary when it's over.

Bill (*to* Shirley, *with undissembled misgiving*). Is thet im you was speakin on?

Shirley. Thats him.

Bill. Im that wrastled in the music awl?

Shirley. The competitions at the National Sportin Club was worth nigh a hundred a year to him. He's gev em up now for religion; so he's a bit fresh for want of the exercise he was accustomed to. He'll be glad to see you. Come along.

Bill. Wots is wight?

Shirley. Thirteen four. (Bill's *last hope expires.*)

Barbara. Go and talk to him, Bill. He'll convert you.

Shirley. He'll convert your head into a mashed potato.

Bill (*sullenly*). Aw aint afride of im. Aw aint afride of ennybody. Bat e can lick me. She's dan me. (*He sits down moodily on the edge of the horse trough.*)

Shirley. You aint going. I thought not. (*He resumes his seat.*)

Barbara (*calling*). Jenny!

Jenny (*appearing at the shelter door with a plaster on the corner of her mouth*). Yes, Major.

Barbara. Send Rummy Mitchens out to clear away here.

Jenny. I think she's afraid.

Barbara (*her resemblance to her mother flashing out for a moment*). Nonsense! she must do as she's told.

Jenny (*calling into the shelter*). Rummy: the Major says you must come.

Jenny *comes to* Barbara, *purposely keeping on the side next* Bill, *lest he should suppose that she shrank from him or bore malice.*

Barbara. Poor little Jenny! Are you tired? (*Looking at the wounded cheek.*) Does it hurt?

Jenny. No: it's all right now. It was nothing.

Barbara (*critically*). It was as hard as he could hit, I expect. Poor Bill! You don't feel angry with him, do you?

Jenny. Oh no, no, no: indeed I dont, Major, bless his poor heart! (Barbara *kisses her; and she runs away merrily into the shelter.* Bill *writhes with an agonizing return of his new and alarming symptoms, but says nothing.* Rummy Mitchens *comes from the shelter.*)

Barbara (*going to meet* Rummy). Now Rummy, bustle.

Take in those mugs and plates to be washed; and throw the crumbs about for the birds.

Rummy *takes the three plates and mugs; but* Shirley *takes back his mug from her, as there is still some milk left in it.*

Rummy. There aint any crumbs. This aint a time to waste good bread on birds.
Price (appearing at the shelter door). Gentleman come to see the shelter, Major. Says he's your father.
Barbara. All right. Coming. (Snobby *goes back into the shelter, followed by* Barbara.)
Rummy (stealing across to Bill *and addressing him in a subdued voice, but with intense conviction).* I'd av the lor of you, you flat eared pignosed potwalloper, if she'd let me. Youre no gentleman, to hit a lady in the face. (Bill, *with greater things moving in him, takes no notice.*)
Shirley (following her). Here! in with you and dont get yourself into more trouble by talking.
Rummy (with hauteur). I aint ad the pleasure o being hintroduced to you, as I can remember. (*She goes into the shelter with the plates.*)
Shirley. Thats the—
Bill (savagely). Downt you talk to me, d'ye eah? You lea me alown, or Aw'll do you a mischief. Aw'm not dirt under y o u r feet, ennywy.
Shirley (calmly). Dont you be afeerd. You aint such prime company that you need expect to be sought after. (*He is about to go into the shelter when* Barbara *comes out, with* Undershaft *on her right.*)
Barbara. Oh, there you are, Mr Shirley! (*Between them.*) This is my father: I told you he was a Secularist, didnt I? Perhaps youll be able to comfort one another.
Undershaft (startled). A Secularist! Not the least in the world: on the contrary, a confirmed mystic.
Barbara. Sorry, I'm sure. By the way, papa, what is your religion? in case I have to introduce you again.
Undershaft. My religion? Well, my dear, I am a Millionaire. That is my religion.
Barbara. Then I'm afraid you and Mr Shirley wont be able to comfort one another after all. Youre not a Millionaire, are you, Peter?
Shirley. No; and proud of it.

Undershaft (*gravely*). Poverty, my friend, is not a thing to be proud of.

Shirley (*angrily*). Who made your millions for you? Me and my like. Whats kep us poor? Keepin you rich. I wouldnt have your conscience, not for all your income.

Undershaft. I wouldnt have your income, not for all your conscience, Mr Shirley. (*He goes to the penthouse and sits down on a form.*)

Barbara (*stopping* Shirley *adroitly as he is about to retort*). You wouldnt think he was my father, would you, Peter? Will you go into the shelter and lend the lasses a hand for a while: we're worked off our feet.

Shirley (*bitterly*). Yes: I'm in their debt for a meal, aint I?

Barbara. Oh, not because youre in their debt, but for love of them, Peter, for love of them. (*He cannot understand, and is rather scandalized.*) There! dont stare at me. In with you; and give that conscience of yours a holiday (*bustling him into the shelter.*)

Shirley (*as he goes in*). Ah! it's a pity you never was trained to use your reason, miss. Youd have been a very taking lecturer on Secularism.

Barbara *turns to her father.*

Undershaft. Never mind me, my dear. Go about your work; and let me watch it for a while.

Barbara. All right.

Undershaft. For instance, whats the matter with that outpatient over there?

Barbara (*looking at* Bill, *whose attitude has never changed, and whose expression of brooding wrath has deepened*). Oh, we shall cure him in no time. Just watch. (*She goes over to* Bill *and waits. He glances up at her and casts his eyes down again, uneasy, but grimmer than ever.*) It w o u l d be nice to just stamp on Mog Habbijam's face, wouldnt it, Bill?

Bill (*starting up from the trough in consternation*). It's a loy: Aw never said so. (*She shakes her head.*) Oo taold you wot was in moy mawnd?

Barbara. Only your new friend.

Bill. Wot new friend?

Barbara. The devil, Bill. When he gets round people they get miserable, just like you.

Bill (*with a heartbreaking attempt at devil-may-care cheer-

fulness). Aw aint miserable. (*He sits down again, and stretches his legs in an attempt to seem indifferent.*)

Barbara. Well, if youre happy, why dont you look happy, as we do?

Bill (*his legs curling back in spite of him*). Aw'm eppy enaff, Aw tell you. Woy cawnt you lea me alown? Wot ev I dan to you? Aw aint smashed your fice, ev Aw?

Barbara (*softly: wooing his soul*). It's not me thats getting at you, Bill.

Bill. Oo else is it?

Barbara. Somebody that doesnt intend you to smash women's faces, I suppose. Somebody or something that wants to make a man of you.

Bill (*blustering*). Mike a menn o me! Aint Aw a menn? eh? Oo sez Aw'm not a menn?

Barbara. Theres a man in you somewhere, I suppose. But why did he let you hit poor little Jenny Hill? That wasnt very manly of him, was it?

Bill (*tormented*). Ev dan wiv it, Aw tell you. Chack it. Aw'm sick o your Jenny Ill and er silly little fice.

Barbara. Then why do you keep thinking about it? Why does it keep coming up against you in your mind? Youre not getting converted, are you?

Bill (*with conviction*). Not M E. Not lawkly.

Barbara. Thats right, Bill. Hold out against it. Put out your strength. Dont lets get you cheap. Todger Fairmile said he wrestled for three nights against his salvation harder than he ever wrestled with the Jap at the music hall. He gave in to the Jap when his arm was going to break. But he didnt give in to his salvation until his heart was going to break. Perhaps youll escape that. You havnt any heart, have you?

Bill. Wot d'ye mean? Woy aint Aw got a awt the sime as ennybody else?

Barbara. A man with a heart wouldnt have bashed poor little Jenny's face, would he?

Bill (*almost crying*). Ow, will you lea me alown? Ev Aw ever offered to meddle with you, that you cam neggin and provowkin me lawk this? (*He writhes convulsively from his eyes to his toes.*)

Barbara (*with a steady soothing hand on his arm and a gentle voice that never lets him go*). It's your soul thats hurting you, Bill, and not me. Weve been through it all ourselves. Come with us, Bill. (*He looks wildly round.*) To brave manhood on earth and eternal glory in heaven. (*He is on the point of breaking down.*) Come. (*A drum is heard in the shelter; and* Bill, *with a gasp, escapes from the spell as* Barbara *turns quickly.* Adolphus *enters from the shelter with a big drum.*) Oh! there you are, Dolly. Let me introduce a new friend of mine, Mr Bill Walker. This is my bloke, Bill: Mr Cusins. (Cusins *salutes with his drumstick.*)

Bill. Gowin to merry im?

Barbara. Yes.

Bill (*fervently*). Gawd elp im! Gaw-aw-aw-awd elp im!

Barbara. Why? Do you think he wont be happy with me?

Bill. Awve aony ed to stend it for a mawnin: e'll ev to stend it for a lawftawm.

Cusins. That is a frightful reflection, Mr Walker. But I cant tear myself away from her.

Bill. Well, Aw ken. (*To* Barbara.) Eah! do you knaow where Aw'm gowin to, and wot Aw'm gowin to do?

Barbara. Yes: youre going to heaven; and youre coming back here before the week's out to tell me so.

Bill. You loy. Aw'm gowin to Kennintahn, to spit in Todger Fairmawl's eye. Aw beshed Jenny Ill's fice; an nar Aw'll git me aown fice beshed and cam beck and shaow it to er. Ee'll itt me ardern Aw itt her. Thatll mike us square. (*To* Adolphus.) Is thet fair or it is not? Youre a genlmn: you oughter knaow.

Barbara. Two black eyes wont make one white one, Bill.

Bill. Aw didnt awst you. Cawnt you never keep your mahth shat? Oy awst the genlmn.

Cusins (*reflectively*). Yes: I think youre right, Mr. Walker. Yes: I should do it. It's curious: it's exactly what an ancient Greek would have done.

Barbara. But what good will i t do?

Cusins. Well, it will give Mr Fairmile some exercise; and it will satisfy Mr Walker's soul.

Bill. Rot! there aint nao sach a thing as a saoul. Ah kin you tell wevver Awve a saoul or not? You never seen it.

Barbara. Ive seen it hurting you when you went against it.

Bill (*with compressed aggravation*). If you was maw gel and took the word aht o me mathth lawk thet, Aw'd give you sathink youd feel urtin, Aw would. (*To* Adolphus.) You tike maw tip, mite. Stop er jawr; or youll doy afoah your tawm (*With intense expression.*) Wore aht: thets wot youll be: wore aht. (*He goes away through the gate.*)

Cusins (*looking after him*). I wonder!

Barbara. Dolly! (*indignant, in her mother's manner.*)

Cusins. Yes, my dear, it's very wearing to be in love with you. If it lasts, I quite think I shall die young.

Barbara. Should you mind?

Cusins. Not at all. (*He is suddenly softened, and kisses her over the drum, evidently not for the first time, as people cannot kiss over a big drum without practice.* Undershaft *coughs.*)

Barbara. It's all right, papa, weve not forgotten you. Dolly: explain the place to papa: I havnt time. (*She goes busily into the shelter.*)

Undershaft *and* Adolphus *now have the yard to themselves.* Undershaft, *seated on a form, and still keenly attentive, looks hard at* Adolphus. Adolphus *looks hard at him.*

Undershaft. I fancy you guess something of what is in my mind, Mr. Cusins. (Cusins *flourishes his drumsticks as if in the act of beating a lively rataplan, but makes no sound.*) Exactly so. But suppose Barbara finds you out!

Cusins. You know, I do not admit that I am imposing on Barbara. I am quite genuinely interested in the views of the Salvation Army. The fact is, I am a sort of collector of religions; and the curious thing is that I find I can believe them all. By the way, have you any religion?

Undershaft. Yes.

Cusins. Anything out of the common?

Undershaft. Only that there are two things necessary to Salvation.

Cusins (*disappointed, but polite*). Ah, the Church Catechism. Charles Lomax also belongs to the Established Church.

Undershaft. The two things are—

Cusins. Baptism and—

Undershaft. No. Money and gunpowder.

Cusins (*surprised, but interested*). That is the general opinion of our governing classes. The novelty is in hearing any man confess it.

Undershaft. Just so.

Cusins. Excuse me: is there any place in your religion for honor, justice, truth, love, mercy and so forth?

Undershaft. Yes: they are the graces and luxuries of a rich, strong, and safe life.

Cusins. Suppose one is forced to choose between them and money or gunpowder?

Undershaft. Choose money and gunpowder; for without enough of both you cannot afford the others.

Cusins. That is your religion?

Undershaft. Yes.

The cadence of this reply makes a full close in the conversation, Cusins *twists his face dubiously and contemplates* Undershaft. Undershaft *contemplates him.*

Cusins. Barbara wont stand that. You will have to choose between your religion and Barbara.

Undershaft. So will you, my friend. She will find out that that drum of yours is hollow.

Cusins. Father Undershaft: you are mistaken: I am a sincere Salvationist. You do not understand the Salvation Army. It is the army of joy, of love, of courage: it has banished the fear and remorse and despair of the old hell-ridden evangelical sects: it marches to fight the devil with trumpet and drum, with music and dancing, with banner and palm, as becomes a sally from heaven by its happy garrison. It picks the waster out of the public house and makes a man of him: it finds a worm wriggling in a back kitchen, and lo! a woman! Men and women of rank too, sons and daughters of the Highest. It takes the poor professor of Greek, the most artificial and self-suppressed of human creatures, from his meal of roots, and lets loose the rhapsodist in him; reveals the true worship of Dionysos to him; sends him down the public street drumming dithyrambs (*he plays a thundering flourish on the drum*).

Undershaft. You will alarm the shelter.

Cusins. Oh, they are accustomed to these sudden ecstasies. However, if the drum worries you—(*he pockets the drumsticks; unhooks the drum; and stands it on the ground opposite the gateway*).

Undershaft. Thank you.

Cusins. You remember what Euripides says about your money and gunpowder?

Undershaft. No.

Cusins (*declaiming*).

One and another
In money and guns may outpass his brother;
And men in their millions float and flow
And seethe with a million hopes as leaven;
And they win their will; or they miss their will;
And their hopes are dead or are pined for still;
But who'er can know
As the long days go
That to live is happy, has found his heaven.

My translation: what do you think of it?

Undershaft. I think, my friend, that if you wish to know, as the long days go, that to live i s happy, you must first acquire money enough for a decent life, and power enough to be your own master.

Cusins. You are damnably discouraging. (*He resumes his declamation.*)

Is it so hard a thing to see
That the spirit of God—whate'er it be—
The law that abides and changes not, ages long,
The Eternal and Nature-born: t h e s e things be strong?
What else is Wisdom? What of Man's endeavor,
Or God's high grace so lovely and so great?
To stand from fear set free? to breathe and wait?
To hold a hand uplifted over Fate?
And shall not Barbara be loved for ever?

Undershaft. Euripides mentions Barbara, does he?

Cusins. It is a fair translation. The word means Loveliness.

Undershaft. May I ask—as Barbara's father—how much a year she is to be loved for ever on?

Cusins. As for Barbara's father, that is more your affair than mine. I can feed her by teaching Greek: that is about all.

Undershaft. Do you consider it a good match for her?

Cusins (*with polite obstinacy*). Mr Undershaft: I am in many ways a weak, timid, ineffectual person; and my health is far from satisfactory. But whenever I feel that I must have anything, I get it, sooner or later. I feel that way about Barbara. I dont like marriage: I feel intensely afraid of it; and I don't know what I shall do with Barbara or what she will do with me. But I feel that I and nobody else must marry her. Please regard that as settled. —Not that I wish to be arbitrary;

but why should I waste your time in discussing what is inevitable?

Undershaft. You mean that you will stick at nothing: not even the conversion of the Salvation Army to the worship of Dionysos.

Cusins. The business of the Salvation Army is to save, not to wrangle about the name of the pathfinder. Dionysos or another: what does it matter?

Undershaft (*rising and approaching him*). Professor Cusins: you are a young man after my own heart.

Cusins. Mr Undershaft: you are, as far as I am able to gather, a most infernal old rascal; but you appeal very strongly to my sense of ironic humor.

Undershaft *mutely offers his hand. They shake.*

Undershaft (*suddenly concentrating himself*). And now to business.

Cusins. Pardon me. We are discussing religion. Why go back to such an uninteresting and unimportant subject as business?

Undershaft. Religion is our business at present, because it is through religion alone that we can win Barbara.

Cusins. Have you, too, fallen in love with Barbara?

Undershaft. Yes, with a father's love.

Cusins. A father's love for a grown-up daughter is the most dangerous of all infatuations. I apologize for mentioning my own pale, coy, mistrustful fancy in the same breath with it.

Undershaft. Keep to the point. We have to win her; and we are neither of us Methodists.

Cusins. That doesnt matter. The power Barbara wields here—the power that wields Barbara herself—is not Calvinism, not Presbyterianism, not Methodism—

Undershaft. Not Greek Paganism either, eh?

Cusins. I admit that. Barbara is quite original in her religion.

Undershaft (*triumphantly*). Aha! Barbara Undershaft would be. Her inspiration comes from within herself.

Cusins. How do you suppose it got there?

Undershaft (*in towering excitement*). It is the Undershaft inheritance. I shall hand on my torch to my daughter. She shall make my converts and preach my gospel—

Cusins. What! Money and gunpowder!

Undershaft. Yes, money and gunpowder. Freedom and power. Command of life and command of death.

Cusins (*urbanely: trying to bring him down to earth*). This is extremely interesting, Mr Undershaft. Of course you know that you are mad.

Undershaft (*with redoubled force*). And you?

Cusins. Oh, mad as a hatter. You are welcome to my secret since I have discovered yours. But I am astonished. Can a madman make cannons?

Undershaft. Would anyone else than a madman make them? And now (*with surging energy*) question for question. Can a sane man translate Euripides?

Cusins. No.

Undershaft (*seizing him by the shoulder*). Can a sane woman make a man of a waster or a woman of a worm?

Cusins (*reeling before the storm*). Father Colossus—Mammoth Millionaire—

Undershaft (*pressing him*). Are there two mad people or three in this Salvation shelter today?

Cusins. You mean Barbara is as mad as we are?

Undershaft (*pushing him lightly off and resuming his equanimity suddenly and completely*). Pooh, Professor! let us call things by their proper names. I am a millionaire; you are a poet; Barbara is a savior of souls. What have we three to do with the common mob of slaves and idolators? (*He sits down again with a shrug of contempt for the mob.*)

Cusins. Take care! Barbara is in love with the common people. So am I. Have you never felt the romance of that love?

Undershaft (*cold and sardonic*). Have you ever been in love with Poverty, like St Francis? Have you ever been in love with Dirt, like St Simeon! Have you ever been in love with disease and suffering, like our nurses and philanthropists? Such passions are not virtues, but the most unnatural of all the vices. This love of the common people may please an earl's granddaughter and a university professor; but I have been a common man and a poor man; and it has no romance for me. Leave it to the poor to pretend that poverty is a blessing: leave it to the coward to make religion of his cowardice by preaching humility: we know better than that. We three must stand together above the common people: how else can we help their children to climb up beside us? Barbara must belong to us, not to the Salvation Army.

Cusins. Well, I can only say that if you think you will get her away from the Salvation Army by talking to her as you have been talking to me, you don't know Barbara.

Undershaft. My friend: I never ask for what I can buy.

Cusins (in a white fury). Do I understand you to imply that you can buy Barbara?

Undershaft. No; but I can buy the Salvation Army.

Cusins. Quite impossible.

Undershaft. You shall see. All religious organizations exist by selling themselves to the rich.

Cusins. Not the Army. That is the Church of the poor.

Undershaft. All the more reason for buying it.

Cusins. I don't think you quite know what the Army does for the poor.

Undershaft. Oh yes I do. It draws their teeth: that is enough for me as a man of business.

Cusins. Nonsense! It makes them sober—

Undershaft. I prefer sober workmen. The profits are larger.

Cusins. —honest—

Undershaft. Honest workmen are the most economical.

Cusins. —attached to their homes—

Undershaft. So much the better: they will put up with anything sooner than change their shop.

Cusins. —happy—

Undershaft. An invaluable safeguard against revolution.

Cusins. —unselfish—

Undershaft. Indifferent to their own interests, which suits me exactly.

Cusins. —with their thoughts on heavenly things—

Undershaft (rising). And not on Trade Unionism nor Socialism. Excellent.

Cusins (revolted). You really are an infernal old rascal.

Undershaft (indicating Peter Shirley, *who has just come from the shelter and strolled dejectedly down the yard between them).* And this is an honest man!

Shirley. Yes; and what av I got by it? (*He passes on bitterly and sits on the form, in the corner of the penthouse.*)

Snobby Price, *beaming sanctimoniously, and* Jenny Hill, *with a tambourine full of coppers, come from the shelter and go to the drum, on which* Jenny *begins to count the money.*

Undershaft (*replying to* Shirley). Oh, your employers must have got a good deal by it from first to last. (*He sits on the table, with one foot on the side form,* Cusins, *overwhelmed, sits down on the same form nearer the shelter.* Barbara *comes from the shelter to the middle of the yard. She is excited and a little overwrought.*)

Barbara. Weve just had a splendid experience meeting at the other gate in Cripps's lane. Ive hardly ever seen them so much moved as they were by your confession, Mr Price.

Price. I could almost be glad of my past wickedness if I could believe that it would elp to keep hathers stright.

Barbara. So it will, Snobby. How much, Jenny?

Jenny. Four and tenpence, Major.

Barbara. Oh Snobby, if you had given your poor mother just one more kick, we should have got the whole five shillings!

Price. If she heard you say that, miss, she'd be sorry I didnt. But I'm glad. Oh what a joy it will be to her when she hears I'm saved!

Undershaft. Shall I contribute the odd twopence, Barbara? The millionaire's mite, eh? (*He takes a couple of pennies from his pocket.*)

Barbara. How did you make that twopence?

Undershaft. As usual. By selling cannons, torpedos, submarines, and my new patent Grand Duke hand grenade.

Barbara. Put it back in your pocket. You cant buy your salvation here for twopence: you must work it out.

Undershaft. Is twopence not enough? I can afford a little more, if you press me.

Barbara. Two million millions would not be enough. There is bad blood on your hands; and nothing but good blood can cleanse them. Money is no use. Take it away. (*She turns to* Cusins.) Dolly: you must write another letter for me to the papers. (*He makes a wry face.*) Yes: I know you dont like it; but it must be done. The starvation this winter is beating us: everybody is unemployed. The General says we must close this shelter if we cant get more money. I force the collections at the meetings until I am ashamed: dont I, Snobby?

Price. It's a fair treat to see you work it, miss. The way you got them up from three-and-six to four-and-ten with that hymn, penny by penny and verse by verse, was a caution. Not a Cheap Jack on Mile End Waste could touch you at it.

Barbara. Yes; but I wish we could do without it. I am getting at last to think more of the collection than of the people's souls. And what are those hatfuls of pence and halfpence? We want thousands! tens of thousands! hundreds of thousands! I want to convert people, not to be always begging for the Army in a way I'd die sooner than beg for myself.

Undershaft (*in profound irony*). Genuine unselfishness is capable of anything, my dear.

Barbara (*unsuspectingly, as she turns away to take the money from the drum and put it in a cashbag she carries*). Yes, isnt it? (Undershaft *looks sardonically at* Cusins.)

Cusins (*aside to* Undershaft). Mephistopheles! Michiavelli!

Barbara (*tears coming into her eyes as she ties the bag and pockets it*). How are we to feed them? I cant talk religion to a man with bodily hunger in his eyes. (*Almost breaking down.*) It's frightful.

Jenny (*running to her*). Major, dear—

Barbara (*rebounding*). No: don't comfort me. It will be all right. We shall get the money.

Undershaft. How?

Jenny. By praying for it, of course. Mrs Baines says she prayed for it last night; and she has never prayed for it in vain: never once. (*She goes to the gate and looks out into the s treet.*)

Barbara (*who has dried her eyes and regained her composure*). By the way, dad, Mrs Baines has come to march with us to our big meeting this afternoon; and she is very anxious to meet you, for some reason or other. Perhaps she'll convert you.

Undershaft. I shall be delighted, my dear.

Jenny (*at the gate: excitedly*). Major! Major! heres that man back again.

Barbara. What man?

Jenny. The man that hit me. Oh, I hope he's coming back to join us.

Bill Walker, *with frost on his jacket, comes through the gate, his hands deep in his pockets and his chin sunk between his shoulders, like a cleaned-out gambler. He halts between* Barbara *and the drum.*

Barbara. Hullo, Bill! Back already!

Bill (*nagging at her*). Bin talkin ever sence, ev you?

Barbara. Pretty nearly. Well, has Todger paid you out for poor Jenny's jaw?

Bill. Nao e aint.

Barbara. I thought your jacket looked a bit snowy.

Bill. Sao it is snaowy. You want to knaow where the snaow cam from, downt you?

Barbara. Yes.

Bill. Well, it cam from orf the grahnd in Pawkinses Corner in Kennintahn. It got rabbed orf be maw shaoulders: see?

Barbara. Pity you didnt rub some off with your knees, Bill! That would have done you a lot of good.

Bill (*with sour mirthless humor*). Aw was sivin anather menn's knees at the tawm. E was kneelin on moy ed, e was.

Jenny. Who was kneeling on your head?

Bill. Todger was. E was pryin for me: pryin camfortable wiv me as a cawpet. Sow was Mog. Sao was the aol bloomin meetin. Mog she sez "Ow Lawd brike is stabborn sperrit; bat downt urt is dear art." Thet was wot she said. "Downt urt is dear art"! An er blowk—thirteen stun four!—kneelin wiv all is wight on me. Fanny, aint it?

Jenny. Oh no. We're so sorry, Mr Walker.

Barbara (*enjoying it frankly*). Nonsense! of course it's funny. Served you right, Bill! You must have done something to him first.

Bill (*doggedly*). Aw did wot Aw said Aw'd do. Aw spit in is eye. E looks ap at the skoy and sez, 'Ow that Aw should be fahnd worthy to be spit upon for the gospel's sike!' e sez; an Mog sez 'Glaory Allelloolier!'; an then e called me Braddher, an dahned me as if Aw was a kid and e was me mather worshin me a Setterda nawt. Aw ednt jast nao shaow wiv im at all. Arf the street pryed; an the tather arf larfed fit to split theirselves. (*To* Barbara.) There! are you settisfawd nah?

Barbara (*her eyes dancing*). Wish I'd been there, Bill.

Bill. Yus: youd a got in a hextra bit o talk on me, wouldnt you?

Jenny. I'm so sorry, Mr Walker.

Bill (*fiercely*). Downt you gow being sorry for me: youve no call. Listen eah. Aw browk your jawr.

Jenny. No, it didnt hurt me: indeed it didnt, except for a moment. It was only that I was frightened.

Bill. Aw downt want to be forgive be you, or be enny-body. Wot Aw did Aw'll py for. Aw trawd to gat me aown jawr browk to settisfaw you—

Jenny (*distressed*). Oh no—

Bill (*impatiently*). Tell y' Aw did: cawnt you listen to wots bein taold you? All Aw got be it was bein mide a sawt of in the pablic street for me pines. Well, if Aw cawnt settisfaw you one wy, Aw ken anather. Listen eah! Aw ed two quid sived agen the frost; an Awve a pahnd of it left. A mite o mawn last week ed words with the judy e's gowing to merry. E give er wot-for; an e's bin fawnd fifteen bob. E ed a rawt to itt er cause they was gowin to be merrid; but Aw ednt nao rawt to itt you; sao put anather fawv bob on an call it a pahnd's worth. (*He produces a sovereign.*) Eahs the manney. Tike it; and lets ev no more o your for-givin an prying and your Mijor jawrin me. Let wot Aw dan be dan an pide for; and let there be a end of it.

Jenny. Oh, I couldnt take it, Mr Walker. But if you would give a shilling or two to poor Rummy Mitchens! you really did hurt her; and she's old.

Bill (*contemptuously*). Not lawkly. Aw'd give her an-ather as soon as look at er. Let her ev the lawr o me as she threatened! She aint forgiven me: not mach. Wot Aw dan to er is not on me mawnd—wot she (*in-dicating* Barbara) mawt call on me conscience—no more than stickin a pig. It's this Christian gime o yours that Aw wownt ev plyed agen me: this bloomin forgivin an neggin and jawrin that mikes a menn thet sore that iz lawf's a burdn to im. Aw wownt ev it, Aw tell you; sao tike your manney and stop thraowin your silly beshed fice hap agen me.

Jenny. Major: may I take a little of it for the Army?

Barbara. No: the Army is not to be bought. We want your soul, Bill; and we'll take nothing less.

Bill (*bitterly*). Aw knaow. Me an maw few shillins is not good enaff for you. Youre a earl's grendorter, you are. Nathink less than a andered pahnd for you.

Undershaft. Come, Barbara! you could do a great deal of good with a hundred pounds. If you will set this gentleman's mind at ease by taking his pound, I will give the other ninety-nine.

Bill, *dazed by such opulence, instinctively touches his cap.*

Barbara. Oh, youre too extravagant, papa. Bill offers twenty pieces of silver. All you need offer is the other ten. That will make the standard price to buy anybody who's for sale. I'm not; and the Army's not. (*To* Bill.) Youll never have another quiet moment, Bill, until you come round to us. You cant stand out against your salvation.

Bill (*sullenly*). Aw cawnt stend aht agen music awl wrastlers and awtful tangued women. Awve offered to py. Aw can do no more. Tike it or leave it. There it is. (*He throws the sovereign on the drum, and sits down on the horse-trough. The coin fascinates* Snobby Price, *who takes an early opportunity of dropping his cap on it.*)

Mrs Baines *comes from the shelter. She is dressed as a Salvation Army Commissioner. She is an earnest looking woman of about 40, with a caressing, urgent voice, and an appealing manner.*

Barbara. This is my father, Mrs Baines. (Undershaft *comes from the table, taking his hat off with marked civility.*) Try what you can do with him. He wont listen to me, because he remembers what a fool I was when I was a baby. (*She leaves them together and chats with* Jenny.)

Mrs Baines. Have you been shewn over the shelter, Mr Undershaft? You know the work we're doing, of course.

Undershaft (*very civilly*). The whole nation knows it, Mrs Baines.

Mrs Baines. No, sir: the whole nation does not know it, or we should not be crippled as we are for want of money to carry our work through the length and breadth of the land. Let me tell you that there would have been rioting this winter in London but for us.

Undershaft. You really think so?

Mrs Baines. I know it. I remember 1886, when you rich gentlemen hardened your hearts against the cry of the poor. They broke the windows of your clubs in Pall Mall.

Undershaft (*gleaming with approval of their method*). And the Mansion House Fund went up next day from thirty thousand pounds to seventy-nine thousand! I remember quite well.

Mrs Baines. Well, wont you help me to get at the people? They wont break windows then. Come here, Price.

Let me shew you to this gentleman (Price *comes to be inspected.*) Do you remember the window breaking?

Price. My ole father thought it was the revolution, maam.

Mrs Baines. Would you break windows now?

Price. Oh no, maam. The windows of eaven av bin opened to me. I know now that the rich man is a sinner like myself.

Rummy (*appearing above at the loft door*). Snobby Price!

Snobby. Wot is it?

Rummy. Your mother's askin for you at the other gate in Cripps's Lane. She's heard about your confession (Price *turns pale.*)

Mrs Baines. Go, Mr Price; and pray with her.

Jenny. You can go through the shelter, Snobby.

Price (*to* Mrs Baines). I couldnt face her now, maam, with all the weight of my sins fresh on me. Tell her she'll find her son at ome, waitin for her in prayer. (*He skulks off through the gate, incidentally stealing the sovereign on his way out by picking up his cap from the drum.*)

Mrs Baines (*with swimming eyes*). You see how we take the anger and bitterness against you out of their hearts, Mr Undershaft.

Undershaft. It is certainly most convenient and gratifying to all large employers of labor, Mrs Baines.

Mrs Baines. Barbara: Jenny: I have good news: most wonderful news. (Jenny *runs to her.*) My prayers have been answered. I told you they would, Jenny, didn't I?

Jenny. Yes, yes.

Barbara (*moving nearer to the drum*). Have we got money enough to keep the shelter open?

Mrs Baines. I hope we shall have enough to keep all the shelters open. Lord Saxmundham has promised us five thousand pounds—

Barbara. Hooray!

Jenny. Glory!

Mrs Baines. —if—

Barbara. "If!" If what?

Mrs Baines. —if five other gentlemen will give a thousand each to make it up to ten thousand.

Barbara. Who is Lord Saxmundham? I never heard of him.

Undershaft (*who has pricked up his ears at the peer's

name, and is now watching Barbara *curiously*). A new creation, my dear. You have heard of Sir Horace Bodger?

Barbara. Bodger! Do you mean the distiller? Bodger's whisky!

Undershaft. That is the man. He is one of the greatest of our public benefactors. He restored the cathedral at Hakington. They made him a baronet for that. He gave half a million to the funds of his party: they made him a baron for that.

Shirley. What will they give him for the five thousand?

Undershaft. There is nothing left to give him. So the five thousand, I should think, is to save his soul.

Mrs Baines. Heaven grant it may! Oh Mr Undershaft, you have some very rich friends. Cant you help us towards the other five thousand? We are going to hold a great meeting this afternoon at the Assembly Hall in the Mile End Road. If I could only announce that one gentleman had come forward to support Lord Saxmundham, others would follow. Dont you know somebody? couldnt you? wouldnt you? (*her eyes fill with tears*) oh, think of those poor people, Mr Undershaft: think of how much it means to them, and how little to a great man like you.

Undershaft (*sardonically gallant*). Mrs Baines: you are irresistible. I cant disappoint you; and I cant deny myself the satisfaction of making Bodger pay up. You shall have your five thousand pounds.

Mrs Baines. Thank God!

Undershaft. You dont thank me?

Mrs Baines. Oh sir, dont try to be cynical: don't be ashamed of being a good man. The Lord will bless you abundantly; and our prayers will be like a strong fortification round you all the days of your life. (*With a touch of caution.*) You will let me have the cheque to shew at the meeting, wont you? Jenny: go in and fetch a pen and ink. (Jenny *runs to the shelter door.*)

Undershaft. Do not disturb Miss Hill: I have a fountain pen. (Jenny *halts. He sits at the table and writes the cheque.* Cusins *rises to make room for him. They all watch him silently.*)

Bill (*cynically, aside to* Barbara, *his voice and accent horribly debased*). Wot prawce selvytion nah?

Barbara. Stop. (Undershaft *stops writing: they all turn to her in surprise.*) Mrs Baines: are you really going to take this money?

Mrs. Baines (*astonished*). Why not, dear?

Barbara. Why not! Do you know what my father is? Have you forgotten that Lord Saxmundham is Bodger the whisky man? Do you remember how we implored the County Council to stop him from writing Bodger's Whisky in letters of fire against the sky; so that the poor drink-ruined creatures on the Embankment could not wake up from their snatches of sleep without being reminded of their deadly thirst by that wicked sky sign? Do you know that the worst thing I have had to fight here is not the devil, but Bodger, Bodger, Bodger, with his whisky, his distilleries, and his tied houses? Are you going to make our shelter another tied house for him, and ask me to keep it?

Bill. Rotten dranken whisky it is too.

Mrs Baines. Dear Barbara: Lord Saxmundham has a soul to be saved like any of us. If heaven has found the way to make a good use of his money, are we to set ourselves up against the answer to our prayers?

Barbara. I know he has a soul to be saved. Let him come down here; and I'll do my best to help him to his salvation. But he wants to send his cheque down to buy us, and go on being as wicked as ever.

Undershaft (*with a reasonableness which* Cusins *alone perceives to be ironical*). My dear Barbara: alcohol is a very necessary article. It heals the sick—

Barbara. It does nothing of the sort.

Undershaft. Well, it assists the doctor: that is perhaps a less questionable way of putting it. It makes life bearable to millions of people who could not endure their existence if they were quite sober. It enables Parliament to do things at eleven at night that no sane person would do at eleven in the morning. Is it Bodger's fault that this inestimable gift is deplorably abused by less than one per cent of the poor? (*He turns again to the table; signs the cheque; and crosses it.*)

Mrs Baines. Barbara: will there be less drinking or more if all those poor souls we are saving come tomorrow and find the doors of our shelters shut in their faces? Lord Saxmundham gives us the money to stop drinking—to take his own business from him.

Cusins (*impishly*). Pure self-sacrifice on Bodger's part, clearly! Bless dear Bodger! (Barbara *almost breaks down as* Adolphus, *too, fails her.*)

Undershaft (*tearing out the cheque and pocketing the book as he rises and goes past* Cusins *to* Mrs Baines).

I also, Mrs Baines, may claim a little disinterestedness. Think of my business! think of the widows and orphans! the men and lads torn to pieces with shrapnel and poisoned with lyddite! (Mrs Baines *shrinks; but he goes on remorselessly*) the oceans of blood, not one drop of which is shed in a really just cause! the ravaged crops! the peaceful peasants forced, women and men, to till their fields under the fire of opposing armies on pain of starvation! the bad blood of the fierce little cowards at home who egg on others to fight for the gratification of their national vanity! All this makes money for me: I am never richer, never busier than when the papers are full of it. Well, it is your work to preach peace on earth and good will to men. (Mrs Baines's *face lights up again.*) Every convert you make is a vote against war. (*Her lips move in prayer.*) Yet I give you this money to help you to hasten my own commercial ruin. (*He gives her the cheque.*)

Cusins (*mounting the form in an ecstasy of mischief*). The millennium will be inaugurated by the unselfishness of Undershaft and Bodger. Oh be joyful! (*He takes the drum-sticks from his pocket and flourishes them.*)

Mrs Baines (*taking the cheque*). The longer I live the more proof I see that there is an Infinite Goodness that turns everything to the work of salvation sooner or later. Who would have thought that any good could have come out of war and drink? And yet their profits are brought today to the feet of salvation to do its blessed work. (*She is affected to tears.*)

Jenny (*running to* Mrs Baines *and throwing her arms round her.*) Oh dear! how blessed, how glorious it all is!

Cusins (*in a convulsion of irony*). Let us seize this unspeakable moment. Let us march to the great meeting at once. Excuse me just an instant. (*He rushes into the shelter.* Jenny *takes her tambourine from the drum head.*)

Mrs Baines. Mr Undershaft: have you ever seen a thousand people fall on their knees with one impulse and pray? Come with us to the meeting. Barbara shall tell them that the Army is saved, and saved through you.

Cusins (*returning impetuously from the shelter with a flag and a trombone, and coming between* Mrs Baines *and* Undershaft). You shall carry the flag down the first street, Mrs Baines (*he gives her the flag*). Mr Undershaft is a gifted trombonist: he shall intone an Olympian diapason to the West Ham Salvation March. (*Aside to* Undershaft, *as he forces the trombone on him.*) Blow, Machiavelli, blow.

Undershaft (*aside to him, as he takes the trombone*). The trumpet in Zion! (Cusins *rushes to the drum, which he takes up and puts on.* Undershaft *continues, aloud.*) I will do my best. I could vamp a bass if I knew the tune.

Cusins. It is a wedding chorus from one of Donizetti's operas; but we have converted it. We convert everything to good here, including Bodger. You remember the chorus. "For thee immense rejoicing—immenso giubilo—immenso giubilo." (*With drum obbligato.*) Rum tum ti tum tum, tum tum ti ta—

Barbara. Dolly: you are breaking my heart.

Cusins. What is a broken heart more or less here? Dionysos Undershaft has descended. I am possessed.

Mrs Baines. Come, Barbara: I must have my dear Major to carry the flag with me.

Jenny. Yes, yes, Major darling.

Cusins (*snatches the tambourine out of* Jenny's *hand and mutely offers it to* Barbara.)

Barbara (*coming forward a little as she puts the offer behind her with a shudder, whilst* Cusins *recklessly tosses the tambourine back to* Jenny *and goes to the gate*). I cant come.

Jenny. Not come!

Mrs Baines (*with tears in her eyes*). Barbara: do you think I am wrong to take the money?

Barbara (*impulsively going to her and kissing her*). No, no: God help you, dear, you must: you are saving the Army. Go; and may you have a great meeting!

Jenny. But arnt you coming?

Barbara. No. (*She begins taking off the silver S brooch from her collar.*)

Mrs Baines. Barbara: what are you doing?

Jenny. Why are you taking your badge off? You cant be going to leave us, Major.

Barbara (*quietly*). Father: come here.

Undershaft (*coming to her*). My dear! (*Seeing that she is going to pin the badge on his collar, he retreats to the penthouse in some alarm.*)

Barbara (*following him*). Dont be frightened. (*She pins the badge on and steps back towards the table, shew-*

ing him to the others.) There! It's not much for £5000, is it?

Mrs Baines. Barbara: if you wont come and play with us, promise me you will pray for us.

Barbara. I cant pray now. Perhaps I shall never pray again.

Mrs Baines. Barbara!

Jenny. Major!

Barbara (*almost delirious*). I cant bear any more. Quick march!

Cusins (*calling to the procession in the street outside*). Off we go. Play up, there! Immenso giubilo. (*He gives the time with his drum; and the band strikes up the march, which rapidly becomes more distant as the procession moves briskly away.*)

Mrs Baines. I must go, dear. Youre overworked: you will be all right tomorrow. We'll never lose you. Now Jenny: step out with the old flag. Blood and Fire! (*She marches out through the gate with her flag.*)

Jenny. Glory Hallelujah! (*Flourishing her tambourine and marching.*)

Undershaft (*to* Cusins, *as he marches out past him easing the slide of his trombone*). "My ducats and my daughter"!

Cusins (*following him out*). Money and gunpowder!

Barbara. Drunkenness and Murder! My God: why hast thou forsaken me?

She sinks on the form with her face buried in her hands. The march passes away into silence. Bill Walker *steals across to her.*

Bill (*taunting*). Wot prawce selvytion nah?

Shirley. Dont you hit her when she's down.

Bill. She itt me wen aw wiz dahn. Waw shouldnt Aw git a bit o me aown beck?

Barbara (*raising her head*). I didn't take your money, Bill. (*She crosses the yard to the gate and turns her back on the two men to hide her face from them.*)

Bill (*sneering after her*). Naow, it warnt enaff for you. (*Turning to the drum, he misses the money.*) Ellow! If you aint took it sammun else ez. Weres it gorn? Bly me if Jenny Ill didnt tike it arter all!

Rummy (*screaming at him from the loft*). You lie, you dirty blackguard! Snobby Price pinched it off the drum when he took up his cap. I was up here all the time an see im do it.

Bill. Wot! Stowl maw manney! Waw didnt you call thief on him, you silly aold macker you?

Rummy. To serve you aht for ittin me acrost the fice. It's cost y'pahnd, that az. (*Raising a pæan of squalid triumph.*) I done you. I'm even with you. Uve ad it aht o y—(Bill *snatches up* Shirley's *mug and hurls it at her. She slams the loft door and vanishes. The mug smashes against the door and falls in fragments.*)

Bill (*beginning to chuckle*). Tell us, aol menn, wot o'clock this mawnin was it wen im as they call Snobby Prawce was sived?

Barbara (*turning to him more composedly, and with unspoiled sweetness*). About half past twelve, Bill. And he pinched your pound at a quarter to two. *I* know. Well, you cant afford to lose it. I'll send it to you.

Bill (*his voice and accent suddenly improving*). Not if Aw wiz to stawve for it. Aw aint to be bought.

Shirley. Aint you? Youd sell yourself to the devil for a pint o beer; only there aint no devil to make the offer.

Bill (*unashamed*). Sao Aw would, mite, and often ev, cheerful. But s h e cawnt baw me. (*Approaching* Barbara.) You wanted maw saoul, did you? Well, you aint got it.

Barbara. I nearly got it, Bill. But weve sold it back to you for ten thousand pounds.

Shirley. And dear at the money!

Barbara. No, Peter: it was worth more than money.

Bill (*salvationproof*). It's nao good: you cawnt get rahnd me nah. Aw downt blieve in it; and Awve seen tody that Aw was rawt. (*Going.*) Sao long, aol soupkitchener! Ta, ta, Mijor Earl's Grendorter! (*Turning at the gate.*) Wot prawce selvytion nah? Snobby Prawce! Ha! ha!

Barbara (*offering her hand*). Goodbye, Bill.

Bill (*taken aback, half plucks his cap off; then shoves it on again defiantly*). Git aht. (*Barbara drops her hand, discouraged. He has a twinge of remorse.*) But thets aw rawt, you knaow. Nathink pasnl. Naow mellice. Sao long, Judy. (*He goes.*)

Barbara. No malice. So long, Bill.

Shirley (*shaking his head*). You make too much of him, miss, in your innocence.

Barbara (*going to him*). Peter: I'm like you now. Cleaned out, and lost my job.

Shirley. Youve youth an hope. Thats two better than me.

Barbara. I'll get you a job, Peter. Thats hope for you: the youth will have to be enough for me. (*She counts her *money.*) I have just enough left for two teas at Lockharts, a Rowton doss for you, and my tram and bus home. (*He frowns and rises with offended pride. She takes his arm*) Dont be proud, Peter: it's sharing between friends. And promise me youll talk to me and not let me cry. (*She draws him towards the gate.*)

Shirley. Well, I'm not accustomed to talk to the like of you—

Barbara (*urgently*). Yes, yes: you must talk to me. Tell me about Tom Paine's books and Bradlaugh's lectures. Come along.

Shirley. Ah, if you would only read Tom Paine in the proper spirit, miss! (*They go out through the gate together.*)

ACT III

Next day after lunch Lady Britomart *is writing in the library in Wilton Crescent.* Sarah *is reading in the armchair near the window.* Barbara, *in ordinary fashionable dress, pale and brooding, is on the settee.* Charles Lomax *enters. He starts on seeing* Barbara *fashionably attired and in low spirits.*

Lomax. Youve left off your uniform!

Barbara *says nothing; but an expression of pain passes over her face.*

Lady Britomart (*warning him in low tones to be careful*). Charles!

Lomax (*much concerned, coming behind the settee and bending sympathetically over* Barbara). I'm awfully sorry, Barbara. You know I helped you all I could with the concertina and so forth. (*Momentously.*) Still, I have never shut my eyes to the fact that there is a certain amount of tosh about the Salvation Army. Now the claims of the Church of England—

Lady Britomart. Thats enough, Charles. Speak of something suited to your mental capacity.

Lomax. But surely the Church of England is suited to all our capacities.

Barbara (*pressing his hand*). Thank you for your sympathy, Cholly. Now go and spoon with Sarah.

Lomax (*dragging a chair from the writing table and seating himself affectionately by* Sarah's *side*). How is my ownest today?

Sarah. I wish you wouldnt tell Cholly to do things, Barbara. He always comes straight and does them. Cholly: we're going to the works this afternoon.

Lomax. What works?

Sarah. The cannon works.

Lomax. What? your governor's shop!

Sarah. Yes.

Lomax. Oh I say!

Cusins *enters in poor condition. He also starts visibly when he sees* Barbara *without her uniform.*

Barbara. I expected you this morning, Dolly. Didnt you guess that?

Cusins (*sitting down beside her*). I'm sorry. I have only just breakfasted.

Sarah. But weve just finished lunch.

Barbara. Have you had one of your bad nights?

Cusins. No: I had rather a good night: in fact, one of the most remarkable nights I have ever passed.

Barbara. The meeting?

Cusins. No: after the meeting.

Lady Britomart. You should have gone to bed after the meeting. What were you doing?

Cusins. Drinking.

Lady Britomart.	Adolphus!
Sarah.	Dolly!
Barbara.	Dolly!
Lomax.	Oh I say!

Lady Britomart. What were you drinking, may I ask?

Cusins. A most devilish kind of Spanish burgundy, warranted free from added alcohol: a Temperance burgundy in fact. Its richness in natural alcohol made any addition superfluous.

Barbara. Are you joking, Dolly?

Cusins (*patiently*). No. I have been making a night of it with the nominal head of this household: that is all.

Lady Britomart. Andrew made you drunk!

Cusins. No: he only provided the wine. I think it was Dionysos who made me drunk. (*To* Barbara.) I told you I was possessed.

Lady Britomart. Youre not sober yet. Go home to bed at once.

Cusins. I have never before ventured to reproach you, Lady Brit; but how could you marry the Prince of Darkness?

Lady Britomart. It was much more excusable to marry him than to get drunk with him. That is a new accomplishment of Andrew's, by the way. He usent to drink.

Cusins. He doesnt now. He only sat there and completed the wreck of my moral basis, the rout of my convictions, the purchase of my soul. He cares for you, Barbara. That is what makes him so dangerous to me.

Barbara. That has nothing to do with it, Dolly. There are larger loves and diviner dreams than the fireside ones. You know that, dont you?

Cusins. Yes: that is our understanding. I know it. I hold to it. Unless he can win me on that holier ground he may amuse me for a while; but he can get no deeper hold, strong as he is.

Barbara. Keep to that; and the end will be right. Now tell me what happened at the meeting?

Cusins. It was an amazing meeting. Mrs. Baines almost died of emotion. Jenny Hill simply gibbered with hysteria. The Prince of Darkness played his trombone like a madman: its brazen roarings were like the laughter of the damned. 117 conversions took place then and there. They prayed with the most touching sincerity and gratitude for Bodger, and for the anonymous donor of the £5000. Your father would not let his name be given.

Lomax. That was rather fine of the old man, you know. Most chaps would have wanted the advertisement.

Cusins. He said all the charitable institutions would be down on him like kites on a battle-field if he gave his name.

Lady Britomart. Thats Andrew all over. He never does a proper thing without giving an improper reason for it.

Cusins. He convinced me that I have all my life been doing improper things for proper reasons.

Lady Britomart. Adolphus: now that Barbara has left the Salvation Army, you had better leave it too. I will not have you playing that drum in the streets.

Cusins. Your orders are already obeyed, Lady Brit.

Barbara. Dolly: were you ever really in earnest about it? Would you have joined if you had never seen me?

Cusins (*disingenuously*). Well—er—well, possibly, as a collector of religions—

Lomax (*cunningly*). Not as a drummer, though, you know. You are a very clearheaded brainy chap, Dolly; and it must have been apparent to you that there is a certain amount of tosh about—

Lady Britomart. Charles: if you must drivel, drivel like a grown-up man and not like a schoolboy.

Lomax (*out of countenance*). Well, drivel i s drivel, don't you know, whatever a man's age.

Lady Britomart. In good society in England, Charles, men drivel at all ages by repeating silly formulas with an air of wisdom. Schoolboys make their own formulas out of slang, like you. When they reach your age, and get political private secretaryships and things of that sort, they drop slang and get their formulas out of the Spectator or The Times. You had better confine yourself to The Times. You will find that there is a certain amount of tosh about The Times; but at least its language is reputable.

Lomax (*overwhelmed*). You are so awfully strong-minded, Lady Brit—

Lady Britomart. Rubbish! (Morrison *comes in.*) What is it?

Morrison. If you please, my lady, Mr Undershaft has just drove up to the door.

Lady Britomart. Well, let him in. (Morrison *hesitates.*) Whats the matter with you?

Morrison. Shall I announce him, my lady; or is he at home here, so to speak, my lady?

Lady Britomart. Announce him.

Morrison. Thank you, my lady. You wont mind my asking, I hope. The occasion is in a manner of speaking new to me.

Lady Britomart. Quite right. Go and let him in.

Morrison. Thank you, my lady. (*He withdraws.*)

Lady Britomart. Children: go and get ready. (Sarah *and* Barbara *go upstairs for their out-of-door wraps.*) Charles: go and tell Stephen to come down here in five minutes: you will find him in the drawing room. (Charles *goes.*) Adolphus: tell them to send round the carriage in about fifteen minutes. (Adolphus *goes.*)

Morrison (*at the door*). Mr Undershaft.

Undershaft *comes in.* Morrison *goes out.*

Undershaft. Alone! How fortunate!

Lady Britomart (*rising*). Dont be sentimental, Andrew.

Sit down. (*She sits on the settee: he sits beside her, on her left. She comes to the point before he has time to breathe.*) Sarah must have £800 a year until Charles Lomax comes into his property. Barbara will need more, and need it permanently, because Adolphus hasnt any property.

Undershaft (*resignedly*). Yes, my dear: I will see to it. Anything else? for yourself, for instance?

Lady Britomart. I want to talk to you about Stephen.

Undershaft (*rather wearily*). Dont, my dear. Stephen doesnt interest me.

Lady Britomart. He does interest me. He is our son.

Undershaft. Do you really think so? He has induced us to bring him into the world; but he chose his parents very incongruously, I think. I see nothing of myself in him, and less of you.

Lady Britomart. Andrew: Stephen is an excellent son, and a most steady, capable, highminded young man. You are simply trying to find an excuse for disinheriting him.

Undershaft. My dear Biddy: the Undershaft tradition disinherits him. It would be dishonest of me to leave the cannon foundry to my son.

Lady Britomart. It would be most unnatural and improper of you to leave it to anyone else, Andrew. Do you suppose this wicked and immoral tradition can be kept up for ever? Do you pretend that Stephen could not carry on the foundry just as well as all the other sons of the big business houses?

Undershaft. Yes: he could learn the office routine without understanding the business, like all the other sons; and the firm would go on by its own momentum until the real Undershaft—probably an Italian or a German—would invent a new method and cut him out.

Lady Britomart. There is nothing that any Italian or German could do that Stephen could not do. And Stephen at least has breeding.

Undershaft. The son of a foundling! Nonsense!

Lady Britomart. My son, Andrew! And even you may have good blood in your veins for all you know.

Undershaft. True. Probably I have. That is another argument in favour of a foundling.

Lady Britomart. Andrew: dont be aggravating. And dont be wicked. At present you are both.

Undershaft. This conversation is part of the Undershaft tradition, Biddy. Every Undershaft's wife has treated him to it ever since the house was founded. It is mere waste of breath. If the tradition be ever broken it will be for an abler man than Stephen.

Lady Britomart (*pouting*). Then go away.

Undershaft (*deprecatory*). Go away!

Lady Britomart. Yes: go away. If you will do nothing for Stephen, you are not wanted here. Go to your foundling, whoever he is; and look after h i m.

Undershaft. The fact is, Biddy—

Lady Britomart. Dont call me Biddy. I dont call you Andy.

Undershaft. I will not call my wife Britomart: it is not good sense. Seriously, my love, the Undershaft tradition has landed me in a difficulty. I am getting on in years; and my partner Lazarus has at last made a stand and insisted that the succession must be settled one way or the other; and of course he is quite right. You see, I havent found a fit successor yet.

Lady Britomart (*obstinately*). There is Stephen.

Undershaft. Thats just it: all the foundlings I can find are exactly like Stephen.

Lady Britomart. Andrew!!

Undershaft. I want a man with no relations and no schooling: that is, a man who would be out of the running altogether if he were not a strong man. And I cant find him. Every blessed foundling nowadays is snapped up in his infancy by Barnardo homes, or School Board officers, or Boards of Guardians; and if he shews the least ability he is fastened on by schoolmasters; trained to win scholarships like a racehorse; crammed with secondhand ideas; drilled and disciplined in docility and what they call good taste; and lamed for life so that he is fit for nothing but teaching. If you want to keep the foundry in the family, you had better find an eligible foundling and marry him to Barbara.

Lady Britomart. Ah! Barbara! Your pet! You would sacrifice Stephen to Barbara.

Undershaft. Cheerfully. And you, my dear, would boil Barbara to make soup for Stephen.

Lady Britomart. Andrew: this is not a question of our likings and dislikings: it is a question of duty. It is your duty to make Stephen your successor.

Undershaft. Just as much as it is your duty to submit to your husband. Come, Biddy! these tricks of the governing class are of no use with me. I am one of the governing class myself; and it is waste of time giving tracts to a missionary. I have the power in this matter; and I am not to be humbugged into using it for your purposes.

Lady Britomart. Andrew: you can talk my head off; but you cant change wrong into right. And your tie is all on one side. Put it straight.

Undershaft (*disconcerted*). It wont stay unless it's pinned (*he fumbles at it with childish grimaces*)—

Stephen *comes in.*

Stephen (*at the door*). I beg your pardon (*about to retire*).

Lady Britomart. No: come in, Stephen. (Stephen *comes forward to his mother's writing table.*)

Undershaft (*not very cordially*). Good afternoon.

Stephen (*coldly*). Good afternoon.

Undershaft (*to* Lady Britomart). He knows all about the tradition, I suppose?

Lady Britomart. Yes. (*To* Stephen.) It is what I told you last night, Stephen.

Undershaft (*sulkily*). I understand you want to come into the cannon business.

Stephen. I go into trade! Certainly not.

Undershaft (*opening his eyes, greatly eased in mind and manner*). Oh! in that case—

Lady Britomart. Cannons are not trade, Stephen. They are enterprise.

Stephen. I have no intention of becoming a man of business in any sense. I have no capacity for business and no taste for it. I intend to devote myself to politics.

Undershaft (*rising*). My dear boy: this is an immense relief to me. And I trust it may prove an equally good thing for the country. I was afraid you would consider yourself disparaged and slighted. (*He moves towards* Stephen *as if to shake hands with him.*)

Lady Britomart (*rising and interposing*). Stephen: I cannot allow you to throw away an enormous property like this.

Stephen (*stiffly*). Mother: there must be an end of treating me as a child, if you please. (Lady Britomart *recoils, deeply wounded by his tone.*) Until last night I did not take your attitude seriously, because I did not think you meant it seriously. But I find now that you left me in the dark as to matters which you should have explained to me years ago. I am extremely hurt and offended. Any further discussion of my intentions had better take place with my father, as between one man and another.

Lady Britomart. Stephen! (*She sits down again, her eyes filling with tears.*)

Undershaft (*with grave compassion*). You see, my dear, it is only the big men who can be treated as children.

Stephen. I am sorry, mother, that you have forced me—

Undershaft (*stopping him*). Yes, yes, yes, yes: thats all right, Stephen. She wont interfere with you any more: your independence is achieved: you have won your latchkey. Dont rub it in; and above all, dont apologize. (*He resumes his seat.*) Now what about your future, as between one man and another—I beg your pardon, Biddy: as between two men and a woman.

Lady Britomart (*who has pulled herself together strongly*). I quite understand, Stephen. By all means go your own way if you feel strong enough. (Stephen *sits down magisterially in the chair at the writing table with an air of affirming his majority.*)

Undershaft. It is settled that you do not ask for the succession to the cannon business.

Stephen. I hope it is settled that I repudiate the cannon business.

Undershaft. Come, come! dont be so devilishly sulky: it's boyish. Freedom should be generous. Besides, I owe you a fair start in life in exchange for disinheriting you. You cant become prime minister all at once. Havnt you a turn for something? What about literature, art, and so forth?

Stephen. I have nothing of the artist about me, either in faculty or character, thank Heaven!

Undershaft. A philosopher, perhaps? Eh?

Stephen. I make no such ridiculous pretension.

Undershaft. Just so. Well, there is the army, the navy, the Church, the Bar. The Bar requires some ability. What about the Bar?

Stephen. I have not studied law. And I am afraid I have not the necessary push—I believe that is the name barristers give to their vulgarity—for success in pleading.

Undershaft. Rather a difficult case, Stephen. Hardly anything left but the stage, is there? (Stephen *makes an impatient movement.*) Well, come! is there a n y t h i n g you know or care for?

Stephen (*rising and looking at him steadily*). I know the difference between right and wrong.

Undershaft (*hugely tickled*). You dont say so! What! no

capacity for business, no knowledge of law, no sympathy with art, no pretension to philosophy; only a simple knowledge of the secret that has puzzled all the philosophers, baffled all the lawyers, muddled all the men of business, and ruined most of the artists: the secret of right and wrong. Why, man, youre a genius, a master of masters, a god! At twentyfour, too!

Stephen (*keeping his temper with difficulty*). You are pleased to be facetious. I pretend to nothing more than any honorable English gentleman claims as his birthright (*he sits down angrily*).

Undershaft. Oh, thats everybody's birthright. Look at poor little Jenny Hill, the Salvation lassie! she would think you were laughing at her if you asked her to stand up in the street and teach grammar or geography or mathematics or even drawing room dancing; but it never occurs to her to doubt that she can teach morals and religion. You are all alike, you respectable people. You cant tell me the bursting strain of a ten-inch gun, which is a very simple matter; but you all think you can tell me the bursting strain of a man under temptation. You darent handle high explosives; but youre all ready to handle honesty and truth and justice and the whole duty of man, and kill one another at that game. What a country! What a world!

Lady Britomart (*uneasily*). What do you think he had better do, Andrew?

Undershaft. Oh, just what he wants to do. He knows nothing and he thinks he knows everything. That points clearly to a political career. Get him a private secretaryship to someone who can get him an Under Secretaryship; and then leave him alone. He will find his natural and proper place in the end on the Treasury Bench.

Stephen (*springing up again*). I am sorry, sir, that you force me to forget the respect due to you as my father. I am an Englishman and I will not hear the Government of my country insulted. (*He thrusts his hands in his pockets, and walks angrily across to the window.*)

Undershaft (*with a touch of brutality*). The government of your country! *I* am the government of your country: I, and Lazarus. Do you suppose that you and half a dozen amateurs like you, sitting in a row in that foolish gabble shop, can govern Undershaft and Lazarus? No, my friend: you will do what pays u s. You will make war when it suits us, and keep peace when it doesnt.

You will find out that trade requires certain measures when we have decided on those measures. When I want anything to keep my dividends up, you will discover that my want is a national need. When other people want something to keep my dividends down, you will call out the police and military. And in return you shall have the support and applause of my newspapers, and the delight of imagining that you are a great statesman. Government of your country! Be off with you, my boy, and play with your caucuses and leading articles and historic parties and great leaders and burning questions and the rest of your toys. *I* am going back to my counting-house to pay the piper and call the tune.

Stephen (*actually smiling, and putting his hand on his father's shoulder with indulgent patronage*). Really my dear father, it is impossible to be angry with you. You dont know how absurd all this sounds to m e. You are very properly proud of having been industrious enough to make money; and it is greatly to your credit that you have made so much of it. But it has kept you in circles where you are valued for your money and deferred to for it, instead of in the doubtless very old-fashioned and behind-the-times public school and university where I formed my habits of mind. It is natural for you to think that money governs England; but you must allow me to think I know better.

Undershaft. And what d o e s govern England, pray?

Stephen. Character, father, character.

Undershaft. Whose character? Yours or mine?

Stephen. Neither yours nor mine, father, but the best elements in the English national character.

Undershaft. Stephen: Ive found your profession for you. Youre a born journalist. I'll start you with a high-toned weekly review. There!

Before Stephen *can reply* Sarah, Barbara, Lomax, *and* Cusins *come in ready for walking*. Barbara *crosses the room to the window and looks out*. Cusins *drifts amiably to the armchair*. Lomax *remains near the door, whilst* Sarah *comes to her mother*.

Stephen *goes to the smaller writing table and busies himself with his letters*.

Sarah. Go and get ready, mamma: the carriage is waiting.

(Lady Britomart *leaves the room.*)

Undershaft (*to* Sarah). Good day, my dear. Good afternoon, Mr Lomax.

Lomax (*vaguely*). Ahdedoo.

Undershaft (*to* Cusins). Quite well after last night, Euripides, eh?

Cusins. As well as can be expected.

Undershaft. That's right. (*To* Barbara.) So you are coming to see my death and devastation factory, Barbara?

Barbara (*at the window*). You came yesterday to see my salvation factory. I promised you a return visit.

Lomax (*coming forward between* Sarah *and* Undershaft). Youll find it awfully interesting. Ive been through the Woolwich Arsenal; and it gives you a ripping feeling of security, you know, to think of the lot of beggars we could kill if it came to fighting. (*To* Undershaft, *with sudden solemnity.*) Still, it must be rather an awful reflection for you, from the religious point of view as it were. Youre getting on, you know, and all that.

Sarah. You dont mind Cholly's imbecility, papa, do you?

Lomax (*much taken aback*). Oh I say!

Undershaft. Mr Lomax looks at the matter in a very proper spirit, my dear.

Lomax. Just so. Thats all I meant, I assure you.

Sarah. Are you coming, Stephen?

Stephen. Well, I am rather busy—er—(*Magnanimously.*) Oh well, yes: I'll come. That is, if there is room for me.

Undershaft. I can take two with me in a little motor I am experimenting with for field use. You wont mind its being rather unfashionable. It's not painted yet; but it's bullet proof.

Lomax (*appalled at the prospect of confronting Wilton Crescent in an unpainted motor*). Oh I s a y !

Sarah. The carriage for me, thank you. Barbara doesnt mind what she's seen in.

Lomax. I say, Dolly, old chap: do you really mind the car being a guy? Because of course if you do I'll go in it. Still—

Cusins. I prefer it.

Lomax. Thanks awfully, old man. Come, my ownest. (*He hurries out to secure his seat in the carriage.* Sarah *follows him.*)

Cusins (*moodily walking across to* Lady Britomart's

writing table). Why are we two coming to this Works Department of Hell? that is what I ask myself.

Barbara. I have always thought of it as a sort of pit where lost creatures with blackened faces stirred up smoky fires and were driven and tormented by my father? Is it like that, dad?

Undershaft (*scandalized*). My dear! It is a spotlessly clean and beautiful hillside town.

Cusins. With a Methodist chapel? Oh do say theres a Methodist chapel.

Undershaft. There are two: a Primitive one and a sophisticated one. There is even an Ethical Society; but it is not much patronized, as my men are all strongly religious. In the High Explosives Sheds they object to the presence of Agnostics as unsafe.

Cusins. And yet they dont object to you!

Barbara. Do they obey all your orders?

Undershaft. I never give them any orders. When I speak to one of them it is "Well, Jones, is the baby doing well? and has Mrs Jones made a good recovery?" "Nicely, thank you, sir." And thats all.

Cusins. But Jones has to be kept in order. How do you maintain discipline among your men?

Undershaft. I dont. They do. You see, the one thing Jones wont stand is any rebellion from the man under him, or any assertion of social equality between the wife of the man with 4 shillings a week less than himself, and Mrs Jones! Of course they all rebel against me, theoretically. Practically, every man of them keeps the man just below him in his place. I never meddle with them. I never bully them. I dont even bully Lazarus. I say that certain things are to be done; but I dont order anybody to do them. I dont say, mind you, that there is no ordering about and snubbing and even bullying. The men snub the boys and order them about; the carmen snub the sweepers; the artisans snub the unskilled laborers; the foremen drive and bully both the laborers and artisans; the assistant engineers find fault with the foremen; the chief engineers drop on the assistants; the departmental managers worry the chiefs; and the clerks have tall hats and hymnbooks and keep up the social tone by refusing to associate on equal terms with anybody. The result is a colossal profit, which comes to me.

Cusins (*revolted*). You really are a—well, what I was saying yesterday.

Barbara. What was he saying yesterday?

Undershaft. Never mind, my dear. He thinks I have made you unhappy. Have I?

Barbara. Do you think I can be happy in this vulgar silly dress? I! who have worn the uniform. Do you understand what you have done to me? Yesterday I had a man's soul in my hand. I set him in the way of life with his face to salvation. But when we took your money he turned back to drunkenness and derision. (*With intense conviction.*) I will never forgive you that. If I had a child, and you destroyed its body with your explosives—if you murdered Dolly with your horrible guns—I could forgive you if my forgiveness would open the gates of heaven to you. But to take a human soul from me, and turn it into the soul of a wolf! that is worse than any murder.

Undershaft. Does my daughter despair so easily? Can you strike a man to the heart and leave no mark on him?

Barbara (*her face lighting up*). Oh, you are right: he can never be lost now: where was my faith?

Cusins. Oh, clever clever devil!

Barbara. You may be a devil; but God speaks through you sometimes. (*She takes her father's hands and kisses them.*) You have given me back my happiness: I feel it deep down now, though my spirit is troubled.

Undershaft. You have learnt something. That always feels at first as if you had lost something.

Barbara. Well, take me to the factory of death; and let me learn something more. There must be some truth or other behind all this frightful irony. Come, Dolly. (*She goes out.*)

Cusins. My guardian angel! (*To* Undershaft.) Avaunt! (*He follows* Barbara.)

Stephen (*quietly, at the writing table*). You must not mind Cusins, father. He is a very amiable good fellow; but he is a Greek scholar and naturally a little eccentric.

Undershaft. Ah, quite so, Thank you, Stephen. Thank you. (*He goes out.*)

Stephen *smiles patronizingly; buttons his coat responsibly; and crosses the room to the door.* Lady Britomart, *dressed for out-of-doors, opens it before he reaches it. She looks round for others; looks at* Stephen*; and turns to go without a word.*

Stephen (*embarrassed*). Mother—

Lady Britomart. Dont be apologetic, Stephen. And dont

forget that you have outgrown your mother. (*She goes out.*)

Perivale St Andrews lies between two Middlesex hills, half climbing the northern one. It is an almost smokeless town of white walls, roofs of narrow green slates or red tiles, tall trees, domes, campaniles, and slender chimney shafts, beautifully situated and beautiful in itself. The best view of it is obtained from the crest of a slope about half a mile to the east, where the high explosives are dealt with. The foundry lies hidden in the depths between, the tops of its chimneys sprouting like huge skittles into the middle distance. Across the crest runs an emplacement of concrete, with a firestep, and a parapet which suggests a fortification, because there is a huge cannon of the obsolete Woolwich Infant pattern peering across it at the town. The cannon is mounted on an experimental gun carriage: possibly the original model of the Undershaft disappearing rampart gun alluded to by Stephen. *The firestep, being a convenient place to sit, is furnished here and there with straw disc cushions; and at one place there is the additional luxury of a fur rug.*

Barbara *is standing on the firestep, looking over the parapet towards the town. On her right is the cannon; on her left the end of a shed raised on piles, with a ladder of three or four steps up to the door, which opens outwards and has a little wooden landing at the threshold, with a fire bucket in the corner of the landing. Several dummy soldiers more or less mutilated, with straw protruding from their gashes, have been shoved out of the way under the landing. A few others are nearly upright against the shed; and one has fallen forward and lies, like a grotesque corpse, on the emplacement. The parapet stops short of the shed, leaving a gap which is the beginning of the path down the hill through the foundry to the town. The rug is on the firestep near this gap. Down on the emplacement behind the cannon is a trolley carrying a huge conical bombshell with a red band painted on it. Further to the right is the door of an office, which, like the sheds, is of the lightest possible construction.*

Cusins *arrives by the path from the town.*

Barbara. Well?

Cusins. Not a ray of hope. Everything perfect! wonderful! real! It only needs a cathedral to be a heavenly city instead of a hellish one.

Barbara. Have you found out whether they have done anything for old Peter Shirley?

Cusins. They have found him a job as gatekeeper and time-keeper. He's frightfully miserable. He calls the time-keeping brainwork, and says he isnt used to it; and his gate lodge is so splendid that he's ashamed to use the rooms, and skulks in the scullery.

Barbara. Poor Peter!

Stephen *arrives from the town. He carries a fieldglass.*

Stephen (enthusiastically). Have you two seen the place? Why did you leave us?

Cusins. I wanted to see everything I was not intended to see; and Barbara wanted to make the men talk.

Stephen. Have you found anything discreditable?

Cusins. No. They call him Dandy Andy and are proud of his being a cunning old rascal; but it's all horribly, frightfully, immorally, unanswerably perfect.

Sarah *arrives.*

Sarah. Heavens! what a place! (*She crosses to the trolley.*) Did you see the nursing home!? (*She sits down on the shell.*)

Stephen. Did you see the libraries and schools!?

Sarah. Did you see the ball room and the banqueting chamber in the Town Hall!?

Stephen. Have you gone into the insurance fund, the pension fund, the building society, the various applications of cooperation!?

Undershaft *comes from the office, with a sheaf of telegrams in his hand.*

Undershaft. Well, have you seen everything? I'm sorry I was called away. (*Indicating the telegrams.*) Good news from Manchuria.

Stephen. Another Japanese victory?

Undershaft. Oh, I dont know. Which side wins does not concern us here. No: the good news is that the aerial battleship is a tremendous success. At the first trial it has wiped out a fort with three hundred soldiers in it.

Cusins (*from the platform*). Dummy soldiers?

Undershaft (*striding across to* Stephen *and kicking the prostrate dummy brutally out of his way*). No: the real thing.

Cusins *and* Barbara *exchange glances. Then* Cusins *sits on the step and buries his face in his hands.* Barbara *gravely lays her hand on his shoulder. He looks up at her in whimsical desperation.*

Undershaft. Well, Stephen, what do you think of the place?

Stephen. Oh, magnificent. A perfect triumph of modern industry. Frankly, my dear father, I have been a fool: I had no idea of what it all meant: of the wonderful forethought, the power of organization, the administrative capacity, the financial genius, the colossal capital it represents. I have been repeating to myself as I came through your streets "Peace hath her victories no less renowned than War." I have only one misgiving about it all.

Undershaft. Out with it.

Stephen. Well, I cannot help thinking that all this provision for every want of your workmen may sap their independence and weaken their sense of responsibility. And greatly as we enjoyed our tea at that splendid restaurant—how they gave us all that luxury and cake and jam and cream for threepence I really cannot imagine!—still you must remember that restaurants break up home life. Look at the continent, for instance! Are you sure so much pampering is really good for the men's characters?

Undershaft. Well you see, my dear boy, when you are organizing civilization you have to make up your mind whether trouble and anxiety are good things or not. If you decide that they are, then, I take it, you simply dont organize civilization; and there you are, with trouble and anxiety enough to make us all angels! But if you decide the other way, you may as well go through with it. However, Stephen, our characters are safe here. A sufficient dose of anxiety is always provided by the fact that we may be blown to smithereens at any moment.

Sarah. By the way, papa, where do you make the explosives?

Undershaft. In separate little sheds, like that one. When one of them blows up, it costs very little; and only the people quite close to it are killed.

Stephen, *who is quite close to it, looks at it rather scaredly, and moves away quickly to the cannon. At the same moment the door of the shed is thrown abruptly open; and a foreman in overalls and list slippers comes out on the little landing and holds the door for* Lomax, *who appears in the doorway.*

Lomax (*with studied coolness*). My good fellow: you neednt get into a state of nerves. Nothing's going to happen to you; and I suppose it wouldnt be the end of the world if anything did. A little bit of British pluck is what y o u want, old chap. (*He descends and strolls across to* Sarah.)

Undershaft (*to the foreman*). Anything wrong, Bilton?

Bilton (*with ironic calm*). Gentleman walked into the high explosives shed and lit a cigaret, sir: thats all.

Undershaft. Ah, quite so. (*Going over to* Lomax.) Do you happen to remember what you did with the match?

Lomax. Oh come! I'm not a fool. I took jolly good care to blow it out before I chucked it away.

Bilton. The top of it was red hot inside, sir.

Lomax. Well, suppose it was! I didn't chuck it into any of y o u r messes.

Undershaft. Think no more of it, Mr Lomax. By the way, would you mind lending me your matches.

Lomax (*offering his box*). Certainly.

Undershaft. Thanks. (*He pockets the matches.*)

Lomax (*lecturing to the company generally*). You know, these high explosives dont go off like gunpowder, except when theyre in a gun. When theyre spread loose, you can put a match to them without the least risk: they just burn quietly like a bit of paper. (*Warming to the scientific interest of the subject.*) Did you know that, Undershaft? Have you ever tried?

Undershaft. Not on a large scale, Mr Lomax. Bilton will give you a sample of gun cotton when you are leaving if you ask him. You can experiment with it at home. (Bilton *looks puzzled.*)

Sarah. Bilton will do nothing of the sort, papa. I suppose it's your business to blow up the Russians and Japs; but you might really stop short of blowing up poor Cholly. (Bilton *gives it up and retires into the shed.*)

Lomax. My ownest, there is no danger. (*He sits beside her on the shell.*)

Lady Britomart *arrives from the town with a bouquet.*

Lady Britomart (*impetuously*). Andrew: you shouldnt have let me see this place.

Undershaft. Why, my dear?

Lady Britomart. Never mind why: you shouldnt have: thats all. To think of all that (*indicating the town*) being yours! and that you have kept it to yourself all these years!

Undershaft. It does not belong to me. I belong to it. It is the Undershaft inheritance.

Lady Britomart. It is not. Your ridiculous cannons and that noisy banging foundry may be the Undershaft inheritance; but all that plate and linen, all that furniture and those houses and orchards and gardens belong to us. They belong to m e : they are not a man's business. I wont give them up. You must be out of your senses to throw them all away; and if you persist in such folly, I will call in a doctor.

Undershaft (*stooping to smell the bouquet*). Where did you get the flowers, my dear?

Lady Britomart. Your men presented them to me in your William Morris Labor Church.

Cusins. Oh! It needed only that. A Labor Church! (*He mounts the firestep distractedly, and leans with his elbows on the parapet, turning his back to them.*)

Lady Britomart. Yes, with Morris's words in mosaic letters ten feet high round the dome. NO MAN IS GOOD ENOUGH TO BE ANOTHER MAN'S MASTER. The cynicism of it!

Undershaft. It shocked the men at first, I am afraid. But now they take no more notice of it than of the ten commandments in church.

Lady Britomart. Andrew: you are trying to put me off the subject of the inheritance by profane jokes. Well, you shant. I dont ask it any longer for Stephen: he has inherited far too much of your perversity to be fit for it. But Barbara has rights as well as Stephen. Why should not Adolphus succeed to the inheritance? I could manage the town for him; and he can look after the cannons, if they are really necessary.

Undershaft. I should ask nothing better if Adolphus were a foundling. He is exactly the sort of new blood that is wanted in English business. But he's not a foundling; and theres an end of it. (*He makes for the office door.*)

Cusins (*turning to them*). Not quite. (*They all turn and stare at him.*) I think—Mind! I am not committing myself in any way as to my future course—but I t h i n k the foundling difficulty can be got over. (*He jumps down to the emplacement.*)

Undershaft (*coming back to him*). What do you mean?

Cusins. Well, I have something to say which is in the nature of a confession.

Sarah.
Lady Britomart.
Barbara.
Stephen. } Confession!

Lomax. Oh I say!

Cusins. Yes, a confession. Listen, all. Until I met Barbara I thought myself in the main an honorable, truthful man, because I wanted the approval of my conscience more than I wanted anything else. But the moment I saw Barbara, I wanted her far more than the approval of my conscience.

Lady Britomart. Adolphus!

Cusins. It is true. You accused me yourself, Lady Brit, of joining the Army to worship Barbara; and so I did. She bought my soul like a flower at a street corner; but she bought it for herself.

Undershaft. What! Not for Dionysos or another?

Cusins. Dionysos and all the others are in herself. I adored what was divine in her, and was therefore a true worshipper. But I was romantic about her too. I thought she was a woman of the people, and that a marriage with a professor of Greek would be far beyond the wildest social ambitions of her rank.

Lady Britomart. Adolphus!!

Lomax. Oh I say !!!

Cusins. When I learnt the horrible truth—

Lady Britomart. What do you mean by the horrible truth, pray?

Cusins. That she was enormously rich; that her grandfather was an earl; that her father was the Prince of Darkness—

Undershaft. Chut!

Cusins. —and that I was only an adventurer trying to catch a rich wife, then I stooped to deceive her about my birth.

Barbara (*rising*). Dolly!

Lady Britomart. Your birth! Now Adolphus, dont dare to make up a wicked story for the sake of these wretched cannons. Remember: I have seen photographs of your parents; and the Agent General for South Western Australia knows them personally and has assured me that they are most respectable married people.

Cusins. So they are in Australia; but here they are outcasts. Their marriage is legal in Australia, but not in England. My mother is my father's deceased wife's sister; and in this island I am consequently a foundling. (*Sensation.*)

Barbara. Silly! (*She climbs to the cannon, and leans, listening, in the angle it makes with the parapet.*)

Cusins. Is the subterfuge good enough, Machiavelli?

Undershaft (*thoughtfully*). Biddy: this may be a way out of the difficulty.

Lady Britomart. Stuff! A man cant make cannons any the better for being his own cousin instead of his proper self (*she sits down on the rug with a bounce that expresses her downright contempt for their casuistry*).

Undershaft (*to* Cusins). You are an educated man. That is against the tradition.

Cusins. Once in ten thousand times it happens that the schoolboy is a born master of what they try to teach him. Greek has not destroyed my mind: it has nourished it. Besides, I did not learn it at an English public school.

Undershaft. Hm! Well, I cannot afford to be too particular: you have cornered the foundling market. Let it pass. You are eligible, Euripides: you are eligible.

Barbara. Dolly: yesterday morning, when Stephen told us all about the tradition, you became very silent; and you have been strange and excited ever since. Were you thinking of your birth then?

Cusins. When the finger of Destiny suddenly points at a man in the middle of his breakfast, it makes him thoughtful.

Undershaft. Aha! You have had your eye on the business, my young friend, have you?

Cusins. Take care! There is an abyss of moral horror between me and your accursed aerial battleships.

Undershaft. Never mind the abyss for the present. Let us settle the practical details and leave your final decision open. You know that you will have to change your name. Do you object to that?

Cusins. Would any man named Adolphus—any man called Dolly!—object to be called something else?

Undershaft. Good. Now, as to money! I propose to treat you handsomely from the beginning. You shall start at a thousand a year.

Cusins (*with sudden heat, his spectacles twinkling with mischief*). A thousand! You dare offer a miserable thousand to the son-in-law of a millionaire! No, by Heavens, Machiavelli! you shall not cheat m e. You cannot do without me; and I can do without you. I must have two thousand five hundred a year for two years. At the end of that time, if I am a failure, I go. But if I am a success, and stay on, you must give me the other five thousand.

Undershaft. What other five thousand?

Cusins. To make the two years up to five thousand a year. The two thousand five hundred is only half pay in case I should turn out a failure. The third year I must have ten per cent on the profits.

Undershaft (*taken aback*). Ten per cent! Why, man, do you know what my profits are?

Cusins. Enormous, I hope: otherwise I shall require twenty-five per cent.

Undershaft. But, Mr Cusins, this is a serious matter of business. You are not bringing any capital into the concern.

Cusins. What! no capital! Is my mastery of Greek no capital? Is my access to the subtlest thought, the loftiest poetry yet attained by humanity, no capital? My character! my intellect! my life! my career! what Barbara calls my soul! are these no capital? Say another word; and I double my salary.

Undershaft. Be reasonable—

Cusins (*peremptorily*). Mr Undershaft: you have my terms. Take them or leave them.

Undershaft (*recovering himself*). Very well. I note your terms; and I offer you half.

Cusins (*disgusted*). Half!

Undershaft (*firmly*). Half.

Cusins. You call yourself a gentleman; and you offer me half!!

Undershaft. I do not call myself a gentleman; but I offer you half.

Cusins. This to your future partner! your successor! your son-in-law!

Barbara. You are selling your own soul, Dolly, not mine.

Leave me out of the bargain, please.

Undershaft. Come! I will go a step further for Barbara's sake. I will give you three fifths; but that is my last word.

Cusins. Done!

Lomax. Done in the eye! Why, *I* get only eight hundred, you know.

Cusins. By the way, Mac, I am a classical scholar, not an arithmetical one. Is three fifths more than half or less?

Undershaft. More, of course.

Cusins. I would have taken two hundred and fifty. How you can succeed in business when you are willing to pay all that money to a University don who is obviously not worth a junior clerk's wages!—well! What will Lazarus say?

Undershaft. Lazarus is a gentle romantic Jew who cares for nothing but string quartets and stalls at fashionable theatres. He will be blamed for your rapacity in money matters, poor fellow! as he has hitherto been blamed for mine. You are a shark of the first order, Euripides. So much the better for the firm!

Barbara. Is the bargain closed, Dolly? Does your soul belong to him now?

Cusins. No: the price is settled: that is all. The real tug of war is still to come. What about the moral question?

Lady Britomart. There is no moral question in the matter at all, Adolphus. You must simply sell cannons and weapons to people whose cause is right and just, and refuse them to foreigners and criminals.

Undershaft (*determinedly*). No: none of that. You must keep the true faith of an Armorer, or you dont come in here.

Cusins. What on earth is the true faith of an Armorer?

Undershaft. To give arms to all men who offer an honest price for them, without respect of persons or principles: to aristocrat and republican, to Nihilist and Tsar, to Capitalist and Socialist, to Protestant and Catholic, to burglar and policeman, to black man, white man and yellow man, to all sorts and conditions, all nationalities, all faiths, all follies, all causes and all crimes. The first Undershaft wrote up in his shop IF GOD GAVE THE HAND, LET NOT MAN WITHHOLD THE SWORD. The second wrote up ALL HAVE THE RIGHT TO FIGHT: NONE HAVE THE RIGHT TO JUDGE. The third wrote up TO MAN THE WEAPON: TO HEAVEN THE

VICTORY. The fourth had no literary turn; so he did not write up anything; but he sold cannons to Napoleon under the nose of George the Third. The fifth wrote up PEACE SHALL NOT PREVAIL SAVE WITH A SWORD IN HER HAND. The sixth, my master, was the best of all. He wrote up NOTHING IS EVER DONE IN THIS WORLD UNTIL MEN ARE PREPARED TO KILL ONE ANOTHER IF IT IS NOT DONE. After that, there was nothing left for the seventh to say. So he wrote up, simply, UNASHAMED.

Cusins. My good Machiavelli, I shall certainly write something up on the wall; only, as I shall write it in Greek, you wont be able to read it. But as to your Armorer's faith, if I take my neck out of the noose of my own morality I am not going to put it into the noose of yours. I shall sell cannons to whom I please and refuse them to whom I please. So there!

Undershaft. From the moment when you become Andrew Undershaft, you will never do as you please again. Dont come here lusting for power, young man.

Cusins. If power were my aim I should not come here for it. You have no power.

Undershaft. None of my own, certainly.

Cusins. I have more power than you, more will. You do not drive this place: it drives you. And what drives the place?

Undershaft (*enigmatically*). A will of which I am a part.

Barbara (*startled*). Father! Do you know what you are saying; or are you laying a snare for my soul?

Cusins. Dont listen to his metaphysics, Barbara. The place is driven by the most rascally part of society, the money hunters, the pleasure hunters, the military promotion hunters; and he is their slave.

Undershaft. Not necessarily. Remember the Armorer's Faith. I will take an order from a good man as cheerfully as from a bad one. If you good people prefer preaching and shirking to buying my weapons and fighting the rascals, dont blame me. I can make cannons: I cannot make courage and conviction. Bah! you tire me, Euripides, with your morality mongering. Ask Barbara: s h e understands. (*He suddenly reaches up and takes* Barbara's *hands, looking powerfully into her eyes.*) Tell him, my love, what power really means.

Barbara (*hypnotized*). Before I joined the Salvation Army, I was in my own power; and the consequence was that I never knew what to do with myself. When I joined it, I had not time enough for all the things I had to do.

Undershaft (*approvingly*). Just so. And why was that, do you suppose?

Barbara. Yesterday I should have said, because I was in the power of God. (*She resumes her self-possession, withdrawing her hands from his with a power equal to his own.*) But you came and shewed me that I was in the power of Bodger and Undershaft. Today I feel—oh! how can I put it into words? Sarah: do you remember the earthquake at Cannes, when we were little children?—how little the surprise of the first shock mattered compared to the dread and horror of waiting for the second? That is how I feel in this place today. I stood on the rock I thought eternal; and without a word of warning it reeled and crumbled under me. I was safe with an infinite wisdom watching me, an army marching to Salvation with me; and in a moment, at a stroke of your pen in a cheque book, I stood alone; and the heavens were empty. That was the first shock of the earthquake: I am waiting for the second.

Undershaft. Come, come, my daughter! dont make too much of your little tinpot tragedy. What do we do here when we spend years of work and thought and thousands of pounds of solid cash on a new gun or an aerial battleship that turns out just a hairsbreadth wrong after all? Scrap it. Scrap it without wasting another hour or another pound on it. Well, you have made for yourself something that you call a morality or a religion or what not. It doesnt fit the facts. Well, scrap it. Scrap it and get one that does fit. That is what is wrong with the world at present. It scraps its obsolete steam engines and dynamos; but it wont scrap its old prejudices and its old moralities and its old religions and its old political constitutions. Whats the result? In machinery it does very well; but in morals and religion and politics it is working at a loss that brings it nearer bankruptcy every year. Dont persist in that folly. If your old religion broke down yesterday, get a newer and a better one for tomorrow.

Barbara. Oh how gladly I would take a better one to my soul! But you offer me a worse one. (*Turning on him with sudden vehemence.*) Justify yourself: shew me some light through the darkness of this dreadful place, with its beautifully clean workshops, and respectable workmen, and model homes.

Undershaft. Cleanliness and respectability do not need justification, Barbara: they justify themselves. I see no darkness here, no dreadfulness. In your Salvation shelter I saw poverty, misery, cold and hunger. You gave them bread and treacle and dreams of heaven. I give from thirty shillings a week to twelve thousand a year. They find their own dreams; but I look after the drainage.

Barbara. And their souls?

Undershaft. I save their souls just as I saved yours.

Barbara (*revolted*). Y o u saved my soul! What do you mean?

Undershaft. I fed you and clothed you and housed you. I took care that you should have money enough to live handsomely—more than enough; so that you could be wasteful, careless, generous. That saved your soul from the seven deadly sins.

Barbara (*bewildered*). The seven deadly sins!

Undershaft. Yes, the deadly seven. (*Counting on his fingers.*) Food, clothing, firing, rent, taxes, respectability and children. Nothing can lift those seven millstones from Man's neck but money; and the spirit cannot soar until the millstones are lifted. I lifted them from your spirit. I enabled Barbara to become Major Barbara; and I saved her from the crime of poverty.

Cusins. Do you call poverty a crime?

Undershaft. The worst of crimes. All the other crimes are virtues beside it: all the other dishonors are chivalry itself by comparison. Poverty blights whole cities; spreads horrible pestilences; strikes dead the very souls of all who come within sight, sound, or smell of it. What y o u call crime is nothing: a murder here and a theft there, a blow now and a curse then: what do they matter? They are only the accidents and illnesses of life: there are not fifty genuine professional criminals in London. But there are millions of poor people, abject people, dirty people, ill fed, ill clothed people. They poison us morally and physically: they kill the happiness of society: they force us to do away with our own liberties and to organize unnatural cruelties for fear they should rise against us and drag us down into their abyss. Only fools fear crime: we all fear poverty. Pah! (*turning on* Barbara) you talk of your half-saved ruffian in West Ham: you accuse me of dragging his soul back to perdition. Well, bring him to me here; and I will drag his soul back again to salvation for you. Not by words and dreams; but by thirtyeight shillings a week, a sound house in a handsome street, and a permanent job. In three weeks he will have a fancy waistcoat; in three months a tall hat and a chapel sitting; before the end of the year he will shake hands with a duchess at a Primrose League meeting, and join the Conservative Party.

Barbara. And will he be the better for that?

Undershaft. You know he will. Dont be a hypocrite, Barbara. He will be better fed, better housed, better clothed, better behaved; and his children will be pounds heavier and bigger. That will be better than an American cloth mattress in a shelter, chopping firewood, eating bread and treacle, and being forced to kneel down from time to time to thank heaven for it: knee drill, I think you call it. It is cheap work converting starving men with a Bible in one hand and a slice of bread in the other. I will undertake to convert West Ham to Mahometanism on the same terms. Try your hand on my men: *their* souls are hungry because their bodies are full.

Barbara. And leave the east end to starve?

Undershaft (*his energetic tone dropping into one of bitter and brooding remembrance*). *I* was an east ender. I I moralized and starved until one day I swore that I would be a full-fed free man at all costs; that nothing should stop me except a bullet, neither reason nor morals nor the lives of other men. I said 'Thou shalt starve ere I starve'; and with that word I became free and great. I was a dangerous man until I had my will: now I am a useful, beneficent, kindly person. That is the history of most self-made millionaires, I fancy. When it is the history of every Englishman we shall have an England worth living in.

Lady Britomart. Stop making speeches, Andrew. This is not the place for them.

Undershaft (*punctured*). My dear: I have no other means of conveying my ideas.

Lady Britomart. Your ideas are nonsense. You got on because you were selfish and unscrupulous.

Undershaft. Not at all. I had the strongest scruples about poverty and starvation. Your moralists are quite unscrupulous about both: they make virtues of them. I had rather be a thief than a pauper. I had rather be a murderer than a slave. I dont want to be either; but if you force the alternative on me, then, by Heaven, I'll chose the braver and more moral one. I hate poverty and slavery worse than any other crimes whatsoever.

And let me tell you this. Poverty and slavery have stood up for centuries to your sermons and leading articles: they will not stand up to my machine guns. Dont preach at them: dont reason with them. Kill them.

Barbara. Killing. Is that your remedy for everything?

Undershaft. It is the final test of conviction, the only lever strong enough to overturn a social system, the only way of saying Must. Let six hundred and seventy fools loose in the streets; and three policemen can scatter them. But huddle them together in a certain house in Westminster; and let them go through certain ceremonies and call themselves certain names until at last they get the courage to kill; and your six hundred and seventy fools become a government. Your pious mob fills up ballot papers and imagines it is governing its masters; but the ballot paper that really governs is the paper that has a bullet wrapped up in it.

Cusins. That is perhaps why, like most intelligent people, I never vote.

Undershaft. Vote! Bah! When you vote, you only change the names of the cabinet. When you shoot, you pull down governments, inaugurate new epochs, abolish old orders and set up new. Is that historically true, Mr Learned Man, or is it not?

Cusins. It is historically true. I loathe having to admit it. I repudiate your sentiments. I abhor your nature. I defy you in every possible way. Still, it is true. But it ought not to be true.

Undershaft. Ought! ought! ought! ought! ought! Are you going to spend your life saying ought, like the rest of our moralists? Turn your oughts into shalls, man. Come and make explosives with me. Whatever can blow men up can blow society up. The history of the world is the history of those who had courage enough to embrace this truth. Have you the courage to embrace it, Barbara?

Lady Britomart. Barbara: I positively forbid you to listen to your father's abominable wickedness. And you, Adolphus, ought to know better than to go about saying that wrong things are true. What does it matter whether they are true if they are wrong?

Undershaft. What does it matter whether they are wrong if they are true?

Lady Britomart (*rising*). Children: come home instantly. Andrew: I am exceedingly sorry I allowed you to call on us. You are wickeder than ever. Come at once.

Barbara (*shaking her head*). It's no use running away from wicked people, mamma.

Lady Britomart. It is every use. It shews your disapprobation of them.

Barbara. It does not save them.

Lady Britomart. I can see that you are going to disobey me. Sarah: are you coming home or are you not?

Sarah. I daresay it's very wicked of papa to make cannons; but I dont think I shall cut him on that account.

Lomax (*pouring oil on the troubled waters*). The fact is, you know, there is a certain amount of tosh about this notion of wickedness. It doesnt work. You must look at facts. Not that I would say a word in favor of anything wrong; but then, you see, all sorts of chaps are always doing all sorts of things; and we have to fit them in somehow, dont you know. What I mean is that you cant go cutting everybody; and thats about what it comes to. (*Their rapt attention to his eloquence makes him nervous.*) Perhaps I dont make myself clear.

Lady Britomart. You are lucidity itself, Charles. Because Andrew is successful and has plenty of money to give to Sarah, you will flatter him and encourage him in his wickedness.

Lomax (*unruffled*). Well, where the carcase is, there will the eagles be gathered, dont you know. (*To* Undershaft.) Eh? What?

Undershaft. Precisely. By the way, may I call you Charles?

Lomax. Delighted. Cholly is the usual ticket.

Undershaft (*to* Lady Britomart). Biddy—

Lady Britomart (*violently*). Dont dare call me Biddy. Charles Lomax: you are a fool. Adolphus Cusins: you are a Jesuit. Stephen: you are a prig. Barbara: you are a lunatic. Andrew: you are a vulgar tradesman. Now you all know my opinion; and my conscience is clear, at all events (*she sits down with a vehemence that the rug fortunately softens*).

Undershaft. My dear: you are the incarnation of morality. (*She snorts.*) Your conscience is clear and your duty done when you have called everybody names. Come, Euripides! it is getting late; and we all want to go home. Make up your mind.

Cusins. Understand this, you old demon—

Lady Britomart. Adolphus!

Undershaft. Let him alone, Biddy. Proceed, Euripides.

Cusins. You have me in a horrible dilemma. I want Barbara.

Undershaft. Like all young men, you greatly exaggerate the difference between one young woman and another.

Barbara. Quite true, Dolly.

Cusins. I also want to avoid being a rascal.

Undershaft (with biting contempt). You lust for personal righteousness, for self-approval, for what you call a good conscience, for what Barbara calls salvation, for what I call patronizing people who are not so lucky as yourself.

Cusins. I do not: all the poet in me recoils from being a good man. But there are things in me that I must reckon with. Pity—

Undershaft. Pity! The scavenger of misery.

Cusins. Well, love.

Undershaft. I know. You love the needy and the outcast: you love the oppressed races, the negro, the Indian ryot, the underdog everywhere. Do you love the Japanese? Do you love the French? Do you love the English?

Cusins. No. Every true Englishman detests the English. We are the wickedest nation on earth; and our success is a moral horror.

Undershaft. That is what comes of your gospel of love, is it?

Cusins. May I not love even my father-in-law?

Undershaft. Who wants your love, man? By what right do you take the liberty of offering it to me? I will have your due heed and respect, or I will kill you. But your love! Damn your impertinence!

Cusins (grinning). I may not be able to control my affections, Mac.

Undershaft. You are fencing, Euripides. You are weakening: your grip is slipping. Come! try your last weapon. Pity and love have broken in your hand: forgiveness is still left.

Cusins. No: forgiveness is a beggar's refuge. I am with you there: we must pay our debts.

Undershaft. Well said. Come! you will suit me. Remember the words of Plato.

Cusins (starting). Plato! You dare quote Plato to me!

Undershaft. Plato says, my friend, that society cannot be saved until either the Professors of Greek take to making gunpowder, or else the makers of gunpowder become Professors of Greek.

Cusins. Oh, tempter, cunning tempter!

Undershaft. Come! choose, man, choose.

Cusins. But perhaps Barbara will not marry me if I make the wrong choice.

Barbara. Perhaps not.

Cusins (*desperately perplexed*). You hear!

Barbara. Father: do you love nobody?

Undershaft. I love my best friend.

Lady Britomart. And who is that, pray?

Undershaft. My bravest enemy. That is the man who keeps me up to the mark.

Cusins. You know, the creature is really a sort of poet in his way. Suppose he is a great man, after all!

Undershaft. Suppose you stop talking and make up your mind, my young friend.

Cusins. But you are driving me against my nature. I hate war.

Undershaft. Hatred is the coward's revenge for being intimidated. Dare you make war on war? Here are the means: my friend Mr Lomax is sitting on them.

Lomax (*springing up*). Oh I say! You dont mean that this thing is loaded, do you? My ownest: come off it.

Sarah (*sitting placidly on the shell*). If I am to be blown up, the more thoroughly it is done the better. Dont fuss, Cholly.

Lomax (*to* Undershaft, *strongly remonstrant*). Your own daughter, you know!

Undershaft. So I see. (*To* Cusins.) Well, my friend, may we expect you here at six tomorrow morning?

Cusins (*firmly*). Not on any account. I will see the whole establishment blown up with its own dynamite before I will get up at five. My hours are healthy, rational hours: eleven to five.

Undershaft. Come when you please: before a week you will come at six and stay until I turn you out for the sake of your health. (*Calling.*) Bilton! (*He turns to* Lady Britomart, *who rises.*) My dear: let us leave these two young people to themselves for a moment. (Bilton *comes from the shed.*) I am going to take you through the gun cotton shed.

Bilton (*barring the way*). You cant take anything explosive in here, sir.

Lady Britomart. What do you mean? Are you alluding to me?

Bilton (*unmoved*). No, maam. Mr Undershaft has the other gentleman's matches in his pocket.

Lady Britomart (*abruptly*). Oh! I beg your pardon. (*She goes into the shed.*)

Undershaft. Quite right, Bilton, quite right: here you are. (*He gives* Bilton *the box of matches.*) Come, Stephen. Come, Charles. Bring Sarah. (*He passes into the shed.*)

Bilton *opens the box and deliberately drops the matches into the fire-bucket.*

Lomax. Oh! I say (Bilton *stolidly hands him the empty box*). Infernal nonsense! Pure scientific ignorance! (*He goes in.*)

Sarah. Am I all right, Bilton?

Bilton. Youll have to put on list slippers, miss: thats all. Weve got em inside. (*She goes in.*)

Stephen (*very seriously to* Cusins). Dolly, old fellow, think. Think before you decide. Do you feel that you are a sufficiently practical man? It is a huge undertaking, an enormous responsibility. All this mass of business will be Greek to you.

Cusins. Oh, I think it will be much less difficult than Greek.

Stephen. Well, I just want to say this before I leave you to yourselves. Dont let anything I have said about right and wrong prejudice you against this great chance in life. I have satisfied myself that the business is one of the highest character and a credit to our country. (*Emotionally.*) I am very proud of my father. I—(*Unable to proceed, he presses* Cusins' *hand and goes hastily into the shed, followed by* Bilton.)

Barbara *and* Cusins, *left alone together, look at one another silently.*

Cusins. Barbara: I am going to accept this offer.

Barbara. I thought you would.

Cusins. You understand, dont you, that I had to decide without consulting you. If I had thrown the burden of the choice on you, you would sooner or later have despised me for it.

Barbara. Yes: I did not want you to sell your soul for me any more than for this inheritance.

Cusins. It is not the sale of my soul that troubles me: I have sold it too often to care about that. I have sold it for a professorship. I have sold it for an income. I have sold it to escape being imprisoned for refusing to pay taxes for hangmen's ropes and unjust wars and things that I abhor. What is all human conduct but the daily and hourly sale of our souls for trifles? What I am now selling it for is neither money nor position nor comfort, but for reality and for power.

Barbara. You know that you will have no power, and that he has none.

Cusins. I know. It is not for myself alone. I want to make power for the world.

Barbara. I want to make power for the world too; but it must be spiritual power.

Cusins. I think all power is spiritual: these cannons will not go off by themselves. I have tried to make spiritual power by teaching Greek. But the world can never be really touched by a dead language and a dead civilization. The people must have power; and the people cannot have Greek. Now the power that is made here can be wielded by all men.

Barbara. Power to burn women's houses down and kill their sons and tear their husbands to pieces.

Cusins. You cannot have power for good without having power for evil too. Even mother's milk nourishes murderers as well as heroes. This power which only tears men's bodies to pieces has never been so horribly abused as the intellectual power, the imaginative power, the poetic, religious power that can enslave men's souls. As a teacher of Greek I gave the intellectual man weapons against the common man. I now want to give the common man weapons against the intellectual man. I love the common people. I want to arm them against the lawyers, the doctors, the priests, the literary men, the professors, the artists, and the politicians, who, once in authority, are more disastrous and tyrannical than all the fools, rascals, and impostors. I want a power simple enough for common men to use, yet strong enough to force the intellectual oligarchy to use its genius for the general good.

Barbara. Is there no higher power than that (*pointing to the shell*)?

Cusins. Yes; but that power can destroy the higher powers just as a tiger can destroy a man: therefore Man must master that power first. I admitted this when the Turks and Greeks were last at war. My best pupil went out to fight for Hellas. My parting gift to him was not a copy of Plato's Republic, but a revolver and a hundred Undershaft cartridges. The blood of every Turk he shot—if he shot any—is on my head as well as on Undershaft's. That act committed me to this place for ever. Your father's challenge has beaten me. Dare I make war on war? I must. I will. And now, is it all over between us?

Barbara (*touched by his evident dread of her answer*). Silly baby Dolly! How could it be!

Cusins (*overjoyed*). Then you—you—you— Oh for my drum! (*He flourishes imaginary drumsticks.*)

Barbara (*angered by his levity*). Take care, Dolly, take care. Oh, if only I could get away from you and from father and from it all! if I could have the wings of a dove and fly away to heaven!

Cusins. And leave me!

Barbara. Yes, you, and all the other naughty mischievous children of men. But I cant. I was happy in the Salvation Army for a moment. I escaped from the world into a paradise of enthusiasm and prayer and soul saving; but the moment our money ran short, it all came back to Bodger: it was he who saved our people: he, and the Prince of Darkness, my papa. Undershaft and Bodger: their hands stretch everywhere: when we feed a starving fellow creature, it is with their bread, because there is no other bread; when we tend the sick, it is in the hospitals they endow; if we turn from the churches they build, we must kneel on the stones of the streets they pave. As long as that lasts, there is no getting away from them. Turning our backs on Bodger and Undershaft is turning our backs on life.

Cusins. I thought you were determined to turn your back on the wicked side of life.

Barbara. There is no wicked side: life is all one. And I never wanted to shirk my share in whatever evil must be endured, whether it be sin or suffering. I wish I could cure you of middle-class ideas, Dolly.

Cusins (*gasping*). Middle cl—! A snub! A social snub to me! from the daughter of a foundling!

Barbara. That is why I have no class, Dolly: I come straight out of the heart of the whole people. If I were middle-class I should turn my back on my father's business; and we should both live in an artistic drawing room, with you reading the reviews in one corner, and I in the other at the piano, playing Schumann: both very superior persons, and neither of us a bit of use. Sooner than that, I would sweep out the guncotton shed, or be one of Bodger's barmaids. Do you know what would have happened if you had refused papa's offer?

Cusins. I wonder!

Barbara. I should have given you up and married the man who accepted it. After all, my dear old mother has more sense than any of you. I felt like her when I saw this place—felt that I must have it—that never, never, never could I let it go; only she thought it was the houses and the kitchen ranges and the linen and china, when it was really all the human souls to be saved: not weak souls in starved bodies, sobbing with gratitude for a scrap of bread and treacle, but fullfed, quarrelsome, snobbish, uppish creatures, all standing on their little rights and dignities, and thinking that my father ought to be greatly obliged to them for making so much money for him—and so he ought. That is where salvation is really wanted. My father shall never throw it in my teeth again that my converts were bribed with bread. (*She is transfigured.*) I have got rid of the bribe of bread. I have got rid of the bribe of heaven. Let God's work be done for its own sake: the work he had to create us to do because it cannot be done except by living men and women. When I die, let him be in my debt, not I in his; and let me forgive him as becomes a woman of my rank.

Cusins. Then the way of life lies through the factory of death?

Barbara. Yes, through the raising of hell to heaven and of man to God, through the unveiling of an eternal light in the Valley of The Shadow. (*Seizing him with both hands.*) Oh, did you think my courage would never come back? did you believe that I was a deserter? that I, who have stood in the streets, and taken my people to my heart, and talked of the holiest and greatest things with them, could ever turn back and chatter foolishly to fashionable people about nothing in a drawing room? Never, never, never, never: Major Barbara will die with the colors. Oh! and I have my dear little Dolly boy still; and he has found me my place and my work. Glory Hallelujah! (*She kisses him.*)

Cusins. My dearest: consider my delicate health. I cannot stand as much happiness as you can.

Barbara. Yes: it is not easy work being in love with me, is it? But it's good for you. (*She runs to the shed, and calls, childlike.*) Mamma! Mamma! (Bilton *comes out of the shed, followed by* Undershaft.) I want Mamma.

Undershaft. She is taking off her list slippers, dear. (*He passes on to* Cusins.) Well? What does she say?

Cusins. She has gone right up into the skies.

Lady Britomart (*coming from the shed and stopping on the steps, obstructing* Sarah, who follows with Lomax. Barbara *clutches like a baby at her mother's skirt*). Barbara: when will you learn to be independent and to act and think for yourself? I know as well as possible what that cry of "Mamma, Mamma," means. Always running to me!

Sarah (*touching* Lady Britomart's *ribs with her finger tips and imitating a bicycle horn*). Pip! pip!

Lady Britomart (*highly indignant*). How dare you say Pip! pip! to me, Sarah? You are both very naughty children. What do you want, Barbara?

Barbara. I want a house in the village to live in with Dolly. (*Dragging at the skirt.*) Come and tell me which one to take.

Undershaft (*to* Cusins). Six o'clock tomorrow morning, Euripides.

THE END

William Golding:

The Brass Butterfly

The play that in this collection precedes *The Brass Butterfly* is, among other things, a paean to technology. In it Shaw suggests that the power that destroys the world can rebuild it, that the munitions maker may redeem humanity, that "the way of life lies through the factory of death," and that when technology has put enough bread in everyone's stomach, we may get a decent morality. In Adolphus Cusins, Shaw sees a union of intelligence with spirit that will make power into a moral force. William Golding is less sure.

Superficially, Golding is Shavian: he offers witty paradoxes, he writes a comedy that examines the contrast between what man is and what he thinks he is, and (like the Shaw of *Caesar and Cleopatra*) he takes the past and lets it speak in the idiom of the present. It will be enough here to give a single instance of the first point, an entertaining paradoxical dialogue. The Emperor is speaking of a steamship to the technologist:

Emperor. You will say I am old—but I prefer a slow boat. We will have nothing but slow boats in the future.

Phanocles. But Caesar!

Emperor. Besides, have you considered how unfair she was to the slaves?

Phanocles. She would have made them unnecessary.

Emperor. Well, there you are, you see. To be a slave-rower is a hard life, Phanocles, but it is better than no life at all. You do not have to think of these things, but I am respon-

> sible for the well-being of all classes. Your fast boats would lead to nothing but a pool of unemployment, and I am not hardhearted enough to countenance that.

Even this fragment, however, reveals that Golding's attitude toward man is not Shaw's. Golding's technologist, Phanocles, has an enthusiasm and a hope for the future that would make him a Shavian hero, but in *The Brass Butterfly* he is the comically imperceptive fool who looks so single-mindedly at one thing—as the comic miser stares lovingly at his gold, or as the comic husband stares jealously at his wife—that his folly is evident. Phanocles has some interesting ideas about the workings of the surrounding world (he invents the steam engine, among other things, and after the play concludes he will invent the compass), but he does not understand mankind. He cannot understand why men are interested in beautiful women ("the bedding of individuals," he calls it) when "there is such an ocean at our feet of eternal relationships to examine or confirm." By eternal relationships he does not mean man's relationship to eternal things, but the relationships of things to things, of cause and effect, or, as he puts it, "the world of substance and force." His desire is to change the universe, to "reshape the whole future of humanity," or, as he elsewhere puts it, to have his way with the universe. The Emperor finds him hubristic. And Phanocles is something of a comic version of Aeschylus' Prometheus, now not sublimely but comically unaware of man's capabilities. Anything like a tragic view is inconceivable to the enthusiastic technologist who sees no limit to his power. Sophocles (whom the Emperor's illegitimate son admires) puts his finger on the trouble. In *Antigone* he includes a chorus that runs in part as follows:

> Creation is a marvel
> And man its masterpiece:
> He scuds before the southern wind
> Between the loud white-piling swell. . . .
> The light-balanced light-headed birds
> He snares; wild beasts according to their kind.
> In his nets the deep sea fish are caught—
> O master mind of Man. . . .
> All fertile in resource
> He's provident for all
> (Not beaten by disease)

All but death, and death—
He never cures.[1]

Phanocles wants to meddle with the surface, but he does not see the central fact that Sophocles sees. The Emperor, however, knows that change is not necessarily progress (if we have cured some diseases, we have created new ones), and that "the universe does not seem to give something for nothing." Shaw, an enthusiastic creative evolutionist, generally sees in change progress; he sees, for example, new economic systems as better than their predecessors, and as aids to a new morality. Golding sees in technological advances a series of adult toys, things not bad in themselves, and sometimes useful, but things that do not minister to man's deepest nature and things that are always dangerous, like a sharp knife in a child's hands. Golding's Phanocles has unbounded confidence in man's goodness and intelligence, but Golding's Emperor has enough insight to distrust man's nature. For Phanocles, intelligence is the whole of man; the Emperor does not argue the point because he knows Phanocles' own nature too well. Even were Phanocles to read Golding's *Lord of the Flies* he would not sense that the Beast is part of man, and that there is darkness in man's heart. Phanocles is left in his absurdity (he is of course not quite absurd; the audience knows that he will ultimately have his way), and the Emperor is left to savor the experiences that time will still grant him. The Emperor's assumption that "life is not organized to make men happy" leads not to despair but to a treasuring of experience: "a wood fire, a healthy tiredness in the limbs, a robust red wine; and if possible, a sense of peril." Phanocles' gods of law, change, cause and effect, and reason, and the consequent clutter of toys that he will manufacture with their aid, cannot draw the Emperor from his delight in song and stars, "the beauty of the common world."

Golding's common world, it must be mentioned, is not so common that Phanocles can see it. For Phanocles the ocean is something to be crossed, but here is how Golding sees it in *Lord of the Flies*:

> Along the shoreward edge of the shallows the advancing clearness was full of strange, moonbeam-bodied creatures with fiery eyes. Here and there a larger pebble clung to its

[1] Translated by Paul Roche, in his *The Oedipus Plays of Sophocles,* New York, New American Library, (Mentor Books) 1958.

> own air and was covered with a coat of pearls. The tide swelled in over the rain-pitted sand and smoothed everything with a layer of silver. Now it touched the first of the stains that seeped from the broken body and the creatures made a moving patch of light as they gathered at the edge. The water rose further and dressed Simon's coarse hair with brightness. The line of his cheek silvered and the turn of his shoulder became sculptured marble. The strange, attendant creatures, with their fiery eyes and trailing vapors, busied themselves round his head. The body lifted a fraction of an inch from the sand and a bubble of air escaped from the mouth with a wet plop. Then it turned gently in the water.

The common world in *The Brass Butterfly* includes "the exquisite beauty of the night," "pools of light," the taste of trout, and the healthy tiredness already mentioned. And it includes even more, for it includes mystery. Phanocles, baffled for a moment by the behavior of one of his toys, can later find an explanation and take comfort in cause and effect, but his sister (responsible for the thing's strange behavior) insists that what she did was as in a dream, guided by God. Against Phanocles' view of changing the world by intelligence, and even against the Emperor's view of leaving the world alone (except to enjoy what it offers), is the woman's view of remaking the world under the guidance of a newly perceived divine power. And she does indeed effect a transformation: the Emperor's illegitimate son, bored at the outset of the play, acquires an enthusiasm that is almost Adolphus Cusins-like. Because the play is a play (Golding is playing with ideas as well as talking seriously), Phanocles can be got safely out of the way. He has found his way back to the Western world, and (under Emperors less wise than Golding's) has pretty much run things as he pleases ever since. Golding's play may remind an audience that real butterflies have their appeal too.

Golding: Biographical Note.

William Golding (b. 1911) was born in Cornwall. In his youth he thought he would become a scientist, but at Oxford he shifted from the study of science to the study of English literature. After being graduated, he served in the Royal Navy during the Second World

War; since the war, he has been teaching and writing. His best-known book is *Lord of the Flies* (1945), but it gained popularity rather slowly. The general public has yet to catch on to his other novels, which include *The Inheritors* (1955), *Pincher Martin* (1956; published in the United States as *Two Deaths of Christopher Martin*), and *Free Fall* (1958). *The Brass Butterfly* was first performed in Oxford, in 1958, under the direction of Alastair Sim, who played the Emperor in this and in the London production. The play is based on Golding's long story, "Envoy Extraordinary," which has been published in a collection called *Sometime, Never* (1956).

Suggested Reference: Peter Green, "The World of William Golding," *A Review of English Literature,* I, No. 2 (April 1960), 62–72.

The Brass Butterfly

Characters

MAMILLIUS
CAPTAIN OF THE GUARD
POSTUMUS
EMPEROR
PHANOCLES
EUPHROSYNE
SERGEANT
ATTENDANTS, etc.

ACT I

Scene I: The Emperor's *villa on the isle of Capri.*

Everything is on a large scale but in exquisite good taste. Perhaps the taste is the least bit too good—in any case the bust of a young and brutal-looking man, Back center, is noticeable as the only sign of an exterior world where life is earnest, real and rather bloody-minded. The bust stands under an opening to the sky.
Entrances: Right, to depths of villa. Left, to the open.
Architect has cunningly suggested on the inside here, what a magnificent front door the Emperor *has to his summer cottage. Bright sunlight.*
Time: Late afternoon some time in the third century A.D. *No one is going to be more specific. It is an unspecific-looking place, except for the bust.*
Mamillius, *a man-boy?—is lying on his stomach on a couch Right center. He is in the throes of literary composition.*

Mamillius. "Darken the five bright windows of my mind,
My soul is stretched out rigid in her bed.
Admit the corpse within. Pull down the blind—"
Pull down the blind . . .
(*Sees bust—springs up, flings cloak over it and returns to the couch.*)
"Admit the corpse within. Pull down the blind."
Pull down—pull down the blind—
(*Pause. Then inspiration comes.*)
"How *long*—"

Officer of the Guard *is heard shouting, off.*

Officer. Halt. Into line. Left turn. By the right—dress! Guard and men with arms—order—arms! Stand at—ease!

Captain of the Guard *comes in, left. Halts. Draws his sword. Stands easy.* Mamillius *pretends he is alone, but each time he paces towards the door the* Captain *comes to attention and reverts to at-ease as he turns away.*

Mamillius. Tell me, Captain, must we continue to play this foolish game?

Captain. Game, sir?

Mamillius. Moving your feet like that.

Captain. It's not a game, sir. Regulations.

Mamillius. And without regulations the empire would totter.

Captain. Yes, sir.

Mamillius. That would be exciting at least.

Captain. Yes, sir.

Mamillius. I am new to the imperial scene, Captain. Tell me, do you jump about just so when my grandfather comes near you?

Captain. Oh no, sir. We stand to attention whenever the Emperor comes in sight.

Mamillius. And when General Postumus—(*looking at cloak on bust which he has forgotten and which he now removes with elaborate unconcern*)—and when General Postumus comes in sight?

Captain. No, sir. Twenty paces for General Postumus—but we extend it a bit for the General, since he takes such a personal interest in discipline.

Mamillius. I am neither the Emperor nor General Postumus; just make yourself as comfortable as that dreary uniform will allow you.

Captain. Sorry, sir. Regulations. Distance makes no difference now. "Whilst addressed by a member of the Imperial Family officers of the guard will remain at attention until dismissed or until the Imperial Personage indicates beyond all reasonable doubt that the officer is no longer the subject of his interest."

Mamillius. How bored I am! How bored you must be!

Captain. No, sir. Used to it.

Mamillius. There's only one Imperial Family.

Captain. Yes, sir. But the regulations are the same in the vicinity of the vestal virgins and at public executions.

Mamillius. So I'm an Imperial Personage.

Captain. Yes, sir. Just, sir.

Mamillius. Only just? How near do I have to come before you give that horrid little jump?

Captain. Five paces, sir.

Mamillius. Because I'm a bastard?

Captain (*shocked*). Oh no, sir. You're not a bastard, sir. You're the Emperor's illegitimate grandson, sir.

Mamillius. Tell me, how does an Imperial Personage dismiss an officer?

Captain. The Emperor does it with one finger, like that, sir. Sorry, sir. I'm not here for you. I had to turn out the guard because General Postumus is coming to say good-by to the Emperor. You're just an accident, sir.

Mamillius. A what?

Captain. Oh—er—what I meant was—well—I certainly didn't mean what you probably thought I meant. (*Sees* Postumus *approaching*.) Excuse me, sir. Guard and men with arms! Shun! Slope arms!

Enter Postumus.

Postumus (*to Captain*). Take up position with the guard and stand them at ease.

Captain. Sir. (*Salutes and exits. Voice off*.) Guard. Order arms! Stand at ease! Keep still in the back there.

Postumus. Did you put him up to it?

Mamillius. If you are talking about the Captain, he gets everything out of a book, Postumus.

Postumus. I'm not talking about the Captain, you young fool. This other business. Someone let them get away. Did you do it?

Mamillius. I'm too bored to do anything.

Postumus. Give me a straight answer! (*Seizes his wrist*.) Did you help them escape or not?

Mamillius. Let me go! Let me go! I shall go back to Sybaris. I shall complain to grandfather. I warn you, Postumus. I warn you.

Postumus. Don't think you'll get away with it, Mamillius. I know what sort of influence you've got with him—

Mamillius. A civilizing influence. Grandfather!

Enter the Emperor *attended*.

Emperor. Ah, there you are, Postumus. Saying good-by to Mamillius? I'm so glad you get on well together. Come and sit for a moment, and drink wine with me.

Postumus. Caesar—(Emperor *halts him with a gesture and signs slaves to leave*). Someone gave them a boat. Who was it? Did he?

Mamillius. I haven't got a boat.

Emperor. No, of course he hasn't. Would you like one?

Postumus. Caesar!

Emperor. He doesn't understand, you know. Mamillius, a dreadful thing has happened. The ends of justice have been thwarted.

Postumus. And I've been made to look a fool.

Emperor. Nothing could do that. Nothing shall do that. You are my Heir Designate, Postumus. Take your fleet to Tripoli and extend the Empire. Go and give the blessing of civilization to the Sahara.

Postumus. I shall do so, and hope to show myself worthy of the imperial inheritance. But these three men—I must be certain that my work here is completed.

Emperor. The Heir Designate, Mamillius, pausing here at Capri to pay his respects to the Emperor, since the wind was contrary, occupied some days in examining the Imperial Household for disaffected persons, of whom he found three.

Postumus. The executions should have taken place this afternoon.

Emperor. But they got away.

Mamillius. What was their crime?

Postumus. They were Christians.

Emperor. Postumus is about the only man left to keep up the good old Roman customs.

Mamillius. Why should he think I had anything to do with it? Christianity is horribly vulgar. I do not care for vulgarity.

Postumus. After the orders I gave, only a member of the Imperial Household could have got them a boat.

Mamillius. Perhaps they simply stole one.

Emperor. They would hardly do that, do you think?

Postumus. And therefore I can only conclude—

Mamillius. —that *I* gave them one?

Postumus *rises.*

Emperor. (*intervening*). Postumus, the boy has only just heard about your Christians.

Postumus. Where has he been these last two days?

Emperor. In Arcadia with the Muse of poetry. Postumus, you and I know so much more than he. We live in a different world—the real one. Accept my assurances to quieten the thought lurking in your head. The boy is, and will remain, a private person. Eh, Mamillius?

Mamillius. Yes, grandfather.
Emperor. He cares nothing for public affairs—does he, Mamillius?
Mamillius. No, grandfather.
Emperor. Have I ever deceived you, Postumus?
Postumus. Yes.
Emperor. But in matters of moment?
Postumus. Perhaps not. Or if you have, Caesar, you have concealed it very cleverly.
Emperor. Come, Postumus, you are too intelligent to be deceived; so you may accept my assurances. (*Pause.*)
Postumus (*suddenly*). Contrary wind or not, I must be going, or there will be none of the season left.
Emperor. You accept my word then?
Postumus. I have your interests at heart—
Emperor. Because they are your interests too.
Postumus. Let the boy remain your companion so long as he becomes nothing more important.
Emperor. Surely.
Postumus. And find out who gave those Christians a boat.
Emperor. The enquiry could not be in safer hands. Good-by, my dear Heir Designate. Come back with the usual laurels on your sword.
Postumus. I shall try to do so.
Emperor. A last cup before you go?
Postumus. No, no.
Emperor. Good-by then. Our thoughts go with you and your gallant men. And remember, Postumus, I shall keep you informed of everything that happens.
Postumus. I shall keep myself informed. For the time being, good-by, Caesar.

(*Exit* Postumus.)

Emperor. Good-by! Good-by!
Officer (*off*). Guard shun! Slope arms! Present—arms!

Fanfare.

Emperor. Good-by! Good-by! Death or victory! But victory for choice, of course!
Officer (*off*). Slope—arms! Order arms! Turning right—dismiss!
Emperor. That was an affecting moment, eh, Mamillius? Good-by! Good-by!
Officers (*distant*). Present—arms!

(*Fanfare.*)

Emperor. My blessing etcetera. Good-by! How many today? (*Turning to petitions.*) Watch him go, Mamillius. It is a splendid ritual. Watch him, Mamillius. Mamillius!

Mamillius (*sulkily*). Caesar?

Emperor. Report his progress, will you? You might wave once or twice. Try to combine affectionate regret with boyish impetuosity.

Mamillius. The Heir Designate is about to step down to the quay.

Officer (*very distant*). Present—arms!

(*Fanfare distant.*)

Emperor. It is very trying to a man of any musical sensibility to have to hear that same old fanfare over and over again. Not that Postumus minds, you know. So long as the instruments are all at the same angle he is perfectly happy.

Mamillius. The Heir Designate is about to go aboard a boat.

Emperor. Why are you not waving?

Mamillius. Why should I?

Emperor. Come away then, and let me. (*Emperor gives some last courtly waves.*) There. I think that will do. And now for these petitions. Will you help me?

Mamillius. I looked at some. They bore me.

Emperor. They bore me, too. Forget him now, Mamillius. Postumus will be gone a long time.

Mamillius. I shan't feel easy till he's off the island. There. At last he's seated in the boat.

Emperor. That will take him out to the fleet. How peaceful everything is!

Mamillius. Too peaceful.

Emperor. Already? Let me think how you can be amused. (*He lifts a finger. In the villa a* Eunuch *begins to sing.* Mamillius *listens for a while.*)

Mamillius. No. (Emperor *switches off* Eunuch.) Even your famous singing eunuch is not what he was.

Emperor (*drily*). He would agree with you, Mamillius.

Mamillius. Is there an imperial recipe for the cure of boredom?

Emperor. Millions of people must think that an emperor's grandson—even one on the left-hand side—is utterly happy.

Mamillius. I have run through the sources of happiness.

Emperor. An hour ago you were eager to help me with these petitions.

Mamillius. That was before I had begun to read them. Does the whole world think of nothing but cadging favors?

Emperor. Write some more of your exquisite verses. I particularly liked the ones to be inscribed on an egg-shell. They appealed to the gastronome in me.

Mamillius. I found someone had done it before. I shall not write on eggshells again.

Emperor. Try the other arts.

Mamillius. Declamation? Gastronomy?

Emperor. You are too shy for the one and too young for the other.

Mamillius. I thought you applauded my interest in cooking.

Emperor. You talk, Mamillius, but you do not understand. Gastronomy is not the pleasure of youth but the evocation of it.

Mamillius. The Father of his Country is pleased to be obscure. And I am still bored.

Emperor. If you were not so wonderfully transparent I should prescribe senna.

Mamillius. I am boringly regular.

Emperor. A woman?

Mamillius (*indignantly*). I hope I am more civilized than that! (The Emperor *rocks with laughter*.) Am I so funny?

Emperor. I am sorry. Mamillius, you are so desperately up-to-date that you dare not enjoy yourself for fear of being thought old-fashioned.

Mamillius. The trouble is, Grandfather, I do not even want to. There is nothing new under the sun. Everything has been invented, everything has been written, everything has been done.

Emperor. Have you ever heard of China?

Mamillius. No.

Emperor. I must have heard of China first twenty years ago. An island, I thought, beyond India. It would take Postumus years to get there with his fleet. Since then, odd fragments of information have filtered through to me. Do you know, Mamillius, that China is an empire bigger than our own?

Mamillius. That is nonsense. A contradiction in nature.
Emperor. But true, none the less.
Mamillius. Travelers' tales.
Emperor. I try to prove to you how vast and exciting life is.
Mamillius. I do not care to go exploring.
Emperor. Stay home then, and amuse an old man who grows lonely.
Mamillius. Thank you for allowing me to be your fool.
Emperor. Boy, go and get mixed up in a good, bloody battle!
Mamillius. I leave that sort of thing to your *official* heir. Postumus is an insensitive bruiser. He can have all the battles he wants. Besides, a battle cheapens life, and I find life cheap enough already.
Emperor. Then the Father of his Country can do nothing for his own grandson.
Mamillius. I am tired of twiddling my fingers.
Emperor. So soon? Have I been very foolish? Be careful, Mamillius. A condition of our unusual friendship is that you keep your fingers out of hot water. Go on twiddling them. I want you to have a long life, even if in the end you die of boredom. Do not become ambitious.
Mamillius. I am not ambitious for power.
Emperor. Continue to convince Postumus of that. Leave the prospect of ruling to him. He likes it.
Mamillius. Yet you would prefer—
Emperor. No.
Mamillius. You would prefer—
Emperor. Be silent!
Mamillius. —that I should inherit the gold fringe on your purple toga.
Emperor. What place do you think this is? Have you read no history? If his agents heard you we should neither of us live another six months. Never say such a thing again! It is an order! (*Pause.*) Listen.
Mamillius. I am listening.
Emperor. Not to me. Do you hear nothing?
Mamillius. I hear nothing. Yes, I do. Like the beating of a heart.
Emperor. It is indeed the beating of a heart, Mamillius—a thousand hearts. They cannot spread the sails, but Postumus is in a hurry. There is a drum in every ship and the slaves keep time to it. They are condemned to the car as I am condemned daily to these merciless

petitions. Life is not organized to make men happy, Mamillius.

Mamillius. What have I to do with slaves?

Emperor. Nothing practical, of course; but your indifference to the idea of them argues a dislike of humanity.

Mamillius. And you?

Emperor. I accept humanity.

Mamillius. I avoid humanity.

Emperor. You must not do that, Mamillius. We must get Postumus to agree to my giving you a small governorship. Egypt?

Mamillius. Greece, if I must.

Emperor. Greece is booked, I am afraid—there is even a waiting list. It is our Roman passion for second-hand culture.

Mamillius. Egypt, then.

Emperor. A part of Egypt. If you go, Mamillius, it will be for your own sake. You would find nothing of me on your return but ashes and a monument or two. Be happy then, if only to cheer an aging civil servant!

Mamillius. What has Egypt to make me *happy?* There is nothing new, even out of Africa.

Emperor. Here is something new for you! They are two of your prospective subjects. You had better see them.

Mamillius *takes the petition and turns so that he can read it in the sunset light.*

Mamillius. Oh, no! It can't be! But Grandfather—what does he mean?

Emperor. I hoped you would explain.

Mamillius. But the diagram! Grandfather, it's indecent! (*He giggles.*)

Emperor. Be careful Mamillius—you are harboring old-fashioned ideas—

Mamillius. No—but look at that! Really! (*They laugh together.*)

Mamillius. Otherwise, I suppose it *could* be some sort of a ship.

Emperor. I get the same impression. At least this one is literate, if somewhat incoherent.

Mamillius. He's mad!

Emperor. They are. Frequently.

Mamillius. Violent?

Emperor. Sometimes.

Mamillius. I know what he wants.
Emperor. What?
Mamillius. He wants to play at boats with Caesar! (*They laugh.*)
Emperor. Oh, very good, Mamillius—very good! Yes—he wants to play at boats! Shall we see him?
Mamillius. Oh, yes please, Grandfather.
Emperor. Very well.

Mamillius *strikes bell. Enter* Captain.

Mamillius. Captain—
Captain. Sir?
Mamillius. The Emperor will—what will you do, Grandfather?
Emperor. Grant an audience, Captain.
Captain. Caesar! (*He takes his station behind the* Emperor's *chair with sword drawn.*)
Mamillius (*coldly official*). The Emperor grants an audience to the petitioners—what are they, Grandfather?
Emperor. Phanocles and Euphrosyne.
Mamillius. —to the petitioners Phanocles and Euphrosyne.
Usher (*off*). The Emperor permits the petitioners Phanocles and Euphrosyne to approach him!
Mamillius. What do I do?
Emperor. Show an interest in something.

Enter Usher. Phanocles *is bobbing behind him. As the* Usher *speaks* Phanocles *gets round him and explores the stage in search of the* Emperor.

Usher. Caesar: The petitioners Phanocles and Euphrosyne! (Usher *can find neither.*)
Phanocles. Caesar! Caesar!
Emperor. So you are Phanocles?
Phanocles. An Alexandrian, Caesar.

Enter Euphrosyne *balancing the model on her head. The* Usher, *satisfied that he has now delivered both petitioners, withdraws.*

Emperor. Mamillius—Mamillius!
Mamillius. Caesar?
Emperor. Ah! I see. You are showing an interest, I believe.

Mamillius. Yes, Caesar.

Emperor. You are guarding my chair, Captain—not eying my guests.

Captain. Caesar!

Emperor. And you, Phanocles?

Phanocles. Phanocles, Caesar—the son of Myron, an Alexandrian.

Emperor. Son of Myron? The Librarian?

Phanocles. Yes, Caesar.

Emperor. I remember him. Did your father finish his dictionary? He had reached B when I left some forty years ago.

Phanocles. He died seven years ago, Caesar. He reached F, but it was too much for him.

Emperor. And you will finish his life's work?

Phanocles. I was an assistant, Caesar—but then—something happened. Look at this, Caesar. (*He realizes he is without the model, then remembers, looks round, and discovers it on* Euphrosyne's *head. After some difficulty he manages to set it up on portable trestles.*)

Emperor. And you want to play boats with Caesar?

Phanocles. There was obstruction, Caesar, from top to bottom. I was wasting my time and public money, they said, and I was dabbling in black magic, they said, and they laughed. I am a poor man, and when the last of my father's money was spent—he left me a little, you understand—not much—and when I spent that—what are we to do, Caesar? There was obstruction and mockery, incomprehension, anger, persecution—

Emperor. How much did it cost you to see me today?

Phanocles. Three pieces of gold.

Emperor. That seems reasonable. I am not in Rome.

Phanocles. It was all I had.

Emperor. Mamillius, see that Phanocles does not lose by his visit. Mamillius!

Mamillius. Caesar.

Emperor. And this lady? Is she your wife?

Phanocles. She is my sister.

Emperor. Your sister?

Phanocles. Euphrosyne, Caesar. A free woman and a virgin.

Emperor. Lady, let us see your face.

Phanocles. Caesar! She—

Emperor. You must accustom yourself to our western manners, Phanocles. We intend no discourtesy, lady. Modesty is the proper ornament of virginity. But let us see your face, so that we may know to whom we speak. (Euphrosyne *with extreme reluctance lowers the veil.*) Lady, you were well named for one of the Graces.

Phanocles. My sister!

Mamillius. Phanocles, you bring us the tenth wonder of the world!

Phanocles. But Lord, I have not explained!

Mamillius. "The speechless eloquence of beauty."

Emperor. I have heard that somewhere before. Has no sculptor seen your sister?

Phanocles. Sculptor?

Mamillius. She should be immortalized as Aphrodite!

Phanocles. Daaah! Forgive me, Caesar—she is too modest—she is too sensitive—she—she—

Emperor. Calm yourself. No harm is intended to you or or to your sister. Mamillius, they are our guests.

Mamillius. Oh, yes, Grandfather!

Phanocles. My model—

Emperor. So you are a sculptor too?

Mamillius. Phanocles and the lady Euphrosyne are the Emperor's guests! (*During the ensuing speeches,* Euphrosyne *is removed in as much grave pomp as the company can muster.*)

Phanocles. My model!

Mamillius. Take great care of her. Go with them, lady.

Emperor. Be happy, lady. You too, Phanocles.

Mamillius. Farewell until a later hour!

Emperor. You speak verses. And now, Phanocles, come, sit down. A cup of wine to celebrate her—and your—arrival.

Mamillius. A toast to beauty!

Phanocles. But my model! My working model!

Emperor. I divine your troubles, my dear Phanocles, and rest assured that they are all over. All, all, over. You shall have all the marble or bronze you want.

Phanocles. Marble is useless.

Emperor. Gold, perhaps.

Mamillius. Warm, flesh-tinted alabaster.

Emperor. No, no. Pay no attention, Phanocles. Bronze. My dear boy, you are making me very happy! I rejoice with you.

Mamillius. What is her voice like?

Phanocles. My sister's voice?

Mamillius. How does she speak?

Phanocles. She speaks very seldom, Lord. I cannot remember the quality of her voice.

Mamillius. Men have built temples for objects of less beauty!

Phanocles. She is my sister!

Emperor. Have you promised her in marriage? Is she betrothed?

Phanocles. No, Caesar.

Emperor. But if you are so poor, Phanocles, has it never occurred to you that you might make a fortune by a brilliant connection?

Phanocles (*blank*). What woman would you have me marry, Caesar?

Mamillius. Has she an ambition?

Emperor. My dear Mamillius, a beautiful woman is her own ambition.

Mamillius. She is all the reasons in the world for poetry!

Phanocles (*angrily. Jumps up*). I cannot follow you, Caesar. I cannot understand men. Of what importance is the bedding of individuals when there is such an ocean at our feet of eternal relationships to examine or confirm?

Emperor. Explain a little further.

Phanocles. If you let a stone drop from your hand it will fall.

Emperor. I hope we are following you.

Phanocles. Each substance has affinities of an eternal and immutable nature with every other substance. A man who understands them—this lord here—

Emperor. My grandson, the Lord Mamillius.

Phanocles. Lord, do you know much of law?

Mamillius. It is my fate to be a Roman.

Phanocles. There then! You can move easily in the world of law. I can move easily in the world of substance and force because I credit the universe with at least a lawyer's intelligence. Just as you who know the law could have your way with me since I do not, so I can have my way with the universe.

Emperor. Confused, illogical, and extremely hubristic. Tell me, when you talk like this do people ever say you are mad?

Phanocles. Always, Caesar. That is why I severed my connection with the Library.

Emperor. I see. *Are* you a sculptor?

Phanocles. No. Am I mad?

Emperor. I think perhaps you are.

Phanocles. The universe is a mechanism.

Mamillius. Are you a magician?

Phanocles. There is no magic.

Mamillius. Your sister is the living proof and epitome of magic.

Phanocles. Then she is beyond Nature's legislation.

Mamillius. That may well be. Is there any poetry in your universe?

Phanocles. That is how they all talk, Caesar—poetry, magic, religion—

Emperor (*chuckling*). Be careful, Greek. You are talking to the High Pontiff of Jupiter.

Phanocles. Does Caesar believe in the things that the High Pontiff has to do?

Emperor. I prefer not to answer that question.

Phanocles. Lord Mamillius, do you believe in your very heart that there is an irrational and unpredictable force of poetry outside your rolls of paper?

Mamillius. How dull your life must be!

Phanocles. Dull? My life is passed in a condition of ravished astonishment! Yet I am destitute. Without your help I must starve. With it I can change the universe.

Emperor. Are you a Christian?

Phanocles. Caesar—I swear—I am willing to sacrifice to you whenever you like—

Emperor. You believe in the gods then?

Phanocles. I—I am indifferent, Caesar, as I think you must be, together with all educated and thinking men.

Emperor. But you are not a Christian?

Phanocles. How should that contradictory mixture of hysterical beliefs appeal to such a man as I?

Emperor. Forgive me, Phanocles, but I like to be certain. I am getting old and perhaps foolish. Executions distress me.

Phanocles. Executions?

Emperor. You were going to change the universe. Will you improve it?

Mamillius. He is mad, Caesar.

Emperor. Phanocles, in my experience changes have seldom been for the better, since the universe does not seem to give something for nothing. Yet I entertain you for my—for your sister's sake. Be brief. What do you want?

Phanocles. With this ship you will be more famous than Alexander. Any one of the rich men I approached could have had that fame had they wanted it. Caesar!

Emperor. Ah, yes. Your ship. What is she called?

Phanocles. She has no name.

Emperor. A ship without a name? Find one, Mamillius.

Mamillius. I do not care for her. Amphitrite, Grandfather, with your permission—

Emperor. I shall see you at dinner and further your education.

Mamillius. I will ensure that our guest is comfortable.

Emperor. Do so. Mamillius!

Mamillius. Grandfather—?

Emperor. I am sorry you are bored.

Mamillius. Bored? I, bored? Yes, of course I am. Very, very, very.

Exit Mamillius.

Emperor. She is unseaworthy, flat-bottomed, with little sheer and bows like a corn barge. What are the ornaments? Have they a religious significance?

Phanocles. Hardly, Caesar.

Emperor. So after all you do want to play boats with me? If I were not charmed with your innocence I should be displeased at your presumption.

Phanocles. I have three toys for you, Caesar. This is only the first.

Emperor. Man, I have tried for the equivalent of at least three normal audiences to understand you. What do you want?

Phanocles. Have you ever seen water boiling in a pot?

Emperor. I have.

Phanocles. There is much steam evolved which escapes into the air. If the pot were closed, what would happen?

Emperor. The steam could not escape.

Phanocles. The pot would burst. The force exerted by steam is titanic.

Emperor (*interested*). Really? Have you ever seen a pot burst?

Phanocles. Beyond Syria there is a savage tribe. They inhabit a land full of natural oil and inflammable vapor. When they desire to cook they lead the vapor through pipes into stoves at the sides of their houses. The meat these natives eat is tough and must be cooked for a long time. They put one heavy dish on top of another, inverted. Now the steam builds up a pressure under the pot that penetrates the meat and cooks it thoroughly and quickly.

Emperor. Will not the steam burst the pot?

Phanocles. There is the ingenuity of the device. If the pressure becomes too great it will lift the dish and allow the steam to escape. Steam could lift a weight that an elephant would balk at.

Emperor (*excited*). And the flavor, Phanocles! It will be confined with the steam! The whole wonderful intention of the comestible will be preserved by magic!

Phanocles. Now in a ship—Let me light this lamp inside the model.

Emperor (*disregarding him*). I have always been a primitive where meat is concerned. To taste meat in its exquisite simplicity would be a return to those experiences of youth that time has blunted. There should be a wood fire, a healthy tiredness in the limbs, a robust red wine; and if possible, a sense of peril—(*pause*). Phanocles, we are on the verge of an immense discovery. What do the natives call their two dishes?

Panocles (*depressed*). A pressure cooker.

Emperor. How soon could you make me one? Or perhaps if we simply inverted one dish over another—Fish, do you think? Or fowl? I think on the whole one would detect the intensification most readily in fish.

Phanocles. Caesar!

Emperor. You must dine with me now and we will formulate a plan of action.

The Emperor *claps his hands. Enter* Valet.

Phanocles. But my boat, Caesar! (*Pause.*)

Emperor. Amphitrite? I could give you anything you want, Phanocles. But come, let us dine.

Phanocles. When the wind fails, what happens to a ship? (*Pause—then shrugs and signs to Valet.*)

Emperor (*indulgently—he is now affable, seeing the value of* Phanocles). She waits for the next one. The master invokes a wind. Sacrifices and so on. Toga!

Valet *starts the change of togas, rosewater, etc., with the help of another* Slave.

Phanocles. But if he does not believe in a wind god?

Emperor. Then I suppose he does not get a wind.

Phanocles. But if the wind fails at a moment of crisis for your warships?

Emperor. The slaves row.

Phanocles. And when they tire?

Emperor. They are beaten.

Phanocles. But if they become so tired that beating is useless?

Emperor. Then they are thrown overboard. You have the Socratic method. (Phanocles *groans.*) You are tired and hungry. Have no fear for yourself or your sister. You have both become very precious to me and your sister shall be my ward.

Phanocles. I do not think of her.

Emperor (*puzzled*). What do you want, then?

Phanocles. I have tried to say. I want to build you a warship after the pattern of Amphitrite.

Emperor. A warship is an expensive undertaking. I cannot treat you as though you were a qualified shipwright when you are only a librarian.

Phanocles. Then give me a hull—any hull. Give me an old corn barge if you will, and sufficient money to convert her after this fashion.

Emperor. Of course, my dear Phanocles, anything you like. I will give the necessary orders. Indeed, it will be the second boat I have given away lately. Now, let us dine.

Phanocles. And my other inventions?

Emperor. The pressure cooker?

Phanocles. No. What I have called an explosive.

Emperor. Something that claps out? How strange! What would be the use of that? What is the third invention?

Phanocles. I will keep it in reserve to surprise you.

Emperor (*relieved*). Do so. Make your ship and your clapper-outer and then surprise me with the third invention. But first of all the pressure cooker. And now let us dine.

Phanocles. Shall I bring the working model with me, Caesar?

Emperor. Amphitrite? No, no. On the whole, I think not. Come, Phanocles.

Phanocles. I could explain the machinery—

Emperor. The circular contrivances?

Phanocles. I call them paddle-wheels—a mode of progression. That globe in the center is a boiler.

Emperor. A pressure cooker? A tiny little pressure—

Phanocles. Oh, no! Caesar! Please try to understand. There is no *frivolity* here. My aim is to reshape the whole future of humanity.

Emperor. Dear me. Then I had better give you an official position at once. Supposing I appoint you my Director-General of Experimental Studies—would that please you?

Phanocles. I? Caesar's Director-General? With leave to experiment?

Emperor. To your heart's content, my friend. But now we go to dine.

Usher. Caesar goes to dine!

Exit Emperor.

Phanocles (ecstatic, as he follows). . . . with leave to experiment:

Exit Phanocles. *Trumpets off.* The Captain *is released by the trumpets. He comes downstage, sheathing his sword as he does so. Pauses. Looks down funnel.* Amphitrite *starts to go—Peep! Peep! chuffa, chuffa, Poop! Poop!* Captain *leaps away. Draws his sword.*

Captain. Sentry! Turn out the guard!

ACT II

Scene: Same as Act I.

Phanocles *is discovered making calculations with the aid of a portable abacus which* Euphrosyne *is holding for him. He also has some sort of sighting instrument along which he squints out to sea from time to time and notes readings and results, etc., on tablets. All this intersperses the rather spasmodic phrasing of the opening speech.*

(*Enter a* Seaman.)

Seaman. Director-General Phanocles, Sir.

Phanocles. What do you want?

Seaman. The Captain's compliments, Sir and beg to report that the magic ship is in all respects ready for sea. (Phanocles *nods. Exit* Seaman.)

Phanocles (*to* Euphrosyne). Is there anything more impenetrable than frivolity? How can I demonstrate the explosive here? Something that "claps out"! I tried to explain again. I was logical and precise; but he is like—I cannot tell what he is like;—what they are all like. Help me. In this mad race of men only you and I know true sanity; and yet sometimes you seem to know these people too. Would the young Lord Mamillius understand, do you think? Euphrosyne, make them understand the heat, the boundless force, the sudden expansion—(*Pause. She shakes her head.*) Why must I waste my time? If I could only brush them aside—or show them my new heaven and new earth!

Enter Captain of the Guard.

Captain. Director-General—Phanocles!
Phanocles. What do you want?
Captain. There is a casket for you outside the door.
Phanocles. Ah, yes, yes. Why are they waiting? Let them bring it in at once. The Emperor may be here at any moment.
Captain. I can hardly do that, Phanocles. If the Emperor wants such a thing brought into the villa he is entitled to. That presents no difficulty. "Guard will reverse arms and assume an attitude of dejection"—and so on. But where are my instructions? Suppose this is not a dead body?
Phanocles. A body?
Captain. Imagine the black I should put up if I reversed arms and assumed an attitude of dejection while those men carried in a concealed assassin. Before the casket comes through that door the body must be examined, and in my presence.

The light dawns on Phanocles.

Phanocles. You want to open—
Captain. Of course I shall have every respect shown whilst confirming the melancholy truth.
Phanocles. Look if you must. But please hurry!
Captain. With your permission then.
Phanocles. Yes, yes—Captain!—On no account touch the butterfly.

Exit Captain.

Captain (off). Guard and men with arms—shun! Reverse arms!

Phanocles. Power in the hands of man. How shall I make him understand? Be merciful, Euphrosyne! What is a vow? You could be the link! You can choose for us —a new heaven and earth, or poverty again, and frustration.

Enter Mamillius. *He stands contemplating* Euphrosyne.

Lord Mamillius!—(*to Euphrosyne*). If only you would help me, Euphrosyne!

Phanocles *approaches* Mamillius.

Phanocles. Lord Mamillius, what happens when lightning strikes a tree?

Mamillius. If the tree is anywhere near the Imperial Precincts, my grandfather offers a sacrifice—How unbelievably ignorant you are, Phanocles! Surely you know that?

Phanocles. Euphrosyne! Explain to him—

Mamillius. Yes—let your sister explain.

Phanocles. No, no—of course she must not. There was a vow . . .

Mamillius. What does he mean, Euphrosyne?

Phanocles. Please let us be, Lord—(*He sees the* Four Slaves). Ah!

Enter Four Slaves *carrying an object which is as much like a coffin as the cast and the public will take.*

Gently—carefully. . . . Round here. Lower that end. It must face this way. (*He dismisses the slaves and examines the horrible box devoutly.*)

Mamillius. How horrible! Lady, you should not be seen in company with so stark a reminder.

Phanocles. Lord, there is nothing to fear.

Phanocles *removes the lid and reveals the black and yellow projectile standing on its stalk. It is the size of a man and more. It is very nasty.*

Mamillius. A new god!

Phanocles. Lord, this is my explosive. The whole mechanism is to be hurled from a catapult at what you wish to destroy. This will make your Empire irresistible.

Mamillius. It is not my Empire!

Phanocles. Here is an arming vane. The pressure of the air makes it spin off—when this rod touches any solid object a compressive shock heats the explosive to the point where it catches fire. What happens then?

Mamillus. Could your sister tell me?

Phanocles. The heat causes a sudden expansion. So what happens to the mechanism?

Mamillius. It will become bigger.

Phanocles. No!

Mamillius. Smaller?

Phanocles. No!

Mamillius. Then, logically, Phanocles, it must remain the same size which is a pity. Any change would be for the better.

Phanocles. The mechanism changes—into vapor.

Mamillius. You are a conjurer after all. Show me, sometime—but not now. I have a message for you. The Emperor is delayed by grave imperial business.

Phanocles. Delayed? You mean he's not coming? But my steamship! She is down there in the bay, waiting! He was to see her!

Mamillius. No one could see much in this heat haze, Phanocles. We shall have thunder. Is your sister afraid of thunder?

Phanocles. This is—this was to be—one of the great days of the world—and he delays—he is signing—business—!

Mamillius. Phanocles, I have just now remembered the second half of my grandfather's message. He wishes you to inspect the north wing of the villa; carefully; by yourself, Phanocles. He particularly wishes you to go by yourself.

Phanocles. What reason—?

Mamillius. Reason?

Phanocles. But then—an Emperor does not always give a reason. . . .

Mamillius. No, indeed. He need not necessarily find a reason.

Phanocles. What must I do there?

Mamillius. Do? Just stay there, I suppose.

Phanocles (*naughty temper*). He made me Director-General of Experimental Studies. Any architect, any builder, any hodman—

Mamillius. He asks you—please—to calculate the number of paving stones of different sizes in the corridors.

Phanocles *registers what might be anything or nothing!*

(*sticking to it*)—and give him your comments if you find any . . . any significant mathematical relationships.

Phanocles. But my ship—my explosive—my sister—

Mamillius. I will take care of them all. It is his Imperial Will, Phanocles.

Phanocles. This is madness! I am lost, Lord. People defeat me. (*Goes, muttering.*) Significant mathematical relationships. . . . *All* mathematical relationships are significant!

Exit Phanocles. Mamillius *gives a gasp of relief, looks furtively towards the* Emperor's *apartments, and then moves cautiously towards* Euphrosyne.

Mamillius. Are they, Lady? But not all human relationships. I have tried to follow you. Did you know that? Did you? (*She nods.*) Have I annoyed you? It would seem so. I cannot confuse this curious and obsessive interest with the enchantment of the blind god. Yet a glimpse of you walking the lawns—even the knowledge as I pace the long corridors that you are lying asleep behind this wall or this—. . . I had a speech prepared, but now you stand near me the words have flown out of my head. This cannot be love; yet I cannot rest. I have written poetry—Greek, of course—and some whose judgment is of value think it good. But your magic fits no verses. I have written and erased till the wax melted. The ache, the frustration—my bewilderment—distil down from blown verses through the single line to one cold drop of truth—

"Euphrosyne is beautiful but dumb."

Silence and mystery are merciless weapons. Cease to be the Egyptian Sphinx. Become a face, a voice with accent, tricks of speech—with laughter and opinion; become an ordinary woman, and either conquer me outright for your empire, or set me free! No words? Must our meeting be this half-measure? (*Pause.*) Oh, Lady, have mercy! I have tried to be honest—(*She looks at him suddenly.*)—a strange lower-middle-class word to hear spoken in an Emperor's villa! Your brother can change this mechanism into vapor. Could he change me too? I have it almost in my heart to wish he could! (*Goes to projectile.*)

Euphrosyne. No!

Mamillius. You spoke! Euphrosyne—you spoke to me! You said "No!" What did I do? (*He has left the box and gone to her.* Euphrosyne *has sunk back into silence, only shakes her head. After a second* Mamillius *rushes back to the box.*)

Euphrosyne (*starting up*). No!

Mamillius (*wreathed in delight*). Oh, but yes! (*His hands fumble happily all over the explosive, keeping his eyes on* Euphrosyne. *She goes desperately over to between him and the box.*)

Euphrosyne. The butterfly—the brass butterfly! It is outside your world. You will kill us all!

Mamillius. Is there a curse on it?

Euphrosyne. Yes—No. Look. This is a charm. He has stored the lightning in this metal egg. Have you ever worn a charm?

Mamillius. All men wear them—to keep off the evil eye or fever.

Euphrosyne. As long as the charm sits there the lightning will not wake; but when my brother hurls the whole mechanism from a catapult the butterfly spins off. Then a touch would make lightning come from the egg, that would push this villa over and throw it into the sea.

Mamillius. Only a touch?

Euphrosyne. Write your verses, Lord. Leave the lightning alone.

Mamillius. You are . . . dawning on me.

Euphrosyne. You made me break a vow—

Mamillius. You are so beautiful—

Euphrosyne. No more than you.

Mamillius. How ignorant I was to think that hearing your voice would cure me of you! Euphrosyne! You said, "No more than you"! (*Pause.*) I haunt you? We haunt each other. There is the honest truth. We are wonderful undiscovered country. Show me your face again.

Euphrosyne. I must go. Let me pass!

Mamillius. I will see you—I must! Our haunting gives me the right to see you.

Euphrosyne. You are a prince.

Mamillius. I? A prince? I am a poor bastard on a string! (*Pause.*) And therefore what have I to lose? Show me your face. Come here. Closer. Your obedience is wonderful, and breaks my heart. Uncover your face. (*She uncovers her face and they look at each other. She is dazzling.*) I am lost. I am killed with kindness. Why would you not speak? Why did you hide this from me?

Euphrosyne. My vow.

Mamillius. Euphrosyne, you are a person. You have been here and there. You have a history. There are things you like—

Euphrosyne. My voice and my face were to cure you.

Mamillius. Do you begin to love me?

Euphrosyne. What good would it do to say yes?

Mamillius. We shall spend our lives together.

Euphrosyne. No.

Mamillius. My grandfather is the Emperor—

Euphrosyne. He would not give you a free woman against her will.

Mamillius. Your vow? Let the Emperor absolve you.

Euphrosyne. No.

Mamillius. You are your brother's ward. I can twist him round my finger. Besides, he would never dare to—

Euphrosyne (*defiantly*). Do not speak like that! My brother is a great man. His name will outlast Caesar's!

Mamillius. A conjuror! A toy-maker!

Euphrosyne. What are you, with your verses, to speak of him? He says, "Let such and such a new thing be"—as though he were—He could throw a chain round the stars!

Mamillius. I could throw a rope round his neck! May he count cobbles till his eyes cross!

Euphrosyne (*suddenly frightened*). Go away. Let me alone. I will have nothing to do with you. You are cruel, like all the rest; you want to harm and humiliate—perhaps to murder him. We might be from another kind of earth, I and my brother . . . your conjurer! He is ignorant in some ways—but you! (*She bursts into tears.*)

Mamillius. Euphrosyne—forgive me! I didn't think what I was saying, nor how it would hurt you—I meant what I said as a joke, Euphrosyne—as a *joke!* I was only joking! (*Pause.*)

Euphrosyne. Oh . . .

Mamillius. Are we friends again?

Euphrosyne. I want to be—more than anything, since the vow is broken. But we are so different. Somehow I have never been able to laugh at jokes the way other people do. I don't think I have a sense of humor.

Mamillius. I love you as you are, so—

Enter Emperor.

—adorably grave, even when you are happy, and you *are* happy now, aren't you? Please, please say you are happy!

Emperor. Well, Mamillius, I have news for you. Euphrosyne—(*she sniffs*) Crying? What a bully!

Mamillius. I did nothing!

Emperor. I was not referring to you, Mamillius.

Mamillius. Tell me the secret of success in love.

Emperor. Decision. It is irresistible. Dear me. . . . Judging by the almost hysterical ugliness of the figure and the mortal overtones of the box, I must assume this to be one of the inventions of my Director-General.

Mamillius. The figure turns into vapor.

Enter Phanocles.

Phanocles. Caesar! At a rough computation, the tiles in the north wing number eleven thousand. I could not count them exactly. (*The* Emperor *awaits further enlightenment.*) However, Caesar, this is a great day in the history of the world. When projected from the catapult which I have placed down there on the quay, the brass arming vane flies off. Then, in contact with a solid object—

Emperor. —Flies off. That reminds me, Phanocles—the demonstration is canceled.

Phanocles (*an outburst*). Canceled? My demonstration? What business—what right—I come to the top—I climb from nowhere with this head and these hands—I come to the peak among men, and you are like the others! Where shall I find someone who can understand? In this—this anthill of blind and indifferent humanity—among these wars and—and catastrophes. . . . Last night there was an eclipse of the moon. I could not see it, but the slave described it to me—the still movement, that fated advance of the copper shadow. . . . Oh, the majestic distances! They are real. We grow up into them. They are man's true empire of the mind—and of the body. . . . But only I of all men—I alone—I by myself—I have no brother—the ants—there is nothing. Nothing. No one. . . .

During this speech the Emperor *takes more and more care*

to be imperial. He does it, perhaps, by being rather than by doing.

Euphrosyne *holds* Phanocles, *pulling him back, both hands on his left arm. She is turned, petrified, towards the* Emperor.

The enormity of the occasion has dawned on Mamillius, *who is acutely conscious that* Phanocles' *raw knees are on his account. He sees the change in grandfather long before* Phanocles *sees it.*

Emperor. Mamillius.

Mamillius. Caesar?

Emperor. There is news from Tripoli.

Mamillius. From Postumus?

Emperor. He has broken off his campaign. He has concentrated his army on the seaport and he is stripping the coast of ships, from fishing boats to triremes.

Mamillius. He is tired of heroics.

Emperor. No, Mamillius. He is a realist, and realists are always frightened.

Mamillius. Postumus? Frightened?

Emperor. He fears your influence.

Mamillius. Postumus—frightened of me?

Emperor. You are too intelligent not to know why; and too inexperienced to appreciate our danger.

Mamillius. But he thinks me an incompetent fool!

Emperor. He is right, of course. But he knows also that incompetence and folly have not prevented a number of my predecessors from attaining to this purple. And he has heard—I think—that the Emperor's affectionately regarded grandson is taking an interest in ships and weapons of war.

Mamillius. What shall we do?

Emperor. I shall go to Tripoli to convince him that I am still Emperor and that you do not want to be the next one.

Mamillius. But that will be dangerous!

Emperor. My dear Mamillius, have you begun to think of other people? Where will this end?

Mamillius. I shall come with you.

Emperor. Bless you, child!—do you want your throat cut?

Mamillius. My throat?

Emperor. I do not think that Postumus would accord you the privilege of committing suicide.

Mamillius. I am a man.

Emperor. Officially.

Mamillius. And therefore I shall come with you to Tripoli. When do we leave?

Emperor. As soon as this heat haze lifts. Towards evening. I—we must get there before Postumus leaves. When Postumus moves, he does so with frightening speed. He was here, on his last welcome visit, two days before I expected him.

Mamillius. I shall *play* the man.

Emperor. What a curious turn of phrase! But apt. Something has happened to you, and I am delighted. But be careful, Mamillius. We are dealing with a superb man of action.

Mamillius. I shall surprise you.

Emperor. You have done that already. (*As if noticing him for the first time.*) Ah, Director-General, here you are at last. The very man I wanted for advice and information.

Mamillius. I shall make my preparations now. Phanocles, take great care of Euphrosyne.

Emperor. Make your preparations?

Mamillius. We are going to the army.

Exit Mamillius.

Emperor. What did he mean by that? Have you noticed, Phanocles, that today the normal means of human communication have seemed to be a little inadequate?

Phanocles. I have noticed it all my life, Caesar.

Emperor. You are a philosopher. What a pity to cancel the demonstration! Now I shall have to try your pressure cooker on my return.

Phanocles. My pressure cooker?

Emperor. Had you forgotten that we were to dine todine together this evening and try your pressure cooker? Politics, administration, dynastic emergencies. . . . Never consent to be an Emperor, Phanocles. To be the servant of all men is a worthy ideal, no doubt, but restless, restless. . . . How *fast* will your steamship take us to Tripoli?

Phanocles. My—?

Emperor. Amphitrite.

Phanocles. My steamship!

Emperor. She is ready, of course. (Phanocles *makes an inarticulate noise.*) You must go aboard her now,

Phanocles, and prepare her for the voyage. Tripoli is hardly a majestic distance, but it is far enough.

Phanocles. She will take you there twice as fast as your fastest ship, Caesar! Oh . . . Caesar!

Emperor. I have an irrational faith in you, Director-General. That is unwise, of course. Go now. But let your sister stay here for a moment. Oh—and Phanocles—

Phanocles. Caesar?

Emperor. Remove this object, will you?

Phanocles. My explosive?

Emperor. Or vaporize it, if you prefer. Could you do that quickly?

Phanocles (*laughing*). I should knock the villa down, Caesar. Let me have it loaded on the catapult down by the quay. Then, perhaps, when you are leaving in Amphitrite—

Emperor. Do so.

Phanocles. You men—take it back to the quay!

Enter the Four Slaves. *They box up the projectile and go out towards the quay during the following speeches.*

Emperor. Twice as fast?

Phanocles. At least, Caesar.

Emperor. I must confess to a perhaps childish delight in the thought of approaching Postumus, of all people, with terrifying speed. Our steamship will take the wind out of his sails, Phanocles.

Phanocles. Yes, Caesar. I shall go now, Caesar. (*Pauses at door.*) Caesar—how far is it to Tripoli?

Emperor. About three days' sail at this season. In winter, of course, it is either much further—as much as eight days—or disastrously nearer.

Phanocles. Pardon, Caesar . . . miles?

Emperor. Well?

Phanocles. To Tripoli, Caesar.

Emperor. Miles to Tripoli? You are a baffling mixture of genius and ignorance. Surely you know we cannot reach Tripoli by land?

Phanocles. There must be a fixed distance.

Emperor. I fail to see why we should interest ourselves in such an academic consideration at this juncture. Tell your captain to be ready to leave when the haze lifts. You *have* a captain?

Phanocles. Yes, Caesar.

Emperor. You chose him carefully?
Phanocles. Yes, Caesar.
Emperor. A lucky and religious man?
Phanocles. I don't know.
Emperor. To what an enterprise am I committing myself! On land, Phanocles, although I am the All Father's High Pontiff, I should be the first to admit that the workings of his divine nature are often inexplicably random and obscure; but once surrounded by water. . . . We must take ample provisions, for frequent sacrifices will be necessary.
Phanocles (*going*). We shall get there twice as fast as your ships can move, Caesar.

Exit Phanocles. Emperor *goes to* Euphrosyne.

Emperor. Still frightened and silent after all these weeks, Euphrosyne? Come! Are you not yet accustomed to our unpretentious little retreat? In Rome, now—ha, Rome! There you might well be overawed, child. Rome is a really intimidating symbol of the Imperial Power.

Usher *enters right; crosses left, and signs with his finger.*

Sentry (*off*). Guard—turn out!
Emperor. But here, at peace, and with the minimum of ceremonial—(Usher *exits right.*)—where I am no more than any other country gentleman, surely you can accept us as the kindly and unaffected folk we are?
Officer (*off*). Left-right left-right left-right—halt! Into line—right turn! Pick up your dressing.
Emperor. Forgive this insistence, Euphrosyne; but the happiness of that golden youth, my grandson, is very near to me. What is your mystery?
Euphrosyne. I cannot tell you.
Emperor. Shall I guess then? This remarkable man who passes as your brother—are you not in fact his wife?
Euphrosyne. No.
Emperor. What are you hiding? Look at me. (*Pause.*) Child, you are frightened of me. That is terrible. Can you not understand what a humiliation that is? I learn now, and for the first time, that the young and charming, the poor and the helpless, see not the man, but the position. They do not see me as the ultimate guardian of justice—and perhaps even mercy. They hear only the fanfares, they are blinded by the purple and the gold.

I beg you, child—for his sake, but also for mine—see what infinite power lies in the soft cheek of a girl! Do not humiliate me.

Euphrosyne. Forgive me, Caesar. I want to tell you—but I have not found the courage. We have lived for so long in fear, my brother and I; here at least we have achieved a sort of peace in your kindness . . . but strange new things have happened—miracles you could call them—

Emperor. What miracles? Do you mean your brother's ingenious toys?

Euphrosyne. Oh no, Caesar. My brother is a great man, but still only a man. . . .

Emperor. Go on.

Euphrosyne. I dare not.

Emperor. But why?

Euphrosyne. Because you *are* Caesar.

Emperor. So I am useless, although they have made me Father of the Country and High Priest of all the gods? And after all, officially I am a god myself.

Euphrosyne (in terror). Be merciful! Let me go now—please, Caesar! (*Pause.*)

Emperor. Oh I see. Or perhaps I think I see.

Euphrosyne (almost inaudible). Yes, Caesar. (*Pause.*)

Emperor. Now, what were we talking about? Strange how completely a recent conversation, with all its implications, can vanish out of mind! As I was saying, my dear Euphrosyne, you will grow accustomed to our little retreat. You may go now, and return when we are leaving in order to bid us farewell. You will hear the Captain of the Guard, even in the women's quarters. He is a very good soldier.

Exit Euphrosyne. *The* Emperor *busies himself with documents. Bustle. Passing of slaves with baggage.* Usher, *among them, announces* Mamillius, *since he sees him off and is transfixed.*

Usher. Caesar—the Lord Mamillius.

Exit Usher. *Enter* Mamillius. *He is dressed in what he conceives to be a truly martial costume. Starting at the ground floor: the soles of his shoes are three inches thick. He got this from Greek tragic acting and it is a good idea if you are used to it.* Mamillius *is not, so that when he moves it feels as though he is lifting pieces of pavement with him. The red and blue leather of the boots comes to just below his knees, but is hidden in front by brass greaves that flare over each knee into knobs and spikes. These are effective and decorative when kept apart by a horse, but* Mamillius *dislikes horses, and in any case has not got one with him. He takes care, therefore, to leave a gap between them since, if he does not, they catch and release with a sudden melodious twang. It is fortunate that spurs have not been invented. Above the greaves is a short skirt of red and blue stripes, partly hidden by brass scale armor, and topped by a belt from which hangs a long sword —much longer than a Roman one. Above the belt again is a brass cuirass, heavily decorated. In the middle of all these decorations is a Gorgon's head whose expression is partly due to her deadly nature and partly to sheer astonishment at finding herself where she is. The arms are covered with scale armor, and the right one is holding against the hip a helmet big enough for a diver.* Mamillius *knows the* Bacchae *of Euripides by heart and this helmet has three crests instead of one—each with plumes on.* Mamillius *advances as casually as his costume will allow him. If he were not intensely civilized he would probably whistle. His red and blue striped cloak reaches to where his spurs would be if he had them.*

It is some time before the Emperor *believes his eyes.* Mamillius *tries meanwhile to convince himself that his recent and haunting suspicion of his own foolishness is nonsense.*

Mamillius. Well, Grandfather, I have made my preparations.

Emperor (pause). Did no one point out the significance of the color to you?

Mamillius. Color, Grandfather?

Emperor. That near imperial purple.

Mamillius. Oh, but I was particularly careful, Grandfather. There is not a touch of purple in the whole costume. Just red and blue stripes.

Emperor. That was very delicate of you, Mamillius. How many people have seen this . . . this regalia?

Mamillius. Only the craftsmen, Grandfather. I designed the whole thing myself. I wanted to surprise you.

Emperor. You have.

Mamillius (gaining a little confidence). As a matter of fact, I've kept it by me for some time.

Emperor. I suppose that thing is a helmet?

Mamillius (losing it all). Thing? You don't really like—

Emperor. Put it on.

Mamillius. This?

Emperor. That.

Mamillius. Oh no, Grandfather. It gives me a headache.

Emperor. You have worn it? Often?

Mamillius. Only in private, Grandfather—perhaps, after all, for a sea voyage this isn't—

Emperor. Put it on!

Mamillius *puts on the helmet. The* Emperor *loses all but a shred of self-control. He laughs silently for what seems to* Mamillius *to be about an hour. He shrinks into his armor and looks, if possible, even sillier. This finishes the* Emperor, *who collapses in cackles.*

Mamillius. You are treating me as a child! I grant you that the costume is unfortunate; but there is a man inside! (*This last remark, taken in conjunction with* Mamillius's *almost total disappearance between cuirass and helmet, sets the* Emperor *off again.*) Am I so funny? (*A curious thing happens.* Mamillius *begins to grin, to giggle and then to laugh. As he does this he begins to emerge.*) It was all right in private, Grandfather but an audience—! (*They are laughing side by side.*)

Emperor. Can you sit down?

Mamillius. I've never tried.

Emperor. Try now.

Mamillius. What a fool was I! There! Achilles can bend in the middle.

Emperor. If only Postumus could see you!

Mamillius. I should not care for Postumus to laugh at me.

Emperor. He is humorless. Do you know, Mamillius, something has come to me. That wonderful costume of yours is the real reason for his return.

Mamillius. But no one knew!

Emperor. My dear man! His agent sleeps under your pillow.

Mamillius. You never told me.

Emperor. I have an old-fashioned belief in the protective powers of innocence. But that applies no longer.

Mamillius. Should I stand up?

Emperor. Do not risk more movements than are necessary.

Mamillius (*takes off his helmet and puts it in his lap*). I must go back and remove all the metal and put it with my hoop and my shuttlecock. And perhaps with my poems.

Emperor. You must give me the poems to keep.

Mamillius. So I shall—all but one. What have I to hide from a man who has seen me in this? I wonder if that haze is lifting? (*He goes clumsily to center and looks through the door.*)

Emperor. You must make a special dedication of the helmet.

Mamillius. To Mars himself! (*Puts the helmet on bust.*)

Emperor. Be careful!

Mamillius. How wonderful he looks! General Postumus—shun! Slo-o-ope arms!

Captain (*off*). Guard and men with arms—shun!

Emperor. You see, Mamillius? You have touched off some automatic response in the military mind.

Mamillius. Guard and men with arms—

Emperor. No, no. You must not make fun of them.

Mamillius. Present arms!

Captain (*off*). Guard and men with arms—present arms!

Enter Postumus. *Longish silence.*

Emperor (*recovering*). Welcome home, Postumus! You have saved us the trouble of coming to see you.

Mamillius. Hullo, Postumus.

Postumus. Mamillius in arms.

Mamillius. For show only, Postumus. I do not want to be an Emperor.

Postumus. You are not going to be. Captain, dismiss the Guard.

Captin (*off*). Sir! Guard! Order arms. Turning right—dismiss!

Postumus. Where are the rest of your men?

Emperor. There may be one or two in the gardens, Postumus. Why do you ask?

Enter Usher.

Usher. General....

Postumus. See that the life of the villa beyond this room is normal.

Emperor. Yes. Do that, Chamberlain. (*Exit* Usher.) What else can we do to make you feel at home? I deduce, Postumus, from your behavior, that something has been worrying you. Let us be frank. What is it?

Postumus. Listen. (*Reads.*) "Ships and weapons of war are being built or converted and conveyed to the island of Capri for the Emperor's inspection. He and the Lord Mamillius are experimenting with large-scale methods of poisoning food."

Emperor. I suppose that refers to the pressure cooker.

Mamillius. You bribed someone to spy on the Emperor!

Emperor. No, no, Mamillius. A man with prospects as brilliant as the Heir Designate does not need to pay cash for anything.

Postumus. "The Lord Mamillius is in a state of high excitement—"

Mamillius. Postumus—I swear—

Postumus. Look at yourself!

Enter Phanocles.

Phanocles. Caesar! They would not let me go on the quay—

Emperor. Who would not?

Phanocles. Soldiers.

Postumus. Where were you going?

Phanocles. To my steamship.

Postumus. So you are Phanocles. Stay where you are! Caesar, you may have an explanation that will satisfy me—I see now that no one could take this boy and his armor seriously—but there are too many strange things going on. In the circumstances, as Heir Designate, I felt it my duty to return. You are growing too old for responsibility, Caesar. We must establish a regency. *I* shall be Regent.

Mamillius. But Postumus! You cannot really suppose that Caesar would be so foolish as to alter the succession for my sake!

Postumus. You may think not. But he would bridge the Adriatic to please you.

Mamillius. And you call yourself a realist!

Postumus. I take no chances, even with fools, Mamillius. They may be fools who are very lucky. Know yourself, then. You are an old man's folly.

Emperor. You have never wanted my affection, Postumus, so you have never missed it. If I have been foolish enough to think that I could enjoy his company without more than the usual scandal, I have been wise enough to know that you are the best man to rule the Empire—however uncongenial I may find you personally.

Mamillius. Let the Greek explain what has been done.

Phanocles. Lord—I am altering the whole circumstance of life. . . .

Emperor. He has this curious manner of speech, Postumus.

Phanocles. My ship, Lord—that was not intended to do you any harm. I am joining the ends of the world together. There will be no slaves, but coal and iron.

Postumus. And men will fly!

Phanocles. Of course. Think of the problem of communication, Lord. You are a soldier. What is your greatest difficulty?

Postumus (*fiercely*). I have no difficulty!

Phanocles. But if you had?

Postumus. Getting there first.

Phanocles. You see, Lord? It has been the same for every soldier. Communications.

Emperor (*agreeably*). Yes, indeed. They should be made as difficult as possible.

Phanocles. My ship would set men free! My ship will—

Postumus. You have no ship. I gave orders for them to burn her.

Phanocles. Burn my steamship! You burnt her!—Oh, Caesar!

Postumus. I don't know what your game was, Caesar, but, as I said, I take no chances.

Phanocles. All that work . . . all that thought. . . .

Mamillius. You still have your explosive, Phanocles.

Postumus. Explosive?

Emperor. He has loaded some new projectile on the catapult down by the quay.

Postumus. I saw the thing. What is it?

Mamillius. He turns it into vapor. Explain, Phanocles.

Phanocles. My ship. . . .

Emperor. Yes. Explain, Phanocles, to please me. We must be quite clear about your inventions, Phanocles. They have troubled the Heir Designate. His projectile digs a hole, Postumus—some kind of spade. Useful!

Phanocles. How can I explain, Caesar? You are all like children!
Emperor. Speak to us as children, then.
Phanocles. Big egg falls on ground and goes—boom! Flames and smoke, and big, big hole! Earthquake! Volcano! Enemy men run away. . . . I can't do it, Caesar! To speak so to grown men—
Emperor. I said speak to us as children—not as babes in arms. . . . You must make allowances, Postumus.
Postumus. This big hole—could you make it in a city wall?
Phanocles. You burnt my ship!
Postumus. If you treat me with disrespect I shall have you burnt yourself. Could you make the big hole in this villa?
Phanocles. I could destroy the whole villa.
Postumus. An army too?
Phanocles. If I made the explosive large enough.
Emperor. Phanocles, what on earth are you saying? It is important that you be serious and truthful.
Postumus. And that was the weapon you had trained seaward, ready for my ships!
Phanocles. I was aiming the catapult at a rock.
Postumus. You see? Lies everywhere! But we'll soon know the truth. You, Greek, come with me. And I'll take the boy too, Caesar—just as a precaution.
Emperor. I forbid him to go with you, and I beg you to think carefully what you do, Postumus. For the last time, no one is trying to deceive you! These things are what they appear—harmless labor-saving devices—

Commotion off.

Sergeant (off). General . . . General Postumus—
Postumus. What was that? Who's there?
Sergeant (off). Sir! Sir!
Postumus (draws sword). All of you stay where you are. Here I am, man.

Enter bleeding Sergeant.

Sergeant. The men, sir! Something horrible, sir!
Postumus. Who sent you? Who is your officer?
Sergeant. The officer's dead, sir. Drowned.
Postumus. Make your report, Sergeant.
Sergeant. We were in the other ship, sir—not yours.

Emperor. *Other* ship?

Sergeant. Yes, Caesar. Our two were in advance of the Fleet. We got orders to burn the magic ship, so we went alongside—

Postumus. Make your report to *me,* Sergeant!

Sergeant. The boarding was dead easy, sir. The Captain shouts "Oars!" and out went the oars, straight and firm and level as a road. We got the word—"Away, boarders!" and we all charges out along the oars and on to the magic ship. There was hardly any crew to speak of for a ship that size, and what there was we knocks on the head with no trouble at all. . . .

Phanocles. I trained these men . . . there are no more like them!

Postumus. Come to the point quickly! What happened to my men?

Sergeant. Well, sir, we set her on fire, sir, like you said —and she burnt like a volcano!

Phanocles. Then you sank her?

Sergeant. Yes, sir—but not before she woke up and went mad. She was alive, sir—I swear it! The few that escaped and are able to talk will bear me out. When the flames got hold, sir, they made her big brass belly scream at us, and those wooden wheels went round. She moved, sir—I swear she did—of her own—moved through the water without rowers or the wind! Those wheels caught us, sir, and we was set on fire, and then she swung round faster and faster and chewed up your own ship, just like as if she was a giant shark, sir! The sea was all full of men drowning and burning and screaming, and she was screaming and I was screaming —we were all screaming—

Postumus (*the fighting leader*). Company Sergeant Pyrrhus, Leading Sergeant of A Company in the invincible Roman Army of General Postumus—*SHUN!* (*The* Sergeant *"shuns" and holds it for some seconds.*) That's better! Now stand easy and tell me how many escaped.

Sergeant (*quietly*). Not much more than a dozen, sir—fighting fit, that is . . . they were burnt a bit, most of 'em—I'm senior.

Postumus (*grimly*). I see. I'm glad you're safe, Sergeant. (*Turning to* Phanocles.) So you were altering the circumstance of life, were you? And you altered it at the cost of nearly two hundred of my men. I shall let their comrades try you. They will know best how to alter what is left of *your* life. (*He turns to the Emperor.*) And you, Caesar, plotted nothing with this Greek monstrosity—or with this little fancy bastard! Of course not! You just wanted to see how fierce your little pet could look in such pretty armor—and with purple frills too!

Emperor. Postumus, a thought has just occurred to me. I am beginning to understand. You have been—how shall I put it?—

Mamillius. —bluffing.

Euphrosyne *appears in the doorway, unseen, and stands listening.*

Emperor. We heard no drums. You are separated from your Fleet. You had only two ships, and now they are sunk.

Mamillius. You've been hurrying on, Postumus—getting there first—moving with terrified speed—

Postumus. What if I have? The Fleet will be here in a few hours, and I've men enough to hold the quay and you haven't even a guard!—ships that go mad—armor—explosives—whatever they might be! Sergeant!

Sergeant. Sir?

Postumus. Could you aim that catapult?

Sergeant. I done fifteen years with the Mark Seven, sir.

Postumus. Train it round away from the sea. Aim it inland. Aim it at this villa, for that matter—

Sergeant. Sir—(Euphrosyne *who has crept up stage, now silently darts off.*) Do I loose it, sir?

Postumus. A big hole, you said, Phanocles? Flames and smoke?

Phanocles. This is a nightmare. . . .

Postumus. No. Let's just train it round, Sergeant. If we fire it we shall wait till the Fleet arrives. We shall let all the troops share in the fun.

Sergeant. Sir.

Postumus. Meanwhile, stand guard within earshot and keep your sword drawn.

Sergeant. Yes, sir.

Exit Sergeant. Postumus *calms down, since he has now the whip hand again.*

Postumus. You know me, Caesar.

Emperor. Indeed, I thought so.

Mamillius. I know him, Grandfather. He's frightened.

Postumus. I? Frightened? There is reason for you to be frightened, Mamillius. I am arresting you.

Mamillius. Try.

Postumus. Do you think you can fight me?

Emperor. Postumus—Phanocles was right. This is a nightmare. Neither I nor the boy wish any harm to you. You are Heir Designate. What more do you want?

Postumus. You had better both prepare to sail with me to Rome. As for the boy—he is under arrest. Give me your sword. (Mamillius *draws his sword.*)

Mamillius. Come and take it.

Emperor. Postumus! This is open rebellion!

Postumus. Is it possible that he *wants* me to run him through? If you are sensible, Caesar, the whole thing can be disposed of with the minimum of fuss.

Emperor. What is your proposal?

Postumus. Consent to the arrest of this boy.

Emperor. And then?

Postumus. Then you may remain in your villa and I shall go to Rome with your signed appointment of me as Regent—or co-ruler, if you prefer the old forms.

Emperor. And then?

Postumus. What then?

Emperor. The boy.

Postumus. Surely you must realize, Caesar—

Emperor. —that he would die quickly—or perhaps slowly....

Postumus. Before that, he would have a fair and unbiased trial.

Emperor. What do you think of my health?

Postumus. Good, for your age.

Emperor. What would you think of it after I signed such a document?

Postumus. Frankly I should cease to think of it.

Emperor. The care of my health would doubtless be given to others. I should have, perhaps, a month to live.

Postumus. I am a ruler, and a Roman. Greek, come down to the quay with me.

Mamillius. No, Phanocles—get behind me.

Postumus. Why, Mamillius! Both I and my agent underestimated you. So much the worse for you.

Mamillius. I intend to live as long as I can.

Postumus. Look out there, Mamillius. What do you see?

Mamillius. Water.

Postumus. Look at the horizon.

Mamillius. Ships.

Postumus. My ships, Mamillius. Nine thousand men.

Mamillius. Coward!

Postumus. For making certain? Enjoy yourself. When the men land I shall sweep this island in form and force. You have rather less than two hours to live.

Emperor. Let us come to some composition.

Postumus. Before he drew his little sword we might have done so. But why should I argue now? My ships do that for me.

Exit Postumus.

Mamillius. What shall we do?

Emperor. Phanocles could not arrange for our sudden transportation through the air to Rome?

Phanocles. No, Caesar.

Emperor. Then we must eat and drink and be quietly merry.

Mamillius. I could not eat.

Emperor. I think with such clarity when eating. Something may yet be done. Mamillius, Phanocles and—and perhaps the girl. Or no. Better not the girl. I am thinking of her safety, Mamillius. No harm will come to her if she stays in the women's quarters. Phanocles, Director-General of Experimental Studies, the canceled demonstration is redecreed. We shall try your pressure cooker! (*He beats the gong.*)

ACT III

Scene: The same.

Phanocles, *detached and brooding.* Mamillius, *at the wall, looking towards the quay.*

Mamillius. He has lifted the weapon towards us like a malicious finger. I can see his ships in dozens crawling down from the horizon. When the wind shifts you can hear them. Can your ideas turn them back? (*No answer from* Phanocles.) At least Euphrosyne is safe. If I were noble and brave, that ought to be a comfort to me. Help me to die! Instead, it makes me sick. She is my happiness, and if I were sure of immortality I'd want to take her with me—to die also. D'you hear that, Phanocles? I tell myself I love your sister, yet here I am wanting her to die. (*Pause.*) Ah, but suppose she insisted on dying with me! How beautiful! Then of course I couldn't possibly allow it. . . . Could I, Phanocles? I must say, for a Greek you are astonishingly taciturn.

Phanocles. What did I do to get myself here?

Mamillius. You wrote a petition. Try it on Postumus.

Phanocles. A petition. A reasonable statement from one man to another. I have asked from men nothing but good will and common sense. Yet the Emperor of the world is preoccupied in there, eating from a toy I would never have thought worth making. And down there a fool's finger is on my own trigger. We build on the expectation of man's goodness and the foundations collapse under us. We reveal to him the movement of the stars, the reasonable miracles of creation—and he buries his nose in filth like a dog!

Mamillius. You are so great and so clever, Phanocles—

Phanocles. I am a fool!

Mamillius. All this cosmic intelligence. . . . Can you keep back those ships?

Phanocles (*kindly*). No.

Mamillius. No! Because there is a truly great man facing us on the quay—a great ruler—a great general. . . . Presently he will prove that greatness for all time and in the established manner by cutting our throats!

Phanocles. Yes.

Mamillius. And you can do nothing?

Phanocles. No. The island is his. I can reveal miracles, Lord; I cannot perform them.

Mamillius. The sword is mightier than the pen?

Phanocles. Yes, Lord.

Mamillius. Think, man! What hope have we but you?

Phanocles. The Emperor, perhaps?

Mamillius. You know he thinks of nothing but the pressure cooker! "While there is still time," he said. He said, "This may be the fine flower of a life's experience." Phanocles, I am devoted to the arts, but that is gastronomy to excess!

Phanocles. Help yourself, Lord. I cannot help you.

Mamillius. We're going to change the universe!

Phanocles. I am incapable.

Mamillius. How? Come here. Suppose you were the Heir Designate—put yourself in his place. He suspects me unjustly . . . well, perhaps I *have* had foolish thoughts of what it would be like to be Emperor, but not, not—

Phanocles. Not to excess?

Mamillius. Exactly. (*Pause.*) If we can understand him perhaps we can defeat him. Think, man. You are he.

You look up at the villa. You think: "The old man is getting senile. The Greek is a magician. The boy is completely helpless by himself." Now, Phanocles, what would you do next?

Phanocles. If I were Postumus?

Mamillius. Yes. (*Pause.*)

Phanocles. I should wish I were Phanocles! (*Proudly.*)

Enter the Emperor *in a high state of excitement and emotion.*

Emperor. Phanocles—my dear, dear Phanocles! Be the first to congratulate me! It worked!

Mamillius. Grandfather—what are we to do?

Emperor. Do, my dear boy? Make one in solid gold!

Mamillius. About Postumus?

Emperor. Ah! The Heir Designate. I had put him out of my mind. We shall deal with Postumus presently.
What a momentous discovery it was! I must sit. . . .

Mamillius. But, Grandfather—

Emperor. We shall bargain. A drink with you, Phanocles?

Phanocles. I shall drink no more. I am sane and I will die sane.

Emperor. Not enjoy what might be our last hour?

Phanocles. Humanity is mad, Caesar, or how could an Emperor be an old man who lives in a cloud of fantasy, and yet rules the world?

Emperor. What else is there in life but these conceptions that you call fantasy? Have at you, Phanocles!

Phanocles. I cannot debate.

Emperor. Life is a personal matter. Alexander did not fight his wars till I discovered him at the age of seven. When I was a baby, life was a single instant; but I pushed, bawled, saw, smelled, tasted, heard, that one point into whole palaces of history!

Phanocles. You say nothing.

Emperor. You do not choose to understand me. Do you think that your pressure cooker was for the satisfaction of a gross appetite? If I read a book now—say the Eclogues—I am not transported to a Roman Arcady; no. I become a boy, as I was when I first read it.

Phanocles. A poor return for reading.

Emperor. Do you think so? The most precious thing in life is a memory. When I tasted the fish from your cooker, I was aware on the instant of a hundred subtle perceptions that time has blunted; and, suddenly, it came back to me—I was young again! Yes—yes! I was lying above her. She was smooth and secret; she quivered, slightly. I was passionately alive—there was a sense of triumph, of domination, of power, of rape! I struck with lion's claws—she was out! She was mine. My first trout.

Mamillius. Grandfather! For the last time—Are we to die and do nothing?

Emperor. Let us first drink a health, Mamillius. I give you—the pressure cooker! The most Promethean discovery of them all!

Phanocles. I cannot understand you, Caesar. You are not a fool, but you talk like one.

Mamillius. This is the Emperor!

Phanocles. For the next hour.

Mamillius. You are insolent!

Phanocles. We are going to die.

Emperor. Shall I be trite, Phanocles, and remind you that we were always going to die?

Phanocles. I had so many things to do. . . .

Emperor. Ah, yes—your toys. But your personal machinery—these levers and catapulting muscles—you did not think them indestructible?

Phanocles. Caesar, I conquered the universe, and yet the ants have defeated me. What is wrong with man?

Emperor. Men. A steam ship, or anything powerful, in the hands of man, Phanocles, is like a sharp knife in the hands of a child. There is nothing wrong with the knife. There is nothing wrong with the steam ship. There is nothing wrong with man's intelligence. The trouble is his nature.

Mamillius. The last lesson.

Phanocles. Intelligence *is* the whole man. You are a fool after all, Caesar.

Mamillius. You—you! dare to talk like—

Emperor. Be quiet, Mamillius. My friend has added to my life.

Mamillius. Another insult like that, and I will subtract from his!

Emperor. The Imperial dignity is adequately safeguarded in my hands. And now to our diplomacy.

Mamillius. What is there to do?

Emperor. Negotiate.

Mamillius. Using what?

Emperor. He has the men. We have the intelligence.

Mamillius. Did you smile, Phanocles?

Phanocles. I, Lord?

Mamillius. I thought you smiled. I am glad you did not smile, Phanocles. Forgive me, Grandfather—you were saying—?

Emperor. Let him negotiate from strength and he will make mistakes that will astonish you. People always underestimate intelligence, do they not?

Phanocles. They do, Caesar.

Enter Captain.

Emperor. Ah, Captain. You have come for the night password?

Captain. No, Caesar. Excuse me, Caesar—

Mamillius. Captain!

Captain. Sir?

Mamillius. We are in danger.

Captain. It is true then, sir?

Emperor. Do not trouble yourself, Captain.

Mamillius. The Father of his Country is in danger!

Captain. In defense of the Father of his Country I would—

Mamillius. Could you defend the villa?

Captain. Sir, I could defend it to the death.

Emperor. What an astonishingly egotistical sentiment! Could you defend it successfully?

Captain. No, Caesar.

Mamillius. Perhaps the Captain could find us a boat.

Emperor. Have you ever seen fugitives arrested in a boat? It is perhaps the most degrading form of arrest. Consider. There is a swift boat—not yours, Phanocles. And there is a small boat—a dinghy. The fugitives row. They are inevitably overtaken. They cannot hide. They are forced at last to lie on their oars, and are finally loaded into the pursuing trireme like mules on a block and tackle. No, Mamillius. Let us not add to our humiliations by attempting to escape by boat. I have another use for the Captain.

Captain. Excuse me, sir—and Caesar. But—

Mamillius. The Emperor has a command for you.

Captain. Yes, sir—but—

Emperor. Well, Captain?

Captain. The lady, sir.

Mamillius. Euphrosyne!

Captain. I believe the lady is sister to the Director-General of Experimental Studies, Caesar?

Emperor. What of her?

Captain. She came to the guardroom, Caesar, in a state of great agitation—and she had such a tale to tell of rebellion—

Emperor. About Postumus?

Captain. Caesar, is it true that he—?

Emperor. Indeed it is.

Captain. In that case, Caesar, I wish to renew my assertion of loyalty.

Emperor. I am delighted, Captain. Provided we survive the day, I shall promote you so high that you will be quite dizzy.

Mamillius. Where is the lady now?

Emperor. The main thing is that she is safe, Mamillius, and we shall send for her presently. Now, Captain, you must take a message from me to the Heir Designate. Tell him I have proposals to make. For example, the shift of power could be effected more easily in Rome, before the Senate. Tell him, Captain, that I am tired of ruling, but not of living. Add that the presence of the Lord Mamillius would be essential.

Captain. Caesar!

Mamillius. Is that all?

Emperor. Tell him, Captain, that we must meet once more, before he does irreparable damage to his prospects of an untroubled reign.

Mamillius. What good would my presence do in Rome?

Emperor. Point out, Captain, that the presence of the Lord Mamillius in demonstrable freedom would ensure that my subjects understood that the proclamation was made by me freely.

Captain. Caesar!

Emperor. Take the message as a Captain and bring back a favorable reply as a Colonel.

Captain. Caesar! Yes, Caesar! But the lady, sir—she's outside. . . .

Mamillius. Euphrosyne!

Emperor. Allow the lady to pass.

Captain. Caesar! All right, lads—let her come in.

Enter Euphrosyne, *still in a dream.*

Emperor. Child, where have you been? There is danger everywhere but in the women's quarters.

Euphrosyne. I came back here earlier, Caesar, when the two soldiers were talking to you. I stayed in that doorway long enough to know that a terrible thing had been done and that you and my brother and the young Lord were in great danger . . . and then . . . something happened to me.

Mamillius. Where did you go?

Euphrosyne. Down to the quay.

Emperor. My child, what possessed you? You took a very grave risk. A young girl, like you, going off alone—among all those soldiers!

Euphrosyne. There was no risk, Caesar—they would not think I was going to hurt them. No one had eyes or thoughts for any but the drowned or the dying. There was no sign of my brother's ship—only wreckage and smoke, and dead men lying in rows at the water's edge. . . .

Mamillius. Oh, Euphrosyne—how terrible for you!

Euphrosyne. I felt nothing. They were like a *picture* of dead men . . . (*astonished*). Do you know, Mamillius, I could think of nothing but you—

Mamillius. Do you love me so much?

Euphrosyne. Nothing but you. They were dead and dying—and—and yet I could only think of you! Oh, Mamillius! (*breaks down*).

Mamillius. Grandfather—we love each other! Before we die, I want to marry her.

Phanocles. Impossible!

Mamillius. What?

Phanocles. Tell him, Euphrosyne. We die today, and all vows are canceled.

Euphrosyne. Must I?

Mamillius. This is the moment for truth. What was your vow?

Euphrosyne (*reciting*). "Not to engage in frivolous conversation with the ungodly; and not to reveal my transitory beauty to the eyes of pagan concupiscence."

Mamillius. Of *what?*

Euphrosyne (*repeating*). —of pagan concupiscence.

Mamillius. Oh. . . . Pagan? Country people? Why should you fear them?

Emperor. It is simple, like all tragedy. She is a Christian.

Mamillius. Is that all?

Phanocles. All? Do you know what General Postumus did to the Christians he found in Clusium? And do you know how I have been driven half across the Empire because she would not give up this superstitious nonsense? She is my ward. I am responsible in law—even for her beliefs.

Mamillius. Let her believe what she will! You have me, too.

Euphrosyne. You are a prince.

Mamillius. My throat is half-cut—what sort of a prince is that? Grandfather—*make* her marry me!

Emperor. She is a free woman in law, and technically a criminal. The situation is one of some complexity.

Mamillius. Change the law, then!

Emperor. Have you forgotten Postumus and his approaching Fleet? The effect of a legal change would be purely local.

Mamillius. The change I want is local. (*To* Euphrosyne.) You love me. Will you change your religion for me?

Euphrosyne. No! Never!

Mamillius. I loved you when you were nothing but a shape for my mind to play with. I loved you before I heard your voice or saw your face. In the same way, whatever comes, I will embrace the hidden future.

Emperor. Wait! Believe me, I should have no objection were the marriage private. I have found that Christians make bad philosophers, but good civil servants. I see no reason why a Christian should not make an excellent wife.

Euphrosyne. Caesar, forgive me! You do not understand. He is a part of the world that is forbidden me. We Christians must remake the world. It is a condition of our belief. I cannot say "Yes." You are a pagan—a believer in the old gods—

Mamillius. But I do not believe in the old gods!

Phanocles. No intelligent man believes in them!

Emperor. But there remains something, nevertheless. We—they—do not believe in Jupiter, Phanocles, but it is a condition of our existence that we should pretend to believe. A pretended belief is better than a belief in nothing at all.

Phanocles. No!

Emperor. Surely!

Phanocles. And there is always something to believe in, Caesar. I give you the names of my new gods: Law, Change, Cause and Effect, Reason—and Reason is the greatest. You could have those gods in place of the old ones.

Emperor. You know, Mamillius, I suspect that Phanocles will survive us all. His gods and those of General Postumus are too alike to quarrel!

Mamillius. Tell me about your gods, Euphrosyne. Do they sound as cold as his?

Euphrosyne. There is only one God.

Mamillius. Can he save us, do you think, from those ships?

Euphrosyne. If it is His will.

Mamillius. If it *should* be his will, he's leaving it rather late. The first of the ships is coming in to the quay. Postumus must be itching to hurl your explosive at us, Phanocles. What will happen? Shall we all be killed?

Phanocles. No, Lord. It could not reach the villa.

Mamillius. Are you sure?

Phanocles. I am sure. At worst a hole in the cliff face some yards below where you are standing.

Mamillius. I suppose he *will* let loose the thing?

Emperor. He could hardly resist it. But not until he has a good audience.

Mamillius. And what then?

Emperor. Assuming that our worthy Phanocles knows what he is talking about, then at least we ought all to be alive after his device has tunneled into our cliffs. Our best hope then lies in the message I sent with the Captain. Postumus delights in telling us he is a realist who takes no chances. We must somehow persuade him that he is taking no chances by allowing you to live, Mamillius.

Mamillius. I will not cringe to him, Grandfather!

Emperor. No, I can see that you will not. Euphrosyne, I fear I must hold you largely responsible for an astonishing change in my grandson—a change which deserves life—not death. He will listen to you. What do you advise?

Euphrosyne. Pray.

Mamillius. How? To what?

Euphrosyne. To God.

Emperor. Ah, but which god? You mean *your* God?

Euphrosyne. What else?

Mamillius. Then you pray, Euphrosyne! No god could refuse a prayer from you!

Euphrosyne. I dare not. But He elects whom He will—or so they said. . . .

Mamillius. Pray, dear Euphrosyne—for love of me!

Euphrosyne. I love you, whatever happens. If it is a sin to love a pagan, then I will pay for it gladly!

Mamillius. And I love you! We should have found out about each other—spent our lives—open towards each other, like a couple of friendly cupboards. . . . My goods should be your goods, my house your house—my life your life!

Euphrosyne. I have nothing to give in exchange.

Mamillius. Yourself!

Euphrosyne. I had nothing but my God. . . .

Mamillius. I will share your gods!

Euphrosyne. If only you could!

Mamillius. If you believe, that is enough for me. Your gods shall be my gods!

Euphrosyne. My *God* shall be thy God.

Mamillius. Very well. Thy *God* shall be my God. Kiss me. (*They embrace.*)

Emperor. Bless you, my children. Because of that wretched man down there I have not the heart to make a longer speech. I should have enjoyed your happiness. . . .

Mamillius. (*the man of action*). Grandfather—pray!

Emperor. Since you propose to be a Christian, Mamillius, it would be better if you did.

Mamillius. But how? Euphrosyne. . . .

Euphrosyne. No. . . .

Emperor (*philosophically*). Yes, Euphrosyne. He is right. Prayer is an admission of human frailty, and therefore, though we may not believe in the object of our prayer, we should at least make the admission. To whom shall we pray?

Euphrosyne. To whom but God?

Emperor. Ah, yes, of course. You have no difficulty there, have you? A womanish answer—but excusable in the circumstances.

Mamillius. Grandfather—you are Jupiter's High Pontiff.

Emperor. Well . . . yes.

Mamillius. Hurry, Grandfather—pray!

Emperor. My dear boy! To think I should have to wait until now to find out that you are fundamentally religious! Very well. Let us accept our probable defeat with the usual dignified forms. Stand, Phanocles.

Phanocles (*as in a daze*). Caesar, I named *my* god. Reason.

Emperor. I think we have enough gods for the moment. Stand, Phanocles.

Phanocles. Reason might have shown us a way. If only I had trusted and invoked—

Mamillius (*fierce*). If you will not stand for Jupiter,

Phanocles, perhaps you will do so for the Emperor.

Phanocles (*stands*). Caesar!

Emperor. Bring me the bowl, Mamillius. Now the lamp. Should you be doing this? I think not. Phanocles, place the lamp on the table—Incense. . . .

Mamillius (*whispering to the kneeling* Euphrosyne). Are you praying, Euphrosyne?

Euphrosyne. When I *saw* them—they were like a picture —yet why when I only *think* of them should they appear so terrible? We must pray for God's mercy on the dying!

Mamillius. But that's not the point. I want *us* to live!

Euphrosyne (*with a look of appeal*). Try, dear Mamillius —try to pray! He is the God of Love!

Emperor (*busy with his rituals, quietly to* Phanocles). See, Phanocles—that is always the way with a young religion. I have no doubt that Christianity will achieve a formal etiquette in time, like all the others. . . . Incense, Phanocles. Pour water over my hands. (Phanocles *does so.*) Gently, Phanocles. The washing is symbolic only. (*He finishes.*)

Mamillius's *attention is uncertainly divided between* Euphrosyne *and the* Emperor *and his own efforts at silent prayer.*

Are we all ready? (*Pause.*) Be absent every unpropitious speech. Let every unhallowed tongue keep silent! (*Tense pause.*) All Father. . . .

Phanocles (*in a great shout*). Great Caesar! Forgive me for a fool! Reason *is* the only god!

A short tense silence.

Emperor. I doubt if your madness can excuse sacrilege, Phanocles.

Phanocles. But the brass butterfly. . . . Think. . . . We could force Postumus to destroy himself by his own hand! . . .

Mamillius, *noticing that* Euphrosyne *has stopped praying and is greatly upset, seizes his sword, and rushes to* Phanocles.

Mamillius. I swear I'll kill you if you make another sound!

(Phanocles *succumbs.*)

Emperor. Let him be, Mamillius. He is calm now. I am familiar with the convulsions of religious hysteria and I can see the fit has passed. Phanocles, I promise you that in a few moments you may invoke your god of Reason to your heart's content, but we must give precedence to Jupiter. In the circumstances, Mamillius, do you mind officiating once more? We need only repeat the symbolic washing. . . . (Mamillius *pours water.*) Now, are we all ready?

Great Jupiter, All Father, Lord of heaven and earth, accept this sacrifice from us and hear our prayer. Oh, Conductor of Souls, deliver us from danger! Oh, Lord of the Lightning, Thunderer, destroy our enemies!

There is a fearful and reverberating explosion. The Emperor *is transfixed.* Euphrosyne *gives a cry and is also transfixed. Indeed, they are all more or less transfixed.*

Mamillius. Thunder! Grandfather! was it on the right hand? Grandfather—there's something wrong—you prayed to Jupiter! There is nothing down there but smoke—I can't see anything—(*looking towards* Euphrsyne). A miracle! But whose miracle?

Phanocles. No, no, no, no, no!

Mamillius. I can see now—that is where the soldiers were standing, but they've all gone! The hedges over the quay are burning—

Phanocles. Impossible! The firing mechanism was foolproof—unless someone removed the—

Mamillius *leaves the wall and runs to* Euphrosyne.

Mamillius. Euphrosyne, my love—we are saved! Jupiter has destroyed our enemies!

Euphrosyne. It was our God! He guided my hand—

Mamillius (*incredulous*). The God of Love?—Striking people with lightning?

Euphrosyne. But He is the God of Battles, too!

Emperor. Not a cloud. Not a cloud anywhere. . . .

Mamillius (*triumphant*). Abandon Jupiter, Grandfather! Grandfather—did you hear? Love and War at one altar! This is comprehensive!

He returns happily to the cliff wall.

During the ensuing dialogue Euphrosyne *takes the brass*

butterfly from her dress and holds it close to her breast in terror.

Why! The statue of Hercules is lying down in pieces by the pedestal! And the trees—how peculiar. . . . The smoke has almost cleared. . . . But there's nobody about —and where are the steps—and the boats that were tied up alongside them?

Phanocles. It could never happen, Caesar. I made certain.

Mamillius. Some of the trees are down, and some are leaning against the others. . . .

Phanocles (to himself). The only possible explanation!

Mamillius. There's a man running—

Phanocles. Some fool removed it—

Mamillius. Grandfather, a man is coming up the steps to the villa, running—

Emperor. Are there any clouds?

Mamillius. Not a cloud in the sky! Only smoke down by the quay—

Phanocles. Yet who—*who* would have tampered with it? What fool—?

Mamillius. I seem to know him—

Phanocles (to Mamillius*).* —unless the Heir Designate himself—

Mamillius. No, it's certainly not Postumus— Why, he's our Captain.

Phanocles. I am not a vengeful man, but that would be a sort of justice—

Mamillius. Phanocles! You *can* smile!

We begin to see in Phanocles *the effect of a grim joke dawning on him.*

Phanocles. The Heir Designate himself!

Mamillius—but it's not! It's our Captain. He'll tell us what happened!

Phanocles (still savoring his private thought). At least only he could have ordered its removal . . . *(a hollow chuckle)*. Divine retribution!

Mamillius (waving). Captain! Captain!

Phanocles (surveying all three compassionately). How can they *not* believe in gods!

Enter Captain.

Captain. Caesar! I tried to give your message to the Heir

Designate—but I was prevented. And now he's dead, Caesar—they are all dead, or dying—

Emperor. Who—is—dead?

Captain. General Postumus, the Heir Designate, Caesar!

Emperor. The Heir Designate?

Captain. —and his officers, Caesar. It was . . . well, I hardly like to say this. There's nothing in the regulations to go by—It was a miracle—an Act of God—

Emperor. God?

Captain. The All Father—praised be his name! The Thunderer—Jupiter. . . . I must start from the beginning—They were all standing by the Mark Seven and laughing, Caesar. The lamented General was bending down to loose the rachet; and then there was a kind of a sort of—there was a kind of white bang, Caesar, and a storm of smoke billowing out. They went to pieces—and in the middle of them the lamented General passed on, leaving nothing behind him but his helmet, which fell on the south wing of the villa. There's nothing left of the distinguished officers who followed him, Caesar. As for the quay, Caesar—there's a smoking hole where the quay was!

Long pause.

Emperor. Captain, go down to the misguided and—irreligious soldiers who are coming in to the quay. Tell them that Jupiter, the All Father, has destroyed the Heir Designate before their very eyes, for the sin of open rebellion against the Emperor.

Captain. Caesar! (*Pause.*) Hail, Caesar!

Exit Captain.

Euphrosyne *swoons. The brass arming vane falls from her hand.* Mamillius *picks her up and comforts her.*
Phanocles *rushes forward, grabs the arming vane.*

Mamillius. Euphrosyne, my love, did you hear? It is as I said—we have all our lives. Jupiter—I mean our God—has protected us. We have nothing more to fear! (Euphrosyne *has opened her eyes. She smiles—then sees* Phanocles *standing, rooted, over her and holding the brass butterfly.*)

Phanocles. My intelligent sister. . . . This was exactly calculated! We owe our lives—

Euphrosyne. No, Phanocles—no! I was guided in all I

did. It was like a dream. . . . I had no fear, no doubts. . . . I did not even try to hide—all those dead men were nothing to do with me. God killed them!

Mamillius. What is that, Phanocles?

Phanocles. The arming vane, Lord—what I was trying to explain—

Mamillius. How did she get it?

Phanocles. God knows!

Euphrosyne *is on the verge of happy tears as* Mamillius *takes her in his arms.*

What did I tell you, Caesar? Here is the brass butterfly—the safeguard!

Emperor (*miles away*). I must adjust my conception of the universe. . . .

Mamillius. Dry your tears. Look up. The sun has risen for us.

Phanocles. She took it off, so of course the weapon would have to explode as soon as he fired it!

Emperor. It is perhaps natural that the All Father should take especial care of his own High Pontiff—but he's never done it before!

Phanocles. So you see, Cause and Effect still holds good, Caesar.

Emperor (*at last focusing on* Phanocles). And you, Phanocles—you with your talk of Law and Change and Reason—you dared to suggest that the universe is a machine!

Phanocles. But look, Caesar! I have just been telling you—

Emperor. You can tell me nothing more. Where is all your logic when the gods take a hand?

Phanocles. I . . . I don't know.

Emperor. We were helpless—condemned to death—with only a glimmer of hope. Yet, out of this limpid sky, his lightning struck your machine, and the elect were elected.

Phanocles. I . . . Yes, Caesar. (*He is defeated.*)

Euphrosyne (*happy now*). Never let me go!

Mamillius. How could I? Keep looking at me!

Euphrosyne. Where else should I look?

Emperor. Mamillius—

Mamillius. Grandfather?

Emperor. They are right after all.

Mamillius. Who?

Emperor. Just they. The simple, the old wives. The mad

philosophers and the frantic priests—even the savage in the desert with his piece of wood. They are right after all. And I was wrong. Hopelessly wrong—Postumus spoke more truly than he knew. It is time for a regency.

Mamillius. Grandfather!

Emperor. Yes?

Mamillius. Postumus is dead. Who is the next Heir Designate?

Emperor. Who but you?

Mamillius. Caesar!

Emperor. Any man can bring about a change—and yet change is the one thing no man can control. Therefore, Mamillius, ruling is necessary, but nonsense. You will make a terrible Emperor—What does that matter since the gods take a hand?

Mamillius. I shall be the greatest of Emperors!

Emperor. Do not remind me too soon of my folly!

Mamillius. —with the Empress Euphrosyne beside me—

Emperor. I forgot—stop—stop!

Mamillius. No, Grandfather, you cannot control us any more than you can control change. Her god may or may not strike out of a clear sky, but he is *her* God, and her God shall be my God. I have sworn it. Come with me, my Empress Designate!

Emperor. Wait!

Mamillius. What for, Grandfather?

Euphrosyne. To receive his blessing, Mamillius. We are right after all. By trusting love we trusted God. Isn't that what you meant?

Emperor. Did I?

Euphrosyne. Oh, but you made everything so clear! There is a time for weeping, a time for rejoicing, and a time to marry. How simple life is after all!

Emperor. Do you mean to marry my grandson?

Euphrosyne. I do!

Emperor. And you, Mamillius?

Mamillius. I do, I do!

Emperor. If my blessing means taking my love with you into the future, then you are blessed already. But the thought of that future is strangely oppressive.

Mamillius. But why, Grandfather? The future is ours now. You have seen to that, and we are eager to alter it together.

Emperor. That is what oppresses me. I must seek guidance; though goodness knows where! Leave me now and come back in an hour.

Mamillius. Thank you Grandfather. Hail and—for an hour—farewell, Caesar! Come, Euphrosyne.

Euphrosyne (*kisses the* Emperor, *then steps back. She speaks with intense emotion.*) God save our gracious Emperor!

Mamillius. Do you really love me?

Euphrosyne. I told you so.

Mamillius. Say it again!

Euphrosyne. I do, I do, I do!

Emperor. Wait, I beg of you, Mamillius!

Mamillius. No, Grandfather—no, no, no! Hail, and for a little while—farewell, Caesar! Now, where were we? Oh yes—(*to* Euphrosyne.) Tell me, do you really and truly love me? . . .

(*They have gone.*)

Emperor. This is the end in every direction.

Phanocles. But we are saved! Now we can go on! The obstacles have been removed by, by—

Emperor. The All Father.

Phanocles. We can build ourselves a bigger steamship, Caesar.

(*The* Emperor *begins to get angry. The day's transactions have left their mark. There is an unwonted readiness in his anger and later, in both anger and excitement, a touch of hysteria.*

Emperor. A bigger steamship! Phanocles, son of Myron, Director-General of Experimental Studies—did you hear what he said?

Phanocles. She is only a girl.

Emperor. Clever man, learned man, genius—what a fool you are!

Phanocles. I?

Emperor. There is no death hanging over them other than the one that waits us all—her God *shall* be his God! He means it and she means it—and what is an Empire to a pretty girl?

Phanocles. But Caesar—

Emperor. Do you see what you have done?

Phanocles. I have done nothing.

Emperor. You did nothing! A steamship that wrecks half a fleet—an explosive that claps out half an army—and now—now—just when the All Father is pleased to signify his personal interest in the succession—*now!* A Christian Emperor!

Phanocles. It is not my fault that she is a Christian!

Emperor. Why did you come here?

Phanocles. To see you.

Emperor. Can you control the elements and not your own sister? What have I done that at my age I should be forced to suffer like this?

Phanocles. When you are used to my inventions, Caesar, the old world will seem like an evil dream.

Emperor. But I like the old world! What has yours to offer? A white bang! Wheels like sharks' teeth! Unrest, ferment, fever, dislocation, disorder, wild experiment and catastrophe! (*The* Emperor *almost feels his way to a seat and lowers himself into it.*) This is a delirium!

Phanocles. Shall I call your physician?

Emperor. Have we dreamed, Phanocles? Are you my indigestion?

Phanocles. No.

Emperor. Let me . . . experiment. This feels like a cup, and you see that though my hand shakes, I can pour straight. Delusions, destruction, ruin, flames, a divine intervention—steamships and clapper-outers. . . .

Phanocles. Caesar—Caesar! Do you feel better, Caesar?

Emperor. Better. Sadder. Wiser. Bang. Boom.

Phanocles. Caesar. . . . The—the pressure cooker. . . . Nyum, nyum!

Emperor. The Promethean pressure cooker—

Phanocles. Trout.

Emperor. Levels of shining water and cataracts from the dark rock on high. Music! Just the harp. . . .

Music. Pause.

The old world returns to me—the old world which is this world. Of course. . . . There is no other.

Phanocles. Trout, Caesar. . . .

Emperor. This libation to the Thunderer—

Phanocles. Think of the pressure cooker—

Emperor. I am myself again. Well, Phanocles—how am I to reward you?

Phanocles. As Caesar will. I was certain that in the long run you would see the sense of my inventions, Caesar.

Emperor. I shall have one made in pure gold. Or would silver be more suitable? There is an excellent field for your ingenuity, my dear Director-General.

Phanocles. Perhaps access to more workmen and a bigger boat—

Emperor. Who was talking about boats?

Phanocles. She was so fast. . . .

Emperor. Blasphemously so!

Phanocles. Have you no use for a fast boat, Caesar?

Emperor. You will say I am old—but I prefer a slow boat. We will have nothing but slow boats in future.

Phanocles. But Caesar!

Emperor. Besides, have you considered how unfair she was to the slaves?

Phanocles. She would have made them unnecessary.

Emperor. Well, there you are, you see. To be a slave-rower is a hard life, Phanocles, but it is better than no life at all. You do not have to think of these things, but I am responsible for the well-being of all classes. Your fast boats would lead to nothing but a pool of unemployment, and I am not hardhearted enough to countenance that.

Phanocles. There is work enough in a steamship—

Emperor. Besides, you cannot find your way without a wind when the stars or the sun are hidden.

Phanocles. I had thought of an instrument that points to the North.

Emperor. What would be the use of that? No one wants to go there.

Phanocles. You have not thought—

Emperor. For the future nothing but slow boats. It is Our Imperial Will, Phanocles.

Phanocles. I bow.

Emperor. Whatever else we do, we must look after the slaves. They are a sacred charge.

Phanocles. Perhaps one day, Caesar, when men are free because they no longer believe themselves to be slaves—

Emperor. You work among perfect elements, and therefore politically you are an idealist. There will always be slaves, though the name may change. What is slavery but the domination of the weak by the strong? How can you make them equal? Or are you fool enough to think they are born equal?

Phanocles. My explosive makes the strong weak.

Emperor. Your explosive is even more unsettling than your ship. Certainly it has—under Jupiter—preserved me this day, and therefore the peace of the Empire. But it has cost the world a merciless ruler who would have murdered half a dozen people and given justice to a hundred million. The world has lost a bargain. No, Phanocles. No more explosives. . . . Your pressure cooker. . . . I shall reward you for that.

Phanocles. Caesar—you will reward me well for this—

Emperor. For what?

Phanocles. You remember the third great invention I was keeping in reserve to surprise you? Here it is.

Emperor. Careful, Phanocles! Put it down! Put it down, I said!

Phanocles. But Caesar—

Emperor. Keep off!

Phanocles. There is nothing to fear. Look, Caesar—touch if you will.

Emperor. Nothing about vapor—no steam—no noise?

Phanocles. Now, how will you reward me?

Emperor. It has no connection with—(*pointing up*).

Phanocles. With silence only. Look.

Emperor. I see nothing but two pieces of paper.

Phanocles. Take them.

Emperor. Poems? You are a poet? That is quite incredible!

Phanocles. Mamillius wrote the lines.

Emperor. I might have known! Sophocles—Aeschylus—How well read the boy is!

Phanocles. This will make him famous. Read both papers, Caesar, for they are exactly the same. I have invented a cheap and noiseless method of multiplying books. I call it printing.

Emperor. Printing?

Phanocles. Think. How many books of mathematics are irretrievably lost that this invention would have saved for us? How much astronomy, medicine if you will—husbandry, essential skills—

Emperor. But this is another pressure cooker!

Phanocles. By this method a man and a boy could make a thousand copies of a book in a day.

Emperor. We could give away a hundred thousand copies of the works of Homer!

Phanocles. A million if you will.

Emperor. A poet will sell his verses by the sack, like vegetables—"Buy my fine ripe odes!" (*He is really excited.*)

Phanocles. A public library in every town!

Emperor. Phanocles—dear Phanocles! Perhaps the world is not too old to learn. Ten thousand copies of the love poems of Catullus!

Phanocles. A hundred thousand of the works of Mamillius—

Emperor. Encyclopedias!

Phanocles. An author in every street, Caesar! We shall set man free by liberating his frustrated desire for self-expression.

Emperor. Self-expression! (*he is suddenly cautious*). Was that the first cool breeze of evening I felt on my neck? Phanocles, let us be very careful. Let us assess this invention of yours *before* it claps out—

Phanocles. How can printing clap-out?

Emperor. Self-expression. Is there genius enough to go round?

Phanocles. Let history convince you, Caesar. In our library at Alexandria there are more books than a man could read in seven lifetimes.

Emperor. That would seem to suggest that we have more than enough books already. How often is a Horace born?

Phanocles. Come, Caesar—nature is bountiful.

Emperor. But supposing we all write books? Each man will be lured to erect himself a small but indelible monument—

Phanocles. Interesting biographies—

Emperor. Diary of a Provincial Governor. . . . I built Hadrian's Wall. . . .

Phanocles. Scholarship, then—

Emperor. Books about books about books—

Phanocles. History—

Emperor. Can you not understand, extraordinary man? A great historian is born less frequently than a great poet! But every man who is indeed so frightened of the future that he can think only of the past will labor at the bald outline. And every person who thinks his own life of cosmic importance will give us a blow by blow description of the fight. I was Nero's Grandmother. I was Nursey to the little Prince Mamillius—

Phanocles. I see a new heaven and a new earth! The masses of information will grow, will swell, will become a torrent. There will be corridors and quarries of books—pillars and pyramids of them!

Emperor. The ceilings will lift, will burst—

Phanocles. Reports, Caesar—a stream of ceaseless facts!

Emperor. Reports! Who will read them? Not you! I shall read them. Reports—military, naval, sanitary—I shall have to read them all! Political, statistical, economical, theological—(*pause*). Let my eunuch sing to me again. . . .

The Eunuch *sings. The* Emperor *touches a pillar, observes what is now the exquisite beauty of the night. A woman is lighting the lamps. The music, the stars, the pools of light, calm them. The play is fading now, slowly and gently as the day has done.*

Forgive me, Phanocles—

Phanocles. What is there to forgive, Caesar? You have done nothing.

Emperor. I touched that factual stone to exorcise the vision. I am too old for these terrors. . . .

Phanocles. Terrors, Caesar?

Emperor. The vistas you show me are too magnificent.

Phanocles. I see no vistas and I feel no terrors.

Emperor. Of course. You are a force of nature, Phanocles—not solely a man. There is no stopping you. I can only divert you. For you will continue invincibly exercising your partial foresight till your inventor pulls out the pin and your mechanism jolts to a stop.

Phanocles. You mean when I die.

Emperor. How exquisite beyond expression is the beauty of the common world! Will you rub it away, I wonder, as I rub the bloom from this grape?

Phanocles. I should change it.

Emperor. But to please me—as a wedding present for your sister—you would not consent to let that frantic brain of yours occupy itself with, say, gardening?

Phanocles. Why not, Caesar? I have often thought that the yield of the earth is scandalously low. I have conceived a number of contrivances—

Emperor. I understand you, indomitable man. Well, Phanocles, I shall reward you for the pressure cooker.

Phanocles. I am in Caesar's hands.

Emperor. Would you care to be an ambassador?

Phanocles. My fondest dream has never reached to such a position of distinction, Caesar! I should be your representative in person!

Emperor. It would be rather a long journey, but of great interest to an enquiring spirit such as your own. Come, let us stroll together in the cool night air. Yes. . . . You can take your explosive and your printing with you. I shall make you Envoy Extraordinary and Plenipotentiary. Phanocles, my dear friend—I want you to take a *slow* boat to China. . . .

(CURTAIN)

Part Two

THE ESSAYS

Oliver Goldsmith:

An Essay on the Theater: or, A Comparison Between Sentimental and Laughing Comedy

The theater, like all other amusements, has its fashions and its prejudices; and when satiated with its excellence, mankind begin to mistake change for improvement. For some years tragedy was the reigning entertainment; but of late it has entirely given way to comedy, and our best efforts are now exerted in these lighter kinds of composition. The pompous train, the swelling phrase, and the unnatural rant, are displaced for that natural portrait of human folly and frailty, of which all are judges, because all have sat for the picture.

But, as in describing nature, it is presented with a double face, either of mirth or sadness, our modern writers find themselves at a loss which chiefly to copy from; and it is now debated, whether the exhibition of human distress is likely to afford the mind more entertainment than that of human absurdity?

Comedy is defined by Aristotle to be a picture of the frailties of the lower part of mankind, to distinguish it from tragedy, which is an exhibition of the misfortunes of the great. When comedy therefore ascends to produce the characters of princes or generals upon the stage, it is out of its walk, since low life and middle life are entirely its object. The principal question therefore is, whether in describing low or middle life, an exhibition of its follies be not preferable to a detail of its calamities? Or, in other words, which deserves the preference, the weeping sentimental comedy, so much in fashion at present, or the laughing and even low comedy, which seems to have been last exhibited by Vanbrugh and Cibber?

If we apply to authorities, all the great masters in the dramatic art have but one opinion. Their rule is, that as tragedy displays the calamities of the great, so comedy should excite our laughter, by ridiculously exhibiting the follies of the lower part of mankind. Boileau, one of the best modern critics, asserts, that comedy will not admit of tragic distress:

> *Le Comique, ennemi des soupirs et des pleurs,*
> *N'admet point dans ses vers de tragiques douleurs.*[a]

Nor is this rule without the strongest foundation in nature, as the distresses of the mean by no means affect us so strongly as the calamities of the great. When tragedy exhibits to us some great man fallen from his height, and struggling with want and adversity, we feel his situation in the same manner as we suppose he himself must feel, and our pity is increased in proportion to the height from which he fell. On the contrary, we do not so strongly sympathize with one born in humbler circumstances, and encountering accidental distress: so that while we melt for Belisarius,[b] we scarcely give halfpence to the beggar, who accosts us in the street. The one has our pity, the other our contempt. Distress therefore is the proper object of tragedy, since the great excite our pity by their fall; but not equally so of comedy, since the actors employed in it are originally so mean, that they sink but little by their fall.

Since the first origin of the stage, tragedy and comedy have run in distinct channels, and never till of late encroached upon the provinces of each other. Terence, who

[a] *L'Art poétique,* III, 401–402: "Comedy, enemy of sighs and tears, admits no tragic sorrows in its lines." [b] sixth-century Byzantine general, alleged to have become a blind beggar in his old age

seems to have made the nearest approaches, always judiciously stops short before he comes to the downright pathetic; and yet he is even reproached by Cæsar for wanting the *vis comica.*[c] All the other comic writers of antiquity aim only at rendering folly or vice ridiculous, but never exalt their characters into buskined pomp, or make what Voltaire humorously calls a *tradesman's tragedy.*

Yet notwithstanding this weight of authority, and the universal practice of former ages, a new species of dramatic composition has been introduced under the name of *sentimental* comedy, in which the virtues of private life are exhibited, rather than the vices exposed; and the distresses rather than the faults of mankind make our interest in the piece. These comedies have had of late great success, perhaps from their novelty, and also from their flattering every man in his favorite foible. In these plays almost all the characters are good, and exceedingly generous; they are lavish enough of their *tin* money on the stage; and though they want humor, have abundance of sentiment and feeling. If they happen to have faults or foibles, the spectator is taught not only to pardon, but to applaud them, in consideration of the goodness of their hearts; so that folly, instead of being ridiculed, is commended, and the comedy aims at touching our passions without the power of being truly pathetic. In this manner we are likely to lose one great source of entertainment on the stage; for while the comic poet is invading the province of the tragic muse, he leaves her lovely sister quite neglected. Of this, however, he is no way solicitous, as he measures his fame by his profits.

But it will be said, that the theater is formed to amuse mankind, and that it matters little, if this end be answered, by what means it is obtained. If mankind find delight in weeping at comedy, it would be cruel to abridge them in that or any other innocent pleasure. If those pieces are denied the name of comedies, yet call them by any other name, and if they are delightful, they are good. Their success, it will be said, is a mark of their merit, and it is only abridging our happiness to deny us an inlet to amusement.

These objections, however, are rather specious than solid. It is true, that amusement is a great object of the theater, and it will be allowed, that these sentimental

[c] comic power

pieces do often amuse us; but the question is, whether the true comedy would not amuse us more? The question is, whether a character supported throughout a piece with its ridicule still attending, would not give us more delight than this species of bastard tragedy, which only is applauded because it is new?

A friend of mine, who was sitting unmoved at one of these sentimental pieces, was asked how he could be so indifferent? "Why, truly," says he, "as the hero is but a tradesman, it is indifferent to me whether he be turned out of his counting-house on Fish-Street Hill, since he will still have enough left to open shop in St. Giles's."

The other objection is as ill-grounded; for though we should give these pieces another name, it will not mend their efficacy. It will continue a kind of *mulish* production, with all the defects of its opposite parents, and marked with sterility. If we are permitted to make comedy weep, we have an equal right to make tragedy laugh, and to set down in blank verse the jests and repartees of all the attendants in a funeral procession.

But there is one argument in favor of sentimental comedy which will keep it on the stage, in spite of all that can be said against it. It is of all others the most easily written. Those abilities that can hammer out a novel, are fully sufficient for the production of a sentimental comedy. It is only sufficient to raise the characters a little; to deck out the hero with a riband, or give the heroine a title; then to put an insipid dialogue, without character or humor, into their mouths, give them mighty good hearts, very fine clothes, furnish a new set of scenes, make a pathetic scene or two, with a sprinkling of tender melancholy conversation through the whole; and there is no doubt but all the ladies will cry and all the gentlemen applaud.

Humor at present seems to be departing from the stage, and it will soon happen that our comic players will have nothing left for it but a fine coat and a song. It depends upon the audience whether they will actually drive those poor merry creatures from the stage, or sit at a play as gloomy as at the Tabernacle.[d] It is not easy to recover an art when once lost; and it will be but a just punishment, that when, by our being too fastidious, we have banished humor from the stage, we should ourselves be deprived of the art of laughing. [1773]

[d] where the noted Methodist, George Whitefield, had preached

Charles Lamb:

On the Artificial Comedy of the Last Century

The artificial Comedy, or Comedy of manners, is quite extinct on our stage. Congreve and Farquhar show their heads once in seven years only, to be exploded and put down instantly. The times cannot bear them. Is it for a few wild speeches, an occasional license of dialogue? I think not altogether. The business of their dramatic characters will not stand the moral test. We screw everything up to that. Idle gallantry in a fiction, a dream, the passing pageant of an evening, startles us in the same way as the alarming indications of profligacy in a son or ward in real life should startle a parent or guardian. We have no such middle emotions as dramatic interests left. We see a stage libertine playing his loose pranks of two hours' duration, and of no after consequence, with the severe eyes which inspect real vices with their bearings upon two worlds. We are spectators to a plot or intrigue (not reducible in life to the point of strict morality), and take it all for truth. We substitute a real for a dramatic person, and judge him accordingly. We try him in our courts, from which there is no appeal to the dramatis personae, his peers. We have been spoiled with—not sentimental comedy—but a tyrant far more pernicious to our pleasures which has succeeded to it, the exclusive and all-devouring drama of common life; where the moral point is everything; where, instead of the fictitious half-believed personages of the stage (the phantoms of old comedy), we recognize ourselves, our brothers, aunts, kinsfolk, allies, patrons, enemies,—the same as in life—with an interest in what is going on so hearty and substantial, that we cannot afford our moral judgment, in its deepest and most vital results, to compromise or slumber for a moment. What is *there* transacting, by no modification is made to affect us in any other manner than the same events or characters would do in our relationships of life. We carry our fireside concerns to the theater with us. We do not go thither like our ancestors, to escape from the pressure of reality, so much as to confirm our experience of it; to make assurance double, and take a bond of fate. We must live our toilsome lives twice over, as it was the mournful privilege of Ulysses to descend twice to the shades. All that neutral ground of character, which stood between vice and virtue; or which in fact was indifferent to neither, where neither properly was called in question; that happy breathing-place from the burthen of a perpetual moral questioning—the sanctuary and quiet Alsatia [a] of hunted casuistry—is broken up and disfranchised, as injurious to the interests of society. The privileges of the place are taken away by law. We dare not dally with images, or names, of wrong. We bark like foolish dogs at shadows. We dread infection from the scenic representation of disorder, and fear a painted pustule. In our anxiety that our morality should not take cold, we wrap it up in a great blanket surtout of precaution against the breeze and sunshine.

I confess for myself that (with no great delinquencies to answer for) I am glad for a season to take an airing beyond the diocese of the strict conscience,—not to live always in the precincts of the law courts,—but now and then, for a dream-while or so, to imagine a world with no meddling restrictions—to get into recesses, whither the hunter cannot follow me—

——Secret shades
Of woody Ida's inmost grove,
While yet there was no fear of Jove.[b]

I come back to my cage and my restraint the fresher and more healthy for it. I wear my shackles more contentedly for having respired the breath of an imaginary freedom. I do not know how it is with others, but I feel the better always for the perusal of one of Congreve's—nay, why should I not add even of Wycherley's—comedies. I am the gayer at least for it; and I could never connect those sports of a witty fancy in any shape with any result to be drawn from them to imitation in real life. They are a world of themselves almost as much as fairy land. Take one of

[a] a London district noted as a sanctuary for debtors [b] Milton's "Il Penseroso," lines 28–30

their characters, male or female (with few exceptions they are alike), and place it in a modern play, and my virtuous indignation shall rise against the profligate wretch as warmly as the Catos [c] of the pit could desire; because in a modern play I am to judge of the right and the wrong. The standard of *police* is the measure of *political justice*. The atmosphere will blight it; it cannot live here. It has got into a moral world, where it has no business, from which it must needs fall headlong; as dizzy, and incapable of making a stand, as a Swedenborgian bad spirit that has wandered unawares into the sphere of one of his Good Men, or Angels. But in its own world do we feel the creature is so very bad?—The Fainalls and the Mirabels, the Dorimants and the Lady Touchwoods,[d] in their own sphere, do not offend my moral sense; in fact, they do not appeal to it at all. They seem engaged in their proper element. They break through no laws or conscientious restraints. They know of none. They have got out of Christendom into the land—what shall I call it?—of cuckoldry—the Utopia of gallantry, where pleasure is duty, and the manners perfect freedom. It is altogether a speculative scene of things, which has no reference whatever to the world that is. No good person can be justly offended as a spectator, because no good person suffers on the stage. Judged morally, every character in these plays—the few exceptions only are *mistakes*—is alike essentially vain and worthless. The great art of Congreve is especially shown in this, that he has entirely excluded from his scenes—some little generosities in the part of Angelica [e] perhaps excepted—not only anything like a faultless character, but any pretensions to goodness or good feelings whatsoever. Whether he did this designedly, or instinctively, the effect is as happy as the design (if design) was bold. I used to wonder at the strange power which his *Way of the World* in particular possesses of interesting you all along in the pursuits of characters, for whom you absolutely care nothing—for you neither hate nor love his personages—and I think it is owing to this very indifference for any, that you endure the whole. He has spared a privation of moral light, I will call it, rather than by the ugly name of palpable darkness, over his creations; and his shadows flit before you without distinction or preference. Had he in-

[c] i.e., censors [d] Fainall in Congreve's *The Way of the World;* Mirabel in Farquhar's *The Inconstant;* Dorimant in Etherege's *The Man of Mode;* Lady Touchwood in Congreve's *The Double Dealer* [e] in Congreve's *Love for Love*

troduced a good character, a single gush of moral feeling, a revulsion of the judgment to actual life and actual duties, the impertinent Goshen would have only lighted to the discovery of deformities, which now are none, because we think them none.

Translated into real life, the characters of his, and his friend Wycherley's dramas, are profligates and strumpets,—the business of their brief existence, the undivided pursuit of lawless gallantry. No other spring of action, or possible motive of conduct, is recognized; principles which, universally acted upon, must reduce this frame of things to a chaos. But we do them wrong in so translating them. No such effects are produced, in *their* world. When we are among them, we are amongst a chaotic people. We are not to judge them by our usages. No reverend institutions are insulted by their proceedings—for they have none among them. No peace of families is violated—for no family ties exist among them. No purity of the marriage bed is stained—for none is supposed to have a being. No deep affections are disquieted, no holy wedlock bands are snapped asunder—for affection's depth and wedded faith are not of the growth of that soil. There is neither right nor wrong—gratitude or its opposite—claim or duty—paternity or sonship. Of what consequences is it to Virtue, or how is she at all concerned about it, whether Sir Simon or Dapperwit steal away Miss Martha; or who is the father of Lord Froth's or Sir Paul Pliant's children? [f]

The whole is a passing pageant, where we should sit as unconcerned at the issues, for life or death, as at the battle of the frogs and mice. But, like Don Quixote, we take part against the puppets, and quite as impertinently. We dare not contemplate an Atlantis, a scheme, out of which our coxcombical moral sense is for a little transitory ease excluded. We have not the courage to imagine a state of things for which there is neither reward nor punishment. We cling to the painful necessities of shame and blame. We would indict our very dreams.

Amidst the mortifying circumstances attendant upon growing old, it is something to have seen *The School for Scandal* in its glory. This comedy grew out of Congreve and Wycherley, but gathered some allays of the sentimental comedy which followed theirs. It is impossible that it should be now *acted*, though it continues, at long intervals, to be announced in the bills. Its hero, when Palmer played

[f] characters in Wycherley's *Love in a Wood*

it at least, was Joseph Surface. When I remember the gay boldness, the graceful solemn plausibility, the measured step, the insinuating voice—to express it in a word—the downright *acted* villany of the part, so different from the pressure of conscious actual wickedness,—the hypocritical assumption of hypocrisy,—which made Jack so deservedly a favorite in that character, I must needs conclude the present generation of playgoers more virtuous than myself, or more dense. I freely confess that he divided the palm with me with his better brother; that, in fact, I liked him quite as well. Not but there are passages,—like that, for instance, where Joseph is made to refuse a pittance to a poor relation,—incongruities which Sheridan was forced upon by the attempt to join the artificial with the sentimental comedy, either of which must destroy the other—but over these obstructions Jack's manner floated him so lightly, that a refusal from him no more shocked you, than the easy compliance of Charles gave you in reality any pleasure; you got over the paltry question as quickly as you could, to get back into the regions of pure comedy, where no cold moral reigns. The highly artificial manner of Palmer in this character counteracted every disagreeable impression which you might have received from the contrast, supposing them real, between the two brothers. You did not believe in Joseph with the same faith with which you believed in Charles. The latter was a pleasant reality, the former a no less pleasant poetical foil to it. The comedy, I have said, is incongruous; a mixture of Congreve with sentimental incompatibilities; the gaiety upon the whole is buoyant; but it required the consummate art of Palmer to reconcile the discordant elements.

A player with Jack's talents, if we had one now, would not dare to do the part in the same manner. He would instinctively avoid every turn which might tend to unrealize, and so to make the character fascinating. He must take his cue from his spectators, who would expect a bad man and a good man as rigidly opposed to each other as the deathbeds of those geniuses are contrasted in the prints, which I am sorry to say have disappeared from the windows of my old friend Carrington Bowles, of St. Paul's Churchyard memory—(an exhibition as venerable as the adjacent cathedral, and almost coeval) of the bad and good man at the hour of death; where the ghastly apprehensions of the former,—and truly the grim phantom with his reality of a toasting fork is not to be despised,—so finely contrast with the meek complacent kissing of the rod,—

taking it in like honey and butter,—with which the latter submits to the scythe of the gentle bleeder, Time, who wields his lancet with the apprehensive finger of a popular young ladies' surgeon. What flesh, like loving grass, would not covet to meet halfway the stroke of such a delicate mower?—John Palmer was twice an actor in this exquisite part. He was playing to you all the while that he was playing upon Sir Peter and his lady. You had the first intimation of a sentiment before it was on his lips. His altered voice was meant to you, and you were to suppose that his fictitious co-flutterers on the stage perceived nothing at all of it. What was it to you if that half reality, the husband, was overreached by the puppetry—or the thin thing (Lady Teazle's reputation) was persuaded it was dying of a plethory? The fortunes of Othello and Desdemona were not concerned in it. Poor Jack has passed from the stage in good time, that he did not live to this our age of seriousness. The pleasant old Teazle *King,* too, is gone in good time. His manner would scarce have passed current in our day. We must love or hate—acquit or condemn—censure or pity—exert our detestable coxcombry of moral judgment upon everything. Joseph Surface, to go down now, must be a downright revolting villain—no compromise—his first appearance must shock and give horror—his specious plausibilities, which the pleasurable faculties of our fathers welcomed with such hearty greetings, knowing that no harm (dramatic harm even) could come, or was meant to come, of them, must inspire a cold and killing aversion. Charles (the real canting person of the scene—for the hypocrisy of Joseph has its ulterior legitimate ends, but his brother's professions of a good heart center in downright self-satisfaction) must be *loved,* and Joseph *hated*. To balance one disagreeable reality with another, Sir Peter Teazle must be no longer the comic idea of a fretful old bachelor bridegroom, whose teasings (while King acted it) were evidently as much played off at you, as they were meant to concern anybody on the stage,—he must be a real person, capable in law of sustaining an injury—a person towards whom duties are to be acknowledged—the genuine crim-con[g] antagonist of the villanous seducer Joseph. To realize him more, his sufferings under his unfortunate match must have the downright pungency of life—must (or should) make you not mirthful but uncomfortable, just as the same predicament

[g] abbreviation of "criminal conversation" (i.e., adultery)

would move you in a neighbor or old friend. The delicious scenes which give the play its name and zest, must affect you in the same serious manner as if you heard the reputation of a dear female friend attacked in your real presence. Crabtree and Sir Benjamin—those poor snakes that live but in the sunshine of your mirth—must be ripened by this hotbed process of realization into asps or amphisbænas; and Mrs. Candor—O! frightful!—become a hooded serpent. Oh! who that remembers Parsons and Dodd—the wasp and butterfly of *The School for Scandal*—in those two characters; and charming natural Miss Pope, the perfect gentlewoman as distinguished from the fine lady of comedy, in the latter part—would forego the true scenic delight—the escape from life—the oblivion of consequences—the holiday barring out of the pedant Reflection—those Saturnalia of two or three brief hours, well won from the world—to sit instead at one of our modern plays—to have his coward conscience (that forsooth must not be left for a moment) stimulated with perpetual appeals—dulled rather, and blunted, as a faculty without repose must be—and his moral vanity pampered with images of notional justice, notional beneficence, lives saved without the spectator's risk, and fortunes given away that cost the author nothing?

No piece was, perhaps, ever so completely cast in all its parts as this *manager's comedy*.[g] Miss Farren had succeeded to Mrs. Abington in Lady Teazle; and Smith, the original Charles, had retired when I first saw it. The rest of the characters, with very slight exceptions, remained. I remember it was then the fashion to cry down John Kemble, who took the part of Charles after Smith; but, I thought, very unjustly. Smith, I fancy, was more airy, and took the eye with a certain gaiety of person. He brought with him no somber recollections of tragedy. He had not to expiate the fault of having pleased beforehand in lofty declamation. He had no sins of Hamlet or of Richard to atone for. His failure in these parts was a passport to success in one of so opposite a tendency. But, as far as I could judge, the weighty sense of Kemble made up for more personal incapacity than he had to answer for. His harshest tones in this part came steeped and dulcified in good humor. He made his defects a grace. His exact declamatory manner, as he managed it, only served to con-

[g] Sheridan was manager of Drury Lane when his *School for Scandal* was first produced.

vey the points of his dialogue with more precision. It seemed to head the shafts to carry them deeper. Not one of his sparkling sentences was lost. I remember minutely how he delivered each in succession, and cannot by any effort imagine how any of them could be altered for the better. No man could deliver brilliant dialogue—the dialogue of Congreve or of Wycherley—because none understood it—half so well as John Kemble. His Valentine, in *Love for Love*, was, to my recollection, faultless. He flagged sometimes in the intervals of tragic passion. He would slumber over the level parts of an heroic character. His Macbeth has been known to nod. But he always seemed to me to be particularly alive to pointed and witty dialogue. The relaxing levities of tragedy have not been touched by any since him—the playful court-bred spirit in which he condescended to the players in Hamlet—the sportive relief which he threw into the darker shades of Richard—disappeared with him. He had his sluggish moods, his torpors—but they were the halting-stones and resting place of his tragedy—politic savings, and fetches of the breath—husbandry of the lungs, where nature pointed him to be an economist—rather, I think, than errors of the judgment. They were, at worst, less painful than the eternal tormenting unappeasable vigilance, the "lidless dragon eyes," [h] of present fashionable tragedy. [1822]

[h] Coleridge's "Ode on the Departing Year," line 145

Sir John Gielgud:

INTRODUCTION TO THE IMPORTANCE OF BEING EARNEST

It is possible to give a performance of one of the great Shakespearean tragedies upon an almost bare stage, with a minimum of accessories, and hold the interest of a large and unsophisticated audience. Shakespeare's comedies, on the other hand, are very much more difficult to perform. In them the qualities of suspense and situation are considerably less strong, and the author has trusted to his powers of word-spinning, local humor, topical jokes, and a balance of speed, and contrast designed for an unlocalized apron stage.

The comedies of the Restoration period, and those of Oscar Wilde, are less imaginative, less free, both in conception and execution, than the comedies of Shakespeare, and written, of course, for a picture stage. Their performance demands, both from actors and directors, a considerable understanding of the period in which they were written, and some degree of urban sophistication from the audience. They are city plays, and, though there are country scenes in them, those scenes represent the country seen very much through city eyes.

Shakespeare lived, probably, as much in the country as he did in London. Many of his comedies are pastoral in scene and atmosphere, but in his day the cities were so small compared to ours that the juxtaposition in his plays of scenes of town and country life, court and woodland, inn yard, castle and seashore, give to their action—especially on the unlocalized stage for which he was writing—a wonderful freedom of movement and variety of atmosphere.

After the Restoration, with the introduction of picture

stage, front curtain, and proscenium, plays came to be written which could be sustained throughout in a single mood. Long acts took the place of short scenes. Audiences became increasingly delighted in seeing people on the stage behaving exactly as they themselves behaved at home (only saying more amusing things) against backgrounds of painted scenery and realistic accessories of every kind.

But playwrights of poetic genius cannot be kept down by convention. The mad scene of Valentine in Congreve's *Love for Love*, Worthing's interview with Lady Bracknell in *The Importance of Being Earnest*, and his arrival in mock mourning in the second act of the latter play, these are flights of poetic imagination—though, of course, they are comic scenes as well. The author, in each case, seems to blossom into a kind of inspired lunacy which is light, poetic, exquisitely original. These moments lift the plays in which they occur to a brilliant peak of nonsense. They are incomparable examples of their kind. They are scenes of classic farce.

We shall never know whether Wilde wrote his last play meaning to keep it as a perfectly "straight" realistic picture of high life as he knew it. It may be that the touches which make the play most memorable only occurred to him as an afterthought. He is known to have been the most wonderful extempore talker, but it is possible, too, that before he went to a party he did a little homework first (as an actor does), and was ready with some of the good things he proposed to say, even if he was not sure of the order in which he was going to say them. No doubt, too, he was stimulated by his own wit, and one good remark suggested another, till the best one, the cherry on top of the cake, came to him suddenly in a flash of inspiration. Certainly the construction of this his best play is careful and precise, though the author does not hesitate to make use of a set of stock characters and several well-worn devices of farce to carry his plot to a satisfactory conclusion. Similarly, Shakespeare and Congreve were not above a good deal of borrowing of plots, slapstick, and conventional misunderstandings, to keep their comedies spinning along to the usual pairing off of all the characters at the end.

The Importance of Being Earnest begins in a quite realistic atmosphere. The characters behave and talk in the languid, pointed, conscious manner of their day. They are witty, cultured, idle, and wealthy. Even Lane, Algernon's manservant, has caught some of his master's wit, added a pinch of his own, and replies to questions with epigrams uttered in tones of deferential gravity. Everybody is solemn, correct, polite. The bachelors only loll or smoke or cross their legs when they are alone. In company they sit with straight backs and conduct themselves with irreproachable exactitude, hitching their trousers before they sit down, stripping off their gloves, shooting their cuffs. Their hats are worn at exactly the right angle, their canes carried with an air of studied negligence. They have never been seen in Piccadilly without top hats and frock coats.

Algy, in the country, is dressed to kill. But he must not kill the comedy by a costume verging upon caricature. A correct country suit of the period will be quite amusing enough to modern eyes. Miss Prism and Doctor Chasuble are stock figures of farce, the spinster governess and the country rector, but they must be simple and sincere in their playing, not exaggeratedly ridiculous. Well acted, they have great charm—Prism, at the end, has even a touch of pathos. The comedy verges upon fantasy and occasionally spills over into farce: it must never degenerate into knockabout. In Act Two it is the tradition of Worthing to produce from his breast pocket a black-edged handkerchief. (We do not know if this was the invention of Wilde, or of George Alexander, who created the part. I suspect the latter, for there is no mention of it in the printed text.) This must not be flourished or handled continually to distract from the dialogue and force the laughter of the audience. Used twice, it is legitimate. Shaken once too often, it becomes a cheap "prop" which may destroy the whole beauty of the author's exquisite invention. The scene with the muffins, at the end of the second act, should be played deliberately and with great seriousness. Here again, the actors must not enjoy themselves too much, nor must they snatch and fight and talk with their mouths full. The decorum, the deadly importance of the triviality, is everything—they are greedy, determined, but exasperatedly polite.

Cecily is first cousin to Alice in Wonderland—the same backboard demureness, the same didactic manner, the echoes of remarks she has copied from her elders and her governess. Gwendolen is perhaps more difficult for an actress to hit off correctly, but we may find her prototype in the cartoons of George du Maurier in *Punch*. But her affectations must be of society, not the "Greenery Yallery Grosvenor Gallery" airs which Gilbert satirized in *Patience*. She is bored and elegant, with an occasional flash of individuality peeping out under overwhelming layers of her mother's condescension and snobbishness, which she frequently echoes in her own remarks.

Lady Bracknell is not called Augusta for nothing. She is never put out or surprised. She is never angry. But she is frequently disapproving and almost always annihilating. If the author were anyone but Wilde, she would be unanswerable. She moves slowly and seldom. She is beautifully dressed and carries herself superbly. Her every accessory—veil, gloves, parasol, chatelaine, bag, and shoes—must be worn with a perfection of detail that has become second nature to her. It is impossible to conceive her (or her daughter either) except *en grande tenue*.

The pace of the comedy must be leisurely, mannered; and everybody must, of course, speak beautifully—but the wit must appear spontaneous, though self-conscious. The text must be studied and spoken so as to arouse a cumulative effect of laughter from the audience. That is to say it may be sometimes necessary to sacrifice laughs on certain witty lines, in order that a big laugh may come at the end of a passage, rather than to extract two or three small ones in between, which may dissipate the sense and retard the progress of the dialogue. There are, if anything, too many funny lines, and the actor may easily ruin a passage by allowing the audience to laugh in the middle. For instance, the following sally in the first act:

Jack. My dear Algy, you talk exactly as if you were a dentist. It is very vulgar to talk like a dentist when one isn't a dentist. It produces a false impression.
Algernon. Well, that is exactly what dentists always do.

If the actors leave time for the audience to laugh after the words "It produces a false impression," Algernon's reply will fall flat and seem redundant. Actors with expert pace and timing will hurry the dialogue, Algernon breaking in quickly with his line, so that the audience may not laugh until he has spoken it.

A certain amount of "business" is surely justifiable. In my productions I have introduced a persistently warbling bird in the garden scene, which is so rude as to interrupt Gwendolen in the midst of one of her most pregnant observations, a church clock to herald Worthing's entrance in mourning and to chime four o'clock as tea is punctually served, and, in the third act, a stepladder to the high bookcase in which Ernest seeks for his Army Lists. He is thus provided with a dominating, if precarious, position for the moment of the final denouement. But such interpolations must be discreetly introduced, and not allowed to disturb the brilliant flow of dialogue or drown an important line with irrelevant laughter.

The play can be mounted either in the correct period, 1895, or, at the producer's discretion, in a slightly later year—but not, I think, later than 1906. The designers who worked for me decided that Lady Bracknell would look more imposing in the great hats of the early Edwardian era, than in the small bonnets worn by the older generation in the 90's, and this was the main reason why we chose the later period for our production. Also the furnishings of the rooms at the later date, heavier and more ornate, seemed to us to provide a more amusingly lavish and crowded background. But Algy's room might well be decorated with blue and white china, Japanese fans, Aubrey Beardsley drawings and spindly bamboo furniture, with the morning room of the last act a comfortable contrast of Mid-Victorian solidity. Certainly the garden must be pretty and profuse with roses, the tea tables groaning with lace, silver, and masses of food, and Worthing must be the only character allowed to use the center entrance, emerging with stately processional gloom upon the sunlit scene.

It is not easy to achieve the style, the lightness, the apparent ease which the play demands. Above all it is hard to act it with a deadly seriousness, yet with an inner consciousness of fun—the fun with which one plays seriously a very elaborate practical joke.

The play must originally have been thought funny because it tilted so brilliantly at society as it then was. The people who laughed at it were many of them laughing at themselves, reproduced with only very slight exaggeration upon the stage. Today we laugh at the very idea that such types could ever have existed; at the whole system—the leaving of cards, chaperons, proposals of marriage, ceremony of meals, the ridiculously exaggerated values of birth, rank, and fashion.

But there is a danger that the actors of today, lacking real types to observe, will turn the comedy into wild caricature, and the audience, even if they may not know the reason, will then find the piece contrived, silly, and overdrawn. The performance needs to be correct though not dry, leisurely but not dragged, solemn yet full of sparkle. Above all it is an agreeable play. The brittle crackling staccato of Noel Coward, the smart rudeness of Frederick Lonsdale, this was not wit as Wilde conceived it. In his plays nobody is nervous, impatient, catty, or ill-natured. The "lower classes" are spoken of patronizingly but not contemptuously. Even Lady Bracknell's stern summons of "Prism!" in the final scene is firm without being cruel. The girls conduct their elegant quarrel with the highest good breeding. Everything depends on no one losing their tempers or their poise. The movement throughout must be smooth, stylish (but not balletic, as often occurs when actors and directors try to create a period sense) and the more elegantly the actors give and take, the more will the intrinsic quality of the wit emerge, as the grave puppet characters utter their delicate cadences and spin their web of preposterously elegant sophistication. [1949]

Kenneth Tynan:

The Angry Young Movement

It all came to a head one May evening in 1956 at the Royal Court Theater in Sloane Square. There had of course been plenty of preliminary rumbles. A group of young British writers had recently published a series of picaresque novels featuring a new sort of hero—a lower-class intellectual with a ribald sense of humor, a robust taste for beer and sex, and an attitude of villainous irreverence towards the established order. A butterfly-theorist named Colin Wilson had written an apocalyptic best-seller about the necessity of being an "outsider." An attack had just been launched by the younger movie critics and directors against the genteel vacuity of the British cinema: their new watchword was "commitment," by which they meant commitment to reality and social truth. A similar rebellion was taking place in the world of painting, where the new "kitchen-sink school" (so called for its alleged preoccupation with domestic squalor) had begun to move into the lead. Even before the events of that May evening it was clear that the postwar generation in Britain had a good deal to say and was in quite a hurry to say it.

Most of the new rebels were leftish-liberal or outright Socialist; a few, like Colin Wilson, had religious aspirations; but on one point nearly all of them agreed. They detested "the Establishment," a phrase that had lately been coined to describe the hard core of top people—professional monarchists, archbishops, press barons, Etonian Tories, and *Times* leader writers—who still seemed, in spite of a war and a social revolution, to be exerting a disproportionate influence on the country's affairs. Protest against these apparent immovables was very much in the air. So it was, of course, in the 1930's. But the intelligentsia of that period were mostly rebelling against their own class; many of them were Etonians and most came from solid Establishment backgrounds. The new malcontents were chiefly state-educated lower-middles. Their feeling about the country-house class, which had survived into their era like some grotesque coelacanth, was not one of filial resentment. It was closer to outraged boredom.

Into this combustible atmosphere John Osborne, a lean, esurient actor in his twenty-seventh year, flung a play called *Look Back in Anger,* which summed up what many of his contemporaries were feeling about their rulers and elders. It opened, unheralded, at the Royal Court Theater; and the explosion of that spring night two years ago is still reverberating through the decorous anterooms of English culture. It was as if, in the tiptoe hush of a polite assembly, someone had deafeningly burped. The theater's press-agent, asked for a description of the iconoclastic young gate-crasher, said he was first and foremost "an angry young man." Before long the phrase, in itself not particularly striking, had snowballed into a cult. It did so because it defined a phenomenon that was nationally recognizable. It gave a name to a generation of young intellectuals who disliked being called intellectuals, since they thought the word phony, affected, and "wet."

There is nothing new in young men being angry: in fact, it would be news if they were anything else. Byron and Shelley were classically angry young men. American writing in the 1930's was on fire with anger: Dos Passos, Steinbeck, and Odets come to mind, all brandishing their fists. The very phrase was used in 1951 by an English social philosopher named Leslie Paul as the title of his autobiography: it is the story of a devout left-wing agitator who lost his faith in Russia during the 1930's and turned, like so many others, to a vague sort of Christian humanism. What distinguishes the modern English "young angries" is that they all came of age around the time that their elders invented the hydrogen bomb. How could they revere "civilization as we know it" when at any moment it might be transformed into "civilization as we knew it"? How could they carry the torch of freedom when to do so meant running with it into the ammunition dump? These unanswerable questions set up feelings of uselessness and impotence, which led in some to apathy, in others to a sort of derisive detachment, and in still others to downright rage. And these feelings were intensified by the knowledge that Britain no longer had a voice strong enough to forbid chaos if, by some horrific chance, it should impend.

Somebody, in short, had to say that many young Britons were fed up; that to be young, so far from being very heaven, was in some ways very hell. Osborne was the first in the theater to say it; and, the theater being the naked, public place it is, the statement caused a considerable bang. What made it even more shocking was that both the author and his hero, Jimmy Porter, came from low social shelves, yet had the cheek to be highly articulate on a wide variety of subjects, including the sex war, the class war, and war itself. There was no mistaking the portents. A breakthrough was beginning. The new intelligentsia created by free education and state scholarships was making its first sizable dents in the façade of public-school culture.

A few months before, in a Christmas message to the readers of the London *Sunday Times*, Somerset Maugham had expressed his opinions of state-aided undergraduates. It was simple and unequivocal: "They are scum," said the Old Party. He was in fact referring to Jim Dixon, the hero of Kingsley Amis' immensely successful novel, *Lucky Jim*. Dixon, who lectures at a minor university, is a frankly comic character, much less ferocious than Jimmy Porter; he keeps his anger in check by drinking and pulling dreadful faces; but he shares with Osborne's hero a defiant provincialism, semi-proletarian origins, and the kind of blithe disgruntlement that inspires such phrases as "the interminable facetiousness of filthy Mozart." By Mr. Maugham's standards *Look Back in Anger* was the apotheosis of scum. The letter columns of the more pompous dailies were soon filled with similar opinions. These young men (said one correspondent) were just envious upstarts: in a decently run society they would have been sent out to work at fourteen with no time to brood about ideas above their station.

Despite his greater violence and dogmatism, it was clear that Jimmy Porter was speaking essentially the same idiom as Lucky Jim and the heroes of John Wain's *Hurry on Down* and Iris Murdoch's *Under the Net*. Both these novels, the work of writers under thirty, had been grouped with Amis' and achieved a comparable celebrity. Wain's hero was a young provincial iconoclast whose occupations included, at various times, window-cleaning and dope-running: Miss Murdoch's was an aimless pub-crawler with a mordant sense of humor and a talent for sponging. Both were obvious forerunners of Jimmy Porter. All the same, to most of the London critics he was a new and unheard-of disease. They reacted to the play with flustered disapproval; while acknowledging Osborne's command of dialogue, they dismissed his hero as "a young pup."

The salient thing about Jimmy Porter was that we—the under-thirty generation in Britain—recognized him on sight. We had met him; we had pub-crawled with him; we had shared bed-sitting rooms with him. For the first time the theater was speaking to us in our own language, on our own terms. Most young people had hitherto regarded the English theater as a dusty anachronism which, as Dylan Thomas said of a certain Welsh museum, ought to be in a museum. Osborne showed them their error; and some of them even began to write plays.

The under-thirties responded to many qualities in Jimmy Porter—his impulsive, unargued leftishness, his anarchic sense of humor, and his suspicion that all the brave causes had been either won or discredited. For too long British culture had languished in a freezing-unit of understatement and "good taste." In these chill latitudes Jimmy Porter flamed like a blowtorch. He was not, like Jean Cocteau, *"trop occupé pour être engagé";*[a] he cared, and cared bitterly. On the one hand, he represented the dismay of many young Britons whose childhood and adolescence were scarred by the depression and the war; who came of age under a Socialist government, yet found, when they went out into the world, that the class sytem was still mysteriously intact. On the other hand, he reflected the much wider problem of what to do with a liberal education in a technological world. In Britain, as elsewhere, the men who count are the technocrats of whom Sir Charles Snow writes. Jimmy Porter's education fitted him for entry into the intelligentsia at the very moment when the intelligentsia were ceasing to matter. He lurks, a ghostly, snarling dodo, in the scientists' shadow.

In Europe as on Broadway, it is difficult to escape *Look Back in Anger*. Nearly every repertory company in Britain has performed it, and it is being played all over Germany and Scandinavia. Osborne followed it up in 1957 with another hit, *The Entertainer*, which repercussed almost as widely. In just eighteen months an obscure repertory actor had become one of the most prosperous playwrights of the century, with a weekly income in the neigh-

[a] "too busy to become involved"

borhood of £3,500. Osborne married his leading lady, Mary Ure, and moved into a smart little Chelsea back-water, at least a class and a half above Fulham, the suburb of his birth, where he and his mother (a contented bar-maid) at one time subsisted on a joint income of less than a pound a week. Once, as a boy, he was out walking with his grandfather, who surprised him by indignantly cutting a passer-by who greeted them. "That man's a Socialist," said grandfather in explanation. "That's a man who doesn't believe in raising his hat." Osborne has never found a better definition of his own Socialism: its emblem is an un-tugged forelock rampant. When a master slapped his face at school, he at once riposted by slapping the master; and this, in Britain, takes preternatural guts.

He is passionate in his refusal to venerate what he calls "the idiot heroes" of patriotic movies; and his fervent re-publicanism recently led him to describe the British royal family as "the gold filling in a mouthful of decay." He will probably always be a bad belonger, to any party or group; his real talent is for dissent. But when his enemies complain that all his opinions are negative, I think they forget that nowadays there is a positive value in merely standing against a current of events which you believe is moving towards suicide. Osborne is a disconcerting, rather impenetrable person to meet: tall and slim, wearing his shoulders in a defensive bunch around his neck; gentle in manner, yet vocally harsh and cawing; sharp-toothed, yet a convinced vegetarian. He looks wan and driven, and is nervously prone to indulge in sudden, wolfish, silly-ass grins. Sartorially he is something of a peacock, and his side-burns add a sinister touch of the Apache. A dandy, if you like: but a dandy with a machine gun.

Unlike Jimmy Porter, Osborne never went to a university. This is about all he has in common with Colin Wilson, the brash young metaphysical whose first book, *The Outsider*, was hailed as a masterpiece by several middle-aged critics who saw in its philosophy of salvation through despair an antidote to their own disillusion. Although a playwright can get along without the disciplines of higher education, a philosopher cannot, as Wilson's book aw-fully proved. As one ploughed through its inconsistencies, repetitions, and flights of paranoid illogic (an experience rather like walking knee-deep in hot sand), all one could state with any certainty was that an "outsider" was any-one whose books happened to have been on the author's recent library list. "We read Anatole France," said a

French critic, "to find out what Anatole France has been reading"; and the same is true of Wilson. He was angry, all right, but his anger was more presumptuously cosmic than that of Osborne and the rest. For him we were not just misguided: we were rotten to the core. As far as I could make out, Wilson's philosophic position was somewhere between existentialism and Norman Vincent Peale; but his talk of a spiritual revival, with an élite of outsiders leading the world out of chaos, exerted a hypnotic charm on the lonely and maladjusted, who are always enticed by the promise of words like "élite." Shaw was posthumously enrolled in the cult: not Shaw the Fabian Socialist and wit, but that later, lesser Shaw whose belief in the "life force" led him to condone dictatorship. This, cried Wilson, was the greatest religious thinker of modern times.

In 1957, fresh from unsuccessful flirtations with acting and playwriting, a twenty-four-year-old Yorkshireman named Stuart Holroyd climbed on the Bund-wagon by writing a philosophical work called *Emergence from Chaos,* which more or less followed the Wilson line. According to Holroyd, democracy was "a myth" and government was best left to "an expert minority"; but by now it was beginning to dawn on many people that such ideas, if not consciously fascist, were certainly the soil in which fascism grew. Wilson's second book, *Religion and the Rebel,* appeared last autumn. It proved to be a road-company version of the first, and was obliteratingly panned.

Not all the prominent young Britons of today are self-taught. Many of them were at Oxford when I was there, during the four years immediately after the war. As undergraduate generations go, it was disorderly and a bit piratical, but full of gusto and wildfire. There was plenty of gaiety about, but not of the fox-hunting, cork-popping, bounder-debagging kind that followed World War I; most of the new undergraduates were ex-servicemen living on government grants, for whom upper-class prankishness held very little appeal. Kingsley Amis and John Wain both come from the Oxford of that period. Neither of them had an Oxford accent, which is ordinary speech pushed through a constipated flute: that sort of "poshness" was emphatically out. Both Amis and Wain were (and are) poets and critics as well as novelists, and after graduation both taught at provincial universities; and it is this all-round academicism that makes their writing at once saner and tamer than, for instance, Osborne's. Another postwar Oxonian was Lindsay Anderson, whose anger with the *status quo* has not been off the boil for at least ten years. A formidable film critic, director, and polemicist, he has done more than anyone else to bring the idea of "committed art" into public controversy. Many Continental critics today speak of Anderson as if he were the dominant force in British cinema. According to one reporter, the party thrown by Mike Todd after the Cannes *première* of *Around the World in Eighty Days* was entirely made up of people anxiously whispering, in eighteen languages: "Lindsay didn't like it." He won an Academy Award in 1955 for *Thursday's Children,* a documentary about the education of deaf-mutes, and a Venice Grand Prix two years later for a forty-minute exploration of life in Covent Garden market; and though he has yet to make a feature film, his position as a critical moralist and spokesman for life-embracing cinema is unique in Britain. Quite apart from its A.Y.M.'s, the postwar Oxford vintage was a heady one. It also produced Tony Richardson, who directed both of Osborne's plays in London and on Broadway; Sandy Wilson, author of *The Boy Friend,* the most successful of postwar British musicals; and Roger Bannister, the first four-minute miler. In Labor politics it turned out the virulent back-bencher Anthony Wedgwood Benn; and on the Tory side, Sir Edward Boyle, who was the youngest member of the Eden cabinet when he resigned as a protest against the Franco-British invasion of Egypt.

The flag-wagging, wog-flogging assault on Suez was a great promoter of anger. Passions long thought extinct flared everywhere; people who had prided themselves on their detachment suddenly found themselves clobbering their best friends. Reasonably enough, those who were anti-Suez also tended to be supporters of *Look Back in Anger*. In the heat of the crisis, while smoke-bombs were bursting in Downing Street and mounted police charged the crowds in Whitehall, Osborne conceived his second play, *The Entertainer*. When it opened last April, the leading role was played—and played to the hilt—by Sir Laurence Olivier. Significantly, it was he who approached Osborne for a part, presumably on the principle of joining what you can't lick. This was the Establishment's first bow to the "angries." It meant that they had officially arrived.

It also established the Royal Court Theatre as the home

of forward-looking British drama. Angus Wilson's first play had its London *première* there; so did Nigel Dennis' Swiftian satire, *Cards of Identity*, and the same author's furious parable, *The Making of Moo*, which is the only overtly atheistic play in the English language. Newcomers like Michael Hastings, the ambitious East End teenager, saw their work conscientiously staged; and the whole venture throve, and thrives still, in a heady intellectual ferment. Its fiscal keystone, however, was Osborne, who has proved against all augury that you can make a fortune by telling an audience the very things about itself that it wants least to hear.

On the other side of the Thames the National Film Theatre has developed into a comparable oasis of progressive cinema, with the pugnacious film magazine *Sight and Sound* acting as its ally and interpreter. Nor have I yet mentioned such associated phenomena as the rhetorical left-wing poet Christopher Logue or the stoutly committed art critic John Berger, whose influence on the graphic arts is roughly commensurate with Lindsay Anderson's on the cinema.

The newest angry is a fleshy Yorkshireman named John Braine, whose novel *Room at the Top*, an analysis of the means used by an amoral young opportunist to break into the upper stratum of provincial society, was among the larger English best-sellers of 1957. Shrewd and deliberate of speech, Braine has the stamina of a youthful J. B. Priestley, plus a vein of bizarre, unfettered humor that will probably seep into his next novel: its title, *The Vodi*, is the name of a monumentally batty secret society which has figured in his private fantasies for many years. He is at heart a plain old-fashioned Socialist with a common-sense regional brogue, but there is wildness in his background. He was connected, during the war, with a mildly anarchist group in Yorkshire that published a mimeographed broadsheet with an unprintable name. (One of its members, hating regimentation, gathered together a number of cans and fixed them with wire to selected lamp posts in the town where he lived. On each can he painted the words: "Please put your Identity Cards in here." Before the police removed the cans he had collected, and subsequently burned, nearly five thousand cards.)

Braine exudes ambition and may easily outlast many of his fellow angries. His egotism is extremely disarming. After a long conversation some months ago he warned me not to be surprised if much of our talk turned up in his next book. "And if you complain of being plagiarized," he said gustily, with his little finger admonitorily raised, "I shall expose you to the world as one who tried to climb to fame on the back of that colossus of letters—*Braine*."

In many directions, a lot of unequal talent is exploding. Certain things, however, seen to be agreed on, certain attitudes towards the relationship of the arts to living. The ivory tower has collapsed for good. The lofty, lapidary, "mandarin" style of writing has been replaced by prose that has its feet on the ground. And the word "civilized," which had come to mean "detached, polite, above the tumult," is being restored to its old etymological meaning: to be civilized nowadays is to care about society and to feel oneself a responsible part of it. The books, plays, poems, films, and paintings that the young Britons are trying to turn out may well be ham-fisted and un-Englishly crude, but they will be based on the idea that art is an influence on life, not a refuge from it or an alternative to it. That, really, is what the anger is all about. It is anger that our kind of world is so chary of that kind of art.

If you object that you have heard this sort of thing before, I urge you to remember that the day you stop hearing it will be the day on which art shrugs its shoulders, gives up the ghost, and dies. Britain's angry young men may be jejune and strident, but they are involved in the only belief that matters: that life begins tomorrow.

[1958]

Suggested References

A great deal has been written about the subject, but the following list can serve as a start. Although several titles mentioned earlier are repeated below, most of the following books are conspicuously broader than those cited after the introduction to each play.

I. General

Agate, James, ed., *The English Dramatic Critics,* New York, Hill and Wang, 1958; London, Arthur Barker, 1932.

Cole, Toby, and Helen Krich Chinoy, eds., *Actors on Acting,* 2nd ed., New York, Crown Publishers, 1954; London, W. Heffer & Sons, 1955.

Hartnoll, Phyllis, ed., *The Oxford Companion to the Theatre,* 2nd ed. rev., New York and London, Oxford University Press, 1957.

Kronenberger, Louis, *The Thread of Laughter,* New York, Alfred A. Knopf, 1952.

Nagler, A. M., *A Source Book in Theatrical History,* New York, Dover Publications, 1960; London, Constable & Co., 1959.

Nicoll, Allardyce, *British Drama,* 4th ed., New York, Barnes & Noble, 1957, with corrections; London, George H. Harrap & Co., 1947.

Nicoll, Allardyce, *A History of English Drama,* 6 vols., Cambridge, Cambridge University Press, 1952–1959.

Prior, Moody, *The Language of Tragedy,* New York, Columbia University Press, 1947; London, Oxford University Press, 1947.

Wimsatt, W. K., Jr., ed., *English Stage Comedy,* New York, Columbia University Press, 1955; London, Oxford University Press 1955.

II. From the Mid-Seventeenth Century to about 1800

Avery, Emmet L., ed., *The London Stage, 1660–1800: Part 2: 1700–1729*, 2 vols., Carbondale, Ill., University of Southern Illinois Press, 1960. (The work, which will comprise 12 volumes, is scheduled for completion in 1965.)

Baker, Herschel, *John Philip Kemble*, Cambridge, Mass., Harvard University Press, 1942; London, Oxford University Press, 1942.

Bateson, F. W., *English Comic Drama, 1700–1750*, Oxford, The Clarendon Press, 1929.

Bernbaum, Ernest, *The Drama of Sensibility*, Boston, Ginn & Co., 1915.

Burnim, Kalman, *David Garrick, Director*, Pittsburgh, University of Pittsburgh Press, 1961.

Dobrée, Bonamy, *Restoration Comedy, 1660–1720*, London, Oxford University Press, 1924.

Dobrée, Bonamy, *Restoration Tragedy, 1660–1720*, Oxford, The Clarendon Press, 1929.

Fujimura, Thomas H., *The Restoration Comedy of Wit*, Princeton, Princeton University Press, 1952.

Green, Clarence C., *The Neo-Classic Theory of Tragedy in England During the Eighteenth Century*, Cambridge, Mass., Harvard University Press, 1934; London: Oxford University Press, 1934.

Harbage, Alfred, *Cavalier Drama*, New York, Modern Language Association, 1936; London, Oxford University Press, 1936.

Holland, Norman N., *The First Modern Comedies*, Cambridge, Mass., Harvard University Press, 1959; London, Oxford University Press, 1959.

Krutch, Joseph Wood, *Comedy and Conscience after the Restoration*, New York, Columbia University Press, 1929 (paperback, 1961).

Loftis, John, *Comedy and Society from Congreve to Fielding*, Stanford, Stanford University Press, 1959; London, Oxford University Press, 1960.

Lynch, James J., *Box, Pit, and Gallery: Stage and Society in Johnson's London*, Berkeley and Los Angeles, University of California Press, 1953; Cambridge, Cambridge University Press, 1953.

Nicoll, Allardyce, *A History of English Drama, 1660–*

1900, Cambridge, Cambridge University Press, 1952–1959, Vols. 1–3, 6.

Nolte, Fred O., *The Early Middle Class Drama 1696–1774,* Lancaster, Pa., Ottendorfer Memorial Series of Germanic Monographs, 1935.

Sherbo, Arthur, *English Sentimental Drama,* East Lansing, Mich., Michigan State University Press, 1957.

Sherburn, George, "The Restoration and Eighteenth Century," in *A Literary History of England,* ed. A. C. Baugh, New York, Appleton-Century-Crofts, 1948.

Smith, John Harrington, *The Gay Couple in Restoration Comedy,* Cambridge, Mass., Harvard University Press, 1948; London, Oxford University Press, 1948.

III. The Nineteenth Century

Beerbohm, Max, *Around Theatres,* New York, Simon and Schuster, 1953; London, Rupert Hart-Davis, 1953.

Findlater, Richard, *Grimaldi,* London, MacGibbon & Kee, 1955.

Hillebrand, Harold Newcomb, *Edmund Kean,* New York, Columbia University Press, 1933; London, Oxford University Press, 1933.

Irving, Laurence, *Henry Irving,* New York, the Macmillan Co., 1952; London, Faber and Faber, 1951.

James, Henry, *The Scenic Art,* ed. Allan Wade, New Brunswick, N. J., Rutgers University Press, 1948; London, Rupert Hart-Davis, 1949.

Lewes, George Henry, *On Actors and the Art of Acting,* New York, Grove Press, 1957.

Nicoll, Allardyce, *A History of English Drama,* Cambridge, Cambridge University Press, 1955–1959, Vols. 4-6.

Reynolds, Ernest, *Early Victorian Drama,* 1830–1870, Cambridge, Cambridge University Press, 1936.

Rowell, George, *The Victorian Theatre,* London, Oxford University Press, 1956.

Shaw, George Bernard, *Our Theatres in the Nineties,* 3 vols., London, Constable & Co., 1932.

Watson, Ernest Bradlee, *Sheridan to Robertson,* Cambridge, Mass., Harvard University Press, 1926.

IV. The Twentieth Century

Agate, James, *The Later Ego,* New York, Crown Publishers, 1951.

Cole, Toby, ed., *Playwrights on Playwriting,* New York, Hill and Wang, 1960.

Donoghue, Denis, *The Third Voice: Modern British and American Verse Drama,* Princeton, Princeton University Press, 1959; London, Oxford University Press, 1959.

Esslin, Martin, *The Theatre of the Absurd,* Garden City, N.Y., Doubleday & Co., (Anchor Books), 1961.

Findlater, Richard, guest ed., *The Twentieth Century,* Vol. 169, No. 1008 (February, 1961).

Kitchin, Laurence, *Mid-Century Drama,* London, Faber and Faber, 1960.

Lumley, Frederick, *Trends in 20th Century Drama,* Fair Lawn, N. J., Essential Books, 1956; London, Rockliff Publishing Corp., 1956.

MacCarthy, Desmond, *Theatre,* New York, Oxford University Press, 1955; London: MacGibbon & Kee, 1954.

Pearson, Hesketh, *The Last Actor-Managers,* New York, Harpers, 1951; London, Methuen & Co., 1950.

Purdom, Charles Benjamin, *Harley Granville Barker,* Cambridge, Mass., Harvard University Press, 1956; London, Rockliff Publishing Corp., 1955.

Shaw, George Bernard, *Shaw on Theatre,* ed. E. J. West, New York, Hill and Wang, 1958.

Taylor, John Russell, *Anger and After: A Guide to the New British Drama,* London, Methuen, 1962.

Trewin, J. C., *Dramatists of Today,* London, Staples Press, 1954.

Tynan, Kenneth, *Curtains,* New York, Atheneum, 1961; London, Longmans Green, 1961.

Weales , Gerald, *Religion in Modern English Drama,* Philadelphia, University of Pennsylvania Press, 1960.

Williamson, Audrey, *Contemporary Theatre, 1953–1956,* New York, The Macmillan Co., 1956; London, Rockliff Publishing Corp., 1956.

Williamson, Audrey, *Theatre of Two Decades,* New York, the Macmillan Co., 1952; London, Rockliff Publishing Corp., 1951.

Wilson, A. E., *Edwardian Theatre,* New York, the Macmillan Co., 1952; London, Arthur Barker, 1951.